Reader's
Digest
Condensed
Books

READER'S DIGEST ASSOCIATION (CANADA) LTD.
CONDENSED BOOKS DIVISION

215 Redfern Ave., Montreal, Que. H3Z 2V9
Editor: Deirdre Gilbert
Assistant Editor: Anita Winterberg
Design: Andrée Payette
Production Manager: Holger Lorenzen

© 1992 The Reader's Digest Association, Inc. (except *Blaze* and *Dead Fix*)
© 1992 The Reader's Digest Association (Canada) Ltd.
© Reader's Digest (Australia) Pty Ltd, 1991.

ISBN 0-88850-287-7

FIRST EDITION
PRINTED IN THE U.S.A.

READER'S DIGEST CONDENSED BOOKS

In this volume

SUCH DEVOTED SISTERS
by Eileen Goudge

Daughters of a famous actress, Annie and Laurel grew up in a glamorous but troubled home. When the tensions became intolerable, they fled in quest of success and love in New York City. They had their talent, their determination and their fierce loyalty to each other. But can that loyalty survive amid the pressures and temptations of the big city? Or will the sorrows and secrets of the past tear the sisters apart? A captivating journey through the worlds of Hollywood, Paris, and Manhattan from best selling author, Eileen Goudge. / Page 7

RULES OF ENCOUNTER
by William P. Kennedy

1916: As war rages in Europe, a young British naval hero, William Day, is secretly shipping American supplies to England on board neutral ships. Dedicated, proudly patriotic, Day knows he is flouting all the rules of traditional warfare. But this, he believes, is a time when rules were made to be broken. Too late he realizes he's a pawn in a ruthless game—and that he's jeopardized the life of the woman he loves. From the author of *Toy Soldiers,* a page turner from the opening sentence. / Page 183

BLAZE
by Robert Somerlott

Cappy Holland breeds and trains German shepherds on his ranch in the rugged mountains of New Mexico. Now he's facing his biggest training challenge ever: Blaze, a handsome young shepherd whom abusive owners have turned into an aggressive fighter. And just as Cappy begins to think he might have met his match in Blaze, an even tougher assignment comes his way: his ten-year-old grandson, who flatly refuses to return to his adoptive parents. Reluctantly, Cappy provides a new home for the boy and the dog…with results that are not at all what he expects. / Page 349

DEAD FIX
by Michael Geller

Jockey Ken Eagle has fought his way to top ranking in the ruthless world of thoroughbred racing. Tricia Martin is just breaking into those ranks and the struggle has left her bitter. But gradually Ken comes to see what is beneath her hard shell and when Tricia is badly injured in a fall from a horse that *had* to have been doped, he is devastated. So devastated, in fact, that after the owner of the horse is found murdered, Ken becomes the prime suspect. An action-packed mystery alive with the sights and sounds of the racetrack. / Page 445

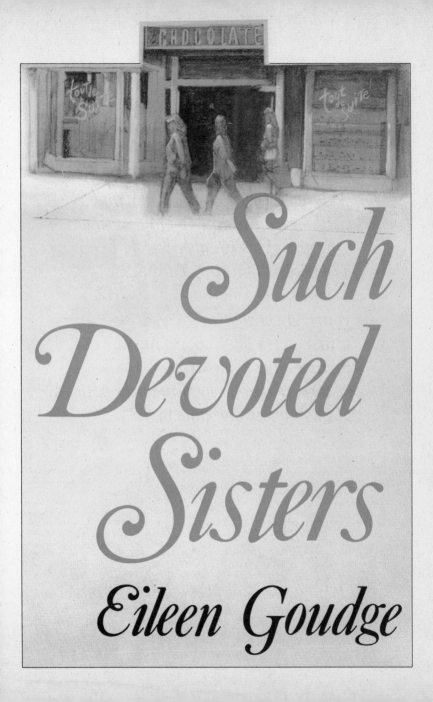

Such Devoted Sisters

Eileen Goudge

*T*rust and unfailing loyalty—
that's what being sisters meant to
Annie and Laurel. Runaways from
a troubled home in California,
they're on their own in New York
City—each the other's only family.
One struggles to carve out a life
as a book illustrator. The other
becomes a chocolatier—a creator of
gourmet chocolates—and is swept
into a world of glamour and high
finance. But what happens to the
sisters' trust and loyalty when both
of them want the same man?

Prologue
California: 1954

DOLLY Drake got off the bus at Sunset and Vine. In the heat-shimmery air the sidewalk seemed to heave as she stepped down onto it in an almost seesawing motion, as if she were standing on the deck of a ship at sea. Her stomach pitched and her head throbbed. Before her the great curved flank of the NBC building reflected the sun back at her in a blast of white light that struck her eyes like hot needles.

Must be coming down with something, she thought. A touch of flu . . . or maybe the curse.

But no, she wasn't sick, she realized with a pang. This was no flu bug. It was a whole lot worse. She felt sick in her soul.

Dolly thought of the letter in her purse. Looking down at the shiny patent leather bag looped over her arm, she saw the letter as clearly as if she'd had Superman's X-ray vision—the long white business envelope folded in half, then again for good measure.

Inside was a single mimeographed sheet, minutes of a meeting of the Common Man Society. The date at the top was June 16, 1944. Ten years ago.

So what? she thought. A fellow-traveler club that broke up years ago, with a bunch of members nobody ever heard of. Except for one. A faded but still legible scrawl on the bottom line. A name almost as familiar to millions of good Americans as their own. A name Senator Joe McCarthy, back in Washington, D.C., would surely want to pounce on. The bottom lines read "Respectfully submitted, Eveline Dearfield, Recording Secretary."

9

But that, of course, was long before Eveline got shortened to Eve, before she won an Oscar and married hotshot director Dewey Cobb. Before she stopped giving two hoots about her sister, Dolly.

Dolly sucked her breath in, a lungful of air that tasted like melting tar. She thought of the air-conditioned Cadillac that Eve rode around in these days—white as a virgin bride, with cherry-red seats and a roof that folded down. Dolly imagined what it would feel like to be in that Caddy now, gliding up Sunset Boulevard with her hair blowing in the warm breeze. People rubbernecking to gape in admiration and envy, and wonder to themselves, Who is she? Somebody famous, I bet.

A car horn blared, and the image was bumped rudely away. Then a group of would-be actresses—too young and blond and doe-eyed to be anything else—jostled Dolly as they walked past, gossiping in low tones. One of them wore a pair of silk stockings that were slightly mismatched—the result of careful scrimping, no doubt. Dolly smiled grimly and thought of the can of Campbell's chicken noodle that awaited her back at her Westwood bungalow. Mixed with two cans of water instead of one, along with a dollop of ketchup and a handful of saltines, a can of soup filled you up right fine. Well, almost. And maybe she'd even treat herself to a Hershey bar for dessert. Chocolate was the one thing that almost always lifted her spirits.

But right now the thought of food was making her stomach knot up. Give Eve the slap in the face she deserved? Could she? But how could she deliberately hurt—maybe ruin—her own little sister?

In her mind, traveling back through the dusty miles and years to Clemscott, Kentucky, Dolly could still hear Preacher Daggett thundering from the pulpit in his syrupy drawl, *"Put on the armor of God, that ye may stand against the devil."*

Yeah, right, Dolly thought. And who was standing up for me while little Evie was out snatching up every decent role I went after? And my guy, too. A town full of men, and she had to get her hooks into mine.

Tears started in the back of her throat. Hard tears that burned like acid. She gave the corner of each eye a swipe with the heel of her hand and sniffed deeply. Damned if she'd get caught bawling in public, showing up at Syd's with her eyes all red and puffy. If Mama-Jo had taught her one thing in this life, it was to keep your dirty linen in your own hamper.

Dolly crossed the street and headed north, up Vine. The hot air seemed to drag at her, as if she were plowing her way through something solid and viscous. She stepped up her pace; Syd got mad when she was late. Then she thought, To hell with Syd. That's what I pay him for. Except, when you got right down to it, an agent's ten percent of nothing was . . . well, nothing. Her last picture, *Dames at Large*, hadn't even gone into general release.

That's the ticket, all right. Dolly Drake winds up with zero, while little Evie has handprints in the sidewalk outside Grauman's.

And now Val, too.

Dolly reached the Century Plaza Hotel, its windows turned to mirrors by the sun. Briefly she saw herself reflected: a pretty woman in her late twenties—she'd be thirty next May—bottle-blond hair unraveling from the combs that held it up in back. A bit on the plump side, maybe, wearing a flowery pink rayon dress—her best.

She thought again of the envelope in her purse and felt her stomach turn. She'd received it in yesterday's mail, along with a note from Syd: "Call me." First time she'd ever heard from him through the mail. His whole life was on the phone. But this was different. Syd had a real axe of his own to grind. Six years ago Eve dumped him—and not only as her agent—a week before they were to be married. Syd had gone on a bender for two weeks, not seeing anyone, not even answering his phone, which for him was like cutting out his tongue. Since then, there had been a new, sour edge to him.

Dolly knew that the last thing Eve wanted was to overthrow the U.S. government. Probably some assistant producer had taken her to the meeting on a date and then asked her to take some notes. By the next day she must have forgotten all about it. Otherwise, wouldn't she have at least mentioned it to Dolly?

But now anybody who had been the slightest shade of pink—or who was just plain accused of it—was getting fired and blacklisted. No work anywhere in town. Like a silent death.

And if she went along with this, one of those poor blotted-out souls could be Eve.

Dolly felt a flash of hot bitterness. *Serve her right, wouldn't it just? Show her what it's like down on the dirty pavement with the rest of us. And then what would Val Carrera think of her?*

All night Dolly had wrestled over what to do, and now she knew why. She hadn't wanted to face the truth, but there it was. *Did Eve think twice before sticking a knife in my back?*

Dolly, her mouth set in a grim line, turned west onto Hollywood Boulevard and into the cool marble lobby of the office building on the corner. Well, she wouldn't definitely make up her mind until she talked it over with Syd. When she called him yesterday, he'd said he had something to tell her, something really big. But what could be bigger than this?

"IT'D be like . . . murder," Dolly said.

Seated on the low Scandinavian couch opposite Syd's kidney-shaped desk, she fingered the envelope she had taken from her purse, regarding it the way she would a nasty little dog that's quite capable of nipping you. Here, for some reason, it seemed more real . . . and more unthinkable . . . than it had on the way over.

Dolly stared at Syd. The kind of handsome Mama-Jo would've called slick as snake oil. Right now, with his feet propped on the desk, his brown eyes boring into her, Dolly felt as if she were staring down the twin barrels of Daddy's 12-gauge Winchester. Syd's eyes, set alongside a jutting Roman nose, seemed almost gleeful.

"Why me?" Dolly pressed. "Why send that thing to *me* when you could've been the big patriot and presented it personally to Senator McCarthy . . . if you hate Eve that bad?"

"You got it all wrong. This is business—*your* business—nothing personal on my end," he said evenly, betrayed only by a cold flicker of his eyes. "Now you're ready to talk, am I right? Are we having a conversation here?"

She leaned forward, trembling a little, hating him for knowing her heart the way a local boy knows the hidden back roads of his hometown. And for giving her a choice she never should've had.

"Okay, but don't you forget she's my *sister.*" Dolly thought of her niece, too—Eve's little Annie. Both of them her flesh and blood.

"First hear me out," he said, his tone reasonable, even soothing. "Then you make up your own mind." He waited until she'd settled back against the spongy sofa. "That's better. Dolly, sweetheart, you know what's wrong with you? You're nice. And in this business, nice is just another word for stupid. Nice and 'a nickel will buy you a phone call. What it *won't* get you is the lead in *Devil May Care.*"

There was a lapse before Dolly made the connection. Then it hit

12

her like a double bourbon straight up. Maggie Dumont, the part every star in town was angling for. But Eve had it sewed up.

"Even if Eve got knocked out of the running, what makes you think the director would consider me?" she demanded.

"*Think*, Dolly, sweetie. *Devil* is Preminger's picture, and he'd turn handstands for Eve Dearfield. He's crazy about her. If he can't have Eve, what's the next best thing?"

Could that be true? Dolly wondered. No question, she and Eve did look alike. Only sixteen months apart, practically twins, except that Eve was beautiful, and she was . . . well, okay, pretty. Eve's hair was naturally blond, almost platinum. Dolly's, under its dye job, was just plain dishwater. And where Eve's eyes were a deep, startling indigo, hers were the washed-out blue of faded denim.

No, she thought. No way would Preminger cast a B-movie look-alike when he could have the real thing. But if Eve was out of the way . . .

She thought of Val, surprised by the keenness of the ache she felt. It had happened almost a year ago, and she hadn't known him more than a few weeks to begin with—certainly not long enough to go around moaning about a broken heart.

It was Eve who had hurt her, she realized. Not Val.

Syd hunched forward, palms flat against the desk top.

"Dolly, sweetie, you still don't get it, do you?" He spoke softly, but each word hit her like an icy drop. "What Eve has that you don't is fangs. She'd *kill* to get a part, any part. You, Dolly, you're too soft." He paused, waiting for her to absorb all this. "Show me how much you want this, baby. Show me you'd do *anything*, and you'll be halfway there. Then"—he smiled—"if something should happen to Eve, like she just happens to get blacklisted . . . Well, what do you think Preminger's gonna say when you walk into his office looking damn near enough like Eve to be her twin?"

Dolly only half heard him. Her mind suddenly was elsewhere. Clear as a Technicolor movie, she was seeing two bleary-eyed girls stepping off a Greyhound bus—Doris and Evie Burdock, come all the way to Hollywood from Clemscott, Kentucky—lugging a single battered suitcase between them, giggling, punch-drunk with exhaustion and high spirits. She could hear Eve's voice ringing across the years: "*It's just you and me from now on, Dorrie. We'll always have each other. . . . Nothing will ever come between us.*"

Dolly squeezed her eyes shut, a pulse throbbing over one eye. When she opened them, she saw that Syd was eyeing her with something close to sympathy. She stood up, the envelope fluttering from her lap onto the carpet.

"I'll think about it," she said.

"You think too much. Anyway, it doesn't have to be the end of the world, you know," he urged, lazily unfolding his lanky frame from the swivel chair, clasping her hand in a moist handshake that made her itch to wipe her palm on her skirt. "This whole McCarthy scare'll probably blow over in a month or two. She might lose out on a few pictures, but knowing Eve, she'll be back on her feet before you can say, 'That's a wrap.' "

Not until she was outside and halfway to Sunset did Dolly realize she was still clutching the letter. She thought about tearing it up and tossing it in a trash can. But she didn't see one, so she shoved it back into her purse and kept walking.

"Aunt Dolly, how did that crack get there?" Annie sat on a high stool in the kitchen of Dolly's Westwood bungalow, swinging her little feet back and forth between its rust-speckled chrome legs.

Dolly, stirring a saucepan at the stove, looked over at her niece, then up at where Annie was pointing, at a plastered-over crack that bisected the ceiling.

"That? Why, honey, that's what you call history. This old place is a map of every earthquake to hit Los Angeles County since the walls of Jericho came tumbling down."

With her eyes glued to the ceiling, Annie wore a look of pinched concern on her face. "Is it gonna fall down on us?"

Dolly went over and hugged her with a little laugh. "Course it's not gonna fall down. It's stayed put this long."

Looking at Annie now, Dolly saw a grown-up in a child's body—a somber little lady with her mother's indigo eyes and her father's dark, straight hair. *Poor thing, she's had enough fall down on her head to know to duck. Her father's getting killed in that plane crash last year and Eve's taking off for Mexico to film* Bandido *before the flowers on Dewey's grave had hardly wilted.* Annie had been raised mostly by nannies—six, or was it seven? Dolly had lost count. The last one eloped just two days ago. Eve had phoned Dolly in a panic. Would she baby-sit tonight? Unless she needed something, Eve hardly ever called her anymore.

Dolly had been on the point of saying no, but then she thought of Annie alone in that big house in Bel Air with some strange baby-sitter, and she relented. She adored Annie, and it just clean broke her heart to think of the loneliness the kid had to put up with.

"When's Dearie coming back?" Annie wanted to know. That funny nickname—Dearie—never Mama or Mommy.

"She didn't say, hon."

"Where did she go?"

"A party, she said. A big star like your mama has to go to a lot of parties. It's like . . . well, sort of like part of the job."

"Is Val part of the job, too?" Annie stopped swinging her legs and stared at Dolly with enormous ink-blue eyes.

Dolly's heart caught in her throat. "Not exactly," she ventured.

"I don't like Val." Annie's face became very tight.

"Oh, sugar, Val doesn't mean no harm. He's just not your daddy," Dolly soothed, hoping to jolly her out of it. She sighed. "Come on now. Help me set the table. Soup's on."

Later, when they'd eaten and the dishes were washed, she tucked Annie into bed in the tiny bedroom and made up the sleep sofa in the living room for herself. Who knew when Eve would roll in—maybe not until morning.

Dolly changed into an old silk kimono and curled up in the sagging club chair by the half-open front window, hoping to catch a breeze as evening cooled into night. Suddenly she felt so heavy and tired. Minutes later she was asleep.

The slamming of a car door woke her. Swimming up through gritty layers of sleep, she squinted at the glowing face of the clock atop the battered footlocker that served as a coffee table. Five after six. Her neck felt cramped from being scrunched against the backrest, and her legs tingled as she stretched them.

Pushing aside the frayed curtain, she peered out the window. Eve had arrived. She was weaving her way up the pathway with the elaborate caution of someone who's drunk too much. In the milky predawn light her strapless, blue satin evening dress appeared almost liquid, and her platinum hair gleamed like polished silver. Reaching the front door of Dolly's bungalow, she swayed against the peeling doorframe, leaning a pale shoulder against it for support.

"You'll never guess. Never, never, never," she burbled excitedly.

Her breath smelled sweet and somewhat effervescent, like orchids and Champagne. Shadowed by the narrow porch overhang, her eyes were huge dark puddles. "I got married!"

"What?"

"It was Val's idea. At the Preminger party he just got the notion, and I said, 'Well, why not?' and we both jumped in the car."

Dolly just stood there, stunned, listening to the crazed ticking of a moth beating itself to death against the dim yellow porch light, her face burning in the cool night air as if she'd been slapped.

Eve wiggled her hand in front of Dolly, and Dolly saw that the finger that had once worn Dewey Cobb's antique gold band now sported a glittering pear-shaped diamond.

At the curb, the horn of Eve's white Cadillac honked impatiently. Then Val stuck his head out the driver's side and called, "Come on, baby. You gotta be at the studio in two hours."

Dolly thought of the first time she'd seen Val. She'd been making her way across the RKO lot to the soundstage where they were filming *Dames at Large*. Crossing a western street, she'd looked up just as a tall man in cowhide chaps leaped off the roof of a false-front saloon. While Dolly watched, her hands clutching her breast, the stuntman landed precisely in the center of a hay-filled cart.

Val Carrera was the most beautiful man she'd ever laid eyes on. When he made his way toward her and asked if she'd join him for a cup of coffee, she didn't hesitate for a second.

After coffee, and then later that day, after drinks and dinner, they'd gone back to his apartment in Burbank. And stayed there for an entire weekend. Dolly didn't know for sure if this was love, but it sure felt like *something*. Val must have thought so, too, because he was with her nearly every day for a month, and the whole time, he could never keep his hands off her.

Until he met Eve.

Dolly, watching her sister yawn and stretch languidly like a Siamese cat that's just finished off a bowl of cream, felt an odd weakness spread through her limbs. Speechless, trembling, she stared, unable to move. *Does she think I have no feelings? That her happiness counts more than mine?* Maybe that was it. Maybe Dolly was supposed to feel sorry for Eve and step aside gracefully because, poor kid, she'd lost Dewey . . . or maybe simply because she was Eve Dearfield—a star, *somebody*.

The memory of the night she'd walked in on them at Val's apartment came crashing back—Dolly screaming at Eve, telling her she was a rotten, selfish bitch; Eve weeping and saying how sorry she was. And somehow, despite her rage and hurt, Dolly had ended up forgiving and even consoling her sister.

Now it all flooded through her again—all the pain and bitterness and resentment. Eve hadn't really cared one bit about her feelings, not then and certainly not now.

"We drove straight through, Vegas and back." Eve flung her arms about Dolly's neck. "Be happy for me, Dorrie. Please be happy for me." When she pulled away, Dolly saw that her cheeks were wet and her eyes were shiny. "Is Annie awake? I can't wait to tell her!"

"It's six in the morning," Dolly replied dully.

"I'll get her." Eve darted past her and returned a minute later, holding the sleepy-eyed little girl by the hand.

Dolly watched them walk side by side down the path, amid the sprinklers' stuttering spray, a gleaming blue blade of a woman and a stalwart little girl dressed in a cotton nightie and clunky orthopedic shoes, clutching her clothes in a bundle under one arm. Dolly felt her heart rip open, letting in a searing-hot pain.

Then Eve half turned, switching on her brightest smile—the one she reserved mostly for reporters and fans.

"Oh, did I mention . . . Preminger's promised me Maggie in *Devil May Care*. But there's a small part he hasn't cast yet: Maggie's kid sister. I told him you'd be perfect for it. Tell Syd to give him a call."

Dolly felt her last thread of loyalty give way.

She waited until the Cadillac's taillights disappeared into the gloom; then, moving like a sleepwalker, she went into her tiny bedroom, still fragrant with Annie's sweet baby smell, and rummaged in her dresser until she found an envelope. She addressed and stamped it, and carried it back into the living room, where she retrieved the mimeographed sheet folded inside her purse.

Still in her kimono and slippers, clutching the sealed letter, Dolly walked to the mailbox on the corner and slipped it inside.

The envelope was addressed to Senator Joseph McCarthy, Capitol Hill, Washington, D.C.

It wasn't until the box clanged shut that Dolly came to her senses as suddenly as if she'd been slapped. She sagged against its cool metal side, all the blood in her body seeming to drain right down into the soles of her slippers.

"What have I done?" she cried in a strangled whisper. "What have I done?"

PART ONE: 1966
Chapter One

A NNIE lay in bed staring at the dragon on her wall.

It wasn't a real dragon, only the shadow of one. Each of the tall posts on her Chinese bed was carved in the shape of a dragon, its tail starting at the mattress and ending at the top in a great snarling head with a forked tongue. She remembered when her mother had sent her the bed, for her fifth birthday, all the way from Hong Kong, where Dearie had been filming *Slow Boat to China*. The moment Annie saw it, she loved it. Dragons weren't afraid of anyone or anything . . . and that's how she wanted to be.

But right now Annie didn't feel quite so brave. She felt small and scared—closer to seven than seventeen.

Lying very still, she listened. All she could hear was the rapid thumping of her heart, then the usual creaks of Bel Jardin settling into itself. Now it came to her—the sound that a moment ago she had hoped she was only imagining: the low growl of Val's Alfa Romeo as it sped up Chantilly Drive and rumbled up the crushed-shell driveway.

Earlier tonight, when she was getting ready for bed, she'd heard her stepfather go out and had felt light-headed with relief. She'd prayed he would stay out a long time, maybe all night. But now he was back. A cold fist of dread squeezed her stomach.

She sat up in bed holding her pillow scrunched against her chest, nibbling on a thumbnail that was already bitten down to the quick. She'd always felt so safe here in this room, and now somehow it was more like a cage—or a baby's barred playpen—a little girl's room full of things she'd long ago outgrown. Had Dearie stopped noticing she'd grown up, or was it just that when her mother drank, she didn't care?

Annie stared at the pale blue bookcase filled with all her favorite childhood books. Nancy Drew would've figured out what to do, she thought. If Val tried to mess with her, she'd climb into her roadster and roar off into the night.

Except Nancy Drew didn't have an eleven-year-old sister. A sister Annie had done everything for since she was in diapers, and whom Annie loved more than anything. The thought of leaving Laurel here alone with Val made her stomach ache even more.

To calm herself, she went over the plan she had been mapping out in her head. Next time Val went out on a date or a job interview, she would pack two suitcases—one for her and one for Laurel. Then the two of them would run away. But where? The only relative Annie had ever heard of—besides Uncle Rudy, who was Val's brother and, moreover, an even slimier creep—was Aunt Dolly, whom she hadn't seen or spoken to in ten or twelve years. Annie had a hazy memory of being at a sunny beach with a smiling lady with lemon-colored hair who was helping her dig a hole to China.

Aunt Dolly.

What had become of her? Long, long ago Annie remembered overhearing Dearie tell Val that her sister, Doris, had gotten herself a rich husband and moved to New York and good riddance. But was Aunt Dolly still in New York? Would she want to see her nieces? Probably not. For Dearie to have been so mad at her, there had to have been a good reason.

And even if they had a place to go, what about Val? Sure, he wouldn't chase after her if she took off—they'd never gotten along. But Laurel was his flesh and blood. Not that he'd ever paid her much attention. She was like a toy to him. Weeks went by when he hardly noticed her; then, suddenly, he'd scoop her onto his lap and tickle her until she cried, or feed her ice cream until she was sick. Still, he was her legal father. Annie's running away was one thing, but if she took Laurel, Annie knew Val would call it kidnapping.

Val might even try to have her arrested and thrown in jail. Annie felt her heart lurch in panic at the thought.

But what else could she do? In Spanish, Bel Jardin meant "beautiful garden," and she loved this great old house, with its Spanish-tiled roof and pale yellow stucco walls festooned in bougainvillea. It made her ache to think of leaving and not being able to start college next week, as she'd planned. She'd been accepted at Stanford but had turned it down in favor of U.C.L.A. so she could stay close to Laurel. But to live here with Val? She'd rather die.

She remembered last night—Val's following her upstairs and sitting on her bed, saying he wanted to talk—and hugged herself tighter, shivering. She had gotten the creeps just looking at him.

"Look," he'd launched right in, "I'm not gonna beat around the bush. You're not a kid anymore." His large hand shot out and closed over her wrist; then to her horror he drew her onto the bed beside him. "The thing is, we're broke."

Annie, shocked, had sat frozen. "You *spent* everything we had?"

His eyes had slid away from hers. "It wasn't like that. It didn't happen overnight. And it wasn't like we had money coming in. Your mother— She hadn't made a picture in twelve years. And when the school folded . . . You know how it is."

Val, who had a black belt, had started a karate school a couple of years before, but like everything he did—being a real estate broker and then a foreign car salesman—he'd screwed it up somehow.

"What's going to happen?" Annie had made herself ask. She hated feeling so powerless, having to depend on him for things. If only she was old enough to be in charge!

He'd shrugged. "Sell the house, I guess. Rudy says we should be able to get a pretty good price for it, but we owe a lot, too, so there won't be much left over."

Val's brother, Rudy, was a couple of years older than Val, short and ugly but a lot smarter—a hotshot divorce lawyer. Val wouldn't make a move without asking his brother's advice, but Dearie had never liked or trusted Rudy, and thank goodness she'd been savvy enough to let someone else handle the trust money she'd set aside for Annie and Laurel—twenty-five thousand each. The only bad thing was, Annie couldn't touch hers until her twenty-fifth birthday. Right now that seemed eons away.

"We can look for something smaller," Val had said. "Something closer to downtown . . . where you can catch a bus to work."

"I'll be in school." Annie was struggling to keep her voice even. "I thought I'd pick up a part-time job on campus."

"Yeah, well, here's the thing. Rudy can set you up with something in his law office. Full time. You can type, can't you?"

Suddenly she understood. Now that he'd run through all their money, he wanted *her* to take Dearie's place. She would go to work, forget about college, support all three of them. And he was so obvious about it! She wanted to hit him, smash her fists into his smug face. But she could only sit there, trembling, speechless.

Val, mistaking her helpless rage for sorrow, had put his arms around her, patting her clumsily. "I miss her, too," he murmured.

She tried to pull away, but he only squeezed tighter. Now the embrace became something more. He was stroking the small of her back, her hip. His rough cheek pressed against hers, his breath warm and quick against her ear.

She felt sick.

Steeling herself, Annie had given him a hard push and jumped to her feet. "I have to brush my teeth," she'd said. Then she rushed into the bathroom and locked the door. She ran a bath and stayed in it for an hour. When she got back to her room, Val had gone.

Today, all day, she had managed to avoid him. But now he was back, and if he felt like coming into her room again, there was no lock on the door to stop him.

Annie heard the front door slam downstairs, then the soft clacking of shoes against the tiled foyer. She could hear him climbing the stairs now, his footsteps heavy, measured, but muffled by the Oriental runner. Just beyond her door he slowed . . . then stopped. Her heart was pounding so hard, she was sure he would hear it.

Then after what seemed to her like an eternity, she heard him move on. Annie let her breath out in a dizzying rush. She felt flushed and weak, as if she had a fever. A swim, that's what she needed. And the pool would be perfect—cool and still.

Annie waited until she was absolutely certain Val had gone to bed. Then in her nightgown she tiptoed out into the hallway.

Reaching the half-open door to Laurel's room, Annie paused, then slipped inside. Looking at her sister asleep on her back, her small hands folded neatly across the blanket that covered her, Annie thought of the print her art teacher had shown in class last year. A famous painting of drowned Ophelia floating face up in the water, her long golden hair drifting like seaweed about her still, white face. Annie's heart caught in her throat, and before she could stop herself, she was listening for Laurel's breathing.

There it was, but so soft it could have been a breeze blowing through the open window. Annie relaxed a little. *Don't worry, Laurey. I'll take care of you.*

That time when Laurel had scarlet fever, when she was two, came back to her in a hot rush. That morning when she'd looked into her baby sister's crib and found Laurel gasping for air, her face purple, her tiny arms thrashing. Annie, only eight and scared out of her mind, had snatched Laurel up and had run through the house screaming for Dearie. She could feel Laurel's frail chest hitching desperately. Despite how little Laurel was, she was still too heavy for Annie and kept slithering from her grasp.

She had finally found Dearie passed out on the living-room sofa, an empty brandy bottle on the coffee table in front of her, exhausted from being up all night with Laurel. Annie, sobbing, more scared than she'd ever been, had hit her, pushed her, shouted in her ear, trying to make her wake up. But Dearie wouldn't budge. There was no one else; it was the maid's day off, and Val was gone. Annie, terrified, had thought, I'm just a kid. I can't do this. I can't save Laurey.

Then a voice inside her head commanded, Think.

She remembered a long time ago, when she herself had had a bad cough and stuffy chest, and Dearie had put her in a steamy bathtub, and how it had made her breathe easier.

Annie had lugged Laurel into Dearie's bathroom and cranked on the tub's hot-water tap. Then, sitting on the toilet with Laurel face down across her knees, she began to pound on her back, praying that whatever was choking her would somehow pop out.

Nothing so dramatic happened, but as steam billowed and stuck Laurel's hair to her scalp in wet clumps, her breath gradually returned and the awful purple color faded.

Then with a tremendous whoop Laurel began to cry. She was going to be all right. Annie's face felt wet—from the steam, she thought. Then she realized she was crying.

And she realized something else—that she was Laurel's real mother, that God had meant for her to look after and protect her sister always.

Annie now pushed her fingers through her hair, still a little shocked by its shortness. She'd hacked it off only last week with Dearie's sewing scissors. For some reason it had made her feel better, seeing all that dark hair clumped at her feet . . . as if she were shedding an old skin and making way for a new Annie—strong, shining, brave.

Downstairs, in the sun-room that opened onto the patio, the moon shone through the palmettos in their huge terra-cotta tubs by the French doors. Stepping outside, Annie could see the pool gleaming darkly, its glassy surface twinkling with sparks of orange light reflected by the electric tiki torches.

She peeled off her nightgown and dived in.

The cool water slicing along her naked body felt wonderful. She stayed under for half a length before she broke the surface, gulping in the night air, fragrant with the scent of honeysuckle and the faint smokiness of a brushfire burning way off in the canyons. She could hear the rustling of the hibiscus hedge surrounding the patio. She had to do something . . . and soon. Or she'd stay stuck with Val, cramped in a tiny house with no place to hide, and roped to a desk typing stupid letters for that troll Rudy.

She remembered, too, how Rudy always seemed to be staring at Laurel, his bulgy eyes fixed on her like a toad's on an iridescent-winged dragonfly. Seldom approaching her, but those eyes—always there, watching. A shiver coursed through Annie. What did Rudy want from Laurel? The same thing Annie suspected Val wanted from *her?*

No, that was too gross, too unthinkable. They just had to get out.

In her mind Annie heard her mother drawl, *"The good Lord is fine for praying, kiddo, but when the going gets rough, you'd best be off your knees and on your feet."*

Annie now felt angry. Oh, yeah? she thought. Then how come you killed yourself?

She pushed off against the slippery tiles with her feet and began furiously stroking her way across the pool. Gradually she felt her anger dissolve into sorrow. If only Dearie had talked to her before she took those pills. Now as Annie climbed out of the pool and pulled on her nightgown—why hadn't she thought to bring a towel?—it hit her like a slap that she really *was* on her own.

Shivering and dripping her way across the sun-room, Annie caught a sudden flicker of movement out of the corner of her eye. She froze, and looked up. Val was standing framed in the archway leading from the living room. For an instant she thought she might pass out. There was no sound other than the soft ticking of water as it dripped from her wet hair onto the tiled floor.

Moving with oiled grace, he glided across to where she stood. He was wearing a pair of navy satin pajamas. In the orange glow of the electric tiki torches filtering in through the wide French doors, his tanned face, striped with shadows, reminded her of a tiger's.

"You oughta put something on," he said. "You'll catch cold."

"I was just going in." She began walking quickly toward the archway. *God, let him leave me alone.* She felt his eyes on her and realized that with her wet nightgown clinging to her, she might as well be naked. She felt herself grow hot with embarrassment.

In the cavernous living room, Annie was crossing the rug in front of the fireplace when she felt Val's hand on her wet shoulder. She spun away, banging her knee against a massive carved chair.

Then she saw that he was only offering her his pajama top, which he'd slipped off when her back was turned. She felt flustered, not knowing how to react. Why didn't he just leave her alone?

She tried to step past, but he caught her roughly. Holding her pressed against him, he stroked the back of her head. "Give me a break, kid. It hasn't been easy for me, either." On his breath she caught an all-too-familiar whiff of booze.

Anger took hold of her, and she tore away, hissing, "It's all your fault! You never loved her! You only married her because she was famous and rich. And then when she . . . she couldn't work anymore, you treated her like she wasn't even there."

"She was a drunk," he snarled, "way before I met her. You know the saying: Once a drunk, always a drunk."

Over Val's shoulder, on the fireplace mantel, light winked off a shiny metal surface—Dearie's Oscar, the Best Actress Award she'd won for *Storm Alley.* Annie remembered how proud she'd felt staying up late to watch her mother on TV, seeing Dearie floating up onto the stage, hoisting the glowing statuette in triumph.

Tears pricked at Annie's eyes, but she bit them back. She wouldn't cry in front of Val. "If my mother drank, it was your fault."

"You little bitch." Val grabbed her, his fingers digging into her upper arms. "You never even gave me a chance. Spoiled brat with your nose in the air. You had it in for me since day one."

His eyes glittered in the darkness—black prisms reflecting a whole spectrum of ancient hurts.

Annie felt shaken. She'd never seen Val this mad. "I'm going up now," she said, shivering. "I'm really cold."

His lips stretching in a cold grin, Val leaned down for his pajama top and tossed it at her. "Put it on." It wasn't an offer.

Annie dropped the bundle of cloth as if it were a snake.

With a low moan Val fell on her.

At first she thought he was going to hit her. It *felt* as if he *had* hit her—a bruising blow to her mouth. Then she realized what it was. He was kissing her.

She tried to scream, to pull away, but he held her tight. *This isn't happening. God, please make this not be happening.*

"I wanted you to like me," he said in a little boy's petulant voice. "I tried, but you . . . you wouldn't let me."

Annie, terrified, struggled to free herself. "Please let me go." She thought of something else. "Laurey might wake up."

"Do you think *I* wanted it to end like this?" he went on as if he hadn't heard. "You don't know what it was like for me."

"Val," Annie pleaded, truly scared.

With one arm he held her tight, while with the other he began touching her. Annie felt as if she were dying.

Summoning all her strength, she somehow managed to rip herself free of him. Ducking past Val, she felt strangely light, her arms seeming to stretch on forever, until finally her fingers closed about something cold and hard—Dearie's Oscar. Blindly Annie swung the heavy statuette like a club. Out of the corner of her eye she saw Val feint to one side as she connected. The impact slammed through her arm like an electric jolt, and she felt as shocked as Val looked.

Blood streamed from a cut over his right eyebrow. He froze, his face the color of cottage cheese. "Oh," he said in soft surprise. He sank down abruptly on the wide leather sofa. A moment later he toppled onto his side and grew still. Frighteningly still.

I've killed him, Annie thought.

Terror was waiting for her somewhere in the back of her mind. But right now she felt numb. Staring down at Val's bloody, sprawled form, she thought calmly, sensibly, I won't pack much. A change of clothes, underwear, toothbrush. And Dearie's jewelry.

Packing was easy. It was waking Laurel that was the hard part. She slept like the dead. And when Annie finally got her up, Laurel wore a glassy look, as if she wasn't quite awake.

"I have to go away," Annie told her. "I won't be coming back. Do you want to come with me?"

The glassy expression was gone; Laurel's face crumpled in dismay. "Where are we going?"

Annie was encouraged by the "we."

She tried to think, but couldn't come up with an answer. "On a bus" was the best she could do. "You'd better hurry and get dressed before . . . before he wakes up."

Then because Laurel looked so worried and scared, Annie hugged her. "It's going to be all right," she said. "In fact, it'll be fun. A real adventure."

Laurel gave her a long look that seemed burdened with far more than any eleven-year-old should have to carry. "It's because of . . . of Val, isn't it?" she whispered. "Something he did?" Not Daddy or Dad; since she could talk, she'd called him Val.

Annie nodded, her throat suddenly tight.

"Annie," Laurel whispered sheepishly as they were leaving, "can I take Boo?" Boo was her old baby blanket, nubby and tattered from a thousand washings. She didn't like to admit she still slept with it, but Annie knew how much Boo meant.

"Course," she said.

At the front door Annie paused, remembering another keepsake: Dearie's Oscar. She was scared of going back in there, but couldn't bear the thought of leaving it behind.

"Wait here," she whispered.

Her heart slamming against her ribs, Annie slipped back into the living room and snatched up the Oscar from the rug where she'd dropped it, quickly averting her eyes from the still form on the couch. Reaching Laurel's side, she saw a horrified look on her sister's face. Annie looked down at the statuette and saw the blood smearing its bright surface.

Then, wordlessly, Laurel took it from Annie, using her precious Boo to wipe it clean. She handed it back to Annie, who quickly stuffed it into her bulging overnight bag. Looking into Laurel's trusting eyes, she found the strength to push open the door.

Minutes later as they made their way in darkness down the long, curving drive toward the wrought-iron gates at the bottom, Annie turned for one last look at Bel Jardin. Above the palms that lined the drive, she saw the first milky light of dawn touch the top of the tiled roof, and she turned away, quickening her step.

At that moment, clutching the heavy overnight bag, Annie's courage seemed to wither. Where on earth was she going? And what was she going to do when she got there? Then, strangely, she felt an invisible hand against the small of her back giving her a gentle push. Inside her head a sweet, throaty voice drawled, *"Once*

you've made up your mind to go someplace, don't waste all your time fiddling with your shoelaces."

Annie straightened suddenly, hitching the heavy suitcase a little higher so she could walk faster. She reached for Laurel's hand. "I hope you wore socks." She spoke briskly to her sister, who trudged listlessly alongside her, hugging a tattered baby blanket smeared with her father's blood, a pale golden-haired stalk of a girl dressed in pink. "You know how you get blisters when you don't wear socks. And we have a long way to go."

Chapter Two
New York City

LAUREL pushed the sausage to one side of her plate. Maybe if she hid it under her toast, Annie wouldn't notice. She felt too sick to eat another bite, but the last thing Laurel wanted was for Annie to start in again about her being too skinny.

Anyway, look who was talking! Annie looked awful with her cheekbones sticking out and those brown smudges under her eyes. Why hadn't she ordered something besides toast? She looked hungry enough to gobble up every stale doughnut in this diner.

But no, they had to save for when they found an apartment. But when would that be? A whole two weeks in New York, and they were still stuck in that smelly dark room at the Allerton.

In the beginning the nine hundred and seventy dollars they'd gotten for Dearie's jewelry had seemed like a king's treasure, but now it was almost all gone. Everything cost so much! Annie hadn't told her they were almost broke, but Laurel had seen the worried look on her sister's face last night when she carefully counted out this week's money for Mr. Mancusi at the front desk. She saw it now, too, in the way Annie nibbled her toast, trying to make it last. Laurel wished she could be strong like Annie.

If only I was older. Then I could look for a job, too, and Annie wouldn't have to do everything herself.

But who would ever hire an eleven-year-old kid, when Annie, who looked older than seventeen, was having a hard time?

Laurel watched Annie break open another plastic container of grape jelly and begin spreading it thickly on her last wedge of toast. She felt a surge of love for her sister. At least she had Annie.

What if she was alone? The thought made her stomach dip crazily.

Annie looked up and said, "I have a feeling this is our lucky day." She sounded so cheerful and determined that Laurel believed her. Then she remembered, Annie said the same thing *every* day.

Laurel pushed her milk glass across the Formica tabletop. "Here, you finish it."

Annie frowned and pushed it back. "You need it more than I do. Anyway, I'm full."

It was a lie. Annie meant well, but Laurel wanted to shout at her sister, plead with her to please, please stop being so nice. But all she said was, "Can I see the paper?"

One thing they had to buy every day was *The New York Times*. Sunday's fat edition, with today's date at the top, October 9, lay next to Annie's plate; she hadn't looked at it yet. Did this mean she was losing hope?

Some of the apartments they'd looked at were nice but way too expensive. Or they were so awful, in neighborhoods where the sidewalks were lined with overflowing garbage cans. In one, when the super switched on the light, a whole parade of cockroaches began scurrying over the kitchen counter.

Where Laurel really wanted to be at this moment was back home at Bel Jardin. She badly missed her room, with its sunny window seat crammed with stuffed animals. In a weird way she even missed her father.

She imagined Val asleep in the bed he'd once shared with Dearie. Then the image dissolved, and all she could see in her mind was blood. Val's blood. And the darkness that had followed her and Annie all the way to Sunset, where in the yellow glow of street-lamps, she'd seen the dried blood on Boo. She remembered dropping her old blanket in the first garbage can they came to, yet feeling as if somehow *she* was the one being left behind.

If only Annie would tell her what Val had done that night to get her mad enough to hit him. Imagining Val dead, lying on the sofa in a pool of blood, she felt gripped by an icy chill.

No, she told herself, Val *couldn't* be dead.

But if he were alive, he might be out looking for them. Annie had said they had to be careful not to get caught, or Val would take Laurel away. And maybe even get Annie arrested for kidnapping.

Annie in jail? Laurel couldn't bear the thought. Nor could she imagine being separated from her sister. So she had to be very careful and not tell anyone too much about herself.

Annie was now buried in the Help Wanted section.

"Listen to this," she said. " 'Gal Friday. Hat company seeks energetic young person for busy office.' I'd be perfect for it."

"But if they give you a typing test—"

Annie cut her off, smiling forcefully. "Last time, I was nervous. The next time, I'll do better. I know I will." She looked down at Laurel's plate, and Laurel saw a worried look on her face. "You didn't finish your breakfast. Are you feeling okay?"

"I ate as much as I could. Why don't you have the rest."

Annie looked up sharply, as if she thought Laurel might just be pretending not to want it. Then hunger won out. Grabbing her fork, she gobbled up the rest of the scrambled eggs and sausage. Then with her last piece of toast she scoured the plate clean. Watching her, Laurel felt the ache in her own stomach ease.

"Will that be all?" The waitress was standing above them. Not waiting for an answer, she slapped the bill down on the table.

Annie paid, then grabbed her purse and slid off her seat. "Come on. I'll bet there'll be something in the *Village Voice*. Let's go look."

On their way out, passing the quick-serve counter, Laurel caught sight of a folded newspaper left on one of the stools. Too small to be the *Times*. Laurel snatched it up and tucked it under her arm.

Outside, pausing on the sidewalk while Annie went into the candy store to look at the *Voice*, Laurel unfolded the paper and saw that it was the *Jewish Press*. Would there be apartments in here? She turned five or six pages, and then she saw APTS. UNFURN. The very first one seemed to jump out at her.

Midwd. 1 bdrm. Top of 2-fmly hse w/grdn. Quiet neighborhood. $290. Shomer Shabbat. 252-1789.

Her heart bumped into her throat. But where was Midwood? At that price it had to be Brooklyn. It sounded perfect.

A funny name, she thought—Shomer Shabbat. But just about everyone in New York had strange names. Like the night clerk at the Allerton, Mr. Tang Bo.

There was a pay phone by the candy store's front door. She dug out a dime and dialed the number from the paper. After one ring it was picked up.

"So don't keep me waiting in suspense," a lady's voice chimed right in. "Refrigerators, I'll bet you he said, don't grow on trees."

Bewildered, Laurel stammered, "H-hello?"

There was a short silence; then the lady laughed—but a nice, jolly laugh. "You're not Faigie, are you? Who is this?"

Laurel felt like quickly hanging up, but the voice at the other end sounded so nice, she forced herself to speak.

"This is Laurel . . . uh . . . Davis." Or was it Davidson? She'd heard Annie tell so many lies she couldn't keep them straight anymore. "Your apartment," she blurted. "The one you advertised. . . . We, my sister and I, that is— It's not taken, is it?"

"How old are you, darling?"

"Twelve." She could get away with one extra year. "But my sister's twenty-one," she added quickly.

"She's got a job, then?"

"Oh, well, yeah . . . she does. In a hat company. In the office. See, we're from . . . uh . . . Arizona, and we really really need an apartment, especially one with a garden."

There was a long pause; then Mrs. Shabbat sighed and said, "To be one hundred percent honest, I don't know if you're the right tenants for me, but you sound like a nice girl. I suppose it wouldn't hurt for you to have a look. So you want to come over now?"

Laurel felt light with relief. "That would be great," she said, trying to hold her excitement in. How long would it take to go by subway to that part of Brooklyn? She took a wild guess. "How about in an hour? Will you be home then?"

"Where else? I'm in my ninth month, Laurel Davis. Only, God bless him, this baby is in no hurry to come out."

Laurel hadn't even met this Mrs. Shabbat, but she couldn't remember when she'd liked anyone so much right off the bat. Quickly, feeling hot with excitement, she got the address and directions, and rushed to find Annie.

Laurel had never felt so proud. She'd show Annie she was grown up, responsible. Everything was going to work out. She was sure of it.

LAUREL and Annie got off the subway at the Avenue J station. They hadn't walked more than two blocks when Laurel began to feel as if they didn't belong, as if they'd been whisked here by a cyclone, like Dorothy and Toto into the Land of Oz.

She couldn't help but gape at a group of boys huddled under a produce-market awning, jabbering in what sounded like a foreign language. They all wore black hats and oversized black suits, and on either side of each boy's head a long curl hung down.

Annie was peering at a street sign. "Are you sure we're in the right place?"

"East Fourteenth. That's what she told me."

They passed a bakery with a mouth-watering display of fruit tarts, and a delicatessen with salamis big as baseball bats.

"I think this is it," Annie said.

Laurel stopped and stared at where her sister was pointing: a two-story wooden house, with a little front porch and a tiny lawn surrounded by a neat hedge. She noticed a tricycle on the front walk, and up on the porch, a cozy jumble of chairs. It wasn't Bel Jardin, but it looked nice . . . and well, homey. A sign over the door read THE GRUBERMANS. Laurel's heart lifted. A real family lived here.

But wait. The name was supposed to be Shabbat, not Gruberman. Could this be the wrong house?

"Don't get your hopes up," Annie warned, but Laurel could see that she was excited herself. "They'll probably say I'm too young."

Even so, Laurel squeezed her eyes shut and prayed, Please, God, let Mrs. Shabbat take us.

Annie pulled her up the path and pressed the doorbell.

"Coming, I'm coming!" someone yelled to them from inside.

After a long minute the front door swung open. A woman stood before them. An apron was tied about her enormous belly, and a round face with crinkly brown eyes smiled at them. "Miss Davis?"

"Yes," Annie answered at once. "I'm Annie . . . and this is my sister, Laurel. She's the one who called you."

"And I'm Rivka Gruberman." She smiled at Laurel. "And you talk lovely on the phone, darling, but I've never seen such young girls as you two looking for an apartment. You understand, I can't have someone who's going to move right back to Mama."

"We don't have a mother," Annie answered quietly.

"Oh," said Rivka, nodding several times, then opening the door wider. "Well, you better look at it."

Rivka gave them a sharp glance as she ushered them into a dim vestibule smelling of cooked carrots, but said nothing more as huffing and puffing she led them up the narrow stairs.

The apartment was small: a tiny kitchen with yellow cabinets, a living room with a faded green carpet, and a bedroom not much bigger than Laurel's closet at Bel Jardin. But the place was clean, and all the walls had fresh light blue paint.

"It's a very nice apartment," Annie said firmly. "We'll take it."

Rivka eyed them carefully. "Before you make up your mind, you would like to see our *shul*, no?"

Something was wrong; Laurel could feel it.

Annie, her face reddening, echoed, "Your *shul?*"

Rivka gave them a long look and said gently, "Come, *shainenkes*, come downstairs with me. Manhattan's a long trip, and you could use some hot tea and maybe a piece of babka, yeah?"

Downstairs, the Grubermans' apartment was a madhouse. Children everywhere—older boys on the sofa, reading aloud to one another in that same foreign language Laurel'd heard on the street; two little ones with toy trucks, scooting about the cabbage-rose carpet; a baby in a playpen, banging a set of plastic keys against its bars.

"*Sha*, everyone, we've got company!" Rivka yelled as she sailed through, but no one paid any attention.

In the big, cheerful kitchen, a dark-haired, pink-cheeked girl about Annie's age was rolling out dough on the counter.

"My oldest," Rivka said, waving a hand in her direction. "My Sarah." The girl nodded shyly, and went back to her rolling pin.

This house, this woman reminded Laurel of the old woman who lived in a shoe, who had so many children she didn't know what to do. Except Mrs. Gruberman seemed so happy. And nice.

Laurel and Annie sat down at a long table. Looking around, Laurel noticed something odd. Everything was in twos: two sinks, two sets of cupboards, even two refrigerators.

"I see you looking at my refrigerators," Rivka observed. "It's because we're kosher, darling. Everything that's meat and everything that's milk we keep strictly separate."

Rivka bustled about the stove, putting the kettle on and lighting the fire under it. Then she turned to face them, hands folded over her fat belly. "So, what shall I do with the two of you? You don't even know what *Shomer Shabbat* means. Am I right?"

Laurel's heart sank.

"We're not Jewish," Annie confessed.

Rivka sighed, and then ruefully nodded. "Darlings, this I saw the second I laid eyes on you. I'm sorry. *Shomer Shabbat* means 'Sabbath observers only.' "

"We won't make one bit of noise on the Sabbath," Annie pleaded. "My sister and I, we don't have a TV, or even a radio."

Rivka shook her head while plunking mugs of steaming tea in front of them. "You seem like nice girls. Please, don't take it personal." She set out a plate of yeasty cake laden with raisins and nuts, which smelled as if it had just come out of the oven.

Laurel's mouth watered. Her eyes were watering, too. Feeling hungry and miserable, she helped herself to a big piece.

"I have money. I could pay you the deposit right this minute," Annie pressed, desperation in her voice. "Cash."

"Please," Rivka replied sorrowfully. "It's not the money."

"But . . ." Annie started to plead; then suddenly her mouth clamped shut. Laurel knew that look—it was Annie's stubborn look. "It's okay," she said briskly. "I understand."

Tears welled in Laurel's eyes. Why didn't Annie tell her that they'd looked everywhere and they were too exhausted to look anymore? Why couldn't she admit she was hungry? Laurel saw Annie eyeing the cake, but no, she was too proud to take any.

Then Laurel had an idea. "I could baby-sit for you," she said softly. "I wouldn't even charge for it."

Shaking her head pityingly, Rivka turned back to her stove, picking up where she must have left off when they'd arrived, flouring chicken drumsticks and dropping them into a hot skillet.

Annie stood up. "Thank you anyway, for showing us the place. Laurey, I think we'd better be go—"

She was interrupted by a wail from the other room. The older girl, Sarah, shot her mother a pleading look and said, "Please, Ma, I have to finish this before Rachel gets here to help me with my algebra."

"And I"—Rivka threw up her floury hands—"have four hands all of a sudden?"

Laurel, guided by instinct, rushed into the next room and scooped the crying baby from her playpen. While the boys on the sofa looked on in fascination she peeled off the baby's plastic pants. Then Laurel saw why she'd been crying—one of the diaper pins had popped open and was sticking her in the side.

She had just gotten the pin out when Rivka rushed in. She hoisted the baby onto her big belly and smiled at Laurel.

"So? You know about babies? You're just a baby yourself!"

"I know a lot about babies." Laurel lied.

"A pin was sticking Shainey!" cried a dark-haired boy. "The girl pulled it out."

Rivka covered the baby with kisses, then said, "By my husband, it's enough already I have the older girls to help out." She sighed. "But with Sarah and Chava and Leah in yeshiva all day and this new one coming any minute, I could use a little more help."

Laurel looked up into Rivka's kind face and saw an uncertainty that hadn't been there a few minutes ago. She felt a surge of hope. We'd be safe here, she thought. Safe from muggers and mean landlords and cockroaches. Safe from policemen and from Val.

"Stay," Rivka said softly. "Meet my husband, Ezra. He'll be home soon. Maybe he meets you, and then he'll change his mind."

Laurel let her breath out, feeling a rush of happy relief. And pride, too. Because she was the one who had made all this happen. She grinned at Annie, who grinned back.

Somehow Laurel felt sure it was going to be okay. For right now, at least. She didn't want to think about going to school in this weird neighborhood or whether or not Annie would find a job.

Later, if they could have the apartment, she'd ask Mrs. Gruberman about the bearded men with the round fur hats and the boys with long curls.

She could see she had lots and lots to learn.

Chapter Three

DOLLY slammed down the phone.

She felt mad enough to spit. Those customs morons at JFK had been sitting on her shipment for four whole days. And the inspectors she'd spoken to were too lazy to find out why. Damn it! What the devil did they expect her to do with two thousand dollars' worth of highly perishable chocolates going soft in some customs shed?

But that's not what's really needling you, is it? You're just using this to let off steam.

Remembering that phone call from Ned Oliver a few weeks ago telling her that Evie's girls had run away from home, Dolly felt a stitch in her gut. Ned, her old friend, had secretly kept Dolly up to date on Annie and Laurel over the years.

Those poor girls! It had to be Val's fault somehow. But why blame Val? When you got right down to it, wasn't *she* the one to blame? If it hadn't been for her knifing Eve in the back, probably none of this would ever have happened.

Dolly began to get that familiar downward-spiraling feeling, and she quickly caught herself. She had to find her nieces somehow.

Itching with impatience, she grabbed the phone and dialed the private investigator she'd hired out in L.A.

"O'Brien," he answered.

"Dolly Drake here," she told him. "You turned up anything on my nieces yet?" The other times she'd called, he'd merely told her to be patient. Why should today be any different?

"Funny you should call. I've been trying to reach you, but your phone's been busy. Look, don't get too excited, but I think I know where they are. I talked to a Greyhound driver who recognized the photos. He says they were headed for New York City. But . . ."

New York? Here! Dolly's heart lurched.

"The chances of finding a couple of runaways in such a big city, I have to tell you, could be a million to one. You're best off sitting tight. They get desperate enough, they'll call home."

No, she told O'Brien, you keep looking. But as she hung up, she felt suddenly leaden. She could not count on O'Brien. One way or another, she would have to find them.

Get busy, she told herself, and maybe an idea will come to you.

In the tiny office above her shop, Dolly squeezed out from behind her desk and walked over to the refrigerated case containing her overstock. Fifty-eight degrees. Not enough to cause condensation, but exactly the right temperature to keep her precious chocolates from melting or from turning gray with bloom. Fine chocolates, she had learned, needed to be coddled, babied. But what good were all her precautions here when her next two weeks' inventory was going stale in some shed at the airport?

Dolly felt the beginning of a headache. Then she remembered something else, something good: Henri's plane was due in at JFK around five. She should've asked him to pack an extra suitcase full of chocolates. In his shop in Paris, the original La Maison de Girod—shortened here to Girod's—they were made fresh daily.

Then it occurred to her—two birds with one stone. Why not? She'd go straight to the top, to McIntyre himself. He was the import specialist. She could personally try to sweet-talk him into releasing her shipment and then afterwards meet Henri's plane.

Her spirits rose. Wouldn't Henri be surprised, and pleased? Usually she waited for him at her apartment, with Champagne on ice and wearing nothing but black silk-chiffon.

Dolly caught her reflection in the refrigerator's glass door. Her dress was a brilliant tomato red with a navy polka-dot panel over her bosom. In her ears she wore the ruby-and-diamond earrings Dale had given her for their fifth—and last—anniversary.

Dolly believed in bright colors. She loved things that glittered and twinkled—rhinestone buttons, shiny patent leather shoes, oversized jewelry. Dale had once joked that the inside of her closet looked like Carmen Miranda's turban. The way Dolly saw it, the world was already gray enough without adding to its misery.

Dolly straightened her upswept honey-blond hair and applied a fresh coat of Fever Red to her lips. Oh, she knew how the blue-rinse dowagers in her Park Avenue building gossiped about her. *"Loud, vulgar, cheap,"* she could almost hear them whispering. *"Her late husband was some oil wildcatter. She was waiting tables when he married her. Lavished a fortune on her . . . as if it did any good. She still looks right out of a five-and-dime."* Well, what did she care? Those antique snoots, with their dreary clothes and taste-ful pearls, what could they offer her that was better than what she already had with Henri?

Henri.

Just thinking about him made her feel as if she were coming in from the cold. And it had been so long, almost three months. Oh, she couldn't wait.

But at the same time she felt uneasy. Tonight she was supposed to give him her answer. She had promised she would.

And if I say yes? If I agree to move to Paris? Dolly let herself imagine the two of them together—nights in Henri's arms, week-ends roaming the galleries on the Left Bank.

But, damn it, Henri was still married. *"You can look at a mule ten different ways, but it's never gonna be a horse,"* Mama-Jo always used to say. And well, no matter how you sliced it, she'd only be what she was now—Henri's mistress.

And what about Girod's? Dolly loved knowing each time she unlocked the iron grate at 870 Madison that the shop was hers, that it couldn't fire her or simply fade away like one more dead-end screen test. She needed Girod's—the chitchat with the customers, the figuring and ordering, the satisfaction of selling, the fun of arranging windows. And of course, all those heavenly chocolates.

Dolly thought back to when she'd first decided to open a chocolate shop. One rainy spring day, some months after Dale had died, when the thought of spending the rest of her life alone had almost sent her reeling back to bed, she'd packed a suitcase, grabbed a battered French phrase book, and escaped to Paris.

On the Rue du Faubourg St.-Honoré, she'd happened upon La Maison de Girod. Within the hour, having sweet-talked her way into a tour of the chocolatier's basement kitchen and sampled flavors that tasted too delicious to have been created on this earth, she'd learned that Monsieur Henri Baptiste was indeed eager to franchise a Girod's outlet in New York. Dolly suddenly knew exactly what she wanted to do when she returned home.

And now, after five years, her little Madison Avenue shop felt more like home than her cavernous Park Avenue apartment. Did she love Henri enough to give it up?

Stop torturing yourself. . . . You can make up your mind when you see him.

Impatient now to get to the airport, Dolly dialed her apartment and told her driver, Felipe, to get over to Girod's as soon as he could, with a bottle of Champagne on ice.

Now she had to come up with some charming way to unbend the import specialist McIntyre—not a bribe, but some kind of *incentive*. He *had* to release that shipment.

Dolly plunged into the closet-size storeroom catty-corner to the office. She'd bring McIntyre some chocolates, she decided, something really special. Her gaze scanned the stacks of flat cardboard yet to be folded into boxes embossed with Girod's gold imprint. Above, lining the shelves, were the special containers, ones she'd collected herself: antique cookie tins and art deco canisters, gaily painted Mexican boxes, baskets studded with seashells.

Gloria De Witt, her assistant, called this room Dolly's magpie's nest. And now, rummaging through her treasures, Dolly wondered what in the world would impress a seen-it-all customs agent.

Then she spotted it. Perfect—a cookie jar in the shape of an apple. She would fill it with rum caramels and Champagne truffles, and play Eve to McIntyre's Adam. It had worked in the Good Book. Why not now?

With the cookie jar tucked under her arm Dolly made her way down the world's narrowest staircase. It had to have been built with a midget in mind, she thought. Definitely not for a size fourteen on five-inch spike heels. Downstairs, Gloria was folding boxes. She looked up at Dolly, her enormous brass earrings tinkling like wind chimes.

"You manage to kick some butts at customs?"

"Better." Dolly held up the apple jar and grinned wickedly. "I'm mounting a personal attack. Death by chocolate."

"Amen to that." Gloria laughed.

Dolly was just finishing filling the cookie jar when she spotted Felipe pulling up across the avenue. She grabbed a shopping bag and threw on her coat. Dashing out into the street with barely a glance in either direction, she reached Felipe—but not before a taxi missed hitting her by a hair.

"You don' watch out, you gonna get youself killed one a these days!" her feisty Guatemalan driver scolded her affectionately as she slid into the back seat. Dolly shrugged. Henri, too, was always after her for her reckless jaywalking.

As the Lincoln inched its way along the Long Island Expressway, Dolly's thoughts returned to Annie and Laurel. Did they have any money? A place to sleep? Enough to eat?

Lord, what it must have been like for them those last years— Eve's drinking more and more out of control, then the drying-out spells, when she'd be gone for months at a time.

Hollywood had buzzed over Eve's stone-faced refusal to give McCarthy one single name and Preminger's snagging Grace Kelly in her place. Her agent, Syd, had been way off about Dolly's prospects, but what she had cared about was making Eve understand how sorry she was.

Dolly had so wanted to help her sister. And there wasn't a day when she didn't regret having sent that damn letter. But every time she called, Eve's Spanish maid would say, "Missa Dearfield no home." Eve never returned one of her calls.

Twelve years. It had taken Eve that long to die. And now, because of what Dolly had done, Eve's girls were out there somewhere, probably scared to death.

Dolly covered her face with her hands and wept. She didn't deserve anything. She didn't deserve Henri. Nor had she deserved the man she'd married—huge-hearted Dale, who had picked her up when she was waiting tables at Ciro's, lavished her with affection, and died leaving her so wonderfully well provided for.

She closed her eyes and allowed herself to imagine being reunited with her nieces. Lord knew, she couldn't replace Eve, but she *could* be sort of like a mother to those girls, couldn't she? She'd longed for children of her own, but the tests had shown that Dale's sperm count was impossibly low. No babies ever . . .

But wouldn't this be almost as good in a way? If she could be a mother to her nieces, wouldn't it in some small way help make up for what she'd done to Eve?

The green approach signs for JFK could be seen up ahead now. Minutes later they were pulling up in front of cargo building 80, and Dolly was dashing in, shopping bag tucked up under her arm. Inside, the place looked even more dreary than it had outside: pea-soup walls, scuffed linoleum floor, furniture that looked as if it belonged in the Bates Motel, right out of *Psycho*.

She found McIntyre's office easily enough; his plastic name tag was in a slot by the door. Though they'd spoken to one another a number of times over the phone, they'd never actually met.

"Dolly Drake," she introduced herself after knocking softly at his open door, and at his sheepish wince, she grinned. "Guess you know why I'm here."

She slipped the apple-shaped cookie jar onto his desk.

McIntyre's smile faded. "Hey, come on. You know I can't take that. You don't want to get me in trouble, do you?" He was a middle-aged man with sallow skin and red hair shot with gray.

She suddenly felt ashamed. But she forced a brilliant smile, exclaiming, "Why, Mr. McIntyre, what a thought!"

"The plain fact is, Dolly"—he held up some papers—"approval on your shipment is being held up until the lab results come back. We do a random check every so often on the alcohol level, to make sure it doesn't exceed regulations."

Dolly felt her neck muscles knot with frustration. Hell's bells, *she* knew the law, and so did Henri. Why, there wasn't enough liquor in Girod's chocolates to inebriate a kitten!

What now? It was McIntyre's rubber stamp and his alone that

would release her shipment. Then it struck her: *Why couldn't they have the test right here and now?*

"Mr. McIntyre, I'm going to ask you to do yourself and me a small and perfectly legal favor. Try one. No one in the history of the United States ever lost their job for eating one chocolate bonbon." She lifted the lid and gently extracted one of the dark rum caramels. As the weary official was opening his mouth to protest, she popped the bonbon in. "Tell me what you think."

A look of annoyance creased his face. But he was chewing it, not spitting it into the ashtray. He kept on chewing, his eyes drifting shut. And now—praise the Lord!—he was smiling.

McIntyre swallowed and then reached for another. "No alcohol in these," he said, grinning. "But wow, they ought to be outlawed."

Dolly felt a rush of triumph that left her a little dizzy.

Five minutes later she was back in her Lincoln, heading out to Air France cargo to pick up her shipment.

After that, Henri.

"Dolly?" Henri called softly in the darkness.

Dolly looked up from the television she'd been staring at. He stood at the entrance to the den—a stocky figure wrapped in a silk dressing gown, his thick pewter-colored hair mussed with sleep. A present from her, that robe—a little fancy for Henri, who was more the plain terry type. Still, he wore it to please her.

"I couldn't sleep," Dolly told him. She'd been worrying about Laurel and Annie.

But now she had to think what to do about Henri.

On the way from the airport Henri had told her that he had come across the most charming flat with a garden view, a stone's throw from Girod's. He had even left a deposit to hold it for a week.

What should I tell him? The thought of being with Henri shimmered in her head like a green oasis in a desert.

But the truth was that things had changed since she'd promised him she'd think about moving to Paris. She couldn't leave now, not until Annie and Laurel had been found. And even after that, there were still, let's face it, Henri's wife and children.

Henri sank down beside her on the deep sofa, tucking an arm about her. He kissed her shoulder, the ends of his mustache pleasantly scratchy. *Oh, was that nice!* After Dale she'd thought she would never again know that sweet tug a woman feels in her belly when her man kisses her.

She thought of the first time she'd laid eyes on Henri, in the kitchen of his shop, bent over a steaming copper caldron, holding a wooden spoon to his lips. Surrounded for the first time in her life by chocolate on all sides—sheets of chocolate, tray after tray of bite-size dollops of *ganache*—Dolly felt as if she'd died and gone to heaven.

Now, snuggled against her, Henri whispered, "Without you, the bed is cold. And I miss your snoring."

"Like hell I snore!"

Henri grinned. *"Exactement."*

"My grandpa used to say, *'You can dress a frog in silk drawers, but that don't stop him from croakin.'* " She elbowed him lightly in the ribs. "Hey, you ever been west of the Mississippi?"

"When I was very young, my parents took me to Yellowstone Park to see—how do you say?—Old Reliable."

She giggled. "Old Reliable? Sounds like the stuff Mama-Jo used to swallow before bedtime. You mean Old Faithful, don't you?"

He rolled his eyes and chuckled.

"You know what I love about you, *ma poupée?*" he said. "You make me laugh." He kissed her, and she felt an almost electric sensation shoot from her lips to her lower belly.

"No," she murmured, pulling away. "Henri, we need to talk."

His slate-colored eyes regarded her from beneath his bushy brows. "But of course," he said, nodding gravely.

It came straight to her then, the decision she'd been holding at arm's length all evening. What surprised her was the pain she felt, the sharpness of the ache gripping her chest.

Dolly took a breath. "I'm not moving to Paris," she told him. "Not now, anyway. It wouldn't be right, not with . . . with the way things are. Your wife . . ." She gulped. Henri started to speak, and she held up her hand to stop him. "Oh, I know you don't love Francine. And I know all your reasons for not divorcing her: your children, your religion, Francine's father. . . ."

Henri's face sagged. He seemed suddenly a decade older than forty-seven. "What you don't know," he finally said, "is how she despises me. If not for her father, she says, I would still be an assistant chef at Fouquet's. It is not true, of course, but until the old goat takes his retirement, I remain under his thumb."

Once, while in Paris on business, Dolly had met Henri's wife—a grim woman who looked as if she'd devoted her forty-odd years to mastering the art of smiling without moving her lips. No denying she was good-looking—or had been, at some point—with her blade-thin figure and chic clothes. But now, twenty years into their marriage, Francine was like some spindly chair in a museum on which one wouldn't dare sit.

Dolly felt resentment growing inside her. *How can he stay with Francine when it's me he loves? Why doesn't he just go ahead and divorce his wife, Papa Girod be damned?*

But Dolly knew it wasn't that simple. If Henri walked away from Francine, he'd have to leave Girod's. And Girod's was more than a business to him; it was his whole life. His son was pretty much grown, but he absolutely doted on eleven-year-old Gabrielle.

"It's not just your . . . situation," Dolly said. Quickly she told him about Annie and Laurel. "So you see, I *have* to stay here. I've got to find them. You see that, don't you?"

Henri frowned, but then he gained control of himself.

"Of course I do. And you will, *ma poupée*," he conceded sadly. Then after a moment he ventured, "But instead of looking everywhere for them, could you not perhaps bring them to you instead?"

"What do you mean?"

"Perhaps an advertisement in the newspaper?"

Dolly thought for a moment, growing excited. Yeah, it could just work. She hugged Henri, feeling a surge of hope. Tomorrow, first thing, she'd see about placing an ad.

"You're a genius. How am I ever gonna get along without you?" She felt a desperate urge to be wrapped up in him, engulfed by his body. "Come on. Let's go back to bed."

Moments later Dolly kissed him and forgot everything but how wonderful she felt. What could be sweeter than this? A man who loved her, who thought she was beautiful. Why, she could die this very minute, and she wouldn't feel she'd missed out.

"Looks pretty foxy," Gloria said.

"If it works." Dolly held up crossed fingers.

She had the *Times* open atop the display case and was staring at the half-page ad. A selection of chocolates was featured at the top, plus the usual copy about Girod's seventy-five years of international awards. And smack in the center, a cutout from an old glossy of Dolly from her Hollywood days—heavy lipstick, tight sweater, cone-shaped brassiere and all—the weirdest chocolate ad in history. But she was hoping—grasping at straws, really—that Annie might see it and recognize her. Her name below it read, big as you please, DOLLY DRAKE, PROPRIETOR.

The important thing now was to get to her nieces before anything happened to them. She shivered, tugging on the arms of the pink sweater draped over her shoulders. The radio had said it might snow this week. She imagined Annie and Laurel shivering on the sidewalk somewhere, and her heart twisted in her chest.

Two days later snow was coming down in earnest, and Dolly had almost given up hope of ever finding the two girls. She was checking over the day's receipts when the bell over the door tinkled. Looking up, she watched a tall, angular young woman hesitate a moment on the threshold, then take a deep breath as she entered the shop. She wore a thin coat, and loafers that looked soaked. Her dark shoulder-length hair wasn't covered, not even with a scarf.

Dolly was about to turn away, leave this one to Gloria, but something about the girl held her. That long neck and those high cheekbones, those startling indigo eyes. The girl looked straight at Dolly, and Dolly felt her heart tip sideways in her chest.

"Annie," she whispered, "honey, is that you?"

"Aunt Dolly?"

Then all at once it struck her: *She's really here.* Dolly started to cry. "Oh, sugar, I was afraid— Well, don't just stand there. Come here and let me give you a hug." She gathered Annie into her arms.

Annie remained stiff at first; then, tentatively, her hands came up and circled Dolly's back, and with a sigh she rested her head against Dolly's shoulder, like a weary traveler easing a heavy burden.

"I saw your picture in the paper." Annie drew away, a thin smile touching her lips.

A thousand questions came to Dolly all at once. But she asked only the most important one: "You okay, sugar?"

"Sure." Annie was glancing fearfully about the shop, as if she half expected someone to spring out and clap a pair of handcuffs on her.

"I don't bite," Gloria called out, moving out from behind the counter. "Hi, I'm Gloria. I guess you two have a whole lot of catching up to do, so why don't I close up and let you go at it."

Dolly led Annie up to her office and plugged in the space heater next to her desk for extra warmth.

"Now slip out of those wet shoes," she told her niece, "and I'll make you a cup of tea. You like chocolate?"

Annie nodded, looking around her. "Please . . . don't tell Val," she pleaded softly. Her clear eyes fixed upon Dolly with a scared, desperate look, but Dolly saw a glint of steel there, too.

She didn't want to make a promise she couldn't keep, but at the same time Dolly sensed that a wrong word now would send Annie bolting like a panicked deer. "Why don't you tell me all about it," she said, "and let me decide. Fair enough?"

Annie was silent for a long moment; then she said, "I guess so."

Dolly made tea on the hot plate and brought it to Annie in a thick ceramic mug. Annie held the mug against her knee, cupping her fingers about it, and began to talk.

Haltingly at first, then with gathering passion, she told Dolly about Eve, how she'd died. And then Val, acting so strange . . . and, finally, the night she and Laurel ran away.

"I couldn't stay," Annie said, leaning forward, her eyes bright and her cheeks a little flushed. "He would have . . . Well, I didn't stop to think it through all the way. I just grabbed Laurey and—"

"He's saying you kidnapped her."

The color drained from her niece's face. "It's not true! Laurey wanted to be with me! And I wouldn't have come to you. Not unless I was really desperate. I—I didn't think you'd want us."

Dolly felt the bare honesty of her words sock home.

"Did your—" She licked her lips. Her heart was doing a crazy riff against her rib cage. "Did your mama ever talk about me?"

"You had some kind of fight, didn't you? She never said what it was about."

Dolly felt her body sag with relief. *Thanks to heaven, she doesn't know the whole story.*

"Sometimes people say . . . or do . . . something hurtful that they're sorry for later. And the more you love that person who let you down, the worse it hurts." She sighed, the old pain surfacing.

Dolly looked into Annie's eyes—so much like Eve's it nearly broke her heart—and found herself saying briskly, "Val doesn't have to know. Now drink your tea, and let's see what we can do about straightening out this mess before it gets any worse."

Chapter Four

"ANNIE, *why* can't we spend Christmas with Aunt Dolly?" Laurel stopped in the middle of the sidewalk, looking up at her sister.

Annie felt a bead of annoyance form in her stomach. *How many times must I go over this with her? Why can't she just trust me?*

But she bit back the harsh words and reached for her sister's mittened hand. "Look, Laurey, we can't go to her apartment, because people would see us and it might get back to Val."

Laurel, dropping her gaze, said nothing. Annie wondered if she was wishing she were at Bel Jardin with Val instead of here. Her insides suddenly felt as chilled as her cold-reddened hands. Should she tell Laurel everything that had happened that night with Val— the real reason she'd had to run away?

No. It was too awful to talk about.

"But you're *working* for Aunt Dolly," Laurel reasoned. "And what's so safe about that?"

"At the shop nobody but Gloria knows she's my aunt," Annie explained. "But her apartment has doormen, nosy neighbors. If we started hanging out there, pretty soon everybody would know." She gave her sister a nudge. "Now come on, or you'll be late for school."

Laurel glared at Annie. "I don't care! I hate it here! It's cold and yucky . . . and . . . and"—her voice wobbled—"we'll be all alone on Christmas!"

"What about the Grubermans?"

"The Grubermans don't celebrate Christmas." Laurel's wide blue eyes glittered with unshed tears. "And we might as well be Jewish if we're not even going to have a tree."

Annie couldn't think of anything to say. She wanted a tree, too. Should she have taken the money Dolly offered? She thought back to that first day at Dolly's shop, her aunt's pressing several folded twenties into her hand and pleading with her to take them. But Annie just couldn't. If she accepted Dolly's charity, wouldn't she somehow be betraying Dearie? Once her mother had referred to her sister as a two-faced snake in the grass. Did that mean that Dolly, no matter how nice she acted, couldn't be trusted?

She'd settled instead for agreeing to work for her aunt, and accepted a small cash advance against her salary. But now it had been three weeks, and she still hadn't saved enough to buy half the things they needed. The list seemed endless: long underwear, warm clothes, heavy boots, dishes, sheets, towels.

She glanced over at Laurel, wearing a Salvation Army duffle coat that didn't quite reach her wrists. Laurel's bright hair spilled like sunshine from under the red knit cap squashed over her head, but her lips and the tip of her nose were tinged with blue.

"Are you warm enough?" Annie shivered inside her own coat, a man's gabardine that flapped at her ankles.

"I'm okay," Laurel said. "I've got a sweater on under this. Rivka gave me one of Chava's that didn't fit her anymore."

More likely Rivka had seen that Laurel needed a sweater and had hunted one up that would fit her. Rivka had practically adopted Annie and Laurel into her big, noisy family, and Annie couldn't help being grateful for the cast-off clothes and extra blankets, the fresh-baked kugel and loaves of challah she sent up to them.

"Guess what?" Laurel said. "After school today Rivka's gonna show me how to sew, and when I get good enough, I'll even make *you* something. . . ." Her voice trailed off, and she peeped up at Annie with a sheepish expression. "Annie, I'm sorry I got mad at you. But it *would* be nice to have a little tree."

"Yeah, it would." Annie forced herself to sound cheery, but inside she felt terrible. The fir trees they trucked into the city were so expensive. Ornaments, too. No, it was out of the question.

At Avenue K and Sixteenth Street, Annie caught sight of P.S. 99, a massive, grim-looking brick building surrounded by a high chain link fence. Annie remembered going to enroll Laurel. She'd been so nervous, saying that she was Laurel's guardian and that her school records had been lost in a fire. But the school secretary hadn't even seemed suspicious, just bored. Now Annie knew it was because a lot of the kids here were illegal, with parents from places like Haiti and Nicaragua who didn't even have green cards.

"Our class Christmas play is this Friday night," Laurel said when they'd reached the graffiti-sprayed doors. "I'm in charge of the scenery. It's going to be really neat."

"I can't wait to see it."

Laurel was so artistic. Annie remembered the wonderful cards she used to draw for Dearie—amazingly lifelike dogs, monkeys,

47

squirrels. And she had such an eye for color, too. Like the other day, rescuing that old paisley shawl Rivka was throwing out, seeing how perfect it would be to dress up their own shabby couch.

"Do you think Dolly would come, too?"

"Why don't I ask her? I bet she'd like that." With forced brightness Annie added, "Look, Laurey, about Christmas . . . Why don't we invite Dolly over to *our* place? We'll get some holly and hang some mistletoe. And we'll sing all the carols."

"The Grubermans will hear us." Annie could see the tiniest smile was prying at the corners of Laurel's mouth.

"Let them," she said, feeling her spirits rise. "So what if everyone in Brooklyn hears us!"

A MINIATURE Christmas tree lit with tiny white lights and tied with gilt-wrapped bonbons twinkled in Girod's front window.

Annie was checking an order form against the merchandise.

>   1 doz. dark-chocolate hazelnut rums
>   1 doz. white-chocolate espressos
>   3 lbs. bitter-chocolate almond bark
>   4 doz. Champagne truffles

All there, cradled in molded Styrofoam trays, in a big brown-and-gold Girod's shopping bag on the counter in front of her.

She glanced at the invoice: Joe Daugherty. The address was a restaurant—Joe's Place—on Morton Street.

Just her luck. All the way down to the Village. And it was snowing like crazy out there. Oh, well, at least she'd be in a warm cab. And maybe, since it was almost four, Dolly would tell her to go on home after she'd delivered her package.

ANNIE didn't look down as she was getting out of the taxi, and by the time she did, it was too late. Her foot slid out from under her on the icy curb, and she landed on her bottom with a hard smack that sent her shopping bag of chocolates flying.

Picking herself up, she prayed that none of the chocolates were broken. She felt like enough of a klutz without having to go through a bunch of explanations and apologies.

Joe's Place turned out to be one of those aged Federal-style brick houses common to the Village, narrow as a chimney, with a few stairs leading up to a paneled door set with an oval of beveled glass.

Buzzed in through a wrought-iron gate, Annie immediately smelled baking bread as she entered the door beyond. Down a dimly lit hallway she could see into the kitchen. She heard voices, the clatter of pots, the hiss of steam.

Then a smashing sound, crockery crashing against a tiled floor. "Damn it!" a voice roared. "You idiot!"

Annie jumped.

The voice coming from the kitchen seemed to reverberate, as if directed exclusively at her. Annie shrank back as a figure appeared— a lanky man in his early twenties, his rangy height making even five-foot-nine Annie feel short. He wore a stained apron over blue jeans, and a faded chambray shirt with its sleeves rolled up over his elbows. His longish hair was pushed back from a sweaty forehead, and his eyes swam murkily behind steam-fogged eyeglasses.

"Yeah, what do you want?" he barked.

"I . . ." For an awful moment her mind went blank.

Before she could get the words out, he blurted, "Look, I'm really busy. One of the ovens just fritzed out on me, and two of my waiters are out sick, so whatever it is you want, spit it out."

Something in Annie snapped. "I don't *want* anything," she said haughtily, thrusting her shopping bag at him. "If you're Joe Daugherty, just sign the stupid invoice, and I'll get out of your way."

The condensed steam on his lenses began to evaporate, revealing eyes that looked gentle, wide, and brown. He looked chagrined.

"I'm sorry. Look, can we start over?" He turned a sheepish grin on her. "I *am* Joe Daugherty, and I've been having a day you wouldn't believe. I guess I just sort of came unglued."

Annie thought of the guy—some poor dishwasher, no doubt—that he'd yelled at back there. She wasn't buying his Mr. Nice Guy act.

"Right." Crisply she handed him the invoice. "Sign here." Then she remembered that the chocolates might be damaged. She swallowed hard and said, "Wait. I slipped and fell on the ice on my way over, and some of the chocolates might be . . . uh . . . broken."

Annie waited for the other shoe to drop, for this guy to explode again, but after a tense moment he surprised her by laughing. It was a low, easy laugh that made her want to smile in spite of herself.

"I guess this isn't your day, either," he observed mildly. "Sorry about your fall . . . and you can stop looking at me like I'm going to cut you up and serve you for dinner. I really *am* sorry I snapped at you. You may not believe this, but I'm actually a pretty mellow guy. I have a long fuse, but when I blow, I *really* blow."

"Great. But what about the poor guy in there you dumped on?"

Daugherty looked puzzled; then he began to chuckle, and in a minute was roaring with laughter. "*I* was the one who dropped those dishes. I was cursing myself out."

Annie didn't know what to say. Then she began to laugh, too.

"Why don't we step into my executive boardroom and assess what damage has been done," Joe suggested wryly. He led the way to a tiny, grungy office, where he gestured for Annie to sit. "You must be new with Dolly," he said. "You're . . ."

"Annie. I just started last week."

"Funny, I would've pegged you for the college type. Vassar or Sarah Lawrence, maybe."

"Well, you'd be wrong, then," Annie answered evenly. College, which she had once yearned for, couldn't have been further away.

"Hey, I'm one to talk. I deep-sixed law school to open this place. My old man is figuring this is temporary insanity. He's even saving a space for my nameplate on the door to his old office: Poth, Van Gelder, Daugherty, and Prodigal Son."

He took his glasses off and began polishing them, and Annie saw that his eyes weren't really brown: they were sort of a cross between green and brown—a shifting mossy hazel. He just missed being handsome—not ordinary handsome, but really knockout handsome, like a movie star.

Annie realized she was staring and jerked her gaze away as he signed the invoice with a flourish. "Stuff the chocolates," he said. "Even if a few of them are smashed, it's too ugly out there for you to make a second trip."

Seeing how hard he was trying to make up for how he'd acted before, Annie actually found herself smiling.

"You haven't been in New York very long, have you?" he asked.

"Why? Does it show?"

"Your smile—it's definitely west of the Mississippi."

"How do New Yorkers smile?"

"They don't."

She giggled. "Does it ever get any easier here?"

"Nope. Only it sort of grows on you after a while. You'll see."

50

Annie stood up. "I'd better go. I have to get home." At the door she stopped and looked back. "Uh . . . well, thanks."

She was making her way out down the hall when he called, "Wait!" He loped past her, and minutes later reappeared holding a large plastic carton. He presented it to Annie as if it held the crown jewels.

"To make up for acting like a jerk," he said. "Merry Christmas."

Annie heard a faint scratching sound and peeked inside. A big lobster scuttled feebly about in some seaweed. She was so startled she nearly dropped the container. She looked up at Joe, at his handsome face so full of good intentions. No, it wasn't a joke.

But what on earth was she going to do with a . . . a *lobster?* She didn't even have a pot to cook it in.

"Uh . . . thanks," she managed, reddening a little. "I'm sure it'll be . . . uh . . . delicious. Well, thanks."

"Don't mention it. And hey, drop by any time."

Trudging through the snow to the subway at West Fourth, Annie spotted a man selling Christmas trees out of the back of his truck. Her heart sank. If only she could afford one. And the irony of it was, this lobster, if she'd bought it in a store, would have cost a lot. With that money she might have been able to buy a small tree.

Then it hit her.

She walked over to the truck. The man—burly and bearded— was nailing a cross of two-by-fours to the trunk of a bushy fir.

"Can I do for you, miss?"

"I was just wondering— Would you be interested in trading one of your trees for . . . for . . ."

"Whatcha got there?" He tossed his hammer down.

Annie opened her box and held it up so he could see inside.

The man looked at her as if she'd just offered him a slice of green cheese from the moon. But after he'd poked the lobster to see if it was still kicking and after she had agreed to accept his skinniest, spindliest tree, she had a deal.

Annie thought of how pleased Laurel would be, and how they would decorate it with paper chains, popcorn, and tinfoil stars. Maybe it would turn out to be an okay Christmas after all.

EVEN in L.A., Val thought, December was a misery.

As he churned his way across the pool at Bel Jardin he tried not to feel how cold the water was or how his head was throbbing, or to think about the real estate broker and her snob clients who right now were tramping around inside his house, peering into closets and pointing out cracks in the plaster.

Instead, Val thought about Annie.

The rotten kid. She'd had no right to clobber him like that. Fifteen stitches.

He didn't care about finding her. But Laurel, that was different. If he could just get his daughter back, there ought to be some way of getting ahold of that trust money of hers.

Fifty laps. Val grabbed the ladder and hoisted himself out of the pool. He was breathing hard now, heart pounding.

"How can you swim in that muck?" A gravelly voice penetrated the red tide surging in his ears. "You oughta get it cleaned."

Val focused his bleary, chlorine-stung eyes on the stubby figure sprawled on a nearby chaise. As always, he felt a tiny prick of incredulity. No one in a million years would guess that Rudy was his brother. A full foot shorter, squat, balding, and ugly. In his Hawaiian shirt and Pepto-Bismol-pink shorts, legs pinkening under a coat of tanning oil, Rudy reminded him of a roast pig at a luau.

"With what?" Val flung himself into the nearest deck chair. "You think the old lady fixed it so I'd be left with anything? If I still had Laurel, things might be different, but—"

His words were cut off by Rudy's jumping up and strutting over to him. "Relax. In another week or two the girls'll run out of money, and you'll find them right on your doorstep, scratching to be let in."

"I don't know." Val fingered the scar over his eyebrow. It still felt tender, and under it was a hard ridge. "If they had somebody to go to, maybe they wouldn't be in such a big hurry."

"Like who?"

"Dolly, maybe. The way she was acting over the phone, I got a funny feeling she might know something she's not telling. If only I had the money, then I'd fly out there and see for myself." He thought about asking Rudy to spot him a few hundred, but then he remembered he was already in the hole to him for almost a grand.

Rudy's grin seemed to slip a notch, and a hard gleam stole into his beady black eyes. "What you need is a drink," he said. "How about I fix us a couple of Bloody Marys."

Later, as they sipped their drinks under the magnolia at the outdoor bar, Rudy said, "Tell you what. Day after tomorrow I'm flying out to New York to see a client and collect some depositions. Afterwards I could drop in on Dolly, check out her story."

Val sat up straighter. "Would you? Hey, that'd be great." Gruffly he added, "Thanks."

Rudy shrugged. "Hey, no sweat. What are brothers for?"

It never even occurred to Val that Rudy was doing this not for him, but for Laurel.

In his mind Rudy saw his niece standing in the doorway at Bel Jardin, hovering just beyond his reach—her sweet face and those big blue eyes. She was spooked by him, he knew. What kid wouldn't be? But now, if he could somehow track her down, things would be different. Never mind about Annie—with her fierce eyes and sharp gestures, she'd always made him want to keep his distance. Sweet Laurel was all he cared about. And if he found her, he'd figure out a way of keeping her to himself, away from Val and his moneygrubbing. He doesn't deserve Laurel, Rudy thought.

Rudy's heart twisted in his chest. What if Dolly *did* know something? She sure wouldn't come right out and tell him her secret. In her mind, no doubt, that'd be the same as telling Val.

Well, if she was lying, he'd see right through her. Yeah, he'd know. And then he'd have Dolly tailed, and sooner or later she'd lead him to Laurel.

He felt better. Two days later he'd be in a cab bouncing over the potholes on his way to Dolly's shop. Could Val be right? Did Dolly maybe know where Annie and Laurel were? He felt excited, hopeful, but his stomach was in knots.

LAUREL peered through the slit where the stage curtain met the wall. From where she stood at a darkened edge of the stage, she scanned row after row, but Annie and Aunt Dolly still hadn't arrived. Where could they be? It was almost six thirty, and the play was half over! Could something have happened to them?

"Group four," she heard Miss Rodriguez whisper. "Laurel, Jesús . . . you're on next. Line up when I give the signal."

Phutt! Phuuuuuut! Jesús had a hand tucked under one armpit and was pumping his elbow, making it sound as if he were farting.

Laurel felt like jabbing him with her papier-mâché scepter, but she didn't dare. Yesterday, when she won the spelling bee, he'd tried to trip her on her way back to her seat.

The teacher scowled in their direction.

Looking past the folding screen that separated her group from the stage, Laurel could see Andy McAllister, who was playing Scrooge, swaggering about the stage. She bit her lip. It'd be her turn to go on in just a minute.

Laurel was the Ghost of Christmas Present. She was wearing a red chenille robe that was so long it dragged on the ground, and a crown made out of plastic holly leaves. She had to speak sixteen whole lines, but if she was thinking about her sister and her aunt the whole time, how would she be able to remember them? And the set—she'd worked so hard on it! Annie would be so surprised when she saw what a great job she'd done.

But Annie wasn't here.

"Who was you lookin' for, Beanie?" a sly voice whispered in her ear. Jesús—ugh! The first day of school he'd named her String Bean, then shortened it to Beanie. "The *Prez*-i-dent, maybe?"

"N-nobody," Laurel stammered. She hated Jesús.

He pressed closer. "Your mother ain't coming neither, huh?" His voice dropped to a conspiratorial whisper. For once he sounded almost . . . well, *nice*.

"My mother's dead." Laurel was somehow shocked into admitting the truth.

"Yeah, so's mine. She always tellin' me that, so I'll leave her alone. She tired all the time."

"Why's that?"

"Workin'. Sal's Pizza in the daytime, and after that, she do the cleanin' up at Sunnyview—you know, where all them old people sit around like mummies. It's 'cause my father's an s.o.b." Jesús' dark eyes flashed with scorn. "And now he's gone."

Jesús stared at the floor, his thick black bangs fanning away from his forehead.

Laurel gazed at him. Suddenly she realized he wasn't faking. All that other stuff—the mean things he did—that was the act.

She touched his arm. "Hey, you okay?"

Jesús jerked his head up as if she'd stuck him with a pin. "I'm glad he's gone," he hissed. "I hate him."

"Sh." Miss Rodriguez frowned at them, raising a finger to her lips. She flapped a hand at Laurel. "You're on!"

Laurel could feel her face going rubbery, her eyes hot. Any

second now she would be crying. With everyone staring at her.

"Behold, the Ghost of Christmas Present," Dickie Dumbrowski trumpeted in his froggy bellow.

"Be-hold, Dickie Dumb," Jesús muttered as Laurel slipped past, shocking her into a giggle. The urge to cry faded.

Gliding onto the stage, Laurel felt almost grateful to Jesús.

RUDY'S voice drifted up the stairs. Where Annie was crouched, in the narrow space between the desk and the wall in Dolly's office, she couldn't hear his words, only his flat growl, like grinding machinery. Any minute now, she'd hear him creaking up these stairs. He'd find her. And then Val would come and take Laurel away.

Thank God she'd been up here when he'd come in. She'd heard the bell over the front door tinkle, then his familiar, grating voice calling out, "Hello, Dolly!" A low chuckle. "Hey, isn't that a song? Bet you're surprised to see me, huh?"

In some ways Annie was more afraid of Rudy than she was of Val. Because Rudy was so much smarter, and Val always listened to him and went along with him. Like the time when Dearie's drinking got so bad, and Rudy convinced Val to commit her to Briarwood. When she got out, she was like a zombie; she'd sit for hours and hours, just gazing at nothing. Six weeks later Annie found her mother on her bathroom floor, cold as ice, an empty Darvon bottle on the sink above her. They buried her two days after that.

And the way Rudy looked at Laurel—it was so creepy. Not talking to her much or even trying to play up to her . . . just staring at her all the time, like a fat carp eyeing a minnow.

Rudy would be a lot harder to fool than Val. Could Dolly pull it off? She wished Gloria hadn't left early; she at least would have kept Annie posted on what was going on down there.

A new thought made Annie break out in goose bumps. What if Dolly told him *everything?* She seemed so good and kind, but Annie still remembered Dearie's saying her sister couldn't be trusted.

Please, God, not now, just when things are starting to go right.

She liked working at Girod's, a lot more than she'd thought she would. And Laurel finally seemed to be settling in at school. All week she'd talked about nothing but her Christmas play. If they didn't leave now, they might miss it. But she couldn't exactly waltz downstairs and remind Dolly of that.

What would Laurel think? She'd be so disappointed . . . and probably worried to death.

I've got to let her know I'm okay.

Rivka. Maybe she could call Rivka and ask her to rush over to the school and tell Laurel she'd be late. But then she remembered, No, it was Friday evening, *Shabbat.* It was forbidden for Rivka even to switch on a light. Annie wouldn't be able to get through to her. At sundown Rivka took her phone off the hook.

Annie made herself stand up slowly. Still shaky, she reached for the phone on the desk and tiptoed with it into the tiny bathroom, where Dolly always took it when Henri called from Paris—as if she and Gloria didn't already know about them.

There *was* someone she could call besides Rivka.

She remembered Joe Daugherty's warm smile when he'd stopped in yesterday to ask her to lunch. Was he just being nice? Maybe, but at the little deli where they'd stuffed themselves on pastrami on rye, and talked and laughed for more than an hour, she'd begun to think that she'd made a friend.

Annie dialed the number quickly, before she could change her mind.

At the other end the phone began ringing over and over.

Then Joe's voice came on, sounding out of breath. " 'Lo. Joe's Place." He sounded rushed.

"This is Annie. Annie Cobb," she gasped. "Joe, I know this is going to sound funny, but—but I need your help."

She took a breath and blurted out enough of the story for him to understand why she felt so desperate. It gave her an awful upsy-daisy feeling, opening herself to him.

There was a long silence, and Annie was suddenly scared he was going to tell her he was too busy. Then he said crisply into the phone, "You're in luck. My whole crew showed up tonight, and we've got our preparation nailed down. I can be at your sister's school in half an hour. I'll take her back to your apartment and wait with her until you get there."

He got directions from her, then hung up.

Annie started to sob, pulling her sweater up over her face so Rudy wouldn't hear. Okay, they weren't really safe yet, but just knowing Joe was willing to help made her feel she'd come to the end of a long road.

LAUREL TOOK HER BOW WITH THE others, ducking her head low so that her long hair fell in front of her face. That way, nobody could see she was crying. She just *knew* Annie wasn't out there.

She crept away, stumbling down the steps that led to the auditorium floor, and was slinking out into the corridor when suddenly a large hand gripped her shoulder.

Laurel turned, looking up at a tall man in faded jeans and glasses. She could see that his eyes were smiling.

"Laurel?" he asked.

She nodded, wary.

He smiled. "I'm Joe. Annie told me to look for the prettiest girl on the stage. She sent me over here to tell you she's okay, and Dolly, too. She'll explain everything when she gets home."

Something clicked in her head: *Joe . . . the lobster man?* It had to be him—those glasses and his wavy blond-brown hair. He was just the way Annie had described him. The cold spot in her stomach eased. "Annie's really okay?" she asked. "And Aunt Dolly?"

"Sure they are. Annie said they just got . . . held up. Why don't I take you back, and we'll wait for her. How does that sound?"

"Okay." Laurel nodded. "Then you can see our Christmas tree. The one you gave us."

"Tree? What tree?"

"The one Annie traded the lobster for."

Joe stared at her for a moment, then started to laugh. "She did that?" He shook his head. "Your sister is really something." He squatted down and placed his hands on her shoulders. "She told me about . . . well, your leaving home and coming here. I think both of you are pretty brave."

Laurel felt cold again. "Are you going to tell?" she whispered.

"No," he said, his eyes steady and serious, "I'm not going to tell." And she believed him.

Now he was rocking back on his heels and rising. He held out his hand, and Laurel took it without hesitating.

She thought about Santa Claus, a fat elf in a red suit, who she used to think was a real person. Now it occurred to her that if Santa were real, he might not look like that. He might be a tall man, and young—not much older than Annie—wearing faded jeans and a blue polo shirt, with glasses that slipped down his nose and eyes that crinkled up at the corners when he smiled.

57

Chapter Five

IT'D been more than two weeks since Nan Weatherby's appearance at Joe's Place; if the review was going to appear at all, Joe knew it had to be in this week's issue of *Metropolitan,* due out today. But Joe had been told by Mr. Shamik at the newsstand that he wouldn't be getting his *Metropolitan* delivery until sometime after four. Hours away! How could he wait that long?

Well, he'd just have to, that's all. And maybe once he read it, he'd wish he hadn't.

No one was supposed to recognize *Metropolitan* magazine's arbiter of the food scene, but Joe knew who she was. Three stars from Nan Weatherby, or even two, would bring him all the bookings he could handle. He began to feel excited, but only for a minute. Nan Weatherby, he remembered with a pang, gave mostly scathing reviews.

His father's voice, dry and measured, droned in his head: *"I can't stop you, Joseph. Your grandmother left that money in your name, and it's yours to do with as you wish. But let me say one thing: You'll fail. Inside a year you'll be out of business. You'll fail us."*

Joe looked around the kitchen. He remembered Dad's seeing it for the first time and declaring, *"What this place needs is a wrecking ball."*

You're wrong, Dad, he thought. I'm not going to fail. But if I do, it's on my head. I'll never come begging to you.

Joe headed up to the dining room. He'd hired Laurel to letter menus for him, and he found her at a booth in back, exactly where he'd left her hours ago. A stack of completed menus was piled at one elbow. At a glance Joe saw that she'd done something extraordinary. He'd only intended for her to neatly write in the appetizers, entrées, desserts, and their prices. But this . . .

Picking up a finished menu from the pile, he saw that every corner and blank space was filled with delicate, exquisite ink drawings: morning-glory vines twisting around the borders, a bird's nest with tiny speckled eggs, a crested spoon with a top-hatted mouse sipping from it. Joe felt a tremor of delight travel through him.

Leafing through one menu after another, he was so awed that he all but forgot about the *Metropolitan* review. Laurel had done this? She was just a *kid.* These looked like the work of a Beatrix Potter.

58

Did she have any idea how talented she was?

Her pictures made him think back to Christmas. After Mom and Dad's annual holiday get-together, Joe had headed for Brooklyn, planning to surprise Annie and Laurel. But the surprise was on him. Walking into that shabby living room, he'd felt so good, instantly enveloped in warmth and Christmas spirit. Dolly had gotten there ahead of him, armed with a mountain of presents. But the way Laurel had looked at him when he handed her the shopping bag of gifts he'd brought for her and Annie—it was as if he'd presented her the moon on a silver platter.

Now, gazing down at her as she sat motionless except for the scratching of her fountain pen, Joe was struck by her loveliness. "Laurey," he called softly, Annie's nickname for her. She looked up at him and blinked. Joe held up a menu. "These are really something. I mean it. Who taught you how to do this?"

Laurel blushed, but he could see how pleased she was. "I learned how myself," she said. "Mostly I just draw what's in my head."

"That's quite an imagination you have."

Her color deepened. "Well, drawing isn't the only thing I can do. I'm learning how to sew. I made this." Proudly she smoothed the front of the plaid shift she was wearing.

He whistled. "I'm impressed. Your sister show you how?"

"Annie?" Laurel laughed and rolled her eyes. "She says she doesn't have the patience."

Joe thought of how restless Annie always seemed—even sitting, she couldn't quite keep still. And those alley-cat eyes of hers . . .

"Somehow that doesn't surprise me." He smiled. "But *you* . . ." He tapped the stack of finished menus. "These should be in a book or hanging on someone's wall. They're too good for this."

Laurel looked down. "Thank you for saying so. It's very nice of you," she said primly, but her smile was radiant. "But it's just for fun, really. When Miss Rodriquez catches me during class, she thinks I'm not paying attention. But you know what? I *think* better when I'm drawing. Know what I mean, Joe?"

"Sure I do. I feel that way when I'm making an omelette."

"Huh?"

"Come on down to the kitchen with me, and I'll show you."

Downstairs, Joe showed her how to crack eggs one-handed, and Laurel expertly whisked the eggs.

Seeing the glow on her face, he could almost—*almost*—forget that his career as a restaurateur might soon be demolished.

The buzzing of the service door cut through the kitchen noise.

Joe went to answer the door, and a tall figure in a dripping coat rushed in. Annie. "Joe, you'll never believe it! It's incredible! Oh, I'm all out of breath. It's pouring cats and dogs. And I ran six blocks without stopping."

Annie's face was flushed as she tore at the buttons of her shabby, sopping coat. Underneath he spotted a copy of *Metropolitan* magazine rolled up, and he felt his heart lurch.

"Three stars!" she cried, throwing her arms around him. "Oh, Joe, I'm so happy for you! Isn't it wonderful?" She drew back, flipping open the magazine. "And just listen to this: 'As soon as you walk through the door, you feel as if you're in a cozy country inn, with deliciously hearty food to match. The grilled salmon and spicy venison stew were worthy examples of regional cuisines elevated to the level of haute. . . .' "

Joe couldn't speak or move. Then in a dizzying rush it came to him: the rent, the payroll, and his overdue wine bills. He'd be able to pay them all and one day, maybe, take another floor.

A sound like wildly chiming bells rang in Joe's head.

"Joe!" Annie was pulling at his arm to get his attention. "Your phone. It's ringing!"

Joe rushed into his office and snatched up the receiver. Probably his first reservation from the review.

"Joseph, is that you?" No one but his mother called him Joseph. He felt himself tense.

"Darling!" She rushed ahead without waiting for him to speak. "Dad and I just saw it. It's marvelous, isn't it? Hugs and kisses and all that. And can you guess who just called me? Frank Shellburne. You know Frank, always looking for a tax dodge. Well, when he read that review, he wanted to know immediately if you'd consider selling out. I told him I'd have a word with you, and maybe you two could set up a meeting. Joseph . . . are you there?"

"I'm here, Mother." But his excitement was gone. "I'm here," he repeated dully.

"Promise you'll at least consider it," she said. "Daddy says it's not too late to squeeze you in next semester at Yale—"

"Mother, I have to go," Joe cut her off. "Look, do you want me to put you and Dad down for one night this week? If you ate here once, you might be surprised. Hell, you might even like it."

"Joseph, there's no need to swear. If your father could hear you . . . And don't pretend you don't go out of your way to needle him. I should think you would want to keep in mind Dad's heart condition. You know, you can be very selfish at times."

"I know," he said softly. "Mother, I have to go. Good-bye."

Slowly, carefully, he lowered the receiver. Standing in his tiny, cluttered office, he looked out the iron-barred window. He felt something brush up against him and jumped a little, startled. It was Laurel. She slipped her hand into his and gazed up at him as if she knew exactly how he was feeling. Was he that transparent?

Joe felt touched. He could hear Annie in the kitchen, her strong voice ringing out, and he wanted to plunge into her bracing presence, as if into a cool shower.

"EIGHT dozen . . . nine . . . ten . . ." Annie stopped counting and looked up from the trays of chocolates. "Dolly, how are we ever going to have these ready in time?"

She picked up a bonbon—chocolate specially ordered for David Levy's bar mitzvah, each one meant to go inside its own little silver foil–covered box. Except the printer had screwed up. He'd sent boxes with FOREVER, JAN AND JEFF, instead of MAZEL TOV, DAVID! And the bar mitzvah was tomorrow!

"We'll have to find *something* to put them in," Dolly said. "Oh, dear, how could this have happened?" She fiddled with her fuchsia scarf. In the two months she'd been working at Girod's, this was the first time Annie had seen her aunt looking so rattled. "I promised the Levys something really special."

"I have an idea," Annie said, feeling herself grow excited as she spoke. "We could wrap these in foil and put them inside three or four piñatas. I'll bet Laurey could make them."

As soon as the words were out, Annie wondered if she should have given her idea more thought. Mexican piñatas at a bar mitzvah?

"Piñatas," Dolly repeated, as if musing aloud. She began to chuckle, and then her chuckling rose into a full-bodied laugh. "I love it! It's brilliant! But I'd better call Mrs. Levy first." Dolly raced up to her office, where she kept her Rolodex.

When she returned, Dolly was bubbling over. "She was a little skeptical at first, but then she started to see how cute piñatas would be. How did you ever think of such a thing?"

Annie leveled her gaze at Dolly. "When I was little, Dearie gave me a birthday party with piñatas." She swallowed hard. "Dolly," she blurted out, "what happened between you and my mother?"

Dolly's sigh was more than a sigh—it sounded like the air being slowly let out of a tire or a balloon.

"Lord . . . it was all so long ago." She tried to smile. "It started with Val, I guess. Though, looking back, I believe your mama did me a big favor, marrying him out from under me."

"Val?" Shock rippled through Annie. "You and *Val*?"

"Oh, well . . ." Dolly's hand fluttered to rest on her full bosom, and this time she managed a weak smile. "Like I said, it was all such a long time ago. I don't honestly remember *what all* I felt for him." She straightened, pulling herself together with what appeared to be a great effort. "Now, what about those piñatas? Why don't you call your sister and see if she's up to the job."

Annie had the feeling there was more to Dolly's falling-out with her mother than just Val, but she didn't press her. Did she want to risk hearing something that might make her dislike her aunt? Annie called Laurel from the storeroom phone and asked if she'd be willing to make the piñatas. Laurel said she'd be thrilled to do it. She gave Annie a list of materials to pick up on her way home.

Annie grabbed her coat and was heading for the door when she stopped and turned back to give Dolly a quick hug. Looking up, she saw there were tears in Dolly's eyes.

"Thanks," Annie mumbled.

"What for?" Dolly seemed genuinely not to know.

"For . . ." She was about to say, For being there, for giving me this job, for being so nice to Laurey and me, but all she said was, "For everything."

SOMEONE was following her.

Annie had first noticed him as she was leaving the shop, a thick-set man in a rumpled khaki raincoat. And now he'd been following her for blocks. Why? What could he want? He had to be connected to Val or Rudy. A private detective, maybe. Or else why would he be following her?

Annie felt a pocket of cold form about her heart.

You're being ridiculous, she told herself. Dozens of people, thronging the sidewalk, headed this way for the subway. Why should she imagine this man was after her?

Annie saw a variety store up ahead and ducked into it. Roaming the aisles, taking her time, she collected some of the items on Laurel's list: balloons, crepe paper, poster paints.

As she stood in line at the check-out counter Annie tried to forget about the man in the khaki raincoat. She had probably imagined the whole thing.

And she believed it, too.

Almost.

SITTING in a darkened East Village revival theater, Dolly felt her stomach knot with tension. She peered at her watch. It was getting close to midnight, the movie almost over.

Was he sitting somewhere nearby, she wondered, or up in one of the front rows? She had failed to spot him when she came in, but he'd probably slipped in after the movie started.

Meet him afterwards in the lobby, he'd said. Weird, his wanting to meet her here. What was he on—some kind of nostalgia kick?

The theater wasn't crowded. Dolly, not wanting to be recognized as the now aging star of the picture up on the screen, had chosen a seat in the back row. Right now she was watching a tightly corseted ten-foot image of herself sob, "How did I get myself *into* this?"

She was laughing, and it felt good. Why, she had about as much in common with that woman up on the screen as a green tomato had with a grackle. Sure, her acting might be a joke, but she'd come a long way since then.

Now the credits were rolling, the lights coming on. People were shuffling to their feet, filing toward the exit.

Dolly didn't budge. She was afraid, worried stiff about the man who supposedly was waiting to meet her in the lobby.

Rudy Carrera.

What could he want this time? She shivered at the memory of his call last night. There had been something in his voice. . . . No, not *something*, but something *missing*. He hadn't seemed desperately curious or terribly eager. It was as if he already knew.

Dolly felt her heart start pounding with dread.

It *had* to be money. Why else would he have called her? Because if he already knew how to get to Annie and Laurel, then what did he need her for?

Now, slowly rising to her feet, Dolly saw that she wasn't alone. A man hunched way down in the first row was getting up, too, making his way up the aisle. There was something about his troll-like body, that strutting cock-of-the-walk gait, that made her feel cold all over.

"Rudy." She almost choked saying it.

He stopped. "Hey, Dolly, nice seein' you again." He was eyeing her calmly, with amusement. "You know, I never saw *Dames in Chains* when it first came out."

"Not many people did."

"Too bad. You were terrific in it."

"Cut the crap," she hissed. "What is it you want?"

Rudy glanced around. "Let's get out of here," he said. "You know a place where we can talk?"

Up the avenue at an all-night deli, Rudy ordered two coffees and a pastrami on rye. Waiting for his sandwich, he lit a cigarette, leaned back, and squinted at her through the drifting smoke.

"I found them," he said.

Dolly felt as if she'd stuck her finger in a light socket. "What are you talking about?" she hedged.

"Look, I had an investigator friend follow Annie home the other day." Rudy patted his breast pocket. "I have the address right here."

"What do you want?" Dolly snapped.

Before he could respond, the waitress arrived with their coffee and an obscenely thick pastrami sandwich. He bit into it with relish, tearing off a huge chunk and chewing for what seemed like an hour. Finally he swallowed and dragged a paper napkin across his mouth.

He stared at her, his piggy eyes boring into her. "What do I want from you? Just a little cooperation." He tipped his chin back, eyes narrowing in concentration. "Set up a meeting with Laurel. I don't want to frighten her by popping up outa the blue."

Dolly was breathing too quickly. He was really scaring her now. It took a minute before she could say, "Why should I?"

"Because you want what's best for her, that's why." He was staring at her in a way that made her itch all over. "Because I'd guess you feel guilty as hell about what you did to Eve, and you want to make it up to her kids. Am I right?"

Dolly felt as if he'd somehow stripped off all her clothes, as if she were stark naked. She wanted to get out of there fast, leave this creep, and never see him again. But she forced herself to sit perfectly still. This was for Annie and Laurel, not for herself.

"What about Val?" she asked. "How come he's not here?"

"Val doesn't know about this, and I intend to keep it that way."

A shiver rippled up Dolly's spine. "Listen, buster, you better not have any perverted . . ."

"Hey, hey there." From the pouches of flesh on either side of his squashed-looking nose, his small eyes peered reproachfully. "You think I'm one of *those* creeps, get it out of your head. I just want to see the kid. Talk to her, get to know her a little. She's my niece, too, you know. I want what you want."

"Why now? I don't get it. And I sure don't see why *I* should help you."

Rudy's face darkened; then he pulled himself up and grinned. "Maybe because of the deal I have in mind. Your silence for mine. Even-steven."

"Wh-what?" she stammered.

"When I *do* talk to Laurel, you wouldn't want it to leak out just *who* it was that handed her mother in to Senator McCarthy, now would you? And in exchange I'll trust you not to say a word to Annie of our little . . . arrangement."

Dolly felt as if every drop of blood had been drained from her body. "You bastard. You're doing this to get back at Val. That's it, isn't it?"

"No, you've got it wrong. It's not that at all." He leaned forward slightly, color rising in his pasty cheeks. "I don't want to get *back* at Val. I just want something of his."

"What about Annie? How do you plan on keeping this from her?"

"Leave that to me."

Dolly knew then that she had lost. And that once again she would be dragged into deceit and betrayal. She'd have to lie to Annie, set up Rudy's meeting with Laurel behind Annie's back. Because if Annie ever found out, she'd grab Laurel and run away all over again. Dolly wanted to weep.

With Henri in Paris with no hope of his ever getting a divorce, she couldn't bear the thought of being without her nieces as well.

I betrayed my sister, Dolly thought, her heart feeling as if it were being ripped apart, and now I'll be betraying my sister's child.

"WHY DOES IT HAVE to be a secret?"

Laurel peered at Uncle Rudy in the watery gloom. The aquarium at Coney Island seemed like a funny place for her to be meeting him. Aunt Dolly had said it wouldn't be any different from going to the park with her. But on the way over here in her chauffeured Lincoln, her aunt had explained that Uncle Rudy wasn't going to hurt her or tell on her—he just wanted to see her and make sure she was okay. But if that was all, then why had Dolly's face looked all puffy and red, as if she'd been crying? And why was Uncle Rudy now making her promise to keep this a secret, even from Annie?

Uncle Rudy had been nice, leading her through the shimmery-green walkways and pointing out the different kinds of fish. He hadn't tried to hug her or even hold her hand—she would've *hated* that. And he hadn't said one word about her and Annie running away . . . until now.

"Trust me," he told her. "It's better this way."

"But if Aunt Dolly knows, then shouldn't Annie know, too?" she asked. "If I told her . . . If I explained that you—"

"Look," he cut her off, "you're a big girl, so I'm gonna be straight with you." He leaned close. "Val . . . your dad . . . that night you ran away— By the time I got him to the hospital, he was out of it. The doctors did everything they could for him, but he . . ." Now Rudy was looking away. "He didn't make it."

Dead? My father dead? Laurel felt suddenly hot and dizzy. Then she remembered, Aunt Dolly had said she'd spoken with Val on the phone. So how could he be dead?

"It's not true!" she cried. "He *isn't* dead! Aunt Dolly would've told me."

"Your Aunt Dolly, she's looking out for you and your sister . . . just like I am. She knows what'd happen if this got out. If the police knew it was Annie that . . ." His voice trailed off.

Laurel shuddered, remembering the blood on Dearie's Oscar and on her blanket. "Annie didn't mean to. I know she didn't!" She was almost sobbing now.

"Sure, *I* know that." Now he was clumsily patting her shoulder. "That's just what I told the police—that it was an accident, that he must've fallen and hit his head on a table or something."

"You didn't tell them about . . ."

"Annie? Of course not. That's what I'm trying to tell you. I'm on your side. From now on, whenever I'm in New York, I'll visit you, and if you ever need anything, all you have to do is just pick up the phone and call me. Collect. But it's gotta be our little secret."

Laurel gulped back her tears. "But why can't Annie know?"

"You want her to know she's a murderer?" His voice was a gravelly whisper. "A thing like that, it could really eat away at a person . . . and maybe wind up pushing them right over the edge."

Like Dearie . . .

Laurel could feel tears running down her cheeks. A manatee swimming close to the glass seemed to be staring out at her, its eyes big and sad and eerily human.

"I won't tell," she said, her voice a ragged whisper.

She didn't feel so dizzy anymore, and the watery dimness of the walkway had settled enough, so she could finally breathe. She actually began to feel a tiny bit pleased with herself.

Even if Annie didn't know, Laurel told herself, *she* would. She'd know that she was doing something important, that she wasn't just some dopey little kid dragging her sister down.

She'd know that in a kind of a way she was taking care of Annie, just like Annie had always taken care of her.

PART TWO: 1972
Chapter Six

ANNIE, curled in the deep, swaybacked mission oak chair in Joe's living room, watched Laurel unwrap the birthday gift she'd given her—a beautiful lacquer box containing watercolor paints and a set of delicate brushes.

"It's Japanese," Annie told her. She remembered the hole-in-the-wall Oriental art store down on Barrow Street where she'd found it, and the elderly Chinese man who had waited on her. When she'd told him it was for her sister, who was turning eighteen, he'd given her a sheaf of handmade rice paper to go with it.

"Oh!" Laurel gasped, staring down at the box, tracing with her fingertip the mother-of-pearl rose on its lid. "It's . . . Oh, Annie, I love it."

She was sitting cross-legged on the Navajo rug near the couch where Joe sat, her shoulder almost grazing his knee. Now she was twisting around, holding the box up for him to see, as if this gift from Annie were something she was offering to *him* instead. "Joe, look, isn't it beautiful?"

"Beautiful," Joe agreed. And then Annie saw that he was looking not at the box, but at Laurel.

Barefoot, in her faded jeans and embroidered Mexican peasant blouse, her bright hair shining about her shoulders, Laurel looked so radiant, unaffectedly lovely, that Annie felt a stab of envy.

"I love it!" Laurel turned and beamed at Annie. "You always pick the perfect thing, and it's something I can really use."

"That's what sisters are for," Dolly piped. "It's up to aunts to give you *useless* things you'd never in a million years buy for yourself. Here." She thrust a small robin's-egg-blue box at Laurel—from Tiffany's, Annie could see at a glance. "Happy eighteenth."

Annie smiled, thinking of the little blue boxes like that one stacked inside her dresser drawer, six of them—one for every birthday since she'd come to New York. She watched Laurel open the box. Inside was a gold heart locket with a tiny diamond in its center.

"You're absolutely right." She laughed. "I never would have bought it. I couldn't have afforded it. But I love it. And I love *you* for thinking of it."

"My Sarah, she has such a locket," Rivka said, "with a picture of her husband." From her seat beside Joe on the sofa, she cast a meaningful glance at Laurel. If Laurel were Rivka's daughter, Annie thought, she wouldn't be going back upstate to finish her second semester at Syracuse University. She'd be getting married, too. Annie, at twenty-four, was an old maid already.

As if she'd read Annie's thoughts, Rivka sighed and said, "I still can't get used to it, you girls living in Manhattan. I should have to ride the subway an hour to see my two California *shainenkes?*" For the past five years Annie and Laurel had been renting an apartment in this building—a tiny one-bedroom, two flights up from Joe's.

"Next time, we'll come to you," Annie promised.

"And next time I come to Manhattan," Rivka teased, shaking her finger at Annie, "it will be to dance at your wedding."

Annie, blushing, fought the urge to glance over at Joe.

Rivka rose from the sofa. "Now, who wants cake?" She had made it herself—kosher, of course—carrying it all the way here in a hatbox on the D train from Avenue J.

"Do I get to blow out the candles first?" Laurel asked.

"Not until you open my present," Joe said. He got up and went into his bedroom, reappearing a moment later holding a small, square package clumsily wrapped in tissue paper.

Laurel unwrapped it slowly, revealing a hand-painted wooden box. Inside was a braided silver band.

"The Indians of Mexico make them," Joe explained. "They're called friendship rings."

Laurel was silent as she stared at it, seemingly mesmerized by the light flashing across its surface. Her head was down and her hair was curtaining her face, so Annie couldn't see her expression. Then Laurel looked up, a quick glance before looking down again, and Annie saw why she wasn't jumping up to hug Joe—her eyes were bright with tears, and her cheeks stained a deep red.

Then it hit her: *She's in love with him.*

After what seemed like an eternity, Laurel got up awkwardly and kissed Joe, not on the cheek, but on the mouth, deliberately lingering a split second longer than was merely polite.

"Thank you, Joe," she murmured.

Joe looked pleased, Annie saw, but also a bit embarrassed.

Images flashed through her head: Laurel, a skinny twelve-year-old, running along the sidewalk to catch up with Joe. Laurel in the kitchen at Joe's Place, kneading bread dough alongside him. Laurel, nestled up against Joe, watching *Invasion of the Body Snatchers* on TV, burying her face in his shoulder during the scary parts.

She's in love with him. The thought repeated itself in Annie's mind over and over. She'd always known it, hadn't she? The difference now was that Laurel was no longer a knock-kneed kid.

But that wasn't what was making Annie's heart bump up into her throat, she realized. It had suddenly occurred to her that Joe might be falling in love with Laurel.

Why not?

At eighteen, Laurel seemed older than most girls her age. Still a little dreamy at times, but so poised, gracious, and adept at doing things, like her artwork and sewing her own clothes. My little wife, Rivka used to call her. And so what if Joe was thirty-one? Lots of guys went for younger women. And lately Joe had been talking more about finding a wife and settling down. What would be so—

Stop it, she told herself. You're being ridiculous. Sure, Joe loves Laurel, but he loves her the way he'd love a little sister.

The way he loves me.

Annie felt a sharp pain in her chest. *Did* Joe look at her that way, as just a good friend—a sister, sort of?

She had first realized she was in love with Joe a few months ago, but she hadn't had the guts to tell him, not yet. Maybe in a few days, after Laurel went back to school.

"Happy birthday to you! Happy birthday to you!" Dolly's robust contralto broke into her thoughts. And now Joe was joining in. And Rivka, too, in a wavery soprano. *"Happy birthday, dear Laurey. Happy birthday to yoooouuuu!"*

Annie watched Laurel take a deep breath and, with her eyes fixed on Joe, blow out the candles on the cake.

I don't need a crystal ball to know what she's wishing. Annie felt guilty for wishing the same thing for herself, but, damn it, why should Laurel have any more of a right to Joe than she did? At Syracuse there had to be dozens of guys chasing after Laurel. In no time at all she'd be mooning over one of them, and Joe would go back to being no more than a big brother.

While Rivka was cutting the rich coconut cake and Laurel was passing out slices, Annie went over and sat down next to Joe. "How did it go last night?" she asked. "You know, with your party?"

Joe's Place had just branched into catering, and she knew they hadn't yet ironed out all the kinks. The restaurant, though, was almost running itself now and was fully booked almost every night. In the past six years it had become a Village institution.

"Not bad," he told her. "Except the lady's oven fritzed out, and we had to sweet-talk the next-door neighbor into letting us use hers. Other than having this ditsy neighbor crash my client's black-tie party in her sweatpants, it went okay. You still so dead set on opening your own shop?" His eyes, behind his round steel-rimmed glasses, were mildly challenging.

"I'd like to . . . if I ever get it together. You know, little details like knowing how to make chocolates and having enough money." She shrugged, keeping her voice light, as for one tantalizing moment she allowed herself to think about an apprenticeship in Paris. What better way to learn how to make her own chocolates than under Henri's Monsieur Pompeau, who had been turning out mouth-watering confections for Girod's for over fifty years? But she didn't want Joe or anyone else to know how desperately she wanted this. What if Henri didn't come through with the apprenticeship? And what if the money from Dearie's trust that she'd been counting on to start her business had somehow vanished, stolen by Val, whose silence all these years worried her almost as much as his lechery once had?

"I'm not worried about you," Joe said. "Anything you really want, you'll find a way of getting it."

Looking into Joe's flashing green-brown eyes, she longed to wrap her arms around him and see if his heart was racing the way hers was right now. *Oh, Joe, if you knew what I was wishing for now, would you still be so sure I'd get it?*

"What are you guys whispering about?" Annie looked up and saw Laurel standing over them, a plate of cake in each hand. She was smiling, but her eyes had narrowed the tiniest bit.

"You, of course," Joe teased. "I was wondering—now that you're eighteen and all—if you're finally going to introduce us to your mystery boyfriend."

"I don't know what you're talking about!" Laurel was trying to laugh, but the color in her cheeks was giving her away.

It was nothing new, this secretiveness of hers, but Annie wondered now, as she had a hundred times before, What is she hiding? All those evenings, getting home from work to find Laurel not home. She'd always say that she'd been doing homework at a friend's house or had stayed late at the library, but she'd cut her eyes away when she said it, and her cheeks would color.

"Then how come you're blushing?" Joe ribbed her, his eyes twinkling.

"I'm not!" Laurel's hands flew to her reddening cheeks, but her smile looked strained.

Joe, probably sensing he'd gone too far, tried to smooth things over. "Okay, okay. Forget I said anything." He wiggled his eyebrows, adding in a low, mock-seductive voice, "Maybe I'm just jealous. Maybe I want you all for myself."

Annie felt herself grow hot. Why was she getting so upset? Joe was just kidding around, same as he'd been doing with Laurel forever. Why should now be any different?

You know, even if Joe refuses to see it.

Enough. She had to tell him how she felt, before Laurel ended up getting hurt.

Now Dolly was standing up, reaching for her purse. "I'd like to make a little announcement," she said, looking straight at Annie, smiling, her face pink with anticipation. "I know this is Laurey's big day, but honey, I have something for you, too." She pulled out an envelope and handed it to Annie. "Go on," she urged, "open it."

Inside the envelope was an airline ticket—to Paris. She stared at it, numb with shock.

"I talked to Henri," Dolly gushed. "It's all arranged. One week from today you'll be working under Monsieur Pompeau."

"It's . . . so soon," Annie managed to get past her frozen lips.

"Sorry I couldn't give you more notice, but the other apprentice starts then, and Pompeau wants you both at the same time."

Now the numbness was beginning to fade, and feeling crept back in. She felt a burst of sudden joy—Paris! She was finally going to be a *real* chocolatier, not just an assistant manager in a shop.

Then her joy wilted. Three and a half months without Joe. Now it didn't matter if she told him how she felt. Either way, they'd be apart. And Laurel . . . Well, Syracuse was a lot closer than Paris. Maybe with Annie out of the way, Joe and Laurel would—

"Well, *say* something, for heaven's sake!" Dolly threw up her arms. "If I have to lose the best manager I've ever had, the least you can do is be happy about it."

"I . . . I don't know what to say." Annie stood up and hugged her aunt. "I don't know how to thank you."

And Annie *did* feel grateful, but at the same time she couldn't help thinking that Dolly had picked absolutely the worst moment to play fairy godmother.

AT THE Air France check-in desk, Annie heard her flight being announced. She turned to Joe. "I'd better go." She bent down to grab her carry-on bag, but Joe got to it first, hefting it easily.

"I'll walk you to the gate," he said.

"You don't have to."

She felt so awkward standing there with Joe in the middle of the international-departures corridor, the two of them acting more like strangers on a blind date than best friends. She felt a sudden urge to grab him and shout, I love you, damn it! Why can't you see that?

But of course, she wouldn't. Instead, she just trudged alongside Joe, sneaking sidelong glances at him. Why didn't *he* say something, *anything*, to let her know how he felt, if he was going to miss her?

He didn't speak until they reached her gate. Putting her suitcase down, he reached up to touch her cheek, his fingers cool and light. "I'm not going to promise to write. I'm lousy with letters."

"Well, I'll probably be too busy to write back, anyway." She looked down so he wouldn't see her disappointment.

"Annie"—he hooked a finger under her chin, tilting her head back—"that doesn't mean I'm not going to miss you." His crooked smile was fading now, his eyes serious.

"Joe, I . . ." She felt a high, throbbing ache in her throat.

Over the PA system the final boarding call was being announced. The lounge, she saw, was nearly empty now.

"I'd better go," she finished weakly.

She was about to turn when he caught her in his arms and pulled her close. He kissed her full on the mouth, a deep kiss that pierced her heart. *Dear God, is this really happening?*

A happy, stunned heat flooded through her, making her feel heavy and light-headed. Pulling back and looking into Joe's eyes, she sensed that under that calm surface he felt as shaken as she did.

Say it, she willed. Say you love me. You want me.

But all he said was, "So long, kiddo."

Annie, moving away from him, toward the ramp to the plane, half hated him for that—for kissing her, for letting her go off to Paris, where she knew she would dream about that kiss for weeks and weeks, not knowing exactly what it meant.

LAUREL stared at the naked man lying in front of her.

Dark hair down to his shoulders, a bandanna knotted about his forehead, his lean muscled torso just a shade lighter than the burnt-sienna pastel crayon she was using to sketch him with.

He looked about her age. There was something about him—an edge . . . a tautness. She sketched furiously, using bold, sweeping strokes. There. She was getting it now.

Laurel found herself thinking of Joe, imagining it was Joe she was drawing. In less than an hour she'd be on a bus heading home. And with Annie in Paris, Laurel, for the first time, would have the apartment—and Joe—all to herself. She prayed that tonight, when she got there, he'd be home.

Would things be different between them now? Could he begin to see her in a new light?

Thinking of Joe, Laurel felt herself blushing, and when she looked back at the model, she saw that he was staring at her with his tea-colored eyes. Stretched languidly on his side on a bench in the center of the classroom, he looked familiar. Was he a student? He wasn't in any of her classes, but she might have seen him on campus.

After class, as she was putting away her pencils and pastel crayons in her box, the boy sauntered over.

"Not bad." Flicking his hair off his shoulders, he stared at the sketch she'd done of him.

"Thanks." Laurel was relieved to see he'd put on some clothes—patched jeans and a dark blue T-shirt. Even so, having him so close, chatting with her after she'd been staring for forty-five minutes at his . . . well, *all* of him—it made her feel weird.

"You're trying to remember where you know me from, but you haven't figured it out yet, have you, Beanie?"

Laurel started and looked up. It hit her then: *The little boy in Miss Rodriguez's who'd made her life so miserable.* "Jesús," she cried, "no wonder I didn't recognize you. Last time I saw you, you were about five feet tall, and—"

"And I was wearing clothes." He grinned, as if he knew his frank, carefree nakedness had made her uncomfortable.

Laurel could feel the heat in her face seeping up into her hairline. Was it that obvious? Could guys tell just by looking at her that she was inexperienced . . . a virgin? Was that why Joe treated her like a kid?

"It's Jess now, not Jesús," he answered. "Jess Gordon."

"I heard you'd gone to a foster home after your mother died."

"You heard right. My foster parents, the Gordons, wound up adopting me. Beats me how come—I was murder in those days." He laughed an easy, rich laugh. "But *you* weren't scared of me."

She shrugged, and glanced at her watch. Ten to four—she'd better get moving if she was going to get down to the Greyhound terminal in time to catch the next bus to Manhattan. But Jess, with his mocking smile, was holding her somehow. "I guess I had bigger things to worry about back then," she told him.

She thought of Uncle Rudy. . . . Uncle Rudy, who had become her "mystery boyfriend."

All through that first year, then junior high, and Music and Art High School, Rudy would just show up there three or four times a year and take her for a ride in a limousine. Sometimes she'd catch him looking at her so hard it made her feel creepy inside. But he never touched her—not a hug, not even to hold her hand.

"Listen," Jess was saying, "me and some others, we're organizing this antiwar rally for next week. You interested?"

"Maybe."

She was against the war, sure, but all she really cared about right now was getting home to Joe. "I could help you out with posters. But I'm in kind of a hurry right now." Laurel saw that Jess was staring at her, his dark eyes hooded. He had an edge that made her blood pump faster. She shuddered, feeling suddenly scared.

Of Jess?

Maybe it wasn't Jess who scared her; maybe it was Joe—the thought of what he might do or say when she . . . when she . . .

But *could* she? Could she really make it happen? Could she make Joe love her *that* way?

Now Jess was shrugging. "No problem, Beanie," he said, tipping her a sly wink, as if he could read her thoughts. "I'll give you a call."

JOE stared at her. "Laurey, what are you doing here?"

She was wearing some kind of Indian smock made of crinkly raspberry-colored cotton. Tiny round mirrors were sewn into the bodice, and they glittered in the light.

"Joe!" She hugged him and kissed his cheek so lightly, so quickly, his senses barely had time to record it. "Surprised?"

"Let's just say I wasn't expecting you."

"Does that mean you aren't going to invite me in?"

"Actually, I was just on my way out." Seeing her look of disappointment, he explained, "My mother. I promised her I'd catch this opening down in SoHo. You want to come along?"

"I'd love to." He saw her eyes light up and felt a short, sharp tug inside his chest.

He knew that look; he had, in fact, been avoiding it for a very long time. He'd pretended it wasn't what he thought it was. And now she was here, and, truthfully, was it such a surprise? Hadn't he known deep down that she *would* come—that he'd have to face this sooner rather than later?

But what was he supposed to do? What could he say that wouldn't break her heart, make her hate him?

"I thought you and your parents weren't getting along," Laurel said as they were strolling toward Seventh Avenue to catch a cab downtown. She tucked her arm into his.

"Well, we're not talking *Make Room for Daddy* here," he countered. "But yeah, I guess things are loosening up a little. Get this—last week my mother and the great Marcus Daugherty finally deigned to eat in my restaurant. I'm thinking of having a brass plaque inscribed and put over the table where they sat."

"Don't make fun, Joe. I think it's nice that they came."

"So do I, actually." He *was* glad . . . or maybe just relieved. This tug-of-war between him and his parents had been going on so long, he didn't feel the least bit smug about the fact that he'd won.

As they reached the corner, Joe watched the neighborhood greengrocer unpacking a box of oranges onto his sidewalk display.

Remembering that Laurel might be hungry, Joe asked, "Have you eaten? There may be some wine at this art show, but not much in the way of edibles."

"It's okay," she said. "I had a sandwich on the bus."

"Come on. That long ride—you've got to be starved." Leaving her on the sidewalk, he ducked into the market and grabbed a handful of the tiny, tart kumquats he knew she loved. On impulse he snatched a yellow rose from a bucket by the register. Returning to Laurel and handing her the fruit and the rose, he saw her eyes widen in delight.

Watching her bite into a kumquat, her mouth puckering at its tartness, he thought, Boy, she's beautiful. Those blue eyes, with their thick dark lashes. And those lips . . .

He realized he wanted to kiss her. Very much.

I must be losing my mind. What about Annie?

Annie. He loved her, he missed her, and, damn it, yes, he wanted her. For months, years even, he'd put off telling her how he felt. It was too soon. He wasn't ready to get serious. But gradually, when the prospect of a wife and kids no longer seemed part of some nebulous future, he began looking at Annie with new eyes. Did she love him? Maybe. But was she really ready for a husband, house, kids? No. She was on fire, needing to *prove* herself somehow. Wait, he'd told himself. Wait until she wants this as much as you do.

But why, if he loved Annie, was it Laurel he felt drawn to now? What was it about her that made him want to hold her, lie down beside her, sink into her as he would into cool, still water?

Get a grip on yourself. This isn't a movie, he told himself. This is real. Somebody could get hurt. Hurt real bad.

But it wasn't until a few hours later, back from the opening, that Joe realized that one of the people who might get hurt could be him.

He'd intended to wind up the evening with a quick good-night peck, but as he was letting himself into his apartment Laurel clung to him and whispered, "Let me stay with you tonight, Joe." Her voice was quiet, controlled, but he could hear the slight tremor in it. He knew her so well; he knew it was when she was scared that she acted the most nonchalant. In that way she and Annie truly were sisters.

Joe felt as if he'd been sucker-punched. Had he heard right?

"Laurey, I . . ." His voice choked up on him. He cleared his throat and took her hand. "Look, I have a feeling that no matter what I say, it's not going to come out right, and I . . ."

I'm in love with your sister. Is that what he meant to say?

But was it even true? How could he be in love with Annie if he felt this attracted to Laurel?

"I don't want to hurt you," he finished, feeling weak, cowardly. Hearing footsteps below, he gently pulled her inside and shut the door. It was dark, but he didn't reach for the light switch.

"You don't love me," she said. "Oh, I know. You love me, but you're not *in* love with me. Is that it?"

She laughed shakily; then with a fierceness she said, "Joe, this isn't some crush. I love you. I always have."

Before he could stop her, or stop himself, she was slipping her arms around his neck, drawing him to her. He felt her flesh against his, cool and silken, and her lips soft and sweet. He wanted to tear himself away, stop her from pulling him in the wrong direction, but her mouth . . . her sweet mouth . . .

She's just a baby, he told himself. He had to stop this before he took a path that would lead him forever away from Annie.

Joe drew away, trembling. "Laurey, this isn't . . . us. It's just, well, things are a little up in the air right now."

"Annie, you mean." Her voice was shaking; he could hear the tears close to the surface. "You think this has to do with Annie being gone. That I'm somehow . . . that I'm just *overreacting.*"

"No. This has nothing to do with Annie." He could tell from the way she was looking at him that she didn't believe him.

"Okay, then." She pulled in a deep breath and reached for the door knob, twisting it sharply. "Okay." Forcing a smile that appeared almost ghastly, she said, "Well, good night."

She opened the door and walked out, her shoes clicking against the stairs with hard, rapid strokes, and Joe, watching her go, ached. He ached to wrap himself around her, make love to her. But if he did that, wouldn't he be hurting her even more?

Chapter Seven
Paris

ANNIE watched as tiny white-maned Monsieur Pompeau peered into the pot of melted chocolate—or *couverture*—she had been stirring.

She held her breath, her heart racing. After two weeks she still had trouble melting chocolate without scorching the bottom or causing the cocoa butter to separate. Gauging the temperature— that was the tricky part.

So far the chocolate looked okay—dark brown and satiny. Still, she felt herself tense as Pompeau dipped a spoon into the pot and raised it to his lips. This afternoon he would tell Henri Baptiste whether she had any promise as a chocolatier. And if the report was bad, Henri would feel he had to dismiss her. Apprenticeships at Girod's were precious, the waiting list endless.

Pompeau's wizened face puckered as he ceremoniously tasted the *couverture*. "*Non, non, c'est gâtée!*" he pronounced sadly. "The bouquet, he has gone away."

Annie felt numb. All around her, figures in starched whites were bustling about the large kitchen. Light sparkled off the copper caldrons, the marble counters, the refrigerator doors.

"You permitted it to make the vapor, you see that? And now he has become like mud. *Regardez cela!*"

Annie peered into the oversized double boiler on the cooktop in front of her. Instantly she saw he was right. The lake of silky dark brown chocolate had begun separating into grainy lumps.

"I'm sorry," she said, struggling against the urge to cry. "I thought I was doing it the way you—"

Pompeau cut her off with a wave of his hand.

"*Non, non!* The words I tell to you, they are only words. The *chocolat,* you must know *here* when it is right." He tapped his breast.

"Let me start over. I'll get it right this time. I—"

Again he cut her off, this time with a flap of his white apron, shooing her away as if she were a stray alley cat that had wandered in.

At the other end of the long cooktop Emmett caught Annie's eye and gave her an encouraging thumbs-up. Thank God for Emmett. Always there with a wink or a smile.

Signaling to her, he lifted a coffeepot from the counter and poured *filtre* into two thick white china cups. Coffee break. At nine thirty Pompeau allowed them a luxurious ten minutes. But could it be that late already? She'd started work at six a.m., and it seemed as if hardly an hour had passed. They'd have to move fast, before the nougat syrup bubbling on the stove peaked.

Annie followed Emmett into a small storage area. He walked with a jaunty stride, broken by a slight limp. He wore a red Henley jersey stretched across a chest as thick and solid as a hickory stump, faded jeans, and snub-nosed cowboy boots that clacked on the tile floor. If he hadn't told her about his crippled foot, she might never have guessed it was more than a slightly twisted ankle. Ask him about it, though, and he'd give her that big smile, wide as Texas, and drawl, "Only handicap I got is these here freckles. Must've stood in front of a screen door too long with the sun shining through."

Annie liked Emmett's freckles. She liked everything about Emmett, from his coppery hair to his faint Texas twang, which he exaggerated when he was kidding around. He'd grown up in Texas, but since leaving home, he'd been all over, working on a beef ranch in El Paso, as an oil-field roustabout in Oklahoma, and in Louisiana as a shrimper, a boat builder, and a cook aboard a merchant ship. He seemed to have lived enough to be fifty instead of only twenty-nine.

They settled into a pair of rickety folding chairs set near a narrow table, and Emmett hiked his leg onto one of the extra chairs.

"You look like a mile of bad road," he told her. "Take a load off, Cobb. Old Pompeau's not so mean. I'll bet he drinks hot milk before bed and sleeps with a night-light. A regular old pussycat."

"An old concentration camp guard is more like it."

Emmett laughed. "Pompeau, he's not the problem. It's *you.* My guess is, whatever's eating you, he's twice as tall and ten times better-looking. Boyfriend back home, right?"

"Are you always this nosy?"

"Fraid so." He grinned.

"Well then, I guess you won't mind if I get a little nosy with you."

"Fire away."

"You never told me how you ended up here. I mean—chocolate?"

He shrugged. "Not much to it. I was working as an assistant pastry chef at Commander's Palace. You heard of it?"

"New Orleans. It's famous, isn't it?" She remembered Joe's mentioning it.

"You could say that. Anyway, turns out Paul Prudhomme, chef at the restaurant, and Henri Baptiste are old friends. Old Paul puts in a word, and next thing I know, they got me munching croissants."

Annie laughed. She found herself staring at him. Somehow she'd always thought of freckles as a flaw, but on Emmett they . . . well, they suited him. Made him even more rugged-looking. With his blue denim eyes and square features she could imagine him leaning against a split-rail fence, the mud-caked heel of one cowboy boot hooked over the bottom rail.

"I still don't quite get it," she said. "Why this? Why here?"

Emmett shrugged, and smiled. "Like you, I was figuring on having my own business one of these days."

"You sound like maybe you're having second thoughts."

"Could be. I'm beginning to think this is gonna be just one more dead end for me."

"Why don't you leave, then?"

"It suits me fine . . . for now."

"And after that?"

He brought his boot heel clopping to the floor and leaned so close she could feel his warm breath. Holding her gaze, he spoke with an intensity that startled her. "Land. Property. Buildings. My old man, he owned zip and was proud of it. Soon as he and Mom got settled in somewhere, it'd be time to move on." His eyes took on a feverish light. "When I do settle down, I mean to sink my roots so deep they'll be pulling them up in China."

"But owning things—that's not a living, not something you *do* every day," Annie persisted. At the same time she thought of Bel Jardin and felt a longing for her childhood home that brought a hot ache to her belly, as if she'd gulped her coffee too quickly.

"Owning," Emmett echoed. "Way I look at it, more you own, the more it'll keep your livelihood from owning you."

Annie understood. Security. That was something she'd never known, not even as a child. She realized Emmett had fallen silent and was staring at her.

"So, what about you? What are you doing here?"

Before she could say anything, they were interrupted by Pompeau's shrill voice crying, "Nougat! Nougat!"

Annie and Emmett rushed in just as Pompeau was pouring the kettle of hot caramel and nuts onto a long marble slab.

"*Allons!*" shouted Pompeau, signaling for the men to hurry.

Emmett rushed to the table, along with the two full-time helpers—Thierry and Maurice. The men descended on the pond of hot nougat with metal paddles, beating at it determinedly to flatten it before it cooled and became too brittle to work with. Then Annie watched Emmett begin cutting the warm, flattened nougat into even squares with the "guitar"—a tool with metal strings that looked like an oversized egg slicer.

Suddenly she became aware that Pompeau was staring at her, his small blue eyes hard as bullets. The despair she'd felt earlier came rushing back, but then something inside her stiffened. "Show me," she said in a firm voice. "Please. One more time. I want to learn."

Pompeau, she was half surprised to see, merely shrugged. "*C'est facile,*" he said mildly. "Come, again I will demonstrate for you."

She followed him over to the cooktop. While Pompeau worked, dropping brick-size chunks of chocolate into the big double boiler, he explained how it was required that the chocolate be heated gently, as gently as you would bathe an infant. Now came the hot cream that would turn the melted chocolate into *ganache*—the truffle's soft center. He poured the cream into a separate pan and heated it. When it was almost hot enough to boil, he strained it through a wire colander into the melted chocolate.

After gently stirring the *ganache* until it was smooth and mocha-colored, the old man carried it over to some horizontal wooden doors, covered in silicone-treated paper, that were resting on metal shelving at one end of the kitchen.

"Monsieur Henri, this is his discovery." Pompeau beamed. "Clever, *non?* We could not find the trays large enough, so we find the old doors rescued from the demolished buildings."

Pompeau was now pouring the *ganache* in a dark, silky river onto the uppermost door. With a broad spatula he smoothed it, coaxing it outward to meet the edges of the paper. Then he stepped back. "*Voilà.* You see? No grains, no lumps. *Parfait.* It will cool, and then we shall do the enrobing."

On the other doors different flavors of *ganache* stood cooling; they would form the centers of Girod's world-famous truffles— bittersweet chocolate with soft mocha-Champagne centers, a puree of fresh raspberries in a smooth milk chocolate *ganache*, white chocolate and fresh-grated coconut dusted with ground pistachios from Sicily. Her own favorite was bittersweet and crème fraîche flavored with an infusion of smoky Lapsang Souchong tea.

An idea came to Annie, a way she might be able to redeem herself. *What if I created a whole new flavor? And did it so perfectly that even Pompeau and Henri would be impressed?*

It might work. It might also backfire. But hey, she'd taken a lot bigger chances than this, hadn't she?

Annie concentrated hard. Then she remembered the little bistro where she and Emmett had eaten the other night. After their cassoulet the waiter had brought a basket of pears—the best she'd ever tasted.

Chocolate and pears, would they go together? Maybe. But what if instead of fresh pears, she combined the chocolate with Poire William? She'd seen a bottle of the liqueur once, with a whole pear inside. The pear was grown that way, she'd learned, with the bottle positioned over the branch while the fruit was still a tiny green nub.

Of course, she'd have to ask Pompeau. But how? *Doesn't matter. Just do it now, or you never will.* Her throat seemed to tighten; then somehow she was telling him. She was sure he'd turn her down, or worse, laugh at her. But after a long moment he nodded.

"*Bien,*" he said. "To create a new flavor, it is more difficult than you imagine. But this way, perhaps, you will understand."

Yes, that I won't ever be any good at this. He's hoping I'll fail. Annie pulled her apron ties even tighter, knotting them so that they cut into her waist, making her stand up straighter. Then despite the panic in her cinched-in stomach, she went into the storeroom to get the chocolate she would need.

EMMETT, hoisting a tub of warm *couverture* from its seat on the tempering machine, winced slightly. His bad leg hurt him, though he'd never let on.

Then as always when his leg ached, he was remembering Atlanta, all those black people marching for what they wanted. Just happening by, Emmett had seen a black kid, no more than twelve or thirteen, pinned to the pavement by a slab-armed man twice his size who was beating him with the butt end of a shotgun.

Emmett remembered roaring as he dived at the man. The next thing he knew he was lying in a hospital bed, his mother's face hovering over him like an Arctic moon.

"Bullet sheared off half your anklebone. And three toes. Some muscles, too. . . . But don't worry. The doctors say you'll walk again." Spoken like it was nothing worse than a sprained ankle.

Emmett was jerked from his reverie by a hand on his arm, firm but gentle. He turned and saw Annie. Thin face, saved from mere prettiness by strong bones. Huge eyes the color of blue ink. No makeup, but then she didn't need any. Skinny as a rail.

"Let me give you a hand with that," she said, reaching for a handle of the heavy tub he was hefting.

He smiled. "Thanks, but I can manage. Just don't offer me your foot. I might take you up on it."

"Not funny." But a corner of her wide mouth curved down in a small don't-make-me-laugh smile.

She didn't move away. She was standing so close, he could smell her perfume—something musky and Oriental—overriding even the pervasive aroma of chocolate. There was a smear of chocolate on one cheek. He thought about licking it off.

Emmett felt panicky. What had come over him? He wasn't some teenager. He'd had plenty of women.

Suddenly he knew that if he took so much as a step in her direction, he could fall in love with Annie.

And, with Annie, he suspected that if he fell, it would be a long, hard fall.

ANNIE stared at the small chilled metal box she was holding. Inside was a single truffle, its glossy black coating of *couverture* dusted with toasted bitter almonds crushed to a fine powder.

Was it any good? Over the week, Annie had made fourteen batches of her pear *ganache,* and everyone around here who'd tasted her Poire William truffle had said they loved it. But Henri would be the judge—the only one who counted.

Annie mounted the narrow staircase leading up from the kitchen to the shop, which faced out onto the fashionable Rue du Faubourg St.-Honoré. Her hands shook a bit, but she forced herself to ascend briskly, one foot after the next.

What if he doesn't like it? What if it really is nothing special?

Even so, she mustn't let it destroy her. She *mustn't*.

At the top of the stairs she passed through a narrow door and into the shop itself. She paused on the threshold, a bit dazzled. Girod's was like no other chocolate shop. It looked more like a reproduced nineteenth-century room in a museum: an Oriental carpet; muted gold-flecked wallpaper above walnut wainscoting; on one wall, glass shelves on which artisans' works were displayed.

What Annie loved best of all were the chocolates themselves—on all sides, displayed on silver trays like precious jewels, and in fluted crystal dishes. But right now Annie knew it was Henri to whom she needed to devote all her attention. He caught sight of her and grinned, his mustache twitching up at the corners, his broad face creasing. "Ah, how does it go, Annie!" he called. Then, looking beyond her, he added, "And Bernard, how is it that you do us the honor of climbing the stairs in the middle of the day?"

Annie realized with a jolt that Pompeau had followed her. Of course, the old fussbudget couldn't resist seeing her make a fool of herself. Her cheeks burned, but she wouldn't give him the satisfaction of seeing how nervous she was.

Behind her she heard Pompeau give a low, raspy chuckle. "I may be of a certain age, but in a few weeks, when I take the baths at Baden-Baden, I will be made young again. And you?"

Henri sighed, and something dark, like a cloud shutting out the sun, flitted across his face.

He misses Dolly, she realized. She knew because she'd so often seen the same sad expression of longing on Dolly's face. They only saw each other every other month, and the letters and phone calls in between were clearly not enough to bridge the gap.

But if Henri was sad, he seemed determined not to let it show. As Pompeau stepped past Annie, Henri strode over and clapped the old man's stooped shoulder. Then he kissed Annie on both cheeks, greeting her as if he had not seen her in years. "Annie, Monsieur Pompeau here—he has not terrorized you, I hope, into losing your voice, hmm?" His gray eyes shone with kindness and good humor.

"Monsieur Henri, I don't wish to impose on your time," Pompeau began, "but Mademoiselle Cobb—"

"It's a new flavor we came up with," Annie abruptly interrupted. "We'd like your opinion." If Henri hated it, she'd take the blame, but until then, she didn't want him to be prejudiced by her inexperience.

She handed him the box, her heart pounding. Henri peered at the lone truffle for a long time, examining it the way a doctor might study a wart. Then as Annie watched, her every nerve strung taut, he popped the truffle into his mouth and chewed thoughtfully.

Just as she thought she couldn't bear the suspense a moment longer, Henri smiled.

Formidable! he pronounced. "It has a marvelous texture, and the taste . . . sublime. Bernard, I compliment you. This is an achievement. And will do well with our customers, I am certain."

He thought the old man had done it! She felt sick. What should she do now?

"I . . . you see . . . it was . . ." She watched Pompeau flush a brick red and begin to sputter.

Then something occurred to Annie. Maybe letting him take the credit could help her even more than if she took it for herself.

"Monsieur Pompeau has a gift like no one else," she put in quickly. "It's such a privilege for me to work with him."

Had she gone too far? Then she saw how the old man was puffing up with pride. The glance he shot in her direction was one of pure delight. Good, she'd made the right choice. It was to Pompeau that she had to answer each day, not Henri. And if Pompeau decided to like her, to take her under his wing, she could really *learn* from him.

Annie felt a surge of happiness that seemed to fill her with bright light. She was magic. Nothing could stop her.

"You're not enjoying this," Emmett whispered.

Annie felt a stab of guilt. Their big evening out—a chamber music concert at the Sainte-Chapelle—and she was ruining it for Emmett. Under the spotlight, the cellist was playing Mozart, the music resounding in this soaring space with a clarity she'd never before heard. But she couldn't concentrate, couldn't keep her mind off Joe.

Two months, Annie thought, and not a phone call. Even now with Emmett she felt a loneliness so deep it ached in the pit of her stomach. It had to be partly this place, too, this heavenly music—too much loveliness could break your heart. Especially feeling as miserable as she did.

"It shows?" she whispered to Emmett.

"We don't have to stay."

"But . . ."

Before she could remind him how much he'd spent for the tickets, she felt him tugging her to her feet. Together they slipped down the narrow aisle alongside their row of chairs. Outside, in the stone courtyard abutting the entrance, Annie turned to him and said, "Em, there's absolutely no reason for you to miss the concert because of me. I can make it home on my own."

"Listen, Cobb, I've got an even better idea." He hooked an arm about her shoulders. "I know a café not far from here. When you're feeling low, a Pernod and a shoulder to cry on beats Mozart any day."

"Stop being so nice! You're making me feel even more guilty."

"In that case, I'll let you pay for the drinks."

"Okay." She laughed. "It's a deal."

As they strolled in the mild summer evening Annie glanced at Emmett. He was wearing gray slacks, and a tan blazer over a white button-down shirt. She couldn't help thinking how handsome he looked; he could have passed for a young lawyer or stockbroker—except for his boots. Annie had never seen him without those old cowboy boots—tanned leather rubbed smooth as driftwood.

She felt a surge of gratitude toward him, for being a friend and at the same time not putting even the slightest romantic pressure on her. After all their weeks of working together so closely, he'd never even kissed her good night. Crossing the Seine at Pont St.-Michel, Annie wondered what it would be like if Emmett kissed her. She felt suddenly, acutely conscious of the warm weight of his arm draped about her shoulders.

The crowded sidewalk café was only a pleasant walk from the bridge. Annie and Emmett waited a few minutes until they spotted a couple leaving and then quickly slid into their seats. "You want to talk about it?" Emmett asked after they'd ordered.

"No," she said. "There's really nothing to tell."

"Let me guess—tall, dark, and handsome?"

Annie felt her face flush. She looked at Emmett and saw that he was wearing a languid smile, his blue eyes flicking over her as if trying to read her. But she sensed the empathy behind that smile.

"There's no reason for him to get sentimental just because I'm here and he's there," she blurted in a firm voice, more to convince herself than Emmett. "I mean, we're just good friends. Why should he suddenly start writing me love letters when he's not in love with me?"

"But you're in love with him." Emmett's gaze fixed on her, mildly challenging.

"No! I mean . . . well, maybe. Oh, Emmett, I don't know anymore. How long can you stay in love with someone who doesn't feel the same as you?"

His eyes narrowed, as if he were gazing into bright sunlight. "A long time, I reckon."

Annie knew he wasn't just talking about her, but before she could probe further, a waiter appeared with their drinks.

Soon, feeling light-headed from the Pernod, Annie said, "I lied before, when I told you I wasn't sure if I loved Joe. I do. Why is that so hard to admit?"

"Because you're afraid of making a fool of yourself," he said. "You're not alone, Cobb. Most folks'd rather be hit by a bus than be made a fool of. Specially in love."

"If only I *knew* how he felt, then . . ." She shrugged.

"You sure it's *him* holding back? Or could it be that it's you?" He tipped his head to one side, eyeing her with some amusement.

Annie, feeling his words hit home, stared into her empty glass. She realized with a ripple of unease that she was a bit drunk.

"I think I'd better be getting back," she said. "I don't know about you, but getting up at five every morning means that by ten o'clock at night I'm ready to turn into a pumpkin."

He laughed. "Now that you mention it . . . yeah, you are looking a little orange around the gills."

Minutes later, recrossing the river, it struck Annie that in just a few weeks she'd be back in New York. And Emmett . . . well, who knew where he'd be? Maybe they would never see each other after that. She felt a pang, and as they stopped to watch a barge decked in fairy lights glide under the bridge, she impulsively leaned over and kissed him lightly on the lips.

Then, unexpectedly, Emmett was kissing her back, holding her so tight she couldn't have gotten away if she'd wanted to—which somehow she didn't.

Annie felt a sharp tug low in her belly. The blood seemed to drain from her head; sparks of light danced on the insides of her eyelids. She felt heat rising in her, collecting in the hollow space where moments before her stomach had been. How could this feel so good when it was Joe she wanted, not Emmett?

Emmett, drawing away, seemed to stagger a bit, and she wondered if maybe he was a little tipsy as well. And whether if they'd been perfectly sober, this would have happened at all.

"Well," he muttered, rubbing his jaw, "where do we go from here?"

"Not my place." She gave a short, breathless laugh. "Madame Begbeder would throw us out."

"That kind of whittles it down, doesn't it?" He stepped back and grabbed her hand, squeezing it hard.

Before she could think it over, they were in a taxi, rocketing along a boulevard on the way to the Place Victor-Hugo, where Emmett was subletting. Annie felt both exhilarated and oddly resigned, as if she'd climbed aboard a roller coaster and now had to see it through to the very end.

Then they were inside the narrow, high-ceilinged salon where Emmett lived. The woman who owned the place would have smiled, Annie thought, to see Emmett, broad and rugged, clumping in his cowboy boots amid the plump satin-covered sofas and spindly Empire chairs.

I should turn around right now, this very instant, Annie thought, but she felt drawn to him. She didn't love Emmett . . . but, damn it, she *wanted* him.

Emmett, who seemed to sense her confusion, came to her and, with his arms loosely about her shoulders, kissed her forehead.

Annie felt embarrassed. "Emmett, I shouldn't have come. This is crazy. I don't love you. And you don't love me."

"And you . . . you're not the kind of girl who'd go to bed with a man just for the fun of it, right?" He was mocking her now.

"Not if I wanted us to stay friends afterwards."

"Is it *us* you're worried about, or this fellow back home?"

"No." She lied. "It has nothing to do with Joe."

He shrugged, and stepped back with an easy chuckle. "Hey, Cobb, you could walk right out of here this minute, and I promise you, there won't be a speck of hard feeling. On the other hand," he added soberly, "if you stay, I can promise you something a lot better."

When he kissed her this time, Annie felt it flash through her like summer lightning. In the heat that followed, she thought, Joe . . . I don't need him. And she felt a small, mean triumph.

Then Emmett was leading her into the bedroom. A massive headboard dominated the tiny space. As if in a dream, Annie lay down on the bed and let Emmett undress her. His callused fingers were rough but surprisingly tender and adept. He kissed her lips, her temple, her throat, causing her to shiver and her heart to race.

Now, watching Emmett sit down on the bed and begin prying off his boots, she wondered how seeing his crippled foot would make her feel.

When she did—its purple, puckered flesh and oddly bent shape—she felt a welling of tenderness. She touched it lightly. "Does it hurt?"

"Only when I'm walking in places I shouldn't," he said with a wry, cockeyed smile.

"Like now?"

He shrugged.

"Emmett, I'm scared."

"It's okay. I'm a little scared, too."

But he didn't seem so. Instead, he seemed utterly unselfconscious, as if this were an everyday thing, their being together like this. And then for Annie it became natural, too.

Chapter Eight

ANNIE looked around Dolly's living room, filled with party guests. Nothing much had changed in the months she'd been away. The white leather sofa faced the fireplace just as it always had. Behind it, the wet bar with its buttoned-down leather base—a relic of the early '60s. She could imagine Rock Hudson in a tuxedo leaning an elbow against the lacquered surface, sipping a martini.

But something has changed. I have.

Watching Dolly, elegant in a low-cut, ruby velvet caftan, darting among her guests, Annie felt as if part of her belonged and part had become a stranger.

She looked about, searching for the one face that would make her feel as if she had truly come home.

Joe.

Where was he? Yesterday she'd been too exhausted to see anyone until she'd had some sleep. Then late this afternoon she was jolted out of a dream by Dolly's telephoning to say that her driver would be picking her up in one hour and she was to put on her sexiest dress. Her aunt, it seemed, was making her a little homecoming party.

Annie caught a glimmery reflection of herself in the huge window. Had she overdone it with this dress? What would Joe think? It was chic, *très parisienne*—this black crepe sheath that skimmed her thighs well above the knee, adorned only by a loop of opera-length faux pearls knotted just below her plunging neckline. She'd worn this on her last night in Paris with Emmett. Remembering the obscenely expensive dinner he had insisted on, the Grand Cru wine they'd drunk too much of, and afterwards going back to Emmett's apartment, Annie, suddenly aware that her face was on fire, quickly slammed her mind shut against the memory.

Emmett. Would she ever see him again? He'd talked about coming to New York, but he didn't say when. And what difference would it make if he did come? Whatever they'd had in Paris wouldn't, *couldn't,* be a part of her life here in New York. Still, at the thought that she might not see him, Annie felt a pang of regret.

Threading her way through a cluster of people at the bar, Annie accepted the dripping glass of Champagne the barman thrust at her. Then she spotted Laurel at the far end of the bar. She looked gloomy, and Annie felt a dart of unease. At the JFK arrivals terminal, her sister had seemed so happy to see her, but in the car driving back, she'd sort of clammed up.

Something's wrong with Laurey. Annie had noticed it right away, but until now, it hadn't fully sunk in.

Annie hiked herself onto the barstool beside her sister. "What's up, Doc? You look a little down. I guess this isn't your kind of party. No Grateful Dead . . . no black lights . . . no body paints."

Laurel shrugged, smiling. "I guess I'm in the wrong place, then."

"It's not my scene, either," Annie confided.

"Hey, you're the guest of honor."

"Listen, I'm sure Dolly meant well. She usually does. But . . ."

"But," Laurel echoed.

"Remember the white stretch limousine she rented for your junior prom?"

Laurel winced. "*Red* seats. I almost died of embarrassment. And a *bar*. On the way to the restaurant Rick Warner just sat there staring out the window. It was *awful*. If Joe hadn't . . ."

"Yeah, I remember." Annie finished with a laugh. "He showed up just in time to rescue you with his beat-up old Ford." She'd heard this story many times—Laurel's coming out of the restaurant and finding Joe, who, with a conspiratorial grin, had tossed Rick his car keys and then climbed into the limo idling at the curb. "Hey, have you seen much of Joe this summer?" She tried to sound casual, but it came out false, pitched too high.

She wasn't prepared, either, for Laurel's reaction. Her sister flushed, and her eyes slid away.

Panic crept into Annie's heart. How stupid of her to have thought that what Laurel felt for Joe was just some silly girlish crush.

"Joe?" Laurel muttered. "Not much. My job kept me pretty busy." She managed a tiny smile. "Though no one ever told me that interning in the creative department of an ad agency means mostly sharpening pencils and fetching coffee."

"I guess Joe must be busy with the restaurant, too."

"I guess so."

Annie waited for her to elaborate, but Laurel seemed far away somewhere, off in her own world.

Out of the corner of her eye Annie caught sight of a familiar face—Gloria De Witt, Dolly's old assistant. She was waving enthusiastically to Annie from across the room.

"I see someone I want to say hello to," she told Laurel. "Talk to you later." She slipped off her stool and made her way over to Gloria, who slung an arm casually about Annie's shoulders.

"How does it feel to be back? You leave your heart in Paris?"

"No, I was too busy being a slave for that kind of thing," she told Gloria. Well, it was partly true. She *had* felt like a slave to Pompeau.

"Hey," Gloria said, looking at something beyond Annie's shoulder, "will you look at who the cat just dragged in?"

Annie's heart gave a little slip-sliding thump, and she turned so suddenly she nearly spilled her Champagne. "Joe," she said with a tiny gasp, but he was too far away to have heard.

He was just stepping into the living room, the lenses of his round wire-rimmed glasses flecked with September rain—rain that had also brought out the curl in his streaky brown hair.

Then his gaze caught hers, and suddenly he was close enough to touch. But she didn't embrace him. She just stood there, an unbearable awkwardness clamped over her like a bell jar.

He doesn't want me. He never did.

She found herself saying the first stupid thing that popped into her head. "I didn't know if you were coming or not."

"I got held up," he said. "Traffic jam. I ditched the cab and walked." He forked a hand through his damp curls, making them spring up in wild corkscrews. "So how does it feel to be back?"

"Good," she told him. "Still a little tired."

"You look wonderful. Fantastic. I mean it."

"Can I get you some Champagne?" She could feel herself running out of small talk. Her voice had a funny, overbright ring.

"What happens if I say no?" Joe seemed to have picked up on her nervousness and was trying to put her at ease.

She smiled. "As soon as Dolly notices you don't have a glass in your hand, the waters of Babylon will flow."

"In that case," he said, seizing her hand, "we'd better get out of here." He tugged her toward the dining room.

The prettily garnished platters of shrimp toast, crab cakes, and stuffed mushrooms that two tuxedoed waiters were passing about the living room had grown sparse. Waiters in crisp white shirts were laying out platters of food for the buffet supper. Annie saw one of them look at Joe and touch his forehead in a jokey little salute.

"I see you got the Belons," Joe addressed him, pointing at a tray of half-shelled oysters on a bed of chipped ice. "Good. I wasn't sure they'd get delivered in time."

"Close call," the youth replied with a shrug.

"*You're* catering this?" Annie whispered. "Dolly didn't tell me."

"She wanted it to be part of the surprise."

"It's wonderful . . . what I've tasted so far, that is."

"The catering is really taking off. Only problem is, the kitchen's too small to handle the extra volume, so I'm expanding."

"Won't that cost a mint? You don't even own the building." Falling back into their familiar habit of talking shop was like slipping into an old pair of loafers. She felt herself relaxing.

"I was getting to that part."

"Joe, you didn't! You actually *own* it?"

"Well, mostly it's the bank that owns it, but the deed's in my name. I was pretty lucky. My landlord was in a hurry to unload it. I would've written to tell you, but I only closed last week." He took off his glasses, wiping them with his handkerchief. "What about you? When are you going to strike out on your own?"

"As soon as I can get the bank to release my trust."

She'd had two letters from Wells Fargo out in Los Angeles, and it was still there—twenty-five thousand plus the interest that had been piling up over the years. And since she was only months away from turning twenty-five, her trustee had agreed to release the money early.

Joe cast a glance at Dolly, who was flitting through on her way to the kitchen. "You wouldn't be moving in on anyone's territory?"

"Dolly's given me her blessing. She says the competition will keep her on her toes."

"Well, of course, you have *my* blessing. Though I doubt you'll need it. You could take on the national debt and come out ahead."

Annie felt a flicker of annoyance. What was that supposed to mean—that she was some superwoman? Because she was determined and capable, she couldn't ever feel weak or scared?

Tears filled her eyes.

Then, suddenly, Joe was pulling her off to one side, through the swinging door into a narrow closet that once upon a time had been a butler's pantry. In the close darkness she felt overwhelmed by Joe's nearness and the heat of his body so close to hers.

He touched her cheek and said softly, "This isn't how I imagined it would be. I guess you can look forward to something so much that when you finally get it, you're too paralyzed to make a move."

"Oh, Joe." She could feel tears pressing like hot nickels against the back of her eyes. "Don't say you missed me, or I'll cry. Buckets. You'll think you never came in out of the rain."

She grabbed a handful of his shirt and whispered with desperate urgency, "No, say it. If you don't say it, I'll cry when I get home. I'll even say it first. Joe, I missed you. I missed you so much I thought it'd eat a hole right through me."

He gripped her upper arms tightly, but he didn't kiss her. She saw there were tears in his eyes, too. "Listen, if I'd told you how much I was missing *you,* it would've come out sounding like I'd cribbed it from *Now, Voyager.*" He added softly, "I wanted to see you first, find out if you . . ."

She began to laugh, leaning against the wall behind her, weak with relief. "And all that time I was thinking—"

"What?"

"It's just . . . Oh, it seems so silly now, but I thought . . . well, that maybe you'd met someone while I was away."

His eyes cut away from hers. "There's no one, Annie."

Was he telling the truth? There had been something in his voice just now . . . and in his eyes.

She felt a stab of jealousy, but told herself quickly, Okay, so what if he went out with someone? Who am I to judge, after Emmett?

"I love you, Joe." There. It was out. She'd said it.

Joe's grip loosened, and his hands slid down her arms, finally capturing her wrists, gently . . . so gently. She felt as if her heart might burst. He brought her hands up and held her palms to his cheeks. His face felt very warm—no, *hot*—as if he, too, were burning up.

She had fantasized about this moment for so long that even now it didn't seem quite real—as if she were in some kind of dream.

"I thought a lot about how it would be when you got home," he said in a low, thick voice. "I thought about this." He brought her palm to his mouth and kissed it, and Annie thought, Yes, it is possible to die from too much happiness all at once.

She wouldn't let herself think about Laurel, about how hurt her sister would be. Later. There would be time to deal with all that later. Here, now, she wanted this moment all to herself.

"Annie?"

Annie was scrubbing the last of the cold cream from her face when Laurel came into the tiny bathroom and perched on the edge of the tub. Sitting there, wearing a man's T-shirt that came down almost to her knees, Laurel looked even droopier than she had coming home from the party an hour ago.

"Hmm?" Annie answered, turning back to the wide pedestal sink where she stood. In the mirror she could see Laurel's reflection, her face a pale oval set above a pair of thin, sagging shoulders. The skin under her eyes looked bruised somehow.

"I'm pregnant." Laurel's soft voice dropped into the stillness like an explosion.

Annie felt a shock travel through her, like touching an exposed wire. "Oh, Laurey." She turned to face her sister, feeling a chill that seemed to rise out of her bones.

"You look worse than I do." Laurel managed a tiny smile. "Maybe you'd better sit down."

"I think maybe you're right."

In the tiny bedroom, Annie sat down on the bed facing Laurel, who was curled up in a flowered easy chair by the window.

"How many weeks?" she asked, determined to be sensible.

"Three *months.* Too far along for an abortion, if that's what you mean."

"Oh, Laurey, I wasn't— Why didn't you tell me?"

"I only saw a doctor a couple of days ago. I know that sounds really stupid, but you know how irregular I've always been. I just kept thinking I'd missed a couple of periods."

"Okay." Annie took a deep breath. "Do you want to tell me how it happened?"

Laurel gave a short, mirthless laugh. "The usual way, I guess."

"You know what I mean."

"You want me to go back to the very beginning? Okay, how about we start with, 'Once upon a time there was a girl named Laurel who loved someone so much she thought she could make him love her back by—' " Laurel broke off, and tears welled in her huge eyes.

She saw the puzzled look on Annie's white face and longed to cry out, I only wanted Joe to love me. And maybe deep down I thought that somehow, by sleeping with Jess, I could make Joe see that I was mature enough for him.

But for some reason she didn't quite understand, Laurel found herself holding back.

Annie longed to go to her sister, to comfort her. But there was something steely in Laurel's expression that warned Annie to keep her distance.

"Does he know?" she asked gently. "Have you told him?"

"You mean, did I make a complete fool of myself?" She sounded angry. "Anyway, it's got nothing to do with him."

"What do you *mean?* Believe me, whoever he is and whatever you think of him, he's in this with you fifty-fifty."

Laurel shot her a hard look that cut Annie to the bone. "You don't know anything about it," she said. It's not Joe, she wanted to say, but again Laurel held back.

"Well, of course I don't. You're not *telling* me anything. If you love this guy so much, why can't you tell him?"

Laurel just shook her head, staring down at the carpet.

Annie felt both hurt and exasperated. "Stop acting as if I'm out to get you, Laurey. I just want to *help* you."

"Well then, maybe *you* should talk to him." Laurel's eyes flashed. "*Who?*"

Even before Laurel answered, Annie sensed she was about to hear something she didn't want to. In the space that stretched between her sister and her, Annie felt an invisible tunnel form, a tunnel down which Laurel's voice seemed to whistle toward her like the coldest of winds.

"Joe," she heard her sister say.

LAUREL couldn't face Annie. She stared down at the carpet, faded in spots, so that it looked sadly frayed. In her mind she could still see vividly Annie's shocked, horrified expression. But it wasn't shame that made her look away from her sister; it was something worse. She had a terrible mean urge to smile.

That was what was making her feel ashamed. What rotten part of her soul could it have come from? How could she *want* Annie to suffer? How could she have led Annie to believe that it was Joe who'd gotten her pregnant? *I saw them at Dolly's party. He loves her. It's Annie he wants. Annie, Annie, Annie.*

"Joe?" she heard her sister repeat, exhaling sharply, as if the air had been forced out by a hard punch to her stomach. "*Joe?*"

Laurel kept her eyes fixed on the carpet's balding swirls.

Should I tell her the truth?

She felt rocked by a sudden swell of shame and love. How could she hurt Annie? She loved her sister. If it weren't for Annie . . . No, she had to tell Annie about Jess.

Laurel let the memory come. She recalled exactly how it had happened. She had wanted Joe, not Jess. But Joe, she remembered, didn't want *her*. He'd sent her away that night after they'd kissed. And hadn't he told her that they couldn't ever be anything more than friends? Friends! She felt the hurt all over again, hurt that made her hollow inside, a great burning shell. Going to bed with Jess, she realized now, had just made it worse. It had been another way of hanging on to Joe, of driving the knife in a little deeper.

Now facing Annie's shocked gaze, Laurel realized something odd—the possibility of getting pregnant had never entered her mind. Not at the time. Unless deep down she had secretly *wanted* something like this to happen, something cataclysmic and final.

She hadn't told Jess, and she didn't intend to. He hadn't written or called all summer. So somehow she'd begun thinking of it as Joe's baby . . . conceived out of her love for him.

Still, she would have to tell Annie how it had really happened.

"Does he . . ." Annie swallowed with what appeared to be an effort. "Does Joe know? Have you told him?"

"No."

"Why not?"

The words were on the tip of her tongue: Because it's not his baby. She wanted to say them, but again something stopped her.

"I haven't told *anyone*," she said, horrified and amazed at her smooth cunning. Stop this! she snapped at herself. It's wrong! It'll break Annie's heart!

The way yours is broken, you mean?

Then Laurel was remembering watching them at Dolly's party, remembering how she'd felt. And how she had felt year after year, always following in Annie's footsteps. And now this—the only thing that she had ever *really* wanted—Annie had taken from her. All her longing and resentment came boiling to the surface.

"I can't think about it right now," she controlled herself enough to say. "I don't feel too good." And as she spoke, Laurel realized how exhausted she was. She felt so tired she could hardly stand.

I'll tell her tomorrow, Laurel thought.

ANNIE, gripping the banister for support, slowly descended the stairs to Joe's floor. She felt weak and frail, as if in the last half hour she'd become an old woman.

Joe's baby. No. Not Joe. Not possible. Only minutes ago she would have sworn to it, bet her life on it. But now . . .

She pictured Laurel, white as a sheet, looking both scared and defiant—almost as if she was protecting him. Why would she lie? Why would she have made up something as horrible as this?

Annie's knees buckled, and she sagged against the banister, covering her face as a sob broke loose. How could he have done this to her? To Laurel? *How?*

Anger rose in her, engulfing her. She reached the door to Joe's apartment, then rang the bell.

Joe appeared, so quietly she was only barely aware of the door swinging open. He was barefoot, holding a coffee mug.

"Annie!" He broke into a grin, which faded just as quickly. "Annie, what's wrong? Are you all right?"

She nodded, but somehow she couldn't speak.

"Is it Laurey? She looked really out of it at the party, like she was coming down with something."

It was as if he'd grabbed her, shaken her, sprung her voice free so that the words tumbled out.

"She came down with something all right." Annie shot him a cold look. "She's pregnant."

"Pregnant?"

Annie shouldered past him into the living room. She heard the door click shut, and glancing back, she saw Joe standing there.

Then in three long strides he was beside her, reaching out. Annie jerked away.

"Don't," she said.

Joe looked startled. Even more than that, shocked. As if she'd pulled off a mask and underneath was a face different from the one he'd always known. A stranger's face.

"Annie, for Pete's sake, what is going on?" He managed to grab hold of her elbow, and she could feel his fingers squeezing. "Listen, you don't think I *knew*, do you? Is that why you're mad?"

"Stop it," she hissed. She couldn't believe he was doing this, lying to her, pretending not to know anything.

"Stop what? What are you talking about?"

"How can you just . . . stand there . . . acting as if . . . as if you didn't know?"

She saw color flare along the side of his neck and his eyes grow shiny, the look he got once in a blue moon when he was about to lose his temper. But then with visible effort he dropped her arm and brought himself under control, stepping back.

"Okay, I can see you're not in any kind of mood to talk about this rationally, but do you mind telling me what you're so angry about?"

"Laurey told me. About you and . . . and everything."

There. That guilty flicker. In his eyes, just now. Unmistakable.

"What's 'everything'? What was there to tell?" His face seemed to close, become unreadable. "I figured that as soon as some good-looking, artistic-type guy took her by the hand, she'd fall in love and forget she'd ever felt that way about me."

"Joe." A huge pressure was building inside Annie's head, making it feel as if her skull might split open. She felt as if she were screaming, but her voice was almost normal. "Joe, I can't believe you're doing this . . . trying to pretend it wasn't you. I *know*, damn it."

"You think I—" He stopped, cocking his head a little to one side, looking at her with stunned disbelief.

"I don't think. I *know*, Joe. How *could* you?" She was sobbing now, her whole body seeming to fold in on itself. "I trusted you! Laurey trusted you! How could you do this to us!"

"I didn't—"

"Stop it! Stop lying!"

"Damn it, will you just *listen?*"

Out of nowhere Joe's fist came looping at her, a rush of air kissing her cheek; then his hand was smashing the wall inches from her head. There was a crumpling sound, followed by small chips that struck the side of her face in a stinging hail.

Annie was too stunned to move. *That blow was meant for me. He wanted to hit me. How had all the sweetness of just a few hours ago come to this?*

Two stairs. Three . . . five . . . seven . . . eight. She counted them as she climbed them. Now she was on her landing, fumbling with her key. When she snapped on the light, Laurel, asleep on the sofa bed in the living room, jerked upright, swollen-eyed.

"Annie," she cried, "what happened? Where have you been?"

Annie collapsed in the chair by the sofa.

"Joe . . . I told him." Her voice came in quick, gasping sobs. "But he . . . he said . . ." She stopped, remembering that look of wounded perplexity she'd seen on his face.

And then she knew this had to be a nightmare because she heard Laurel cry, "Oh, Annie! I didn't mean to make you think it was Joe. Not really. It just came out that way. Joe . . . he never . . . ."

Annie couldn't believe what she was hearing. She looked up, trying to focus her stinging eyes on her sister. "Are you saying Joe is *not* the father of your baby? That you and he *aren't* lovers?"

"It was someone from school," Laurel said. "Jess Gordon. I knew him in Brooklyn. It was just . . . Well, I'm not in love with him."

"But you *are* in love with Joe."

Laurel held her gaze. "Yes." No apology. No excuse.

"Why did you lie, then? Why did you tell me . . ." She started to choke and clamped her lips shut before a sob could escape.

I didn't even give him a chance to explain. I didn't believe him. Will he ever forgive me? Will he?

In a clear voice that held no regret Laurel replied, "I didn't tell you he was the father, Annie. That's just what you *heard.*"

Anger flared in her—sharp, galvanizing. "Damn it, Laurey, don't you put this on me! Don't you dare! You said the words. You wanted me to believe it was Joe!"

"I didn't mean to. But when I realized that you'd misunderstood, well . . ." Now Laurel's voice caught, and her eyes narrowed. "You love him, don't you? You want him for yourself. It's not *me* you're upset about, the fact that I'm pregnant. It's just Joe. Isn't that right? Well, *isn't* it?" Her voice rose to an alarming shrillness.

Annie, before she could stop herself, was lunging forward, grabbing Laurel's thin shoulders and shaking her. "How could you? Damn it, how could you? Haven't I always watched out for you, done everything for you? How could you do this to me? How?"

Framed by the absolute whiteness of her face, Laurel's large, clear eyes seemed to cut right through Annie's. "You never asked," she said with a bitterness that seemed utterly unlike the Laurel she had always known. "You just assumed that wherever you went, I'd follow. But Annie, you never asked. You've always done just exactly what *you* wanted. Maybe for once I'd like to be first."

Annie stepped back, stunned by the force of the sudden hate she felt. How could she hate her own sister so? Right now she had to keep her arms locked at her sides to keep from striking her.

"Do what you want, then," she snapped. "Just don't expect me to be there when you *do* need me."

Chapter Nine

ANNIE stared at the empty coffee shop with the FOR LEASE sign in its boarded-up window. Ninth Avenue between Fourteenth and Fifteenth—definitely not a great neighborhood. Could this be the right place? Shivering as gusts of wind whipped around her,

Annie glanced at the address Emmett had given her. This was it, all right. But what a dump! She noted the empty half-pint bottles littered in front of the door, and her heart sank even further.

Annie glanced at her watch. Quarter to twelve. Emmett would be here any minute. All of a sudden she couldn't wait to see him. She marveled at how lucky it was that at what had to be the lowest point in her life, Emmett Cameron had shown up. She remembered his calling a couple of weeks after that awful night with Joe. He was in New York and had gotten a job in a real estate firm. Could she meet him for dinner that night at the Chelsea Hotel?

Seeing him waiting for her, beer in hand, at El Quijote's massive old-fashioned bar, wearing that cowboy grin, she'd felt something in her let go. And then Emmett was walking over, hugging her, so solid. She'd felt safe, grounded, and at the same time oddly charged, every circuit in her body suddenly alive and crackling.

Since then she'd seen him a lot. And Emmett, thank goodness, was putting no pressure on her. That was a relief because these days all she had in her to give him was some companionship. It was Joe she still wanted, needed . . . and yes, missed. An ocean even wider than the Atlantic separated them now—an expanse of icy politeness she found herself drowning in each time she passed him on the stairs or mumbled hello to him at the mailboxes.

She'd twice tried to apologize in the past four months, but she knew her being sorry just wasn't good enough. She sensed she had broken something precious, something that could never be made solid again.

"Hey there, early bird."

Annie turned to find Emmett walking toward her, his red hair flecked with snow. She felt warmed just seeing him. He fished a ring of keys from his pocket and unlocked the metal accordion gate, then the front door.

"Don't look so gloomy, Cobb," Emmett told her when they were inside. "It's second class, but it's not the South Bronx."

Annie eyed the empty circular holes in front of the counter, where stools had been ripped out. Cigarette butts and cellophane wrappings littered the worn-down, warped vinyl tiles. "It's not exactly what I had in mind," she began gently.

"Look, it's a rathole. But a good cleaning crew and a few coats of paint, and you'd be halfway there."

That might be true, she thought, but even with this place fixed up, it was a far cry from Madison Avenue. On the other hand, she reminded herself, she couldn't afford Madison Avenue.

And there was Emmett, looking so confident, as if one slap of a paintbrush would do it all. She could see how he might have talked that syndicate of doctors into buying the loft building his boss hadn't been able to sell. Already Emmett's commissions had to be substantial. Soon, she bet, he'd be buying property on his own.

No more funky clothes, either. He was wearing a rich-looking camel-hair coat over a finely tailored gray worsted suit. The only memento of the old Emmett was his cowboy boots—tanned and creased with age, but saddle-soaped and newly heeled.

Annie ran a finger along the grimy counter. "Oh, Em, I don't know. . . ." She looked around again. "Well, I'll definitely think about it. And I'll want to look at it again with a contractor."

"While you're thinking about it, how about grabbing a bite with me? I know a great deli just a few blocks from here."

Annie was tempted. But she'd planned on dropping by Joe's restaurant to see the new addition, which had to be nearly finished by now. An excuse—really, she just wanted to see him. And at the restaurant he couldn't duck away or ignore her.

Still, she couldn't help feeling torn. She liked Emmett enormously. In a way she even loved him. Or at least she thought she *could* have loved him . . . if it hadn't been for Joe.

"Thanks, Em, but I've got another appointment." She cut her gaze away from his, suddenly unable to look him in the eye. "I'm supposed to meet this confectioner who's selling his equipment. I may be able to get a good deal on some of the stuff I need."

Emmett shrugged. Outside, as he was locking up, he asked, "By the way, how's your sister? Isn't she about due?"

"Not until the end of next month." Annie didn't want to talk about Laurel or the baby. Just talking about her sister, she could feel the tiny spur of anger buried in her heart begin to chafe and burn.

"Is she still thinking of—" Emmett stopped himself, seeming to hesitate about bringing up a sore subject.

"Giving the baby up for adoption? She's talked about it, but she hasn't made up her mind." Annie didn't realize how tightly clenched her hands were until she felt her nails—the chewed-down remains of them, anyway—digging into her palms.

103

"Hey, Cobb, relax, will ya?" She became aware of Emmett touching her arm. "No need for you to be taking on the whole world's problems. Right now, shouldn't you just concentrate on getting this business of yours going?" He smiled. "If you're busy for lunch, how about dinner? My place?"

She shook her head. "I'd like to, but I'm going to a *Bris*."

"A *what*?"

"My friend Rivka's daughter Sarah just had a baby. Her third. A boy. A *mohel* does a circumcision, and there's a little party afterwards. You want to come?"

Emmett arched a brow. "Not me. The whole idea of somebody's snipping away at the family jewels makes me a little nervous."

"I always close my eyes."

"Yeah, well, you can afford to."

Annie thought about Laurel's baby. Boy or a girl? She might never even *see* it, she realized. And that would probably be best, though she didn't know how Laurel was going to live with herself.

Lately a lot of things about Laurel had been bothering her. Like her asking Joe to be her Lamaze coach. With Joe there, Laurel said, she fit in with the other couples. *Married* couples.

And Joe, damn it, had agreed. But who was Annie to say it wasn't right? What claim did she have on Joe anymore?

Annie looked at her watch. "I'd better get going, or I'll be late." She felt guilty about lying to Emmett.

Out on the sidewalk, Annie watched Emmett amble to the curb to hail a cab. When it pulled over, he held the door for her.

"Good luck," he said.

"Thanks," she said, thinking of Joe. "I'll need it."

THE framing for the walls looked complete. In some places they were already sheetrocked. The sharp, sweet smell of sawdust filled Annie's nostrils, bringing her a glad, hopeful feeling.

"I can't believe it," she said, turning to Joe. "Last time I was here, this area was just a weed patch."

He took her elbow lightly and steered her around a big coil of conduit. "We should be ready for plaster and paint in a week or so."

Annie nodded. She couldn't take her eyes off Joe. She felt as if she hadn't seen him in years. He looked the same. So what was different? And then she got it: *He's keeping his distance.* He stood close to the wall, one hand braced against an exposed stud, leaning away from her, his brown hair flecked with sawdust. Whose permission did she need to cross the three steps that stretched between her and Joe? But Annie could not bring herself to make the move.

Then he caught her gaze and said cheerily, "Listen, it's pretty noisy out here. Let's go inside where we can hear ourselves think. You feel like a cup of coffee?"

In the kitchen, Joe poured coffee into two mugs and carried them upstairs to a booth in the deserted dining room. "Everything okay with Laurey?" he asked cautiously, sipping at his coffee.

I didn't come here to talk about Laurel, she felt like shouting.

"Laurey's fine," Annie said. "Joe, I . . ." She set out to say how much she'd missed him, but the words wouldn't come.

"How's the search for shop space going? Have you found anything yet?" he asked quickly—a little too quickly.

"I think I may have," she replied. "But I haven't made up my mind yet. It's a little grungy."

"You should've seen this building before I took over," he told her. "It looked like the morning after a Hell's Angels' bash."

What Annie was seeing in her mind, though, was a hole punched in a living-room wall. A hole the exact size of Joe's fist, with bits of plaster clinging to its ragged edges and hairline cracks radiating out into the wall around it like tiny thunderbolts.

And then she became aware that Joe was leaning forward, frowning slightly. "Annie, are you all right?"

"Yeah, sure—" She caught herself. "No, I'm not okay, Joe. I don't think I've been okay since September. You don't know how many times I've wanted— Well, I *did* try to talk to you about it, to explain, but maybe it was too soon. Maybe . . ."

A strange expression crossed Joe's face.

"Look," he said, "if it means anything, I . . . I shouldn't have blown up the way I did."

"How could you *not* have?" she cried. "How could you . . . after the way I acted, the things I said?"

"You only said what you thought was true." He shrugged. "I forgave you a long time ago. But forgiving isn't the same as forgetting, Annie." His mouth curved down in a slow, sad smile. "Please, don't misunderstand me. I think maybe it happened for the best."

"The best?" she croaked. "How can you say that? Joe, I *need* you."

"You don't need me, Annie. You don't need anyone. Not really." He gave her a look of infinite sadness. "Annie, it wouldn't have worked, you and me."

She felt like a brittle eggshell about to crack. Tears flooded her eyes. She wanted to tell him, *insist* that he was wrong . . . dead wrong. But the look in his eyes said it was too late.

"I love you, Joe," she told him instead. "More than you know."

His face seemed to contort with pain; then he straightened himself and shook his head. "No, you *think* you do. But don't you see . . . love and trust, they come together in the same package. And if you try to separate them, the whole thing comes apart."

It hurt, but at the same time she thought, He's right. That was the awful part. Except for one thing. If she had never loved him, then why did she feel as if she were being stabbed in the heart?

"I think we've both said enough for now," she told him. "I'd better be going." She slid off the bench and rose to her feet.

Joe didn't try to stop her.

"Tell Laurey I'll pick her up at seven tomorrow," he said.

Right. Their Lamaze class. She felt a swift, unexpected thrust of resentment. Then it struck her: *Suppose Joe is falling in love with Laurel? She's beautiful, talented, lovable. Why shouldn't he?*

Because if she were to lose Joe to Laurel, that would mean losing Laurel as well—the only two people she really loved. And how could she keep going after that?

ANNIE watched the *mohel* squeeze the clamplike device over the baby's tiny penis, severing its foreskin with a single neat snip. Out of the corner of her eye she saw Sarah hide her face against her husband's shoulder. Annie knew how Sarah had to be feeling . . . wishing she could take away her son's pain and make it hers.

"See how brave he is! Hardly a peep," Rivka whispered to Annie. Her round face was beaming. "Forgive me if I'm kvelling, but from this boy we'll take great pleasure. He'll make us proud. I can feel it."

Then with a big intake of breath, baby Yusseleh began to shriek. Annie watched as the *mohel* calmly wrapped a bit of gauze about the newly circumsized penis and deftly pinned on a clean diaper. He handed the baby to his nervous-looking grandfather Ezra and began intoning the blessing.

Every eye in the group seemed to be on the little star of the show, but Annie was noticing Laurel, standing off to one side. She looked haggard, morose. Was she thinking that she might never hold her own baby the way Sarah would cuddle little Yusseleh?

In spite of herself, Annie wanted to go to her sister. How awful she must feel!

Then a wave of bitterness welled up in her. Why, she asked herself for the thousandth time, had Laurel wanted to hurt her by pretending her baby was Joe's?

Why?

But now Dolly was sidling over to Laurel, hooking an arm about her thin shoulders. Annie watched as the two of them went off down the dim hall leading to the bedrooms. She hesitated, then threaded her way across the crowded room and followed them.

She found them in Shainey's room, perched on the edge of the bed. In one corner stood a crib that Rivka kept for her grandchildren. Annie paused in the doorway, feeling awkward, as if she might be intruding. But how could that be? Didn't she know Laurel best?

Dolly looked up at her with a bright welcoming smile. Laurel didn't even glance up.

"Why, it's enough to make *anybody* upset." Dolly plunged into the awkward silence. "That poor little thing lying there on that table, getting snipped at like a leg of lamb."

"That's not it." Laurel's head snapped up. "That's not it at all."

"Why don't you tell me, then?" Dolly asked gently.

"It's *my* baby." Laurel locked her hands over her stomach. "I don't want to give it up, but I'm afraid to keep it. I don't feel ready to be a mother." Her voice caught. "I don't know what to do."

Annie opened her mouth to speak, but no words came out. She felt so torn, both irritated with Laurel and sorry for her. For months she'd been trying to talk to Laurel about the baby.

"Oh, you poor thing." Now Dolly was fluffing up like a mother hen while Annie watched. And then her annoyance with her aunt faded. There were *tears* in Dolly's eyes. "I've been so worried about you. About this . . . this awful choice you're having to make."

"What do *you* think I should do?" Laurel asked.

Dolly chewed her lip. "The mess I've made of my life, I wouldn't dare tell another living soul what he or she ought to do. All I know is what I would do if I were in your shoes . . . how I'd feel if I were somehow blessed with the miracle of a baby."

"You think I should keep it?"

Dolly blinked away the brightness in her eyes. "Oh, sugar, if you *did*—and I'm not saying you *should*—it would be the most loved little baby in the whole universe. Between you and me and Annie . . . why, I can't think of a blessed thing it'd be wanting for."

Annie felt a sob rising in her. Somehow, with all her bumbling, Dolly had found exactly the right thing to say.

"Dolly's right," she told her sister, managing to keep her voice clear and steady. Now she found herself walking over, sinking down beside Laurel. "We'll manage somehow. Haven't we always?"

Laurel shot her an odd, flat look. "You have. *You* always manage somehow, Annie." Her voice held a note of accusation, but only a faint one. Mostly she sounded sad. She stood up. "Excuse me, but I have to use the bathroom."

When she was gone, Annie felt defeated somehow. Weren't she and Laurel supposed to be on the same side?

Annie became aware of Dolly touching her arm, and she turned to face her. "Why didn't you ever have kids?" she asked, suddenly curious. "I mean, you and your husband."

"We tried. But Dale . . . I guess there must've been a cog loose somewhere. And later with Henri—" She broke off with a shrug.

"You miss him, don't you?" Annie said softly.

Dolly shrugged again, but Annie saw her lips tremble. "Oh, well, us Burdock gals, we don't give up so easy."

"Guess I'm pretty stubborn, too," Annie said with a laugh.

"It must be hard for you," Dolly said. "Taking the back seat this time when you're used to being up there at the wheel."

"Something like that."

Dolly surprised her by clutching her hard, squeezing so tightly Annie could hardly breathe.

"I made a mistake once," Dolly said in a fierce, hoarse whisper. "And I'll never forget the lesson it taught me. You and your sister—don't let anything . . . or anyone . . . ever come between you, or you'll regret it for the rest of your life."

RUDY stared at the bright mobile dangling over the empty crib. It was the most elaborate one in the store—an array of small gingham teddy bears, each one holding a tiny fishing pole with a nylon string attached to it, from which another teddy bear dangled.

108

Beside him Laurel said softly, "I like to come here sometimes in the afternoon, when I'm too tired to do any more drawing. It makes me feel . . . I don't know, connected somehow. Like I'm really having this baby. Like I'm really going to be a mother."

Rudy felt his heart catch. With her stalwart expression not quite hidden, Laurel reminded him suddenly of her mother—how Eve had looked when she was pregnant with Laurel.

As he thought about what he had to talk her into, Rudy's heart began to pound. He'd have to be careful how he put it to her. Because if she knew he wanted the kid for himself, she'd never buy it.

He felt a sharp longing, like a stitch in his side. A child. His own kid. Somebody who'd look at him and see not a fat little pygmy, but just good old Dad.

"You like to come here just to look or what?" he asked, praying she wouldn't say she had already bought a bunch of this stuff and had it back at her apartment sitting there ready for the baby.

"Just looking. I mean, what's the point of buying stuff if—" She stopped, sucking her breath in sharply. In a low voice she added, "I've been thinking . . . What if I kept it? The baby, I mean. Oh, I know it'd probably be horribly selfish of me. I mean, a baby should have a mother *and* a father, but well . . . I can't help wanting it, can I?" Her blue eyes shimmered, and she caught her lower lip in her teeth, as if to keep her tears from spilling over.

Rudy leaned close. Here was his opening, his chance. "Listen," he said, "I might be able to help. I have someone who would be interested—*real* interested."

"You mean . . . in adopting?" Laurel's voice dropped to a whisper. Her eyes looked back at him, huge, scared-looking.

"Yeah, that's right."

"A family?"

Rudy felt himself beginning to sweat.

Tell her it's you. Explain how you'd be the best dad any kid could have, that he . . . or she . . . would lack for nothing in this world.

"Well, see . . ."

"Because it'd have to be," she said. "Otherwise, I wouldn't even consider it. I mean, if my baby wasn't going to be part of a family—a real *family*—what would be the point?"

Rudy took a deep breath. "They don't have any kids, so they're not a family *that* way . . . but the sweetest couple you'd ever want to meet," he began. "Husband's a real estate developer; wife raises dogs. Puppies running around everywhere. They've been trying for years and years to have a kid, but the doctors tell them it doesn't look too good. Nice people. They'd be terrific parents."

"Did you tell them about me?" She looked stricken.

"Hell, no. I wouldn't do that. Not without talking to you first."

He could tell Laurel was struggling. "I don't know. . . ." Her gaze drifted off in the direction of the teddy-bear mobile. She pushed at it gently, making the little bears dance. She was trying very hard, he could see, not to cry.

Now, he told himself. He had to really pitch it before she backed away. "You'd be doing it for the baby, not for that couple," he told Laurel. "And for yourself. You're young. Why go and mess up your life now? Think about it, Laurel. I mean, *seriously*."

"I *am*." Whipping around to face him, she said sharply, "I think about it every day. And do you want to hear something really crazy? For the first time I'm glad my father is dead. I'm sure it would've hurt him to know I was somewhere out there where he couldn't reach me."

Rudy felt a prickling under his wool scarf. He wanted to tell Laurel that there was no need for her to mourn Val, but how could he without admitting that he'd lied to her all those years?

"You wouldn't be giving it away," he told her instead. "Not like that, not like giving away something you didn't want. You'd be giving him something good, a chance at a normal life."

Now Laurel's eyes were narrowing suspiciously. "Why are you doing this? Why do you care so much?"

Easy, he told himself. Don't push or you'll blow this.

Rudy shrugged. "Hey, if it's a crime to care about somebody," he said lightly, "then call me guilty."

She touched his arm. "Uncle Rudy, I didn't mean . . ."

"I know." He smiled. "It must be tough, what you're going through." He watched her chew her lip, and felt a flicker of hope.

"Can I think about it?" she asked.

"Sure," Rudy told her. "This couple, they'll stay right where they are until you decide."

"Okay," Laurel said, "let's get out of here."

Outside, on Seventh Avenue, Rudy squinted against the sun burning its way through a milky haze. "Buy you a cup of coffee?" he asked.

"Thanks, but I'd better be getting back," she told him. "Did I tell you about those drawings my art teacher sent to a publisher friend of hers? Well, this publisher wants me to illustrate a children's book. I have to get home and start working on some sketches."

"Hey, that's terrific. I mean it." Rudy was happy for her, but he suspected her real reason for being in such a rush to get home just now was so she could be alone. "I'll give you a call sometime tomorrow," he told her. "Think about what I said."

"I will," she told him. She was looking directly at him, her eyes full of pain, and he knew she was telling the truth . . . that she would think about it. And think hard. He'd made it this far at least.

Chapter Ten

ANNIE watched Emmett stamp on the doormat as he came in, small rivulets of water cascading off his boots. She waved to him from behind the display case where she was waiting on a customer.

"I'll have one of those. Just one." The plump woman in a raccoon coat pointed a gloved finger at a tray of dark, lumpy chocolates. Not dainty like Girod's—these were the size of golf balls. A mistake Annie had made with her very first batch, which strangely, wonderfully, had turned out to be a success. The woman gave a nervous laugh. "I'm supposed to be dieting."

Annie glanced up and saw Emmett now leaning against the old marble-top shaving stand on which sat the cash register. He caught Annie's eye and winked. She quickly looked away, busying herself with wrapping the single bourbon truffle in flimsy crimson tissue and placing it in a small crimson bag embossed in gold script with the name she'd given her shop: TOUT DE SUITE.

She handed it to the woman, who was smiling delightedly. Annie felt both irritated with Emmett and happy to see him. She'd agreed to meet him for dinner, but at Paolo's, not here. It was only a quarter to six, and she wouldn't even be closing for another fifteen minutes. And after that, she'd still have to tally the day's receipts, take inventory, and check to see if her assistant Doug had really fixed the tempering machine. So why was Emmett giving her that impish smile—as if she didn't already know!

Warmth crept into Annie's cheeks as she remembered Emmett,

earlier this week, inviting her to go away with him for the weekend. She'd told him no, but he'd merely shrugged, as if he felt confident it was only a matter of time before she would cave in. After all, what was holding her back?

Annie couldn't have explained it to him. She wasn't even sure she understood it herself. When she was with Emmett, she felt this urge—a compulsion almost—to touch him, to feel the span of his broad hand covering hers, to stroke the underside of his jaw. But it wasn't love, what she felt for Emmett. It couldn't be, because how then could she still feel so strongly about Joe?

If it weren't for Emmett, she knew she'd never do anything in the evenings but drag herself home and crawl into bed. After getting up at five each morning to pick out fresh fruit at the wholesale market, then coming here, setting up in the kitchen, constantly checking that her two assistants, Doug and Louise, didn't burn anything or fall asleep stirring the huge pots of *ganache,* then racing through the rest of the day, waiting on retail customers or hailing cabs to get to a meeting, Annie was usually ready to drop. Yet Emmett's popping in was like a cool breeze on a hot day. It revived her somehow.

"You're early," she told him when the plump woman left.

"I was showing a loft in Tribeca, and I thought I'd drop in, see if you needed a hand with that tempering melter."

"Doug supposedly fixed it before he left."

"Mind if I take a look?"

"In those clothes?" As he was shrugging off his overcoat she took in his muted cashmere blazer and silk tie. "You know you're going to get chocolate all over you."

But Emmett's blazer was already off, and he was rolling up his sleeves. "Good. I'll taste irresistible, then. Make it twice as hard for you to say no to this weekend." He winked at her again, then came around to her side and hooked an arm about her shoulders. "And even if you do, I may shanghai you. For your own good. Before you work yourself to death."

Annie drew away. "Em . . ." she started to say.

He held a finger to her lips. "Later. We'll talk about it over dinner." He stepped back with a smile as slow and sure as a sunrise. "Now you close up the joint while I go check on that melter."

Grabbing her clipboard with order forms for bulk supplies from the shelf, Annie was seized by a sudden exhilaration. Tout de Suite had happened so fast—was *still* happening so fast—that even when she slept, she dreamed she was working.

She remembered her revulsion the first time she'd seen the place. Now, seeing the walls with their gay, strawberry-trellis paper and the floorboards painted country white and covered with colorful hooked rugs, she felt a rush of satisfaction. Across the front display window she'd hung white eyelet-lace curtains and fixed antique gaslight sconces to the walls. Along the top of the display case she'd placed white wicker baskets filled with slivers of almond bark for customers to nibble on while they waited.

Annie remembered how she'd feared that no one who could afford to buy fancy chocolates would ever venture into this grungy neighborhood, even if the word ever got out about how good her stuff was. And on the three wholesale accounts she'd managed to land, the profit margin was so low at first that she thought she'd never keep afloat. But since opening up six weeks ago, her retail trade had grown steadily. Hard to believe that now people were sending their drivers from as far away as Sutton Place.

Annie, suddenly too tired to stand, sank down onto the old piano stool that stood between the wall and a secondhand sewing stand crowded with jars of candied grapefruit and orange peels dipped in chocolate. From the kitchen came the dreadful broken-sounding clattering of the melter starting up. Obviously, Doug hadn't fixed it properly. But would Emmett have better luck? Maybe she'd need a new one—not that she had money to buy it.

She sighed. *I miss Joe.* The thought gripped her with sudden force, leaving her weak and breathless.

Since that day at the restaurant they'd hardly spoken. He was busy with Joe's Place and she with Tout de Suite. They smiled and nodded to one another in the hallway. Once in a while he'd chat for a moment about Laurel, who was due any time now.

These days Joe saw more of Laurel than she did. One night a week he took her to her Lamaze class, and on other nights, when he wasn't too tired, he'd phone and she'd go down and practice her breathing exercises at his apartment.

Laurel had grown secretive. She hardly talked to Annie about anything other than the book she was illustrating or Tout de Suite. Never about Joe. It was almost as if the two of them had formed some kind of . . . well, an unspoken pact.

113

Six months ago Annie could not have imagined she'd ever be jealous of her sister, but weirdly, she was.

So what right have I to be jealous of Laurel? Especially now. At least I have Tout de Suite, but what does she have, really? A make-believe husband, a baby she's about to lose?

Annie could hear the melter's clattering smooth to a steady hum. Relief swept through her. Well, at least she wouldn't have *that* to worry about, not for the time being. Emmett had once again pulled a rabbit out of his hat.

PAOLO'S, on Mulberry Street, was a Little Italy institution, every inch of wall space covered with autographed eight-by-ten glossies of celebrities who'd dined there. At a table against the rear wall Annie spotted a swarthy barrel-chested man in a double-breasted suit wolfing down a big bowl of spaghetti, while a couple of younger men, clearly his thuggish bodyguards, occupied a smaller table near the entrance, their eyes roaming the packed dining area.

"Are they for real?" she whispered jokingly to Emmett.

He leaned across the table and whispered, "That's Cesare Tagliosi. He's right up there in the Bonnano family. I met him through this warehouse deal my boss and I are putting together. Tagliosi and Ed Bight—the guy who's selling the warehouses—are business partners. But my guess is it's the kind of business where Tagliosi does the talking and Ed listens . . . if you get my drift."

"You mean, it really happens that way, like in the movies?" Annie asked. "I think I'd die." She caught herself and frowned. "No, I wouldn't. I'd tell him where he could shove it."

Emmett shook his head, smiling. "Sure, and the next day they'd be fishing you out of the East River. Face it, Annie, there are some things you just *can't* fight."

"I haven't come across one yet." She thought of Joe.

"Yes, you have." Emmett paused, watching as their waiter poured the wine he'd ordered. Then he looked at Annie and said, "Me. You can't fight me."

The easy smile had dropped from his face, and Annie could see now how much she meant to him. How could she have missed it before? Wasn't this exactly how she felt about Joe?

"Look, Em, I'm sorry if . . ." His hand closed over hers firmly, shutting off her words.

"No," he said, "no more excuses. Look, I'm not stupid . . . and I'm not so crazy about you I can't see straight." A corner of his mouth curled up slightly. "Not yet, anyway. I'll say it just this once, Cobb . . . and if you don't want to hear it, I won't say it again." He picked up his wineglass, gripping it so tightly Annie had a sudden vision of it shattering. "*Yes,* I'm in love with you. I *know* you're not in love with me. But if you think there's a chance you *might* be someday, even a *slim* chance, then, damn it, take it."

"Emmett, what are you asking?" Anne forced herself to meet his steady gaze. "What exactly do you want me to say?"

"Say you'll go away for the weekend with me. Just that. I'm not asking for the moon, Annie Cobb."

"Just the sun and the stars," she replied lightly, suddenly too exhausted to argue.

He smiled faintly. "Yep. That's about the size of it."

Annie stared at his sturdy hands, at his knuckles big as knotholes in fence posts. She thought, So why is it so terrible to want him even though you don't love him? It's been so long . . . and what am I saving myself for anyway? Not Joe, that's for sure.

Thinking of Joe, she felt her heart bump. She looked down, feeling Emmett's gaze on her.

"Don't lead me on, Cobb," he said mildly. "If you don't want to, now or ever, just say so."

"Em, I'm afraid," she told him, leaning forward on her elbows. "And a little confused. I don't know what to tell you."

"How about the truth?" he said. His blue eyes peered at her, bright and sharp, over the rim of his glass.

"Okay," she told him, "the truth is, I have orders to fill by Monday, so I really can't get away. But I—" Even before the words were out, she wondered, Am I making a mistake? "I wouldn't mind having you ask me another time."

"Maybe I'll do that," he replied without a trace of rancor.

Their pasta arrived—steaming noodles piled with tomato, mushrooms, peppers, olives, all in a fragrant red sauce. After he'd eaten half of what was on his plate, Emmett was once again his old cocky self. "Hey, Cesare," he called over to the big man in the rubout suit, "how was your pasta? Good, eh?"

The man frowned at him; then recognition dawned, and he gave Emmett the barest of nods, wiping his greasy chin. If he thought

Emmett was being flippant with him, he gave no indication of it.

Annie ducked her head, hiding her face in her napkin to muffle her laughter. She felt shocked by Emmett's boldness. But then why should it surprise her? Since she'd known him, when had Emmett Cameron ever been afraid of anything or anybody?

LAUREL was soaking in the bathtub when she felt a tightness in her belly again.

It didn't hurt much—she couldn't call it a pain. Definitely not a *labor* pain. Actually, she'd been having feelings like this all morning, but she was pretty sure they were no big deal.

She remembered her Lamaze teacher saying that false labor— contractions that didn't hurt much and came at irregular intervals— was common. Earlier she'd timed a few of these, and they were jumping all over the place: ten minutes, then six, then ten again. She was tense—that was it. She decided a bath would relax her.

But to be on the safe side, maybe she should call Dr. Epstein.

Laurel started to pull herself up, and the tightness eased. She let herself sink back into the water's warmth. Why bother the doctor when it's probably still a long way off. Don't think about it, she told herself. It was as if an alarm had jangled in her brain, warning her to keep all thoughts of the baby out of her head. *They'll take it away. . . . I won't even get to hold it.*

Her head tipped back; tears slipped sideways down her temples, pooling in her ears. My choice, she reminded herself. No one was forcing her to give up her baby. Rudy had merely persuaded her that it was for the best. She remembered his phoning her the day after they'd met in the baby store. How relieved he'd sounded. Over and over he'd assured her she was doing the best thing. But now she wasn't so sure.

Again she found herself thinking, If only this were Joe's baby . . .

Maybe he did love her after all . . . just a little. And maybe he'd love her a lot more if it weren't for Annie. Tears filled her eyes, and she pressed her hands to her belly, fingers spread like starfish.

For one sweet interlude she imagined how it would be if she changed her mind and kept the baby. She'd buy that homemade-looking oak cradle she'd spotted in the window of the Salvation Army store on Eighth Avenue and put it right by her bed. Whenever he cried, she'd pick him up. And when he was older, she'd point out the evening star—the way Annie had once pointed it out to her—so every night he could wish on it.

Laurel yanked out the tub stopper. Then she heaved herself to her feet and stepped out onto the fluffy pink rug. Reaching for a towel, she felt that tight sensation across her middle again. She stood still, gripping the towel rack until the pain passed. A cup of tea was what she needed. Then she'd finish the last drawing for that book.

Laurel toweled off and slipped into her old chenille robe. With a steaming mug of chamomile she curled up on the big red hassock by the window with her sketch pad. In the drawing she was working on, a bear was rearing up on his hind paws in fury, having just found out that his bride had unwittingly betrayed him. She'd gotten the bear's enraged expression just right. But the bride seemed all wrong. Wouldn't she have jumped to her feet to beg his forgiveness and declare her love? This bride was . . . oh, face it, a *wimp*.

Suddenly it came to Laurel how the bride should be. She grabbed an eraser and with a few swipes rubbed out an arm, a leg, half a face. Then she began to sketch. Her pencil flew, her mind filled with visions of a frightened but determined woman . . . determined to get her prince back.

She lost all track of time and was only dimly aware of the contractions rolling through her like mild ocean waves.

But then a hard contraction, harder than any of the others, gripped Laurel so fiercely that she dropped her pencil. Shuddering from the pain, she hunched forward, clutching her belly. Damn, it hurt. This one really *hurt*.

She'd better call Dr. Epstein. No more fooling around.

She waited for the contraction to pass. It felt like an excruciating eternity. But when she tried to stand up, her legs collapsed underneath her like warm butter. They'd gone numb, she realized. She began to feel panicky. Now something was happening. *Definitely*.

The circulation in her legs gradually came back, but Laurel was still too shaky to stand up. She managed to get onto her knees and began crawling toward the phone. She could feel another contraction coming on, this one more racking than the last.

She pulled herself up, clutching the phone receiver in one hand. As she began to dial, the contraction seized her. She crumpled in agony, and the phone pitched to the floor with a crazed jingling.

"Oh!" she cried, clutching herself.

Something had to be wrong, she thought. It was not supposed to hurt this much, not this soon. Knives. It felt like knives.

The pain finally ebbed, but by then Laurel was no longer thinking about calling Dr. Epstein. Or Annie. There was one person, only one, she wanted now. *Needed.* She dialed the number and waited in sweaty panic while the phone rang and rang and rang.

"Joe's Place," announced a harried-sounding voice, *his* voice.

She forced herself to take a slow, even breath. "Joe? It's me, Laurey. Listen, I think I'm just about to have this baby."

THE front door was unlocked and slightly ajar. With a swift backhand stroke Joe knocked it wide open. "Laurey!"

No answer. His heart dropped. "Laurey!" he called again.

"Joe?" From the bedroom came her faint reply.

Laurel lay on her side on the bed. Her long hair hung in damp tatters over the edge of the mattress. Her face was very white.

Joe crouched at her side. He felt his heart lumbering in his chest. "Laurey, I'm here. It's going to be okay." He struggled to clear away the fear that cobwebbed his mind. "How far apart are the pains?"

Laurel shook her head, forcing her words through gritted teeth. "All . . . together."

No intervals at all between the contractions. That meant she was in the final stage of her labor. Why hadn't she called him sooner?

Joe felt a low swell of resentment. Why did she have to call him at *all?* How had he gotten into this? Why, when she asked him to be her Lamaze coach, hadn't he turned her down? At the very least, couldn't he have had the guts to admit that the main reason he'd ever agreed to it was to hurt Annie?

All right, he had been concerned about Laurel. He still was. But mostly he was so angry at himself he could barely concentrate.

Laurel gripped his forearm with all her might. "Joe . . . I'm scared," she gasped.

Me, too, kiddo.

"What did the doctor say?" he asked.

"I . . . I haven't talked to him. After I called you, I had to . . . to lie down. It hurts so much!" She hugged herself tighter, her face crumpling into an agonized grimace.

"Where's his number?"

"In the . . . the little blue book . . . under the phone."

"I'll be right back. Hang on, Laurey."

He found the blue address book and dialed Dr. Epstein's number. The doctor told him what he already knew: get Laurel to St. Vincent's, pronto. Epstein said he'd phone for an ambulance—it shouldn't be more than five minutes.

Next Joe tried the number at Annie's shop. A girl who sounded very young informed him that Annie was out. He left a message saying that he was on his way to the hospital with Laurel, and the girl breathlessly promised to do her best to find Annie.

Waiting for the ambulance to arrive, Joe returned to the bedroom and found Laurel on her back, clutching a knee in each hand.

"The ambulance'll be here any minute," he told her. "And Dr. Epstein will be waiting for you at the hospital."

"I . . . don't think . . . I can . . . Oh, damn."

Joe strained to remember the breathing exercises they'd practiced in Lamaze. Fine coach he was turning out to be.

"Pant," he urged. "Shallow breaths. That's it."

Laurel kept up the panting for another minute or so, then fell back. "No!" she screamed. "I can't do this. . . . Please don't make me do this!"

Instinctively Joe gathered her into his arms.

"You *can*," he told Laurel. "You can do it."

"Joe." He was close enough to feel her lips move under his. "I never . . . stopped loving you. Please . . . I'm sorry. I . . . I didn't mean to lie to Annie. It's just that I wanted it to be yours . . . *our* baby. Do you hate me?"

"No, Laurey, I could never hate you." He stroked her hair, which felt damp and hot. What *did* he feel?

He didn't know, couldn't sort out all the emotions Laurel summoned up in him. *In* love with her? No. But what he did feel was certainly more than brotherly affection.

"I didn't love him," she panted. "Jess. He . . . he was just somebody." She gasped, and her mouth dragged down in a horrible grimace. "It's coming, Joe! I can feel it!"

"The ambulance . . . ." he started to say, as if this birth were something she could put on hold. But it was going to happen, he realized, whether the ambulance was here or not.

Laurel screamed. Blood had rushed up into her face, turning it a dark crimson. He realized that now she had to be pushing.

119

"It's okay," he heard a calm stranger speak. "Push if you have to."

Between Laurel's hiked knees he spied a dark, wet circle—the baby's head. Joe grew dizzy, as if a part of him were standing at a distance from all this, high up, watching himself. The dark circle widened. He could hear Laurel grunting as she pushed again . . . then again. He saw his arms stretch out, hands cupped to receive the infant's head. But something was wrong. The baby seemed stuck.

Then he dimly remembered something in a film they'd seen in Lamaze class about the baby needing at this point to be rotated a bit. Carefully, as carefully as if this child were a butterfly cupped in his palms, he turned the baby until he felt its shoulders loosen and finally slide free. Now came a long torso, a pair of rumpled red legs. Joe let his breath out with a whistling rush.

With one hand supporting the infant's head, Joe shouted, "It's a boy!"

The baby gave a choked, startled cry, then began to wail, thrashing his arms and legs. Feeling the infant's tiny wet body squirm in his hands, Joe was so thrilled that he started to laugh. Then, seemingly for no reason, he began to cry. He saw that Laurel, too, was laughing, and had tears streaming down her face.

Joe looked at the baby boy in his arms, tied to Laurel by its ropy cord, and for the first time in all his thirty-two years, he felt connected to something larger than himself. To God? The mysteries of the universe? No, smaller than that—a heartbeat, a new life, a measure of grace.

The baby had stopped crying. A pair of indigo eyes stared fixedly into his, and a tiny mottled hand locked about his finger. Joe felt a rush of unexpected joy that nearly knocked him over.

Before he was even aware he'd thought of it, Joe found himself saying, "Adam. His name is Adam."

VAL stood in the lobby of St. Vincent's Hospital and asked the lady behind the reception desk which room Laurel Carrera was in.

While she riffled through her alphabetized index cards he glanced around. What was he even doing here? His little girl, all grown up, a mother herself now, and he was probably the last person she'd want to see. Hadn't she made it clear how she felt about him all those years ago, when she took off without so much as a kiss-my-foot? If he hadn't seen that article in the Los Angeles

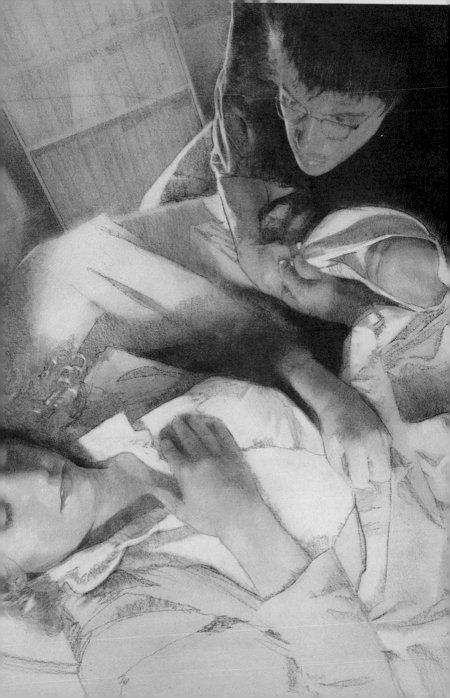

Times Magazine on Annie's chocolate shop, he wouldn't have known either of them was still alive.

No Laurel Carrera listed, Big Mama behind the desk told him. "Sorry, mister."

But he'd come all this way, blowing his last hundred on a low-fare red-eye to New York. He *couldn't* just walk away.

"What about Laurel *Cobb?*" A long shot, but worth a try.

Big Mama thumbed her card index and then looked up at him quizzically. "Third floor. Room three twenty-two."

Val tried to swallow, but his mouth felt dry as an old sock. It was close to noon, but he'd been up all night—five hours from Los Angeles International, and the whole time, he hadn't shut his eyes once. Thinking about Laurel. Wondering what she'd look like, if she'd be glad to see him.

The door to room 322 was propped open. There were two beds inside, but one was empty. In the other a slender woman sat propped up with pillows, her long blond hair tied back in a loose ponytail. She was staring out the window and didn't see him, so he had time for a good long look at her.

Laurel? That beautiful young woman, his little girl?

"Laurel? Baby?" He took a step inside.

She turned and stared at him, her eyes huge and uncomprehending. Then recognition dawned, and the blood drained from her face.

"Val," she croaked, "is it you?" She clapped both hands over her mouth and spoke through white fingers that dragged at her cheeks. "But you're . . . I thought you were *dead.*"

Now Val felt himself reel. "Dead? Where did you hear that?"

"Uncle Rudy t-told me that you'd d-died that night. That Annie—" She gulped. "H-he m-made me p-promise not to t-tell."

Rudy? *Rudy* had told her that? But why? Val felt as if he'd had the wind knocked out of him.

"How . . . how did you find me?"

"I read about your sister in the paper." He kept his voice even, while his thoughts continued to tumble. It hadn't occurred to him when he was reading that article, but from the very beginning Rudy had to have known where Laurel and Annie were living.

"*Annie* told you I was here?" Laurel's voice was hollow with disbelief.

"Not exactly. I . . . uh . . . followed her home from her store. Your super's wife told me where to find you."

Was she glad to see him? He couldn't tell.

"You're looking good," he told her. "I hear you had a kid."

"That's right. A boy." Her eyes welled with tears. Had he said something wrong?

Val grinned. "Hey, that makes me a grandfather." He paused, his grin fading. "It's been so long. I thought you'd forgotten about me."

"I would've written, but . . ." Her voice trailed off.

"Hey," Val said, "how about giving your old man a hug?"

Val sat on the edge of the bed and pulled her into his arms. She seemed to resist a bit, but then he felt her sag against him, the tension going out of her. He wondered if it was too late to try being a father to her. And for a fleeting instant it crossed his mind that maybe it wasn't too late to get his hands on some of that trust money.

Laurel drew back. "Uncle Rudy is handling the adoption," she said, sniffing. "He . . . he found the couple." She paused to take a deep breath. "That's why they put me here instead of in the maternity wing. I'm not supposed to be around the other mothers."

It all tumbled into place. The baby . . . the one Rudy had said he was adopting. Val had thought it was pretty weird anyone's letting a middle-aged loner like Rudy adopt her kid, but he'd figured that Rudy had to have all kinds of connections. But all the time it was Laurel's kid he'd been yakking about. *His* grandchild.

Val squeezed his eyes shut. *All this time Rudy knew where Laurel was, and he kept it from me.* Rage rose in him, and his hands closed about the bed's metal side rail, hard enough to cut off his circulation. He imagined it was Rudy's neck he was squeezing, and he could almost hear the separate crunch of each vertebra.

Then he realized something important: *Laurel didn't know Rudy was planning on keeping her baby for himself.*

When he finally spoke, Val was amazed at the steadiness of his voice. "Let me tell you a few things about good old Uncle Rudy."

"Bring me my baby."

Laurel felt as if she were shouting, but the nurse didn't even look up from the thermometer she was squinting at. "Well now, I don't think that's such a good idea," she said.

Laurel's eyes felt swollen and scratchy. And now this nurse had come bustling in to take her blood pressure and temperature, not even asking if she minded.

But worse than this nurse was the awful *emptiness* inside her.

Uncle Rudy. How could he have done something like this to her? Not just trying to take Adam for himself, but before that, making her believe her father was dead.

She recalled her shock at seeing Val walk in. She hadn't known what to feel. For so many years she'd thought of him as dead. They'd sat and talked for close to an hour, and every so often she'd found herself staring at him, noticing how much older he looked. He was still a sharp dresser, with his expensive silk jacket and Gucci loafers, but the jacket had to have been at least ten years old, and the cuffs were beginning to fray. And he hadn't once mentioned a job or what kind of house or apartment he was living in.

What he *had* talked about, besides Uncle Rudy, was the night she and Annie ran away. He'd told her how upset Annie had been about Dearie, and how when he tried to calm her down, she'd gotten furious at him, hysterical almost. Tears had welled up in his eyes. All he'd wanted, he'd said, was for them to be a family.

Now, thinking it over, Laurel realized that apart from being glad to see him and glad that he was alive, she felt sorry for Val. Even so, she was sure that there had to be another side to his story.

Look at all Annie has done for you. If you want the real story about that night, ask Annie.

But what did any of that matter now? All she knew, all she cared about was that her baby had been taken from her.

Laurel began to get a tight feeling in her chest. She was pretty sure she hadn't signed any papers or anything, so maybe it wasn't too late. But she had to see Adam again first. Until she actually held him in her arms, she didn't want to make up her mind. Laurel hadn't seen Adam since a nurse whisked him upstairs to the nursery two whole days ago. Now her milk was coming in. But that was a small hurt compared to the ferocious, aching need she felt. She could no longer bear it. She *had* to see Adam, to hold him.

"I don't care what you think," she told the nurse. "I want to see my baby. Get him for me, or I'll go get him myself."

The nurse frowned. "Well, honestly, I don't . . ."

Laurel swung her legs out of bed. She was trembling. Dr. Epstein had warned her against getting up. But right now she didn't care. The baby, her baby—the only thing she cared about was him.

"Get out of my way," Laurel commanded.

"Why don't you wait here while I see what I can do." The nurse bustled out.

Laurel waited a minute; then she followed the nurse out into the corridor. Bright fluorescents stabbed at her eyes, and the floor tipped to one side like a banking airplane. There was something wrong with her balance. She had to walk with one palm scooting along the wall to keep from falling into it.

She reached an elevator door and felt a burst of elation. Just another minute or two, and she'd be there. The door slid open, and a harried-looking man in a white doctor's coat stepped out. "Excuse me"—she snatched at his starchy sleeve—"which floor are the babies on?"

He gave her a curious look but appeared to be in too much of a hurry to give her bedraggled appearance any thought. "Eight," he said, jabbing a finger upward as he brushed past her.

Seconds later she was stumbling into a bustling corridor, with residents, nurses, and orderlies scurrying past. Taking slow sliding steps, she forced herself to keep moving. She saw something up ahead—a long pane of glass set into the wall, almost like a brightly lit shopwindow. That had to be the nursery. She made herself go faster despite the pain.

And then she was peering through the glass at rows and rows of spotless white bassinets, in each one a tiny, precious baby. One of those was hers. Her baby. Her son.

She tried the door marked STAFF ONLY and found it unlocked. She pulled it open and walked in. There appeared to be only one nurse on duty, a tall black woman. She looked up from diapering a red-faced infant on the changing table against the far wall.

"This area is restricted to hospital personnel," she informed Laurel in a clipped West Indian accent. "I'm afraid I am going to have to ask you to leave."

Laurel squared her shoulders and said, "I've come for my baby. Cobb . . . Adam Cobb."

"The babies are not scheduled for feeding for another hour," the nurse snapped. "Please return to your room, Mrs.—"

"*Miss* Cobb," Laurel interrupted, sticking her chin out. "And I'm not going anywhere until you let me have him."

The nurse's brown eyes sparked. "We have *rules* around here, young lady. We cannot have just anyone marching in here—"

"I'm not just anyone. I'm his mother." Saying it aloud caused something to crumple inside her chest. Her eyes filled with tears. "I'm his mother," she repeated. "Please, I only want to hold him."

The nurse stared hard at her, then relented. "All right. But you will have to stay here. I cannot let you take him back to your room."

"I don't care about that," Laurel told her, nearly swooning with relief. "Can I sit down?"

The nurse pointed to a rocking chair in the corner. Laurel sank into it gratefully, closing her eyes for a moment. When she opened them, she saw a pair of slender black arms extending a fleecy white bundle. Tightly wrapped in folds of flannel, a squashed red face peered from an opening at the top. Her heart turned over.

"Oh," she breathed. She held her arms out. Where she had felt unsteady before, her muscles now seemed springy with new strength. With the warm weight of her child something dropped into place inside her. Tears slid from her chin and splashed against the blanket. "Adam," she whispered.

She tried to imagine handing him over to some stranger and then walking away, going back to school, forgetting about him. But she couldn't see herself doing those things. She had thought that not having Joe's love was bad, but this would be much worse. It would kill her.

Adam had turned his downy head into her chest and was rooting against the front of her gown. Laurel opened it and felt his mouth instantly fasten onto her nipple and begin to suck. She sat back and closed her eyes, feeling a strong pull as the milk flowed into him.

She began to understand it . . . this mother-love. If she could paint it, she would need a canvas bigger than the Milky Way. And Adam would be right in the middle of it, like the first star of the evening, the one you wish on.

Chapter Eleven

EVEN before she could hear a voice on the phone, Dolly, listening to the crackling of the transatlantic line, felt her heart leap. "Henri," she cried, "that you?"

It had been so long . . . weeks since he'd last called; months since she'd seen him . . . months that seemed like a hundred years.

"*Ma poupée,* did I wake you?" came his voice, faint and crinkly with static. All at once it seemed as if no time at all had passed.

"Not a chance," she told him, though a glance at the faintly glowing malachite face of the clock on the mantel told her it was half past one in the morning. "I couldn't sleep to save my life. Must be something I ate." Only the second part was a lie.

Actually, she was sitting here in the dark, looking out her big window at the million fairylike lights of Tavern on the Green, far away across Central Park, and sipping a Cognac that she knew would probably make her feel worse later on. How appropriate that Henri should call just when she was thinking of how much she missed him, loved him, but still dancing around the thing that was really eating at her: that after eight years Henri wasn't any closer to getting a divorce than he had been in the beginning.

I have to tell him. No more. I can't do this anymore—sneaking around behind his wife's back, seeing him only five or six weeks out of the year. I love him too much.

"As a matter of fact, I'm having myself a pity party," she told him. "*Pardon?*"

"A pity party. You sit around feeling real sorry for yourself, preferably when there's nobody round to slap you on the back and say, 'Hey, lady, snap out of it.' "

"I wish I were there," he said, sounding amused.

"Then it wouldn't be a pity party. It'd be a . . . Well, I'm too much of a lady to say what it'd be."

She prayed it was good news he was calling with; for one week, she'd had just about all the upheaval she could take.

The baby—Laurel's deciding to keep him—was a blessing, but it sure had knocked her for a loop. And Val Carrera's turning up after all these years, pouncing on Laurel when she was at her lowest, probably looking for ways to rake up trouble—why, it gave her chills just thinking about it.

Henri was chuckling. "*C'est ça.* But I did not call you at seven thirty in the morning—for you, I know, it is the middle of the night—just to say hello," he told her. "*Alors,* where to begin?"

"Why not skip over the beginning," she told him, feeling herself begin to tense. "I know it by heart."

"Well then—how do you say it?—the happy finishings."

Inside her chest Dolly's heart did a crazy bump-and-grind.

"Henri, what exactly are you trying to tell me?"

There was a pause, and she could hear his unsteady breathing. Finally he said, "Dolly, come to Paris."

"Henri, we have been through this again and—"

"*Non, non,* this time, it is different. Francine and I, we have now separated."

Dolly nearly dropped the receiver. "What did you say?"

"Francine, she has shown me the door," he said softly, but with a small note of triumph. "It appears my wife has taken a lover." He sounded gleeful; then his voice grew serious. "I must be honest with you, though. There will be no divorce. Francine will not accept that."

Henri's voice seemed to be fading, and then Dolly realized it was her pulse pounding in her ears that was making it hard to hear. "Henri, what exactly are you proposing?"

"That you and I . . . that we live together. It is the modern way, *non?* After that . . ." His voice trailed off. He didn't have to say what they both knew: that he would marry her in a minute if he could.

"What about your father-in-law? Does he know?"

"Yes. We now have a new agreement. I am to receive his controlling interest upon his death. Of course, I am obligated to continue supporting Francine. But it is all completed with witnesses, signatures, and the notary. This is for me a great contract, a deliverance."

"Oh, Henri!" Tears of happiness filled her eyes.

"*Chérie,*" Henri continued soberly, "you have not answered my question."

Dolly's head was spinning. She didn't know *what* to think. The chance to be with him all the time, to live with him!

But she would have to move to Paris.

Paris was beautiful, and she loved it, but New York was her *home.* How could she leave—especially now? Laurel was going to need all kinds of help. And how, if she were three thousand miles away, could she be a proper granny to that precious little baby?

As much as she longed for Henri, she also longed for a real family; this baby would bond her to Annie and Laurel in a way that nothing else had. And her business? It had become more than just a means of making money—it was a cozy place where she and the people who came there felt at home.

"Henri, I've got to sleep on this," she said firmly. "Now don't go thinking I'm too chicken to say what's on my mind. The fact is, I don't know *what's* on my mind. Can you wait until tomorrow?"

He sighed. "Do I have a choice?"

"Nope."

"In that case, sleep well, *chérie,* and I love you."

As Dolly hung up, she thought there was about as much chance of her sleeping well now as there was of her walking on the moon.

ANNIE was gazing through the viewing window of the hospital nursery when she turned to find her aunt, brilliant in an emerald-green bouclé wool suit, dabbing at her eyes with a handkerchief. A gold bracelet jingled at her wrist, and on it Annie recognized the charm she and Laurel had given Dolly last Christmas: a tiny gold candy box in the shape of a heart.

"I think he looks like Dearie," Annie said, turning her attention back to the nursery. "Look at his chin, the way it's rounded." All the other babies were asleep, but Adam was wide awake. He waved his fists, and a tiny pink foot kicked loose from his blanket.

She felt Dolly stiffen beside her, then give a small sigh. "Why, maybe so. . . . I guess it's tough to tell at this age, isn't it?"

"I wish Dearie were here. I wish she could see her grandson."

Her own sudden longing for her mother came unexpectedly. It had been a long time since she felt even a distant ache at the thought of her.

Then Annie's thoughts turned to Joe, and she felt her tight grip on her emotions slip a little. Maybe, just maybe, it's still not too late for me and Joe, she thought. Everything would be different from now on. With Adam to mother, Laurel wouldn't have time to hang around Joe so much. She had even talked about moving out, finding her own place. At first Annie had been against it, but now she was starting to think it might not be such a bad thing. It was as if Joe were her center, her core; without him she'd fly off in a million directions.

And what about Emmett? Where did he fit in? That night after dinner at Paolo's they had gone back to his apartment. How could anything that good be just a fling? She knew she didn't love Emmett the way she loved Joe, but what she *did* feel was certainly more than mere fondness.

"Carnations," Dolly was saying. "I remember when you were born, your father filled Evie's room with pink carnations."

Annie smiled. "I think it's feeding time," she said, watching a nurse bend over Adam's bassinet and lift him out.

Dolly turned to Annie, her blue eyes bright and a high flush making her rouged cheeks even pinker. "Do you think they'd let me hold him? Just for a minute. I wouldn't get in the way."

"Why don't you tell the nurse you're his grandmother? You practically are, anyway."

Dolly looked as if she were going to kiss her, and Annie instinctively found herself sidling away.

"I'll go see if Laurey's ready," she told Dolly. "Give Adam a kiss."

Annie was on her way back to the nursery when she saw one of the elevator doors slide open and a tall, spectacled man step out, his head bent low, as if he were used to ducking through doorways. She felt her heart leap.

"Joe," she called softly.

"Hey, Annie. How's Laurey?" he asked.

"Fine. We're taking her home. Joe, I . . ." She swallowed hard and felt her throat clench. "I guess I ought to thank you. For getting Laurey safely through this. I'm glad you were there."

He shrugged as if it were no big deal. "Any kid in that big a rush to get born doesn't need much of a hand."

"He doesn't look a thing like Laurey."

"The eyes," he said, solemnly touching the corner of his own eye with his index finger, "they remind me of yours."

Annie felt herself grow warm. Did he know what he was doing to her? Why, if he was going to keep his distance, did he have to remind her of what they'd come so close to sharing?

But all she could do was smile. "His father is Puerto Rican. Laurey actually knew him back in Brooklyn, it turns out. Then they met up again at Syracuse. Quite a coincidence, huh?"

Joe flushed, and as he looked away, she thought she saw something in his eyes—a flash of emotion that came and went so quickly she wasn't sure whether she'd imagined it or not.

Jealous? Could he be jealous that he's not the father?

A strained silence settled between them. Finally he gestured toward the dreary-looking lounge. "Can I buy you a cup of coffee?"

Annie thought a cup of coffee right now could well burn a hole right through her stomach. Nevertheless, she found herself nodding. "Just a quick one. I promised Laurey I'd be right back."

The visitors' lounge was empty. Joe led her over to a pair of molded plastic chairs, where they sat side by side, hands folded about the steaming Styrofoam cups. Annie felt like a statue carved out of ice, yet her heart was racing.

"How's it going?" he asked. "The business, I mean."

"Too good," she told him. "I hired a new girl to help Louise in the kitchen. If it keeps up like this, I'll have to put on a swing shift. We can barely keep up with all the orders." She set her cup down. "How are things at the restaurant? I mean, with the new addition and all."

"Bursting at the seams already." He smiled. "Thanks in part to my parents. Would you believe they eat dinner there at least once a week? Miracles never cease, huh?"

She found herself smiling, in spite of her tenseness. "I'm glad."

"Annie." She felt Joe's eyes on her, but she didn't look at him. She didn't know why, but she sensed he was going to say something she didn't want to hear.

"There's something you should know," he went on in a quiet, almost hushed voice. "I'm glad I ran into you, but I just want you to know I would have called you anyway. I haven't said anything to Laurey. I wanted to talk to you first."

She tugged her gaze upward, forcing herself to meet his eyes. And what she saw in them was terrible. Pity. He was *sorry* for her.

"What is it, Joe?" she demanded. "For pity's sake, what is it?"

"I'm going to ask Laurey to marry me."

Her mind seemed to separate from the rest of her and float above her body. "What?" she heard herself say, but the word seemed not to be connected to her.

"Annie . . ." He tried to take her hand, but she whipped back so violently she banged her elbow against the back of her chair.

"I don't want to hear it," she said. "Please, don't make me listen to this."

Slowly he removed his glasses and rubbed the bridge of his nose. His eyes were bloodshot, as if he hadn't slept in days.

"Are you in love with her?" she forced herself to ask. "Is that what this is all about?"

He paused.

She felt a piece of her injured heart rejoice. How much could he love her if he had to stop and think about it?

"You could say that," he responded, seeming to choose his words carefully. "I don't want to hurt you or insult you. But let me say that there really *are* more than one or two kinds of loving, and there's a whole lot of gray shading in between."

"I hope you're not planning to put it to Laurey that way," she said bitterly. "You're not doing her any favors, you know."

"It's more complicated than that, don't you see? Damn it, I wish it weren't! I wish I could say I was just being Joe Samaritan, and then let you talk me out of it."

"Do you *want* me to talk you out of it?" She stared at him.

He didn't answer. "I don't know," he said. "What I *do* know is that what I feel for you hasn't changed."

Annie struggled against the tears swelling at the back of her throat. She should tell him how she felt, she thought. She should beg him not to do this thing. But something was holding her back. Pride? She didn't know. All she knew at this moment was that she hated the man sitting beside her, hated him and loved him with all her heart and soul. She'd felt this way once before—the dreary afternoon she stood in the cemetery watching Dearie's coffin being lowered into the ground. Except that this time it was worse. The person who had died was herself.

"Go," she told him, her voice flat. "Go to Laurey."

LATER that day Dolly dialed Henri's number and waited patiently while the line beeped and buzzed its way to Paris. She was in her office, upstairs at Girod's, where she felt more in control, more in charge of herself than at home. Even so, she felt sick at the thought of what lay ahead.

"Henri?"

"Ah! *Chérie,* you must have been reading into my thoughts. I could not wait any longer. I was just now going to call you."

The sound of his voice caused her to grow light-headed, as if she'd drunk Champagne. How, in the few hours since they'd spoken, could she have forgotten the effect his voice had on her?

Dolly faltered. But then she remembered how that little baby had felt in her arms. She could feel the warm imprint of his body against her bosom still, the firm pressure of his tiny fist wrapped about her finger. Adam was just a part of it, she knew . . . but he seemed to embody it all, everything she stood to lose.

"Henri, I can't. I just can't do it," she told him, a great aching hollow opening inside her. Tears streamed down her cheeks faster than she could mop them up with her handkerchief. "I'm a great-aunt now. Laurel's had a darling baby. His name's Adam, and he's just beautiful. And Laurel needs me, and the baby does, too. And I guess I need him."

For the longest time, except for the rustling of long-distance static, the line was silent.

Finally Henri said, "Just now I was remembering our last time together . . . how we never said good-bye, not the words. Perhaps we knew one day there would come a time for speaking them."

She smiled through her tears, surprised at the keenness of the hurt she felt. Her heart had been broken so many times, she'd have thought there'd be nothing left of it.

"I love you," she told him. "Oh, Henri, what do I say now?"

There was a long silence in which Henri seemed to be losing his struggle. At last he spoke, but his voice had the choked, tinny sound of a man close to tears.

"Just say *au revoir*. After all these years who can tell what tomorrow will bring us?"

Dolly knew it was time to hang up, but she clung to the receiver. If she let go, she felt she'd be severing some vital artery that could never be made whole again. But even as she held on, she could feel it all unraveling, everything they'd shared.

"*Au revoir*," Dolly spoke softly into the receiver. A tear dripped from her chin onto the coiled phone cord.

"*Au revoir, ma poupée.*"

Dolly placed the receiver gently, gently in its cradle.

PART THREE: 1980
Chapter Twelve

THE maître d' led Annie to a window table in the Grill Room. Slipping into her seat, she breathed a sigh of relief that she'd gotten there ahead of Felder. The Four Seasons was too grand a place to dash into with your hem flapping, which she knew was how she arrived at most places these days. So although she didn't usually care much about being seen in the right places or about what she looked like, today it might make a difference—because today, somehow, she had to get this man to save her.

She probably ought to have brought a lawyer with her, or one of Emmett's Wall Street buddies. What did she know about making major financial deals? If she hadn't been such an overconfident idiot in that department, she wouldn't even be here now.

"Shall I bring you something from the bar while you're waiting?" the maître d' inquired.

"Perrier," she told him. It would help settle her stomach.

She glanced at her gold watch, a present from Emmett a month ago, on her thirty-second birthday. Felder would be arriving at any moment; should she have waited before ordering her drink?

Watching her waiter thread his way among the well-spaced tables, Annie grew disgusted with herself. If she couldn't do a simple little thing like ordering a drink without worrying, how on earth could she expect Felder to make a million-dollar deal with her?

"Miss Cobb?"

Annie looked up at the stocky middle-aged man with bristling gray hair who stood over her. Felder? But he didn't look at all the way she'd imagined. Except for the beautifully fitted muted-plaid suit he was wearing, the man standing before her might have been a plumber or a butcher or a housepainter—not someone who'd parlayed his way up to ownership of a hugely successful chain of discount department stores.

"Annie. Please, call me Annie."

She started to get up, smiling brightly, but he didn't smile back. Already she felt she was blowing it.

How she *needed* this to work. On top of the absurd rents she was already paying on her shops on Madison Avenue and now in Southampton, she'd known she was sticking her neck out by leasing at Glen Harbor's new, elegant Paradise Mall. To date, less than half of the mall's pricey pickled-oak-paneled stores had been leased. Her ground-level shop was *bleeding* money.

And that was just the tip of the iceberg. With the new plant in Tribeca she had to admit she'd overreached herself. Financially, she was perched atop a precarious sandcastle that could be about to cave in. If she couldn't restructure her finances, and do it fast, Tout de Suite might be going down the tubes *tout de suite*.

She'd read in *The Wall Street Journal* that Felder's was planning to revamp some of its departments into small, intimate boutiques—including a gourmet-food section—and she'd sent samples and literature that very same day. Then, just a week later, Hyman Felder himself had called and invited her to lunch.

He eased his bulk into the chair opposite her. A waiter materialized with her Perrier, and Felder ordered a Dewar's with soda.

"You're younger than I expected," he began. "You mind my asking how old you are?"

"I'm thirty-two," she told him, adding with a laugh, "But it's not the age itself I mind. What bothers me is not knowing how I got there from twenty-five in what feels like about two weeks."

He chuckled. "Please, I got *daughters* older than you. I was around when they built the Brooklyn Battery Tunnel." He fished a mini ice cube from his newly arrived drink and popped it into his mouth. "But one thing you learn after a lotta years in business is what's successful today usually ain't successful tomorrow. I opened my first store after the war, when discount was the name of the game. Now everything is designer. It's a whole different ball game."

"Did you like the samples I sent you?" she asked.

"Wish I could say I did. Truth is, I can't touch the stuff." He pressed a hand to his bulging midsection. "Some fancy doctors tell me that if I don't take some of this off, I'm gonna make Mrs. Felder a very rich widow in the near future."

"But—"

He held up a hand. "Hey, what I like is that you called. And the same day it all hit the press. But you see, for Felder's Pantry I was thinking, well, smelly French cheeses, high-end Colombian coffee beans, that kind of thing. Candies, too, but they'd have to be in boxes, like in the supermarket, only better quality."

"It's a wonderful idea, but what I had in mind for you is a whole separate boutique," she told him, swallowing hard. "Sort of a . . . a miniature version of Tout de Suite."

She leaned forward, locking her gaze on him. "You're a very smart man, and you're right—these days people want quality, and they're willing to pay more for it. Last year Tout de Suite grossed three million. This year it looks like we'll be up forty percent."

"With half a million plus in unsecured debt, a sixty percent jump in your payroll, mortgage payments on your new plant, and a lease commitment in that new ghost town of a mall in Glen Harbor. But hey, it could be worse." The jovial Felder of a minute ago was now transformed into the flint-eyed Felder of legend.

He held up his hand like a traffic cop. "But you shouldn't get the wrong idea. I'm not knocking you. You think I built Felder's with a triple-A bank account and solid-gold bricks?"

"Then what sort of arrangement did *you* think we might make?"

"Look, we just met. We gotta feel our way."

"You do understand that I don't feel I'm asking for any favors. Tout de Suite's chocolates are the best."

"I like your chutzpah. 'The best.' Sounds great, but says who? You? How do *I* know you're the best?" He stared at her, challenging her with an expression halfway between a smile and a shrug.

Her mind was racing. *Come on, Annie. You've been in tight spots before.* An idea came to her. *Gourmand* magazine's annual chocolate fair at The Plaza was a week from Saturday. Chocolatiers were coming from the world over, the biggest names—Godiva, Kron's, Perugina—and all the tiny great ones like Girod's. As always, there'd be a banquet, dancing, speeches, prizes. Going up against those heavy hitters would be a bit like David versus Goliath, but for a fairly new operation like hers to win the general excellence award would mean manna from heaven: great free advertising, a tremendous boost in retail, and lots of new contracts with hotels and gourmet outlets.

"I'm competing in the *Gourmand* chocolate fair a week from Saturday. In my business that's the equivalent of the Academy Awards," she told Felder. "If I take one of the prizes, will that be enough to convince you?"

"First prize?"

"You're really pushing me."

"*You* said you were the best."

Annie swallowed hard against the knot in her throat and said, "All right. First prize. But what then?"

He laughed, shaking his head as he picked up his menu. "You bring home the trophy, and we'll talk turkey."

LESS than an hour after her lunch with Hyman Felder, Annie stood in the small test kitchen in Tout de Suite's Washington Street factory peering over Louise's shoulder while she put the finishing touches on a cinnamon-truffle cake—four layers of rum-soaked chocolate *génoise* filled with cinnamon-chocolate *ganache* and praline buttercream, the whole thing frosted with *ganache*, then coated with a bittersweet glaze and ringed with toasted hazelnuts. "Mmm, looks perfect," she told Louise. "Maybe a few more hazelnuts?"

"Come on. You said it was perfect." Louise stopped frosting her cake and looked at Annie.

"Well . . . *practically* perfect."

Louise laughed. "That line probably ought to go on your tombstone: Here Lies Annie Cobb, Practically Perfect." She licked a dab of frosting from the back of her thumb. "Oh, Joe called. He said just call him back when you get a free moment."

"You mean sometime in 1993?"

Annie laughed at her own joke, but inside she felt a tug. Six years, and yet when she heard his name—or worse, when she saw him—a sudden lick of heat, followed by light-headed panic. Sure, everything was fine these days. Good friends, just as they'd always been, nothing more. Now and then Joe stopped by for coffee. Mostly, though, she saw him on family occasions.

But still, whenever he greeted her with a hug or touched her hand to make a point, something inside her stirred. Did Joe feel it, too? If so, he kept it hidden. They kept it light and jokey, especially in front of Laurel. Sometimes the whole thing *seemed* real. But Annie knew it wasn't; it was an act, as elaborate as Kabuki theater.

If only . . .

Annie resolutely shut her mind against the thought that seemed always to be crouching there. She could not, *would* not, let herself imagine what her life would be like now if *she* had been the one to marry Joe. He was her sister's husband—end of story.

I should call Emmett instead, she thought. Remind him to pick up his new suit so he'll have it for tonight. The party they were going to was to celebrate the publication of Tansy Boone's newest dessert cookbook, which included several of Tout de Suite's recipes. Tansy had persuaded Stanley Zabar, an old friend, to let her hold the party in his store, and Annie had offered to supply the desserts.

Lost in her work, she didn't hear the footsteps behind her.

"Annie?"

She turned, startled. "Joe!"

"Sorry, I didn't mean to sneak up on you." Smiling that slip-sliding smile of his, he put out a hand, palm up, in a conciliatory gesture. "Have a minute? You feel like taking a walk?"

Annie had about nine hundred things to do, but she found herself nodding. "Sure, why not?"

Once she got outside, she was glad she'd said yes. Fall was here, really here, and until now she'd hardly noticed. Leaves from the catalpa tree outside her building littered the sidewalk, and the sky was the crisp menthol blue of after-shave.

They walked side by side down Washington Street without talking. Joe was so quiet that Annie began to worry. Finally he turned to her and said, "It's my father. He's getting worse."

"Joe, I'm sorry." Marcus *had* gone downhill since Joe's mother died last May; Annie had seen that much herself. He was having weird mood swings and memory lapses. The doctors called it Alzheimer's.

"Even with half his mind gone, he's impossible." Joe sounded angry, but she could see the lines of weariness in his face . . . and yes, the caring. "I've had three nurses quit on me in the last month and a half." He gave a short, incredulous laugh.

"What are you going to do?"

"Well"—he took a deep breath—"last week I made an appointment with that counselor I told you about. She assesses people—families, really—in this kind of situation. She visited Dad the other day, and then she came to see me today at the restaurant."

"And?"

"She's recommending that he be placed in a home." He turned to Annie, a sad smile surfacing on his face. "The other night when I was tucking Adam in, he looked up at me and said, 'You know, Dad, sometimes second grade stinks.'" Joe laughed, this time with genuine amusement. "That about sums it up, don't you think?"

I sure do, Annie thought, but she wasn't thinking of old age. Just of how unfair it was that you could love two people as much as she loved Joe and Laurel, and know that one love must cancel the other. Unfair to Emmett, too. They'd been together so long—sometimes it felt like they were already married—but she hadn't ever been able to take that final step. Maybe she never would. Not until she truly believed that Joe wouldn't care or that she wouldn't.

It's been six years, so isn't it about time you accepted reality?

"I haven't told Laurey. It'll really upset her. From the start she and Dad really got along. She's crazy about him." He looked down, but not fast enough. Annie had seen something in his eyes . . . something dark and unsettling.

"Joe, is . . . is everything okay between you and Laurey?"

He paused a beat too long. "Sure. Why do you ask?"

"I don't know. Forget it. It's none of my business anyway."

He smiled. "Well, well, you *have* changed."

Annie, relieved by his change in tone, quipped, "Only during business hours. Evenings I turn back into a yenta. Rivka says I'm so good at it I could give lessons." She paused. "Joe, about your father—if there's anything I can do . . ."

He shrugged. "Thanks. I'm okay. Just needed to unload on someone, I guess. You know, sometimes I think it'd be easier on all of us if the old man would just die." He stopped, looking rueful. "I've never admitted that to anyone."

"It's okay," she told him. "I'm not shocked. In fact, I think your father would prefer it that way, too."

He touched her arm and said softly, "Thanks."

Joe took her hand, and they walked back that way, as if they had been doing it all their lives. For the first time in years she felt relaxed with him, and oddly content. But still, something dark stirred inside her. An expression of Dearie's nibbled at her mind: *"Let sleeping dogs lie."* But how were you supposed to do that once they woke up?

In Zabar's mezzanine, under a ceiling hung with bright enamel kettles and triple-tiered wire baskets filled with tea towels and pot holders, Annie worked the room, kissing a cheek here, shaking a hand there, stopping to chat with those she knew.

By nine, waiters dressed in crisp chef's whites were setting out coffee and trays laden with Annie's desserts. And lots of people seemed to be snatching them up.

But something wasn't right. Suddenly she didn't feel "on." As the raves for her tiny white-chocolate dessert cups filled with brandied mousse came at her, she wasn't getting her usual surge of triumph. All she was getting was a headache.

She was making her way over to the dessert table when Emmett came over and slipped his arm through hers. "You've got that look," he said affectionately, smoothing back her short dark hair.

"What look is that?"

His blue eyes sparkled. "Like General MacArthur storming Corregidor. Relax, Cobb, it's just a party. You don't have to conquer everyone here with your charm."

Annie stared at him and felt a mixture of affection and exasperation rising in her. He could be such a pain sometimes, but she never grew tired of him. Right now, in his new suit—a soft, charcoal gray with faint burgundy stripes—he looked quite distinguished, as befitted a new partner of a major real estate firm.

"I wouldn't *be* here if it wasn't good for the business," she told him. "Just now, when I was talking to Ed Sanderson, he said he'd like to do a whole spread on me for *Chocolatier* magazine."

"I'll bet he would." Emmett winked lasciviously.

"Em, if you don't stop making fun of me, I'll—"

He caught her upper arm, drawing her close. "You'll what? Kick me out of bed?"

"Just the opposite. I'll keep you there until you beg for mercy."

He rubbed his lips lightly against her temple and whispered, "What do you say we head off to my place so we can get started?"

Annie felt herself grow warm. Damn him, why did he *do* this to her—tempt her when she least wanted to be? Tonight she'd wanted to sort out her thoughts, replay her conversation with Joe.

She shook her head. "In a little while. There're a few people I want to talk to that I haven't gotten to yet."

A dark expression flitted across Emmett's square, seasoned face, but he merely released her and gave a light shrug. Annie felt a dart of worry. She was putting him off, and he knew it. I don't want to lose him, she thought. Yet how could she tell him that she loved him, *adored* him . . . but not enough to marry him?

"Em, I'm sorry."

"No big deal." He glanced at her, a sharp, assessing gaze. "But look, I'm beat. Mind if I cut out on my own?"

"Only if you promise to have dinner with me tomorrow night."

He winked. "You got yourself a deal."

Watching his broad back as he wound his way toward the stairs, Annie felt her gloom deepen. How long, she wondered, how long before he walked away for good?

Suddenly she felt tired. She wanted to run after him, tell him she'd changed her mind, but her feet seemed bolted to the floor. She found herself thinking of all the movies she'd seen with people running alongside trains they had no hope of catching, the teary-eyed love object peering anxiously, fruitlessly, from the window. Though she hadn't moved an inch, Annie felt short of breath, and there was a throbbing in her temples, as if she, too, had been running to catch a train she'd already missed.

Chapter Thirteen

Laurel caught the softball and tossed it back to Adam. She watched him jump for it, arms straining skyward, his Big Bird T-shirt pulling away from his grass-stained jeans. The ball grazed the top of his glove, landing with a thump against the back of the house and scattering small flakes of paint, like confetti, over the grass below.

The place could use a new paint job, Laurel thought. It seemed just months ago that she and Joe had had the whole exterior primed and painted. But that hadn't been since they first moved in. Adam was just starting to crawl then. Six years . . . Could it really be six years? Her gaze scanned upward, taking in the two-story Cape Cod with its charming blue shutters and big, screened sun porch. For almost a year she and Joe had knocked themselves out fixing it up. But it had been worth all the sweat and hassle. Bayside was only a half-hour train ride to the city, and yet they had flowers, a vegetable garden, and this good-sized grassy backyard for Adam to play in.

"Mo-o-o-ommm."

Laurel saw him standing by the line of tall hydrangeas dividing their yard from the Hessels'.

"Watch out, Mom. This'll burn a hole right through your glove!"

"But I'm not wearing a—"

Laurel was so struck by the look of manlike determination on his small amber-skinned face that the words died on her lips. The ball flew upward and seemed to hang in the air before crashing down through the branches of the old apple tree under which she stood. Bending to retrieve it, Laurel thought how much like his real father Adam looked just a second ago, his dark eyes glittering. She remembered the airmail letter she'd gotten from Jess the year Adam turned three. He'd joined the Peace Corps and was living in Mexico. Then he'd met a local girl, and they were going to be married.

The memory of her own hasty marriage at city hall came flooding back. No white dress or veil, no bouquet, no rice even. But she'd been so over the moon she hadn't cared one bit. She had everything she wanted standing right next to her.

But Joe, had he felt such happiness? Kneeling on the grass, Laurel froze, her fingers clenched about the ball.

Don't cry. You mustn't. Not in front of Adam. But the tears were already starting, and with them came the image her mind had been replaying over and over since yesterday: Joe and that woman at the restaurant. She'd dropped off the finished drawings for *Sally, the Silly Goose* at the publisher and then stopped by the restaurant to surprise Joe. Coming up into the dining room, she'd spotted him with his back to her, in a booth with a pretty auburn-haired woman whom Laurel didn't recognize. They were both bent forward, so absorbed in each other that neither one noticed her standing there. The woman was holding Joe's hand tightly between both of hers. Joe's face was hidden, so Laurel couldn't see his expression, but she could tell he was upset. An apology? A lover's quarrel? A farewell?

And now, all over again, she was feeling the horror she'd felt then. All day today she'd been trying hard not to imagine the two of them telling each other little jokes, kissing, making love. What if there was some innocent explanation for what she'd seen?

Okay, maybe there was. But it wasn't just the woman in the restaurant. Lately Joe had seemed so distant and preoccupied. He hadn't made love to her in weeks. And this distance wasn't something that had just cropped up in the last month or so.

You knew. Even when he said the words, you knew when he married you that he didn't love you, not passionately, totally, the way you love him . . . and you took him anyway. So if he's having an affair, why should it be such a shock? At least it's not An—

"Did you see that? Wow-ee, Mom. Did you see how high it gotted? Right up to *space* prac'ly!"

Adam's voice yanked her back to him. Raking her knuckles across her wet eyes, she stood and went over to her son.

"If I were a talent scout," she said, hugging him, "I'd sign you up for the Yankees . . . or maybe NASA. The way you snagged that ball, I'll bet you'd be good with rockets, too."

Adam pulled away from her, saying, "Kids can't be scientises."

Her heart caught. *His world is so orderly. Color inside the lines, and you can't go wrong.*

Laurel wished life *were* that easy. Joe's love—all the years she'd struggled to win it, she'd been so sure it was only a matter of time. Now she wasn't so certain.

"Mommy?"

Now Adam was running in crazed circles about the lawn, flapping his arms.

"Brrrrrrrrrrrr . . . I'm a rocket! Watch me go!"

"Where are you going?" she asked him.

"Mars!"

"Oh, that's too bad. I live on Jupiter. I was hoping you could drop me off on your way back."

Adam giggled. "Mommy, you're silly."

"Look who's talking."

"What if you *really* lived on Joopder? Who would tuck me in?"

"Daddy, of course." A tight, hot band formed about her heart.

"Annie, too!"

"Oh, I don't know. Your aunt Annie is pretty busy."

"But not too busy for *me*."

"Of course not." Annie, though frantic with her chocolate business, always managed to find time for Adam.

"She's coming today, isn't she? Isn't she?" Adam demanded.

"Later," Laurel told him. "After your nap."

"Ahhhhh . . . only babies take naps." He rose, adding slyly, "I bet Annie wouldn't make me take a nap."

"Well, Annie isn't here, so you'll have to do what your mean old mommy says." Laurel steered him in the direction of the house.

When she had him settled in his room, she went downstairs, made herself a cup of tea, and carried it into her studio. It had a window that gave her wonderful morning sun to paint by, and in the afternoon she sewed on the old Singer in the corner. Right now she was working on Annie's dress for the chocolate fair. Her sister had spotted this particular dress in an Italian *Vogue* and had fallen in love with it. And naturally, bigmouthed Laurel had to offer to make it for her.

She slid onto the stool that faced her drawing board. There were several ideas for the next drawing in the story she was working on, and she wanted to sketch them while they were still fresh in her mind. She tore a fresh sheet from her sketch pad, looked at it, but then her mind went blank. A wave of tiredness swept over her. Like all the times she'd been pregnant: drowsy, drugged almost.

Laurel felt her chest squeeze tight. Those babies—three of them—no bigger than the heads of pins, but losing each one had been terrible, almost as terrible as if she had lost Adam.

Joe's babies, his sons and daughters.

If she'd carried even one of them to term, would things be different now between her and Joe?

Inside, Laurel felt herself spiraling downward, and she took a deep breath, steadying herself. Why had she volunteered to make that dress for Annie? Why was she always trying so hard to please her sister? Sometimes it felt as if . . . well, as if she were struggling to make amends for some terrible injustice she'd inflicted on Annie.

And it wasn't Annie who was making her feel this way, either. Annie was terrific. And so great with Adam. It was just that she could be so *overwhelming* at times. Like a tornado—blowing in through the front door, high heels clacking, gold earrings flashing. After Annie's visits things seemed duller somehow. This house, with its bright quilts and woven wall hangings and stripped-pine furniture, seemed to lose its color.

Did Joe feel that, too? He must . . . and sometimes it drove Laurel crazy with jealousy. At times, seeing how happy and . . . well, *charged* he was around Annie, Laurel would feel as if she were fading right into the walls. She had to remind herself that she, too, was an interesting person. Besides taking care of Adam and this house, two of the books she'd illustrated had been nominated for the Caldecott Medal, the prestigious children's book award. Her show at that gallery on Spring Street had gotten two respectful notices and one glowing one, and she'd even sold six paintings. So why on earth should she feel second-rate?

An image of Joe and the pretty auburn-haired woman stole into Laurel's mind, and a knifing pain surged low in her belly.

Annie. What would she do if she were in my place?

Oh, why did it always have to come back to Annie? This was *her* life. She didn't need Annie or her butting in. *Remember how she hit the ceiling when you told her about Val's coming to visit?*

Laurel now imagined how outraged Annie would be if she knew about the money she'd been sending her father. It had started years ago—Val's phoning and explaining sheepishly about this bind he was in, just temporary, but could he "borrow" enough to tide him over? Somehow, though, the loans were never repaid. Laurel didn't really mind. She felt sorry for Val.

Oddly, it was Rudy she missed, though she hadn't answered any of the dozens of letters he'd sent. She knew she ought to really hate him for what he'd done, but she sensed that his lying to her wasn't born of malice. And if it hadn't been for Uncle Rudy, she might have actually given Adam up for adoption.

Thinking of Adam, Laurel badly needed to talk to someone. Should she tell Annie about this thing with Joe? If she didn't talk to somebody, she felt as if it would burn a hole right through her.

Maybe somehow she'll be able to help.

Thinking of how good it would feel just to unburden herself, Laurel straightened up and with pieces of masking tape began fixing a clean sheet of thick drawing paper to the table's tilted surface. With a charcoal pencil she roughed out a sketch of a unicorn. Not an ordinary unicorn—this one had wings, iridescent wings, like rainbows—and it was flying, soaring among the stars.

"A LITTLE higher, I think," Annie told her. "Just above the ankle."

Laurel, on her knees on the living room's braided rug, removed the pins clamped between her lips and gazed up at her sister, glorious in the gown that until a few minutes ago had been just a hank of fabric sagging from its hanger. On Annie it rippled, it glowed, it *danced*—rubbed velvet, the pinkish gold of hammered copper, supple as silk, with a subtle drape that softened her angular shoulders and emphasized her small breasts. Laurel thought it looked spectacular. She stuck a few more pins in and stood up. "There. Go take a look. Try the mirror in the bedroom, only promise not to look at anything else. The room's a mess. I haven't even made the bed."

The whole house, in fact, was a mess. Laurel looked about her, at the cushions scattered with crumbled saltines, at the sticky ring a juice glass had left on the drop-leaf table.

Then Laurel realized that Annie had made no move to leave, and was staring at her with her I-know-something-is-wrong look.

"I don't give a damn about the bed," she said sternly. "It's *you* I'm worried about. Laurey, you look like hell. What's wrong?"

Laurel felt as if there were sandbags tied to her arms and legs. She was so tired. "Nothing," she said. "I took a nap before you came. That's why the bed isn't made."

Annie peered at her with new sharpness. "You're not sick . . . or anything?"

"You mean, am I pregnant?" Laurel snapped. She thought of Joe's not touching her night after night. "If you want to know the truth, it'd be a miracle."

For a moment Annie stood silent. She looked shocked.

145

Then she said, "Is something going on between you and Joe?"

"Nothing a good faith healer couldn't fix." Laurel gave a short, dry laugh.

"Is it something he did?"

Laurel felt as if she was slowly losing her grip. It would be so easy just to let go, to let Annie comfort her. But no, better not.

"I'm glad you like the dress," she said brightly. "Velvet is harder than silk to work with. I don't know how many times I had to rip out that left seam and do it over." But then her control broke, and a sob slipped out. "Oh, Annie, he's having an affair."

She told Annie about the woman at the restaurant, about how awful it had been . . . and how she'd wanted to die. Even now, just talking about it, she felt some little piece of her shrivel up. Tears were rolling down her cheeks.

Stop it, she commanded herself. But she couldn't.

And then Annie started to laugh. She was *laughing.*

Laurel's face stung as if she'd been slapped.

Annie came over and grabbed Laurel's hand. "Laurey, you've got it all *wrong.* Joe isn't having an affair. That woman you saw is a counselor. Joe told me the whole story—about his father's not being able to manage anymore with just a nurse . . . about this counselor's recommending a nursing home. You can imagine how upset Joe must have been. She had to have been *comforting* him, don't you see?"

Oh, yes . . . Laurel saw. Everything, clear as day.

Joe had made this momentous decision about his father, and he hadn't once mentioned it to her. And it was Annie he'd confided in. Not her, his wife, but Annie.

Now it was Annie who looked ill, the color draining from her face. "Laurey, what's wrong? What *is* it?" Annie sounded frantic.

Laurel stared at her sister, feeling an avalanche of love, grief, sorrow, and resentment. "You," she said, the rushing in her ears so great she had to shout to be heard over it. "*You're* what's wrong."

Annie jerked, a hand flying to her mouth. "What?"

Laurel glared at Annie. "How can you pretend when we both know it's *you* he wants? And you want him, too. Isn't that why you've been stringing Emmett along all these years? Stop being so damn noble and *admit it.*" She felt herself unraveling. "Admit you want him for yourself!"

A thundering silence filled the room.

"Mommy?"

Laurel jumped as if she'd been struck. She looked over at Adam, standing frozen at the bottom of the stairs. The front of his shirt was streaked with paint, and he held a paintbrush in one fist. His eyes were huge and scared. How much had he heard?

She wanted to run to him, but she couldn't seem to move. Annie swooped across the room and took Adam by the hand.

"My goodness, look at you! More paint must've gotten on that shirt than on the paper. Do you want to show me what you've done?" She was upset, too, her voice ragged, but she was hiding it well. She was protecting Adam, just as she'd once protected little Laurey.

With a quick, sharp glance over her shoulder at her sister, Annie steered Adam up the stairs. Laurel stared after them for a moment, then sank down on the sofa, determined not to cry.

JOE swung his Volvo into the driveway, crunching over a blanket of fallen leaves. The house was dark except for a light in the upstairs hall. Nearly midnight. Laurel and Adam were probably fast asleep by now. And that's where he longed to be. What a night. With orders stacking up and everyone working double time, the dishwasher had to go on the fritz, flooding the kitchen floor.

But none of the restaurant headaches compared with what he had tomorrow—a two-o'clock meeting with the director of the St. Francis Center. And then he'd have to do what he'd been putting off for days: break the rotten news about Dad to Laurel. She'd probably insist they take the old man in, and he'd end up sounding like a grade-A louse for saying no. Damn, what a mess.

But as he got out of the car and started along the concrete path by the side of the house, Joe began to feel calmer. He could feel the night air against his cheeks, and he could see his breath puffing out in wispy plumes. He found his way easily in the dark to the side door that opened into the kitchen. But at the back of his mind he sensed something was out of place. Then it hit him: *The light wasn't on.* When she knew he'd be getting home late, Laurel always left the light on over the little wooden porch where he was now standing.

Had something happened to her? As he turned his key in the lock and stepped inside, he felt a vague unease. He cut through the kitchen, which he could see hadn't been cleaned up. Dishes piled up on the counter, toast scraps and crumpled napkins scattered over the pine table in the breakfast nook—that wasn't like Laurel.

He made his way through the dining room, with its round oak table and carved breakfront filled not with fine bone china, but with Mexican pottery in bright, primary colors and Laurel's precious knickknacks—lopsided clay animals Adam had made, an intricately painted Russian box, a pair of pewter candlesticks, a small basket heaped with bright marbles.

Laurel's house, he thought. He lived here, but it was really hers, her creation. It struck him that he'd never fully appreciated how restful it was. When he arrived home each night all wound up, just walking in, he felt soothed.

Now he was climbing the stairs, quietly and quickly taking them two at a time. Reaching the second floor, he popped his head through the open door to Adam's room. Adam lay curled on his side, fast asleep, most of the covers kicked off. Joe felt his tension ease a bit. *You see? If anything had happened to Laurel, would Adam be here sleeping so peacefully?*

He tiptoed over and kissed his son's damp, toothpaste-smelling cheek, and was gripped by longing, as if he were somehow hoarding moments with his son and his wife, storing them up against the day when they'd be gone and he'd be left only with memories.

Joe felt the stitch in his gut tighten once more. How had it come to this? With Laurel he'd tried so damn *hard* to keep things together. But it was like running in sand. He always seemed to be going too slowly. Could he be trying *too* hard?

True, he hadn't been *in* love with Laurel when he married her. Bewitched, bothered, and bewildered, yes, but not the deep love he felt for her now, that had needed time to grow.

Still, deep down she had to have suspected that he loved Annie, too. Wasn't that the root of their problem now? Wasn't that why he couldn't touch her in bed anymore without feeling guilty?

But he didn't want to lose her.

When he looked at her, what he saw was a beautiful, smart, talented woman, a ferociously devoted wife and mother.

Joe gently pulled the covers over Adam and slipped out. His and Laurel's bedroom was next to Adam's, but when he peeked in, it was dark. The bed was empty.

Heading downstairs to Laurel's studio, he saw a sliver of light under its closed door. Standing outside, he knocked softly. "Laurey?"

No answer.

He eased open the door and saw her perched on the stool before her drawing table. In the white cone of light cast by the lamp clamped to the side of the table, her hand, madly sketching, seemed to glow with a light of its own.

"Laurey?" he called again, stepping inside.

Her head jerked up, and she swiveled to face him. She was wearing a loose silk robe, and its shimmering folds hung on her. It struck him how thin she'd gotten, seemingly overnight. She looked ill. Joe felt his heart turn over. What was going on?

"Hi. Sorry if I scared you," he said. "Deadline?"

She nodded. "They need it by Monday." Her voice sounded flat, toneless. "It's not working, though. It's the unicorn. He's not . . ." She swallowed.

Joe stepped closer, peering over her shoulder. The nearly finished drawing of a winged unicorn seemed to leap out at him, all fluid lines and supple movement. Extraordinary. She was so talented.

"What I wanted." She frowned, and stared down at the floor. "He's just a horse with wings and a horn."

"Is there a difference?"

She looked up at him, as if surprised that he couldn't see what to her was so clear. "He has to be . . . magical." Now there were tears in her eyes. "Don't you *see?* When I draw, no matter how fantastic the thing is, I believe in it. That's what makes it work."

"And you don't believe in unicorns? Or is it just this unicorn?" He smiled, hoping intensely to lighten her mood.

She stared at him, an expression of terrible sadness passing over her delicate face. Joe felt suddenly as though he were skidding, skidding all out of control, into the lonely future he'd feared.

"I can't seem to believe in either." A shudder passed through her, and she hugged herself, pressing her knees together tightly. Softly she said, "Joe, I want us to . . . to be apart for a while. Please don't argue. I don't think I could stand even talking about it right now." She took a deep, gasping breath.

Joe stared at her, not believing what he was hearing, yet at the same time feeling curiously relieved—as if he'd known this was going to happen and had been waiting for it. "Laurey, what is it?" He took a step toward her, but she held out her hand to stop him.

"Look," she told him, "it wouldn't do any good to start throwing around accusations. When Annie told me about your father, I felt so . . . so . . . Well, but then I realized it wasn't anything new—my feeling left out. What's new is that I . . . I don't believe in us anymore. All the things I hoped for . . . they just aren't going to happen, are they?"

A great drowning sorrow flooded through Joe. With every fiber of his being he wished that he could convey somehow to Laurel how desperately he loved her, needed her.

"I'm sorry I didn't tell you about Dad. I was going to—" He broke off. "But that's not really what this is about, is it?"

"No."

The look on her face told him what she was thinking, and before Joe could stop himself, he was saying it: "Annie?"

Laurel looked straight at him. "Yes."

"Laurey, I—"

"Joe, will you just *go*." Her look was hot and furious.

He didn't want to go away. If he insisted on hashing it out right here and now, Laurel, he knew, would probably give in. Things would be smoothed over—for a few days, anyway.

But in the end nothing would change. Maybe in some way she was being wise. And didn't he owe her this, honoring her wish? And who knew . . . maybe doing this would somehow help them.

But if this was the right thing, why did it have to *hurt* so damn much?

"I'll pack a few things," he said, his words thudding in his ears.

"Will you be staying at the apartment?" She cast him a forlorn glance, then quickly added, "Adam will want to know."

"Yeah, sure." Apartment? For a second he had to think. Then he remembered the old place on Twenty-first Street. He'd hung on to it because his rent was so cheap, and he could crash there when he was too bushed to drive home. But to live there again?

"What should I tell Adam?" Laurel was asking.

Joe hesitated. It occurred to him that much more than Adam's security might be at stake. Maybe his and Laurel's whole future. He did not want to lose all that. Not even one bit of it.

Joe did then what he'd wanted to do the minute he saw her. He crossed the room, catching her in a hard embrace.

"Tell him I'll be back," he murmured, then quickly let go.

Chapter Fourteen

Emmett, standing in a large workstation near the second-floor entrance of the Tout de Suite factory, breathed in the rich, dense aroma of chocolate. Funny thing, he thought, how a certain smell could trigger a memory. Years from now, when he smelled chocolate, would he remember Annie at one in the morning tumbling into his bed after a long night at the factory, the scent of chocolate on her skin, her hair, her lips? Or would it make him think of this night . . . of having to tell her good-bye?

Don't, he told himself sharply. You haven't left yet. You haven't given her a chance to change your mind. He'd tell her about the offer he'd gotten—sales manager at Fountain Valley, ninety million dollars' worth of luxury houses just outside of La Jolla. He'd tell her the time had come for her to fish or cut bait. He needed her once and for all—to become his wife. Or he'd best forget about her and move on.

He watched her now, working alongside Doug and Louise, her hair damp and spiky, her hands and the front of her apron covered with chocolate. They were dipping plastic leaves into melted *couverture* for the tree—made entirely from chocolate—that would be the centerpiece of Tout de Suite's display at tomorrow's *Gourmand* chocolate fair. When the *couverture* on the leaf was dry, it could be peeled off and, using a warm chocolate paste, "glued" to a branch of the tree. Four feet high, its trunk and branches carved from solid chocolate, it was more than ambitious—it was a masterpiece.

"I've never heard of anyone being able to make a whole tree from scratch . . . except maybe God," Emmett joked.

"Yeah." Annie sighed. "Except God created the whole world in six days. If I stopped to think about how long I've been getting this display together, I'd probably pass out."

"Maybe it's time you *did* pass out," Doug volunteered. "We started at six thirty this morning, and it's now midnight."

"Thanks so much, Douglas." Annie shot a withering glance in his direction, a smile nonetheless tugging at her lips. "How would I ever keep track without you?"

"Anything I can do to help?" Emmett asked.

"Yeah." Louise shot a worried glance at Annie. "Get her out of here. Please. Just for an hour. She's been here longer than any of us, and won't take even a five-minute coffee break."

"Fat chance!" Annie yelled as she was carrying a tray of finished leaves over to Doug. Then her foot caught on something, and she staggered, the tray nearly sliding from her grasp.

Doug caught the tray, and Annie, with a loud exhalation of breath, rocked back on her heels. Placing her hands on her hips, she glared at Louise. "If I don't get this display finished by tomorrow and looking good enough to win first prize, I might as well just retire. Because unless I make that deal with Felder, there may not *be* any excuse left for busting my buns."

In her jeans and chocolate-smeared apron, her forehead shiny with sweat, she looked ready to collapse.

"There really isn't that much more to do," Doug told her. "Lou and I, we can handle the rest on our own. Trust us."

"I don't know. . . ." Annie was weakening, but she still resisted.

"Either you go, or we go on strike," Louise threatened.

"You wouldn't!" Annie gasped.

"Try me," Louise replied, plainly in earnest.

Then Emmett, surprising himself almost as much as her, grabbed Annie around the waist and hoisted her over his shoulder.

"Sorry, Miss Kitty, but it's for your own good," he drawled. Glancing back over his shoulder, he saw Louise gaping at them.

"Em, stop it. Put me down! I won't be carried out of here like a sack of potatoes! I have to . . ." Annie stopped struggling and started to giggle as Emmett reached the door. With a grunt he set her down, using his body to hold her against the door. "Can I trust you? Or do I have to tie you up?"

"Em, you're crazy." She clapped her hand over her mouth to stop herself from laughing.

"Crazy about you." He pulled her hand away and kissed her mouth, feeling her resist, then grow still and soft. He felt the ache in his belly deepen. How could he walk away from her?

She drew back. "Okay, okay, you win." She sighed, and let her head rest against his shoulder. "But promise me one thing."

"Anything."

"That you'll stop talking like Matt Dillon. It's starting to make me nervous."

"Why's that?"

" 'Cause at the end of every *Gunsmoke* episode, there was always a showdown."

Was she worrying about tomorrow's fair, or was she maybe sensing that the time had come for a showdown with him?

Minutes later they were strolling up Washington Street toward an all-night pizzeria on West Houston. Hell, Emmett thought, maybe I should get this thing off my chest here and now.

I'm thirty-six, Annie, and sick of waiting. Tired of being on hold. I make a nice living selling apartments and houses, and I still don't own one of my own. Like a drifter with more dreams than brains, I've been waiting for when we could buy one together.

Now, looking at Annie beside him, he knew her affection—her love, if you could call it that—was what kept him going, in spite of what she felt about Joe Daugherty. For half her life she'd been in love with the guy. How could he compete with an obsession?

Emmett touched her elbow. "You nervous about tomorrow?"

"Better now." She smiled at him. "I'm sorry, Em. I know I haven't been around much lately. There's just been so much going on." She let out a breath that left a faint wisp of smoke in the chilly air. "Anyway, you haven't exactly been lounging around these past few weeks. Did you close on that building on Mercer?"

"Not yet, but it's going to go. Just tonight, as a matter of fact, I had dinner with the guy who's organizing the limited partnership."

Annie, caught in the midst of yawning, shot Emmett an apologetic look. "Sorry. I didn't get much sleep last night."

"Working?"

"No. I was on the phone with my aunt. We're really worried about my sister."

"Laurel? She sick?"

Annie shook her head and looked away. "Not exactly. But Dolly says she's really broken up. Joe . . . well, he's moved out . . . back to his old apartment. Laurey asked him to."

Emmett slowed his steps. "You think they'll work it out?"

"I don't know."

Did she mean she hadn't a clue . . . or was she hoping they *wouldn't* get back together? Thinking of Joe and Annie having a clear shot at what he, Emmett, had wanted for so long made his stomach wrench. Suddenly he felt worn down.

"Annie, there's something . . ."

But before he could get the words out, Emmett saw that they were nearing Arturo's, with its garish sign advertising pizza and calzone.

"What?" She half turned toward him with an expectant smile.

No, he thought. Better wait. Right now she needed to relax.

"It'll keep," he told her. "I'll tell you later."

After the fair, he thought, when she wasn't feeling so pressured. He'd explain how New York was making him feel hemmed in, and that unless she gave him the reason to do so, he couldn't see himself sticking around. Because this time, after he asked her to marry him and she said no again, he knew he'd need to be miles and miles away from her. Or how else would he keep from turning right back around and making a damn fool of himself all over again?

ANNIE came to a halt in front of the building where she and Laurel had once lived. She'd been walking, lost in thought, and had no idea how she'd ended up there. The sidewalk was deserted; it had to be three or four in the morning.

She remembered going to Arturo's, wolfing down two slices of pizza, then Emmett's forcing her into a cab, ordering her to go home and get some sleep. Exhausted, she'd let the cabbie take her to her homey but messy apartment. There, too tired even to switch on any lights, she must have fallen onto her bed, clothes and all. Vaguely she recalled waking up a couple of hours later, her heart pounding, feeling trapped. Dying to get out . . . get some fresh air.

Then, as if in a fog, not really seeing where she was going, walking . . . walking . . . walking.

It occurred to Annie that in some deep part of her she must have known all along that this was where she'd been heading.

To Joe.

She saw the lights blazing on the second floor, and somehow she wasn't surprised.

She had to see him, had to find out if Laurel was right . . . if *she* had something to do with Joe and Laurel's splitting apart. What if it was true? Did she *want* it to be true? Now she was mounting the building's stone step, pushing open the heavy glass door to the narrow lobby. Her hand went almost automatically to the bell for Joe's apartment, and she jammed her thumb against it.

The intercom crackled; a distorted voice echoed in the stillness. Joe. He sounded as if he'd been expecting her . . . or somebody.

Annie climbed the stairs. This is crazy, she thought. I shouldn't be here. I'll probably only make things worse for Laurel.

Nearing the top of the stairs, she saw Joe waiting on the landing in front of his open door, the light at his back. She kissed his cheek and walked passed him, through the door, and into the bright living room. Turning, she saw him standing in front of her, looking mildly baffled.

"Annie, what are you doing here?"

"Would you believe I happened to be in the neighborhood?"

He rubbed his face with his hand. "At four in the morning?"

"I couldn't sleep."

"Yeah . . . me, too." He blinked, shaking his head as if to clear it. "Coffee? I made enough to keep the whole city wired."

"No, thanks." She looked around. It had been years since she was here, but it was exactly the way she remembered it. "It's strange," she said, "being here again. Seeing you in this place. It's like you never moved out."

"It doesn't feel that way. Somehow it just doesn't fit. It feels like I'm trying to cram myself into something I've outgrown."

Annie touched his forearm. "Joe, what's going on with you and Laurey? The other day when I was out there, she seemed pretty upset. But I never thought—"

"What did she say?"

"She seemed to think . . . well, that maybe you were having an affair. She'd seen you with that woman at the restaurant—that counselor. But when I told her she had it all wrong, she . . . she got really angry. Said a lot of crazy things. About me . . . and you."

"Maybe they're not so crazy. Maybe *we're* the ones who are."

He was looking at their reflections in the darkened window, wearing an odd, distant expression.

Suddenly Annie felt weak, as if she couldn't trust her legs to support her. She sank onto the hard leather sofa, her heart leaping inside her. "Joe, you and Laurey aren't thinking of . . ."

"Divorce?" He stared at her, his eyes bleak. "Hell, no, not that. Laurey just wants some time alone. To think. See where we're headed." His mouth twisted in a bitter smile. "Euphemisms. What she's really saying is, You let me down, you s.o.b."

Maybe you did. But I'm partly to blame, too.

Outwardly Annie had let go of Joe, but not in her heart. There she held fast to her love, secretly tending it, using it to keep Emmett at arm's length . . . and maybe using it, too, to punish Laurel for taking Joe away from her.

But if that was true, she hadn't meant to.

"Laurel's just hurt. She'll get over it," Annie said.

"No, it's more than that." Joe sank onto the sofa beside her, his forearms resting on his knees. "She's . . . different. I married a kid. Now that kid is grown up. She loves me, but she doesn't really *need* me anymore, not the way she used to. And that's okay. But, you see, the thing is . . . *I need her*." His voice choked on the last words.

"Then *why*? Why all this?"

"Because she knows how I feel about you."

Annie felt cold deep in her bones.

"We haven't done anything wrong," she said.

Joe let his breath out with a whistling noise. "Sometimes I think *everything* we've done was wrong. All our pretending."

She wanted to cover her ears, shut out his voice. "No!" she cried. "I wanted . . . *honestly* wanted you and Laurey to be happy."

Joe looked up at her, the pain in his eyes unbearable. "Sometimes I think," he began slowly, "that if we'd only made love, you and I—just once—then I wouldn't have felt so . . . cheated."

Silence seemed to be swallowing them. There was only the throaty murmuring of a pigeon outside the window.

"Do you want to make love with me now?" The question slipped out of her before she realized she was saying it. She sat back, shocked, breathless, her heart galloping.

Yet she also felt strangely calm. She'd traveled forever to get here, and maybe now the journey would be over. Wasn't this what she'd come here for? To quench a desire so old it had become part of her, her bones, her flesh?

Joe stared at her, his eyes holding her with the tenderness of an embrace. Then he stood up and walked into his bedroom.

Annie, as if in a trance, followed him.

The room was dark except for the glow from the yard, giving everything an oddly stark look. Joe said nothing while she undressed, his eyes fixed on her, unreadable. Then he pulled off his sweater and stood before her, his long torso stippled by the shadow of an ailanthus tree.

An image of Laurel edged its way into her mind, but she blocked it out. This belongs to me, she told herself fiercely. To us.

They stood before one another, not touching. Yet Annie felt as if she were gripped in an electrical field, the air around her charged with static. There was a high humming inside her head. She felt scared, weak, and trembly, barely able to stand. But if a speeding train had been thundering right at her, Annie could not have moved.

Joe began to touch her. Her hair, her face, his fingertips brushing lightly over eyelids, nose, lips, ears. It was as if he were mapping her out, memorizing her. They were joined at so many points, it was strange to realize how much there was still to discover. A universe.

"Oh . . . Joe."

Finally he kissed her. No, not just a kiss. It was more . . . so much more. Bright heat filled her. The room swayed, tilted. Now she was lying on the bed. He was beautiful.

She began to cry silently, tears running from the corners of her eyes. She wanted him—oh, she wanted him—but she didn't want this to end, either. She longed for this to go on forever.

LYING there afterwards, Annie thought, Is it possible to let go and still go on living?

Yet even if she did let go of him, she felt as if a circle inside her had finally closed. She felt strangely at peace.

The world began to trickle in. Muted voices drifting up from below. Outside, the rattle of a garbage can.

Morning.

She turned to Joe, who lay curled by her side, one long leg hooked over hers, an arm looped about her middle.

"I love you." The words came easily, like a line she'd rehearsed countless times inside her head.

Joe brushed a tendril of hair from her cheek.

"It was easier than it ought to have been," Annie said.

"Don't say that." He placed a finger against her lips. "I can't feel guilty. Maybe I should, but it seems like in trying to be honorable and upright, we've both done more harm than good."

"Joe, do you think if we had . . ." She tried to sit up, but Joe held her gently pinned.

"Annie, I don't know what's going to happen tomorrow or the next day or next year. But I know one thing—I love you."

The image of Laurel flickered, then died. Tomorrow she would face it. The guilt, too. Couldn't this one moment be hers?

"Again, Joe," she whispered. "Make love to me again."

But she could feel it—the moment falling away even as she clutched it to her, as if she were drinking from a cup with a hole in the bottom, trying desperately to quench her thirst before all the water trickled away.

Chapter Fifteen

DOLLY swept into the reception area outside the ballroom and was enveloped at once in a haze of cigarette smoke. So many people! The narrow, high-ceilinged room was jammed—tuxedoed men, gowned women in fluttery silk and glittering sequins. Looking around, Dolly found herself remembering other years, other chocolate fairs, when she and Henri had held hands under the dinner table, almost counting the minutes until they could go back to her apartment and snuggle up.

She felt an ache in her chest and brought her hand to her bosom above the scooped neck of her emerald satin gown. Henri. Damn it, where was he? He *had* said he'd be here, hadn't he? But the message on her answering machine had been so garbled, so much background noise. He'd been calling from Charles de Gaulle Airport, and he'd said he'd be in New York for the fair. And—at this point her heart had taken a plunge into ice water—he'd said he needed to speak with her about something very important.

Funeral—was that a word she'd really heard in all that static? Could old Girod have died? And if he had, did that mean Henri was finally free? She *had* to find Henri. She had to *know*. Maybe he was in the ballroom checking on Girod's display.

But when she entered, the ballroom was devoid of people except for hotel staff putting finishing touches on the tables and *Gourmand* judges scribbling notes about the displays. Later the judges would sample and evaluate the edible entries.

At one end of the main ballroom there was a stage framed in great swags of rose-colored velvet; in front of it, the chocolate displays sat on long white-clothed tables. Each display was set slightly apart, and on a small gold card was the name of the chocolatier it represented. She saw a chess set—its board and carved pieces made entirely of dark and white chocolate. Next to it, a chocolate replica of a Spanish galleon, complete with a life-size ship's log, spyglass, and bag of gold-foil-wrapped "doubloons." And in the center of the big table—a fairy castle made out of chocolate puff pastry, surrounded by a moat of whipped cream.

Then she saw the tree.

It was the centerpiece of Tout de Suite's display, ringed by exquisite-looking cakes on rustic wooden plates, and truffles spilling from baskets made of chocolate twigs. A "picnic"—how clever of Annie! Walking over for a closer look, Dolly saw that the trunk and branches of the tree were molded from the darkest bittersweet, studded with crushed nuts and feathered with a sharp knife to give it the look of rough bark. And suspended from its branches were dozens of small, mouth-watering marzipan pears.

A triumph—and Annie, her own Annie, had made it. Dolly felt pride welling up in her. First prize. Annie had said she had to win, and Dolly now felt sure she'd get it.

Her mind turned back to Henri as she inspected Girod's display—an array of small tortes, bonbons, and truffles, set at varying heights, like a garden in bloom. She saw that in the middle of their display an area the size of a serving platter had been cleared—as if at the last minute Pompeau had decided to make room for an addition. But if he'd wanted to include something else, wouldn't he have done so? Unless . . .

Dolly buttonholed a judge she knew. "Do you know Monsieur Baptiste from Girod's? Have you seen him?"

"Henri? Sure. He's in the kitchen working on something."

He's here. Dolly's heart was thumping, and all of a sudden the room turned warm. "Thanks," she said. She was about to hurry off toward the kitchen when she spotted Annie.

Her niece, wearing a full-length velvet dress the color of hammered copper, was deep in conversation with an older man—stocky, florid-faced, gray crew cut. Hyman Felder. Dolly could see the tension knotting Annie's shoulders. Winning first prize meant so much to her. Dolly knew that Tout de Suite needed it merely to stay afloat. *Please, let her win.*

Dolly was angling her way over to Annie when a tuxedoed man up on stage spoke into the microphone. "Please . . . everyone find your seats. Dinner is being served."

Dolly felt a rush of dismay. Now she'd have to wait and just hope that Henri was going to be at her table. She gritted her teeth in frustration. *Henri, where the devil are you?*

159

"You've got guts," Felder said. "Taking a chance on something so risky. A chocolate tree?" He shook his head admiringly.

"Taking chances is what it's all about, right?" Annie sipped her Champagne while trying to look relaxed. But, suddenly, Annie felt she didn't want to smile anymore, talk anymore, be here in this crowd. Images of last night with Joe flitted through her head like grainy frames from a worn-out movie print. As if it had happened years and years ago. Not the beginning of a love affair. More like something remote, from another era.

Was that what it had been . . . a good-bye?

She felt a sweet sorrow rinse through her.

They probably had both known it was the end. Now, no matter what happened with Laurel, she and Joe would never be more than what they'd always been—friends who had loved one another; lovers who had loved others better. She felt sad but somehow complete.

Across the crowded esplanade she caught sight of Emmett and felt a wobbling sensation inside her chest. She ought to be with him right now, working things out with him, not Felder.

He hadn't approached her in the reception area. But now he began working his way over. He wasn't smiling.

"Would you excuse me a moment?" she said, giving Felder her brightest smile. "I see someone I must talk to."

Felder bobbed his head, dismissing her with a genial wave. "Sure, sure. You go ahead."

When she turned, she was treated to a closeup view of Emmett in a dark blue tuxedo. "Annie," he said, "may I talk to you—alone?"

She nodded, her heart plunging with a sharp downward twist. *Something is wrong. Very wrong.*

Now Emmett was guiding her swiftly into the reception area, where only a few stragglers lingered. As he turned to face her his blue eyes were cool and flat. Why was he looking at her that way?

He knows, she thought.

There was so much she wanted to tell him, things that should have been said years ago. But oh, that look . . .

"Annie—"

"Em, I know what you're going to say," she broke in, her heart banging against her rib cage. "Please, don't say it. Not yet. We'll talk later, when we get home . . . when all this is over."

"It *is* over. This. Us. I've had enough." She heard no anger in his voice, only sorrow and regret. "Look, I'm not blaming you. I knew what I was getting into, and like a dumb rodeo cowboy, I figured the guy who stays on the bronco's back longest is the one who wins. In life, though, I guess nothing's that simple."

She watched his lips move and wanted him as eagerly and hungrily now as she had wanted Joe the night before.

"I love you," she told him, and for the first time she knew that she meant it.

His blue eyes, flickering like neon, cut into her. "I was worried about you last night after I left you. So this morning I stopped by to check up on you. Five o'clock, and you weren't home. . . . And then I remembered about Joe." His big hands, she saw, were clenching and unclenching at his sides. He shook his head. "I realized something last night. I always thought of love as something infinite, like the stars or God. But it's not. You can run out of love just like a car running out of gas. I'm tired, Annie. I've got nothing left."

Annie felt stunned. Tears rose in her eyes and began spilling down her cheeks. She had to make him understand. She had to make him *know* how much she wanted him . . . now . . . and tomorrow . . . and forever.

"Em . . ." Her voice cracked and then faded. She wanted to beg him, but she was stuck with her stiff spine just as Emmett was with his crippled foot. Something held her back.

"Anyway," he went on, "I wanted to let you know I'm not sticking around for the banquet. I really just came to say good-bye."

"Dressed in a tux?" She managed a wobbly smile.

One corner of his mouth tipped up in a smile. "Couldn't ride off into the sunset looking like a deadbeat, could I?"

Ride off? "Are you going somewhere?"

He shrugged. "I'm pulling up stakes here. Moving out west." He grinned. "There I go sounding like Matt Dillon again."

"Matt Dillon didn't make a living selling real estate." She sniffed hard and pushed her tears away with the heel of her hand, angry at herself, angry at him. It was wrong. He had no right leaving her. "I don't want you to go. You know that, don't you?"

Emmett looked at her a long time, and as a shadow passed over his face she thought he might change his mind. Then he kissed her lightly and said, "There's a difference between not wanting someone to go and wanting them to stay."

For a long moment he lingered, and his gaze held hers. Then he touched her cheek briefly, sadly, and turned.

Watching him walk away—a big rusty-haired man with one crippled foot and one good one, and more heart than she'd ever deserved—she felt like crumpling onto the carpet under the gilded ceiling and crying until she had no more tears.

But no, she couldn't. Not now. Later, when she was alone.

Feeling cold and numb, she turned and started back toward the ballroom. Though she yearned to chase after Emmett, she knew that if she didn't stay here and win Felder over, she might lose not only Emmett but her business as well.

She'd have nothing.

Blinking away her tears, she swept in through the doors, holding her head up like a queen proceeding to her coronation.

"Damn!" Henri swore as the sheet of chocolate he was cutting in The Plaza kitchen broke in two.

His hands were shaky, but he forced himself to work slowly. The thing had to be perfect, flawless . . . a way of showing her how much he still loved her. Just a few more pieces, and it would be finished—the lake in the Bois de Boulogne, where all those years ago, on their first outing in Paris, he'd taken Dolly.

The lake itself he'd fashioned from a thin oval of chocolate brushed with white chocolate to give it the look of a rippled surface. Around the edges of the lake, slender dagger-shaped wedges formed tall reeds, some dusted with cocoa to give a textured look. There were lily pads made of milk chocolate, blooming with white-chocolate flowers, their petals thin as eggshells. And in the center a chocolate rowboat with two figurines in it—a man and a woman.

Would she recognize it? Would she remember? Even if she did, she might not want him anymore.

So many years wasted.

As Henri worked, his thoughts traveled back to events that were still fresh in his mind: his father-in-law's death and the reading of the will. The old man had kept his promise. Thirty-five percent, in addition to the twenty he already owned, gave Henri an uncontested controlling interest. But then there had been a catch. If for any reason Henri and Francine divorced, the interest would revert in its entirety to Francine.

Henri had felt as if a brick had crashed down on his head. Had he heard correctly? He had forced himself to look at Francine, saw her smug self-satisfied expression, and knew then that it was true. They had planned it, the two of them—fashioned the chain link by link— to shackle him to Francine for the rest of his life.

Non. If Dolly would have him, they would begin again. Here. Together. He had some money put aside, and there were his shares of Girod's, for which Francine—if she wished to keep them in the family—would have no choice but to pay a good price.

Girod's. The thought of never again stepping into his beautiful, beloved shop was almost unthinkable. But he could do it.

So yes, this replica of a lake was more than just pieces of chocolate cut out and glued together. It represented all he knew, the skill his hands possessed. And what better way of expressing his feelings to Dolly? His heart had gone into every lily, every reed.

After applying the last of the leaves and spraying the entire model with confectioners' glaze, Henri tore off his apron and stood back to admire his creation. Yes, she would recognize it.

Henri checked his watch. *Mon Dieu,* already half past eight! Carefully, carefully Henri lifted his masterpiece, which sat on an acrylic board like some magical storybook island. His throat thick with longing, he balanced his great gift to her with one hand while he pushed open the kitchen's padded door with the other.

A WAITER raced past Annie with a little rush of warm air. Up on the velvet-curtained stage at one end of the ballroom, a portly man in a tuxedo was making an announcement. Now that dinner had been served, he said, the prizes would be announced, and then dessert.

Annie, seated between Felder and Dolly at a table near the stage, knotted her fists in her lap, where no one could see them, and watched the president of the Confectioners' Association approach the microphone. "I'm delighted to announce the judges' number one choice in the category of general excellence—"

She held her breath. *Please, please . . . I need this so much.*

"Le Chocolatier Manon."

Annie felt a rush of heat to her cheeks, as if she'd been slapped.

Applause filled the room, nearly drowning the next words, "And in second place, let's give a nice hand to Tout de Suite."

Dolly saw the look on Annie's face, and her heart sank. As Annie

163

rose to her feet Dolly's eyes filled with tears. The room blurred, and Annie seemed to take on a starry corona, red sparks glinting in her hair, the folds of her dress spilling pockets of light as she moved forward, chin high, to claim her prize.

Then, across the room, seated at the table nearest the stage, Dolly spotted Henri. He'd come. He was here! Their eyes met. Henri didn't smile or wave. He just stared, and though he hadn't moved a muscle, she felt as if he were rushing toward her. Then she saw he was pointing at the Girod display table right near her. Why? She half rose to get a better look, and oh, blessed Lord . . . reeds, lilies, a lake, a boat . . . Why, it had to be . . .

The Bois de Boulogne. That first day they'd spent rowing. Dolly felt an exquisite warmth spread through her.

He still loves me.

Then she turned and saw that Felder had gotten up and was heading toward the exit. Annie would be devastated!

Dolly, torn between Henri and her niece, hesitated only a moment before leaping from her chair and following Felder into the lobby. She caught sight of him as he was disappearing down the wide marble staircase that led to the main floor below.

Anxious now, Dolly dashed after him. She was nearly out of breath by the time she reached the ornate lobby with its cascading chandelier. Not waiting for the doorman, she pushed open the heavy glass door and ducked outside. Once again she caught sight of Felder. He was crossing the street toward a stretch limousine. With scarcely a glance in either direction Dolly ran after him.

"Mr. Felder!"

Too late, she heard the squeal of brakes. Something was slamming into her; she felt herself crumpling, the sky tipping over onto her head. Disjointedly she thought, How silly of me.

Jaywalking. How many times had Henri warned her?

Now a bright white light was seeping into her head, blocking out her pain, making even the rumble and screech of traffic fade. And oddly, Dolly wasn't scared anymore. She felt as if this was where she'd been heading all along . . . ever since the moment she'd let that hateful letter slip from her fingers into that mailbox.

A chill sank into her bones. She felt herself slipping . . . slipping away. Her gaze was drawn upward by a peculiar light—the sun glinting on a wave as it combed toward shore.

The wave broke. A young girl's delighted laughter rang in her ears. She could smell salt air, hear sea gulls.

Dolly saw her sister running along the beach at Santa Monica.

Look, Dor, we made it! Cali-for-ni-yay. We're here! Can you believe it? All that other stuff—it's all in the past. Clemscott's just a bad dream. From here on, I'm somebody. I'm a . . .

"Star," Dolly whispered, and felt herself sink down, the warm sand closing over her head.

Lilies?

An enormous bouquet of them, stiff and white as candles, swam into her view. In the light seeping through the shuttered blinds they seemed to glow. But lilies were for funerals. . . .

Dolly tried to press her eyes open wider, but it felt as if sandbags were sitting on her eyelids. "I'm not . . ." She started to say she wasn't dead, not yet, that the lilies didn't belong here, but the only sound she could make was a gargled croak.

Out of one slitted eye she saw Henri's shadowy form unfold itself from a darkened corner. Then arms were encircling her, lips pressing against her cheek, her forehead. She could feel him—his warmth, his solidity, the prickling of his mustache.

"Henri?" She tried to lift her arms—one of them appeared to be hooked up to an IV—to embrace him, but the effort sent a rocket of pain exploding through her rib cage.

"Non . . ." She could feel Henri lightly pressing her shoulders. "You must not move. It is better if you remain still."

"Where . . ." She opened her eyes, and he came into focus.

"Lenox Hill. It is a good hospital, they tell me."

"How long have I been here?"

"Since yesterday night."

"You mean, all this time I've been out like a light?"

"You do not remember last night, your niece's being here?"

"Annie?"

"Yes. And Laurel, too. She telephoned last night two times and came to see you this morning. You opened your eyes, but we could not know if you saw her. We had so much fear . . . but now the doctors, they have reassured us. Four broken ribs and a bad concussion, very bad, but you are strong. You will get better."

Dolly clutched Henri's hand. "Lilies," she slurred, knowing it had to be the sedatives that were making her feel this woozy. "They've got no color. I can't abide lilies."

"Oui, ma poupée. Mr. Felder does not know you as I do. When we are married, you shall have roses—bright red and yellow ones—and you shall wear red. . . ." His voice caught. "A red dress, like the one you were wearing that first day you came into my shop."

What was he saying? Was he really asking her to marry him?

"Henri, are you . . ."

"No, please . . . let me say it. I know I have waited much too long for this, and you may no longer wish to hear it. But yes, I wish you to become my wife. I have quit Girod's, and that means you must quit also. Do you think we could ever start again from the beginning?"

Dolly was now struggling against the tide of wooziness, struggling to tell Henri what she'd been waiting six years to say. How no other man had ever measured up to him. How it didn't matter that they'd have to start over from scratch; she'd love every minute of it. And yes, she wanted him . . . in her apartment, in her bed, his toothbrush next to hers, his robe hanging on the back of the bathroom door.

Her heart was thumping like crazy, each thump bringing with it a wallop of pain, but that didn't matter. What mattered now was getting it straight, getting the words out.

But all Dolly could say was, "Try me."

THREE days later Dolly was sitting up in bed—sipping a ginger ale and wondering if her being so impatient to get out of this place meant she was getting better—when Annie walked in.

"Hi," her niece greeted her, depositing several glossy magazines on the table beside Dolly's bed before dropping a kiss onto her forehead. "You look as if you're feeling better."

"Heaps," Dolly told her. Annie had visited her every day, always bringing her some little thing to brighten her up—a bouquet of chrysanthemums, a basket of raspberries. If there was a silver lining to this ordeal, it was spending these precious hours with her niece.

But still, something inside Dolly twisted and turned. The time had come to put an end to this eternal gnawing inside her, this guilt—to tell Annie the truth about what had come between her and Eve.

For now, though, Dolly sidled onto a safer topic. "How did your talk with Felder go?" she asked.

Annie brightened. "He says he's still interested in making a deal with me . . . that if my aunt thinks highly enough of me to go dashing out in front of a taxi for me, I must be something pretty special." She grinned. "But you know what I think?"

"What's that?"

"That you're the special one." Her eyes turned suddenly bright. "I don't know if I should be thanking you for almost getting yourself killed for me, but would it help just to tell you I love you?"

Dolly felt a jolt. Not in all the years she'd known her, had Dolly ever heard Annie say those words to her. Her eyes filled with tears. "Oh, sugar, it does me a world of good, your saying that. But . . ."

Now was the time. Before the moment slipped past. The truth about dear, self-sacrificing Aunt Dolly.

"Annie," she began, capturing her niece's moist hand and tugging her gently down onto the bed beside her, "there's something that's been on my mind for a long time. If I don't get it off my chest now, I don't know when I'll ever again get up the nerve."

"It's about Dearie, isn't it?"

Dolly nodded, her throat suddenly thick.

"Your mama was a good person," she began. "And I did a terrible thing that ruined her career and broke her heart. I just want you to know—"

"You don't have to say it," Annie broke in, squeezing Dolly's hand. "For a long, long time I wondered what had happened between you and Dearie. And now"—she paused—"I know that whatever it was, nothing can change how I feel about you. And whatever it was that made you think you're responsible for the way things turned out . . . Well, she made her own choices, too. I loved her. She was my mother. But she wasn't perfect."

Dolly felt relief, like a vast ocean wave, sweep through her.

"I loved her, too," she said. Oh, how good it felt to be able to say those words aloud without feeling like the worst sort of hypocrite!

"I know," Annie said. "Why else would I be here?"

Chapter Sixteen

LAUREL eyed the flowers Dolly was clutching as she made her way up the aisle of the sedate church. No traditional bridal bouquet for her aunt, just a single spray of orchids—deep purple striped with yellow. Her dress, too—not white lace, but a red silk suit. A huge cartwheel hat was tilted at a jaunty angle atop her platinum hair, giving her the look of a '40s movie siren. Dolly's gaze was fixed on the altar where Henri, in a pearl-gray cutaway and vest, stood waiting.

Sitting on her hard pew right up in front, Laurel felt her throat tighten. She was happy for Dolly. No one deserved this happiness more. But Dolly was not the reason she was choked up right now.

She glanced over at Joe, seated across the aisle. Beside her, Adam squirmed and whispered, "Why can't Daddy sit with *us?*"

"Because," she whispered back.

This was hardly the time to go over it again with Adam.

Eleven and a half months, and I still break out in goose bumps whenever I see you. I'll catch myself setting an extra place for you at the table . . . or I'll be calling Annie or Dolly and realize I've dialed your number by mistake.

Can I go on like this? Can I keep on living without you?

Well, you have, for almost a whole year, she told herself.

She'd gotten through those first weeks of misery by imagining her life as a painting she was gessoing over, preparing a blank white canvas on which she would paint something new, something better.

And she'd managed to pull it off, hadn't she? More commissions than she could handle. And now a book she'd both written and illustrated on the *Publishers Weekly* young reader's best-seller list.

But if she'd grown so strong, how was it that all her carefully cultivated independence crumbled the second she laid eyes on Joe?

Laurel, swallowing hard, focused on Annie, seated on her left, next to Adam. *Please, God, give me some of Annie's strength.*

But Annie, she saw, was weeping. Was she thinking about Emmett, missing him . . . or was it Joe?

Laurel tried to concentrate on what the bald-headed, hawk-nosed minister was saying, but she found herself thinking of Uncle Rudy, remembering that L.A. lawyer phoning three months ago. "Your uncle has died," he'd said. Cancer. How sad she'd felt, then how shocked. He'd left her and Adam a fortune—a house in Malibu, not to mention checks every month from partnerships in shopping malls and office buildings. He'd given her financial security. Now she would never need Joe's money, or any man's.

But this isn't about money, is it?

Laurel looked around, recognizing a number of the guests: col-

leagues from the Confectioners' Association; Dolly's housekeeper; her driver, Felipe; Gloria De Witt, who'd once managed Dolly's shop. And Rivka, wearing a modest blue sweater dress, had come, too. Religious Jews, Laurel knew, weren't supposed to enter churches, but for Dolly, Rivka had made an exception.

Laurel had promised herself while Dolly and Henri were exchanging their vows that she would not look at Joe. But now, like an alcoholic too weak to resist, she sneaked a sidelong glance.

Joe's gaze also wasn't on the altar—he was looking straight at her. Laurel felt guilty, as if she'd been caught cheating on an exam. She could feel blood rushing up into her face.

And he wasn't just looking; it was the *way* he was looking at her: puzzled, as if she were a stranger he thought he might have met and was trying to place.

Excuse me, madam, but you look awfully familiar. Are you sure we weren't married at one time?

Laurel, feeling a giggle about to erupt, had to clamp the tip of her tongue between her teeth. No matter how bad things got, she had Adam . . . and Annie, too. No matter how mad at Annie she sometimes got, they were joined forever. Sisters.

Even so, thinking ahead to when Joe would be free to marry someone else, Laurel felt gripped by a queasy weakness. That had to be why she'd put off discussing their getting divorced. Was it because she was afraid he'd marry Annie?

No, he couldn't. She'd give anything for another chance with Joe. But Joe had to want it, too. She couldn't make him want her. She'd already tried that, and look where it had gotten her.

ARRIVING at Dolly's apartment, a bit late after being stuck behind a double-parked delivery truck, Laurel found the wedding reception in full swing. She deposited Adam with Henri's eight-year-old twin grandsons and watched him immediately drag them off to the guest bedroom, where Dolly kept a box of toys. Then she walked over to the bar and poured herself a drink.

"Laurey."

At the sound of his familiar voice she turned too quickly, vodka splashing over the rim of her glass. She looked up into a pair of round steel-rimmed glasses, at reflected images of herself flickering in his lenses.

"We need to talk," Joe said in a low voice. "The terrace. We'll have some privacy out there. I'll get your coat."

Laurel didn't argue. Just nodded, and waited quietly.

He's going to tell me he's seen a lawyer, that it's time we got divorced. Oh, he's right, of course . . . but can I bear it?

Outside, she didn't bother to button her coat. The October wind was whipping at her hem, but she wasn't cold.

Don't wait for him to say it. Get this over with while you still have a shred of dignity left.

"I think I know what this is all about, Joe, and I don't want it to be any harder than it already is. You know, the way couples end up fighting over dumb things like who gets the martini pitcher."

Joe smiled. "We don't have a martini pitcher," he pointed out.

"Well, you know what I mean."

"Yeah, I think I do."

"I mean, things aren't the issue here, are they? Oh, I suppose we'll have to do some . . . sorting out. You know, like with Adam." She took a deep breath. "It's just as well, I guess, I never had those other babies."

"Don't say that." Joe grabbed her by the shoulders. "Don't ever say that." He sounded angry.

"Why not?" She glared at him, her hurt welling to the surface. "It's true, isn't it? Another child would've been one more thing standing between you and . . . and what you really want."

"What makes you so sure you know what I want?"

"How can I know when you never tell me anything! Damn it, Joe, you should have told me. About your father. About Annie. Everything. You should have told me in the very beginning that you were only marrying me because of Adam!"

"That isn't true."

"Of course it's true. I knew it then, deep down, and I wanted you badly enough to marry you anyway."

His eyes filled with tenderness. "Laurey . . ."

Say it, she pleaded silently. Please just say it and get it over with.

"I love you."

She pulled away, trembling. "That's not fair!" Tears were running down her cheeks. "Joe, please stop this. Just *stop*."

Laurel, feeling desperate, walked away from him, going all the way around the terrace to the Park Avenue side. Blindly, savagely, she wrenched the gold wedding band from her finger and flung it over the wrought-iron railing. She watched it arc toward the street, twelve stories below. She imagined it simply dissolving into the air—a sorcerer's spell, which she had now broken forever.

Looking back at Joe, she saw that the blood had drained from his face. Suddenly he bolted across the terrace, flung open the sliding glass door, and disappeared inside the apartment.

Where had he gone? What did it mean?

Then in a dizzying rush it struck her: *Her ring. He had gone after it. Like Jason charging after the Golden Fleece.*

She leaned over the wrought-iron railing, peering down. Vehicles the size of Adam's toy cars were streaming in opposite directions along Park Avenue. Then she spotted him—a tiny figure darting out from under the apartment building's green-and-white canopy. At the curb he appeared to be hesitating; then he was plunging headlong into the ongoing traffic. Laurel, her blood drumming in her ears, watched him stride before the oncoming cars, arms extended like a cop's, bringing some to shrieking halts, while others swerved and fishtailed around him. A cacophony of angry horns blasted her ears.

Joe, like a man obsessed, ignoring them all, hunkered down—right there in the middle of the chaotic avenue.

"Joe, come back! Come back here!" She knew he couldn't hear her, but she couldn't stop herself from screaming.

With the traffic now surging around him, she lost sight of him. At last she spotted him. He was standing in the middle of Park Avenue on the dividing strip, legs apart, holding what had to be her ring up to the sky, as if it were an Olympic gold medal.

"Joe . . . you idiot," she choked.

Minutes later he returned to her side, his eyes bright with triumph. "Laurey," he panted, "I can't change what happened back when we got married. All I know is how I feel now. I love you. I can't fall asleep at night without you next to me. I can't get through a single hour without missing you. Laurel Daugherty, will you marry me?"

She stared at him, too stunned, too overflowing with happiness to know quite what he meant or what she should say. "Are you sure it's me you want . . . not Annie?"

"You, my sweet Laurey." He touched her cheek. "Only you."

Joe snatched up her left hand and eased the ring back onto her finger. Then he was kissing her hand, holding it to his lips.

"Say I do," he murmured, pulling her into his arms. "Quick, before I do something really nuts, like throwing myself over this balcony."

Laurel pulled in a deep breath of frosty air. "I do!" she cried, loud enough for all of Park Avenue to hear.

BACK inside, while Joe went off to look for Adam, Dolly came over and slipped an arm about Laurel's shoulders. "Anyone with eyes can see I don't have the market cornered on happiness today," she said, smiling.

"Joe and I . . ."

"You don't have to say it. It's written all over your face. Oh, sugar, you've just given me the best wedding present I can think of." Dolly hugged Laurel, then gave her a little shove. "Now go on, get out of here. Get on home, where you can celebrate properly." She winked and gave Laurel another little push. "And don't worry about Adam. I'll have Felipe take him home later on . . . after you and Joe have had a chance to get reacquainted."

Laurel kissed her aunt and said good-bye to Henri, but she didn't see Annie. Probably she was in the dining room checking on the triple-layer white-chocolate cake she'd made for the occasion. Laurel felt the tiniest bit relieved. She didn't really feel like talking to Annie right now. Joe had gone to get his Volvo, parked a few blocks away, and would meet her in Bayside. She could hardly wait to get home.

Outside, walking briskly east toward her own car, Laurel became aware of the staccato tapping of heels behind her.

She turned and saw Annie hurrying toward her. Laurel waited. Seeing her sister, as always, brought forth a grab bag of feelings: love, resentment, guilt. What now? she wondered.

"Dolly told me," Annie panted when she'd caught up, "about you and Joe. I wanted to tell you how happy I am for you." Laurel searched her face, but Annie's expression was sincere.

"Thanks," Laurel told her, feeling suddenly awkward, not knowing what else to say except, "You're not leaving, too, are you?"

"No. I'm going back now to help serve the cake."

"I saw it. It's beautiful. It looks like the ceiling of a Victorian parlor . . . all those rosettes and swags and curlicues."

173

"That's where I got the idea, actually. From a mansion in Newport." Annie laughed. "I showed Hy Felder a picture of a cake just like Dolly's, and he ordered one for his daughter's wedding."

"How's it going with Felder's?"

"Looks like it'll be another few months before the grand opening, but I'm gearing up to go into production."

"The rate you're going, you'll need a factory the size of Brooklyn before too long." Laurel glanced at Annie. "By the way, have you heard anything from Emmett?"

Annie looked away, but not before Laurel had seen the hurt in her eyes. "Not a thing. You know what they say, A clean break heals the quickest." Then she added lightly, "I guess I'm just not cut out for marriage. Or maybe I'll end up like Dolly, marching down the aisle when all my friends are having grandchildren."

"What about kids?" Laurel asked.

Annie was silent for several long minutes. "I was just remembering," she said at last, softly, "those first weeks in New York, when you used to cry all the time. I felt like I'd done this terrible thing that you'd hate me for."

"I didn't hate you," Laurel said. "I just felt so uprooted. Like Dorothy in *The Wizard of Oz.* And all the time I was scared."

"Say it, why don't you?" Annie gave Laurel a sharp, wounded look. "You blame me for taking you away."

A deep calm flowed through Laurel. "No, Annie, I don't blame you. You did what you had to do. And I followed. . . . What choice did I have? Without you there, it would have been awful."

"We're sisters," Annie stated matter-of-factly. "Sisters look out for each other."

"But don't you see? It was always you looking out for me. Never the other way around." She touched Annie's arm. "I'm sorry about the way things have been. It's just that with Joe gone . . ." She let her voice trail off, not sure what, exactly, she wanted to say.

"I know." Annie's eyes, shining with emotion, met Laurel's, and Laurel felt as if they'd just made an unspoken pact.

"Well, I guess I'd better get going," Laurel said. "Joe'll be wondering what's kept me."

"Joe? Oh, yeah . . . sure. Well . . ."

Laurel watched her sister start to step back, looking suddenly awkward and slightly forlorn. Not watching where she was going, she caught the side of her heel in a deeply indented crack in the sidewalk. Thrown off balance, she lurched forward.

Laurel started to catch her, but her stance was somehow wrong, and she went sprawling onto the sidewalk with Annie on top of her.

After the first shocked moment, Laurel was able to sit up, pushing Annie up with her. As they sat there Laurel felt overcome, realizing how much she loved her sister. How much she still needed her in all sorts of little ways.

Suddenly she found herself giggling.

Annie, laughing a little, too, and wiping her eyes on her sleeve, said, "Don't look now, but there's a woman over there who thinks one of us is getting mugged."

Pulling herself up, Laurel helped Annie to her feet.

To the woman staring at them openmouthed, Laurel called, "It's okay. We're sisters!"

Epilogue
California: 1983

ANNIE handed her car keys to the parking valet and started up the canopied walkway leading into the Beverly Hills Hotel. Driving in from Los Angeles International Airport, she'd felt tense. But here in this lovely shade, tubs of pink azaleas and ruby rhododendrons flanking her on both sides, she felt herself begin to unwind. She glanced at her watch. Twelve forty—she had hours until her meeting. Time for a short nap, and maybe afterwards a swim.

Then she thought of *who* she was meeting and why, and she felt her stomach tighten.

Emmett.

More than a year and a half since she'd seen him, and in all that time not even a postcard. Then last week the shock of his voice over the phone drawling, "Hey there," as if it had been merely days, not ages, since they'd last spoken. He had his own real estate agency now, he told her, in Westwood. He was "doin' okay," which, given Emmett's laid-back way of putting things, could have meant anything from a hole-in-the-wall with an answering machine to some swank address with a dozen employees. But he hadn't just called to shoot the bull. He had something he thought she might be interested in.

Bel Jardin. It was on the market, and he had an exclusive listing.

Annie, so close now to her childhood home, felt her heart begin to race. That she might once again actually live in Bel Jardin seemed like a fairy tale too good to be true.

Suppose it's way more than I can afford. What's the point of flying out here just to take a stroll down memory lane?

Face it. Bel Jardin was not the only reason she'd come.

She imagined Emmett's sharp blue eyes crinkling in amusement. Could he possibly know that after he'd called, she had to soak in a hot bath—in the heat of July—to stop her shivering?

No, no way. By now he was probably married. He hadn't mentioned a wife, but then why should he? It was just a business call.

"May I help you, ma'am?"

Someone was speaking to her, Annie realized, a white-jacketed young man behind the desk.

"A reservation for Annie Cobb," she told him.

"Do you have any luggage?" he asked after she'd signed in.

"Just this." Annie hefted her single suitcase, and the bellhop, who looked like a former Olympic athlete, deftly took it from her and led her across the wide lobby.

Upstairs in her room, Annie kicked off her pumps and sank down on the bed. Despite the air-conditioning, her silk-and-linen suit felt as uncomfortable as thick wool. Well, if she moved out here, she'd have to buy a whole new wardrobe.

She'd been toying with the idea of keeping her apartment in New York and living in L.A. part of the year. The opening of Tout de Suite on Rodeo Drive next month would keep her hopping out here for a while anyway. And now, with Dolly and Henri supervising the manufacturing, the stores, and Felder's boutiques, she could scout out some other West Coast locations as well.

But Annie couldn't help feeling that coming out here would somehow be running away. But not from Tout de Suite—the business was now even more successful than she could ever have dreamed. And not from Laurel—she felt closer to her sister than she ever had. And Laurel, in her sixth month—already big as a house, radiant, bubbling over—didn't need her next door.

Might the running be not away, but *toward* something—the happiness that was always just beyond her reach? How many times had Rivka told her she ought to be married. Thirty-four. In Rivka's world she was an old maid.

But the men since Emmett—tied to their mothers, their therapists, their jobs. Most of them were nice, fun for an evening or a weekend. But for a lifetime?

Why, when she had him, hadn't she valued Emmett more? Why hadn't she begged him to stay, to give her another chance?

ANNIE, seated at a redwood patio table on the deck of the Crow's Nest in Santa Monica, overlooking the Pacific, sipped her white zinfandel and waited for Emmett. The tables around her, she noticed, were filled mostly with people even younger than she. Hip Californians. Annie felt overdressed, out of place. Would Emmett take one look at her and notice how she didn't belong?

A shadow fell across her, and she looked up, shading her eyes. Then he was bending down—warm, dry lips brushing her cheek.

"Hey there, good-looking." He dropped into the redwood chair opposite hers. "You beat me to it. I was gonna have vintage Champagne on ice when you got here."

She was feeling all wrong, her heartbeat picking up, her breath growing suddenly, alarmingly short. She folded her hands about the stem of her wineglass. "Hi, Em. It's good to see you."

"You're looking prettier than ever. Success agrees with you, I see. Congratulations. I hear you're opening up a store out here."

"Is that why you thought I'd be interested in Bel Jardin?"

"Naw. I'd have called if I'd heard you were moving to Borneo. I know how much that old place meant to you."

"Who said anything about moving?" She heard the defensive edge in her voice and immediately wanted to kick herself. Was she trying to convince Emmett or herself?

"Let's just say that for whatever reason, I figured you'd be interested." Emmett now was squinting out at the Santa Monica pier, and she noticed little sun lines radiating from the corner of his eyes. But otherwise, the same old Emmett. He hadn't gone native, thank heaven. She looked down and saw those same old cowboy boots of his. More weather-beaten, maybe, but obviously cared for. Seeing them, Annie felt an absurd happiness steal through her.

"I ought to be congratulating you, too." She had to change the subject. "I called your office to confirm our appointment. A very nice lady told me you were out, but would I like to speak to one of the other salespeople. Hey, Em, how many do you have?"

"Just two," he said. "But yeah, I'm doing okay. I like it out here."

And you . . . How are you? she longed to ask. In love?

But all she said was, "Well, I'm not surprised." A waiter, she saw, was approaching.

Emmett pointed at her glass. "You want another wine?"

"No, thanks. I'd probably fall asleep on you."

"Well then"—he pulled himself to his feet—"let's roll."

"Okay." She watched a volleyball shoot into the air and over the deck railing, Emmett catching it easily and tossing it back, as if he were one of the players.

Right now, if he'd asked her to, Annie would've gone with him to the moon.

"YOU still haven't told me a thing." They were in Annie's rented Ford, and she was turning off Sunset Boulevard onto a narrower tree-lined road leading up into Bel Air. She could feel her stomach fluttering. "I mean, if they're asking the moon, I have no business even looking at it."

"It won't cost you a thing," Emmett said.

Annie nearly slammed on her brakes. "What?"

"Just what I said."

"Em, if this is some kind of joke . . ."

"It's no joke. Annie, I didn't want to say anything before . . . but Bel Jardin's been sold."

Now she *was* slamming on the brakes, hard enough to fishtail off the road onto the shoulder.

"I'm sorry, Annie." She felt his hand on her arm and jerked away. "It just came up this morning. Listen, if it makes you feel any better, you were probably right about not being able to afford it. It went for over three million."

She turned to Emmett, sitting there calmly beside her, as if this was just some minor inconvenience. "Would you mind telling me what we're doing here? I mean, if Bel Jardin's been sold, what's the point of me looking at it?"

"You're here, aren't you? What's the harm?" He grinned. "I nearly forgot that temper of yours. Hell, Cobb, once you got a notion into your head, you always did like to hang on to it."

"As if I'd have gotten anywhere in this world if I hadn't!" Annie, oddly, was starting to feel better.

"Who says," he asked gently, "there's anything wrong with the way you are?"

"*I* do! Maybe I just should've been happy with what I had. Maybe I was a damn idiot not to see what was right in front of me the whole time." A pressure was building behind her eyes.

"Are we still talking about Bel Jardin here?" He spoke quietly, yet his voice seemed to echo inside her head.

"No," she said sharply, "we're not." With a wrench of the steering wheel she turned the car back onto the road, knowing that if she didn't get going, get *moving*, she'd probably do something dumb, like telling Emmett she was in love with him.

Then she was winding her way up Chantilly Drive, and there, gliding out from behind a tall oleander hedge, was Bel Jardin. The house, at the end of the long crushed-shell drive lined with steeple-high palms, glowed in the setting sun.

Oh, how good to see it! Annie could feel her annoyance at Emmett fading, and she was gripped by an excitement. Pulling to a stop at the end of the drive, she got out and sucked in a deep breath. Lemon blossoms and jasmine. And look how the bougainvillea had climbed up around the porch. She stared at the heavy, carved door and felt her heart turn over in her chest.

Home. She was home.

Annie turned to Emmett. "Are they home?"

"No. But I have the keys. Want to go in?"

"Oh, Em, I don't know. Maybe I'd be cheating myself. Seeing it the way it is instead of the way I remember it."

"Why don't you describe it to me while we take a look around? Who knows, maybe the new owner would like a few suggestions."

"Why should he?"

"I don't know. Why don't you ask him?" Emmett draped his arm around her shoulders. "He's standing right here."

Annie stepped away, her knees buckling a little.

"You?" she gasped. "*You* bought Bel Jardin. But why?"

Emmett's blue eyes seemed to blaze with an almost unnatural brightness.

"Because for almost two years I've been trying to get your own sweet, stubborn self out from under my skin, Annie Cobb, and I haven't had a helluva lot of luck. When this listing fell into my lap, I sort of figured it was fate. And then after I talked with Laurey—"

"You called Laurey? What did she say?"

"That you'd once told her that not marrying me was the biggest mistake you ever made. So I figured, well, maybe you'd be interested in sharing Bel Jardin with a reformed drifter like me."

"That's about the nicest thing you've ever said to me." Tears filled her eyes, and her vision blurred. Her relief and joy were so vast she could not have put them into words. "Now, will you shut up and kiss me."

He did. A kiss that made her remember everything good she had ever longed for in her entire life. A sweet, golden warmth filled her. Rapture. There could be no other way to describe this feeling . . . this dazed lightness, this heart-struck bliss.

In her mind she heard Dearie say, *"Grab it, kiddo. . . . A second chance like this one may never come your way again."*

"Let's go inside," Annie said, pulling back and taking Emmett's hand. "And I'll show you where we'll put my mother's Oscar."

Walking into Eileen Goudge's Manhattan town house makes the noise and bustle of the city seem far away indeed. Tapestried walls and carved Victorian antiques create a sense of elegance and history. And seated in the midst of it all, Eileen Goudge looks as if she's been here all her life.

Eileen Goudge

Actually, that couldn't be further from the truth. This prolific author started out, at twenty, as a divorced mother living on welfare in California, where she grew up. "It was the worst year of my life," she recalls. "There is a shame that comes with poverty. It's humbling in a devastating way."

A second marriage rescued her from welfare, but only barely. However, it was during this time that the author began to write—first magazine articles, then young adult fiction. (She was one of the original writers for the much praised Sweet Valley High series.) This newfound success gave her the self-confidence to end a marriage that had turned unbearable. She took her two children and, like Annie and Laurel, moved to New York. There she continued to turn out her teen books—one every six weeks—until she finally achieved some financial security.

Eileen Goudge is now married to literary agent Al Zuckerman, and between them they have five children. In spite of the demands on her time, Goudge is able to devote herself to the writing she likes best: adult fiction. In 1989 she published *Garden of Lies,* an enormous best seller.

For *Such Devoted Sisters,* Goudge drew largely from her own life experiences. Her love of cooking desserts inspired the chocolate angle, and with four sisters, she found herself very familiar with sibling rivalry.

Though her early struggles are now past, she still remembers them clearly. "I really am blessed," she says. "Whenever I see people on the street, I always give them something. I have to think how close I came to ending up almost the same."

RULES OF ENCOUNTER

WILLIAM P. KENNEDY

The time: the dark dawn of World War I. German U-boats are sabotaging Britain's North Atlantic shipping lanes. To Winston Churchill, young First Lord of the Admiralty, it's clear that England must bring a reluctant America into the war. His desperate plan: provoke an incident so heinous, so outrageous that the Americans must respond. But there are rules against the sort of encounter Churchill envisions, rules that must now be broken.

Fall 1914

CHAPTER 1

London. "The United States is a peace-loving nation, committed to peace throughout the world. President Woodrow Wilson is pledged to keep our country neutral in this terrible world war, a friend to every nation involved on every side. And it is as a friend of England that I present his proposals for an honorable peace."

Colonel Edward House was Woodrow Wilson's personal friend and confidant, his handpicked emissary to the warring nations of Europe. He had come to London with Wilson's idealistic plan to bring the war out of the trenches and to the more civilized setting of the conference table, and was in the process of presenting it to the leaders of His Majesty's government.

No one was really listening. What England needed to end its war with Germany was not a peacemaker, but an ally.

Germany had struck into France with incredible swiftness. England's army crossed the Channel to aid its French ally, but the British were driven back by the German onslaught. Then when it seemed defeat was inevitable, the ragtag Russian army attacked Prussia. One of the German armies was sent to deal with the Russians, which turned the German advantage into a stalemate, and the war dug into a line of trenches across northern France.

The standoff wouldn't last forever. Once the Russians were defeated, the Germans would return. The only hope of victory that British generals and admirals had was that their own lines could be strengthened before the Russians collapsed. And their only source of new strength was the United States. They needed America in the war, on their side. Not at the head of a conference table.

"And therefore the President proposes freedom of the seas, guaranteeing to the ships of all nations access to the ports of any nation," Colonel House droned on.

Absurd, the British leaders thought. Their most effective weapon was their naval blockade across the North Sea, cutting off all maritime commerce with Germany. They had no intention of letting any ship get within a hundred miles of a German port.

There was polite applause as House finished his presentation. He poured a glass of water from a pitcher on his lectern and sipped it as he waited for questions.

"Colonel House." The questioner was a cherubic-faced young man of barely forty. He wore the gray morning attire that was the uniform of civilian government officials.

"Yes, Mr. . . ."

"Winston Churchill," the young man said. And then with a mischievous grin, "I believe I'm First Lord of the Admiralty."

"Yes, of course," House pretended.

"While we are most respectful of your President's commitment to neutrality," Churchill said, "I wonder if there is anything that might persuade him to take a more active role in the war?"

"More active?" The President had offered to serve as the architect of a lasting peace. What could be more active than that?

"To declare war on Germany," Churchill said, clarifying any ambiguities.

The colonel stiffened. "Mr. Churchill, there is nothing that will bring the United States into this war."

"Nothing?" Churchill pressed, blinking in astonishment.

"Well," House reconsidered, "if the Germans were to attack American citizens, then certainly we would be forced to fight. But of course, that would be highly unlikely."

"Highly unlikely," Churchill agreed, settling back into his chair. He was buoyant as he walked from the meeting.

General John French, commander of the British armies in France, caught up with him. "Not much hope from that quarter."

"Oh, I think we can count on the Americans."

French was stunned. "I thought he made it quite clear that there would be no help from across the Atlantic."

"Unless the Germans attack American citizens," Churchill reminded the general. "What we have to do is assemble some Americans and then persuade the Germans to attack them."

"You can't be serious," French said. "How would you ever get Americans in front of a German gun?"

"I was thinking of a ship," the First Lord of the Admiralty answered.

The North Sea. Daylight. A pale knife-edge cut through the mist, separating the night from the distant outline of the Dutch coast. The west wind seemed suddenly to die, and from the east came the first squawking of the gulls. Standing on the wing of *Aboukir*'s bridge, Commander William Day could suddenly make out the bow of his own ship and the white foam that washed out of its way.

"Sunrise, Quartermaster," Day called as the small leaden arc of the sun appeared. The North Sea was colorless in the fall, and in the rain even the tint of the sun was difficult to discern.

"Sunrise at 0614 hours," the quartermaster chanted as he made the appropriate entry in the log. He leaned out of the wheelhouse and looked up at the signal bridge. "Morning colors," he ordered, and in response the Union Jack slid up the signal mast.

They were steaming north by northeast, parallel to the coastline, in a broad triangle. *Hogue* was closest to the beach, and *Cressy* was up front in the van. Day was just able to make them out.

"Number One." Captain Drummond always addressed his officers by their billet titles. He came and stood beside Day.

"Good morning, Captain."

"Nothing much good about it," Drummond mumbled, sniffing at the heavy air. "Where's the barometer?"

"Holding at twenty-eight and a half," Day answered.

"Looks like we're in for another day of this muck." The captain rose up on his toes, pressed his hands into the small of his back, and leaned backward. A chain of cracks sounded from his spine. "The dampness gets into everything."

As the two men stood side by side, they seemed to be from different planets. At the age of thirty, Day towered over his commanding officer. He was over six feet, with broad shoulders and powerful arms inherited from his longshoreman father. Drummond was a short, slight man, whose physique suggested scholarship more than hard work. Day had a dark complexion, with

187

angular features and deep-set, brooding eyes. Drummond's thin white hair blended easily into a soft, pink face.

"Any orders from the flag?" Drummond was asking whether the squadron commander, who had his flag aboard *Cressy*, had sent any signals.

"Turn to two eight five at 0700," Day answered.

"Why in hell are we steaming in circles off the Dutch coast?" Drummond cursed. "If the German fleet comes out, they won't be heading in our direction. They'll go north." He looked into the wheelhouse and focused on the chronometer. "I'll take my breakfast before the maneuvering starts, Number One."

"Aye, sir."

Day looked toward the coastline. He could now make out the superstructures of *Hogue* and *Cressy*—the masts streaming their wireless antennas—and the four stacks that rose above each hull. They were ancient ships, but they were the only ones available for patrolling the northern approaches to the English Channel. All the British dreadnoughts were needed for patrols north of the Orkneys to keep the German fleet from breaking out into the Atlantic. Heaven help us, Day thought, if the German High Seas Fleet ever does come out. *Cressy*-class cruisers had only nine-inch guns as their main battery. The new German cruisers, with their fifteen-inch guns, could drop shells on *Cressy, Hogue*, and *Aboukir* for half an hour before the English ships could even bring them into range.

Day checked the chronometer: 0625. In thirty-five minutes the signal flags on *Cressy* would drop, ordering the squadron to turn to the west. He stepped into the wheelhouse and pulled the cap from one of the voice tubes. "Engine room, this is the bridge."

"Engine room, aye." The voice came from deep within the ship.

"We're going to be maneuvering in a few minutes," Day said. "You might want to bring up your steam now."

"Aye, aye, sir," the hollow voice responded.

Day raised his binoculars and scanned the horizon. To the east, there was a faint trace of light, broken by the flat landfall of Holland. To the north and west, still nothing but murky darkness.

Suddenly the ship lurched, as if struck by a giant hammer, its steel side crashing like a cymbal. Day toppled and slid across the deck until he smashed against the wheelhouse. He looked up to see a wall of black water rise high above the port wing, followed by a cloud of hissing steam. Instantly fire alarms began clanging deep within the hull.

"A torpedo!" screamed the helmsman, who had been slammed to the deck by the violent twisting of the ship's wheel.

"Hold her on course," Day yelled as he struggled back onto his feet. He ran into the wheelhouse and uncapped the voice tube. "Engine room, this is the bridge."

A voice shouted back above the howl of escaping steam. "We're taking water into the boiler rooms. We've got a hole clean through the portside bunker. And we've got busted steam lines."

Day was suddenly aware that the deck was tilting to port. "Open the starboard sea cocks," he screamed back down the voice tube. "Flood the starboard coal bunkers."

"We're already taking on more water than we can handle."

"Flood them. Now!"

There was a pause, and then, "Aye, aye, sir."

The explosion, Day realized, had blown a hole through the port bunker to the sea. Now seawater was filling the half-empty bunker. The imbalance would roll the ship over in a matter of minutes. He had to open the starboard bunker to keep *Aboukir* upright.

He charged out of the wheelhouse and up the ladder to the signal bridge. "Signal to *Cressy*," he screamed above the deafening alarm bells. " 'Struck by mine or torpedo. Losing speed, and listing.' "

"Aye, aye, sir," the signalman acknowledged as he tore the weather cover off the carbon-arc signal lamp.

"Number One!" Captain Drummond had staggered out onto the wing. "What happened? Do we have damage reports?"

"A torpedo," Day snapped. "Our port coal bunkers are open to the sea. I've ordered the starboard bunkers flooded. I'm going to tell the black gang to vent steam."

Drummond nodded. Once one bunker was open, *Aboukir* was doomed. All they could do was prolong the death agony until the crew could make it safely over the side.

"Message from flag!" the signalman screamed. " '*Cressy* . . . coming . . . alongside . . . to . . . render . . . assistance,' " he mouthed as he read the flashing light on *Cressy*'s bridge. " '*Hogue* . . . will . . . provide . . . protective . . . screen.' "

Drummond and Day watched as *Cressy* leaned into a tight turn, swinging her bow at the stricken *Aboukir*.

Forty feet below, the engineers waded waist-deep in inky black water as they went from valve to valve, venting away the ship's steam. In the boiler rooms, the stokers were raking out the fires.

"Bridge, this is the engine room," the chief engineer shouted through the voice tube. "We've got all the sea cocks open. It's no good. The starboard bilge must be out of the water."

"Get all your men topside," Day said.

They only had a few seconds left. Within the ship everything loose was falling toward the port side. Heavy machines would soon begin to tear free. Any moment the ship would roll over and die.

Captain Drummond was looking straight down from the port wing, waiting for the rush of water along the side of the ship to slow. He wanted the ship dead in the water before he ordered the boats lowered and his crew over the rail. But even as she moved forward, the ship was twisting over onto her side. He made his decision.

"Abandon ship!"

"Cut the lifeboats free," Day screamed. He couldn't lower them. The boats on the port side were hanging ten feet away from the ship. No one could reach them. Those on the starboard side were hanging in over the deck.

Crewmen formed fire lines, passing life jackets out from their lockers. As quickly as the men were able to fasten on jackets, they jumped over the port rail into the sea.

"You, too, Number One," Drummond said.

"We'll go together," Day said.

Drummond shook his head. "I'll stay until *Cressy* comes."

"You don't have time," Day began, but his words were lost in a screech of tearing metal. The number one stack broke and fell like a tree, crashing down on the seamen struggling in the water.

Day wrapped his arms around Captain Drummond and wrestled him over the lifeline. As *Aboukir* continued to roll, the rising sea lifted them off the bridge and floated them clear. The ship paused on its side for only an instant before its decks and superstructure fell under. She turned completely over, the whalelike curve of steel broken only by the propellers, which slowly rose into the air.

For a half mile behind the sinking ship, its crew was stretched out in a line of bobbing heads. Choking men struggled toward the overturned boats. Others screamed out in pain. Some were still and silent, blank faces kept afloat by the life jackets.

Commander Day held Captain Drummond in his arm as he kicked out toward the floating flag cases from the signal bridge. The older man struggled for a handhold, and then Day vaulted him onto one of the cases. Drummond reached back to help haul Day on top, but the commander was already swimming back toward a signalman who was thrashing in the water.

The signalman pounced on Day as soon as he was near, and for a moment they struggled before Day got an arm around the boy's neck, turned him over onto his back, and started kicking back toward the floating flag cases. It was then that he saw *Cressy* as she appeared around the capsized hull of *Aboukir*.

The flagship had slowed toward the line of men who were screaming and waving frantically to be rescued. Aboard *Cressy*, crewmen lined the rail, lowering nets and ropes over the side. Then well behind *Cressy*, Day saw *Hogue*. She was moving at full speed, belching clouds of thick smoke as she searched for a submarine that might be lurking beneath the water.

Drummond reached down and caught the signalman by his shirt collar. Day got his shoulder under the boy, and together they were able to lift him up next to the captain. "Get aboard," Drummond called to Day. The commander was reaching up when the sky suddenly flashed with light, and the air vibrated in a thunderclap.

"Good God," the captain prayed. In the distance *Hogue* shuddered beneath a billowing cloud of smoke. She seemed to skid sideways, kicking up a wave of white water as she stopped dead. Then there was a second flash, this one near her stern. The old ship began to roll to starboard, her decks and then her gun mounts disappearing into the sea. Her crew fell like raindrops into the water.

Aboard *Cressy*, the crew scampered away from the railing, abandoning the nets and lines. The flagship moved away from the drowning men, rushing off toward the sinking *Hogue*.

Cressy had no choice but to attack. If she stopped to rescue *Aboukir's* crew, she would be an easy target. The submarine had to be somewhere beyond *Hogue*. As soon as she had gathered enough speed, *Cressy* began zigzagging. In the water around *Hogue*, sailors waved deliriously at what they thought was approaching rescue. Their calls turned to screams of horror as *Cressy* charged through their midst, her wake tossing them aside like bobbing corks.

Drummond and Day watched *Cressy* race a thousand yards

north, then turn back toward the rising steam of *Aboukir*. Screams came from the water around them. *Aboukir*'s crewmen had seen *Cressy* steam over *Hogue*'s survivors in her frantic chase toward her invisible tormentor. Now she was coming straight toward them.

And then she exploded. The blast threw a waterspout up along her starboard side, and a cloud of coal dust belched from her shattered hull. Immediately she began to lean to starboard. Her coal bunker, like those of her sister ships, was flooding quickly, its weight dragging the ship into a roll from which there was no hope of recovery. *Cressy*'s whistle sounded her death groan. Then she began to settle into her own black stain, joining *Hogue* and *Aboukir*, which had already vanished.

Now there were a thousand men thrashing in the water, struggling toward bobbing pieces of debris. Cries echoed across the flat surface of the still water.

Day identified one of the voices, slid down from the flag box, and struck out toward the helmsman, who was pleading for help. As he was pushing the man up next to Captain Drummond, he heard another voice nearby. A pale face bobbed up a few yards away, and Day was able to reach out, seize the man's life jacket, and drag him alongside. In just a few minutes he gathered six of *Aboukir*'s crew— three on top of the floating flag locker, three with him in the water.

Then through the pained wail that blended hundreds of voices, he heard a new sound—the dull throbbing of an engine.

"The murdering bastard." It was Captain Drummond, sitting on top of the flag locker, who saw it first. Day turned and saw the ghostly shape of a submarine cutting through the mist. The droning noise grew louder, and the details of her structure began to take shape. He could see the top of her bow as it sent up a misty spray. And then he saw a man standing atop the conning tower, looking around in disbelief at the destruction he had caused.

The submarine came closer, and as it moved, the air around it became deathly still. Voices stopped in the throats of the men in the water as they came face to face with the image of death, moving like a shark through their midst.

"Bastard," Drummond suddenly screamed.

The submarine captain raised his hands in a gesture of helplessness. As the U-boat drifted past he stretched out his arms, embracing the tiny size of his craft. How, he seemed to be asking, can this little boat rescue so many? The beat of the engines suddenly quickened, and the ghostly craft disappeared into the low-lying mist.

Day tightened his grip on the edge of the locker. He was exhausted, and the weight of his clothes dragged him lower in the water. He could taste the sulfur in the coal slick floating under his chin.

London. Alfred Booth raised the glass of port to his lips, pausing for a moment so that he could savor the sweet bouquet. His cousin George looked on apprehensively from across the table.

"Very nice," Alfred pronounced. He sipped, then closed his eyes to block out all distractions. "Very nice, indeed."

"I'm so glad you like it," George said. He signaled the waiter, who approached with a wooden chest of cigars.

Alfred reached for a cigar, but his eyes looked over the top of the box and fixed suspiciously on his cousin. Though they each ran half of the family business, they didn't generally socialize together. As chairman of the Cunard line, Alfred was involved with the shipping barons of the great port of Liverpool, while George, as the family's financial genius, spent most of his time in London. It had been over a year since George had last invited Alfred to dinner at his club, and his solicitude was alarming to his cousin.

George cleared his throat. "I suppose you've guessed that there is something I need to discuss with you."

"I thought there might be," Alfred said, lighting his cigar.

"Well, in truth, it's not just me. One of my associates is going to be joining us." George glanced at his watch. "Any minute, in fact."

"Who?" Alfred demanded, his eyes narrowing.

"Winston." George watched Alfred's jaw tighten. "Please. I wouldn't have done this if it wasn't absolutely necessary."

Alfred pulled back from the table. "This is outrageous," he fumed. "You know my opinion of that . . . upstart."

"It's about the war effort," George tried.

"It's about *Lusitania*," Alfred fired back.

"Well, yes. As a matter of fact, it is."

"Then the First Lord of the Admiralty can make an appointment during business hours," Alfred said, jumping to his feet.

"Sit down, Alfred," George Booth ordered. *"Sit down."*

Alfred's jaw slackened, as if he had been slapped. No one spoke to him in that tone of voice. He settled slowly back into his chair.

"I'm sorry," George said, "but the truth is, I arranged this meeting for your sake, not for his. Churchill doesn't have to ask for your cooperation. He has the authority to order it."

Alfred Booth nodded slowly. "I know that," he admitted. "If the Admiralty wants *Lusitania,* it has the right to take her. Probably best if it did. Cunard can't afford to keep her in operation. Maybe it's time she did her tour as a cruiser."

Lusitania had never turned a profit. The great liner had been built to Admiralty specifications that called for twice the engine power of her transatlantic competitors. Her advanced turbines gave her more speed than any vessel afloat, but the twenty-five giant boilers that fed them steam consumed more coal in a one-way passage than most liners used in the round-trip.

The moment her keel had been laid, she was intended to be converted into a naval cruiser in the event of war. Mounting rings for eight long-range naval guns were already built into her decks. Valuable cargo space was given over to ammunition magazines and to elevators to hoist six-inch shells up to her gun mounts.

George Booth shook his head. "Winston wants to keep her in regular passenger service," he answered.

Alfred's blank expression showed that he didn't understand.

George leaned over the table confidentially. "It all has to do with the supply of war materials. We're firing more shells in France each day than we can make in England in a week. And there's guncotton. We have all the mines we need to lock the German navy into the North Sea. But we have no explosive guncotton to put into the mines. Our only chance is to buy what we need in America. So I've set up a purchasing commission there, and we've hired the Morgan Bank to finance our purchases. We can buy just about anything we need. But our biggest problem is getting the supplies across. That's what Winston wants to talk to you about."

As if on cue, Winston Churchill strode into the dining room, his short, round physique impeccably turned out in white tie and tails. He paused to order a bottle of Champagne from the maître d' and to select a cigar, then walked up to the table. "George."

George Booth rose and gestured Churchill into a chair.

"Alfred," Churchill said as he held the cigar up to the light that the waiter struck. "How good"—he puffed a few times—"to see you." One more puff, and then a brisk exhale of smoke.

194

"A pleasure," Alfred managed as Churchill turned away to examine the bottle of Champagne the wine steward held.

"That will do nicely," Churchill told the steward. "George, shall I put this on your bill?" George nodded. Alfred winced.

"Alfred," he began, "has your cousin explained our problem?"

"About transporting war materials? Yes, he has. But I was still a bit confused as to Cunard's role. It would seem you would need freighters rather than passenger ships."

"For special cargoes we need fast passenger ships," Churchill said. "You're familiar with the maritime rules of encounter?"

"Of course," Alfred responded.

These rules of encounter were recognized by all nations. In time of war, warships were entitled to sink commercial vessels, but only after providing for the safety of all civilians aboard. They were also entitled to stop them, board them, and search for contraband. If they found nothing, the commercial vessel was entitled to pass. But if they found war materials or military personnel, they were entitled to seize the vessel as a war prize. Or they could simply sink her after placing civilians into lifeboats.

"We plan to use passenger ships to carry munitions from America," Churchill explained as he sipped his Champagne. "Submarines can't simply fire torpedoes at passenger ships. According to the rules, they have to surface and order them to stop. And they can't very well board and search *Lusitania*, because there's no way they can catch her. And even if they did, they couldn't sink her. How could they provide for the safety of two thousand passengers?"

"Submarines?" Alfred asked. "I thought you were concerned about the German fleet."

"The German fleet isn't the problem," Winston said, hunching over his cigar. "If it comes out, we'll sink it. It's the U-boats. Last week we lost an entire squadron of cruisers in half an hour, all sunk by a single submarine twelve miles off the Dutch coast."

Alfred was stunned. "I hadn't heard."

"We're not talking about it," Churchill said. "No point in stirring up a panic. The fact is, all the ships in the King's navy can't keep the sea-lanes open." He set an ashtray in the center of the table. "Here's England." He put his Champagne glass beside it. "Here's Ireland. Every pound of war materials that George buys in America has to come through here to get to England." He moved the tip of

195

his cigar around the bottom of the glass and into the space between the glass and the ashtray. "Across the southern coast of Ireland and up through Saint George's Channel. Put half a dozen submarines in the area, and you can shut down England."

Alfred looked up, and instead of the smug little man who had ingratiated himself in high places, he saw a statesman who was plainly frightened. "They could do it to us," Alfred mumbled.

Winston nodded. "This war won't be won or lost in France." He pushed the wet end of his cigar down on the tablecloth. "It will be fought right here, off the Irish coast."

"But if *Lusitania* carries munitions, then she gives up her rights under the rules of encounter," Alfred Booth said.

"The munitions will never appear on her cargo manifest," Churchill answered.

"But if the Germans even suspect—"

"The ship will be carrying civilian passengers, many of them Americans. Even if the Germans suspect she's carrying munitions, I don't think they'll want to invite the Americans into the war."

"But where will she carry the ammunition?" Alfred questioned.

"You're going to pull her out of service for a brief overhaul," Churchill answered. "Basically, we're tearing out everything below the main deck and forward of the number one boiler room. The entire bow of the ship will become a magazine."

Alfred Booth looked at Churchill's cherubic jowls. "You're asking me to be a contrabandist," he said.

"We're asking you to be a patriot," Churchill answered.

Alfred sat in stunned silence. A munitions ship disguised as an ocean liner, with innocent passengers unaware that their lives were being offered to protect the deadly cargo. It was unthinkable. Absolutely immoral. Then he looked at the ashtray that represented England and the cigar stain that marked his country's lifeline. "Yes, yes, of course," he finally managed. "It all makes perfect sense."

CHAPTER 2

New York. Strings. Definitely strings. There was no doubt about it. He had made the right choice.

Even from the terrace of his estate on the North Shore of Long Island, Sir Peter Beecham felt a tingle of excitement as he listened to the musicians tuning their violins in the ballroom. He had toyed with the idea of something trendy. Maybe a shirtsleeved trio playing ragtime. After all, the party was for Jennifer, and the music was for her and her friends. But he had reminded himself that no matter what the occasion, the party was always for the Americans. And in the company of Europeans, Americans pretended to prefer strings.

He couldn't explain Americans. They were the most independent, decently democratic people in the world, but he had closed dozens of deals simply by hinting at the opportunity for them to meet an English princess.

No doubt about it. Strings were definitely the right choice. Sir Peter looked out onto a hillside that rolled from his manor house down into Long Island Sound. It was fall, and the countryside was ablaze with color, the trees in tones of orange and yellow. If he looked west, he could see the fledgling skyline of New York City. He had made his fortune helping to build the industries of America, where the new world was pushing the old aside. Now he was calling on those industries to come to the rescue of England.

The invitations to Jennifer's coming out had been written from a list of America's power brokers. Among others, there were the chairmen of two steel companies, both considering contracts for two million shell casings. There was the president of the nation's largest chemical concern, a manufacturer of nitrate explosives. There were two shipping magnates. All these men were free to sell equally to the Germans or the English, and they would manufacture victory for the highest bidder.

To stay ahead in the bidding, Sir Peter needed vast supplies of credit. So J. P. Morgan had been invited, along with two of his top lieutenants. Morgan had refused—he detested social events—but his lieutenants had accepted.

And then there was government. Authorities had to be persuaded to look the other way as contraband was being loaded, and to scratch their signatures on cargo manifests that they knew were false. Dudley Malone, customs collector for the Port of New York, had therefore received an invitation. And Germany could certainly be expected to file protests with the Department of State over America's outrageous breach of its obligations as a neutral power. Which explained why Robert Lansing, counsel to the State Department, was listed as a guest of honor.

The invitations were not entirely cynical. In the ten-year course of Sir Peter's business dealings in North America, he had befriended at least half of these men. And when George Booth had asked him to head up the British purchasing agency in the United States, Beecham had gone out of his way to make the acquaintance of all the others.

Beecham's guests began arriving. His wife, Anne, stood beside him as he welcomed each couple. She was a marvelous asset—dignified, more vivacious than her fifty years would suggest, and with beauty that made a mockery of youth. She not only put a name with every face but made even the most formal relationship seem like a lifelong friendship.

Robert Lansing arrived with his wife, the daughter of a former Secretary of State. He was a tall man, with his full head of gray hair nicely styled, his mustache carefully contoured. His eyes twinkled as he smiled an elaborate greeting to Anne.

"Strings," he noticed. "I love an evening of strings."

The guests broke into small groups—the manufacturers in the center of the room, the financial men near the orchestra, and the steamship owners by the French doors that looked out over the sound. Jennifer's young guests, who seemed to laugh more than talk, stayed close to the bar. Waiters circulated with trays of Champagne and hors d'oeuvres.

And then came Jennifer's moment. The orchestra played a spirited fanfare, and all heads turned in anticipation toward the staircase, where Jennifer suddenly turned into view. She was tall and thin, the perfect figure for the narrow floor-length underskirt and blousy tunic that had been the spring revolution in Paris. Her deep complexion complemented the almond white of the brocade. She wore her dark hair up, showing a long neck and soft shoulders.

Sir Peter crossed to the bottom of the stairs and extended his hand. Jennifer descended the steps. When he turned, with his daughter on his arm, there were tears of joy in his eyes. He led her into the ballroom, where his guests exploded in applause.

Jennifer was his life, a fact that his wife understood better than he did. Peter thought of himself as a thick-skinned businessman, but Anne knew him to be an apprehensive father who caved in to his daughter's every wish.

Sir Peter introduced her to each of his guests. It was a rite of passage—the moment when he admitted publicly that his little girl had become a woman. Anne relished the moment. The two people she loved the most seemed so happy.

The conductor turned to his musicians and whispered the name of a waltz. Peter led his daughter to the center of the ballroom and circled the floor to smiles and applause. Then Jennifer asked the others to join them, and the ballroom came to life.

Peter handed his daughter to one of the young men and did a turn around the floor with Anne. "Can you give me a few minutes before we serve?" he asked. She nodded without losing her smile.

He carried two whiskeys to the library, where he had a rendezvous with Robert Lansing.

"You're a very lucky man, Sir Peter." Lansing tipped his glass in a toast. "Your daughter is lovely."

"Thank you, Robert." Peter gestured toward one of the leather chairs, and Lansing's expression grew grave as he sat.

"Ambassador von Bernstorff was in this morning," Lansing began. "He brought Franz von Papen with him."

Beecham nodded. The German ambassador and his military attaché were overdue. The true nature of the cargoes Sir Peter was loading aboard neutral vessels and passenger ships would never be officially acknowledged. But in the course of arranging passage and loading and unloading cargoes under the noses of port commissioners, it was impossible to keep his activities secret.

"They're warning us of their right to sink any ship carrying war materials," Lansing continued. "Von Papen said Germany could assume no responsibility for American citizens who travel on passenger ships carrying contraband." He shook his head in despair.

"Outrageous," Sir Peter sympathized. "I know of no government more diligent in checking cargo manifests than your own."

"That's exactly what I told them," Lansing agreed. But there had been no candor. He knew perfectly well that the British were loading cargoes after they had filed official manifests. American law allowed for supplementary manifests, covering last-minute cargoes, which were handed to the pilot as their ships departed. Port commissioners and customs inspectors had no way of verifying whether the supplementary manifests were true.

"Robert, I assure you that we are abiding by the laws of your country. Oh, mistakes are made. But to suggest that there is contraband on passenger ships . . ." Peter lifted his hands in a gesture of helplessness. "Ridiculous."

Lansing rose and paced toward the fireplace. "The problem is that this is just the thing Bryan would love to believe." William Jennings Bryan, the Secretary of State, distrusted the British. He was anxious to assure that the administration's neutrality policy wasn't tipped in favor of Britain.

"Robert, I'm well aware how difficult this is for you. All of us respect your loyalty to your government's policy."

"It's just a matter of time. Americans are clearly behind the Allies. President Wilson has to begin to see the national will."

"Or his successor. There are a number of very powerful people in England who are hoping you might aspire to the job, Robert."

"The presidency?" Lansing tried to look shocked at the suggestion. "That's not even remotely possible," he protested.

"My purchasing committee is dealing with the biggest men in this country," Beecham countered. "These men are not neutral. They want to help the British cause. When they look to Washington, you're the only man they can agree with."

"But still—" Lansing started.

Peter held up a hand. "I'm wrong to even raise the issue. Suffice it for me to say that many of us hope to see a change in American policy by the next election. A change much along the lines of your own thinking." He rose to escort his guest back to the party.

Beecham knew perfectly well that Lansing thought of little else but the presidency. Sir Peter's hint of support from powerful friends was really a promise—if Lansing helped them get rich selling war materials to England, they would have enough money to buy him the White House.

The music grew louder as they walked toward the ballroom. "Ah, Cinderella has found her Prince Charming," Lansing said.

Jennifer was in the center of the room, swaying in the arms of a tall naval officer in full-dress uniform.

"My new aide," Peter said. "He's officially attached to our commercial delegation, but he'll be working with me."

"He seems captivated by your daughter."

"Nonsense," Sir Peter protested. "He's much older than Jennifer. Let me introduce him to you. A most interesting chap. One of the survivors of *Aboukir*."

He got them together as soon as the music stopped. "Counselor Lansing, may I present Commander William Day."

"An honor," Day said as he offered his hand.

"My honor," Lansing insisted. "I heard about your ship. Three of them, if I remember. A terrible tragedy."

Day nodded. "They were very old ships," he said. "The tragedy is that they were sailed by very young men."

Sir Peter had been careful in arranging the seating for dinner. Dudley Malone, the collector of customs, was to be parked between a young lady who never stopped giggling and Commander Day. Since Day would be loading contraband right under Dudley's nose, Sir Peter wanted them to get acquainted. Given the childish noises that would come from the young lady's side, Malone would certainly turn all his attention to the commander. Jennifer was to be at the center of the table, flanked by two young men.

Jennifer destroyed his plan. She brought William Day to a place beside her, sending one of the young men across the table to Day's place. That trapped Dudley Malone between the giggling girl and a young man who was determined to amuse her. Throughout dinner they leaned forward and talked under Malone's chin.

Sir Peter should have been furious with his daughter for her outrageous breach of etiquette. Instead he was thrilled he had provided a uniformed prince for her entertainment. She had claimed for herself the most interesting man of the evening.

The ladies withdrew at the end of the meal, and the servants brought brandy and cigars. Everyone was anxious to hear from the young British naval officer. To Americans the war was a championship fight, and now, in its early months, the fighters had only just climbed into the ring. The bell would sound when the German High Seas Fleet came out into the North Atlantic to challenge the English first line. The question that all of them waited for William Day to answer was which one was going to win.

He laughed at the question and shook his head slowly. "I don't think my opinion is worth very much. My total combat experience was the two or three minutes it took my ship to turn over."

"But is the Admiralty confident?" a banker pressed.

"Confident? Yes. If the High Seas Fleet comes out, there's a good deal of confidence that our navy will be up to the test."

"If?" one of the shipping barons asked. "They have to come out."

"I'm not sure," Day responded. "I think this may be a war of supply. And they can win that with their submarines. If the Germans starve us out, they don't need their High Seas Fleet."

"But can't the Royal Navy deal with a few submarines?" asked one of J. P. Morgan's bankers. "If it can't, why would anyone finance cargo vessels sailing into English waters?"

"Surely you're being too pessimistic," Sir Peter said, realizing that his suppliers might begin to think of England as a lost cause. "There has to be something we can do."

"The answer may be a large number of small ships rather than a small number of large ships," Day answered. "Submarines can only stay down for a few hours. They have to come up to replenish their air supply and charge their batteries. If we could blanket the shipping lanes, submarines wouldn't be able to operate there."

"Is that Admiralty policy?" an electrical manufacturer asked.

"No," Day admitted immediately. "It's just my own thought. I've had a lot of time to think about submarines lately."

There was an appreciative chuckle as the butler made the rounds with more brandy.

The North Sea. Was it smoke? Lieutenant Feldkirchner couldn't be sure. The way the boat was rolling, he couldn't steady his binoculars. And with the height of the seas, he was able to get only occasional glimpses of the horizon.

The timing was right. Submarine Flotilla Commander Bauer's sources had confirmed *Glitra*'s sailing from Oslo at noon the previous day, headed around the Orkneys, past the Hebrides, and down the North Channel, to Liverpool. Feldkirchner rechecked his watch: 0730. It had to be the freighter *Glitra*, right on schedule.

U-17 had left its home port, Emden, three days earlier, heading past the Frisian Islands and breaking out into the North Sea. She then ran due north to her patrol box, a hundred-and-twenty-mile square from the southern tip of Norway, across the Skagerrak, and down the west coast of Jutland. Bauer scattered his submarines into patrol areas surrounding England. Then he waited for information. He had informers in nearly every European and American port.

Feldkirchner stood on the conning tower, nine feet above the sea. The narrow hull rolled continuously, slamming to a stop each time the bow plunged into a wave, then shooting forward the instant the bow broke free. He was constantly ducking beneath walls of water and then struggling for balance to keep from being battered against the iron rails.

Belowdecks, the battering was even worse. The U-17's hull was only a hundred and twenty feet long and less than ten feet across. Packed into that small tube were two diesels, coupled to a motor-generator set. There were banks of lead-acid batteries, hundreds of yards of copper cable, water pumps, water tanks, and fuel tanks. To turn the boat into a weapon, there were five eighteen-foot torpedoes. There were compressed-air firing tubes and a firing computer, an ingenious arrangement of cams and gears that could take the speed and relative course of a ship and calculate the exact moment of fire. There were ammunition magazines and shell hoists.

And then there were the men, squeezed into the small, awkward spaces that were left over. To escape their hellish world of damp mildew, choking air, and glaring electric lights, they climbed out onto the decks whenever the boat was running on the surface. But with the heavy weather the decks were too dangerous.

The bow plunged, and Feldkirchner ducked behind the conning-tower shield. The ocean roared over his head, spilling torrents down on top of him. For an instant the boat seemed to be stuck motionless in the sea. Then the bow broke through on a wave, and there ahead of him was the freighter, plowing across his bow. Feldkirchner raised his range finder and took a reading on his target, still several miles away. He opened the hatch at his feet and dropped down the ladder, pulling the hatch closed over his head.

"Dive," he ordered his executive officer. He stepped to a plotting board to calculate his course to the intercept point, where he would break surface beside *Glitra* and put a shot across her bow.

At the executive officer's command, a series of orders passed through the boat. Engineers uncoupled the motor generators from the engines. The chattering diesels suddenly stilled, replaced by the whine of the motors, which now used battery power to drive the propellers. Seawater flooded the ballast tanks, and the boat slowly began to sink.

Suddenly there was silence. The boat fell from the wild, pitching surface to the dead stillness below.

"Turn to one one zero," Lieutenant Feldkirchner ordered.

"One one zero," the helmsman echoed as he swung the wheel.

"All ahead flank," the commanding officer intoned.

"All ahead flank." The chief of the watch rang the command on the engine telegraph, and the engine room responded.

"Rig for surface attack." The gun crew began loading three-inch shells into the ammunition hoist. A machine gun, already armed with a cartridge belt, was brought to the conning tower.

"How long?" the executive officer asked Feldkirchner.

"Eighteen minutes. Check her again in ten minutes."

They stood quietly. The preparations were completed. The gun crew hunched at the foot of the ladder to the after hatch, and the boarding party, their hands on the frame of a collapsible boat, waited beneath the forward hatch. The gunner was already at the top of the conning-tower ladder, his weapon cradled in his arms.

"Time." It was the executive officer, reminding Feldkirchner that the ten minutes had elapsed. Feldkirchner nodded, and turned to the periscope as his second-in-command pulled down on the counterweight cable. The polished steel tube rose inside its track.

For a moment all Feldkirchner could see was a moving hill of water. Then as the spray cleared, he saw the freighter bearing toward him, its bow pitching as it fought through the white-capped crests.

He called out the bow angle and fixed the image within the brackets of the range finder. Then he pushed the scope down. "Right on course," he announced. "Looks about one mile."

"About five minutes," the executive officer commented.

They waited again, hearing their own nervous breathing above the hum of the electric motors, and then there was a new sound, like distant thunder. It was *Glitra*'s screw as it cut through the sea.

Feldkirchner pointed at the periscope. "Let's take another look." Once again he eased the scope up. *Glitra* appeared off his port quarter no more than one hundred yards astern.

"Right to one six zero," he ordered, pushing the periscope down.

They listened carefully for any change in the sound of the propeller. If *Glitra* had spotted the periscope, then the freighter would probably make a sudden turn. But there was no change. The throbbing continued, growing louder.

"Surface," Feldkirchner ordered, starting up the ladder.

The bow planes were tilted upward. Compressed air was fired into the ballast tanks, making the boat slightly buoyant. The bow and conning tower exploded out of the sea at the same instant.

The gunner threw open the hatch and charged upward through the torrent of water that poured down into the tower. Feldkirchner followed behind him. He saw *Glitra,* running on a parallel course, no more than fifty yards off his port quarter. "Switch to the engines," he shouted through the hatch as he slammed it closed.

The instant the decks cleared the surface, hatches opened fore and aft of the conning tower. The gun crew sprang from the after hatch, each man connecting a safety line from his belt to a track in the deck. The boarding party climbed through the forward hatch, dragging the collapsible boat up behind them.

Feldkirchner watched his gunner bolt the machine gun into its stanchion. Then he looked at *Glitra.* These were his most vulnerable moments. His guns weren't armed. He was switching from the electric motors to the diesels. His crew was standing in plain sight. A gunner aboard the freighter could rake his boat with machine-gun fire, dropping his men like ducks in a shooting gallery. Or the freighter might cut his boat in half with her bow.

But there was no activity at all aboard *Glitra* as she pounded through the sea. No one on the ship had yet seen the submarine.

The gunner's mate at the deck gun held up his hand. Feldkirchner raised his own arm and then let it drop. A second later the deck gun fired with a sharp crack, and a column of water exploded into the air and broke across the freighter's foredeck.

Suddenly there was a face on the bridge, wide-eyed under a seaman's cap. The man looked in disbelief at the submarine, then disappeared toward the wheelhouse. An instant later another man, this one wearing an officer's cap, appeared on the bridge.

"Heave to," Feldkirchner screamed in English through his megaphone. "Prepare to be boarded."

The officer peered down incredulously. The boat was only a third as long as his ship and seemed barely afloat. He hesitated.

"Take the cargo rigging," Feldkirchner told his gunner. The machine gun chattered, and a stream of tracers reached out across the sea. Ropes frayed, and wooden blocks shattered. One of the cargo booms crashed down on the freighter's foredeck.

"Heave to," Feldkirchner screamed again.

The man disappeared into the wheelhouse. *Glitra* was still making good speed, but U-17 had begun building momentum as soon as she had switched to the diesels. Now the submarine was matching the steamer's speed, the two craft moving side by side.

A new figure appeared on *Glitra*'s wing, again in officer's cap, but shorter and older-looking than the watch officer. As soon as he saw the submarine, his hands flew into the air.

"Prepare for boarding," the lieutenant ordered. "Put a ladder over the side. My executive officer will come aboard."

Glitra's captain nodded vigorously. The freighter was already slowing, and the submarine had to slow its engines to stay abreast. Then when *Glitra* was nearly stopped, U-17's executive officer, who had climbed up onto the U-boat's foredeck, ordered the collapsible boat into the water. He followed two seamen aboard, and the small craft bobbed toward the ladder that was lowering along the steamer's side. The executive officer jumped onto the ladder and scrambled up and over the ship's rail.

"First Officer Otto Marx." The executive officer saluted when he reached the bridge.

"Captain Morrissey," the old man answered. He couldn't bring himself to salute the bearded young man.

"May I see your cargo manifest?" Marx asked politely. Morrissey led him through the wheelhouse to the chart room, where he opened the ship's safe and found the cargo manifest.

Marx shook his head at the first entry. "Stainless steel bars," he said with genuine sadness. The rest of the items included ball bearings, electrical wire, and optical lenses. "Half of these items are war materials," he continued. "Captain, I must claim my right to destroy this cargo. We will allow you ten minutes to put your crew in the ship's boat and stand clear. We intend to sink your ship."

"We won't be safe in a small boat in these seas."

"Safer than you'll be staying on board," the German said, then saluted and walked back through the wheelhouse.

Morrissey followed him down the ladder from the bridge to the main deck and watched as he climbed over the rail.

The small collapsible boat pushed off from *Glitra*, the two seamen struggling to get some rhythm into their oars. The sea was tossing in swells, making it difficult to keep the boat on a steady heading. Just as it reached U-17, a wave caught it, lifted it up, and tossed it over the top of the deck. Then the boat slid down the back of the wave and smashed against the conning tower, where Feldkirchner was standing. He grabbed the boat's bowline and took one turn around a cleat, hauling the small boat against U-17's deck.

Meanwhile, *Glitra*'s crew had swung out the ship's boat and were lowering it over the side. Her captain jumped aboard as the lifeboat dropped below the deck.

"Stand clear," Feldkirchner called through his megaphone as soon as the lifeboat was in the water. The crew pushed away from the hull and began rowing frantically past her stern.

The lieutenant turned to his gun captain. "Below the waterline, directly beneath the funnel. Commence firing," he ordered.

The gun crew aimed the rifle carefully, but the rolling of the deck made it impossible to fix their elevation precisely. The first round tore through the hull plating three feet above the surface of the sea and exploded inside. The second round hit short and exploded in a geyser along the ship's side. The third shot blew a hole right at the waterline. The next shot hit just below the surface, splitting one of the riveted seams. *Glitra* immediately took on a list.

"That should do it," Feldkirchner called to his gun captain. "Get your men below." He was interrupted by a metallic blast within *Glitra*'s hull. Cold seawater had reached one of her boilers, which had exploded. Bulkheads collapsed, allowing water to rush forward. Within a few minutes her stern lifted out of the sea, its enormous weight putting an unimagined strain on the ship's keel. With a sickening screech of metal the ship tore in half.

"All ahead two thirds," Feldkirchner called down to the control room. "Come to course one seven five." He looked up as the last edge of *Glitra*'s transom disappeared under a swell. Then he saw the lone lifeboat, its crew thrashing their oars about in heavy seas.

"Come topside, Otto," Feldkirchner shouted down to the control room below. Marx climbed up to join him.

"They're not going to make it." The commanding officer nodded toward the lifeboat. "We better give them a tow ashore."

Marx laughed. "First we put them in the water. Now we're getting them out. Does this make any sense to you?"

"Why should it?" Feldkirchner said, shaking his head. "These are English rules we're playing by." He maneuvered U-17 close to the lifeboat. At first the English crew sat hunched over their oars, fearing a mass coup de grace from the machine gunner, who still held his position on the conning tower. But when they saw the German sailor uncoiling a heaving line on the submarine's afterdeck, they scrambled for the line and secured it to a bow cleat. Feldkirchner then made for the Norwegian coast, with his enemies in tow.

Insane, he thought as he looked back at the small boat bobbing in his wake. The international cruiser rules insisted that he act like an armed cruiser, firing a shot across the bow of his prey and ordering the ship to heave to for searching. But his submarine didn't fit the traditional cruiser rules. Lurking beneath the waves, he was more than a match for any ship afloat. But when he surfaced, he became a weakling.

The Norwegian coast loomed up ahead. Feldkirchner could see the waves breaking on a rocky shore. He ran parallel to the coast until he sighted a break in the rocks. Then he ordered his boatswain out on the afterdeck to haul the lifeboat alongside.

"This is as far as we can take you, Captain," Feldkirchner shouted.

Captain Morrissey saluted. "Thank you, Captain," he said. "I'll make a full report on your proper conduct."

Feldkirchner returned the salute and watched as the men rowed toward the beach. A full report, he thought. That should have the English admirals holding their sides in laughter.

CHAPTER 3

New York. News of *Glitra's* sinking hit the Manhattan shipping offices like a torpedo. Suddenly it was dangerous to carry war materials to the British Isles. Foreign steamship companies that days before had been courting Sir Peter Beecham's cargoes suddenly wanted no part of the nitrates, the shell casings, and the generators that he was buying from American manufacturers.

Insurance rates for ships bound for England were suddenly doubled. And if the ships were carrying anything that might be used to bludgeon a German, the rates were doubled again. Beecham was suddenly spending more to get his war materials across the ocean than he was to buy them.

"One ship!" he protested to Commander William Day. "A few rounds into the side of a rusting steamer, and the Huns are able to bankrupt England right out of the war."

"It may get worse," Day cautioned, "once the Germans give up the cruiser rules and start fighting by the submarine rules. They'll declare the Western Approaches a war zone, just as we've declared the North Sea a war zone. They'll sink anything that comes across their bow."

"Innocent passengers? Without warning? Preposterous," Beecham insisted.

"Naming it a war zone is all the warning they need."

Sir Peter saw war as a duel between gentlemen. There were strict procedures, dictated by good breeding. Day saw war as mindless brutality, a jungle game of kill or be killed. English mines didn't pause to allow innocent passengers to take to the lifeboats on ships traveling to Germany. Why should the submarine commander go through the niceties of the rules of encounter before firing?

Beecham spent every hour trying to find neutral ships to supplement the fleet of English steamers he had commandeered, and William Day was his constant companion. He used Day almost as a patriotic poster, shamelessly displaying him in front of shippers and insurers to wring out concessions.

"We're not really discussing tonnage, you know. We're discussing the lives of fine young men. Like Commander Day here, one of the few survivors of the *Aboukir* outrage. What we're talking about is giving these brave men a chance to fight back."

The steely eyes would soften as they looked up from the contract. "I understand the submarine rammed the lifeboats and ran over the men in the water. It must have been terrible."

Before Day could explain what actually had happened, Beecham would turn back to the contract. The agent, who could have demanded three times the going rate, would settle for twice.

Day's experience and his uniform were particularly important in dealing with Dudley Malone, the New York customs inspector. Malone was far too shrewd to be fooled by repackaging and relabeling cargoes. But even though he lived in a world defined by clerical forms and rubber stamps, his imagination traveled out over the dangerous seas. He had admired Commander Day when he first met him at Jennifer's party. The officer in the gold-trimmed uniform had become his alter ego. As he plied Day for information on warships and their tactics to feed his heroic fantasies, he signed and stamped forms that he couldn't bother reading.

Secretly Day wished that Malone would challenge his last-minute cargoes and supplementary cargo manifests. Would passengers sail aboard ocean liners if they understood the explosive force that was resting against their keels? He protested to Sir Peter about orders to load rifle cartridges on *Lusitania*. "Do you know what would happen to the passengers if a German submarine put a torpedo into that cargo?"

"They wouldn't dare fire on a passenger ship," Beecham countered. "That's why the passengers are perfectly safe, and the cargo."

If the young commander was essential to Sir Peter's workday, he was almost as important to Beecham's evenings. Jennifer had followed her prince from Long Island to Manhattan. She had moved into the family town house on Washington Square, leaving her mother's watchful eye for her father's more casual supervision.

During her first days in New York, Sir Peter would find her waiting up for him when he came home late, ready to serve him tea and his favorite biscuits. He would listen eagerly as she recounted all the things she had done during the day. Jennifer could take an hour describing dinner with Commander Day at Delmonico's.

"Every eye was on him," she rejoiced. "In his uniform he was quite the most handsome man in the room."

"I'm sure they were looking at you," Beecham teased.

"No. It was the women who stared. The lady at the next table almost fell off her chair, sniffing at his cologne. Just to drive her mad, I reached across the table and took his hand."

"You didn't," he protested. "Not in public?"

She laughed mischievously. "I most certainly did. You should have seen her expression. She stiffened like an old schoolmarm."

"Positively scandalous," Beecham censured. But he was smiling as he climbed the stairs to his bedroom. Such spirit! Such daring!

Weeks later it was he who was sitting up by the teapot waiting for Jennifer to come home. Commander Day would see her to the door, stepping in just long enough to pay his respects to Beecham.

Jennifer would explode the minute the door closed behind Day. "Oh, Father, William was simply wonderful."

"William is it?" as he poured the tea.

"Well, you can't keep calling someone Commander while you're dancing."

"You were dancing? Where?"

"At the Winter Garden. There was a wonderful orchestra."

Beecham was happy to see Jennifer so happy. And grateful to Day for being so understanding of his daughter. With his aide watching her, Peter didn't feel guilty for leaving Jennifer so much on her own.

Anne began hearing about Jennifer's escapades from friends in the city. "I saw Jennifer just the other evening," one woman told her. "She looked so lovely in her bare-shouldered dress."

"How she's grown," another harpy cooed. "I couldn't believe it was Jennifer dancing with that wineglass in her hand."

"Anne, is it serious?" a friend begged. "Between Jennifer and that handsome naval officer? They're seen everywhere together."

Anne went to the telephone, rang the operator, and asked to be connected to New York. "I want to know about Jennifer," she told her husband. "Have you been keeping a close watch over her?"

"Of course. She's having a fine time here in the city."

"Too fine a time from what I hear," Anne fired back. "One friend tells me she's appearing in public half naked. Another says she's drinking. And she's too young to be keeping serious company with anyone, much less a sailor who's years older than she."

Sir Peter sighed. "Commander Day is simply looking after her for me. He has no interest in her. How could he? He's a commoner."

Anne groaned at her husband's density. "He's tall, handsome, and a war hero. Your daughter is an impressionable child who likes to rush into things. And the next thing she's scheduled to rush into could leave her with a warm bun in the oven."

Sir Peter gasped. "That is the most outrageous thought," he said. "Commander Day wouldn't think of . . . of . . ." He wanted to slam the telephone down.

For the rest of the day he eyed William Day suspiciously. Not that he thought for a moment that there could be anything serious between him and Jennifer. But she was only eighteen. There was no reason for her to charge so enthusiastically into adulthood. It was probably a good idea for her to spend more time with her mother. He would explain that he and Commander Day would be quite busy over the next few weeks. Then he would help her pack, and see her personally to the train in the morning.

London. To Winston Churchill it seemed so obvious. He had explained it in broad terms, and Captain Hall, head of naval intelligence, had filled in the details. Why couldn't the First Sea Lord, Admiral John Fisher, grasp the concept?

"It's illegal! A blatant violation of international law." Fisher's voice was tired and gravelly. The old man who sat hunched in a wing chair no longer had the vitality that had carried him to the very pinnacle of the Royal Navy. Nor did he particularly care for Churchill and Hall. He knew that the two younger men would do exactly as they wished, whether he agreed with them or not.

Churchill sat behind his desk at the Admiralty offices in Whitehall, his pink complexion darkening to red with mounting anger. Reginald Hall sat on a chair drawn up beside the desk, so that he and Churchill were facing Fisher as a team.

Churchill didn't need Fisher's advice, but he did need his support. When he went to brief the Prime Minister on his strategy for dealing with the submarine menace, he needed to be able to say that Fisher approved. He tried again. "The submarine is writing its own laws on naval warfare, Admiral. You yourself have said a submarine commander would be insane to adhere to the rules of encounter."

Fisher's puffy eyes widened. "But I never said that would give us the right to fly foreign flags on our merchant ships."

Churchill glanced in despair at Captain Hall. "Sir," Hall explained, "we know from our radio intercepts that the Germans are taking great pains to avoid involving neutral countries. They have set up extensive spy networks to track British ships with military cargoes and to avoid neutral ships. By flying our own flag on our merchant ships, we simply make their job easier for them."

"Then fly no flag at all," Fisher growled.

Hall looked at Churchill. The Admiral was worrying about flags and their proper use according to the rules of chivalry and about what history would say if he hid his ships under foreign colors. He couldn't understand that modern warfare was a struggle for survival and that the real issue here was the very existence of the British Empire.

"That simply won't do, Admiral," Churchill said. "The absence of a flag will be just as much a giveaway as the presence of a British flag. What we have to do is fly the flags of neutral nations."

"Then the Germans will have to attack everyone," Fisher argued. "Neutrals and British ships alike."

"Exactly," Churchill nearly shouted, thrilled that Fisher had finally gotten the point. "Or avoid attacking anyone. If they can't tell what is a British ship, they will have to treat them all alike."

"Then they'll simply stop each ship, board it, and demand its papers," Fisher argued. "That will tell them which ships are British."

Churchill's eyes closed in despair. Hall came to the rescue. "That's why we need the second part of the plan, sir. British merchantmen will be forbidden to obey a submarine's order. Instead they will ram any submarines that challenge them. We're installing guns on their fantails. Concealed, of course. The U-boats will have to inspect the ships to be sure they're British. And if they are British, the submarine is going to find itself under attack."

Fisher's dark expression began to brighten. It wasn't just a matter of flags. It was a counterattack that would blunt the submarine threat. "Which flags are you planning to use?" he asked.

"Principally the U.S. flag," Hall responded. "The Germans are particularly determined to keep the Americans neutral."

"And Washington will go along with this?" the admiral asked.

"We're not planning on asking them," Churchill responded through clenched teeth. "We'll change flags at sea and switch back to the British flag when we enter port."

"But surely they'll find out," Fisher protested.

"The only ones who could possibly see the flag would be German submarine captains," Hall said. "But suppose one of them knows the ship. Suppose he is able to positively identify it as one of ours flying a foreign flag. What can the German government do other than raise a protest? We will simply deny the charge."

Fisher nodded slowly. "Well," he gasped as he lifted himself out of the chair, "I suppose I'm in favor of anything that could make life more difficult for Admiral von Pohl."

The mischievous twinkle returned to Winston Churchill's eyes. "Wonderful," he said. "I do hope you understand how grateful I am for your counsel on this matter." He jumped up to assist the admiral.

Fisher brushed the helping hand aside. He retrieved his hat and walking stick from the rack next to the door and let himself out.

"Tell me, Captain," Churchill said, "which of our codes are the Germans reading?"

Hall looked shocked. "Absolutely none that I'm aware of."

"That's comforting news," Churchill allowed. "But I'm afraid I can't buy it. If they haven't got through one of our ciphers yet, it's only a matter of time before they do."

"You want them changed more frequently?" Hall asked.

Churchill shook his head, a conspiratorial smile slowly spreading across his face. "To the contrary. I want to find one code they are reading, and then I want to make sure that we never change it."

Hall's eyes narrowed. "You want to get information to the Germans. Information they'll assume is classified. About ships."

"Not ships. A particular ship." Churchill could see that his intelligence officer was baffled. "When our ships begin turning on the submarines, what do you think the Germans will do?"

"Begin firing without warning. They'll have no choice." Then Hall's eyes glowed in recognition. "And you have a particular ship you'd like them to fire at." Churchill nodded. "You'll use the compromised radio code to direct them toward the ship you want them to attack," Hall went on. "May I ask which ship you have in mind?"

"Of course," Churchill answered. "A ship that will bring the Americans into the war. On our side."

New York. The city stopped and turned to face the Hudson River as *Lusitania* appeared around the tip of Manhattan. In downtown offices, clerks and brokers slipped away from their desks and pressed against the windows. On the docks, longshoremen left crates they were loading, and wandered to the water's edge. On the streets of the West Side, pedestrians ran toward the waterfront to get a better look.

New Yorkers called her the Greyhound, which seemed a more fitting name for the fastest ship afloat. She was not the largest ship in the world. *Olympic,* sister ship of *Titanic,* was both longer and beamier. But the Greyhound seemed to be the tallest. The rapier-shaped black hull climbed five stories from the waterline. Three more decks, painted glistening white, were built above that. And then there were the four enormous funnels rising another seven stories. As she slipped past lower Manhattan, she was one of the tallest buildings in the city.

William Day heard the Greyhound's mournful whistle signal to the tugboats that came alongside to assist her. Slowly they began swinging her bow in toward the Cunard piers. She would spend the next two days loading her cargo and filling her coal bunkers. Then the passengers would come aboard, and she would head back to the cold, hostile waste of the North Atlantic.

Day watched as the black hull slid along the dock, blocking out the sun and casting the Cunard offices into shadow. High above his head, on the bridge, he could make out the ship's master as he kissed *Lusitania* cautiously against the pilings. Caution was Captain "Fairweather" Dow's trademark, and it was his caution that had summoned Day to Cunard's New York offices.

Charles Sumner, the Cunard line's American representative, looked up from behind a cluttered desk as Day was shown into his office. "Ah, Commander!" He began digging through stacks of correspondence until he found the typed copy of the wireless message that had preceded *Lusitania* into port. "What am I supposed to do with this?" He pushed the message toward Day.

> Upon arrival, demand briefing on all structural changes made to *Lusitania*. Demand full access to all areas of ship closed off by Admiralty order. Have no intention of sailing until I am fully satisfied as to safety of ship and cargo. Captain Daniel Dow, Master.

"It's not as if *Lusitania* weren't causing me enough problems," Sumner chattered while Day read. "Alfred Booth is constantly haranguing me about costs. Everything from coal to oysters."

"What does this mean?" Day asked, giving the message back.

"Just what it says," Sumner answered. "The man is responsible for everything on the ship. He can't accept that responsibility unless he's fully informed."

"What kind of man is he?" William Day asked.

Sumner began to snicker. "He's a little old lady—that's what he is. He got the name Fairweather because he'll take a ship a hundred miles off course to avoid a rainsquall."

"Can he be trusted?" Day asked.

"Trusted? You mean—"

His secretary interrupted him. "Captain Dow is here."

Fairweather Dow marched into the office. He was a slight man, seemingly too small to command a ship. Even before he was seated, his eyes darted apprehensively between Sumner and Day.

"Commander William Day, from the Admiralty," Sumner said.

Day offered his hand and took care not to crush the thin, manicured fingers that he grasped. "I've seen your wireless, Captain," he said. "Is there something wrong with *Lusitania?*"

"Something?" Fairweather Dow said sarcastically. "Everything is wrong. Since you put her in the yard, she's a different ship."

"Ridiculous," Sumner snapped, dismissing the charge.

Dow directed his comments to Day, a fellow sailor. "*Lusitania* was always a roller. But when the sea put her over, she snapped back into trim. Now she's unsteady, unsure. I'm steaming with coal bunkers only half full. That makes her top-heavy. Even worse is the yawing of the bow. She doesn't track in a straight line."

"Are the problems just westbound, when you're traveling empty?" Day asked.

"It's certainly worse when she's light," Dow said. "The cargo we take back to England helps keep her tighter. But that's another problem—these last-minute cargoes that are sealed into the holds before I can inspect them. How can I assure the safety of my ship when I don't even know what I'm carrying?" He turned to Sumner. "Well, I won't have it. I demand to be shown the holds."

"Captain Dow, may I remind you that we are at war," Sumner began to scold. "Those cargoes—"

"I agree with Captain Dow," Day interrupted. He turned to the ship's master. "I have the keys for all of the areas that the Admiralty has secured. Would you like to inspect them now?"

Dow was stunned by the Admiralty's acquiescence. Sumner was flabbergasted. Even he was forbidden from venturing beyond the new hatchways that the Admiralty had installed.

Day and the captain boarded the ship and walked forward, around the great rotunda that rose like the dome of a statehouse above the first-class dining room. They passed the two caged elevators that waited to carry passengers down two levels to their staterooms or up two levels to the lounges, libraries, and music rooms. Farther forward, Captain Dow led Commander Day down a stairwell into the lower decks of the ship, descending two levels, past the third-level saloon, until their passage was blocked by a heavy steel door secured by a padlock. A small metal sign warned SECURED BY ORDER OF THE ADMIRALTY. Day took out a ring of keys, selected one, and opened the padlock. He pulled the door open. Dow stepped through the hatch and turned into a passageway that he assumed would lead him to the third-class cabins on the main deck. He stopped so abruptly that Day charged into him.

There were no cabins. Before him stretched nearly a hundred feet of open cargo deck. Sixty cabins, with accommodations for nearly two hundred passengers, had vanished.

"The deck below is exactly the same," Day told him.

"What about the athwartship coal bunker?" Dow asked.

"Removed," Day answered. "It was valuable cargo space."

Dow looked around, mentally measuring depths and dimensions. "All the bulkheads," he calculated, "and portions of six decks have been removed. There's nothing left but a hollow shell."

Day nodded. "That's the yawing motion you're noticing when she's empty. We use these holds to carry war materials."

"What kind of war materials?" the master persisted.

"Artillery shells. Rifle cartridges. Range finders— "

"Artillery shells?" Dow's thin face was turning ashen.

"They're not particularly dangerous by themselves," Day assured. "We store the explosive materials well above the waterline. It would be impossible for a torpedo to score a direct hit. And nothing short of a direct hit would pose any significant danger."

Dow shook his head in disbelief. "If it's all so safe, then why all this damn secrecy?" he demanded.

"Because it's completely illegal. American law doesn't allow us to ship any war materials on passenger ships."

"I've seen enough," Dow said, and he started back.

They were at the companionway leading to the pier when Dow announced his conclusion. "I'll take her out." He stopped and turned. "I appreciate the truth. I've heard nothing but lies from the Admiralty and from the owners of my company."

"They were simply trying to protect you," Day answered. "What I've told you is a top Admiralty secret. If you should ever breathe a word of what you now know to anyone, you can count on spending the rest of the war in a naval prison."

It was midafternoon when Beecham's motorcar picked up Day from the Long Island railroad station. By the time they reached the house, the winter sky had already darkened.

The two men ate their supper off trays in the library while they worked before the fire. Beecham had delivery schedules for hundreds of orders he had placed with American manufacturers, and Day had lists of ships on which cargo space had been requisitioned. They had to match delivery dates with scheduled sailings.

Jennifer paced the hallway outside the closed library door. Each time she passed it, she stopped and listened for an indication that the meeting might be adjourning. All she heard was the mumble of dull business.

"Jennifer!" Anne had come downstairs to make tea, and caught her daughter with her ear pressed against the library door.

Jennifer rolled her eyes in exasperation. "William has come all this way to see me, and Father has him locked up in the library for the whole evening." She followed her mother to the kitchen.

"Commander Day didn't come to see you," Anne said. "He came to see your father. They have important business to discuss."

"What's so important that it can't wait until tomorrow?"

"That's not your affair," Anne scolded.

"William *is* my affair," Jennifer yelled, stopping her mother in her tracks. They stared at each other, Anne stunned by her daughter's rude outburst and Jennifer choking back tears. Then Jennifer turned and rushed off to the music room. Seconds later there was the sound of a lullaby being banged out on the piano.

Anne brought a silver tray with a teapot and cups into the library and tried to be unobtrusive as she set it on the desk. When her husband took his tea, she always served it herself. It was a gesture of caring that she couldn't leave to the servants.

"We've just about finished," Sir Peter said. Anne had left the door open. "What is that infernal banging?"

"That's your daughter enjoying a cultural moment," Anne said. "She was anxious to see you, Commander," she said to Day. "Perhaps she thinks the ruckus will drive you out of your meeting."

Day looked from Anne to Beecham. "Will you excuse me, Sir Peter?" Beecham nodded as he closed his briefcase.

Anne brought Peter his tea. "I don't suppose the commander will want any."

"Probably not. Pour for yourself, and join me."

They sat quietly with their tea while Anne tried to think of the best way to introduce the subject that was bothering her. Finally she decided to plunge right in. "I suppose you've noticed that Jennifer is very much taken by your naval officer."

Peter chuckled. "I think infatuated is a better word. After all, she's just a girl."

"She's eighteen," Anne answered. "I was nineteen when I became infatuated with you."

"A different situation," Peter said. "We were from the same stock. Good heavens, it was our parents who introduced us."

"And you think your daughter is concerned over Commander

Day's stock? I hope you're not underestimating what may be happening between them."

"Believe me," Sir Peter said lightheartedly. "I work very closely with Commander Day. If he were in love with my daughter, I would certainly know it."

DAY followed the furious tempo of the lullaby to the music room and walked to the piano, where he stood beside Jennifer.

For a few moments she played on. Then she jumped up and threw her arms around him. "Oh, William, I've missed you."

"I've missed you, too," he admitted. He tried to wring a smile from her tearstained face. "In fact, the whole city has missed you. Delmonico's is thinking of shutting for the season."

"I don't care about the whole city. I care about you. I thought surely you would come out to see me."

"I couldn't. I have work to do," he reminded her.

"I know you don't have much time. That's why I should be in the city, so that I'm there when you're free."

To make sure they were alone, Jennifer took his hand and led him toward the French doors that opened out onto the terrace. "Come outside," she said.

He felt the cold draft as soon as she opened the door. "Jennifer, you'll catch pneumonia out there."

They walked to the stone wall that marked the edge of the lawn. Day took off his jacket and slipped it over her shoulders.

"I have a friend who lives in Manhattan," she whispered. "She'd take me in. Then we could be together when you weren't busy."

"You can't wait weeks on end for me to have a few hours off. There are so many wonderful things you should be doing."

"Nothing is wonderful without you," she argued, her voice rising.

He tried for a change of subject. "Does your father approve of your going back to Manhattan and staying with a friend?"

"He doesn't know yet," she admitted. She looked up at him anxiously, waiting for his approval.

"Do you always get exactly what you want?" he asked.

Her eyes widened in surprise. "I thought that was what you wanted, too," she said softly.

He leaned on the wall and looked out over the water. "I want so many things. I want a ship. I want to get back into the war. And . . .

I want very much to be with you." He looked back at her. "All those things are beyond my reach. I don't suppose I'll ever have them."

"You think I'm selfish," Jennifer concluded.

"No. I think you're impatient. I think you want your whole lifetime right now."

"I don't need everything right now," she decided. "Tell me that I should wait for you, and I will, no matter how long it takes."

She was looking up at him, waiting for his answer. He took her in his arms and kissed her gently.

PETER Beecham raked the coals with the poker until he was sure that the fire would die. When he looked up, he saw Jennifer and William Day outside. They were at the edge of the terrace, outlined in the light that came through the French doors from the music room. His daughter was in the officer's arms.

He should have been furious. But instead, something about the way that Day was holding Jennifer filled him with a great sadness. She looked pathetically small in the oversized jacket with gold braid and buttons. And Day, despite his brutal strength, was holding her carefully, as if she were a precious crystal. Their kiss was soft—a shared breath of life rather than an urge of passion. Beecham suddenly understood what his wife had seen so clearly. It was not that Jennifer was in love with her prince. It was that Commander Day was hopelessly in love with his daughter. He felt heavy with grief, because it was all so futile.

Later Beecham and Jennifer walked Day out to the car, which was waiting to bring him back to the station. He had to catch the train back to the city. Jennifer leaned against her father as the car disappeared. He suddenly took her hand and held it as if they both were sharing some great loss.

In the middle of the night he climbed out of bed and walked to the library. There, he sat at his desk and in the dim light of a shaded lamp penned a letter to the First Lord of the Admiralty.

My dear Winston,

May I ask, as a personal favor, that you recall Commander William Day, naval aide to our delegation here in New York.

Commander Day has been an invaluable asset to our activities and is to be highly commended for his intelligence, energy, and

professionalism. My request is made for reasons of harmony within my household and should in no way affect his career adversely. I hope that he can be assigned to an important, yet *safe*, duty station. I would regard his loss as the loss of my own son.

Sir Peter folded his letter into an envelope, sealed it, and addressed it to Churchill. The next day it would be included in the diplomatic pouch headed for London, and put aboard *Lusitania* just before sailing.

CHAPTER 4

Washington. "Ambassador von Bernstorff and Captain von Papen," Robert Lansing's secretary announced.

Lansing could abide von Bernstorff. The man was a bore, but he was well meaning. It was his military attaché who was unbearable. A youthful miniature clone of Kaiser Wilhelm, Franz von Papen was convinced that the German officer was the final evolution of the human species and that he himself was its perfect specimen. He was never seen without his full uniform—a dark blue jacket with a three-inch-high collar of gold brocade, fringed shoulder boards, and an array of medals across the chest. A scabbarded sword invariably hung at his side. And squared on his head he wore a spiked brass-encrusted helmet, its point adding a full four inches to his height.

Captain von Papen was always on duty. Rarely did he engage in genuine conversation. Instead, he spoke orders. On any issue there was only one correct position, which was, of course, his own.

"Count von Bernstorff, how good to see you," Lansing oozed, stepping around his broad mahogany desk.

The count responded with a trace of a smile.

"And Captain von Papen. A pleasure."

The captain's response was a window-rattling click of his heels. His body snapped downward from the waist in a formal bow that aimed his spike at Lansing. Then he ratcheted back up.

Lansing pirouetted back around his desk, gesturing to the two armchairs across from him. "Please be seated, gentlemen."

The ambassador settled into a chair. It was more difficult for von Papen, who had to fit his sword under the arm of his chair before he could lower himself to its edge in perfect attention.

"To what do I owe this honor?" Lansing began.

"Most distressing information concerning the maritime policy of the British government," von Bernstorff began. He turned to his aide. Von Papen opened a leather briefcase, withdrew a gray folder, and snapped it down on Lansing's desk.

"These are Admiralty orders just found on a British steamer stopped by a German military vessel," von Papen said.

Lansing, frowning earnestly, opened the folder, and began to read. Simultaneously von Bernstorff delivered an analysis. "The first order instructs British merchant captains to fly the flags of neutral nations, which is a flagrant violation of international law. Note the preferred neutral flag is that of the United States."

He waited until Lansing had turned to the next page.

"The second document forbids British merchant captains from obeying the lawful search orders of German submarines. When confronted with a submarine, they are to attack her."

"Most disturbing," Lansing agreed. He turned to the third paper, which required each merchant ship reaching certain ports to be held over for several days so that a naval gun could be installed on its fantail. He closed the folder, already organizing his defense. "I will bring this to the attention of His Majesty's ambassador. If such an order had been issued, I'm certain my government would protest the use of the flag."

"The order was issued," von Papen corrected. "Obviously, the British government is abandoning the rules of encounter."

Lansing pursed his lips. "I'm not quite sure I would come to that conclusion."

"There is no other conclusion," von Papen pressed. "If British passenger ships and merchantmen ignore a submarine's warning shot, then the submarine is left with no alternative but to attack."

Lansing's eyes flashed with anger. "Captain von Papen, these few papers, even if genuine, in no way constitute an excuse for German submarines to attack ships without making provision for civilian passengers."

"England is attempting to embroil our submarines with neutral nations," von Papen said. "We must insist that you warn the English that you will hold them strictly accountable for any loss of American lives."

It took all of Robert Lansing's decorum to stay in his chair.

"Captain," he said slowly, "we cannot hold England accountable for events that have not occurred."

The attaché leaned across Lansing's desk and pressed a white-gloved fingertip against the gray folder. "These orders have already occurred, Herr Lansing. If the neutral nations cannot convince the British to retract these orders, then Germany must follow England's lead and abandon the rules of encounter."

Lansing looked at von Bernstorff. "Your aide, sir, is threatening citizens with submarine attack."

The count looked in confusion from one man to the other.

Von Papen snapped to his feet. "The threat, Herr Lansing, comes from England, not from Germany. Will you be so kind as to convey our views to your Secretary of State."

He placed the briefcase under his arm. The ambassador, realizing that his aide was adjourning the meeting, stood up from the chair. Lansing rose as well, his eyes burning at the miniature Prussian warlord. Von Papen's heels clicked like a rifle shot. He marched out of the office, with the ambassador stumbling at his heels.

"Damn," Lansing cursed as soon as the door closed. He picked up the gray folder and slammed it down on his desk. What could have ever prompted the British to put such blatantly illegal decisions into writing? Of course the documents were genuine. If William Jennings Bryan took this folder to the President, then Wilson would have no choice. He would have to prohibit Americans from traveling on British passenger ships and deny the use of American ports to England's armed merchantmen. He would have to demand that England give up the use of American flags. It would mean the end of all material support that America was providing to the side it unofficially favored. It would also mean the end of Lansing's usefulness to the industrialists and bankers who were profiting from filling the British arsenals and whose support was important to his heady political ambitions.

Lansing slipped the documents into his bottom drawer. At his next meeting with Secretary Bryan he would casually mention the "forged British orders" that had gotten von Papen into an uproar.

London. When Captain Reginald Hall entered Churchill's office, Winston was at his desk poring over estimates of the navy's reserves of critical war materials. The information had sunk his generally optimistic outlook into a sea of despair. All mining in the English Channel and along the North Sea coast would have to be suspended in three months because the supplies of guncotton had been exhausted. Everywhere he looked, scarcities of supplies were proving to be a more lethal enemy than the Germans.

"I hope you have some good news for me," he mumbled without looking up to greet his guest.

"I think so," Hall said as he settled into a chair. "I think we've found that mailbox in Germany that you were looking for."

"A communications channel?" the First Lord of the Admiralty asked. "Where?"

"Ireland," the intelligence officer said. "The Germans seem to be reading our traffic through the radio station at Crookhaven."

Churchill's face showed its mischievous smile. "I might have known. The damned Fenians. How did you find it?"

Hall smiled broadly. "We invented a ship and then broadcast messages to it using different radio channels and different ciphers. Of course, we continued listening in on the German submarine frequencies. The first time we used the Crookhaven transmitter, we picked up a German broadcast referencing our fictional ship. Then we invented other ships and radioed to them through Crookhaven, using different ciphers. No matter which code we used, the Germans learned about it."

"Then it's not our codes that have been broken. The Germans seem to have found a spy in Ireland."

"Precisely."

"Any ideas?" Churchill asked.

"That's a bit sticky," Captain Hall confessed. "We deliver our Irish traffic to Admiral Coke, in Queenstown. We use telephone lines between Queenstown and our communications center at Crookhaven. There are two possibilities: the Irishers have a tap on our phone lines"—Hall grimaced—"or it's one of our own people."

Churchill lit a cigar carefully, then puffed it like a steam engine. "For the time being," he concluded, "let's leave things alone. I'd like to find out who the spy is, but I want to leave him in place."

Hall nodded. "And feed him bogus information."

"No. I think the information should be valid," the First Lord answered. "I'd rather not give the Germans any reason to suspect that we're on to the Crookhaven leak."

"Then I won't look too hard for the spy. But still, for appearances, I should send someone out there to look into the matter."

Churchill brightened. "Perhaps an officer with impeccable credentials." He opened his desk drawer, fumbled about briefly, then withdrew a letter and slipped it across to Hall. "I was asked to find a position for this man. Something that wouldn't get him killed."

"William Day," Hall said as he read Sir Peter's letter. "Isn't he the chap who rescued half a dozen shipmates from *Aboukir*?"

Churchill nodded. "A fine officer. We could assign him to Admiral Coke, in Queenstown, and then have Coke put him in charge of the southern coast."

Hall stood and walked to the door. Then he turned back. "You appreciate that if we use Crookhaven, we risk handing the Germans one of our own ships. It could be disastrous."

Churchill lifted his cigar from the corner of his mouth. "If we pick the right ship, it will be disastrous. For Germany."

New York. "You'll be joining us for Christmas?" Sir Peter asked as he pushed an enormous stack of papers into his briefcase.

Commander Day was standing by the window of the British purchasing board's fourth-floor office, looking out at the snow that was beginning to accumulate in the street below. He turned to Sir Peter. "If you're sure it won't be an intrusion."

"Nonsense. You're one of the family." He suddenly looked up, embarrassed at his choice of words. They both knew it was not true. William Day was most certainly not one of the family.

Day's recall orders had come the day before, and Beecham had launched into a tirade, complaining that the Admiralty had no right to rob him of such a valuable assistant. But William knew his transfer had been requested, and guessed that it was precisely to ensure that he would never become one of the family. "That's very kind of you," he said.

"Not kind at all," Beecham said, trying to recover from his gaffe. "We both could do with a holiday."

They had been working long hours and had had only modest success. They had gotten a respectable buy on twenty thousand time-delay shell fuses. But the order for eight thousand bags of black powder had slipped through their fingers when German purchasing agents topped their final price. And then there was the guncotton. Twice they thought they had a contract for Du Pont's entire production of the highly explosive material, only to have the company quote a new and higher price.

"You should have better luck in the new year," Day consoled the older man. "The Germans will run out of credit before we do."

Beecham had slipped into his topcoat. "I'm sure you're right. Things have to get better. But that guncotton would have made a great Christmas present for Winston."

Day stayed by the window until he saw Sir Peter cross the street below. He went to Beecham's desk and found the unsigned agreement for the guncotton. Then he took his cap and greatcoat, and locked the office door behind him.

The snow, which had begun falling at midday, was turning into a blizzard. Day set his head into the wind and walked up Broadway. He could only hope that Harry Sinclair was still in his office.

He reached the Nassau Building and rode the elevator to the Du Pont offices, on the fifth floor. He entered the reception area, where a matronly secretary led him back to the executive offices.

"Commander Day. Did we have an appointment?" Harry Sinclair was a bullet-headed man, with a mournful expression.

"No, we didn't," Day answered, crossing to the uncomfortable leather chair that faced across Sinclair's oak desk. "I just dropped in on the chance that you might spare me a minute."

"That's about all I have. Sir Peter isn't with you?"

"As a matter of fact, he's not. But I thought you and I might be able to wrap this up without him."

"The pyroxylin?" Sinclair said, using the technical name for guncotton. "Are you entering a new bid?"

Day pulled out the unsigned contract. "No. I was simply hoping that we might come to an agreement on the outstanding bid. I've been called back to sea duty, and I'd feel a good deal better if I knew we had the pyroxylin instead of the Germans."

"Commander Day, we are a neutral country, and this is simply a business transaction," Sinclair said. "I don't care who gets the pyroxylin. I do care about getting the best price."

Day opened the contract. "I thought our offer was very generous. It's sixty percent higher than your list price."

Sinclair rose from his chair, signaling the end of the meeting. "I can see you don't know a great deal about business."

Day remained in his chair. "I'm sure you're right. On the other hand, I don't think you know a great deal about war. You're talking about your associates' getting rich. I'm talking about my associates' getting killed." He set the contract on the desk. "Sir Peter has already signed. All we need is your signature."

Sinclair looked down at the document, then looked back up in disbelief at Day. "I have no intention of signing anything."

"That's very brave of you, Mr. Sinclair." Day rose slowly from the chair, walked back to the door, and turned the key in the lock. Then he walked across the room and threw open the window.

Sinclair recoiled from the icy blast that rushed into the room. "Are you crazy? What the hell are you doing?" he demanded.

Day responded with two strong hands that grabbed the astonished businessman under the arms, snapped him off his feet, and lifted him steadily toward the open window. "Diplomatic immunity," the commander explained patiently as he tilted Sinclair's head into the opening. "All they can do is send me back to England. And without that guncotton I'll be safer in jail."

"You can't do this," Sinclair screamed.

Day dropped the man's back down on the windowsill, grabbed his knees, and began pushing him out over the edge. Sinclair let out a bloodcurdling scream, but it was hardly a whisper into the snowy wind that was rushing along the side of the building. Sinclair's hands were flailing in space. Day's grip slipped down to his ankles.

"I'll sign. For heaven's sake, I'll sign!"

Day hesitated for a moment of exaggerated indecision. Then he dragged Sinclair back through the window and set him carefully into his chair. The man sat wide-eyed. Melting snow dripped from his bald head down over his face.

"Close the window," Sinclair panted.

Day nodded toward the contract, scattered on the desk. Sinclair opened his desk drawer and found a pen. He scribbled a shaky signature across the bottom of the agreement.

Day lowered the window. "You've made a wise decision," he commented as he gathered up the contract. "You can tell your people that the Germans never met the price. And I'll tell mine that you wanted us to have it."

"You're crazy," Sinclair blurted, his eyes still wide with terror.

"Desperate," Day answered after a thoughtful pause. "I think desperate is a better word." He unlocked the door. "We'll have our check to you right after the holiday."

"You would have done it—dropped me out the window."

"What kind of a way is that to conduct business?"

PETER Beecham was the Christmas elf, determined to bring magic to the holiday. At home he had supervised everything. The sprigs of holly that were affixed to every door. The candles, one carefully placed in each of the house's windows. The stockings that hung above the fireplace. And of course, the Christmas tree.

"Not another like it in all the world," he had said. It was a thick blue spruce, reaching to the fifteen-foot ceiling in the music room and decorated with the traditional ribboned fruit and candy canes. Delicate candles were set at the tips of the branches and filled the room with a warming glow on Christmas Eve.

He rubbed his hands in anticipation as Anne found her gift under the tree, a small package containing an antique silver ring, which she slipped on her finger and modeled with great joy. Then it was his turn to unwrap the box Anne had given him. It was a gold tiepin, which he pronounced the most beautiful he had ever seen.

"Well now, what have we here?" Sir Peter handed a box to Day. "Saint Nick seems to have left a gift for you, William."

Day carefully removed the paper despite Jennifer's urging him to tear it. He found a small ebony chest, fastened with a gold clasp. He opened it and from its soft felt interior lifted a snowy white meer-schaum pipe.

"Peter says that sea captains need a good pipe to smoke on the bridge," Anne explained. "And we all know that you'll soon have your own command."

Day held the pipe as though it were a relic. "It will take a fine ship to deserve such a pipe on its bridge," he told her.

He found under the tree a small flat box, which he gave to Anne. She opened it, lifted out an embroidered handkerchief, and thanked him as though it were the one thing she had wanted since childhood. Then he took an envelope from his jacket pocket. "Merry Christmas, Sir Peter."

Beecham's eyes widened. He ran his finger under the flap and drew out an official-looking document.

"You said it would be a fine Christmas present for Mr.

Churchill," Day reminded him. "I thought you deserved it more."

Peter glanced at the familiar guncotton contract, then flipped to the last page, where he found Harry Sinclair's signature.

"We have it all," Day said. "Delivery by the first of May."

"But how—"

"I appealed to his best instincts," Day said.

Beecham could see that his wife and daughter were bewildered. "A very important contract that I thought I had lost," he told them. "William has saved it for me." He turned back to Day. "William— " Sir Peter tried to begin. But the best he could do was shake his head. "I think there are many men who would want to thank you," he finally managed.

William saved his gift for Jennifer until they were alone, walking on the packed-snow path that led to the carriage house. He had stripped his bank account to find a gift that would tell her how much she meant to him. And yet that was exactly the wrong message he should be delivering to someone whom he would probably never see again.

She opened the package eagerly and gasped when she saw the string of pearls. "Put them on me," she said, handing him the pearls and turning her back to him. "I don't think I'll ever take them off."

He laughed when she turned back to him, the pearls hanging outside her coat.

Jennifer reached into her pocket and produced a small, square package trimmed with lace. "And this is for you, William."

He examined it curiously and took out a heavy gold signet ring, his initials cut into it. "Now this is something *I'll* never want to take off. It's beautiful." He began slipping it onto his ring finger.

"Read it. It's inscribed." She turned it in his palm and pointed with her fingertip: I'LL ALWAYS LOVE YOU. JENNIFER.

Slowly he closed his fist around the ring. His muscles tightened, as if he were fighting against an intense physical pain. She took his strong hand in hers, and slowly his grip on the ring relaxed.

"It's true. I'll always love you. You do love me?" she asked.

Day looked down at the ring in his hand. "If I were half the man your father wants for you, I'd be able to tell you, No, I don't love you. That would be the right thing for me to say."

"Then you do love me," she answered joyfully. "We're in love, and love changes everything, doesn't it?"

He looked at her, then shook his head. "No. Not everything."

She launched into a speech that she had been rehearsing for days. "I know you'll be away and that I won't see you for months on end. But thousands of women are waiting alone. Something could happen to you. And then we would never be together. That's why we should be together now. While we can."

Carefully he took the ring and slipped it onto his finger. He took her hand, and they began walking toward the carriage house.

"A year or so ago," he began, "all the officers in the navy were from important families. I became an officer because with the war they needed people to command their ships. The war will end," he went on softly, "and we'll all go back to where we belong. There are rules among people. Rules that none of us can change. Jennifer, my father is a longshoreman. He carries heavy cases up the sides of ships on his back. The house that I'll go back to after the war is smaller than that carriage house."

"I'd be happy with you in a carriage house," she insisted.

"And when would you wear your pearls?" he asked.

She pulled her hand away angrily. "You're making fun of me!"

He reached for her, but Jennifer backed away, tears showing on her cheeks. "I'm not making fun of you," Day insisted.

"Then trust me. Trust that I can make everything work."

He answered the only way he could. "No, I can't do that."

Her eyes filled with rage. She turned away, lifted the hem of her coat, and began running back toward the house.

"Jennifer!" He tried to call her, but the sound died on his lips. He had ended it. And whether now or later, he knew it had to end.

When he finally returned, the music room was empty, the Christmas tree pretending to a joy that seemed to have fled the house.

Winter 1915

CHAPTER 5

Schull. Emmett Hayes narrowed his eyes behind his wire-framed glasses and bounced the ruler in the palm of his hand. He stared down at the red-haired boy, whose face was rapidly draining of color. "Terrance, is this the best you can do?"

"Yes, sir," the alto voice answered in a whisper.

Hayes looked down at the penciled page that rested on his desk.

He studied it for a moment, then pushed it aside in disgust. "Well, your best isn't good enough. And what does that mean?"

The boy shuffled his heavy shoes. "That I have to do better."

Hayes picked up the paper, jamming it into the small hand. "So do it again. Tonight. Without a single mistake. Is that clear?"

"Yes, sir," Terrance whispered. The boy turned, and tiptoed a few steps before he broke into a run. As he flashed through the doorway he nearly collided with Father Brendan Connors.

The priest sauntered into the room, his biretta square on top of his close-cut white hair, the buttons of his cassock turning in a detour around his ample paunch. "I thought it was a murder he was seeing, Emmett."

The schoolteacher slipped on his topcoat and took his umbrella from the clothes tree. "The boy is lazy."

"You're too hard on them," the priest advised. "They're just tenants. In Ireland it's enough if we can teach them their prayers."

Emmett gathered up his books. "We've been using prayers for five hundred years, Father. It's time we started using our heads."

Connors laughed. "You're on your way to sainthood. You've got no faith and not a drop of charity. But I've never met a man so blessed with hope." He waited as Hayes locked the schoolhouse door, then started down the narrow street.

"Father," Hayes called after him, smiling. "I don't have hope. I have plans."

Emmett was an oddity in Schull, always dressed in a jacket and tie in a population of rough shirts and shapeless sweaters. He was small and delicate, while most of the men were brawny. He was always armed with books, which were a curiosity to neighbors who could neither read nor write. Only forty years old, he carried himself like the village patriarch. And yet they loved him. Hayes represented intelligence to people buried in ignorance.

"Nasty weather, Mr. Hayes," James Corcoran said from behind the counter as Emmett entered his store.

"Nasty indeed, Mr. Corcoran," Hayes echoed.

"Terrible for the rheumatism," Corcoran said.

"Just a bit of cheese today." Emmett hung his umbrella on the counter while he dug for his wallet. "And a pint of milk."

Corcoran lifted a cheese wheel onto the counter, positioned his knife to outline a wedge, and cut down.

Hayes counted out the coins while Corcoran wrapped the cheese in paper and stuffed the package and the milk bottle into a paper bag. Hayes pushed his books into the bag and retrieved the umbrella. "I hope your rheumatism is better, Mr. Corcoran." He swung the door closed behind him.

He walked to the end of the main street, then turned down a row of small stone houses that led up the hill, away from the water. His house was at the end of the row. There were two steps up to the door that opened into a parlor, with the kitchen behind.

Hayes set the paper bag on the kitchen table, unwrapped the cheese, and carried it with the milk to the icebox. He then took the cheese wrapper with him upstairs to his bedroom.

Emmett lifted the small brass key that hung from his watch chain and unlocked the armoire. He took a starched white shirt from a stack on one of the shelves, unfolded it, and removed the shirt cardboard. With the cardboard in one hand and the cheese wrapper in the other, he sat down at a desk beneath the front window. Carefully he copied the words written on the wrapper.

Steamer *Edmund Hampton*. Dep. Philadelphia 8 January. Arr. Liverpool 19 January. Escort rendezvous 180 Fastnet 10 miles, 2300 GMT 18 January. HMS *Juno* assigned.

He opened the fold in the shirt cardboard and removed a code table that substituted random letters for each letter of the alphabet. Over the next two hours he calculated the proper substitutions until he had translated the message into gibberish.

When he finished, he folded the shirt around the cardboard, replaced it with the other shirts, and locked the armoire. He crumpled up the cheese wrapper into an ashtray and struck a match to it. Then he carried the coded message down to the cellar.

The radio was built into a sewing-machine cabinet. Hayes lifted the top and swung the radio up into position. As he sat rocking his feet on the metal treadle, the sewing-machine belt turned the armature of a generator. The needle climbed into the required power range. Then he tapped out a call sign on the telegrapher's key. Immediately the signal was repeated, telling Hayes that a German operator was ready to receive.

He keyed his coded message, and then he signed it with his identification name, Leprechaun.

Crookhaven. "Attention on deck!"

Chief Radioman Richard Gore rolled off the dilapidated sofa and sprang to his feet, buttoning his uniform jacket. Radioman Tommy Halliday, who had shouted the order, stood at ramrod attention, still holding the teapot he had been pouring from when Commander Day pushed open the door.

"Stand down," Day responded. He shook the mist from his cap.

"Welcome to Crookhaven radio station," Gore said. "We wasn't expectin' you till tonight. We would've tidied up a bit."

"I got an early start," Day explained, offering his hand. "Commander William Day. It's good to be here."

"Radio Chief Richard Gore," the petty officer responded, shaking Day's hand. "This is Radioman Halliday. Get the commander a cup," he ordered the radioman.

"Not yet," Day said. "I'd like to have a look around first."

Crookhaven station stood atop a rocky mountain that rose two hundred feet out of the sea at the southwestern tip of Ireland. On its western end was Mizen Head Light, the first point of warning for ships coming in from the Atlantic. The gate to the station was just outside the tiny village of Crookhaven, where the road from Skibbereen ended. The station's two buildings were identical to any of the stone cottages that dotted the coastline. It might have been a farm except for the two towers that stabbed a hundred feet into the sky, above the land line.

The cottage Gore stepped out of with Day served as the communications office. It housed the transmitter and receiver—giant boxes filled with glowing vacuum tubes—and two desks, with telegraph keys and telephones. One bedroom served as the coding room.

The other cottage served as the crew's quarters. The loft was fitted out with a row of narrow beds and footlockers. The sink, stove, and kitchen table functioned as the mess hall.

"We've got six men out here," the chief explained as they walked through the deep, wet grass. "Myself, two radio ratings, and three able bodies who stand guard watches."

"Only three guards? Is that enough?"

"I think so, Commander. For show mostly. The locals aren't fond of us, but they mind their business. Shiela McDevitt, our coding clerk, keeps 'em in line. She's Irish and was raised around here."

"Isn't she on duty?" Day asked.

"Oh, she's always on duty. Only coding clerk we have. But she can't live out here, you know, with six men. She lives near Schull and comes out every morning. She's doing some shopping today. We wanted a nice table in the mess. In honor of your arrival."

They walked to the edge of the station, where a sheer wall of stone dropped down into the crashing sea. They were at the western tip of Europe, looking at the sea-lane that carried the blood England needed to stay alive. The radio tower was essential to keep that blood flowing. Yet all Day had to keep it in operation were a few seamen and a coding clerk doubling as a housekeeper.

Day started back toward the communications office, the chief scurrying to keep up with him. As they turned the corner of the cottage Day saw a woman on a bicycle riding up the path from the guard gate. "Looks like our coding clerk is back from her shopping," he said to Gore.

Shiela McDevitt pedaled hard to move the bicycle, with its basket full of packages, into the face of the wind. She wore a wool hat, and a heavy sweater over a long skirt. She was breathing hard when she stepped down. She pulled off the hat and let long red hair fall down around a fair Celtic face with striking green eyes. "You must be Commander Day."

"Our new area commanding officer," Chief Gore added.

"Well, I hope you like fish, Commander," she said, "because there isn't a piece of beef in any store in Schull."

"Fish will be perfect." Day smiled.

"We'll get it started." The chief reached for the packages.

"In the meantime," Day asked Shiela, "I wonder if we could take a look at your coding operation."

Inside, Shiela took off her sweater, revealing a long-sleeved white blouse tied at the collar with a green bow. She was an athletic-looking woman in her late twenties. She had a businesslike appearance, which she confirmed by asking Day to produce his security authorization before she unlocked the door to the coding room.

The room was bare except for a rolltop desk and an iron safe. Messages, Shiela explained, were delivered in plain language from Queenstown over an Admiralty telephone line. She used the code books, kept in the locked safe, to translate them into the day's cipher and then gave the coded copies to the radioman for transmission. Incoming messages were handled in the same way: the radioman copied a coded transmission, and Shiela translated it into plain language before the message was telephoned to Queenstown.

Day saw immediately that the system was anything but secure. Anyone tapping the phone line would have access to the plain-language text. "Why use a telephone?" he asked. "Couldn't the traffic be handled by a messenger?"

"I suppose you've driven the roads," Shiela answered. "You could spend a whole day getting here by car from Queenstown."

Day nodded grimly. "Then we have to be damn sure of that line. Chief Gore tells me you know this country."

"I lived here as a child. Until I was twelve. Then the family picked up and moved to Liverpool, looking for work. I suppose that's why the Admiralty assigned me here. I've been away for seventeen years, but nothing has changed."

"Maybe I can borrow you for a few hours each day?" he asked. "I'd like to get to know the area. Particularly the coastline."

"You're the commanding officer," Shiela said.

HE WAS wearing a civilian suit when he met Shiela next morning at the station. "What do you want to see first?" she asked.

"The fishing harbors. I'm hoping to put a fleet together to help us with the German submarines." She glanced across at him and smiled, wondering if he had any idea what he would find.

It was a motley group of battered boats, tied to a sinking pier. Wooden dories with pegs for oarlocks. Rusted bumboats with single-cylinder steam engines and woodburning boilers. Ancient gaff riggers with patches on their canvas.

They stood on the main street looking down a grass slope, over the harbor at Schull. Beyond it was Roaringwater Bay, dotted with barren rocky islands, and Cape Clear, set into the distant mist.

"They could do it," he told Shiela.

"Battle submarines?" she asked incredulously.

"They don't have to fight the submarines," he answered. "All they have to do is keep them from surfacing. Submarines have to come up for air every few hours and recharge their batteries."

Day and Shiela had spent most of the day touring the weather-beaten coastal towns stretching along the southern cliffs from Glandore all the way to the western tip of Mizen Head.

"There's some fishing," Shiela had explained. "And some of

them carry small cargoes down from Cork. But it's all coastal traffic. None of these boats would ever venture out into the ocean."

But Day hadn't been thinking of long voyages. He had been thinking of the coastal waters that ships inbound from America passed through on their way to Coningbeg Light and Saint George's Channel.

Shiela pointed down to a twenty-foot sloop that was struggling into the harbor, its rails nearly in the water. "A submarine would be afraid to surface next to that?"

Day nodded. "Yes. A submarine is helpless when it first breaks the surface. It's completely unarmed until its crew can get out on deck and man the guns. Any of these boats with a single machine gun could get the crewmen before they ever cleared the hatches."

"But they don't have guns," she said, dismissing the idea.

"I can get the guns," Day said. "And some sailors to man the guns. What I need are the boats, and the people to sail them. Three or four towns could supply all the boats we'd need."

"These people?" she said. "Irishmen? You expect them to give up their livelihoods to help the British navy? We're the enemy, you know. The Germans are their liberators."

"We'd pay them. There are people making a fortune out of this war. Why shouldn't the Irish get a bit of it?"

Shiela smiled and shook her head. "I don't think you'll have much luck. A man who took money from the English would have a hard time finding a friend in Schull. Or Glandore or Baltimore."

They climbed back into Day's canvas-topped touring car. He drove carefully through a throng of gawking children and started down the town's single main street.

"If we could recruit one town," he said, "and people were making money, the other towns might want their fair share, too."

Shiela turned to him sympathetically. "I don't think you know what you're up against. The Fenians would come down hard on anyone who helped you."

He nodded. "I don't expect to win over the radicals. But what about the rest of the people?"

"I was born here," she answered. "But I became English, and now I've come back working for the English. I have cousins in Schull who won't speak to me."

"Insanity," he said.

They were on the main east–west road that ran along the coast from Skibbereen to Crookhaven.

"Could we go right here?" Shiela asked as they reached a small intersection. "There's something I want you to see."

Day turned inland, driving through treeless country—large mounds of stone, with occasional green pastures between the rocks. There was a stark desolation to the landscape.

Shiela leaned forward as they came to a bend in the road. "You can stop anywhere along here."

"Here?" He braked the car. "There's nothing here."

Shiela got out and started up a slope, into a grassy field.

Day caught up with her. "Where are we going?"

"A cemetery. It's right ahead of us."

He was bewildered. There was no trace of a wall, a gate, a monument, or even a headstone. And then, half buried in the grass, he spotted a small stone marker leaning awkwardly to one side.

As she walked, Shiela pointed at the marker, which bore no inscription. Day hesitated at the stone, then ran a few steps to catch up. There was another headstone. And then another behind that. Now Day could make out uneven rows of stones, stretching out into the distance, their tops hardly visible over the swaying grass.

"The children's cemetery," she told him.

"Children? Only children?"

"Three hundred of them. Most of them never had headstones. They were buried sixty-five years ago, during the famine."

He was angered by the sight. "Why in heaven's name doesn't someone take care of this place?"

"Who?" she challenged. "They have no families. No one even knew their names. See—the stones have no names. Just a year: 1851."

"They all died in the same year?"

"At the worst of the famine. There was no food, so the families gave whatever they could scratch from the ground to their children. The parents ate grass. And when they died, there were hundreds of orphaned children roaming the countryside. The English governor, who visited here once or twice a year, left one of his relatives in charge. A cousin from London, if I remember."

He looked at the tiny stones. "We didn't feed them?"

"Parliament tried," Shiela said. "They allocated money and gave it to the cousin. But he put it in his pocket and never left London. The children died in the fields, trying to graze like cattle."

William dropped to one knee and brushed the dirt from one of the stones. "What happened to the cousin?"

"I understand he made quite a success in finance. They tell me he was knighted."

Day walked slowly down a row of stones. He found one fallen, and bent to straighten it. When he reached the end of the row, he turned and walked down the next one, twisting his cap in his hands. Finally he stopped and looked at Shiela.

"I should be getting back," she told him. "There may be messages waiting to be coded."

"Then I'll wait until you finish, and take you home." Day went to her, took her hand, and led her back to the car.

They drove in silence. When they reached the radio station, they left the car at the gate and walked up to the radio cottage. "It has to be difficult for you," he said, "working for the English in a place where Irish children are buried."

"I have a job to do," Shiela answered.

"So do I," Day said. "And I have to have those boats."

Shiela nodded. "I'll do everything I can, Commander. I just wanted you to know what you're up against."

CHAPTER 6

The Irish Coast. Lieutenant Walter Schwieger raised his binoculars and scanned the crystal night air, tracing a horizon illuminated into a silver line by thousands of stars. Still no sign of the British steamer *Hampton,* due from Philadelphia, with a cargo of smokeless powder and electrical apparatus. But he had to be patient.

He had been vectored to his position southwest of Mizen Head by Flotilla Commander Bauer. An Irish agent named Leprechaun had relayed orders intended for the cruiser *Juno,* assigning her to meet *Hampton* ten miles south of Fastnet Light. Bauer had ordered U-20 to take up station thirty miles farther west. To meet up with her escort, *Hampton* would have to steam across U-20.

The temperature was below zero. Schwieger ran his hand over his face, scattering the ice crystals that his breath had formed in his beard. Then once again he began the slow scan with his binoculars.

He saw her—so clearly that he wondered how he could have missed her on his last search. *Hampton* seemed to have jumped up from the horizon—a black hull, with her funnel and masts etched clearly in the light sky. He bent down toward the open hatch behind him. "Haupert, she's here," he called to his executive officer in the control room below. "Let's dive." He dropped through the hatch and spun the locking wheel to secure it.

The clatter of the diesel engines stopped, replaced by the hum of the electric motors. Seawater gurgled into the ballast tanks. Water closed over U-20's deck, and then everything was silent.

"Come to two eight zero," Schwieger told the helmsman, turning his boat toward the target. He guessed that *Hampton* was five miles away; he should wait fifteen minutes before raising the scope.

"You want the boarding party ready?" Haupert asked.

Schwieger shook his head. "She's British, Willi. We just tell the crew to get off, and then sink the thing."

"I hope they have warm coats," Haupert commented idly.

They waited in silence. Schwieger checked his watch, then pointed to the periscope. He bent over to catch it as it came up from its tube. As soon as it broke the surface, he saw *Hampton* dead-on framed against the sky, no more than two miles away. Then he juggled the range finder to bracket the ship from the waterline to the top of its mast. "Three thousand yards."

He stepped back from the scope as it lowered. "Come left to one eight zero." The helmsman spun the wheel. They would run five minutes to the south of *Hampton*'s course line and then come about. That would bring the freighter about five hundred yards across his bow. Schwieger watched the time tick past on the chronometer. "Full left rudder. Come about to north." When the compass settled at north, he signaled Haupert to raise the scope.

Hampton was to port, running in a straight line. Schwieger pushed the scope down. "Right on schedule."

"This is almost too easy," Haupert said.

They heard the propeller, a faint throbbing.

"Stand by for surface attack," Haupert shouted down into the hull. Two seamen charged up into the conning tower, one carrying a machine gun, the other a battery-powered carbon lamp. They took positions under the hatch.

Schwieger exchanged a glance with Haupert. "Surface!"

There was a whistle as valves were opened to release compressed air into the ballast tanks. The lightened boat began to rise immediately, and then there was a crashing sound as the conning tower broke through the surface. Schwieger waited until the gunner had thrown open the hatch cover.

"Surface running! All ahead one third!" Schwieger scampered up the ladder, with Haupert at his heels.

Hampton was still to port, steaming directly across his bow. "Right standard rudder," Schwieger ordered, bringing U-20 to a parallel course. He looked aft. His gun crew was already on deck, swinging the machine gun out toward the target. The first round of ammunition was being passed up toward the breech.

A searchlight switched on aboard *Hampton*. Its beam swung abruptly down the gray hull of the U-boat. Schwieger ordered his own light turned on and aimed directly at *Hampton*'s bridge. He lifted his megaphone. "Heave to! This is the German submarine U-20. I order you to heave to immediately."

The beam of *Hampton*'s light found the submarine's conning tower and lifted until it hit Schwieger in the eyes.

"Turn off that light," he ordered.

The beam painted the tower, then dropped down to illuminate the gunners, who raised their hands to shield their eyes.

"Get the light," Schwieger ordered the machine gunner.

The chatter of the gun exploded through the still night. There was a puff of flame, and then the light went black.

"Heave to!" Schwieger ordered again. The freighter was pulling ahead of him. "All ahead full!" he shouted down into the hatch.

"She has a deck gun!" The frightened scream came from Weiser, his gunnery officer. "On the fantail."

U-20's light snapped to the freighter's transom to reveal a five-inch deck gun, its muzzle swinging toward the U-boat. At the same instant, Weiser's crew was bringing U-20's gun to bear.

"Fire!" Schwieger ordered. Then into the hatch, "Hard right rudder!" He was turning his boat to present the smallest possible target to the freighter.

U-20's gun flashed. There was no explosion aboard *Hampton*. The shell had sailed over the steamer's stern. Endless seconds passed. *Hampton*'s deck gun was now aimed over Schwieger's head, its barrel slowly depressing toward his face.

The steamer's gun roared—a sound twice as deafening as the crack of U-20's deck weapon. The sea just beyond the submarine's hull leaped up into a frothy geyser. The round had passed just inches over U-20's deck.

Haupert cursed as the submarine's gun fired again. *Hampton*'s afterdeck house flashed into flame.

"She's turning on us," the machine gunner screamed.

The freighter's prow was quickly swinging toward them.

"She's going to ram us," Haupert gasped.

"Clear the deck," Schwieger screamed at his gun crew. "Hard right rudder," he yelled into the opening. "Dive! Emergency dive!"

The gun crew had disappeared down the hatch and Haupert was jumping into the hole when *Hampton*'s deck gun roared again. U-20 lurched with a metallic ringing. Schwieger dropped through the hatch and pulled it down on top of him.

"We're hit!" The scream came from the control room below.

Schwieger looked down and saw jets of water flying across his control room. He pushed Haupert toward the lower hatch. "Get me a damage report." Haupert disappeared down the ladder.

Schwieger was suddenly aware of a new sound. *Hampton*'s bow was cutting through the sea almost directly over his head. He cringed from the roar of the charging steamer.

There was a terrifying howl of metal as *Hampton*'s hull grazed across the conning tower. U-20 lurched suddenly onto its right side. The impact smashed Schwieger against the tower wall. Screams echoed through the hull. The entire crew had been tossed from their stations and had fallen against the bulkheads. The deafening pound of the propeller cut through the water inches above the hull.

Schwieger opened his eyes, to find his world totally disoriented. He was lying on one of the walls of the tower, looking up at the other wall. The ladder to the overhead hatch ran from side to side instead of vertically. U-20 was spiraling into a deadly dive even though it was lying on its side. The rudder, locked in a hard right turn, was increasing the angle of dive.

"Amidships," he screamed, crawling up the inclined deck until he could see down through the hatch. "Rudder amidships." But the wheel was unmanned. Streams of water were still firing into the control room.

Schwieger pushed his legs through the hatch opening and scrambled along the ladder. He grabbed the helm and began cranking the wheel to the left. A seaman was fighting his way up the nearly vertical deck toward the bow-plane control. "Neutral," Schwieger yelled to him. "Neutralize the bow."

Haupert had dragged himself forward to the ballast-control levers. "Lighten the starboard tank. Carefully," the commanding officer ordered. Haupert tapped the lever to a slightly open position. Instantly the boat began bringing itself to an upright attitude. The bow was slowly lifting out of its dive, but water was still pouring in through the port bulkhead. Schwieger had to get the boat back up to the surface to relieve the pressure on the hull.

The control-room crewmen were back at their posts. Schwieger checked the depth gauge. The boat had dived a hundred and sixty feet—nearly to its safety limits—but now was rising slowly.

"Take us up to thirty feet," he told Haupert. He couldn't break the surface until he was sure of his distance from *Hampton*. If he came up under its deck gun, he wouldn't be up for long.

Schwieger scrambled up the ladder to get to the periscope. There was an inch of water on the conning-tower deck, fed by a jet from the periscope packing. He pulled down on the counterweight cable. The periscope started to slide upward, then suddenly stopped. It had been bent at the point where it passed through the packing and out through the top of the tower. It was useless.

He cursed and went back down into the control room, where Haupert had ordered the torpedo crew to shore up the leaking bulkhead. It was then that Schwieger heard the distant throbbing of a propeller growing louder—*Hampton* was hoping to finish off the submarine she had crippled.

"Level. Come left to zero nine zero," Schwieger ordered his helmsman. Haupert's eyes widened. Schwieger was turning the U-20 toward *Hampton*.

The propellers pounded directly overhead, but Schwieger ignored them. He was still too far below *Hampton*'s keel to be in any danger, and he had more pressing matters to deal with.

"Steady on zero nine zero," the helmsman called.

"Take her up to twenty feet," Schwieger ordered. The bow struggled upward. Water that had spilled into the forward torpedo room poured back through the hatch into the control room. As the bow lightened, it began to swing into a climb.

"We're going to make it," Haupert said with a smile of relief. "We should get out of here, surface, and pump her out."

"Not while that s.o.b. is still afloat," Schwieger whispered. Haupert's eyes narrowed. U-20 was crippled and, without its periscope, blinded. Schwieger was noted for his caution. It was frightening that he was even considering an attack.

"She'll make one more pass looking for us," Schwieger said softly, as if he were talking to himself. "Then she'll get back on course and head for Fastnet. And that's when we'll take her."

"How will you aim?" Haupert asked cautiously.

"From the surface," Schwieger answered.

"You're going to *surface?*" Haupert asked. Despite his best effort, his disbelief was obvious to everyone in the control room. Schwieger's eyes darted in his direction. Haupert turned away.

"Leveling at twenty feet," a seaman intoned. Schwieger listened carefully. There was no sound from *Hampton's* propellers. *Hampton's* captain, Schwieger figured, would have turned in a circle and recrossed the point where he had seen the submarine dive. He'd run another minute or so and then give up the hunt and turn back to his original easterly course.

In the intervening time, U-20 would have moved perhaps fifteen hundred yards down *Hampton's* course. If U-20 turned back toward her, he could surface dead ahead of her as she ran to the east. Then *Hampton's* captain would have two choices: he could keep coming, hoping to ram the submarine, or he could turn away, opening up the distance and bringing his deck gun to bear.

"He'll turn," Schwieger said aloud. "The bastard will turn."

It was eight minutes since *Hampton* had thundered past above his head. If he was right, she would be charging back now.

"Steady at twenty feet," the seaman said.

"Very well," Schwieger answered. "Steady as she goes."

Haupert stepped away from a voice tube. "The gun crew is ready," he reported.

"Very well," Schwieger acknowledged. But he wouldn't need his deck gun. When the boat came up, only he would go topside. This was a matter between himself and *Hampton's* captain. The man had broken the rules. Schwieger could envision the steamer's crew searching for debris to confirm their kill. Would they lower the lifeboat that he had been prepared to afford to *Hampton's* crew?

He doubted it. They were the ones who had turned the gentleman's game into cold-blooded murder. And he would make them pay.

"Prepare to surface," he ordered. Silently the control-room crewmen eyed one another. "Haupert, open the outer doors and get on the firing board. I want to be ready to fire torpedoes."

"Aye, aye," Haupert answered softly. Schwieger climbed the ladder and opened the hatch into the tower, ignoring the water that poured in on top of him. He closed the hatch and moved up the next ladder. When he felt the tower break the surface, he popped the hatch to the deck and rushed up into the cold night air.

The tower had buckled, the periscope fixtures had been cut away, and the life rails were cut and twisted. Schwieger had to squeeze himself through a tangle of steel. He saw *Hampton* no more than five hundred yards away, headed across U-20's port bow.

"Surprise," he whispered. "Now what are you going to do?"

Hampton did nothing, and continued in a straight line.

"Full ahead," Schwieger called down through the hatch.

He heard *Hampton*'s emergency whistle sound. Then he saw a white spray kick up from the steamer's bow. *Hampton* began turning to starboard, trying to bring its deck gun around.

"Left ten degrees rudder," Schwieger screamed into the hatch. "Stand by to fire one and two." His bow began to swing, until it pointed to the open sea ahead of his target.

"Fire one." He heard the hiss of air and saw the explosion of bubbles at his own bow as the torpedo was blown out of the tube.

"Right ten degrees rudder." The swing of the boat was immediately checked. At the same time, *Hampton* was turning, presenting its port beam. Behind its damaged afterdeck house Schwieger could see the five-inch gun coming into view.

"Fire two," he ordered. He could see the trace bubbles of his first torpedo, pointing ahead of the British ship, in case she broke off her turn. The second trace was aiming directly at her hull.

"Dive," he screamed. He was starting down the hatch when he heard the roar of *Hampton*'s big deck gun, and the sea exploded twenty yards off his starboard beam. As he pulled the hatch cover shut, the ocean washed over the top of the tower.

He lifted the next hatch and dropped into the control room. Anxious faces looked up at him. "Hard right rudder. Take her to fifty feet." He was aiming to get below the impact of the next shell.

They listened in silence. The seconds ticked by like hammer blows on an anvil.

And then there was the muffled sound of a distant explosion. Haupert's face broke into a broad grin. Schwieger responded with the thumbs-up signal. One of the torpedoes had found its mark.

"Come to zero nine zero," Schwieger ordered. "Surface." He nodded to Haupert. "Come with me. You'll want to see this."

They rushed up to the deck as soon as the conning tower broke the surface. The horizon to the south was glowing brightly. At its center *Hampton* was ablaze, spewing jets of white fire.

The torpedo had hit either in the boiler room or the engine room. Secondary explosions were racking the ship.

"Should we get closer?" Haupert asked. If a target didn't sink immediately, they would finish it off with their deck gun.

"Not this one," Schwieger answered. "She's carrying black powder. We don't want to get too close."

As if on cue, *Hampton* exploded in a blinding flash of light, causing the officers to cover their eyes. The thunderclap was nearly deafening. When they looked back, the steamer had vanished, leaving a scattering of burning debris across the surface.

Washington. "Barbaric," President Woodrow Wilson said sadly. "Simply barbaric." He shook his head slowly in despair. "I can only hope we never become involved."

"Let's be sure that we don't," Secretary of State William Jennings Bryan advised. "It's an English ship sunk by a German ship. The United States has nothing to do with it. I don't see any reason why we should file a formal protest."

Wilson bent over the document that had been delivered by His Majesty's embassy only a few hours earlier.

The steamer *Hampton* was torpedoed without warning. No challenge was given, nor was there any attempt to inspect her cargo. Constant cannon fire from the attacking submarine prevented *Hampton* from launching her boats. No assistance was offered to her crewmen, who were left helpless in the water.

"The point here," said State Department counselor Robert Lansing, "is one of international law. As the Secretary advises, there would generally be no reason for our government to become involved in actions between foreign belligerents. But when confronted with such a flagrant violation of international law, we have a duty to protest in the strongest terms. We must remember that the rules of encounter protect American ships from being accidentally attacked. We can't simply ignore the wanton murder of an unarmed commercial vessel's crew."

"Robert has a point," the President said to his Secretary of State.

Bryan was pinching an enormous handkerchief against his nose. He blew furiously, then stuffed the handkerchief into his trouser pocket. "Are you sure it was unarmed, Robert?" he challenged. "There were two English ships in New York last week that had gun mountings on their fantails, and von Papen is telling anyone who will listen that the Admiralty is arming merchant ships. He mentioned some documents that he had left with you."

"Crude forgeries," Lansing fired back. "Who told you there were gun mountings on English freighters?"

The President knocked gently on his desk. "Gentlemen, please. The issue is how to keep our country out of this madness."

"I think, Mr. President," Lansing offered, "that whatever we do must be solidly grounded in international law. You have spoken eloquently on the rule of law as our only hope for peace. Perhaps I should prepare a brief on the legal precedents involved."

Bryan's eyes rolled. The legal precedents would be as crooked as the people who had written them. Why couldn't this fool President understand that we had no business trying to play the world's peacemaker or—what was that idiotic phrase of Wilson's?—making the world "safe for democracy."

"Robert, how long will it take you to pull something together?" Woodrow Wilson asked.

"A few days. Certainly no more than a week."

"Good," Wilson said, jumping up from his desk. "We'll review Robert's brief. Then we'll decide on the proper course of action."

Lansing flashed his most enthusiastic smile. He'd write a legal brief tracing the righteousness of the rules of encounter all the way back to Henry VIII. He would prove that there was no more honorable principle among men than respect for the right of an unarmed merchant ship passing through hostile waters. When he was finished, the President would have no choice but to call the Germans to task.

Wilhelmshaven. *Friedrich der Grosse,* the flagship of the Imperial Fleet, rose like a castle in the great northern German naval harbor. Topped with colorful flags and bristling with twelve-inch guns, she was a floating military pageant. But the heavy links of iron that chained her to the bottom of the harbor belied the impression of a fearsome naval warrior. Like the rest of the great German High Seas Fleet, *Friedrich der Grosse* was going nowhere.

Submarine Flotilla Commander Bauer hated his visits to the flagship. As he stepped onto the companion ladder he heard the ceremonial boatswain's pipe announce his arrival. Why did his every coming and going require that hundreds of sailors stop work and render a ceremonial salute? He had forbidden the ridiculous piping aboard his beloved submarines. If it had been up to him, Bauer would never have left the submarine docks at Emden, where his little gray boats came and went. But this visit to Wilhelmshaven was different. Bauer was on a mission.

When he entered the conference room, Admiral von Pohl was already holding court, surrounded by his staff of admirals and captains. Bauer took his place at one of the tables, nodding an apology to von Pohl for his tardiness. As he listened to the bland recital of facts and figures he fidgeted with the report he had brought with him. "Captain Bauer," he heard von Pohl's adjutant say.

He was on his feet instantly. "I regret that I must ask permission for my command to depart from the international rules of encounter." Nodding heads snapped to attention. "British merchantmen are now attacking our submarines instead of obeying their challenges."

There was a gasp, followed by a rumble of murmuring. Admiral von Pohl slapped his hand on the table to restore order. "You know this for a fact?" he demanded.

Bauer held up the report from Lieutenant Schwieger, commanding officer of U-20. "The British steamer *Hampton* was challenged by U-20 three nights ago. *Hampton* responded with cannon fire from a five-inch gun mounted on her fantail. Then she turned toward the submarine and rammed her."

"Our boat was lost?"

"Fortunately, no, sir. U-20 can't submerge without taking on water, but I'm pleased to add that she carried out her mission. *Hampton* and her cargo of war materials were sunk."

"I can't believe the English would depart from their cruiser rules," a supply officer said.

"We can't fire without warning," a staff admiral shouted. "It would bring the whole civilized world down on us."

"And I can't ask my crews to expose themselves to five-inch cannons and to ramming," Bauer fired back.

Shouts rang from every corner of the room. If Bauer's boats could fire without warning from beneath the surface, there was little need for the Imperial Fleet's dreadnoughts. Without the rules of encounter, submarines were the most lethal weapon afloat.

Von Pohl's hand exploded on the table, followed by a deadly silence. "The business of this meeting is concluded," he whispered as he rose. The room snapped to attention. And then, almost as an afterthought, he told Bauer, "May I see you in my quarters."

The fleet commander was undoing the top button of his tunic when Bauer was saluted into his stateroom. Von Pohl settled into a chair and gestured Bauer toward a sofa. "One ramming could mean nothing," he said. "It could be a merchant captain panicking at the sight of a submarine. But the deck gun—that's a different story. If they are arming their merchant ships, then they are abandoning the rules of encounter."

"Exactly," Bauer agreed. "Which is why we should no longer be bound by them. It's suicide for a submarine."

The fleet commander wagged his head. "I have no problem when it comes to English freighters. But what about passenger ships carrying Americans? Or English ships flying American flags?"

"The Americans are no better than the English," Bauer answered. He handed von Pohl a page from the report he had prepared. "This is an intercept from our Irish agent. He has direct access to British radio traffic from Queenstown. It orders an escort for an American ship inbound from New York. Why would they be escorting it if it weren't carrying contraband?"

Von Pohl read the message. "My dear Bauer," he said, "you are getting into issues of national policy. The Emperor has personally forbidden me to risk attack on an American ship. You want permission to fire without warning. And you may not always be able to determine whether the target is an English ship flying the American flag, which I would love to sink, or an American ship, which I am forbidden to sink. You see the position you are putting me in."

Bauer nodded. "I believe it is exactly the position that the Admiralty wants to put you in."

"Do you have any suggestions that I can bring to the Emperor?"

"I would declare the waters around Ireland and England a war zone," Bauer said. "I would warn all neutrals that all ships entering the zone do so at their own risk."

"A war zone," von Pohl considered. "I wonder how President Wilson would respond to a war zone."

"It's fair warning. It should certainly encourage him to make certain that English ships aren't flying the American flag."

Von Pohl lifted himself from his chair and paced his stateroom. "For the time being," he concluded, "I will allow underwater attack on merchant ships you can positively identify as English."

Bauer tapped the page of his report. "And here, where an intercept tells us a neutral ship is carrying contraband?"

"Not until I have the Emperor's permission," von Pohl said.

"War materials will get through," Bauer warned.

Von Pohl nodded. "I know that. And I will make exactly that point to the Emperor. Perhaps together with the idea of a war zone . . . Who knows what his Imperial Majesty will decide."

Bauer didn't have much hope. But as far as the British merchant fleet was concerned, the rules of encounter had been repealed.

CHAPTER 7

Schull. The lifeboat staggered into Roaringwater Bay just after daybreak, carrying a cargo of battered, frightened men, with white eyes staring from behind coal-blackened faces. Their hands shook on the cups of hot tea that the people of Schull rushed down to the landing.

They were survivors of the British steamship *Ikeria*, which had been torpedoed and then riddled by gunfire during a night of unspeakable terror. The ship, on course for Liverpool, was carrying artillery shells. She had cleared Mizen Head Light when the U-boat surfaced no more than a hundred yards off her port beam. It attacked without warning, causing explosions that echoed like thunderclaps, bouncing people out of bed all along the Irish shore. From Crookhaven to Baltimore, people with coats pulled over their nightshirts hurried to the beach. They could make out the shape of a ship at the base of the towering column of flame. Then there was a white flash, so brilliant that for an instant the flames were invisible. The impact hit them with the roar of a whirlwind. A moment later the flames were gone.

"Poor lads," the women allowed, even though the survivors were English. Even the men, raised on a venom of hatred for their English oppressors, nodded in sympathy. "Hun bastards," they agreed when they heard of the Germans who had fired without warning and then disappeared without any concern for the survivors.

The bodies began washing ashore the next afternoon. They were scorched black, and bloated with seawater. Some had lost limbs.

"BARBARIC," Father Connors said. He reached for the tea that his housekeeper was serving, then turned to William Day and Shiela McDevitt, who were sitting across from him. "I'll do everything I can to encourage the people to cooperate with you, Commander. Now, I can't promise anything. There's no great sympathy here for the English. But we're all outraged by what the Germans did."

"There are dangers," Day repeated. "I wouldn't want your people to underestimate them."

Father Connors nodded. "I understand. And I wouldn't underestimate the attractiveness of the wage you'll be paying. That kind of money can do a great deal for these poor people."

There was a tap on the door, and a small bespectacled man in an ill-fitting suit peeked into the parlor.

"Ah, Emmett," Father Connors announced. And then, turning to Day, "This is our schoolteacher, Emmett Hayes. And this is Commander Day. You already know Shiela." Day rose and shook hands. Hayes bowed toward Shiela.

"Emmett enjoys great respect in our community," Father Connors told Day. "I think he could be a great help in your efforts."

Day explained his plan for using the town's boats in his submarine patrols. Hayes seemed enthusiastic. "But I wonder," the teacher asked, "how you'll fix the positions of the boats. It would take a great deal of organization. These are not highly educated people."

"A grid based on lines of bearing from the shore," Day said. "Something that any seagoing man with a compass would know."

Emmett Hayes smiled. "Well, I could help you there. I'd be happy to rehearse each group on the bearings you assigned."

Day nodded his appreciation.

"Then you'll help persuade the community to take part in the commander's efforts?" Father Connors concluded.

"Certainly," Emmett Hayes volunteered.

The priest adjourned the meeting with a reassuring smile.

Day was buoyant as he and Shiela walked back to his car.

"Easier than I expected," he told her.

"Much easier," she agreed. "I think the Germans did our work for us when they sank that ship."

His flagship was *Hugh O'Neill,* a thirty-two-foot yacht with a white lapstrake hull, gleaming brightwork, and a woodburning steam engine. His fleet was an assortment of peeling work barges and gut-stained fishing boats, some with engines, some with sails; his crew, a gathering of withered old men and cherub-faced boys.

Shiela and Emmett had done Day's recruiting, with Father Connors standing in the background to nod his approval. They organized into three fleets, so that all in all, they were denying the U-boats fifty miles of hunting grounds, from Fastnet Rock all the way to the Old Head of Kinsale.

In Schull, where one fleet was based, they used Hayes' schoolhouse for meetings. Day had drawn a grid on a chart of the coastline, with one boat positioned at each intersection. All the captains had to do was hold a position at the intersection of the two bearings.

While Day laid out the battle plan, British sailors from Queenstown armed the boats. Machine guns were installed on the bows of boats that had enough good wood on their decks to hold screws and bolts. Rifles were put aboard the others. Day had been able to get only enough sailors to man a few of the guns. On the others they trained Irishmen as the gunners.

And now they were putting to sea for the first time. Thomas McCabe, owner of the long-idled *Hugh O'Neill,* cast off and stood behind the polished teak wheel. His nephew opened the throttle, and the yacht moved away from the pier. Then there was the choking of oil engines, which sent clouds of smoke into the air, and the screeching of wooden blocks as drab sails were hoisted up dozens of masts. The Schull fleet fell into line in the wake of Day's flagship.

They charged out into Roaringwater Bay, heading toward their stations. Captains leaned out over the prows, breathing in the adventure that had suddenly turned the routine of daily voyages into the excitement of the hunt for dark shapes and probing periscopes.

Day watched from the bow of *Hugh O'Neill,* amazed at what he saw. The tattered sails on the sailboats that hung like dead skin at their moorings flexed with muscle when they reached the open sea. Engines that were coughing and sputtering in the safe harbor of Schull began pounding with energy. Voices called from boat to boat with a new camaraderie.

There were mistakes, just as Day had anticipated. Three of the boats rushed up to the same station, nearly colliding as none of them would give ground.

"Do you have any idea where you are, Peter Farley?" an angry Tim Sheehy called.

"I'd be on my mark if you'd get that washtub out of my way."

Hugh O'Neill steamed from station to station, arbitrating disputes and checking on the bearings. But boredom came with the sun. Once they reached their stations, the crews had nothing to do.

Then just before noon the masts of a freighter appeared on the horizon. They sent up a cheer as the ship slipped safely through their formation. And then the endless waiting began again.

One of the sailboats dropped a fishing net over the side, and then a powerboat took to the idea and wandered off its bearings to set its nets in a more promising quarter. Other boats did the same. Day went after them, urging them back to their stations. But by mid-afternoon there was no trace of the pattern he had on his chart.

A flare suddenly exploded in the sky to the west. Day snapped his binoculars to his face. One of the distant sailboats was coming about smartly, its crew waving wildly at a nearby powerboat. Then another flare shot up from the powerboat as it suddenly kicked up a wake and began rushing toward the sailboat.

"Submarine!" Day heard from a workboat that was drifting off his starboard quarter. The boat roared off to the rescue.

McCabe's nephew began tossing armloads of wood at the base of the boiler. The captain of *Hugh O'Neill* swung the wheel to give chase. "We've got one," he screamed at Day.

In an instant every boat in the formation was charging toward the flares. Throttles were pushed to the stops. The crews leaned into the wind, urging more speed out of their boats.

Through his glasses Day could see that the fleet was beginning to crowd together around the same spot. It was all wrong. A U-boat would have no trouble slipping away in just the few minutes that it would take the fleet to gather. And then if she surfaced, she would have all the boats in one place—a perfect target for her deck gun.

Their safety, he had explained, depended on keeping their stations, giving the submarine no safe place to surface. But there was action at hand, and no one wanted to be left as a bystander.

Day heard a blast of machine-gun fire. On one workboat a crewman was aiming a deck-mounted gun into the gap between the two boats that had launched the flares. His second burst of fire sent the boats scattering in fear of their lives.

Within a fifty-yard radius Day suddenly had ten boats turning in all directions, cutting dangerously across one another. A rifleman was squeezing off round after round into the churning water at the center of the chaos.

"Cease fire!" Day screamed through his megaphone, punctuating his order with blasts on *Hugh O'Neill*'s steam whistle. As suddenly as it had begun, the attack on the submarine ended. The whistle caught the attention of the boat crews, and every head turned toward *Hugh O'Neill*.

"It *was* a submarine," the captain who had fired the first flare announced sheepishly to his neighbors.

"Let's go home," Day said. And *Hugh O'Neill* led its sullen squadron back toward the tilting pier of Schull.

In Emmett Hayes' schoolhouse, Day handed out the assignments for the next day's grid and spent a moment with each of his captains to argue the importance of holding his station. Later he drove in the darkness to Ballydehob, where he met with the officers who commanded the other two fishing-boat fleets—one at Baltimore and one farther east, at Courtmacsherry, near Kinsale. Their reports were similar to his own: a morning burst of enthusiasm, followed by a deterioration in station keeping as boredom set in.

"It's falling apart after one day," one of the officers said. "What's it going to be like after a week?"

Day shrugged his shoulders. "Keep after them," he said. "As long as they're out there, the U-boats have a problem."

He dismissed his officers and motored back to Crookhaven, and spent an hour with Shiela McDevitt and Chief Gore reviewing the day's radio traffic. Messages had gone out to six incoming ships—two British and four neutral. Only three could be assigned escorts.

Rules of Encounter

The others were advised that a fleet of fishing boats would be on station to discourage submarine operations. Day allowed himself a smile of satisfaction—Queenstown was already counting on his Irish navy.

He drove Shiela back down the dark road to Schull, telling her about the day's adventure.

"Was it really a submarine?" she asked in disbelief.

"Probably not." He laughed. "Maybe the shadow of a cloud."

He pulled up to her house, a small old stone cottage on a long-abandoned farm.

"Let me make you a cup of tea," Shiela offered.

Day followed her into a small brightly painted parlor, with a freshly covered sofa and soft chairs. He dropped wearily onto the sofa while Shiela raked the coals in the cast-iron stove and set a kettle of water over the embers. She spooned tea into a porcelain pot and put cream into a small pitcher. Then she set a tray with two cups and carried it back into the parlor.

Day was fast asleep. Shiela set the tray down and whispered his name. When there was no response, she brought in a blanket and spread it over him, then lifted his feet onto the cushions.

At the edge of the town, Emmett Hayes tapped out the coded details of Day's patrol plan for the next morning on his radio. He signed off, "Leprechaun."

"Stop here for a moment," Shiela said. There was a smile playing across her lips.

Day pulled the car to the siding. "What are you up to?"

Shiela jumped out and lifted the basket she had placed on the back seat. "Lunchtime," she answered.

"Lunch?" he asked, as if it were an unknown word. "We haven't time."

"You never have time," Shiela answered. "But today you're going to have lunch. In the most beautiful dining room in all of Europe. And you can watch your fleet while you eat." She started up the rocky hill that led to a bluff beyond the harbor. Day hung back for a moment, thinking of all the places he had to be. Then he shrugged in resignation and started after her.

They walked out onto a point of land that held Roaringwater Bay to the west and the sea to the south and east. The warm spring sun sparkled off the waves. Shiela opened her basket, handed Day a tablecloth to spread, and began unpacking the basket.

They had been together for the past two weeks, touring the coastline during the days and working at the radio station at night. Their days began in the darkness, when William turned his car up the path to Shiela's cottage. They drove first to one of the harbors, arriving before the boats set out, so that Day could talk to the officer, deliver new instructions, and review the day's sailing plan.

They stopped at the towns and paid calls on the local leaders. Sometimes they met in the drawing room of an English landowner, who acted as Day's paymaster, handing over the wages when the crews docked at night. In other towns the leader was the parish priest. Wherever they went, Shiela took care of the social necessities, her Irish conversation winning friends and making Day seem more the ally than the area commander for an occupying force.

At night at the radio station, Day checked the afternoon traffic while Shiela translated any coded messages. Then he would drive her to her cottage and continue on to his quarters at a boarding-house to catch a few hours' sleep.

They took their meals wherever they happened to be. Sometimes it was as the car bounced along the roads, or in a pub or a rectory. Often it was at the mess in the radio station.

Now Shiela spread the picnic fare on the tablecloth. She had sandwiches made with thick cuts of cheese and thin slices of lamb, a salad of pickled vegetables, a dessert of raisin cakes, and two bottles of dark beer. Day's eyes widened when he saw the food.

"You must have been working all night," he said.

She smiled at the compliment. "It's the first quiet meal we've had in a month. I wanted it to be special."

"Special it is. I've worked you very hard," he told her, "and I've never said thank you. Do you understand that I'm very grateful for all the help you've given me? I wouldn't be anywhere without you."

She broke a sandwich and shared it with him. "I understand that you've thrown yourself into this with your whole heart. You're doing a wonderful job, but I'm terribly afraid that you're letting yourself in for a disappointment."

"There are still ships being sunk," he said. "Fourteen freighters last month. And as many more this month."

"You can't stop it. The ocean is too big for you to make it safe."

Day shook his head in despair. He tasted the beer and began devouring the sandwich, but he noticed Shiela wasn't eating.

"You need a ship," she told him. "They owe it to you."

He smiled. "Sounds as if you'd be happy to be rid of me."

"No," she said, looking away from him. "But I'd be happy to see you out of Ireland. This country is a bog that swallows up good men. The jealousy and the hatred are in the air. We take it in with every breath. Sooner or later it destroys everything that's good."

"The Irish are helping me," he argued.

"You're paying their wages," she said. "But heaven help you if a few of them should get killed by one of the U-boats. Then they'd turn on you in a minute because you're English."

"You're English," he reminded her.

"Yes," Shiela said bitterly. "The worst kind. I was one of them, and I left. So I'm not just their enemy. I'm a traitor. But I'm also Irish. I have no place to go."

He reached out to her. "I'll be careful," he promised.

"Careful isn't enough." She pushed his hand away. "There are things happening all around you that you can't understand."

"What things? Tell me."

Shiela looked at him and then jumped up and ran to the edge of the bluff. He went after her, but she turned her back to him. He realized that she was crying.

"Please, tell me what's wrong," Day begged her.

He could hardly hear her answer. "I'm afraid."

"Afraid of what?"

"Afraid for you," Shiela said. She turned to face him, her eyes red. "Make them give you a ship. Get away from here while you can."

He took her in his arms and held her. He could feel her trembling.

"I'm sorry," Shiela finally managed. "I wanted this to be a happy afternoon for you. And now I've spoiled it." She ran back to the tablecloth and began gathering up the remains of the picnic.

They drove back to Crookhaven, where Shiela disappeared into the coding room. While she worked, Day reviewed the day's traffic with Chief Gore. There were eight ships approaching the Irish coast within twenty-four hours. Coded messages had to be prepared for each. It was already dark when she handed her last message to the radioman for transmission.

Day navigated carefully back down the dark road to Schull, with

Shiela sitting silently by his side. They had always filled their journeys with chatter about their work. But now their relationship was changed. *"Afraid for you,"* she had said. And he understood that because of him, she was frightened for herself. He suddenly understood how alone and helpless she was, caught in the no-man's-land of hatred that separated England and Ireland. In her tears, she had shown him how deeply she cared for him. Now he knew how deeply he cared for her.

He swung the automobile to a stop in front of her doorway. On other nights they had continued talking for a few moments before she jumped down from the car. But tonight Shiela said a simple "Thank you" as she reached for her basket. She was stepping out onto the running board when he caught her hand.

"Thank you for the picnic," Day said.

She started to pull away, but he held on to her hand.

"Don't worry about me," he told her.

"I can't help it," Shiela admitted. "Please ask them for a ship. Something that will take you away from here."

Day shook his head slowly. "I can't leave you here alone." He was still holding her hand, leaning across the empty seat as she stood outside the car.

"We shouldn't be holding on to each other," Shiela warned.

"We have no one else to hold on to," Day said.

Shiela leaned across him and raised the magneto lever behind the steering wheel. The engine stuttered and then was silent.

They lay together in her small bed, her head resting on his shoulder, her long hair flowing across his chest. In the faint lamplight he could see the white curve of her shoulder. And the sparkle of the signet ring on his hand, which rested softly on her arm.

Day tried not to think of the inscription that it bore.

New York. Jennifer read the newspapers every day, searching out the most optimistic reports of the war. If she came upon a more pessimistic report, she tried to dismiss it. Surely William had meant that their marriage was impossible only because of his military duty. He was simply trying to protect her from the war.

But even she couldn't ignore the grim reports from the windswept waters off the Irish coast. Reports of British ship losses were appearing every day. She assumed that William had his own command, probably one of the destroyers that were frequently reported to be hunting the submarines.

"I shouldn't be surprised if he were commanding one of those," her father told her, although he insisted he had no way of knowing where Commander Day had actually been stationed.

During the week, when her father was away in the city, Jennifer wrote letters constantly, beginning them early in the week and then hurrying to finish them by the weekend so that her father could take them back to the city and include them in the diplomatic pouch for London. She addressed them just as Sir Peter had advised—to Commander William Day, in care of the Admiralty. "The navy will see that he gets them," he assured her.

But there were no return letters. Not that Jennifer expected William to match her output of trivial news, coupled with expressions of concern. But still, she longed for an acknowledgment that he was getting her letters and that they were important to him.

As Anne watched her daughter's inexhaustible devotion, her hopes that Jennifer would outgrow her attachment to Commander Day faded. She tried to offer new interests, involving Jennifer in her charitable work, encouraging her to join other young people in their social circle. Jennifer complied, but always with half a heart.

"We're going to have to tell her," Anne finally confronted her husband in the late night quiet of their bedroom.

"Tell her what?" he answered in despair. "That I've been lying to her all along? How will that make things any better?"

"They can only get worse. She's in love with him."

But they didn't tell her. There was never the perfect moment. Sir Peter began to think of writing a frank letter to his former aide requesting that he write Jennifer and put an end to her misunderstandings. He knew where Day was stationed. But each time he was about to take up his pen, he remembered the night when he had seen them together on the terrace and realized that the man was in love with his daughter.

"Do you think that it might work out between them?" he suggested one evening to Anne. "I mean, the world is changing. The old rules—I wonder if they're still so important?"

"I've been asking myself the same question. I wonder if Jennifer will ever meet a more honorable man."

Sir Peter pounded his fist against his stuffed chair. "We carry these blasted class distinctions too far, I tell you. There are young men dying for England who wouldn't be welcome at my table. What is the matter with me?"

Anne placed her hand over his. "I think we should forward her letters. It's their future. They'll have to make their own rules."

Beecham's eyes brightened. "I'll take them on Monday."

He was away from the house when Jennifer recalled an article on British naval operations that she had cut from the *Herald* and given her father. She entered the library. Beecham's huge rolltop desk was open. She glanced across the mail slots, looking for the collection of clippings that she knew he kept. When she didn't see them, she slid open the top drawer. The clippings were there. She lifted them out carefully. It was completely by accident that she noticed the pale yellow envelopes that were her private stationery.

William Day's name was written on the top envelope in her own hand. Beneath it was another, again addressed with William's name. She tossed through the entire stack. When she finally understood, she felt a flash of rage. And then she began to feel sick. She closed the drawer and rushed out of the room.

Jennifer didn't come down for dinner that evening. Early the next morning she walked into the library, where Sir Peter was already hard at work. She carefully placed the letters on top of a document that he was reading. "You sent him away," she said.

Sir Peter looked up helplessly at her. He couldn't bring himself to admit his crime. He could only nod, and then he noticed with horror that her eyes were worn from crying. "Please," he begged. "Let me try to—"

"I'll be going to join him," Jennifer answered.

He knew that she would, and he could scarcely breathe as he watched her walk out of the room. Like all fathers who have ever lied to a child, he realized that he had forfeited his special place in her life and that he would never be welcomed back.

CHAPTER 8

Coningbeg Light. "Lightship two points off the port bow" came the message from the crow's nest.

Captain Daniel Dow smiled and raised his binoculars. He could feel the coiled muscles in his back begin to unwind.

To save coal, Cunard had shut down one of *Lusitania's* four boiler rooms, reducing her flank speed from twenty-six knots to a hair over twenty knots. It was still fast enough to outrun any submarine, but not nearly fast enough for Fairweather Dow. He had been frozen in terror during his passage along the Irish coast.

He had welcomed the sight of his escort *Juno* when she had appeared, but had begun to worry again when he was forced to shave two knots off his speed so that *Juno* could keep up. The sight of Day's fishing fleet had eased his anxiety, but then *Juno* turned off to her anchorage at Queenstown. For the past three hours he had been running alone.

His passengers were completely unconcerned since sighting land. Now the women were in their staterooms, compressing their wardrobes into steamer trunks, while the men were in the lounges, ordering their last drinks before the bars shut down.

The Coningbeg lightship was now clearly visible, no more than fifteen minutes ahead. Dow would swing around her and send the Greyhound charging into Saint George's Channel. The dangerous part of his crossing was behind him, he thought.

He left the wheelhouse and walked out to the bridge, where he stood beside the lookout and looked straight down at the bubbling wash five stories below. Every bit of space forward of where he stood, from three stories above the waterline down to the keel, was given over to the Admiralty's secret cargo. During the entire crossing Dow had worried about what it might be. Now he didn't particularly care. He turned back toward the wheelhouse.

"Submarine! Submarine! Periscope to port!" The scream came from behind him, from the lookout he had just left.

"Hard right rudder," Captain Dow screamed into the wheelhouse. Then he rushed back out to the bridge. The periscope was only five hundred yards on his port beam.

Immediately *Lusitania* began turning to starboard, away from the U-boat, her slender hull leaning into a sharp list. In the cabins below, steamer trunks crashed into bulkheads. In the lounges, glasses slid onto the Oriental carpets.

Dow saw the periscope swinging toward his stern as *Lusitania* turned away. He watched until the periscope disappeared under his fantail. "Rudder amidships," he ordered. The giant ship began to right itself as it straightened into a southerly course, away from

Coningbeg lightship. He shut his eyes and began to count the seconds it would take a torpedo to overtake his Greyhound.

There was no explosion—only a cacophony of voices as the enraged passengers rushed out onto the weather deck. They had picked themselves up from the force of the sharp turn, realized that something was wrong, and came to see for themselves.

"Submarine!" voices shouted. Hands pointed toward the stern, where the periscope had matched *Lusitania's* turn.

Dow looked over his stern. The periscope was still there, but it was falling behind. Another minute, and he would be out of range.

The lookout was searching beyond the wake with his binoculars. "She's gone now, Captain." But Dow was anything but relieved. How could he come about and head into the channel if the submarine might be lying there, waiting for him?

He dashed to the chart room. If he ran to the east for an hour, he could open up fifteen miles between *Lusitania* and the submarine. Then if he turned to the north, he could probably beat the U-boat back to Coningbeg. "Left fifteen degrees rudder," he ordered. "Course zero nine zero."

Dow quickly dictated to his wireless operator a report of the submarine sighting to relay to the naval station at Milford Haven, on the western tip of Wales. The naval station, he reasoned, would forward the report to the patrol ships. They would come out and search the area, preventing the submarine from running on the surface. All he had to do was wait until they were at the lightship.

But the high tide at the Liverpool bar wouldn't wait for him. If he missed the tide, he would be forced to circle outside the port until the next day, exposing himself to daylight attack. He had to move north soon enough to catch the tide.

His first mate was standing beside him. "Captain, there's a delegation of passengers. They insist on speaking with you."

A panic among the passengers was the last thing Dow needed. He ordered the mate to plot the point at which he had to turn north in order to reach the Liverpool bar at high tide. Then he stepped back to the officers smoking room, where five men in formal dinner dress had assembled.

"Thomas Astin," their spokesman said. "Apparently, we're in some danger."

"No danger at all," Dow reassured. "All is quite in order."

"That submarine was close enough to touch us."

"We're well away from her," Dow answered with a forced smile. "And now if you gentlemen will excuse me . . ."

He started for the door, but Astin stopped him. "But don't we have to go back toward her to get to the channel?"

"We're taking a different approach to the channel," Fairweather said. "And there are Royal Navy ships coming to escort us. So there's really nothing to worry about."

But there was, the first mate informed him back in the chart room. They had to turn north within the hour, in full daylight, to catch the tide. And there was no response from Milford Haven.

"Have wireless resend our message," Dow ordered the mate. "Tell Milford Haven that we need an escort ten miles east of Coningbeg by 1630." He paced the bridge as he waited.

Half his allotted time had elapsed before the wireless operator rushed onto the bridge with the message from Milford Haven: CONFIRM RENDEZVOUS, 090 CONINGBEG, 10 MILES, 1630.

Dow stepped back into the wheelhouse and ordered a turn to the north. He doubled his lookouts and ordered all his off-duty deck officers to lookout stations. Fifteen pairs of binoculars searched the sea, already beginning to redden from the western sun.

"I'll tell the lookouts to keep a sharp eye for the escorts," the first mate suggested.

"To hell with the escorts," Captain Dow snapped. "We'll see the escorts. Look for the periscope!"

But they didn't see the escorts. The telltale traces of smoke didn't appear on the western horizon. The first thing Dow was able to make out was the distant blinking of Coningbeg Light.

"Where in heaven's name are they?" he shouted.

"We could circle a bit," the first mate said. "They may be running a bit off schedule."

Dow nodded grimly. That was one of his alternatives. He had two other choices: turn back out to sea and add another costly day to his voyage, or rush through the gap between the lightship and the submarine he had imagined in his panic to be lurking ahead. There was no submarine in sight.

"We're going through," he finally concluded. "Break out the zigzag instructions."

The zigzag was a series of turns designed to prevent a submarine from plotting a ship's heading. Without knowing a target's exact heading, the submarine couldn't aim its torpedoes. *Lusitania* headed for the channel, and its bow began carving quick turns.

In the first-class dining room, Thomas Astin noticed his lobster bisque rolling to one side of his soup bowl. The ice in his water glass began to rattle. He glanced at one of the gentlemen from his passengers' committee. The man's expression was as white as his tie.

"Submarine!" the lookout on the port wing sang out. Dow ran to his side and focused the glasses. The periscope was high out of the water, a thousand yards off.

He was past the U-boat but still well within her firing range. Now speed was his best hope of escape, and the zigzag turns were costing him speed. He made his decision instantly. "Steady on course zero two zero."

If the U-boat captain realized that *Lusitania* had settled on a straight course, and fired immediately, the torpedo could overtake the liner. But if he hesitated, then the Greyhound's speed would carry her safely out of range.

"Captain Dow."

Fairweather followed the voice down to the boat deck, where Thomas Astin was standing with one of his associates.

"Where are our escorts?" Astin shouted.

Dow ignored the question, refocusing his glasses on the periscope.

"Escorts ahead," the first mate called. Dow wheeled around. He made out the masts of two ships steaming south toward him. When he turned back, the periscope had disappeared. He stepped to the rail. "Dead ahead, Mr. Astin."

For one horrifying hour it had all come together—the innocent passengers, the deadly cargo, and the submarine. Dow had no intention of presiding over the slaughter that such a deadly mixture was sooner or later bound to cause. The next morning he walked into the offices of Alfred Booth and resigned his command.

"I'll make sure that you never get another command," Booth screamed at his captain. "Nothing. Not even a rowboat."

But even as he was blustering, the Cunard chairman knew Dow didn't want another command. He wanted out of the war. Booth regained his composure. "Who can replace you?" he asked frankly.

"Bill Turner," Dow answered without a second's pause.

"Bowler Bill," Alfred Booth gasped in horror, thinking of

Turner's habit of wearing a bowler hat on top of his uniform jacket. "The man's a savage. He puts ketchup in his consommé!"

"Find someone else to dine with the passengers," Dow advised. "Put Bill Turner on the bridge. He's the best seaman you've got."

Schull. Day's makeshift fleet was doing its job, much to the surprise of Admiral Coke, who commanded the Irish coast from his flagship at Queenstown. The workboats and fishing vessels, armed with nothing more than rifles and light machine guns, were accomplishing off Ireland what His Majesty's mighty armada was failing to achieve in the other waters surrounding the British Isles. Since Germany's proclamation of a war zone, twenty-five British merchantmen had been sent to the bottom—in the North Sea, the North Channel, Saint George's Channel, and the Western Approaches—with nearly half a million tons of war materials. Only one had been sunk in the stretch of coast that Commander Day patrolled, and that at night, when the Irish boats weren't operating.

But Day didn't need to see the figures on ship losses. He could see the results in the faces of his crews. They had perfected their simple formations. They were in the war, doing honorable work, and that seemed more important to them than the fact that they were shoulder to shoulder with their centuries-old enemy.

Often in the mornings he sailed out with one of his fleets, racing back and forth through the formations, shouting encouragement to his captains. Mostly he was just showing a military presence, reminding the crews of the importance of their mission.

And then there was the time he spent working with Shiela McDevitt. Shiela and Day were careful, but it wasn't easy living under watchful eyes only too eager to see their failures. Her isolation, if anything, was worse than his. The women of the villages were outspoken in their scorn for her. And it was they who first sensed the personal interest the two had in each other. "He's living in her cottage," one of them told a parish priest after Day's car had been seen early one morning parked beside Shiela's house.

One day Shiela was vulgarly insulted by a woman in the docks at Baltimore. She and William went straight to her cottage, without checking back at the Crookhaven station. Day held her throughout the night and then faced Chief Gore's suspicious glances with her in the morning.

IT WAS WHILE DRIVING TO SHIELA'S house at the end of an exhausting day that Day first raised a problem that had been troubling him. "Do you think the Germans are reading our coded traffic?"

"The coded traffic? How?" she asked with an expression of fright. "It's a daily cipher. It changes every day."

"Lots of ways. A tap on the line from Queenstown. Or a leak somewhere—at Queenstown or even our people at Crookhaven."

Shiela went white at the suggestion. "I can't believe it," she said. "Do *you* think we're being compromised?"

"I'm not sure," he said. "But there are too many coincidences. Every U-boat attack over the past weeks has been on an unescorted ship. And they've also hit the most important cargoes. I just can't believe that the Germans are that lucky."

They were silent, Shiela seeming to weigh his conclusions.

"The Germans also seem to know where our fishing boats are operating," he continued. "For example, when we move to the western end of our area, they attack to the east."

Shiela was shaking her head. "But we never broadcast our fleet instructions. We hand the assignments right to the crews."

Day smiled grimly. She was correct, and he knew it wouldn't take her long to realize the implications—there was a spy in their midst. Probably the same spy who was tapping into the radio traffic.

"What about the Fenians?" he asked. "This wouldn't be one of our fishermen. Tapping phone lines and running a radio." It would take a bit of sophistication and the kind of organization that the Irish nationalists could provide. "Do you think any of the brothers might be close to us?"

Shiela shrugged. "They're everywhere. I don't know of anyone, though, who does more than talk."

When they reached the cottage, Day raised a fire in the stove for their tea. "What are you going to do?" Shiela asked.

"Inform the Admiralty." He set the kettle on the fire. "Recommend that they stop sending traffic through Crookhaven."

"And our local problem? You can't just abandon the fleets."

"We won't give out the day's patrol areas until just before the boats leave the dock. That will give the submarines less time to act."

Shiela fixed the tea and carried it into the parlor. "If they close down Crookhaven, they'll have no need for me here."

"I thought of that, too," he admitted.

"I won't leave you here alone," she said. "It's dangerous. You should be asking for a transfer."

He reached out to take her into his arms. "You're the only danger," he teased. But she pushed his hands away.

"Don't be making fun of me," she said, a sudden hurt showing in her eyes.

"I'm sorry," he told her. "Why is it dangerous?"

"Because you're asking questions," Shiela said. "They won't want you to have the answers."

London. Captain Reginald Hall rose from behind his desk as Lieutenant Peter Grace was shown into his office. Lieutenant Grace was no ordinary officer. He wore civilian clothes, had never been aboard a ship, and had no intention of ever accepting a naval command. His services to the crown were in other capacities.

"Everything tidy on the India docks?" Hall asked as soon as he had guided his guest to a chair.

"I think so," Grace answered. "Loughton's friends have been arrested. And Mr. Loughton himself is no longer operative."

Loughton, a stevedore who had been selling cargo information to a German, had been crushed under a six-ton pallet that inexplicably broke free from a cargo hoist.

Accidents seemed to follow close behind Lieutenant Grace wherever his work in counterintelligence took him. His efficiency and discretion had earned him the respect of the Admiralty.

"What do you know about southwestern Ireland?" Hall asked as a way of getting into Grace's next assignment.

"Admiral Coke's area," Grace responded. "We have a radio station there, don't we? Traffic in and out of Queenstown?"

Hall nodded. "Crookhaven. Important traffic. Arrival messages for all ships coming across the south coast." He picked up a folder from his desk. "It's run by Commander William Day, one of our best young officers. He sent this to us. Quite an accurate analysis."

Hall sat quietly while Grace flipped through the pages. "Looks as if he's on to something."

"He is," Hall answered. "We've known we had a leak at Crookhaven for quite some time, but after reading this, it looks as if there's a fair-sized operation down there."

"So you want me to check it out," the lieutenant concluded.

"As soon as possible," Hall answered. "You won't need a cover. Simply go out to Crookhaven and report to Commander Day. While he's watching the coast, you'll be watching for spies."

Grace nodded. "Seems simple enough. In fact, too simple."

"There is one complication: we'd like to know who's causing the leaks. But we don't want him to become . . . inoperative."

Grace was clearly confused.

"We need an open channel to Germany. We want them to read certain traffic that they assume we are trying to keep secure. We would like certain ships brought to their attention."

Grace's lips spread into an understanding smile. "Commander Day's discoveries aren't in the national interest."

"They could prove inopportune," Hall corrected. "With you there to follow up on his suspicions, he'll probably focus his attention on his other duties."

Grace handed the folder back to his commanding officer and stood. "You'll cover my assignment with Admiral Coke."

"Of course," Hall promised.

CHAPTER 9

Schull. Thomas McCabe's nephew tossed more logs into the firebox and watched the steam-pressure gauge inch up. He opened the throttle valve, and steam hissed into the cylinder heads. "Ready to go, Commander," he said to William Day. Day's flagship, McCabe's *Hugh O'Neill*, fell in line with the small flotilla heading out into Roaringwater Bay.

Since he had begun holding the patrol assignments until minutes before sailing, Day had gone to sea with his boats every morning. By denying the submarines that information, he was making the entire coast a high-risk area. He knew the submarines wouldn't abandon their hunting grounds. Sooner or later they would have to come to grips with his civilian navy. He wanted to be there when the danger struck.

He had done all that he could to prepare for the eventuality. A heavy machine gun was mounted on top of *Hugh O'Neill*'s wheelhouse and manned by an experienced gunner. He had also scrounged a simple foot soldier's mortar and placed it on the bow.

The boats quickly took up stations on the western edge of the patrol area, where steamers from America would first appear. The flagship began making its rounds, steaming past each of the boats.

"Not a lot of air out here, Commander," old Mike O'Sullivan said, pointing to the ripples in his sail as *Hugh O'Neill* came alongside. "Hope you won't be expecting me to go anywhere in a hurry!"

"Let's hope not, Mr. O'Sullivan," Day answered.

Three miles southwest of Mizen Head he suddenly saw a trace of soot on the horizon. "This first one through is a Yank," he said to Captain McCabe. They began the wide easterly swing beyond the seaward edge of the formation, Day keeping an eye on the American freighter until it had moved into the safe protection of his fleet. Then he searched ahead, hoping to pick up the Baltimore fleet.

They had been moving eastward for over an hour when McCabe pointed south, where a dark shape was kicking up a wake on the horizon. Day raised his glasses. "Come about," he yelled. "That's not ours."

As the yacht was turning, Day could make out the crashing spray of a bow. "Good heavens," he whispered. "It's a submarine."

"Get me all the pressure that this thing will hold," he yelled at McCabe's nephew. He screamed up to the machine gunner, "Load, and stand by to fire."

The mortar crew, on the bow, had heard the commotion, and were already prying the cover off the container of mortar shells.

"Stand by to fire!" Day ordered.

The gunner turned the crank, tipping the mortar to a thirty-five-degree angle. Day raised his hand.

"Fire!"

With a muffled *pop* the first shot he fired in the war exploded into the water ahead. It was only a fraction of the distance between *Hugh O'Neill* and its target.

"Fire!" Day ordered again.

A second explosion shattered the sea halfway to the submarine.

The U-boat commander couldn't ignore mortar fire moving closer to his boat. He would have to dive or turn his attention toward the onrushing *Hugh O'Neill*. Either way, he would be distracted from the murderous attack he was aiming toward the helpless boats in Day's flotilla. But the U-boat wasn't responding. Instead, it continued at top speed toward the boats.

A puff of smoke appeared above the submarine, followed in

seconds by the crack of its deck gun. A tall geyser of water exploded next to a small engine-powered fishing boat.

"Keep firing," Day screamed to the mortar crew. He saw the submarine's deck gun flash again. The geyser lifted the fishing boat out of the water, and the crewmen spilled out into the sea.

Hugh O'Neill's young engineer had the firebox nearly glowing. But the yacht wasn't moving nearly fast enough.

The submarine had the first row of boats at point-blank range. Its machine gun was now chattering, kicking up spray just short of its targets. The next crack of its deck gun splintered a wooden sailboat and tossed it like pieces of kindling into the air.

As soon as Day's first mortar round had exploded, the boat captains had turned to close in on the submarine, not realizing that she had approached on the surface with her gun crews ready. At the first cannon shot, they had turned in panic, nearly colliding with one another in their rush to escape. But they didn't have a chance. Running on the surface with its powerful engines, the U-boat was quickly overtaking them. They looked over their sterns, caught in a deadly lottery as the German gun crew randomly selected its victims. Within a minute, four of the Irish boats were gone, leaving frantic figures struggling in the water. Day could only watch helplessly, the action still beyond the range of his pathetic guns.

The submarine turned and took aim at the second line of the patrol, where O'Sullivan's sailboat was. O'Sullivan appeared on his transom. Defiantly he raised his English rifle toward the oncoming U-boat.

"Nooo!" Day screamed uselessly as the old man tried to steady the rifle against the sway of his own boat. O'Sullivan fired, the recoil lifting the muzzle into the air. The U-boat's gun crew dropped to the deck for cover. Suddenly the submarine commander was jabbing his finger toward the sailboat, where O'Sullivan was trying to strip a new round into the rifle chamber.

Day watched in horror as the U-boat's machine gun swung toward the old man. A hail of bullets ripped into the sailboat's transom. Suddenly O'Sullivan flew backward, tossing the gun into the air as he disappeared over the side.

Hugh O'Neill's mortar popped again, launching another shell. This time the explosion was less than fifty yards from the target. Immediately the U-boat broke off its attack and turned toward the yacht.

271

"The engine's overheating," McCabe's nephew yelled.

"Full speed," Day screamed back. It didn't matter whether the engine could destroy itself in another minute. The yacht's fate would be decided in the next twenty seconds.

The submarine's deck gun fired, and the sea exploded just off the starboard bow. The yacht pitched off its course, sending Thomas McCabe spinning across the wheelhouse. Day grabbed the wheel and twisted the bow back toward the U-boat. Whoever got off the next shot would probably be the survivor.

Above his head Day heard his machine gun begin to chatter. Bullets began ringing off the U-boat's hull, up toward the gun crew. His crew on the bow dropped another round into the mortar. The instant the round exploded out toward its target, Day spun the wheel to the right. At the same instant the U-boat's deck gun fired.

The three-inch shell ripped into the water where the yacht would have been had she continued on a straight course. A waterspout blasted into the air, pitching *Hugh O'Neill* over on her starboard side. As she struggled to right herself, rounds from the submarine's machine gun began tearing into her wheelhouse. There was a scream from overhead as the bullets raked Day's gunner, blowing him over the side. The last rounds from his machine gun had knocked down two of the German gun crew.

The mortar round was falling toward its target. Warned by its whistle, the U-boat commander ducked behind the conning-tower shield just as the shell exploded a few feet from his hull.

Day turned the yacht back toward the submarine, hoping to get off one more mortar round before the U-boat's machine gunner cut him to pieces. But there was no machine-gun fire. The submarine commander was clearing his decks, preparing to dive.

McCabe, who had been knocked down and dazed by the first shot of the submarine's deck gun, staggered to his feet. "Hold this course," Day told him, pushing him against the wheel. Day climbed up to the machine-gun position.

Through the gunsight he saw crewmen scampering down the submarine's hatches. He threw the bolt and squeezed the trigger. Instantly bullets clanged across the hull. One German dropped before he could reach the deck hatch. Another, halfway into the hatch, threw up his arms and fell into the opening.

In a cascade of bubbling water the U-boat's decks disappeared.

Day fired at the periscope. Bullets ricocheted off the steel weather shield. But with them came pieces of tubing that protected the delicate lens of the periscope. He was still pouring rounds into the U-boat's eye when she disappeared under the sea.

It was then that he realized *Hugh O'Neill* was doomed. The heat from the engine had set the afterdeck on fire; seawater was pouring in through the bullet holes that had raked the hull.

Many of the fleeing Irish boats turned back toward him and toward the crews of the sunken boats, who were struggling in the water. *Hugh O'Neill* was down to her rails when a small workboat came alongside and lifted the crew to safety. There was no satisfaction in the faces of the seamen, even though the first submarine to challenge them had been driven off. Some of their neighbors were not to be found among the survivors.

Day waited on the Schull pier as the day's toll became a reality. Five men were unaccounted for, their wives and families wandering in a daze among the survivors, crying out when their worst fears were confirmed. Two of the men were given last rites by Father Connors, then rolled carefully in sailcloth and carried by their friends toward the church.

William stood aside, the outsider to the town's grief. He saw O'Sullivan's wife, old and frail, standing on the slip where the sailboat had tied up each night. He went to her, touching her hand. When she looked up and recognized him, she screamed, her bony hands flailing out and striking at his face. "Damn you," she cursed in a shrill voice. "What good will your devil's money do him now!"

The people watched while she sagged under the effort of striking him. She fell to her knees, shaking in muffled sobs. Emmett Hayes stepped out of the crowd and helped her to her feet. He led her back to her people, and they all walked slowly toward the village, leaving Day alone on the dock.

SHIELA was waiting in the cottage doorway. She had been at the radio station when she heard of the U-boat's attack, and had begged a ride on a truck that was leaving Crookhaven.

"A bad one?" she asked as Day stepped out of the car.

He slowly nodded. "Jeremy Duke," he began, "the English sailor, shot by the submarine gunner. Pat O'Donnell and the Farley kid, lost over the side. And old Mike O'Sullivan—"

273

Shiela's hands shot to her face. "Oh, no," she groaned.

"The s.o.b. came right at us. He wasn't after a ship. He was after the boats. We drove him off. But it was a slaughter."

Shiela wasn't listening. She had collapsed sobbing onto the sofa. Day tried to take her into his arms, but she pushed him away and rushed into her bedroom. He had lost good men to the cruelty of war. But she had lost neighbors who had been part of her childhood. She needed her moment of mourning.

Pouring a heavy measure of whiskey into a glass, Day ran the dead men through his mind, forcing himself to see their faces. Had he betrayed their trust? They had died fighting his war. But no matter whose war it was, his Irish volunteers had stopped the submarines. Old Mike O'Sullivan, standing there on the transom of his sailboat, facing off against a machine gun, wasn't a fool. He was a brave man, doing what he had to do.

"It's not your fault." Shiela was standing in the doorway, her dress wrinkled, her eyes red. "It's the damned senseless war."

"I know," Day answered. "But I'm sorry for them." He turned toward her. "I'm sorry for you."

Shiela walked to him and took his hand. "We shouldn't be alone," she said. "Not tonight."

They lay together quietly. The first sounds of morning found them still in an embrace.

WHEN William Day pulled to a stop at the foot of the pier, only a few men were waiting by the boats. Day took a deep breath and tried to look confident as he walked toward them. Then he saw Emmett Hayes start down the pier to meet him.

"I don't think you'll be patrolling today," Hayes said. "Mike O'Sullivan's body came in with the tide. We're waiting on the others."

Day nodded that he understood. "I'll wait with them. I'd like to help bring them to the church."

"We'd appreciate that," the schoolteacher agreed. "But then give us a day by ourselves. We'll decide what to do next."

"NEW officer's aboard," the sentry told Day as he was being saluted through the security gate at the radio station.

"New officer?" Day stopped short.

"Yes, sir. A Lieutenant Grace. Replacement for Miss McDevitt."

Day's confusion was obvious. He turned and started up the hill. Chief Gore was waiting for him in front of the cottage.

"Did you know Shiela was leaving?" Gore asked.

"I had no idea, Chief," Day answered.

Gore threw up his hands in disgust. "Why would they move her? Don't they know how important she is to us?"

"Maybe the new lieutenant can tell us. Where is he?"

The chief pointed to the quarters cottage. "Having his lunch. Looks like he's fresh out of school. Brand-new uniform."

The boyish-looking officer sprang to attention as soon as Day stepped through the doorway. "Lieutenant Peter Grace, reporting for duty, sir," he chanted. He had a plate of kidney stew and a pot of tea set in front of him. He looked uneasily at the food and then back at the commander.

"Finish your lunch," Day offered as he dropped his cap on the table and sat opposite the officer.

Grace talked between bites. "Heard you had a bad day yesterday. This probably isn't a good time for me to be starting."

The commander nodded. "A very bad day. But a good time to have you aboard. We need help." He waited while Grace swallowed some tea. "But a bad time to be losing Miss McDevitt. Do you know when she's scheduled to leave?"

"No rush," Grace said. He glanced around, confirming that there was no one else in the cottage. "Fact is, my assignment is just a cover. I'm with naval intelligence." He pushed another kidney onto his fork, ignoring the shock in Day's face. "Nice coincidence, actually. You tell the Admiralty you suspect your radio traffic is being compromised. The Admiralty tells intelligence. So intelligence has to find a way of getting me in here without kicking up a fuss. Then Miss McDevitt asks for a transfer back to England. What's more logical than for me to arrive as her replacement?"

"She requested a transfer?" Day's surprise was obvious.

Grace shrugged. "That's what they told me." He nibbled the kidney off his fork. "Best if you can keep her awhile. Changes tend to make spies suspicious. Wouldn't help our investigation."

"Who are you investigating?"

"Everyone," Grace said. "In this business the last person you'd suspect generally turns out to be the one you're after."

Day didn't enjoy being lectured by a junior officer. "You're an old hand in intelligence, I suppose."

"I've had a few assignments," Grace said. He carried his dishes to the sink, walked back to the table, and leaned down on two strong hands. "Commander, you're the only one who knows why I'm here. And as long as I'm just a snotty brat out of officer training, we'll be able to keep it that way. Believe me, I'm very good at what I do. Every bit as good as you are in your work. I won't get in your way. Don't you get in mine."

Day looked long and hard into eyes that were suddenly cold. Then he nodded in respect. "You'll keep me informed?"

"You'll know everything I know," Grace answered.

Day stood up quickly and picked up his cap. "Let's get you introduced," he said as he started for the door.

"Aye, aye, sir." Grace stepped along behind.

He had no intention of keeping Day informed. If he had, he could have told him that he had already established that no one was tapping the telephone lines. He could have told him that the teacher who distributed his sailing orders, Emmett Hayes, had spent two years writing inflammatory editorials for a Fenian newspaper. Or he might even have warned him that the coding clerk who shared his bed was the daughter of a Free Irish labor agitator.

Lieutenant Grace was already convinced that the Crookhaven station was surrounded by Irish conspirators. He knew he could get the names anytime he wanted them. But he was in no hurry. His assignment was to keep the station operating until it delivered its critical message to the Germans. Then he would shut it down. And when he did, there would be no witnesses.

New York. Sir Peter Beecham had come to dread his weekends. From Monday to Friday he was caught up in the market for war materials. He now owned most of Du Pont's black powder and a whole production line of General Electric's motor generators. He was a bigger customer for heavy shoes than the Sears, Roebuck catalogue. True, not all his supplies were getting through. But he had passed the crisis in keeping his country outfitted.

On Saturday mornings, however, as his car drove through the gates of his home, his spirit blackened. His well-meaning lies to his daughter had destroyed the joy that once sounded through the estate like strings playing in the music room. He and Anne were sick with guilt.

A servant opened the door and took his hat and briefcase.

"Missus Beecham?" Sir Peter inquired.

"In her room, sir. I'll tell her you've arrived."

"And Jennifer?"

"Out for a walk, I believe."

"Ah, yes. Lovely morning for a walk," he said as he started into the library, which had become his own silent prison.

He went to the French doors that opened out onto the terrace. The trees, which only last week had been yellow with new buds, were now green with young leaves.

Anne entered and set down a tray with tea. "Welcome home," she said. He embraced and kissed her. He listened as she catalogued the week's events while she poured the tea and settled into a chair. Then he told her the news that had been weighing on him.

"Jennifer has booked passage to England."

Her teacup sagged against her lap. "Good heavens."

"Second class on *Atlantic,* one of the small Cunarders. Sumner just happened to come across her name on the booking register. He thought it was a mistake and called me for clarification."

"What did you tell him?"

Peter sighed. "Well, oddly enough, they're in the process of transferring the passengers to other ships. *Atlantic* is being held in England for Admiralty alterations. I asked him not to notify Jennifer. Told him that I'd take care of it."

"She was going to leave us without even saying good-bye," Anne guessed. "How she must hate us."

"Nothing of the sort," Sir Peter lied, even though he had thought exactly the same thing. "Just a show of independence."

"You'd let her go?" Anne challenged.

He held out his arms, gesturing to the silent household. "Hasn't she already gone?"

"At least talk to her," Anne begged, near tears.

His opportunity came within the hour, when Jennifer stepped through the front door and crossed toward the stairs.

"Jennifer," he called from the library doorway. She stopped abruptly, hesitating while she decided whether to acknowledge her father. "May I have a word with you? It's important."

She walked slowly into the library, never glancing in his direction, and sat down as he closed the door behind her.

"I understand you've decided to go back to England."

Her eyes widened in shock.

"I wasn't prying," Beecham hastened to reassure her. "I just happened to learn that you've booked passage."

"Even Cunard does your bidding," she said coldly.

"Nothing of the sort. It's just that the ship you booked is being pulled out of service," he said, walking to his chair.

She smiled at the irony. "The one ship I was able to get aboard is being removed from service?"

Peter reddened in embarrassment. "Now really! I don't have the power to order ocean liners about."

"No. Only people," Jennifer answered.

For an instant he thought he might explode with rage at her effrontery. But he realized that her wound was even greater than his. "I suppose I deserve that," he admitted. "I doubt I'll ever forgive myself, much less expect forgiveness from you. But if you're determined to go, at least let me help get you there safely."

"I think you've helped enough."

"For heaven's sake, Jennifer, there's a war on. Ships are being sunk right and left. At least let me get you aboard a safe ship."

She eyed him suspiciously.

"All your life your mother and I arranged things for you. It was the right thing to do. Then suddenly it was the wrong thing. We hurt you terribly. But that doesn't mean we can stop loving you."

"You'll arrange my passage?" she asked, not sure that she wasn't being led into some sort of trap.

He nodded. "*Lusitania* sails on May first. It's only one day later than you were scheduled. And she's the safest ship afloat."

"Thank you," Jennifer said. She stood and started for the door.

"You'll want to let William know that you're coming," he called after her. "I'll make sure your letter gets into Monday's pouch."

Jennifer turned and looked back at him.

"I will," Sir Peter said. "I swear I will."

Schull. The bodies of the Irish crewmen were carried into the church in plain pine boxes. Widows and mothers, their grief hidden in black veils, were led into the front rows; then the townspeople, with Shiela in their midst, filed in. William Day and his English sailors, in full-dress uniform, came in last and stood in the back.

Father Brendan Connors had decreed a High Mass. His sermon pulled together the myriad mysteries of Irish theology to prove that their fallen comrades were already in the company of the Blessed Virgin. "But these men are more than saints," he concluded. "They are also heroes in God's army. And their earthly commander is here with us today." He looked to the back of the church. "Commander Day, will you say a word?"

Even when he reached the pulpit, Day had no idea what he could say. All he could tell them was what he believed. He began with a litany of all the ships that had passed safely down the Irish coast. When he finished, he had counted more than a thousand people who had sailed under the protection of the Irish boats.

"I believe that we are all brothers," he said. "When we find ourselves caught up in a war, I believe the best of us do what we can to save one another from the slaughter. These men offered safety to a thousand of their brothers. They are the best of us."

The English sailors formed an honor guard on the steps as the bodies were carried out. After the coffins had been secured on a wagon and the procession had disappeared toward the cemetery, Emmett Hayes came out of the church and walked up to Day.

"Thank you," Hayes said. "We all appreciated your words."

"Will the men go back on patrol?" Day asked.

"I'm not sure," Hayes said. "Father Connors will know when it's time to raise the subject. Perhaps in a few weeks."

The English contingent returned to Crookhaven, where Shiela disappeared into the code room, while Day began reviewing the day's traffic. But after a short while he walked out to the edge of the cliff. He looked at the empty ocean and realized that his work in Ireland was nearly over. He had demonstrated conclusively that a fleet of small boats could keep the submarines out of the sea-lanes. But Day doubted that the Irish fleet would ever sail again. Even if the men could erase the image of the U-boat, the women would never forget the line of coffins down the center of the church.

Perhaps the Admiralty would organize a new fleet, operating from English ports. But that wasn't his affair.

Even his personal attachment to Ireland would soon be broken. Shiela's request for transfer back to England had been genuine.

She believed that Peter Grace was her replacement and that in all probability she would be gone before summer.

"I think I'm finished here," he told Shiela as they drove together back to her cottage. "I want to get back into the real navy."

"I'm glad," she said as they turned into her road. "You're better off out of here." As they opened the door to her cottage she added, "They won't forget the men they buried today. You've overstayed your welcome, if you were ever all that welcome."

They worked in silence preparing a simple supper, the question of their future hanging over them. They had come together in a moment of need, when their loneliness had driven them into each other's arms. But now the truth was upon them. Could they simply walk out of each other's lives?

Day mulled the question until they were getting ready for bed. He puffed his pillow and sat up under the comforter while she changed into her nightgown. "Can I ask you something?" he tried cautiously.

Shiela glanced at him, looking suddenly defensive.

"You never mentioned your transfer. We could have talked about it. What you're thinking, what you decide—it's important to me."

Shiela slipped under the comforter. "You would have asked why."

"And you couldn't have told me?"

"All I could have told you was that I loved you."

"And that's why you want to leave me?" Day asked.

"That's why I have to." She touched his face with her fingers. "Sooner or later these people will hurt you. I don't want to be here when it happens."

"I don't understand what you mean," Day told her.

"I know," she responded. "And I can't make you understand."

Day slipped down in the bed beside her. "Maybe we should get transferred together. I think I need to be close to you."

She kissed him gently. "You're close to me now."

"But when you leave?"

"What will happen, will happen," Shiela said. "If we're meant to be together, then we'll find each other."

"Then this is only for now?" Day asked.

Shiela looked up at him, and in the soft light of the lamp he could see that she was crying. "Now is all we have," she told him. She pulled him toward her with all her strength.

Spring 1915

CHAPTER 10

London. Reginald Hall was splendid in his full-dress uniform, his traditional fore-and-aft hat pinned under his left arm. He had just left a party at the Italian embassy, where he had talked with one of his agents. Hall had been given information that he was sure would interest Winston Churchill.

He took a cab to Whitehall, where the light was still burning in the window of the First Lord of the Admiralty.

"You smell of mothballs," Winston Churchill said when he saw Hall's full-dress uniform. "On the diplomatic circuit, I see."

"Visiting one of our sources, actually," Hall answered. "I think the Germans are about to go after our passenger ships."

"All of them?" Churchill asked, his gaze suddenly sharpening.

"Anything that comes into the war zone."

Churchill closed the folder of papers that he had been scanning. "Captain, you know what's at stake here? One insignificant American, lost in a sinking, isn't going to change their national policy."

Hall nodded. It was going to take a truly barbarous provocation to tip the United States out of its official neutrality and bring it into the war. "What we need is a prize valuable enough so that the Germans will try for a ship carrying a number of prominent Americans. Something that will make the risk acceptable."

Churchill opened the folder, took out one of the papers, and pushed it across his desk. "Something like this?" he asked.

It was a wire from Sir Peter Beecham, in New York.

HAVE SIXTY TONS OF PYROXYLIN AVAILABLE FOR SHIPMENT, BUT UNABLE TO SECURE WATERTIGHT CONTAINERS AT ANY PRICE. DU PONT ADVISES IT IS HIGHLY DANGEROUS TO LOAD PYROXYLIN WITHOUT CONTAINERS. I RECOMMEND THAT SHIPMENT BE DELAYED UNTIL CONTAINERS CAN BE FOUND.

"The Germans are absolutely determined to keep us from getting the guncotton," Hall said. "They had their agents planning to bomb the train when it reached the New Jersey piers."

"Then they'd find it an irresistible target no matter what kind of ship it was aboard," Churchill concluded.

"Why don't I respond to this," Hall offered.

Churchill turned back to his papers. "I hoped you might."

Crookhaven. Commander Day looked at the plain-language copy of the message that Chief Gore had just received by phone line from Queenstown. It was addressed to WMPB in New York.

> Embark cargo of pyroxylin on *Lusitania,* departing New York, May 1. Assure material in dry holds above waterline. Greatest secrecy imperative.

Day knew the WMPB call letters belonged to Sir Peter Beecham's War Materials Purchasing Board. And he knew the cargo. It was the guncotton he had given Sir Peter as his Christmas present.

"Call Queenstown and request a confirmation," he said to Gore. "I don't believe they want this broadcast from Crookhaven."

He had told the Admiralty of his suspicions that the station was being compromised. Now they were telling Crookhaven to send a message linking a critical cargo with a specific ship. If the message was genuine, they would be putting their guncotton—not to mention the passengers of *Lusitania*—at enormous risk.

Day stuffed the message into his pocket and walked to the quarters cottage. Peter Grace, as he suspected, was inside, stirring his breakfast in a skillet.

"How's your investigation progressing?" Day asked.

"A few leads, but nothing definite," Grace said. He slid his eggs from the skillet onto a plate and sat down in front of it.

"Then traffic through Crookhaven is still being compromised?"

"Yes, as far as I know."

Day took out the message and unfolded it. "Then why would they send us this to forward to New York?"

Grace glanced at the message. "Looks routine to me."

"Do you know what pyroxylin is?"

Grace swallowed his bite. "Haven't the foggiest."

"It's guncotton. The stuff we use in our mines. We're out of it, and this is the only supply we'll get for the next six months."

"An important cargo, I take it. I suppose that's why they're putting it aboard *Lusitania.* Safest ship afloat, from what I hear."

"But why broadcast it over a station that the Germans are probably listening to?" Day asked.

"Does sound silly. Why not query the Admiralty on it?"

"That's what I've done," Day said. "I just wanted to be sure that this wasn't part of your investigation."

Grace shook his head. "Nothing to do with me. All I'm doing here is poking around, asking questions. Routine investigation."

Day smiled sarcastically. "Is that how you hurt your hands?"

Grace looked down. The knuckles of both hands were swollen. "Oh, these. Thought I'd try getting about on a bicycle. Went right over the handlebars. Lucky I didn't break my neck."

When Day got back to the radio cottage, Chief Gore was hanging up the telephone. "No mistake, sir. I ended up talkin' to an officer in naval intelligence. He wasn't exactly pleased that I was questioning his instructions. 'Code the damn thing, and send it,' he tells me."

"Naval intelligence?" Day couldn't figure it out. It made sense that they would put the pyroxylin aboard *Lusitania*. It was their most valuable cargo and their safest ship. But why was naval intelligence involved?

"What do you want me to do?" Gore asked.

"Send it, I suppose," Day said. "Is Shiela here to code it?"

"She should be back any minute. Trouble down in Schull. Some poor bloke she knows tied on a snootful and fell into his well."

New York. *"Lusitania?"* Sir Peter could scarcely believe what he was reading. He held the decoded Admiralty message that answered his query concerning the guncotton. It instructed him to load the lethal cargo without the protective watertight cases into the ammunition hold of *Lusitania*. "Is that safe?"

Captain Guy Gaunt, naval attaché to His Majesty's embassy, raised his eyebrows as he read the cable. "Really no way to ship guncotton that's perfectly safe. But I suppose they're right. *Lusitania* is the safest ship we have."

"There could be fifteen hundred passengers aboard."

"Which is exactly why the U-boats won't dare go after her," Gaunt countered. He stood and retrieved his cap from the coat rack. "Safest place in the whole war, if you ask me."

Well, I'm not going to put Jennifer at risk, Peter decided. Send her off on top of a cargo of guncotton? Out of the question.

He rehearsed his words as he rode out to his Long Island estate. A temporary delay. Just long enough until he could book another ship. Why? Well, we're loading a rather dangerous cargo aboard *Lusitania*. . . . Except Jennifer would raise the logical question of why he was allowing *any* passengers aboard a ship carrying a deadly cargo. How could he explain that he was using civilians to shield contraband? Or why she was an exception?

But it had to be the truth. His family had scarcely survived his lies. He couldn't risk that again. The first glimpse of civility had returned to his home since he had agreed to let her join William Day. Jennifer was allowing Anne to help her pack. There were even bursts of laughter as the two women worked together.

When the car dropped him at his door, Anne was waiting. "Jennifer's new dresses have arrived. She wants to model them for you."

"For me?" Beecham couldn't conceal his delight.

He sat in the library applauding the outfits that Jennifer modeled. And when she spun around in an evening dress well off her shoulders, he said, "My goodness! Would you wear that in public?"

"Really, Father." Jennifer laughed. "You're falling hopelessly behind the times. Everyone is showing their shoulders."

Anne watched with delight as her family came back together before her eyes. "What a wonderful evening," she said to Peter after Jennifer had rushed out of the room in her final outfit.

"Wonderful, indeed," he agreed. But there was a distracted vagueness to his enthusiasm.

"Is something wrong?"

"Oh, no." But then after a pause, "It's just the danger, I suppose. Traveling through the war zone. There have been several incidents."

"Sinkings?" Anne was suddenly frightened.

"I was thinking of suggesting a slight delay. Just until the navy gets control of things." He saw Anne's eyes narrow with concern. "Or perhaps a different ship."

"Not *Lusitania*? But you've said she's the safest ship afloat."

"She is. It's just that now, with all the submarine activity . . ."

"Peter, is there something you're not telling me?"

What could he tell her? That he had been using passengers to protect his military cargoes for the past six months? That he was about to use their daughter as a screen for sixty tons of explosives? That he was weighing the risk of her losing her life against the risk of their losing her affections?

"Peter, if we're going to disappoint her, I have to know why."

"Oh, needless worry, I suppose," he finally answered, squeezing her hand. "In a war nothing is perfectly safe. But *Lusitania*—she's the fastest ship afloat. No submarine would dare try for her."

Emden. *"Lusitania?"* Captain Bauer looked up from his plotting table at submarine flotilla headquarters. "Where did we get this?" he asked his communications officer, who had just brought the message.

"Crookhaven," the officer replied.

"Genuine?"

"Most certainly, Captain. It was signed by Leprechaun."

Just yesterday Bauer had received a report from his New York harbor watchers. The Admiralty's guncotton, they said, was sitting on a railroad siding in New Jersey. Now, if his Irish agent was correct, the Admiralty was ordering it loaded aboard *Lusitania*.

"Contact Admiral von Pohl: 'Imperative I meet with you this evening.' Then get me a car and driver for Wilhelmshaven." The officer saluted, and Bauer returned to his plotting table.

The table was a twenty-foot-square chart, with the western coast of Europe projecting from one edge and the Atlantic approaches to the British Isles disappearing off the opposite edge. Lines of latitude and longitude were drawn in blue. Superimposed was a red grid that marked off the operating sectors for his submarines.

Each U-boat was represented by a miniature wooden model painted white. Ships were represented by other models, colored according to nationality. They were placed on the table as soon as they entered the war zone, and were moved along their course at their best projected speed. By glancing at the table, Bauer had a complete picture of the battlefield and all the information he needed to vector a specific U-boat toward its target.

Lusitania would normally pass about twenty miles off Mizen Head and then about fifteen miles south of Fastnet. Bound for Liverpool, she would move up the Irish coast toward Coningbeg Light, then turn and run up Saint George's Channel.

If he were going to set a trap for *Lusitania*, Bauer thought, he should try for the three most logical points of interception. One boat would cover her most likely course of approach from the Atlantic. Another would wait off Fastnet in the hope that she slowed to fix her position before her escorts from Queenstown arrived. The third boat would cruise completely around Ireland—to avoid the mines in the English Channel—and move directly to Coningbeg, by which time the escorts would have fallen behind and *Lusitania* would not have reached the escorts from Milford Haven.

One of the U-boats should get a clear shot at the Greyhound.

But should he tie down three submarines just to get a shot at a single difficult target? There was no certainty that *Lusitania* could be sunk. Her speed would turn the slightest miscalculation into a clear miss. And should he be attacking *Lusitania* at all—the world's most beloved ship, carrying the cream of the upper class of a half-dozen neutral nations? But he had proof that she would also be carrying the most important munitions cargo that had crossed the Atlantic since the beginning of the war.

To Bauer's logical mind it was the British who were tossing their prize ship, with all its innocent passengers, onto his plotting table. But war was anything but logical. The answers, Bauer knew, would have to come from someone more adept at politics than he was. He would show von Pohl the Irish message to prove that *Lusitania* was carrying the guncotton. Then he would show how his boats could be moved into intercept positions. But as they talked, von Pohl would know they weren't discussing the important question: whether *Lusitania* was a legitimate target. And to get the answer, von Pohl would probably look all the way up to the Kaiser.

Schull. Father Connors led the procession out of the church, then stood aside as the pallbearers struggled to carry James Corcoran down the steps. Across from the priest William Day stood at attention with a small contingent from the radio station.

"A sad day, Commander," Connors said as the coffin was pushed up on a wagon. "Corcoran was a fine man. Bitter, I suppose, since he lost his dear wife. But always a kind word for anyone who went into his store. Will you be walking with us to the cemetery?"

"I have to get back to the radio station," Day explained. "Miss McDevitt will be there for us."

The priest nodded. He led his parishioners and the wagon up the hill toward the grave site.

Day said to Grace, "You come with me." The lieutenant followed Day to the car, and they drove away.

"What happened to him?" the commander asked as soon as the car reached the edge of the village.

"I'm told he was drunk," the lieutenant answered.

Day nodded. "That's what the doctor said. But he also told me that he took one hell of a battering in his fall. Broke all the fingers on both hands, and ribs on both sides of his body. How do you suppose that happened? The well's only fifteen feet deep."

"I suggest you accept the official verdict, Commander. Mr. Corcoran fell into his well. That's all there is to it."

"The same night you fell off your bicycle, as I recall. Isn't that how you bruised your hands? Now, what happened?"

Grace sighed. "He was a Fenian. Someone was dropping off your radio traffic at his store, someone else picking it up."

"So you killed him?"

"I interrogated him."

"And he died under questioning?"

"Apparently."

Day slammed his foot on the brake, and the car screeched to a stop and stalled. "Damn you. He was a decent man."

"He was the same decent man, Commander, who called a submarine in to attack your boats."

Day was stunned into silence. He looked openmouthed at the junior officer, then restarted the car and continued toward the radio station. After a long silence he asked, "What did he tell you?"

"Nothing much," Grace said. "If he had, he'd still be alive."

"You still don't know who's broadcasting to the Germans?"

"Nothing positive. It takes a bit of time, Commander."

Day nodded. "I'm sure it does. But while you're 'interrogating,' Captain Bauer is reading our coded messages. I think the best thing for me to do is to take Crookhaven off the air. Shut it down."

"I wouldn't recommend that," Grace said.

Day looked startled. "I wasn't asking for a recommendation."

"Then without your permission, sir, I'm going to give you a bit of advice." Grace's tone was polite but with an edge of anger to it. "You don't know a thing about intelligence work. That's my specialty. Just follow the Admiralty's orders. You may not like it, but there are more important issues involved than just a few coded messages."

Day started to respond but stopped himself. The little blighter was right. It was an intelligence matter, and that wasn't his field.

When they reached the radio cottage, Day went to his desk and thumbed through the messages. There was nothing that couldn't wait for Shiela. Then he opened the weekly pouch of correspondence from Queenstown. His eyes went to a pale yellow envelope addressed in a flowing hand.

My dearest William,

I have thought of nothing but you since you left, and have written to you constantly. But my parents thought we might not be suited for one another, and have tried to keep us apart. Father never forwarded the letters that I wrote to you.

But now all that is in the past. I am free to live, and for me there is no life except my life with you. I am coming to be with you because, as my parents now understand, we belong together.

I have passage on *Lusitania*, sailing from New York on May 1st, and arriving in Liverpool on May 8th. Please write me, care of Cunard in Liverpool, with arrangements for my coming to you. I shall wait in Liverpool until I hear from you, even if it is forever.

I love you,
Jennifer

Berlin. America's ambassador to Germany, J. W. Gerard, and the German Foreign Minister, Alfred Zimmermann, didn't care much for each other. Zimmermann, despite his diplomatic training, was quick-tempered, given to issuing orders. Gerard was emotional and took the rough edge of Zimmermann's personality as an affront to the United States.

But today's request from Zimmermann had been cordial to a fault. "Would Mr. Gerard be so kind as to stop by at his convenience to discuss a matter of some urgency?" Gerard's curiosity had been piqued, and he had rushed straight to the meeting.

"Mr. Ambassador," Zimmermann said, rising from behind his massive desk. "How good of you to come."

"Nice to be asked." Gerard dropped into a chair with a nonchalance that he knew would infuriate his host.

"I regret to say," Zimmermann began, "that we have information that the British are loading contraband aboard their passenger vessels. Specifically, that they are loading high explosives aboard *Lusitania*."

"*Lusitania?* You can't be serious." Gerard was stunned.

"This message," Zimmermann said, handing him a paper, "was intercepted by the Imperial Navy. I believe it speaks for itself."

Gerard read the paper quickly. "There has to be some mistake. We require a complete cargo manifest of every departing ship."

"Manifests can be falsified," Zimmermann countered. "I'm sure the English have no intention of registering this particular cargo as 'sixty tons of high explosives.' "

"You'll appreciate," Gerard said lamely, "that we can't inspect every package loaded in a port as busy as New York."

"Naturally," Zimmermann agreed. "Just as you will appreciate that we must regard English passenger ships as legitimate targets of war. Perhaps your government will want to advise your citizens against traveling aboard them."

Gerard stood awkwardly, fumbling for his hat, and left.

His dispatch was already composed by the time he reached his office.

> Germany in possession of Admiralty message indicating cargo of high explosives to be carried aboard *Lusitania*'s May 1 sailing. Germany considers *Lusitania* legitimate war target and suggests Americans be prohibited from booking passage. Please advise.

He scribbled out the message and handed it to his coding officer for transmission. He knew that Great Britain and the United States were involved in a conspiracy of lies, and he was their spokesman. But now Zimmermann had thrown the lies back in his face. The German Foreign Minister had presented Washington with two choices: either enforce its own laws preventing military cargoes from being loaded on passenger ships or warn American citizens that their own government had placed their lives in danger. Gerard never suspected his government would concoct an even more deadly lie.

But that was precisely what he learned the next evening, when Washington's response was decoded.

> The United States government appreciates the concern of the Imperial German government for the safety of United States citizens who travel aboard British ships. But the Imperial German government has been misinformed as to the loading of contraband cargoes in the Port of New York. Cargo manifests of all departing ships are carefully scrutinized. We feel that any documents to the contrary in the possession of the Imperial German government are questionable and do not constitute a sufficient reason for denying United States citizens their right to sail aboard any ship of their choosing.

It was signed by Robert Lansing, counselor to the Department of State.

Gerard was infuriated. Cargo manifests are scrutinized, Lansing had written. But that wasn't the issue. It was the cargo that should be scrutinized, and Lansing was offering no indication that the United States would search *Lusitania*'s cargo with extra care.

Gerard remained silent as he placed his government's answer on Alfred Zimmermann's desk and watched him read it.

Zimmermann looked up. "This is not responsive."

"My government feels that it is," Gerard whispered.

"You know, of course, that we intend to attack *Lusitania*."

Gerard nodded. "I think it's apparent that my government will regard such an attack as unwarranted and barbarous."

"*Barbarous?*" Zimmermann hissed the word as if it were a profanity. "And what would you call the actions of a government that loads women and children on top of a cargo of guncotton?"

"Officially, there's no guncotton aboard *Lusitania*."

"If your wife and children were boarding the ship, would you tell them that 'officially' they were safe?"

"I'm not here as a husband and father," Gerard answered. "I'm here as a representative of the United States government."

After a long and heavy silence Zimmermann asked, "Then you will not warn your countrymen?"

Gerard indicated the note on the desk. "I think not."

Emden. Lieutenant Walter Schwieger boarded U-20, which was tied to the pier, and began his inspection. He started at the bow, between the two torpedo tubes. He noted that each tube was loaded and that the two replacement torpedoes, hanging in overhead racks, were tightly secured.

He moved aft, squeezing between the compressor and the tanks of air, and passed the water pumps and the crew's compartment. He lifted the deck boards and looked down at the storage batteries—steel containers of lead plates, filled to the top with acid. They were his only source of power once the boat dived. He inspected the officers quarters, then the control room and, farther aft, the engine room and the after torpedo room.

Schwieger returned to the control room. "Let's take her out," he said, starting up the ladder into the conning tower. The tower was his command post. He climbed one more ladder to the conning-tower bridge, an open deck behind a steel windscreen. It was from here that the watch officer maneuvered the boat while it was on the surface, shouting his commands through a voice tube to the control room two levels below.

"Take in all lines," Schwieger called into the voice tube. He heard the rattle of the idling engines turn into a throaty growl. Seamen on the pier lifted the docking lines from their cleats and tossed them across the widening space of water to the U-20's crewmen. The boat was under way, heading out to the North Sea.

U-27 had left just hours before, the first boat in the series of traps that Captain Bauer was setting for *Lusitania*. U-27 was to head north and take a station twenty miles west of Mizen Head. U-30, already on patrol off the southwestern tip of England, would pause at Fastnet during her return journey. U-20's orders sent it around Ireland to a position southwest of Coningbeg.

Bauer's instructions to his captains had been incomplete. During the night of May 6 and the day of May 7, a large British cruiser, operating as a troop carrier and ammunition ship, would be making her way toward Liverpool. But the U-boats were not yet authorized to attack, pending decisions of national policy. Authorization would be sent by later broadcast.

It hadn't taken Schwieger a second to fill in the missing details. The ship had to be *Lusitania*. Her sailing schedule could be read in every major newspaper. She was the only ship listed in official publications as a cruiser sailing the Atlantic. He could guess at the "reasons of national policy." Along with stores of ammunition, *Lusitania* also carried many passengers of neutral countries.

But Schwieger had no compunctions about the legitimacy of *Lusitania* as a target. Nor did he have any intention of surfacing and putting a gentlemanly shot across her bow. He had done that with *Hampton,* and it had almost cost him the lives of his crew.

It was a two-hour run to the North Sea. Schwieger dropped down into the tower and checked the course that his executive officer, Willi Haupert, had laid out. They would go north, then north-northwest, to a point midway between the heavily patrolled Orkneys and the Shetlands. They would pass between the two British strongholds in the middle of the next night.

Schwieger tested his radio, sending a message of random words that identified his boat to the radio station at Emden. The response "Good hunting" meant that his signal had been received. When his charts indicated that he had fifty feet of water under his keel, he began the routine diving test.

When the boat leveled at thirty feet, Schwieger ordered the periscope raised. Quickly he scanned the horizons to check that he had clear lenses and full mobility.

He felt a drop of water splatter against the peak of his cap. "Dammit!" he cursed. There was a slow drip of seawater from the packing around the scope. The housing, crushed by the *Hampton,* had been repaired twice, but the repairs had obviously been faulty.

"What's wrong?" Haupert asked, climbing up through the hatch.

Schwieger pointed up to the packing, and Haupert illuminated the wet rubber gasket with his flashlight.

"This is the last thing we need," Schwieger snapped. The periscope was his most important weapon. The leak wasn't a good beginning to his hunt for the fastest ship afloat.

Schull. Their separation was approaching. Shiela was expecting her recall to England at any moment. There was no commitment between her and William. Shiela still hadn't explained why she had asked for a new assignment without telling him. Nor had she suggested that they leave together.

And yet William Day was living a lie. He was taking Shiela into his arms, with the words of Jennifer's letter fixed in his mind. Jennifer's words had cut through his despair and filled him with hope. He couldn't deny that she was part of his life.

He had to tell Shiela. But tell her what? That once, in a different world, he had fallen in love? William Day wasn't sure why he had left Jennifer behind. Most likely it had been his blind adherence to the social rules of encounter: they defined which relationships were proper and which were entirely unacceptable. And yet all the canons of behavior were being shattered by the cannons in France and by the deadly gray wolves that roamed the Atlantic.

"There's something I have to show you," Day said to Shiela when they reached her cottage at the end of the day. He led her to the sofa and took the small envelope from his jacket pocket. Then he went into the bedroom, leaving her alone while she read.

"I had to tell you about this," he said when he returned.

Shiela handed the letter back to him. "What will you tell her?"

"What I told her when I left—that it's just not possible." Day sank slowly into the chair opposite her. "We're in two different worlds. I knew it. Her father knew it. Jennifer was the only one who didn't understand."

Shiela stood up. "I'll get dinner started."

But Day caught her hand as she passed. "I thought of not showing you the letter. But that didn't seem honest."

"I don't think we're talking about a letter," Shiela answered. She pulled away and went into the kitchen. He followed at her heels.

"At the time, I loved her very much."

"And now?"

"Now I don't know. I thought it was over."

She answered softly, busying herself with the food. "If it were over, there would have been nothing to tell me."

He nodded. "I'm sorry."

"For telling me the truth?"

"Yes."

Shiela set down the food she was preparing. "It's good that I'm going away," she said. "I don't think I can live with the truth." She walked into the bedroom, closing the door.

Day waited the rest of the evening without disturbing her. Then he fixed a tray with a cup of tea and brought it to her.

"I think I should leave," he said.

"Is that what you want?" Shiela asked.

He couldn't answer her.

"Because I'll be alone soon enough," she continued. "And I'll be alone for a long time."

He put the tray aside and held her in his arms.

May 1915

CHAPTER 11

New York. Thirty feet below the Hudson River, *Lusitania*'s stokers began pumping life into the great ship. An army of men, stripped to the waist, were shoveling huge piles of coal into the furnaces that fired the ship's nineteen operating boilers.

Sixty feet above on her shelter deck, in a gold-encrusted blue uniform, Staff Captain John Anderson greeted the arriving first-class passengers. Each received a salute and a broad ivory smile.

Sir Peter Beecham flashed Jennifer's ticket to the porters. Anne and Jennifer walked ahead as he completed the arrangements for Jennifer's trunks.

"Sir Peter!" It was a reporter from the New York *Sun*. "Are you planning to sail?"

"My daughter is boarding. A visit home," Beecham explained.

"And you're letting her sail aboard *Lusitania?*"

Beecham's expression reflected his confusion. "Of course."

"Have you seen the German advertisement?" The reporter was already unfolding the New York *Sun*, pushing it under Sir Peter's nose. "Do you think it's safe?"

Beecham read the advertisement placed adjacent to *Lusitania*'s sailing notice.

> Travellers intending to embark on the Atlantic voyage are reminded that a state of war exists between Germany and Great Britain; that the zone of war includes the waters adjacent to the British Isles; that vessels flying the flag of Great Britain, or of any of her allies, are liable to destruction in those waters and that travellers sailing in the war zone on ships of Great Britain or her allies do so at their own risk.

Sir Peter handed the paper back without comment. He pushed past the reporter and headed directly for Charles Sumner's office, on the upper level of the pier building.

The area was packed with passengers and newspaper reporters, pressing against the entrance of Sumner's private office. Beecham elbowed his way through the crowd to where Sumner's secretary was barring the entrance to his office. He glowered at the man, stepped around him, and walked through the door.

Captain Bowler Bill Turner was standing next to Sumner's desk. "Of course the manifest is complete," the Cunard official was screaming into the telephone. "*Lusitania* will sail exactly on schedule." He listened impatiently to the comments from the other end of the line. Then he yelled, "She's been cleared by customs in New York. If the State Department wants to inspect her cargo, they can talk to the port officials." He slammed the phone down.

"Well?" Captain Turner asked.

"You heard," Sumner answered. "We're cleared to sail."

"And what do I tell the passengers?" Turner persisted. "They're all asking about the advertisement."

"Tell them that it's nothing more than German propaganda. *Lusitania* is the safest ship in the world."

"I've already told them that," Turner said. "That wasn't enough. Alfred Vanderbilt is still sitting in the first-class entryway, with his steamer trunks stacked beside him."

"Captain Turner, *Lusitania* sails exactly at noon! With or without Mr. Vanderbilt."

Turner lifted his bowler, which he had placed on Sumner's desk. "Any special sailing orders?" he asked.

"There is nothing special about this crossing," Sumner fired back. "It is absolutely routine. And Captain, please leave by the side door. I'd rather if you didn't give any interviews to reporters."

He watched while Turner exited quietly. Then he turned his attention to Peter Beecham. "A madhouse," Sumner complained. "Out of nowhere I'm told that the Department of State is sending an envoy to inspect *Lusitania*'s cargo."

"Have you notified Lansing?" Beecham asked.

"I have," Sumner answered. "He says we're to get the damn ship out of port. Under no circumstances are we to await any inspection party from the State Department."

Beecham nodded. "Is the advertisement authentic?"

Sumner waved his hands helplessly. "The German embassy claims to know nothing about it, although they agree the warning is timely. The *Sun* says the ad came from a group of concerned German American citizens here in New York."

"So maybe it is just propaganda," Beecham thought aloud. "But why now? Why on this trip?"

Sumner snatched the cargo manifest from his desk. "How would I know? I don't even know what the ship is carrying." He looked down the list of items. "Maybe it's this sixty tons of cheese. Do you suppose the Germans are suddenly in need of cheese?"

Beecham lowered himself into a chair. "Charles, my daughter is sailing on *Lusitania*." He looked imploringly at Sumner.

"And you want to know whether you should take her off," Sumner said. He walked to the window and saw passengers filing up the companionway. "You're the only one who can answer that question, Sir Peter. If it's really cheese, there's no reason the Germans should single out *Lusitania*. But if it's something else . . ."

Beecham rose slowly. "I'll use your private exit, if you don't mind." He shuffled toward the door.

As he climbed the companionway he made up his mind. The "cheese" was the most important cargo he had ever sent across the ocean. The German warning was too timely to be a coincidence. Somehow they knew. They were going after the guncotton, and they didn't want any American passengers standing in their way.

"Ah, Sir Peter!" It was Captain Anderson. "Miss Beecham has already gone to her cabin. Our chief steward will lead you there."

Damn, Beecham thought. He followed the steward inside to the elevators on the main deck and rode up one level to the promenade deck, then walked forward to one of the parlor suites on the starboard side. When he stepped in, Jennifer and her mother were already unpacking.

He waited until his daughter had disappeared into the bedroom. Then he turned to Anne. "You've seen the German ad?"

She seemed surprised that he should mention it. "Yes, of course. Captain Anderson told us that it was just propaganda."

"I'm very concerned," Peter whispered. "Perhaps a different ship. It would only take a few extra days."

"Not *Lusitania*?" Anne questioned. "Is anything safer?"

"Of course not," he snapped. "It's just the damned timing."

Anne's expression sank. And then Jennifer's voice called cheerfully from the bedroom. "Did you hear about the German advertisement, Father? Isn't it the most ridiculous thing?"

He looked around the cabin, already littered with Jennifer's belongings. He glanced back at Anne, whose expression was pleading with him not to upset her parting moments with her daughter. "Ridiculous, indeed," he called into Jennifer's bedroom. He felt Anne touch his hand, and he flashed her a reassuring smile, even though his thoughts were locked on the awful cargo below them.

Jennifer walked with them to the companionway. The deck was alive with feigned gaiety. Sir Peter watched as his wife and daughter fell into each other's arms, Anne rocking Jennifer gently, as if she were a child. Then Jennifer turned to him. "I love you, Father," she whispered in his ear as she embraced him. "Even when I hated you, I loved you." He squeezed her until his arms ached.

They stood on the dock looking up at the tiny figure that waved down at them. Then *Lusitania*'s massive whistle shook the sky, and the black wall of steel began easing away from the pilings as she backed out into the river, her bow finally clearing the end of the dock. An instant later she began to ease forward.

She passed the tip of Manhattan, out into the broad harbor, heading toward the open sea. All along her rails the passengers stood in silence watching the land disappear behind them.

Emden. "Damn," cursed Captain Bauer. He crumpled up the message from U-27 and hurled it at the wall chart in the flotilla headquarters' operations room. U-27 had radioed that she was turning back to port.

"Bow planes," he whispered. He turned to his operations officer. "Klaus, how many boats have had failures to their bow planes?"

Captain Klaus Schopfner searched through his memory. "None that I recall, sir."

"Not one," Bauer agreed. "Until now." He shook his head in despair. The boat's captain had no choice. With the bow planes inoperative he couldn't dive, and his only option was to return on the surface, running far north, around the Shetlands, to avoid the British fleet.

"God be with them," Bauer said. He walked slowly to the plotting table and pointed the miniature of U-27 back toward Emden.

The loss of the boat punched a gaping hole in the snare he had stretched across *Lusitania*'s line of approach. It left him without a boat on the western approaches to Mizen Head. That meant that U-30, on her way to a station near Fastnet, would be the first boat to get close to the Greyhound. But U-30 couldn't stay on station very long. She was already at the limit of her fuel, and he had to leave her enough to get home.

"It won't work," Bauer said.

"Marginal at best," Schopfner agreed.

The flotilla commander walked around the table. He lifted the model of U-30 and moved it up to Fastnet. Then he picked up U-20. "What do you think, Klaus?"

Schopfner tapped the table just below Fastnet. "Perhaps both boats here, with five miles between them."

Bauer nodded. "But there could be an escort waiting." He set the U-20 model where Schopfner had indicated. "Besides, U-30

297

can't hold station very long. If *Lusitania*'s arrival changed by even a few hours, we'd have only one boat left for the trap."

Schopfner shrugged. "I suppose Coningbeg Light would be my next choice. But U-30 would be too far from home, unless you let her come right up Saint George's Channel and through the Irish Sea instead of going all the way around Ireland."

Bauer pointed to the narrow North Channel, at the top of the Irish Sea. "Would you send a boat through there?"

"Ordinarily, no. Too dangerous. But this is no ordinary prize."

Bauer knew Schopfner was right. One submarine for the Greyhound was an exchange even a novice chess player would make. Hold U-30 at Coningbeg, take his best shot at the incoming *Lusitania*, and take his chances on U-30's making it through the North Channel past the British patrols. But still he might be able to set the trap at Fastnet. Then U-30's chances of returning to Emden would improve dramatically.

"We need more information, Klaus," he decided. "There must be some instructions to *Lusitania* on rendezvous times and locations. Nothing from our Irish friend?"

"Nothing for several days," Schopfner said.

"Can we reach him?"

"I think so. He's supposed to be listening for us 2300 to 2315, their time." Schopfner went to the communications room and returned with a radio officer.

"This is for Leprechaun," Bauer began. He dictated, " 'Imperative we have all traffic directed to *Lusitania*. Forward as soon as copied. We will stay up on your frequency all hours.' "

Schull. Emmett Hayes took a stack of school papers with him into the basement, lit the oil lamp, and turned its flame low. He had picked the late hours of the evening to guard his radio frequency because no one would come knocking at his door.

He waited for the vacuum tubes to get warm, and peaked his gauges at his assigned frequency. Then he spread the pencil-written essays out on the sewing machine's workbench and started to correct them.

The radio came to life, sounding out a group of letters that he knew as well as his own name. Hayes threw open the sewing-machine door and began pumping the treadle furiously, trying to generate enough power to respond. The needle reached the green band, and he keyed his call sign.

As the message began coming through, he turned over one of the essays and began frantically writing down the clusters of letters sounding from his radio. As soon as he had them all, Hayes rushed up the steps in the dark. In his bedroom he fumbled the key into the lock of the armoire and felt through his shirts. With the laundry cardboard in hand, he rushed back to the basement and began breaking the message. When he finished, he had Bauer's request printed out across the back of a little girl's essay.

LIEUTENANT Grace recognized the sound of Tom Duffy's truck long before it crested the hill behind him. Even in idle, the engine sounded consumptive. Now, climbing the hill that led south, toward Colla, it was blasting out a series of random explosions.

Grace had been following Duffy, one of the two names he had been able to beat out of James Corcoran. But he had been following at a distance. Despite his broad smile and explosive laugh, Tom Duffy was a frightening man. He was enormous in stature, barrel-chested, with a great belly that rolled over his belt buckle. His arms and hands were massive. Tufts of thick white hair protruded around his ears. His nose bore the scars of several shattering breaks.

Duffy's strength was legendary. He and his truck earned their livelihood by moving things that were too heavy to move, like the boulders that were dumped into the harbor to serve as moorings for the boats. But even more legendary was his viciousness. He had earned his way into the Fenian brotherhood as a leg breaker, sent to coax the uncooperative and punish the disloyal.

Corcoran had mentioned Duffy's name as a threat. As his battered body was being tipped into the well he had gurgled through a bloody mouth, "Tom Duffy will get you for this." Grace had made it a point to find Duffy, and when he did, he returned to the radio station and strapped a large-caliber pistol to his belt. He wanted to be armed if he and the giant man should cross paths.

Grace froze in the tall grass as the truck rattled by him. He lifted his head only when the engine sound had faded in the distance. Then he jumped up and lifted his bicycle over the stone wall. He pedaled out onto the road and began following at a safe distance.

Something was up. He had been watching Emmett Hayes—the

other name that Corcoran had delivered—and observed several whispered meetings between the teacher and Duffy. It figured—the Fenians were an unlikely combination of intellectuals and dockworkers, and the two men represented both wings of the brotherhood. When Grace had reached the schoolhouse to take up his daily vigil over Hayes, he'd found the school closed. "He was called away," one of the children had said. "To Colla." Grace had taken up his post on the Colla road, and only minutes later Duffy appeared.

At the Colla dock, the truck turned away from the harbor and headed toward the poor inland farms. When Grace reached the turn, he could see the truck's smoky trail leading up to a nearly toppled barn. He left his bicycle in a hedgerow. Then he moved on foot toward the back of the barn and looked in through the space between two weathered boards.

There were four of them. Emmett Hayes was facing him, looking down at someone who was sitting in a chair. Tom Duffy's broad back was blocking his view of the person. Another of the townsmen was standing beside Duffy. Grace could hear Hayes' voice clearly.

"I haven't seen you since poor Jimmy Corcoran's funeral," Hayes was saying. "I've missed you." Grace couldn't hear the reply, but then the schoolteacher continued. "I told you that you could leave things with Father Connors' housekeeper."

Duffy walked away from the interrogation, and Grace got a look at the spy who was compromising the Crookhaven radio traffic.

Shiela was sitting in the chair, wilting under Hayes' eyes.

"I just can't do it anymore," she answered. "When we buried Mr. O'Sullivan . . . the others . . . The information I was bringing you was killing people."

"That wasn't your doing," Hayes reminded her. "Commander Day handed me the patrol schedules. We didn't need you for that."

"But the others," she protested. "The bodies from the ships. I was telling you what ships were coming."

"English ships," Hayes snapped. "Have you forgotten who the enemy is? The Englishman in your bed may be decent enough. But you're not whoring for the whole country, are you?"

Shiela jumped up. "You've no right to talk to me that way. I've worked for the cause. But it's over. I'm leaving all this behind me."

"It will be over when we own our own country," Hayes said calmly. "Until then, the only way you leave the movement is in your best dress, with your rosary wrapped around your fingers." He walked away from her, then turned abruptly. "There's something we need right now. Something only you can bring us. Just once more, and then you can take yourself back to England."

She looked at him suspiciously. "What do you need?"

"*Lusitania*," he answered. "She'll be arriving in three days. I need to know every message that is sent out to her."

"You can't be serious," Shiela answered.

"Dead serious, lass. Everything since the last message you gave us—the one about loading the cargo aboard her."

"I don't think there's been anything since," Shiela said.

"There will be. And I need it the instant you have it."

Shiela shook her head slowly. "I can't."

Hayes glanced from her toward Tom Duffy, who was leaning against the barn door. "There's two places he can take you," he told Shiela. "I was hoping it would be back to your radio station."

Shiela knew the other place. It was a root cellar behind a deserted farmhouse. They used it as a holding cell while a tribunal was convened. The brotherhood didn't hang women. They turned them over to the ladies, who stripped them, doused them in tar and feathers, and paraded them through the villages. It was worse than hanging. At least the dead men didn't have to live with their shame.

She pushed back her growing terror and tried to think carefully. "Just this once?" she asked. "And then I'm out?"

"Out of the country, yes. We won't try to stop you. And we won't turn you in to your English masters, either."

She stood looking at him, weighing her choices. "All right," she concluded. "And I'm to bring it to the rectory housekeeper?"

He nodded. "Mr. Duffy, would you be so good as to bring Miss McDevitt back to Crookhaven?"

The Atlantic. "I think perhaps the pheasant," Alfred Vanderbilt told the waiter who hovered near his elbow. "Miss Beecham will have the filet of sole amandine."

Vanderbilt turned his attention back to Staff Captain John Anderson, who was explaining the importance of fixing the ship's position immediately when they raised their first sight of land.

"How can you be certain of your exact position?" asked a plump woman encased in lace.

301

"Ah." Anderson, arranging the salt and pepper shakers as props, began an explanation of a two-point fix.

"Does this interest you?" Alfred Vanderbilt whispered to Jennifer. He rolled his eyes in boredom, bringing a smile to her face.

"I don't care how he gets us there," she admitted.

"You seem distracted," he said. "I hope you're not worrying about the German warnings."

"Not at all," she answered. "It's just that I was expecting to be met. But now perhaps the arrangements . . ."

Vanderbilt understood immediately. This was something that even Sir Peter Beecham couldn't arrange. "A young man?"

Her skin flushed red. "A naval officer," she answered. "I have no idea where he might be stationed."

Vanderbilt leaned close to Jennifer and said, "I wouldn't give it a moment's thought. If I were your naval officer, I would take my ship right up onto the beach in order to be waiting for you."

She smiled at his kindness. But it didn't really help. It had all seemed so simple when she had written William Day about her arrival in Liverpool. Now, with each mile closer that *Lusitania* carried her, her doubts grew stronger. He was fighting a war. Was there any room left to shelter a memory of a love that he had left behind? How ridiculous to expect that he would be waiting.

Anderson droned on, explaining every aspect of the crossing, until the fruit compote had been finished. Then he rose to indicate to the first-class dining room that dinner was over. Jennifer rode the elevator with her dinner companions to the boat deck. But as the women headed forward to the library and the men moved aft to the smoking room, she stepped out into the open night and found a space where she could see the Atlantic sliding past.

Jennifer wondered what was waiting for her. The image she took to bed each night was of William looking up from the pier and then waving wildly when he caught sight of her looking down from the railing. But it vanished each morning, with the light of day. Most likely there would be a letter with places and names of people who would make her welcome until they could meet.

Her thoughts turned darker in the afternoon. A letter courteous to a fault but restating why their lives could never fit together.

Her worst fears, however, came in the evening. What if he had found someone else? What if there was no letter at all? Oh, William, she thought. Don't leave me hoping for things that will never be.

"You'll catch a death of cold." Jennifer was startled by Alfred Vanderbilt's voice as he stepped up beside her. He placed his topcoat over her shoulders. "You shouldn't be outdoors on the Atlantic until at least the middle of July. Let me walk you inside."

Jennifer took his arm and started across the deck.

"Still worried about your young man, I imagine."

She smiled. "The one you're so certain will be waiting."

"And you're not? Why?"

"We quarreled," she admitted.

"Then he'll certainly be waiting. To apologize for what he said."

"What he said was that he wasn't from an important family."

"And that concerns you?"

Jennifer laughed. "No. But it concerns him. He thinks that after the war we'll all have to go back to where we belong."

Vanderbilt stopped as they reached the door. "I don't think so," he told her. "This damned war may finally teach us that we all belong together. It has broken all the rules. I think the old ways are finished, and good riddance."

Jennifer looked pleasantly surprised.

He opened the door. "Take my word for it. He'll be waiting."

CHAPTER 12

Crookhaven. "There's coded traffic," Chief Gore told Shiela when she stepped out of Day's car in front of the radio station.

She felt the fear tighten in her throat. "Who's it for?"

"Two ships," he answered. "Don't remember their names."

She breathed easier. The chief would certainly remember the name *Lusitania*. Shiela had been given another reprieve.

Since the previous morning, when Tom Duffy had dropped her at the station, she had thought of nothing but the next message that would go out to *Lusitania*. The Germans knew the Greyhound's call letters. They would spot the message and then ask Emmett Hayes for its contents. She would have to deliver it to him first.

But Shiela knew that she couldn't. She had reached the decision to break from the Fenians when she finally admitted to herself that William Day was the center of her life. That was when she had requested her transfer, hoping the Admiralty would end her deceit by

303

taking her out of Ireland even though it would mean leaving William.

The fact that it was *Lusitania* reinforced her decision. Left with no alternative, Shiela might well have pointed her finger at one more insignificant steamer. But she knew about the special cargo, and this ship was also alive with passengers. Shiela couldn't betray them to the madness that was gripping the world.

And then William had shown her the letter. The thought of another woman's coming to him had crashed the fragile hopes she had been protecting. It was obvious that Jennifer was very important to him. Yet while Shiela wished she had never learned about her, she knew that placing Jennifer in danger would be a betrayal of the decency she was trying to reclaim.

The chief's words had bought her perhaps another day.

Day had taken his coffee and stepped outside the cottage, walking to the edge of the cliff near the radio tower. His eyes searched the horizon where the Greyhound would appear, but his mind was locked on the letter that he had mailed to Liverpool.

He had written twenty pages, tearing them to shreds as he read them. His meaning was simple. She had to go back to America. But the explanation baffled him.

Because he couldn't take care of her. He was a soldier at war. That was true enough. But it was entirely beside the point. A million women were waiting without knowing.

Because there was someone else. True again. But the someone else was leaving. He knew Shiela was telling him that it could never be. And Shiela wasn't the reason he was telling Jennifer to go home.

Because he didn't love her. These were certainly words that would leave her with no reason to stay. But the lie was so transparent that he knew she would see through it. How could he make her understand that there were barriers dividing people into different worlds?

He had finally realized that a letter couldn't tell her what he felt. So it had been short. His delight that she was visiting England. His excuses that he couldn't be there to meet her. His advice that she go to stay with family friends. His promise that as soon as he was able, he would come to England to see her. It said nothing that would answer her question. That was an answer that he had to deliver to her face.

He walked back to the radio cottage.

It was the chief who picked up the Queenstown telephone when it buzzed. "One for *Lusitania*," he said absently when he set down the telephone. He was still filling in the message form. Day walked around him and read over his shoulder.

Rendezvous elements Cruiser Squadron E, 7 May, 0600 hours, 260 Fastnet, 40 miles, then elements Destroyer Squadron A, 1800 hours, 120 Coningbeg, 7 miles.

"Good grief," Day whispered. He reread the message. Squadron E was the patrol ships out of Queenstown that met incoming vessels at Fastnet and escorted them up the coast. It was normal to send arriving ships the time and coordinates for the rendezvous. But the details of the second rendezvous—with the Squadron A ships, from Milford Haven—were never broadcast. That information was signaled over to the ship by the Squadron E vessels.

"Get me a confirmation," Day ordered.

The chief sighed and lifted the telephone.

"Where's Lieutenant Grace?" Day asked.

"In his quarters, I think," Gore answered.

Day took the message pad and pulled out the carbon copy.

Grace was at his washstand, hunched over a shaving mirror. His chin was hidden in a thick lather. "Good morning, Commander," he said to the image that suddenly appeared behind him.

"Do you know anything about this?" Day responded, thrusting the copy of the message into his line of sight.

Peter Grace set his razor down, took the message, and read it. "The Queenstown lads meet *Lusitania* at Fastnet, and then they turn her over to the Milford Haven fleet at Coningbeg." He gave the paper back to Day. "Makes sense to me."

"That's the problem," Day countered. "It will make sense to the Germans, too. With these two points I can plot her course all the way up the coast. We never send anything this specific."

Grace went back to his shaving. "I have no idea," he concluded. "Escorting ships is really not my cup of tea."

"No, but security is. This message will be coded and on the air in less than an hour. Can I be sure that the Germans won't read it?"

"Sure?" Grace chuckled. "Commander, in my line of work we're never sure of anything. Even that you're not working for von Pohl. But I doubt that you have to worry."

"There are civilians aboard that ship."

Grace toweled off the lather. "The Admiralty knows that."

Day stormed out of the cottage, back to the radio building. "Who sent it?" he demanded of Chief Gore.

"Dammit, Commander, I got routed to naval intelligence again. 'Send it,' he tells me. 'And be quick about it.' "

"Where is it?" Day asked.

"Miss McDevitt is translating it right now."

Day still had time to think. Why was intelligence involving itself in routine traffic? And why had Queenstown broadcast the coordinates of the second rendezvous? There were no answers that made sense. Except the one answer that had been drilled home during officer training—you don't question orders; you carry them out.

"Message is ready." It was Gore calling from the open doorway of the coding room. Shiela was standing beside him.

"Send it, Chief," Day said.

London. Reginald Hall, head of naval intelligence, sat alone in his conference room staring up at a map of the war zone and sipping slowly from a glass of deep red port. It was nearly midnight, and the windows throughout Whitehall were darkened.

It was all quite simple, really. Like a chess game. You watched the enemy move and tried to deduce his plan. He and Flotilla Commander Bauer were at the opposite ends of Europe. But they might as well have been sitting across a chessboard from each other. Hall had made his move, pushing *Lusitania* out into the center of the board. Bauer had then countered by moving his submarines toward the sacrificial queen. Now Hall was studying Bauer's response.

What were Bauer's options? He had every reason to take *Lusitania*. But he was making no effort to hide the presence of his U-boats. The boats already on station weren't lying low. Four ships had been sunk off Lands End in the past two days. He might be making us think he's going after the cargo of guncotton so that he can have a field day sinking everything else. Not a bad plan, Hall thought.

Hall might counter by moving the escorts away from *Lusitania*. But Bauer was no fool. If *Lusitania* were suddenly left open, he would certainly wonder why. So what move should Hall make? He had to make *Lusitania* appear to be an impossibly well-protected target. But would Bauer attack in the face of an escort of warships? Probably not, unless he could find a gap in the coverage. And if Hall were going to open a gap, he needed a convincing reason. Like the one on the map in front of him: the sinkings off Lands End. Bauer was raising hell there, off the southwest tip of England. Maybe, Hall thought, the logical response, the one Bauer might be hoping for, was to pull the Milford Haven fleet out of Saint George's Channel and send it south. And that would create an opening for the U-boats.

"All right, Herr Bauer," Hall whispered to the map. "I think I know what you're up to."

STAFF Admiral Oliver stood next to the wall chart, a pointer held under his right arm. He stared blankly at the First Sea Lord, Admiral John Fisher, who had just asked an embarrassing question.

"Why in heaven's name is the Milford Haven fleet rushing down to Lands End? What are they supposed to do down there?"

Oliver stammered as he aimed his pointer toward the area off the southwest tip of England. "Well sir, the submarine activity. Four ships sunk in two days. Our thinking—"

"Whose thinking?" Fisher demanded. He glanced around the room at the other officers of his staff. To his mind none of them had ever had a useful thought in his life. Then his squinting eyes found Winston Churchill and Captain Reginald Hall.

"Sir John," the First Lord of the Admiralty answered, "we can't just sit back while German U-boats run unchallenged ten miles off our coast. We have to do something."

Fisher shook his head. Gestures, he thought. He turned his attention back to Oliver, who was delivering the daily briefing.

"The day after tomorrow we have *Lusitania,* due off Fastnet at dawn," Oliver continued. "Squadron E will provide the escort to Coningbeg. From there . . ." His voice trailed off. With the Milford Haven ships out of position, there would be no further escort.

"She'll be escorted part of the way," Winston Churchill added. "And if there seem to be unusual dangers, we can pull her into Queenstown. But I think we can protect her."

"I'm sure," Fisher agreed. "Escorts don't do much for *Lusitania* anyway. She has to slow down so that they can keep up."

Hall smiled. "An excellent point, Admiral. We don't want to slow her down. The U-boats can't hit what they can't catch."

Fisher rose, signaling the end of the briefing. He turned to Churchill. "You'll be on call during the weekend?"

"No," Winston said. "There's a meeting in Paris. General French asked me to attend. Captain Hall will be here."

The First Sea Lord left, his staff following like a family of ducklings. Churchill and Hall stayed behind, along with Admiral Oliver.

"I suppose the First Sea Lord is right," Churchill pondered aloud. "Who would Squadron E send as an escort? Probably *Juno*— smoky old bucket. All she'll do is give away *Lusitania*'s position and slow her down in the process."

Hall nodded. "She's certainly no match for a submarine."

"Then perhaps we should cancel the rendezvous," Oliver suggested. "I mean, if she adds nothing to *Lusitania*'s safety."

"An excellent observation," Winston Churchill said. He looked toward Captain Hall.

"I certainly agree with Admiral Oliver," Hall responded.

Churchill looked back to Oliver. "Then you'll see to it, Admiral."

Oliver was pleased to have made a contribution. "I'll draft a message to all parties right away."

"I don't think I'd broadcast it," Hall offered. "*Lusitania* will be in radio silence and won't be able to confirm. I think if you would just advise Admiral Coke to recall the escorts."

"Of course." Oliver gathered his papers and left the room.

"Should raise one hell of a row," Churchill said to Hall. "And if the Germans manage to kill an American or two, then Mr. Wilson will fall right into our lap."

The Irish Coast. "Fastnet," Walter Schwieger told Willi Haupert. He glanced down at his watch. "And right on schedule."

"I didn't think we'd make it," Haupert answered.

U-20 was finally making a good cruising speed, making up the ten hours they had lost turning the northern tip of Scotland. Twice they had been forced to dive at the approach of a British patrol. They had been three hours late reaching the Orkneys, and this had cut down the length of darkness available for passing through the British stronghold. When the sun rose, once again Schwieger had taken U-20 under in order to avoid being seen. He had been tempted to raise the periscope to search around him, but the leak in the packing worried him, so he had decided to make minimum use of it.

But for the past day and a half they had been lucky. There had been a blanket of fog for cover, and they had been able to stay on the surface, covering the five hundred miles from the Hebrides in thirty-five hours. That left them a day and a half to reach Coningbeg, only a hundred and seventy miles away. It would be an easy passage.

Bauer had promised to confirm his order to attack the large troop transport and to give the precise position of the intercept. But so far, the flotilla commander had said nothing. Schwieger couldn't send a message asking for instructions—the U-boats went into radio silence as soon as they entered British coastal waters. All he could do was wait until he was on station, then send his call sign. That would tell Bauer that he was in position.

Schull. Father Connors was pacing in his garden, mouthing the words of the breviary he held. He looked up as Day approached, but finished the verse. Then he closed the book. "Good evening, Commander." The priest settled onto a stone bench, leaving a place for Day to sit beside him.

"I'm sorry to interrupt you, Father," Day said. "But I need the fleet out on their stations by dawn tomorrow."

Connors' eyes widened. "Tomorrow? That's difficult."

"There's a ship coming in tomorrow—a passenger ship. I think it may be in danger."

"Passenger ship?" The priest was startled. They had never been concerned with passenger ships before. He climbed to his feet and began walking the path. Day fell in next to him.

"Have you spoken with Emmett Hayes?" the priest asked.

"I can't find him. I thought you might know where he is."

"No," Connors said. "I haven't seen him, either. But it would be good if we could find him. The people respect Emmett."

"They respect you, too, Father. They listened to you before."

"That they did," Connors agreed. "But I was telling them that it was all right to help themselves to English money. Then their neighbors began washing up on the beach. And now I'd be telling them that they should risk their lives again for the English."

"But there are women and children on the ship."

"Ah, yes. Women and children." He nodded his sympathy and turned to face the British naval officer. "You're a fine man, Commander Day. I remember your words at the funeral: *'The best of us do what we can to save one another from the slaughter.'* That's what you're doing now, and that's why I'll try to help you."

It was growing dark when Day headed back toward the Mizen Head road. As he passed Shiela's cottage he was surprised to see a dull lamp glowing in the window. He braked, and turned through the gate. Shiela was startled when he opened the front door. She stood in the middle of her parlor unable even to mouth a greeting.

"I thought you were still at the station," Day said. He looked into the bedroom. Her suitcase was open on the bed, with her clothes stacked beside it. Shiela followed his eyes. "I'm leaving," she said.

Day looked bewildered. He knew that no orders had come in for her. "You can't," he said. "Not yet."

She rushed into the bedroom, where she began pushing the clothes into the suitcase. "I have to. I can't stay here any longer."

"Why? Another few days. Your orders will come through."

"I don't have another few days," Shiela answered.

He watched her as she tried to close the suitcase. Then he bolted into the room and pulled her hands away from the valise. "What are you talking about? What's wrong?"

She tore away from his grasp and backed into a shadowy corner. "Leave me alone," she shouted. Then her hands came up to her face, and the fight drained out of her. Sobbing, she slid down the wall until she was sitting with her knees drawn up in front of her.

"Shiela, what's happened? Is it me? Did I do this?"

Her face lifted slowly. Through the racking sobs she said, "It's me. I did it to myself." Her eyes glistened in the lamplight.

He watched as Shiela struggled to her feet. "Please let me help you," Day whispered.

"You can't." She was speaking more to herself than to him.

"Why?"

He could hardly hear her when she said, "I'm Grace's spy."

For a second he didn't understand. Then it was all perfectly clear. Every word he had spoken to her, every thought he had shared in the night, had been heard in a German officers mess. She had used him.

His eyes fired, and his fists clenched. He took one murderous step toward her. But then he stopped. Shiela was standing helplessly, not even bothering to raise her hands to defend herself. Nothing he could do could hurt her anymore. His rage subsided as quickly as it had flashed. He backed away and sat on the bed. "Everything?" he asked. "Did you tell them everything?"

"Oh, no!" Shiela rushed to him, dropping on her knees. "Not what you said to me. Just the radio messages. I couldn't have told them anything about you. I love you."

"And I—" he started.

She pressed a finger to his lips. "Don't. You love her, and you always will. It would be worse if I believed you loved me."

He stood and took her hand. "I won't leave you like this. We'll go to Queenstown together. We'll make them understand."

"It's not the English I'm running from," Shiela said. "It's the Irish. They want something, and I'm not giving it to them. I can't let them find me. You don't know what they do to their traitors."

"What is it they want?" he asked.

"*Lusitania*," Shiela told him.

Instantly he remembered the message—the coordinates that gave away *Lusitania*'s position mile by mile along the coast. He had handed the information to Shiela.

"But I didn't give it to them," she continued. "I couldn't."

Day tried to think, but it was all happening too fast. "You've got to come with me," he decided. "We have to get this to Peter Grace. He's with naval intelligence. He'll be able to help."

"Peter Grace knows," Shiela said. "He's been watching me."

Day was stunned. "He can't know," he insisted. "He was the one who told me to send the message. He knew I would give it to you. If he knew about you—"

His words stopped. The station was compromised. Peter Grace knew it, and he knew that Shiela was the agent. Yet he had given her the information that would sink *Lusitania*. Which meant . . . "They want her sunk," he whispered.

She read the horror in his eyes. "The English?" she asked.

"The English want the Germans to sink *Lusitania*. It's the Americans they want killed." He focused on her. "You've been used. Not just you, all of us, to set up a shipload of Americans."

Now the shock was in Shiela's eyes. She understood.

"You've got to tell me everything. Who gets your messages? Who talks with the Germans?" Day asked.

"Emmett Hayes," Shiela said.

"Come on," he ordered. "They're not going to kill the people on *Lusitania*. We're not going to let that happen."

She ran with him toward the car.

The Irish Coast. U-20 ran slowly, hiding under the cover of darkness. Schwieger had moved twenty miles south of the shipping lanes that converged at the entrance of Saint George's Channel.

He had a pressing matter to deal with: the periscope had to be repacked. In the few times he had brought the periscope up, gallons of water had poured into the boat. If he was going to stalk *Lusitania*, he might well need to use the scope over and over again.

His engineers had fashioned a new rubber gasket. To install it meant he had to stay on the surface for two, perhaps three hours. He didn't want any ships stumbling on him while his men were working and he was unable to dive.

And then there was the radio. To mount the jack that would force the packing into position, the men would have to disconnect the boat's low-frequency antenna. He would be without communications until the repair was completed. Schwieger had sent his call letters the minute he was on station. Seconds later the call letters had been returned, acknowledging that Emden knew where he was. But there had been no order to strike at the large troop carrier. He had waited as long as he could before starting the repair, but the work had to be finished before daylight, even if it meant that he couldn't receive Bauer's message.

"They'll keep resending," Haupert encouraged him.

It was true. Emden wouldn't consider the message delivered until they received an acknowledgment. But at some point if U-20 didn't respond, Bauer would have to discount her as part of his trap.

"Let's get moving," Schwieger snapped at the engineers, who had brought their tools to the tower. "I want this finished in one hour."

Their glances told him he was demanding the impossible.

CAPTAIN Bowler Bill Turner stood at the window of *Lusitania*'s wheelhouse, in one hand a cheese sandwich, in the other a mug of tea. He hadn't been able to get an evening fix on their approach to

Fastnet because of the fog. And even when the fog lifted, the horizon had remained an indistinct blur, and the haze had obscured the first stars. Now he was in the clear, with a hundred stars overhead to choose from. But without a horizon they were useless.

He walked to his speed indicator: twenty-one knots, the best speed he could make with the number four boiler room shut down to save coal. "Fastest ship afloat," the passengers told one another whenever the subject of the German warning was raised. But Bill Turner knew that with one boiler room shut down, *Lusitania* was just another passenger ship. The accountants at Cunard had taken away her best weapon.

If he made his rendezvous with Squadron E, then things would be relatively simple. But the weather conditions promised more fog in the morning. If he couldn't find Squadron E, he would have to turn north in hope of sighting land and then head toward Coningbeg on his own. He felt safer with escorts. But without them he could at least run at his best speed.

"Home tomorrow," the first mate said as he stepped up beside the captain.

Turner grunted. "I certainly hope so."

CHAPTER 13

Schull. Day parked the car at the edge of town, and he and Shiela turned toward Emmett Hayes' house. They found a dark doorway across from Hayes' front door. Then they waited.

During the short drive into Schull, Shiela had spilled out her involvement with the Fenians. In the first days of the war the Irish patriots had gone over to the Germans, hoping that the defeat of England would bring freedom to their country. German submarines had smuggled them guns, and a radio the Irish could use to organize coast watches, keeping track of the English ships that patrolled the Atlantic approaches. With this information the U-boats could operate safely off the coast of Ireland.

Shiela's arrival had been a godsend. An Irish woman working inside the English radio station! Now they could know the ships' movements days in advance. All they had to do was get the woman working for the movement. After all, her parents had been forced into exile on the docks of Liverpool by English landlords.

Shiela had resisted Emmett Hayes' first overtures. The Germans, she told him, weren't liberators. She was sympathetic to the centuries of Irish poverty and slavery, and wished the Irish patriots well. But she was English now. Then Emmett made it impossible for her to be English. He had taken her to the children's cemetery. He described the little girls and boys who had died lying on the ground with their mouths full of grass. She looked about sadly, but then the sadness was pushed aside by rage. She had never hated anything as much as the people who could do this to children. And right there she had joined the movement.

Then the fresh bodies floated ashore. At first the bodies of English sailors, then Irish bodies—those of her townsmen. She understood that past murders couldn't be undone by new murders, and she decided to break away.

Now Day understood why Shiela had warned him that Ireland would destroy him. It was destroying her. But if she could help save *Lusitania,* she could undo the treachery in her past.

They saw Hayes as he passed under the light of a house window. He vanished in the darkness, only to reappear on his front steps. Day darted across the street as Emmett turned the lock in his door. He grabbed the teacher by his coat collar and threw him into his parlor. Shiela followed, and closed the door behind them.

Hayes' shock gave way to indignation. "What in hell do you think you're doing?" he demanded of the naval officer.

"Stay back," Day ordered. He pulled the shades in the window, then touched a match to the wick of a lamp.

He took Hayes by the shoulders and placed him firmly in a soft chair. Then he set a straight-back chair directly in front of him and sat down. Shiela remained standing near the window.

"I know who you are and what you've been doing," Day said.

Emmett's eyes widened. He looked at Shiela, then at Day. "I don't know what you're talking about. What have I been doing?"

"Sending information to Germany. You're a German agent."

Hayes started to get up. "That's ridiculous."

Day shoved him back into the chair. "Right now I don't give a damn what you've been doing. I need your help. Whoever your contact is, I need to get him on your radio."

Emmett blinked in bewilderment. He turned to Shiela. "For heaven's sake, what's he talking about?"

314

"We've been used, Emmett," she answered.

"Listen carefully, Emmett," Day began, "because we don't have much time. Right now there's a flotilla of submarines waiting for *Lusitania*. And she's steaming right into their trap. The Germans asked you for information about *Lusitania* because they know she's carrying a valuable cargo. And the English provided the information because she's also carrying nearly a thousand American passengers. The English want the Germans to attack the Americans. Can you understand that?"

Hayes' pretended confusion began to disappear.

"England wants America to come into the war," Day went on. "Don't you see? The English know all about your little nest of spies. They're using it to bring America into the war."

Hayes turned to Shiela for confirmation. She nodded.

Day took a copy of the *Lusitania* rendezvous message from his pocket and handed it to Hayes. "There's an English intelligence officer at Crookhaven. He knows that Miss McDevitt has been giving you messages. Yet he gave her this to code, knowing that you would send it to Germany."

Hayes fumbled for his glasses and read the message. "Sweet Mother Mary," he whispered.

"That's why we have to raise Germany," Day concluded. "To convince them they're walking into a trap. *Lusitania* arrives off Fastnet in about five hours."

Emmett handed the message back to Day. "There's just one thing wrong with all this, Commander. You're English. If this is a trap for the Germans, then it's your trap."

"We all have to draw the line somewhere, Emmett," Day said. "I draw it short of women and children."

Hayes turned to Shiela. "There's paper and pencils on the kitchen table. Write what you want to send to the Germans."

They huddled together in the kitchen as Day wrote.

> Cargo not repeat not aboard *Lusitania*. England wants Germany to kill American passengers. High-placed Americans ready to declare war. Sources are within Royal Navy. Most reliable.

They rushed upstairs, and Emmett pulled out the shirt cardboard and began translating the message. He worked for nearly half an hour, retranslating each coded phrase back into plain text to

315

make sure of its accuracy. Then he locked the code back in the armoire. They ran downstairs, and were halfway across the parlor when they stopped short.

Peter Grace was lounging casually in the kitchen doorway. His large-caliber revolver was dangling from his fingers. "Well now, this is a surprise," he said. "You two, I expected." He gestured with the pistol toward Shiela and Emmett. "But you, Commander?"

"Peter, we're setting up *Lusitania* for sinking," Day tried.

Grace shook his head. "That's not our affair, Commander. Higher-ups, you know." He reached for the papers that Hayes was holding. "May I?" Reluctantly Hayes handed them to him. Grace let the page of code drop to the floor and read the plain-language version. "No, this will never do. I think we should send the original version. You have a copy, don't you, Commander?"

"No," William Day lied.

Grace pointed the revolver into Shiela's face. "You have a copy, don't you, Commander?" he repeated. Day remembered James Corcoran's broken body. He took the message out of his pocket.

"Give it to our unassuming German agent," Grace said.

Emmett took the message.

Grace smiled. "Now Emmett, why don't you run upstairs and put that into code. I'll give you exactly twenty minutes."

Hayes looked at Day, who nodded. He started for the stairs.

"And Emmett," Grace called, "bring the code down with you. I'll want to be sure you haven't made any mistakes."

Upstairs, Hayes unlocked the armoire and carried the code to his desk. But before he began working, he lifted the lamp from his desk and placed it carefully in his window, making sure that it was far to the left. Then he raised the shade.

Emden. Captain Bauer was up from the dayroom bed at flotilla headquarters the instant he heard the tapping at his door. He stepped into the operations center. "Message from Leprechaun," his communications officer told him.

It was the information he had been waiting for: the coordinates of *Lusitania*'s two rendezvous with her escorts—one off Fastnet, the other near Coningbeg Light. He took the message to his operations officer. "Plot these, Klaus," he ordered.

The officer leaned over the plotting table and marked small circles at each coordinate. He stretched a tape measure between the two circles and laid out *Lusitania*'s course into Liverpool.

Bauer looked down at the Irish coast. He moved the models of the Squadron E ships out of Queenstown and aimed them toward the Fastnet rendezvous. He twisted the model of *Lusitania* until it was headed for the same point. Then he took the marker for U-30, under Lieutenant Rosenberg's command, and moved it from Lands End toward Fastnet.

"How long will it take Rosenberg to reach here?" He touched the table at a point to the west of the Fastnet rendezvous, where *Lusitania* would still be traveling without her escorts.

The operations officer did a quick calculation. "Too long," he answered. He drew another circle on *Lusitania*'s course line, due south of Cape Clear. "This is the best intercept U-30 can make. Half an hour after *Lusitania* meets her escorts."

"Just so!" Bauer said. He stepped toward Coningbeg. The small U-20 marker was alone, surrounded by open water. "Then this is where we will have to attack."

He turned to his communications officer and began dictating messages. One was for Lieutenant Rosenberg, on U-30. It gave his intercept point and authorized the attack. But it cautioned that *Lusitania* could be heavily escorted. Rosenberg was not to risk his boat if enemy warships were close at hand. The other went to Lieutenant Schwieger, on U-20, giving him an intercept point southeast of Coningbeg Light. It advised that when *Lusitania* reached that point, she should be steaming unescorted. Each of the boats had been given the best opportunity for attack.

Schull. Peter Grace smiled. "Nicely done, Emmett. You should have taken a position with naval communications."

They were in the cellar, Hayes seated at the sewing machine. He had just received acknowledgment of the message he had sent to Germany. Day and Shiela were standing against the back wall.

"We won't be needing the radio any longer," Grace told Hayes. "Just pull it free, and set it down on the floor."

Hayes pulled the antenna wire and the power cord from the sheet-metal box and placed it carefully on the hard dirt floor.

"Now smash it," Grace ordered.

Hayes looked horrified at the suggestion, but he did as he was told, kicking at the instrument until the hollow back panel collapsed and the glass vacuum tubes burst.

"Come to think of it, we won't be needing you any longer, either, Emmett," Grace said.

Hayes had barely understood the meaning of the words when he felt a hot flash burn into the center of his back. As he fell forward over the ruins of his radio, Day and Shiela saw the handle of a knife sticking out of his coat.

Shiela screamed. Day started toward the dying man, but stopped as Grace cocked his pistol. He saw the satisfaction in the young lieutenant's face—another assignment completed with the usual efficiency. Day backed up to the wall, next to Shiela.

"We'll be leaving together," Grace announced. "I'm going to back up the stairs, and you two are going to follow me. Miss McDevitt first." He backed onto the first step. Shiela fell into line in front of him, and Day followed behind Shiela. "We're going to walk to your car, and then we'll drive to the radio station. The code room should hold you nicely until the military police come for you."

Grace was halfway up the stairs, with Shiela and Day following. "Not much I'll be able to do for you," he said to Shiela. "Fenian. German agent." He backed up another few steps. "But in your case, Commander, I think we may be able to buy a bit of leniency. Taken in by the wiles of a seductive woman. Not really a traitor. Of course, I wouldn't count on getting your own ship. . . ."

He was still taunting when a massive fist fired across the doorway. Grace's head flew sideways, and he staggered and then fell across the parlor floor. Tom Duffy's giant form moved in front of Shiela, across the doorway, in pursuit.

Grace skidded on his back. He raised his head, and his clouded vision caught the enormous shape lumbering across the room toward him. He lifted the gun, firing wildly. He got off three shots before Duffy's hands closed around his neck. He felt himself being lifted into the air. The revolver dropped to the carpet.

"Let him down," Day screamed as they rushed up into the parlor. He dove for the gun. But Duffy wasn't taking orders. He had come in response to Emmett's signal, only to find his leader murdered. Now the murderer had to be executed.

Duffy held Grace high in the air. Then with a quick shake of his arms he snapped the head like a whip, breaking the English officer's neck. Duffy turned, walked to the cellar door, and tossed the limp body down the steps. He took a deep, discouraged breath. Then he started downstairs to retrieve his fallen field commander.

Shiela was on her knees, bending over the discarded warning message that Hayes had been going to send to Germany.

"Are you all right?" Day asked as he got up.

"I can send this from the radio station," Shiela answered. "The call letters are here. And Emmett's identification letters. We can still warn them."

"Can you drive my car?" He helped her to her feet.

"I think so." Then she added, "But Mr. Duffy can drive me."

"Then go!" Day said. "I'll get down to the dock. Father Connors is trying to get the fleet together." He saw that Shiela was not steady on her feet. "Are you all right?"

She nodded at him. "I'll be fine. Get to the dock."

Day rushed out through the front door. When he was gone, Shiela reached around to her back and touched the point of pain that had nearly made her faint. When she brought her hand back, it was stained with blood.

The Irish Coast. Schwieger looked at the message that the radioman had brought to the top of the conning tower. He smiled and passed the clipboard to Haupert. "She's ours," he said.

Haupert read the orders from Captain Bauer. "Unless Rosenberg gets to her first."

"Not likely," Schwieger told his executive. "With the escorts, he'll never get close enough. We're the ones who are going to get her if this damned periscope is working." He glanced to the east, where the morning horizon was brightening. "Let's try her out!"

His engineers had finished their work less than an hour earlier. The fabricated gasket had been sealed against the periscope casing, and the deck plate had been refitted and the low-frequency antenna restrung. And now they had the message. Everything was falling into place. Schwieger shouted the order to dive to forty feet.

He stood inside the tower and listened to the sea close over his head. He looked up at the packing. It stayed dry. He followed the boat's gradual descent, letting the pressure build on the new gasket. Even at forty feet no water was leaking in. So far, so good. The real test would come when he tried to raise the periscope.

They took the boat back up, to fifteen feet. "Let's try it," he told Haupert, and the executive officer reached for the counterweight cable. Nothing happened. The periscope didn't budge.

"It's jammed," Haupert said in horror. "The deck plate must have squeezed it too tight."

"Of all the luck!" Schwieger ripped off his cap and fired it at the deck. "Surface," he screamed into the control room, and scampered up into the tower.

The sun was rising, and there was light in the sky. Schwieger spun quickly in the tower, checking the sea around him. He was still alone. "Repair crew topside," he shouted down to Haupert.

How long would it take? An hour at most. The problem was that in a few minutes he would be in open daylight and, while the repair was in progress, unable to dive.

The two machinists squeezed through the hatch and dragged their tools up behind them. Schwieger stepped to the edge of the deck to give them room, reaching for the radio mast to steady himself. He nearly toppled over the edge—the radio mast was gone.

The stub of the low-frequency antenna was flapping from the insulator near the end of the deck. The mast had not been fully secured. It had torn away in the dive and trailed the antenna out behind the boat, and when it reached its full length, it had snapped.

U-20 had no communication with Germany.

Crookhaven. Chief Gore jumped up as the radio-station door blasted open. Shiela came in with a giant man, squeezing through next to her so that he could keep his arm around her waist.

"Miss McDevitt," Gore said. But his eyes locked on the man's round red face. He thought of the pistol resting in his desk drawer.

"I've got a message to send," Shiela said. She pulled away from Duffy and came toward Gore, unfolding a paper. "It's priority."

Gore looked from Duffy to Shiela and, finally, to the paper she was holding. He took it and read it. "Whose call sign is this?"

"It's German," Shiela said. "Please, Chief. Just send it. Commander Day wants it on the air immediately."

Gore reached behind him and began easing the desk drawer open. "Where is Commander Day?" he demanded.

"In Schull. At the dock." Shiela's voice was fading. "He's sending the boats out to escort *Lusitania.* Please send the message. That's what it's about—saving *Lusitania.*"

Gore's hand found the pistol. He eased it slowly out of the drawer and then snapped it in the direction of Tom Duffy. "All right, both of you, back up," he ordered. "I'm not sending any messages to the Germans. Not until Commander Day gets here."

"There isn't time," Shiela begged. Instead of backing away, she began walking toward the chief. But her step faltered. She staggered, then fell against his desk.

Gore saw with horror the dark, wet stain down the side of Shiela's dress. He put down the pistol and rushed to help her. But Duffy was already there. He lifted Shiela in his arms as if she were a doll.

"What happened to her?" the chief asked.

"Your Lieutenant Grace shot her," Duffy said. Then he screamed at Gore, "Send the damn message. She's been bleedin' to death just to get it here."

"She needs a doctor," Gore said to Duffy.

"I'll get her to a doctor," he yelled. "You send her message."

Gore nodded, and Duffy ran out the door with Shiela in his arms.

The chief's hand trembled as he dialed in the frequency. He peaked his power gauge, and then he tapped in the strange call letters. A response came back immediately, loud and clear.

Carefully he began sending the coded letters. He was soaked in sweat when he finished the message. He signed off the coded characters that spelled Leprechaun.

It was the first time Gore had received a coded acknowledgment from a German operator. But when he saw the bloodstain on his desk, he knew he had done the right thing.

Emden. "It wasn't sent by our agent," the communications officer was telling Bauer. "It didn't come from Leprechaun."

"But it's his code," Bauer argued. "And those are his call letters."

"But it didn't sound the same. It wasn't his hand, sir. We know the way Leprechaun keys his letters. And it was a different radio. Much more powerful."

Bauer was angry. It was a vital message, and he had barely an hour to act on it. By now *Lusitania* should be past Fastnet, headed up the coast. U-30 should be racing to intercept her. But his communications officer was telling him that the message might not be genuine.

As soon as they realized it was a complete reversal of Leprechaun's earlier message, they tried for a confirmation. They sent out Leprechaun's call letters and waited for a response. Nothing happened.

"What do you think, Klaus?" Bauer asked his operations officer.

"I think it's a trick," Schopfner answered. "It says that the guncotton isn't aboard *Lusitania*. But our agents in New York saw it put aboard. Why would the British—"

"To make us do exactly what we're doing," Bauer said. "To make us attack American passengers."

He walked away to a corner of the room, where he stood alone. Then he turned abruptly. "It can't be the English. Don't you see? If they sent this message to trick us, they would be standing by to confirm. To send this, the English would have had to capture Leprechaun. How else would they have his call sign and his code? If they've gotten to this man," he continued, "and sent us a hoax, then why don't they answer to confirm their message?" Bauer frowned. "Who's more likely to be away from his radio? A single agent? Or a British communications station?"

He dashed over to his communications officer, snatched the message pad, and began writing. "Something happened in Ireland," he said. "Between the first and second messages something changed. I don't know what, but I think this warning is genuine."

He tore off a message addressed to U-20 and U-30: "Do not repeat not attack large troop carrier. British trap. Stand clear."

"Get that off immediately."

He paced back and forth, rerunning the decision he had just made. Did the British know that he was reading their traffic? Did they know that he would get the message that gave *Lusitania*'s rendezvous points? They were either very stupid or very cunning. And if they were cunning, then he had been played for a fool.

His communications officer rushed back into the room. "We can't raise either boat," he announced, panic in his voice.

Bauer went to the plotting table. U-30 was close to the escorts. More than likely she was submerged. But U-20 was still hours away. She should be on the surface. She should be answering.

"Keep sending," he told the communications officer. "Just keep trying to raise them."

CHAPTER 14

The Irish Coast. *Lusitania*'s great horn bleated out into dense fog. She was moving slowly, feeling her way across what Captain Turner hoped was the rendezvous point. But there was no answering call from Squadron E. He had already lingered too long. Without a fix he could be as much as fifteen miles away from *Juno* and her destroyers, and they would never hear him.

"Full ahead," he decided. "Steer course zero six zero." His plan was simple. Turner knew he was at least twenty miles off Fastnet. Later on in the morning the fog would burn away, and he would get a positive fix. In the meantime, he would be closing in on his second rendezvous, near Coningbeg Light.

And maybe the escorts would realize he had missed the rendezvous, and would start up the coast in the direction they knew *Lusitania* would have to take. There was a chance, Turner thought, that they would see one another when the fog lifted.

But *Juno* had already broken out of the fog. Admiral Oliver's order, recalling *Lusitania*'s escorts, had been received two hours earlier. *Juno* had no intention of meeting up with the Greyhound. She was thirty miles to the east, heading back into Queenstown for an easy weekend tied up to the pier.

ABOARD U-30, Lieutenant Rosenberg saw *Juno* through his periscope. Something was terribly wrong. She was still supposed to be well to the west of her rendezvous with *Lusitania*. But *Juno* was five miles inside her course line, and much closer to the beach. Perhaps there had been some new information from Emden, information he couldn't know, because he had been running under the surface.

"Down scope," he snapped to his executive officer. *Lusitania* was probably coming in right behind *Juno*, he thought. His best chance was to move in toward the beach. Ideally, he would have preferred to keep his periscope up so that he would see *Lusitania* the instant she appeared. But that damned Irish fleet had reappeared.

"All ahead full," he ordered. "Take her down to thirty feet."

His batteries were low. He had just one chance: get to *Juno*'s course line, and then take one quick look through the periscope. If *Lusitania* was there, he would take her. If not, he would get out before the Irish boats spotted him.

WALTER SCHWIEGER SCREAMED in frustration. It was another freighter, the second in the past hour—this one no more than three miles off his port quarter. But he couldn't dive to avoid being spotted. His machinists were just now tightening the bolts on the deck plate that protected his periscope.

"The s.o.b. is probably on his radio right now," he told Haupert. "The whole English navy will know we're out here."

In running out of the shipping lanes while he made the repairs, Schwieger could not have guessed that he was moving into the path of two meandering tramp steamers. Now there was no way he could head back to his intercept point. The whole Milford Haven squadron would probably be waiting for him.

"Finished," the machinist announced proudly.

Schwieger nodded. "Let's hope it works this time." He looked at the sea around them—clear and bright, marked by small patches of hazy fog. "We might not be finished yet," he said. "*Lusitania*'s still coming toward us. Somewhere in the next few hours our paths could cross." There was a chance that by midday his target would appear on the horizon directly on his bow.

"Bring her to three zero zero," he told Haupert. "Flank speed. We'll give it one more try."

London. It was all coming apart, Reginald Hall admitted to himself. Two freighters had reported sighting one of Bauer's submarines thirty miles southwest of Coningbeg Light, well off the route that *Lusitania* would be taking into Saint George's Channel. What was she doing so far out of position? And there had been the panicky phone call from Admiral Coke, in Queenstown: the Irish fishing boats, operating out near Fastnet, had spotted a periscope only ten miles from shore. That was well inside *Lusitania*'s course, and with the boats all around her, Bauer's second submarine probably couldn't do anything even if she sighted the Greyhound. Why in hell were the Irish out there anyway? He had counted on Grace's keeping that situation under control. But Grace was obviously having difficulties. He hadn't even reported in.

Worse, the sighting reports had brought the Milford Haven fleet back up from Lands End. That was exactly what they should have done when they learned that there was a submarine operating near the Irish coast. He certainly couldn't order them to stay away. Now

Admiral Coke had figured out that *Lusitania* was in great danger. He had wired Admiral Fisher requesting permission to divert the Greyhound into the safety of Queenstown's harbor. Fisher would undoubtedly agree and order *Lusitania* to turn inland, out of harm's way.

So the chess game with Bauer was a stalemate, Hall supposed. He had failed to draw the United States into the war. Bauer had failed to stop the guncotton from reaching England. It was time to reset the board. There would be other matches, Hall consoled himself. But this one had been so perfect.

The Irish Coast. Suddenly William Day was caught up in the hunt. The image of the brutality in Emmett Hayes' cellar had quickly faded at the sight of a periscope that sneaked up only a hundred yards from Tim Sheehy's boat.

"There," Day had screamed, pointing to the glass lens. He had launched a flare, and immediately the closest boats converged on the periscope.

The U-boat's captain had seen them coming, and dived to safety. Day could see the huge dark shape fall away below him. He pointed in the direction that the submarine was headed. Sheehy followed, keeping the boat directly over the fleeing submarine.

Day looked up to the west, where a low wall of fog still obscured the horizon. *Lusitania* would be coming out of that fog at any moment. But where? He wanted to maneuver his fleet between the submarine and her target.

"Spread out," he screamed over the water. The dark form below him was no longer visible. The U-boat had gone down deep and could now turn in any direction.

Where would she go? If she had come for *Lusitania,* then she would probably try to break out into the open sea, where she had the most room to maneuver into an intercept position. Day pointed south, and Sheehy turned the boat seaward. "There's *Lusitania,*" Sheehy shouted. There was no doubt it was *Lusitania* in the distant haze, riding high above the water, with four funnels towering above her decks.

Day calculated that she would pass well out to sea of them. To have a chance for attack, the submarine would have to run to the south, the direction in which they were already heading.

"Slow her down a bit, Mr. Sheehy," Day advised. "We don't want to get too far ahead of our friend down there." The Irishman tapped his throttle back, and his old boat slowed to a leisurely speed, to match the probable speed of the U-boat.

Day thought of Jennifer, probably standing on an open deck looking at the coast. Then for an instant Shiela's frightened eyes reappeared. And he felt a pain of guilt.

ROSENBERG glanced at the clock. Ten minutes had passed. If he had guessed right, he had escaped a mile or so out into open water, and the Irish boats were all far behind him. "Let's take a look," Rosenberg decided. "Take her up to fifteen feet." U-30 began rising up from the depths.

The instant the scope broke the surface, he swung it to the south and gasped as the lens filled with the image of *Lusitania*.

"We've got her!" he said. He began twisting the range finder to calculate his firing commands when a small boat cut across his field of vision. It was one of the Irish boats that were waiting for him to show his periscope.

"Damn!" Rosenberg screamed. He dropped the scope down into the hull. "Dive," he yelled into the control room. "Dive!"

As his boat started back down, he turned to his executive officer. "That devil. He read my mind. He was waiting for me. We had her. We had *Lusitania* right in our sights." He pounded his fist against the bulkhead. "To lose her! To a rowboat!" By the time he could get free to come up for another look, all he would see was her stern as she raced away from him. "Let's go home," he said.

CAPTAIN Turner read the message that his wireless operator had rushed to the bridge: SUBMARINE ACTIVITY SOUTH OF CONINGBEG LIGHT. DIVERT TO QUEENSTOWN TO AWAIT FURTHER INSTRUCTIONS.

Bowler Bill bounded out onto the port wing and raised his binoculars. The coastline was still hazy, but he had no trouble finding the Old Head of Kinsale. It stood like a mountain on the end of a finger of land. He could run in toward the beach and put the lighthouse atop the Old Head off his port beam, at perhaps fifteen miles. From there he could plot a direct line to Queenstown, less than an hour's steaming ahead. With a bit of luck *Lusitania* would be tied up in Queenstown in less than three hours.

"KEEP A SHARP EYE," SCHWIEGER screamed down to the lookout on his foredeck. They had raised land directly off the starboard bow, ten miles to the east of the harbor entrance to Queenstown. He was entering the home waters of the British fleet that guarded the Irish coast, a very dangerous place for him to be running on the surface. He guessed that he was fifteen miles offshore.

Haupert climbed up through the hatch. "Are we there?"

"On her course line and turning toward her," Schwieger answered. "If we're going to find her, it will be someplace between here and the Old Head of Kinsale."

After a while Haupert pointed to a shape of land coming into sight off the starboard beam. "Old Head of Kinsale."

Schwieger nodded in agreement. He swung his glasses slowly toward the bow and saw a haze of smoke on the horizon. "There they are! Squadron E!" he told Haupert. Then he asked, "What do you make out? Two ships? Or is it three?"

"Looks like two. Two big ships. Probably both cruisers."

"In a tight formation," Schwieger said. "Or— Look, Haupert, it's one ship with four stacks. It's *Lusitania!*"

"Headed into Kinsale?" Haupert asked.

"Not if we can get there first," Schwieger said. He called into the voice tube, "Right standard rudder. All ahead full." The diesels growled, and the bow began swinging toward the landmark as the boat quickly added speed. "Steady on new course three one zero."

"Do we have a chance of catching her?" Haupert wondered.

Schwieger could see that his relative bearing to *Lusitania* was slowly changing. The damned Greyhound was too fast. "We can try," he answered. "Maybe something will happen. We're overdue for a bit of luck.

JENNIFER Beecham stood on the portside boat deck, a scarf wrapped over her head against the twenty-knot wind that *Lusitania*'s speed was generating. The shoreline was coming into focus. She could see gray rocks, and patches of deep green where farm fields bent over the cliff tops. Ahead was the jagged edge of a mountain, and if she squinted, she could make out a lighthouse on its crown.

"Beautiful, isn't it?" Alfred Vanderbilt stepped up behind her. "What is it?"

"Ireland. The Old Head of Kinsale. There's a harbor behind it that used to be a refuge for Spanish pirates."

"It looks so peaceful. Like paradise!"

"Hardly that." Vanderbilt laughed. "I was just taking a stroll. Would you care to join me?"

Jennifer took his arm, and they started toward the fantail, along the first-class promenade.

"SHE'S getting away from us," Schwieger snapped at Haupert. He had to stay up, hoping that her lookouts were concentrating on the shoreline. Then when he got into range, he would fire his torpedoes. The odds of one of them finding its mark were slim. But it was better than doing nothing.

He studied the towering bow and the blasts of white spray it threw as it cut through the sea. "She's turning," Schwieger shouted. "She's turning toward us." Apparently she was headed farther up the coast.

"Queenstown." He nearly laughed. "She's going into Queenstown. We've got her, Willi." Then he scampered down the right hatch behind his executive officer. "Dive! Dive!" he screamed.

Schwieger leveled off at twenty feet. "Bring the periscope up," he ordered. Haupert reached for the cable, hesitated for just an instant, and then tugged it down. The periscope rose through the repaired packing. The two officers smiled at each other.

"Our luck is changing, Willi." Schwieger dove to the eyepiece. As soon as he saw daylight, he saw *Lusitania* racing toward him. He was on her starboard bow.

"Set the torpedoes for eight feet," he said. That would put them a full deck below *Lusitania*'s waterline. If she held course, she would pass less than seven hundred yards across his bow.

He knew a torpedo hit couldn't finish her off. But if the first one slowed her down, then maybe he could put a second one into her propellers and rudder.

Haupert cranked his firing orders into the calculator. "Twenty seconds," he announced. Schwieger lowered the periscope.

JENNIFER and Alfred Vanderbilt had passed beneath the soaring second stack and were walking up the starboard side, toward the ladder that led up to the bridge.

They were startled by a sharp crash from up ahead. The deck lurched beneath them, and Vanderbilt heard Jennifer scream as she slipped and fell against the bulkhead. An instant later he lost his footing, staggering across the sloping deck until he landed beside her. A torrent of water began pouring down on top of them. The sea had exploded into the air, and the giant waterspout was washing down the side of the ship.

Suddenly the deck was pitching in the opposite direction, and they were both sliding toward the rail. Vanderbilt grabbed Jennifer's jacket and reached out frantically for the base of the davit that held the first lifeboat. He caught it with one arm, but Jennifer broke free and crashed against a collapsible lifeboat fastened to the deck. Then Vanderbilt lost his grip and rolled on top of her.

"What's happened? What's wrong?" Jennifer cried.

He struggled to his feet, lifting her up with him. "An explosion, I think. But we're all right." He tried to lead her up the angle of the deck. The ship had first lurched to port, but now it was listing too far to starboard.

"Are we going to sink?"

Vanderbilt could see that she was close to hysteria. "Of course not. They'll be able to right her. It will only take a few moments." He clutched at a handrail fastened to the bulkhead and began leading her toward the doors. "Everything will be all right," he kept repeating. But he was battling his own fears. *Lusitania* still seemed to be falling to starboard. Whatever it was—a mine or possibly a torpedo—it had obviously opened that side to the sea.

"A HIT!" Schwieger told Haupert, his eyes fixed to the periscope. "Forward of the number one funnel. There's a hole in her side. I can see flames inside. She's listing ten, maybe twenty degrees to starboard. She looks as if she might roll. Only one torpedo!"

Below the waterline the torpedo had blown its way into the front end of the nearly empty starboard coal bunker, instantly drowning the buoyancy along *Lusitania*'s starboard side. Seawater rushed in. But the heat of the explosion had ignited the coal-dust fumes that filled the bunker, and as the gas was compressed by the rising seawater, it burst into flames. The fire roared through the bunker and climbed past the torpedo hole, licking against the giant cases of guncotton that were stacked in the cargo hold two decks above.

VANDERBILT HAD REACHED THE door and was trying to push Jennifer inside. But he couldn't get any footing against the slope of the water-slick deck. He was suddenly aware of a distant rumbling, a sound like a freight train running through the hull of the ship below. It quickly grew louder. Then there was a flash of light, blue-white, like lightning on a dark summer's night. The deck lurched violently, tossing him off his feet. He caught the edge of the door and held on for dear life. Jennifer spun through the doorway and was tossed into the passageway inside.

SCHWIEGER watched in horror as an enormous explosion tore through *Lusitania*'s bow. A white flash lifted her foredeck right off the hull, and the graceful schooner mast shot into the air and disappeared over the far side. "Brace yourself, Willi," he screamed.

The shock wave slammed against U-20 like an enormous fist, stopping her dead in the water and driving her bow to port. There were screams from the control room below. Haupert spun against the bulkhead and grabbed a cable rack to keep from falling. "What the hell happened?" he demanded.

Schwieger turned from the periscope, wide-eyed with fright. "The whole front of the ship," he said. "It just . . . blew off."

CAPTAIN Turner had heard his starboard lookout scream, "Torpedo! Torpedo wake!" He had barely looked up from the chart table when he felt the ship shake. First he was slammed against the table. A moment later he had to hold on to the table to keep from tumbling across the listing wheelhouse.

He knew immediately what had to be done. The starboard bunker was flooding, and the ship was in mortal danger unless he could stop its roll. "Call the engine room," he bellowed to his watch officer. "Order them to flood the port coal bunker."

Two of the small red lamps on the damage-control board were blinking furiously. He had a fire in the transverse coal bunker, but he knew there was no longer a coal bunker—it had been ripped out to make room for cargo. He threw the toggle switch that would close the enormous watertight doors, separating the bow from the boiler rooms. Then he turned on the fire extinguishers that would pump smothering steam into the forward cargo spaces.

Turner started out to the starboard wing, moving carefully from

one handhold to another. The ship was already over by about fifteen degrees, and he knew that if it rolled past twenty-five degrees, it could never right itself. "Call out the list. Every degree,"
he ordered the quartermaster. "Tell wireless to send out a plain-
language signal. All stations. 'SOS *Lusitania*. Come quickly.' "

He was nearly to the bridge when his whole world exploded.
There was a deafening blast, which knocked him down as if he had
been hit with an axe. He felt ice-cold hail pouring down on top of
him. It was a moment before he realized that it was the shattered
glass from the wheelhouse windows. Lying on his back, he could
see the control board blinking crazily. The forward-boiler-room
bulkhead had been incinerated, and the whole front of the ship had
been opened to the sea. Turner climbed to his feet. "Sound abandon ship," he said.

The ship was still rolling, and he doubted that anything could
check its list. But there was a more immediate danger. *Lusitania*
had no bow, no foredeck. Yet she was still racing ahead, the full
force of the sea pounding into her forward boiler room. When the
next bulkhead gave way, the ship would sink instantly.

Turner needed to keep her afloat long enough to launch her
lifeboats. But he had to stop the ship. He staggered back to the
wheelhouse, took the handles of the telegraphs, and threw them to
full astern.

"HER engines are exploding," Schwieger announced, his face still
pressed in morbid fascination against the periscope. Angry clouds
of steam were suddenly blasting from *Lusitania*'s funnels. "The
whole ship is coming apart, Willi. She's twisting herself into the
ocean. Like a screw!"

VANDERBILT knew from the staggering explosion that *Lusitania*
was doomed. Already the bow was beginning to dive. He stumbled
into the passageway and found Jennifer crumpled on the floor. He
reached under her arms and lifted her to her feet.

"Come with me," he told her, the gentleness gone from his voice.
"We have to get you to a lifeboat. This damn thing is sinking!"

"It can't," Jennifer protested feebly.

"It can, and it is," he said, pulling her after him through the door
and back out onto the boat deck.

The ship's officers and groups of seamen were already rushing toward the boats. Overhead, there was the repeated blasting of the ship's whistle.

The starboard lifeboats were directly ahead of them, and Vanderbilt led Jennifer toward them. Crewmen were lifting the boats from their chocks. But *Lusitania* was now listing twenty degrees to starboard. The instant the boats were free, they swung out almost ten feet from the side of the ship—too far for the passengers to reach. Each boat weighed several tons, and with the list of the ship, no number of men could pull them back.

"Stay here," Vanderbilt ordered Jennifer. He pushed through the crowd of passengers assembled next to the first boat and scampered up the sloping deck. He picked up a deck lounge and carried it back to the boat. He and an officer turned the lounge chair over and stretched it like a gangplank from the ship's rail to the gunwale of the boat. A crewman began handing life jackets to the women.

Vanderbilt helped Jennifer into her jacket. "Get aboard," he said.

She stepped to the rail, then looked down at the angry wash of

white water that raced past almost fifty feet below. She jumped back into Vanderbilt's arms. "I can't," she screamed.

"Get on that chair, and get into the boat," he ordered. "If you go, the other women will follow. If you don't, they'll all drown."

The ship lurched another degree to starboard. The boat jumped inches farther away, and the crude gangplank shook for an instant. "Go!" Vanderbilt told her. "Go before it's too late."

Jennifer stepped up to the rail. A seaman took her arm to steady her as she reached out and grabbed the edges of the lounge chair. Then she pulled her dress up above her knees and knelt on the back of the chair. Don't look down, Jennifer reminded herself. Slowly but steadily she began to crawl out into the gaping space between the ship and the lifeboat. In a few seconds she was able to catch the gunwale of the boat. Then she threw herself aboard.

A seaman stretched another lounge chair over the abyss, and within seconds other women were following Jennifer's lead. Within two minutes the boat was filled with women and children.

One crewman went to the stern of the boat to tend the rope falls.

Another went to the bow. "Lower away," the officer ordered. The lifeboat began to sink toward the rushing sea below.

Vanderbilt touched a finger to his forehead in a salute to Jennifer. "He'll be waiting," he called. Then he turned away to tend to others. Vanderbilt had no intention of trying to save himself. This, he thought, was as good a place to die as any.

High above them, Turner climbed to the signal bridge on top of the wheelhouse. Having backed his engines, he could do nothing more to slow the ship. He guessed she might have a minute left, two at the most.

He turned aft to look after his passengers and screamed in rage at the slaughter he saw. Unlike the boats on the starboard side, the portside boats had swung inward, crushing the crewmen tending their falls. Then the boats had dropped onto the deck and slid forward, cutting like a scythe through the waiting passengers.

Seeing there was no escape from the port rail, passengers had rushed across to the starboard side, pushing into those who were waiting to cross out onto the deck chairs and into the boats. In the confusion two chairs had been jostled off the rail and fallen into the sea, carrying passengers with them. *Lusitania* was down to her last moments, yet only one lifeboat had been lowered.

The first boat had almost reached the water. After the swaying journey down, the sea seemed like a safe haven. The terrified passengers felt themselves breathing again. Then the bow dropped and hit the water while the stern was still suspended on the ropes. It swung wildly with the flow of the sea until the boat broached.

Jennifer felt herself being tossed through the air, with bodies flying all around her. She slammed into the water, and was buried in darkness as the huge lifeboat came down on top of her.

"THERE she goes," Schwieger said. His voice had become a monotone, as if he were commenting on a lawn-bowling match. "Her stern is high in the air, swinging back and forth. Now she's settling, rolling over on her starboard side." Haupert endured a long, tense silence. Then Schwieger continued. "She's slipping under rapidly. She's gone."

He remained crouched against the periscope for another minute, watching a sea that was clotted with bodies, some thrashing about wildly, others staring openmouthed at the afternoon sun. He panned from side to side, finding nothing but an ocean of human devastation. There wasn't a single lifeboat anywhere.

"Down scope." Schwieger stood silently a moment and then dropped slowly down the ladder into the control room. "Take her down to thirty feet," he whispered to his silent crewmen. "Set course for Fastnet. All ahead two thirds. We'll stay under until sunset." He stepped forward through the men and went to his cabin, unable to look any of them in the eye.

CHAPTER 15

Schull. With U-30's disappearance and *Lusitania*'s crossing safely behind them, Day took his fleet home. He saw his car waiting before Sheehy's boat reached the dock. He jumped over with the first line and ran to Tom Duffy.

"The message is sent," Duffy told him. "But Miss McDevitt was hit in the shooting at Emmett's place. I took her to Dr. Tierney. She's in a bad way, I think."

Then Day saw the awful stain on Tom Duffy's sleeves and the smear across the belly of his shirt. "Take me there. Please!"

As they sped off, Duffy explained, "She sort of fell as we were gettin' into the car on the way to the radio station. Then I saw the blood. I wanted to take her straight to the doc's, but she wouldn't hear of it. She said they'd never be sendin' the message if a stranger brought it to them. She had to take it to them herself."

Finally Duffy skidded the car to a stop in front of a row house with a fresh coat of whitewash. The lamps in the windows were still bright, left burning from their all-night vigil. Dr. Tierney had thrown his trousers and a collarless white shirt over his nightshirt. He smiled, but there was no joy in his eyes.

"I'm sorry, Commander," he said. He turned to lead Day into one of the bedrooms. "It was such a terrible wound. I couldn't close it. All I could do was take away the pain."

When the door opened, Father Connors turned away from the bedside. "I gave her the last rites," he told Day as he folded his purple stole. Then he stepped out of the room.

Shiela's white face was staring at the ceiling. She heard Day enter, and her eyes flashed with fear. "Don't let them take me," she begged in the little voice that was left to her. "Please."

He rushed to her side and reached for her hand. It was icy cold. Day knew who "they" were. The English. The Irish. Everyone in her life. She thought she had betrayed them all.

He fell to his knees beside her bed. "You saved them," he told her. "The message got through. You saved them."

Her eyes brightened. "Oh, thank God. Then there'll be no more children for the cemetery," she whispered.

"No," Day told her. "No more children. You saved them all."

There was a moment of peace in her smile. And then her breathing stopped.

If heaven was a land of peace, Day thought, then Shiela was surely there. The razor-edged loyalties that were cutting her to pieces no longer mattered. In death she had found a place she could call home.

Father Connors was waiting in the parlor. "Will you tell them?" Day asked him. "I want her neighbors to know that she died trying to save people. No matter whose side they think she was on."

The priest sighed. "Maybe you'd like to tell them yourself."

"I won't be here," Day answered.

Father Connors looked stunned.

"I'm a traitor, Father. It *was* a message to the Germans. The British sent a man to stop me. They'll be sending another."

"But where will you go?"

Day shrugged. "Someplace where Shiela would have gone. I'm a man without a country." Then he said, "Father Connors, could you bury her in the children's cemetery?"

"The deserted place, where the little orphans are?"

"It was important to her."

"Yes, we could do that."

Day walked out to his car, started the engine, and drove the short distance to Shiela's cottage. He found her suitcase still on the bed, where she had left it. It was open, with her few things flowing out. He packed them carefully and set the suitcase next to the closet. Then he began throwing his own things into a bag.

There was a pounding on the front door. "Commander Day! Commander Day!" It was Chief Gore.

Day bolted to the door and snapped it open.

"It's *Lusitania*," Gore screamed. "She's been sunk. We got the SOS at the station."

"Where?" Day demanded. "Where did she sink?"

"Off the Old Head of Kinsale. There are no lifeboats. Everyone's in the water."

Kinsale. Small boats from all along the coast converged on the Old Head of Kinsale. The first arrived at twilight and began sorting through the floating debris in search of survivors. It was after dark when the boats from Schull reached the scene. They could see nothing beyond the small circles of light that fell from their lamps.

Day was on the bow of Sheehy's boat. They motored into a drift of debris—the random artifacts of a world that had disappeared. There were upholstered chairs, a broad-brimmed lady's hat. Wine bottles bobbed like buoys, and deck chairs, still folded to a comfortable angle, lay inches beneath the surface. Life jackets were everywhere, floating empty.

Day asked Sheehy to shut down the engine. "Hello!" he called, waving the lamp. But the only response was the sea slapping against the boat. The motor coughed, and they chugged on.

They saw a man's body, face down and spread-eagled, the tails of the jacket pointing in opposite directions. They dragged it up over the side and laid it gently in the bilge. As they searched the dark water, they saw a colorless face staring back up at them. It was a matronly woman with a jeweled necklace resting on her shoulders. The top of her body was formally attired, but someone had torn her skirt off at the waist to make it possible for her to swim.

"They're all dead!" Sheehy said, looking around at the desolate waters. "The earlier boats must have gotten the survivors."

"Let's keep searching," Day said.

He was thinking of Jennifer, as he had every moment since Chief Gore had pounded on the door of the cottage. He had sailed from Schull with the thought of her trembling in a lifeboat. He had to get to her. But now he was afraid of finding her. He fought against the image in his mind of her still face staring up at him from the water.

They stopped the engine again, and Day was about to call out when he heard a gasping voice from the darkness off his starboard bow. Using an oar as a paddle, he moved the boat toward the sound.

It was a cork raft with two men clinging to its edge. Across the rope netting that served as its deck, two women were sprawled.

Day and Sheehy pulled the raft alongside. One of the women was alive, weak with shock. The other was dead. They hauled them aboard, then the two men.

All through the night they cruised back and forth. At first light they headed for the dark shape of the Old Head. They carried five living passengers from *Lusitania* and six dead bodies.

The sun was up when they turned into Kinsale Harbour. The docks were a confusion of seamen, some with old blankets wrapped around their wet clothes. There were faces animated with tales of rescue and expressionless faces stunned by images of sudden death. A British naval officer rushed to the dock as Sheehy tied up his boat. He gathered the survivors and hurried them up to the shore.

Day worked his way up the pier, questioning the seamen who were able to talk. "Were there many survivors?"

There were. Most of them had been brought in early and taken into family homes. The British were rounding up all they could find and bringing them to a church and a schoolhouse.

"And the dead?"

There was a morgue in a warehouse by the harbor head. One of the seamen pointed out the building.

Day started at the church. A British sailor with a rifle guarded the door. No one was being admitted, and Day was referred to the officer in charge.

"Name?" the lieutenant demanded.

"Her name is Beecham. Jennifer Beecham."

"No. Your name. I need the name of anyone who inquires."

Were they already hunting for him? he wondered. The Royal Navy had a disaster on its hands. He was a witness who knew that England had played a role in the atrocity.

"Day. Mr. William Day. I'm a personal friend of Sir Peter Beecham's. It's his daughter I'm looking for."

"Oh, excuse me, Mr. Day." The officer was suddenly solicitous. "There are reporters, you know. We don't want them talking to passengers." He was flipping through a list of survivors. "Jennifer Beecham doesn't seem to be here. Or at the school." His expression turned solemn. "Have you tried the warehouse?"

The navy, Day understood, had already begun its cover-up. They were frantic to find the passengers before they could speak with the press. They didn't want any witnesses to the absence of escorts. And they wouldn't want witnesses to the messages sent through the compromised Crookhaven radio station. He guessed there were navy people looking for him.

He used another name when he reached the warehouse. A naval officer led him inside, where a medical officer escorted him up and down the rows of bodies laid out on the floor.

He walked quickly, embarrassed to stare at people who had been reduced to carnival displays. There had been no time to compose the bodies. Mouths were gaping open, hair was tossed wildly, and limbs were scattered at awkward angles.

He slowed only once, when there was a slim young woman in an ivory-colored gown. The hands seemed familiar. Still secure around the neck was a string of pearls. He raised his glance. Long dark hair was matted over the face.

"You recognize her?" the doctor asked.

Day couldn't speak, but his stare said that he did.

The doctor bent over the body and gently parted the hair.

Day's breath escaped. It wasn't Jennifer.

"There's still hope," the doctor said as they finished their search. "Hundreds are unaccounted for. Many of them are being cared for in homes all along the coast."

"Thank you," Day answered, and he went outside. There was certainly reason to hope. But he knew that many would float in with the next tide. And many more would forever be locked in the steel coffin that rested at the bottom, fifteen miles from the beach.

"William! William!" He turned and saw Father Connors—the dark stole of the death rites flapping from his neck—coming toward him. Connors wrapped an arm around his shoulders and led him forcefully away. "They're looking for you," he whispered. "There are naval officers in Schull asking for you."

"I was expecting them," Day said, showing little concern.

Connors was frightened. "They've taken over the radio station. There are two armed guards standing in front of Emmett's house. They found him this morning. Him and your young officer friend. You can't go back, William. You've got to get out of here."

"I'm looking for someone, Father," he answered angrily. "I have to find her. Her name's Jennifer Beecham."

Connors shook his head furiously. "Don't be daft, man. We'll find her for you. We've got to get you off the streets."

He ushered Day into one of the narrow streets that climbed

339

the hill. "I have friends here in Kinsale. They'll take you in. And they can find anyone you're looking for. Believe me, lad, we'll find her." He pushed on the picket gate of a small whitewashed house.

Day stopped at the doorstep. "Your friends could get in trouble, Father. I'm a fugitive."

"My friends have been in trouble for three hundred years." He tapped on the door. "Now get inside. I'll be coming back for you."

Washington. President Woodrow Wilson wore his bathrobe into the Oval Office, where the Secretary of State and his counselor were waiting. He had been relaxing in his bed, reading the afternoon papers, when news of the attack on *Lusitania* had reached Washington. Now he was about to hear the grim details.

"Mr. President," Lansing said, rising as Wilson entered. William Jennings Bryan tried to clear his lap of papers, but Wilson was already seated before he could get up.

"Americans have been killed?" the President asked, referring to the note that had been brought upstairs to his bedroom.

"That seems to be the case," Bryan reported. He had a cable from the ambassador to the Court of Saint James's. "There are over a thousand passengers dead or unaccounted for. At least a hundred of them are U.S. citizens."

"Dear Lord. How could so many— Weren't there lifeboats?" Wilson was stunned by the count.

"Apparently she sank very quickly," Bryan said.

"There seems to have been several submarines," Lansing explained. "If they were all firing torpedoes—"

Bryan interrupted. "Our ambassador is simply relaying what he was told by the British. He hasn't had time to verify any of this. I don't think we'll have all the details for several days."

"But I'll have to say something," Wilson reminded them. "The American press will be calling for a statement."

"Perhaps you should simply lament the loss of life and tell them we are trying to ascertain the facts," Bryan offered.

The President looked toward Lansing. "Do you agree, Robert?"

"With all due respect," Lansing began, "I think something much stronger is required. The Germans have knowingly attacked American citizens. To my mind that constitutes an act of war."

Bryan's round face swelled with outrage. "Rubbish," he snapped.

"The Germans have sunk an English ship known to be carrying ammunition."

"Ammunition?" Wilson's eyes widened beyond the wire frames of his glasses. "*Lusitania* was carrying ammunition?"

"Ridiculous," Lansing said. "I can assure you, Mr. President, that there is no ammunition listed in *Lusitania*'s cargo manifest."

"If there were ammunition aboard *Lusitania,* we certainly should have known about it," Wilson mused. "If we didn't, then we're terribly stupid. And if we did, then we certainly should have prohibited Americans from boarding her. Either way, we stand indicted." A tight smile appeared. "So our position has to be that there was no ammunition aboard *Lusitania.* Isn't that so?"

"I agree completely," Lansing said.

Bryan was shaking his head in protest. "The Americans were sailing into a war zone aboard a belligerent ship. It isn't as if the Germans had shot them down in the streets of Berlin."

Wilson stood and paced behind his desk, his chin high, his hands behind his back. "As I see it, we have two choices: either deny the German right to attack ships carrying Americans and call them severely to task, or grant their right and prohibit Americans from sailing on English ships."

"We can't force the Germans to assure that there are no Americans aboard, before attacking an enemy ship," Bryan said.

"We can't prohibit Americans from their constitutional rights," Lansing countered.

But Wilson wasn't weighing legalities. He was guessing at public reaction. He turned to his advisers. "I think we have to condemn this barbarous assault on U.S. citizens," he decided. "I think we have to hold Germany strictly accountable."

Bryan folded the papers in his lap. "If that is your decision, Mr. President, then I must respectfully ask you to accept my resignation. I simply can't support such a one-sided policy."

Robert Lansing tried to look humble. He was the obvious choice to be the new Secretary of State. His political star was rising.

Paris. Winston Churchill folded the cable he had just been given and turned to General John French. "I'm afraid, General, that I have to get back to London immediately. *Lusitania* has been sunk."

"*Lusitania?*" The general went white. "How? Where?"

"Off the Irish coast. I don't have the details. Just that it was submarines and that there is a considerable loss of life."

"The audacity," the general said, rising to console his friend. "The damned audacity." He placed a hand on Churchill's shoulder. "I'm just thankful that you were here, not back at the Admiralty, at the helm. There will be hell to pay for this."

Churchill shrugged. "I can't say that it much matters where I happen to be. I bear full responsibility. An old navy tradition."

"You're not going to resign?"

"I suppose I'll have to."

Churchill went to his bedroom to pack his things while General French summoned a staff car. The general was waiting in the foyer of the mansion when Churchill came down the curved stairs, ahead of the corporal who was carrying his luggage.

"You should reconsider, Winston. The King will need your services now more than ever."

"I have considered," he answered, holding out an arm so that a private could help him on with his topcoat. "But there's a bright side, General. The stalemate in the trenches? I think you'll soon have Americans to tip the balance in your favor. I think that at this very moment, for the first time, you can count on winning the war."

"Americans?" French questioned.

"*Lusitania,*" Winston Churchill reminded his host. "She's a favorite with American society. It wouldn't surprise me if some of Woodrow Wilson's closest friends were aboard."

He winked at General French, whose expression showed that he was beginning to understand.

"So try not to take this too hard," Churchill recommended. "I'll be back!"

Kinsale. Day jumped up from the parlor chair as soon as he heard the squeak of the front gate, and rushed to hide behind the door to the basement. The soft tap on the front door told him that the caller was a friend.

"Father Connors sent me," a man's voice whispered.

Day heard the door close quietly, and then the landlady stepped toward the cellar and called his name. He came cautiously out of hiding and found a tall young man, scarcely through his teens, standing in the center of the room.

"Tom Downey." They shook hands. "Father Connors has a boat waiting for you in Courtmacsherry. He said that he'll be meetin' you there." He held the front door open for Day.

It was long after midnight now. Downey led the way up the narrow street, to a flat horse-drawn wagon. Day stopped short when he saw the six newly made wooden coffins that were stacked on the back.

They lifted one of the coffins aside, and then Downey pulled the lid off one in the bottom row. Day climbed up onto the wagon and then squeezed himself into the coffin.

"You should be able to push up the lid a bit to change the air," the young man guessed as he fitted the top of the coffin over Day's face. Then he replaced the box that had been on top.

Day felt the wagon jerk, and they began moving in time with the slow, steady metronomic pace of the horse's hoofbeats. Crushed into the dark tomb, Day had no image of the new world he was moving toward. He could think only of death. Of Shiela, her shrouded body now waiting alone in the church for burial. Of Jennifer, the horror frozen on her blinded eyes as she was lifted out of the sea. He tried to think of them as martyrs to some cause, to find a purpose more important than the first glimpse of the new day's sunrise that had been taken from them. But they weren't martyrs—only victims. Victims of the holy causes of great men determined to reshape the world in their own likenesses. In their global strategies *Lusitania* was just a small, expendable piece. The people who would die aboard her or die trying to save her had no significance at all. No more than the soldiers in the trenches, whose names weren't as important as the names of the battles that tortured them and killed them. But from the darkness of his coffin Day couldn't see anything more important than life.

They had been traveling for hours when he heard hushed voices, then felt the wagon stop. There was a shuffling of the board over his face and then a crack of pale morning light.

"Good as new," Tom Downey said as he lifted the lid away from the coffin. He helped pull Day free, then steadied him while he tried to find his balance. Day was standing on a rotted pier, next to a small decrepit schooner. The crewmen were leaning along her gunwales—dark figures who stared at him curiously.

"She's Portuguese," Downey said. "You're her new deckhand."

343

The schooner's captain swung himself over the rail, onto the dock. "This him?"

Downey nodded.

The captain took Day's measure. "Then get him aboard. I'm missing the tide."

"Where's Father Connors?" Day asked Downey. "He was going to find someone for me—one of the *Lusitania* passengers."

Downey looked around, then lifted his hands helplessly. "He'd be the one to try. But there's so many of them."

Day turned toward the schooner and saw that the captain was climbing aboard. He heard him bark an order in a strange tongue. The crewmen began taking in the schooner's lines.

Day took a step, then stopped. "I can't," he said to Downey. "Not without knowing."

The young man looked shocked. "There's no goin' back, Commander." The mooring lines were slipping across the pier toward the boat.

The grind of an automobile engine broke the morning stillness. A black car bounced around the curve of the harbor, heading toward the pier. "It's him," Downey said. "Wait here." He ran up the pier. Day waited for only a second and then ran after Downey. He saw Jennifer as soon as she stepped from the car.

She rushed toward him, bursting into tears before he could get his arms around her. She said his name over and over again as he rocked her in his strong embrace.

"You're safe. Thank God, you're safe," Day kept repeating. He looked over her shoulder at Father Connors, who was beaming like an angel.

"In the hospital," Connors explained. "Right there where you'd expect her to be. Asking everyone did they know Commander William Day. And still the Brits couldn't find her."

Day stepped back and held her at arm's length. She looked ridiculous in a borrowed oversized dress and big work shoes. "You're beautiful," he told her, and then he took her back into his arms.

"The tide," the captain shouted from the fantail of the schooner. He waved his arms in frustration. "The tide!"

"He has to get aboard," Downey told the priest.

"I need a minute," Day begged. "Just a minute."

Connors nodded. He looked at Downey. "Run and tell that savage I'll excommunicate him if he sails without Commander Day."

"A minute?" Jennifer was suddenly frightened. She looked at the boat and at Day. "Where are you going? Why?"

He pulled her close to him and walked her slowly down the pier. "I have to go away," he began.

"Why?" She broke his grasp and turned to confront him.

"Because I know things—things that England has to keep secret. I betrayed them, Jennifer. They're hunting for me."

"Betrayed them? What are you talking about? What things?"

He pulled her close to him. "I can't explain. There isn't time. And it would be dangerous for you to know. Just believe that there's no other way. I have to go into hiding."

She pushed him away and looked at him with sudden determination. "Then I'm going with you."

"No," he said with a hard edge to the word. "No. You're going back to your home. To your parents. That's where your life is."

"But my life is with you." She threw her arms around his neck. "I won't let you go."

"Commander"—Father Connors was standing beside them— "he has to cast off. He can't miss the tide." Day saw that the sails were already hoisted, luffing in a breeze that came over the schooner's bow. He reached behind his neck and broke Jennifer's grip. Then he placed her hands in Father Connors'.

"Go home, Jennifer," William told her. "You have a life to live."

"I'll take care of her," Connors promised.

Day turned away and jumped aboard the boat. The captain took in the last line, the crew hauled the sails across, and the schooner began sliding forward.

"I love him," Jennifer whispered helplessly.

"And he loves you," Connors said. "That's why he's doing what's best for you."

She looked at the priest, her eyes suddenly flashing in anger. She broke away from him and rushed down the pier, stumbling on the hem of the borrowed dress. When she caught up with the boat, she saw Day standing at the gunwale, slowly drifting away from her as the schooner moved off the pilings.

"William," she screamed, "do you love me?" She was running to keep up with the boat.

He knew he should lie to her. Only by denying what was true

would he be able to send her away. But it was as impossible now as it had been when he'd left her once before.

"I love you," he called back, his face dark with despair.

Jennifer ran to the edge and leaped out over the water, just reaching the boat. Day's face exploded in laughter as he caught her hand and pulled her aboard.

The schooner heeled as her tired canvas locked onto the breeze. She gathered speed and headed out into the ocean, passing due south of the Old Head of Kinsale.

* * *

July 21, 1915

Dearest Mother and Father,

I am so sorry for not having written to you immediately to tell you that I am well and blissfully happy. But that was not possible. As Father may explain, there were circumstances involved in the sinking of *Lusitania* which must forever remain secret. William knows the details of England's involvement and has been made a fugitive from his own country.

Because I love him, I am going with him into exile. I won't tell you where, nor shall I be able to write you. Knowing where he can be found would pose great difficulties for you and great dangers for him. But please believe that at every moment I will love you both and regret the sorrow that I have caused you.

I don't know what our future will hold. I can only hope that some day our world will find the peace and joy that I have found, and that William and I will be able to come home to you again.

With all my love,
Jennifer Day

William P. Kennedy has always been intrigued by cases in which an individual is caught between political necessity and personal morality—very much the position young William Day finds himself in in *Rules of Encounter*. In fact, the author's next book will pursue a varia-

tion on this theme. It will be set on an American army base where young people are taught methods of torture and resistance—necessary to combat enemy counterinsurgency but which conflict with their inherent sense of decency.

The idea for Kennedy's current novel came to him during a visit to Ireland, when he found himself in a small churchyard looking down upon the graves of an "unknown girl" and an "unknown boy." According to the markers, both children were "victims of the *Lusitania* outrage." He knew right away this could be the basis of an intriguing tale.

William P. Kennedy

Years of experience as an economist and business journalist have made Kennedy an expert at teasing the real story from masses of deceptive statements. "Time often blurs the distinction between fact and fiction," he says, "and that is certainly true of the *Lusitania*." Passengers did dine and dance in luxury unaware that tons of contraband were stashed below. But whether or not Winston Churchill truly played any part in the sinking of the ill-fated liner remains a moot point at best.

Creating exciting fiction competes for time with the author's career as president of a Connecticut advertising and public relations firm specializing in high technology. The devoted father of five children, Kennedy may at times find his life hectic, but he manages. *Rules of Encounter* is his fifth novel and the third to appear in Condensed Books. Previous selections were *Toy Soldiers*, which has been made into a motion picture, and *The Himmler Equation*.

BLAZE

ROBERT SOMERLOTT

The dog was vicious.
Too dangerous to keep but
too beautiful to destroy...

This was the dilemma
that Cappy Holland faced.
He knew he was too old to
start again with a "problem"
dog — too old, too tired, too
bitter about the past.
Yet he also knew that he
must try, that he had to meet
this one special challenge.
What he didn't know
was that the help he needed
could come from a very
unlikely source.

CHAPTER 1

IN JUST a few miles the road had plunged from the mountains into the Mojave Desert, and the truck was in barren, hostile country offering neither water nor shelter when the hitchhiker began to suspect that the old man driving the vehicle was demented.

The hitchhiker, a college student, had felt doubtful when he accepted a ride in the cab of this rattletrap camper van; he had realized that both the vehicle and its driver were odd.

He had been stranded near a crossroads hamlet, the last mountain village on the northwestern rim of the Mojave Desert. Slowly the heat of the afternoon had risen until it became uncomfortably warm. Taking his backpack off, he sought refuge in the shade of a mesquite tree, and had almost despaired of ever encountering traffic on this road when he heard in the distance an angry grinding of an engine and three sharp backfires. Then the vehicle itself came into view, rounding a long curve, an ancient Ford utility truck that had been converted into an oversize camper van by the addition of plywood walls and a tin roof, an awkward, boxy

351

construction that jutted out behind both sides of the cab and loomed high above it.

The hitchhiker waved his thumb vigorously. The truck slowed, and came to a halt a few yards beyond him. He ran to the passenger door. The van had once been painted in flamboyant pinks, reds, and yellows, but the colors were now faded and peeling. There was a pale shape of some huge insect and a name had been neatly stenciled on the side: THE GREEN HORNET.

The door swung out suddenly, and the hitchhiker found a fierce-looking old man leaning across the seat. Sharp blue eyes raked the hitchhiker, eyes set in a face as weathered, wrinkled, and tanned as the bark of a live oak tree. His thick hair and short-cropped pointed beard were iron gray except for two silver streaks at his temples. On the back of his head, cocked at a jaunty angle, he wore a blue cap with a sun visor that made him look like a sea captain.

"Need a ride?" asked the old man gruffly.

"Yes, thanks," said the hitchhiker. Then he added, "Where you bound, sir?"

"East," came the noncommittal reply.

"I mean are you crossing the desert?"

"Such is my hope and intention." The old man arched a pessimistic eyebrow. "God willing, we shall be delivered from the wastes of California and reach the promised land."

The hitchhiker put his backpack on the floor of the cab and climbed in. The old man, meanwhile, was busy fumbling with loose wires under the dashboard. When he touched two wires together, the engine roared to life, a roar that quickly subsided to whines, coughs, and grindings. The clutch, being released, emitted an ear-splitting screech, and the Green Hornet gave a lurch, then limped forward.

The glass had been removed from the rear window of the cab and replaced with a mesh of steel set in a wooden frame. The screened opening was not large, a little more than a foot wide and half as high, but looking over his shoulder, the hitchhiker could make out the shape of a large wooden box—no, not a box, he decided, a big cage with wooden sides and a door made of a metal grating. And an identical cage stood next to this one. What could be imprisoned in these? Animals for a zoo? Just then from the rear came a savage snarling, followed by bangs and crashes as some animal hurled itself at the door of a cage.

When the snarling reached a pitch of frenzy, the hitchhiker asked loudly, "A wolf?"

"What?"

"That big animal back there. Is it a wolf?"

"Good Lord, no!" said the old man, then added sternly, "Wolves, young fellow, are not big animals except in the north. Wolves of this region wouldn't be much bigger than a malamute or a sammy. I am returning a dangerous juvenile delinquent to his original home, you might say. It's not a job I wanted or expected."

It was then that the hitchhiker began to wonder if the old man might be a little crazy. The sounds of attack subsided, and even the engine quietened on the long downgrade into the desert. They rode without speaking, and some dark mood had settled on the old man. He seemed unaware of the hitchhiker, who leaned back in the seat and tried to doze.

He drifted into sleep for some minutes then slowly awakened. Drowsily, he found himself looking into the rearview mirror. Jiggled by the motion of the truck, it had come to rest in such a way that the hitchhiker saw a reflection of the mesh-covered window, and, suddenly, the face of a child, a small boy, who gazed silently through the wire into the cab. The hitchhiker had an impression of a fall of thick dark hair, pale cheeks, and large gray eyes.

The impression dissolved, and the hitchhiker sat up, blinking, startled awake, feeling that what he had just seen was not part of a dream, yet there was a curious unreality about the strange and unexpected appearance of the watching child.

He turned his head and tried to peer through the mesh, but the boy had vanished. The driver had said he was transporting a juvenile delinquent. This little boy?

The old man began to sing, and his voice, curt and crusty when

353

he spoke, rose with surprising warmth. He was not singing to himself. With his head slightly turned toward the wire mesh, he appeared to be singing to the rear of the vehicle, to the van that imprisoned the boy and the animal. He finished the song, and still directing his voice over his shoulder, he said, "Only a few miles more, boy, and we'll be at the Arizona line. We'll be glad to be out of California, won't we, boy?"

The old man, noticing the dubious expression on the hitchhiker's face, said, "They all like to be talked to, it's part of socializing them. You talk or you sing. Maybe I'm getting through to that fellow back there." He gestured toward the rear of the van with his thumb. "Unless he's just too far gone—turned crazy from mistreatment." The old man's fist suddenly banged the steering wheel. "People! Most of 'em aren't fit to be called animals, much less humans."

"That's a good-looking boy you've got back there."

"Good-looking?" It was a snort. "In my life I've seen few of God's creatures that were so beautiful. That's the pity of it. Why, he's sheer fire! Blaze! Fire and steel and quicksilver. A panther could envy the way he moves . . . But how do you know what he looks like? You haven't seen him."

"I had a glimpse of him a few minutes ago—when he looked through the window."

"Looked through the—?" The old man cast a doubtful glance at the hitchhiker. "What the devil are you talking about?"

"The little boy who's in the van. I saw him in the mirror."

"Well, you've been dreaming. There's nobody there but Blaze."

"Sure. Dreaming," said the hitchhiker uncertainly.

They were well into the Mojave now, and the landscape on all sides was a panorama of harshness and hostility. Dark mesas walled off the sky, their shale and sandstone smoldering in the sun. It was late spring and the desert bloomed, the bitterbrush was tipped with yellow, scorpion weed displayed a delicate lavender that belied its sinister name, and wherever a little earth covered the rock floor orange flowers of ocotillo struggled to seize the ground from the sky-blue lupine.

354

But the flowers could not disguise the gaunt land, a place of struggle so fierce that even the plants were spiked, armored, and bristling.

The old man lifted his voice above the rasping engine, half-speaking, half-singing. ". . . In the midst of the valley which was full of bones. Our bones are dried and our hope is lost." He sighed, and said quietly, "The words don't much matter. It's the sound of your voice that means something. It has to be strong and caring. And always, above everything else, it has to sound like love . . ."

BLAZE crouched in the deep shadows on the floor of the cage, disturbed, wary, and as alert as a sniper.

He was only ten months old, but he already had the lithe, powerful body of an adult German shepherd dog. His magnificent body had outdistanced his brain. His mind, his emotions, remained confused and unformed. Blaze had as yet no notion of his place in the world. He was familiar with abuse, but had no experience of kindness, and as his strength had grown, so had his anger. Never had he run free across a meadow, or prowled the woods, or even known the companionship of a human or of his own kind.

Only vague promptings of instinct, the collective experience of generations, kept him from savagery; he was undeveloped except as a weapon superbly designed for attack and destruction, but a weapon without guidance or control. And unlike a weapon, Blaze had felt pain and longing.

Yesterday morning the invariable routine of his life had been suddenly disrupted; he had been taken away from everything he had known, and in this new and unexpected strangeness the cage had a certain familiarity, seemed to offer security, protection—his own lair.

Blaze's conscious memories spanned eight months of his ten-month life, and all of this time had been lived in a suburb of San Francisco. It was a town of small, individual houses on small, identical plots. There were neither paths nor pavements since no person was expected to go about on foot and no dog was allowed to. The shallow front yards of the houses ended at cement curbs bordering the asphalt.

Blaze had spent his entire daylight life pacing on a chain attached to a ring that slid along a heavy wire cable that stretched between a corner of a house and an electricity pole at the edge of its front yard. The sliding ring permitted him freedom of movement to "defend" his dominion, the only ground his paws ever touched, running diagonally to the street, exactly twenty-two yards long and six yards wide.

By running wildly the length of the cable and back again, as he did several hundred times each day, he covered the equivalent of several miles. His shoulders grew powerful and the hip muscles that propelled him on his endless beat back and forth hardened into steel springs.

All this time Blaze suffered physically as well as emotionally. The dog's strong natural affection went unreturned and ignored, a confusion of emotions welled in him, and he became indifferent before he turned angry. He did not feel that he belonged to anyone or lived with anyone, but rather that the house behind his territory was coincidentally occupied by two humans, the Jasmine Woman, who smelt like a harsh imitation of a plant that grew across the street, and the Onion Man who smelt like the vegetable growing wild behind the carport. The Onion Man or sometimes the Jasmine Woman provided him with food, and there was enough of it except on days when the house reeked of alcohol. At such times they forgot he was there.

He was unaware that they had names, that they were George and Wilma Blount. The Blounts never spoke to him and seldom spoke to each other, finding it easier to communicate a few essential needs by nods, grunts, and unfinished gestures.

George Blount, who had never before possessed a dog, acquired this costly German shepherd puppy by accident. He worked as the foreman of the shipping department at a food-processing plant in the city and one day he was having lunch in the company cafeteria with several fellow workers when a salesman named Arthur Wheeler joined their table. This was flattering to George because Wheeler ranked as one of the more important younger men in the company, a chief vendor of its products throughout a vast territory. He was seldom seen in the cafeteria, but when he did drop in, his attitude was always jovial and comradely.

Over coffee, talk at the table was about the sudden increase of crime in formerly safe suburbs, and George, who was concerned about this, told of two daring daylight burglaries in his own neighborhood, when Arthur Wheeler interrupted him.

"George, this is your lucky day. I have the perfect answer to your problem."

George looked questioning.

"A guard dog! My wife's little nephew has been living with us since his parents were killed in a car accident. Just yesterday the boy's grandfather sent a puppy, a first-rate German shepherd from one of the country's top kennels. A dog worth a lot of money."

"You're selling it?" George sounded alarmed.

"Certainly not! My nephew's grandfather is crazy about these dogs. He breeds them on a ranch in the Rocky Mountains, trains them, judges them in some kind of competition. He's famous among people who like that sort of thing. Maybe you've heard of him—Cappy Holland?"

"No. Odd name for a man, Cappy."

"A nickname. He's Captain Elias Holland. Long ago he was in the army, I think he was a founder of the Canine Corps—you know, they train dogs for military duty. Everyone calls him Cappy. Anyway, he sent David—that's my nephew—this puppy. But we can't keep it in our apartment, the lease says no dogs in the building. I can't send it back or sell it without offending the old man. He's coming to California next spring and the first thing he'll ask is to see the dog. So I'm hoping to find a good home for it in the suburbs, a place where my nephew can visit it once in a while. And you seem to need a guard dog . . ." Arthur Wheeler made a gesture indicating their mutual problem was solved.

Something stirred in George's dormant imagination. He saw himself as possessor of an animal of great distinction, a costly canine bred to guard the treasures of the rich and famous. "I'll take the dog," he said, and suddenly found himself shaking hands with Arthur.

Three days later the puppy, Blaze, was shackled in George Blount's patch of grass. Arthur Wheeler, beaming a smile, bade George good-bye, promising to bring his nephew to play with the dog at some indefinite date. But Arthur and his wife, Nadine, had already agreed the night before that such visits would be upsetting to the boy, who might become too attached to the puppy.

During the months of growing up Blaze lived a life without variation. Every weekday morning George Blount would release Blaze from the kennel and immediately attach his collar to the chain in the yard. Usually George remembered to fill Blaze's water dish, but when he did not, the afternoons brought the parched torment of thirst.

Even when the water dish was filled, a hot day meant suffering. Since there was no shade, Blaze dug pits in the yard so he could lie closer to the cooler earth. He groveled in these, panting and perspiring through his lolling tongue and through the pads of his feet. Blaze was only three months old when George Blount came home to find the lawn ruined, and he beat the puppy with a leather strap. The dog did not resist because George, the Onion Man, was the bringer of food. Yet when the sun began burning again, Blaze was compelled to dig once more. Eventually George gave up, deciding the dog was stupid. The thought of shade never crossed his mind.

The torments of heat, thirst, and confinement were hard to bear, but no less brutalizing was Blaze's loneliness. The pain of loneliness was vague and formless, undefined pangs that drove him to rage.

And at times when he drowsed in the yard, he dreamed that he ran free, wild and joyous, dashing from lawn to lawn as he had seen the squirrels do. This dream of freedom was his greatest pleasure, just as his greatest punishment was the torment inflicted by his enemies, the three children. The children came often in the late afternoons. The first time Blaze saw them approaching the yard, he instinctively felt gentle, an inner voice assuring him that these smaller creatures were not to be harmed or frightened.

But he soon learned painfully that they came only to make a game of hurting him. Staying safely out of reach, they hurled stones and sticks. One of them had a bow and target arrows hard-tipped with metal, blunt yet hurtful. Blaze snapped the fallen arrows with one crunch of his jaws.

The children came close, stepping onto the lawn just beyond the limit of his chain, and the eldest little boy, knowledgeable about matches, lit rolled-up newspapers, then hurled them flaming at the maddened animal, screaming with triumph.

The children returned often, and slowly Blaze's besieged mind narrowed and focused: they were the enemy, and he learned to hate them.

Now and then people came to call at the house in the evenings or at weekends. The dog sensed the Onion Man's delight when callers could not step into the drive until the Onion Man had put his hand masterfully and showily on Blaze's collar; also, the Onion Man conveyed pleasure when these guests were unable to leave unless he escorted them across Blaze's dread preserves.

"A born killer!" the Onion Man bragged. "I can only handle him because I feed him."

Blaze could not comprehend the words, but he recognized the pride, the approval in the man's voice, and knew what he had done to terrify the callers was right.

Then, one spring evening, a woman came to call. She wore jangling silver jewelry and a cloth coat that flared and billowed behind her. The woman left her car on the street, as callers always did, and reached the foot of the driveway as the Onion Man stepped from the house into the carport and called, "Just a minute, Marian, till I see to the dog."

"Oh, who's afraid of a dog," she retorted, coming forward with her chin high. "Shut up, mutt!"

Blaze, snarling and with fangs bared, lunged at the intruder, hurling himself with all his strength. Crying out in panic, the woman leaped backward, stumbled, and fell on the cement driveway. She lay out of his reach, but he caught her coat in his jaws and ripped a long strip from it.

"Vicious!" she cried, then made small wailing sounds.

Blaze, responding to her cries, lunged again, barking furiously.

"Quiet! Quiet!" shouted the Onion Man, thoroughly frightened. "I'm so sorry, Marian. Let me help you. Come inside and wash, and I'll make you a drink. Oh, I'll punish the dog, I promise you. I'll beat him within an inch of his life."

"I would hope so!"

"Please don't let this spoil our evening. Wilma has supper ready. Here, take my hand."

The woman scorned his assistance. "My new coat's ruined! Do you have any idea what this coat cost? Somebody's going to pay for this and pay plenty, I can tell you. You invited me here, you're responsible for what that vicious cur does, George Blount! I'm seeing my lawyer tomorrow." She hopped to her car, still making whimpering cries of distress.

After she had gone, the Onion Man went into a frenzy. He cursed and kicked Blaze, chasing him up and down the cable, waving his arms and shouting. Blaze endured the punishment, thinking he was being beaten for allowing the woman to escape, and he knew that in the future he must leap more quickly.

Two days later the woman's lawyer reached George Blount by telephone at work, demanding a huge sum of money, warning him of impending legal action, and threatening criminal prosecution of George for harboring a vicious animal. Frantic, George tried to reach Arthur Wheeler, but the salesman was on the road and George had to wait three days in fear.

On the fourth morning Arthur, resplendent in a checked suit, found George at work near the great bins of onions and other vegetables.

"Congratulate me, George boy!" said Arthur, beaming. "I'm going to become a father. After six years of waiting, Nadine and I had given up hope. But now a blessed event is expected!"

George mumbled congratulations, then burst into his story. "The dog's crazy, just naturally mean," he explained. "I'll have him put away tomorrow. I'll call a vet—or do the police handle such things?"

Arthur's usually sunny face had darkened. "Just a minute! I told you long ago that my nephew's grandfather was coming to San Francisco. Well, he'll be here in two weeks to judge some kind of dog exhibition, and he's going to want to see the pup. After that, I don't care what you do. I'll call the woman and calm her down, but you keep that dog two more weeks, understand?"

Two Sundays later a camper van chugged into the street, halted at the house, and an old man with very bright blue eyes climbed from the cab. Blaze challenged him, racing back and forth on the wire, uttering dire threats, but the old man did not seem perturbed. He stood quietly at the curb and studied Blaze closely, watching every move, every leap and thrust. At last he nodded his head and gave a long sigh. He dropped slowly to one knee and began to talk gently, easily, his voice almost a singsong.

Caught by the soft sound and suddenly curious about the man's immobility, Blaze stopped barking and listened, puzzled because no one had ever spoken more than a few words to him before. Both the man and the camper van behind him gave off an old aroma of dogs, and the man's boots carried newer scents of strange animals, animals Blaze had never seen. Another strange thing, the old man conveyed no scent of fear, even though Blaze growled savagely.

"You're beautiful no matter how crazy they say you are! Too beautiful to be put to sleep, if it can be helped. But what can I do with you? I'm too old to start with another dog. Too old and too tired—and too hurt."

The man reached into his shirt pocket and drew out a little ball of meat. With a slow, smooth gesture he tossed it at Blaze's feet. Pleased by the tempting perfume of hamburger, Blaze swallowed the offering at one gulp.

"Was that good, Blaze? It had medicine in it, something to make you feel very peaceful and just a little sleepy."

The door slammed as George Blount came out of the house and crossed the lawn, smiling.

"Captain Holland?" The old man gave a curt nod.

"I read that piece about you in the *Chronicle* yesterday." George was at pains to be affable. "Nice picture of you, too. Seems you've done everything there is to do with dogs."

"No, sir. Not everything. I have never brutalized one." Cappy Holland stared at the chain and cable with a baleful eye.

George blinked at him. "Well, Captain, this is the dog. I trained him to be a guard. Guess I trained him too well. I put out a fortune to feed him, then he turns vicious and attacks a woman."

Blaze, meanwhile, had stopped growling. Gradually he felt a sense of calm and well-being pervading his body.

When the old man came to him, he stood serene while the studded leather strap that served as an imitation of a spiked collar was removed from his neck and replaced with a light slip chain. Blaze saw the Onion Man retreating hastily toward the house, and then he went docilely to the van and entered the open cage with no protest.

He slept then, and when he awoke in mid-afternoon he still felt quietly secure, but the sharpness of his senses was returning. Since he could not see outside the van, it was a while before he understood that they were in motion. He knew this because of the sudden retreat of smells and sounds, a changing feast of odors such as he had never known before. He heard the old man talking in the cab, meaningless words, although one was repeated over and over: "Blaze . . . Blaze . . . Blaze . . ." A soothing sound, yet a sense of unease, a suspicion, came to him, and finally he realized that he was not alone with the old man, that another human was present in the camper van, one who made not the least sound or movement and was revealed only by scent.

A little later he saw this hidden passenger. They stopped at a place that smelled powerfully of gasoline and of oil drippings. The old man left the cab, slamming the door behind him, and in a moment there was a soft rustling in the far end of the van, followed by cautious footfalls.

Then Blaze saw him through the grating. It was a young boy, and he revealed the scent of fear as he reached for the big plastic water jug on the floor near Blaze's cage.

Blaze drew back, then hurled himself forward, snarling, against the door of the cage. The boy fled back into hiding as Blaze tore at the grating with his nails and teeth, all the while in his mind attacking another boy, one who hurled painful stones and threw flaming newspapers.

Finally, when they were again on the highway, the sound of the old man's voice in the cab lulled him, and as it grew dark, he slept. But it was a fitful sleep, for he knew he must remain alert. Soon the boy would attack the cage, would come to hurt him. Blaze was ready.

Night fell and still they continued southward, down the long central valley of California. Very late they halted at a place near a river. The old man left the cab to sleep a few hours in a tourist lodging, but returned a little before dawn. In the night the boy had again taken water from the jug, but this time, instead of challenging him, the dog lay quiet, pretending sleep, ready to hurl himself forward with rending fangs.

That morning they drove south again, south into the pale yellow dawn as they curved eastward. At length the old man halted the truck on the roadside and gave Blaze another pellet of meat. When the feeling of peace and calm overcame Blaze's anger, the man opened the cage and put in food and water, taking a few minutes to clean the floor.

In the afternoon they left the main highway and took a road into the mountains. "It's out of the way a little, and it's winding," Cappy Holland told Blaze, speaking cheerfully from the cab. "But near the end of this road we'll see the nicest and prettiest lady in California."

Later he said, "Look, there's a hitchhiker, Blaze. We'd better stop for him. Another hour in this sun and he'll dehydrate. We can't let that happen."

And now, with the hitchhiker, they moved deeper into the desert as Blaze lay quiet but alert, absorbing the journey.

CHAPTER 2

THE road wound along the southern slopes of the saw-toothed Providence Mountains, skirting the edge of a harsh and desolate valley. The Green Hornet plunged into sudden dips, jolted, shook, and shuddered on the buckled and broken roadway.

In the rear of the van, concealed by a doorless cupboard behind a hanging Navajo blanket, the boy David tried to stay at least half asleep and also tried to dream of snow.

He had seen snow, real snow, only once, two years ago when his father, realizing David had reached his eighth birthday without knowing true winter, took him and his mother to the high sierra in March. They spent three days at a ski lodge. His mother usually remained inside near a log fire, but he and his father almost lived on the slopes, sledding, making a giant snowman, and exploring white stands of pine trees. Only three days—but ever afterward it seemed to David that he and his father had spent weeks in the dazzling whiteness.

His life had changed completely at the end of that weekend. While they were returning to San Francisco, their car collided head-on with a truck. David's mother was killed instantly; David himself spent a year in various hospitals, learned to walk again, and was sent home the same month his father, Ben Holland, died from side effects of the accident.

In the last two years, ever since the accident, he had learned how to be patient. He had learned this lesson held fast in traction, in hospital beds, and then in a wheelchair. He had been strapped and braced and pinioned. For what seemed to him a very long time he had been free of these restraints; he had even learned to run, although not very fast yet. But he knew how to hold still.

The van dipped into another arroyo, bumping and rattling, and David's head bounced on the thin pillow he had made by folding the checked jacket his Aunt Nadine had insisted he wear when early yesterday morning she laid out his clothes for the bus trip to Redwood Ranch Boys' Camp. There was a big safety pin in the lapel of the jacket with which his aunt had attached a white card bearing a message: *Dear Mr. Bus Driver, This is David's first trip alone. Please be sure he gets off at Ukiah where people will meet him. Have a nice day! Nadine Wheeler.* A stupid note! It made him appear babyish, seeming to say he could not read signs in the stations himself, although he was over ten years old.

But he did not argue with Aunt Nadine, knowing he would tear up the note the moment he was out of her sight. At the time she pinned the note to him it was still possible that he would really go to Redwood Ranch Boys' Camp.

That morning, yesterday, had been a terrible time. For nearly three hours David had pretended he was willing to go to the camp, while at the same time his aunt was trying to hide her joy at her own plans to leave the city the moment David was gone. To complicate matters his grandfather was expected to pay a brief visit. "Today of all days!" Aunt Nadine said bitterly.

His clothes, tagged with name tapes, and the other things he would need for three weeks were packed in a blue and white striped duffle bag. "Just like sailors always carry!" exclaimed his aunt gleefully, covering her nervousness with enthusiasm.

David knew better. Recently he had paid secret visits to the San Francisco embarcadero to scout possibilities of stowing away on a ship. He had seen many sailors, and they carried a variety of things, but he had observed no striped duffle bags.

"There, David!" she said gaily. "Your bag is ready, a big delicious lunch is packed. The bus ticket is pinned in your pocket, and the note on your jacket. You have your taxi fare and spending money. So you're all set to go!"

He gazed at her silently, unable to speak because he knew how happy she was that her own suitcase was packed and waiting in the bedroom, ready for her to leave to join Uncle Arthur at Lake Tahoe. "A second honeymoon!" she had said, describing it to a friend on the phone. "Just Arthur and I! Just the two of us." David had been listening on the extension.

He had also been listening when she and Uncle Arthur had decided not to tell him about this vacation. They had said they

365

did not want him to feel left out, but Aunt Nadine added, "I just can't face another scene with him right now."

The scenes she spoke of were usually moments of silent savagery, and they came after he had heard her talking rapturously about "the new baby that's coming in November." He had never been what they wanted, he had been a substitute, and now he was an unneeded one.

When such thoughts came to him, he felt choked. His father had been dead for a year. Aunt Nadine had taken him into her house and had tried to help him forget the loss of his parents. But now that she was going to have a baby herself, it often seemed as if she had to force herself to be friendly toward him.

Then, the night before he was to leave for the camp, Uncle Arthur had called from Denver and David listened again. "You know, Nadine, we haven't been away together since David came to live with us," his uncle had said, and it seemed to David that there was a resentful note in his voice, a sound that had not been there before the announcement of the baby's coming.

In the morning at breakfast his aunt kept looking at her watch, anxious, he supposed, for time to pass quickly, for him to leave. But it was his grandfather she talked about.

"The most inconsiderate man in the world! He's been in town almost a week, and he waits until the last second to come here. I told him you had to catch an early bus, and that I have a million things to do. He just doesn't care! Oh, the trouble Alice had with that man!"

Alice was David's mother and Aunt Nadine never concealed the lack of affection between Alice and Cappy Holland. David knew very little about his grandfather, but in his mind the old man was a figure connected with disaster and tragedy. As far as he remembered, he had seen his grandfather three times. Long ago, when he had been too little to understand, he had been with his parents and his grandfather in a park, and hundreds, perhaps thousands, of barking dogs were in an open field.

Then, long afterward when he and his father were in different rooms in the same hospital, his grandfather had come to see them, but David remembered nothing about the visit except three red balloons tied to the foot of his bed.

The last visit was a year ago, at the time of his father's funeral. The old man had looked down at him from a great height and said, "You look better than the last time I saw you. No more braces and crutches?"

"No," said David. "And I run better every day."

Later that day his grandfather thrust a small package into David's hands. He started to speak, then shook his head, and turning on his heel, stalked away.

The package contained a strange present, a ball not quite as large as a tennis ball and made of very hard rubber. If you dropped it, the ball made a ringing sound like a muffled chime. The ball was very old, pitted and scarred, with only traces of a green coating remaining.

Aunt Nadine looked at it with distaste. "Tooth marks!" she exclaimed. "Heaven only knows how many dogs have chewed on this thing—and what germs they had." She carried it to the kitchen, holding it gingerly with her thumb and middle finger. David never saw the ball again.

He thought, although he was not quite sure, that it was on that same day Uncle Arthur and Aunt Nadine had told him that he was to live with them always now; he was to be their own son—which was wonderful for them, they explained, because they had always wanted a son and now they had the perfect one.

David hardly thought about his grandfather until the end of the summer when Aunt Nadine, at lunch, made a grim announcement. "Your grandfather has sent us a dog."

"A dog?" A flicker of excitement made David's eyes widen. "Where is it?"

"Still at the airport, but they're sending it here. Thank goodness your uncle will be back tomorrow."

"Can we keep it?" David held his breath. "Oh, David, you know very well we can't," she said gently. "We can't have dogs in this building, it's in the lease. Believe me, David, I'm sorry."

David saw the puppy only once. The dog had been delivered

and was being kept in the basement of the building in a crate made of fiberglass with a barred door. Its lonely howling filled David with strange and disturbing emotions. He approached cautiously. When he put his fingers between the bars, the puppy stopped his howls. A small, red tongue kissed David's fingers.

Two days later, when Uncle Arthur told him that the dog had "a wonderful home in the suburbs," tears suddenly dimmed David's eyes. Uncle Arthur realized he was about to cry.

"Now you mustn't be selfish," Arthur Wheeler said firmly. "The puppy will have a big yard to play in! He can be outdoors all the time on soft grass. How can you be sad when you know what a happy life he'll have and how cooped up he'd be here?"

The puppy was never mentioned again, but now David sometimes thought about his grandfather and about the mountain ranch where the puppy had come from. "He lives surrounded by dogs. Dogs on the couch, dogs in his bedroom, even dogs in the kitchen, I suppose."

Two days after David's tenth birthday in March, a package from his grandfather arrived. It contained a long narrow whistle made of shining steel and attached to a sturdy chain.

But the whistle proved defective. No matter how hard David blew, it made only the faintest sound. Aunt Nadine bought him fancy dominoes to make up for the disappointment.

David put the whistle away in the cigar box with his broken compass, the battery-powered model racing car that would not run, the keyless padlock, and other valuables. He sensed some mystery about the whistle, a feeling that his grandfather had sent more than just a broken toy.

He forgot about his grandfather until one day Aunt Nadine said, "Your grandfather's coming to San Francisco but I don't know how you'll have much time with him. You have rehearsals for the school pageant, then the performance on Friday and the end-of-term picnic on Saturday. Then on Sunday morning you leave for camp."

But his grandfather's arrival was practically forgotten in the days that followed, and even on the Sunday morning when he was expected at any moment, other matters loomed in David's mind. Was Redwood Ranch Camp really just a camp or was it an orphanage, a home for unneeded children who had been replaced?

But then his grandfather arrived. When he said, "Hello, Nadine, how are you?" his voice brought the outdoors inside, and the room, big a moment ago, was suddenly cramped.

"Cappy, how good to see you!" Aunt Nadine shook the extended hand.

"Hello, David. I gather you've been a busy fellow this week. Too bad. We had a fine obedience trial yesterday. I hoped you'd see it, but your aunt said you'd be heartbroken to miss the school picnic."

David looked up at the weathered face as they shook hands. Because he could think of nothing else to say, he said, "Thank you for the whistle, even if it doesn't work."

"Doesn't work?" His grandfather frowned. "How would you know? That's a whistle only dogs can hear. When I sent the whistle, I thought you still had a dog. I have since learned by telephone that I was mistaken."

"Would you like some coffee?" said his aunt, her voice tense. "I'm sorry Arthur isn't here. I told you he's in Denver, didn't I?"

Over coffee his aunt and his grandfather talked of people and times David did not know. It was an uneasy conversation, punctuated by awkward silences. David was afraid of his grandfather—afraid and in awe. Yet he felt a yearning for the old man's acceptance. He tried to think of something to say that would draw attention to himself, something clever that would make the old man smile or even nod admiringly. He just sat staring dumbly at his own shoelaces. But as he listened, he recognized a quality in Cappy's voice that was hauntingly familiar. He thought of his father; he thought again of the snow.

Aunt Nadine looked at her watch. "Oh, dear, I'm afraid David has to hurry or he'll miss the bus."

They all stood up. David knew the moment of expulsion had come. He resisted a sudden, wild impulse to throw himself on

369

the floor, to kick the carpet with his heels while he shouted rage and defiance. He would not go!

"I'll be on my way too, Nadine. There's a long trip ahead of me. But first, I'll need the address of this fellow who has my dog."

"Your dog?"

"Of course. The papers are still in my name. Actually, I'm co-owner with David. I never sign away a fine dog until I feel sure."

"Of course. I'll give you a map of how to get there, just as soon as David's on his way."

David solemnly shook hands with his grandfather. "Come back soon," he said in a whisper.

"No, I'll not be here again," said the old man. "Maybe some day you'll come to Spirit Canyon."

Aunt Nadine was bombarding David with last-second worries and brushed his cheek with a kiss. Carrying his duffle bag, he went down to the lobby and then to the street. The click of the latch behind him was like a signal. He tore the note from his lapel, ripped it into tiny pieces, and let the breeze carry them away.

David moved a few steps, then halted suddenly, his attention caught by the ancient truck. The sunflowers painted on the sides were faded but gay, and they smiled at David. Could a man as cross as his grandfather have done this painting, even have imagined the great emerald green insect with long-lashed pink eyes that hid among the blossoms?

Without thinking, David turned the knob of the back door of the van, and he was startled when the door opened invitingly at his touch. Then, still without conscious thought, he put his striped duffle bag on the floor inside, and knowing this was what he was meant to do, he mounted the two steps.

NEAR a giant saguaro cactus Cappy Holland pulled the van cautiously onto a narrow shoulder.

He reached under the seat, found a wide-mouthed vacuum bottle and, opening it, took out three small gray cubes of cooked meat. "Fried liver. It's still the best bait in the world."

"Bait?" The hitchhiker looked doubtful.

Cappy took a bottle of pills and a Swiss army knife from the dashboard. He broke a pill in half, expertly cut a slit in one of the liver cubes, and inserted half a pill.

"A tranquilizer," he explained. "I want to take that boy back there out for a little run in about twenty minutes, and I don't want to take any foolish chances."

The hitchhiker gave him an apprehensive look. So the little boy was being kept drugged.

The old man left the cab, opened the rear door of the van and returned a moment later. "He went for it like a starved crocodile." Quite contented, he sat himself behind the steering wheel and continued the ride.

They approached an ancient road sign. Just 30 Miles to Miss Myrna's Best Beer & Wine!

The old man pointed to the sign. "I'll be stopping there for the night. You can probably hitch a ride there."

"Fine."

Half an hour later the truck shuddered to a halt.

"Time for the next round with Blaze—and I hope that pill is working," the old man said with a sigh.

"I'll just stretch my legs," said the hitchhiker, reaching for the door handle.

"Hold it right there, young fellow! If you have an urgent natural need to leave the cab, do it now while he's still locked up and I'll wait for you. But once he's *out*, you stay *in!*"

The hitchhiker nodded quickly and denied he needed to leave the cab at all. When the old man stepped down and carefully closed the door behind him, the hitchhiker turned backward on the seat to peer through the mesh-covered window. The door of the van opened and sunlight flooded the interior.

The old man sat on the threshold near the first of the boxlike cages and leaned toward the bars. He was greeted by snarls and growls. But he talked quietly to the caged animal. When the snarling ceased, he reached out slowly and unlatched the door. The hitchhiker gasped, not knowing what to expect.

The animal's head and part of its body emerged, and the hitchhiker recognized the beast as what he called a "police dog." He felt deathly afraid of such dogs. But he had to admit that the dog was oddly beautiful. The animal radiated an alert appearance, a look of being poised for action. The thick coat gleamed, and the back, which at first glance appeared to be jet black, was actually shot with threads of fine silver; on the throat, below the long muzzle, a patch of white stood out. As the dog moved, slowly and suspiciously out of the cage, the hitchhiker saw that its legs and lower chest were coppery.

Startled by the appearance, by the flash of silver and white, the gleam of dark gold, the hitchhiker momentarily forgot to be afraid, and watched in fascination as the old man slipped a light chain over the dog's head, all the while continuing a soft, soothing patter. "That's my boy, Blaze, we'll take a walk in the flowers . . . but you don't know about walks, do you? Or about leashes or slip chains . . . Let's go now, Blaze . . . Oh, you don't know about steps either, do you? What a terrible education you've had! . . . See what I've got here, Blaze? That's liver. Doesn't it smell good? Come and get it . . . Ah, that's a boy!"

Then the two of them were walking side by side toward a marigold patch. And suddenly, to the hitchhiker's surprise, the old man began to run, his strides very long and smooth.

The dog, despite being confused by the leather leash attached to the slip chain, moved briskly at his heels, then raced ahead. The old man dropped the leash and sat on the ground, panting and wiping his forehead while the dog bounded in great circles, joyfully barking. With a yelp of pure abandon, he hurled himself straight into the air, flipping over as he fell to the ground, landing on his back and kicking for sheer happiness. Then, upright once more, he raced and capered and cavorted, chasing a butterfly, plunging after a locust, giddy with freedom.

A few moments later the old man returned, the dog following him and seeming content to go back to its cage. When the old man entered the cab, he was carrying a hat full of marigolds. "For a lady," he said, and started the engine.

"It's a nice police dog, isn't it?" said the hitchhiker.

"No," replied the old man sternly. "He's a German shepherd dog—and he's the best damn dog you're ever likely to see, young man." Then he relented a little. "Of course, they're used for police work too."

The hitchhiker thought of the second cage behind him. "Do you own a lot of those dogs?"

"No," said the old man gruffly. "Not any more."

Thunderclouds were piling up in the southwestern sky when they arrived at a junction. An hour remained before twilight, but the day had lost its brightness and turned cool quite suddenly. On the left huddled a cluster of small ramshackle buildings dominated by a huge sign.

AT LAST MISS MYRNA'S!
Cabins Restaurant Curios
Famous 1 Pump Gas Emporium
Drinks Iced Tires Checked Fortunes Told

A truck stood parked near the lone gas pump and a man, apparently the driver, prowled around the vehicle, squinting at the tires.

"I suggest you approach that gentleman for a ride," Cappy told the hitchhiker. "If he turns you down, I'll take you on to the main highway. Lots of traffic there."

"Thanks," said the hitchhiker, hurriedly picking up his backpack. He darted from the cab, spoke briefly with the driver of the truck, then waved good-bye to Cappy.

Cappy parked the van where it would not block the gas pump or the entrance to the restaurant, then for a moment sat quietly leaning against the steering wheel, gazing at the desolate but dearly familiar place. In the five years since he had last stopped here little seemed to have changed. The buildings were slightly older, slightly shabbier—just as I am, he thought.

Why expect great changes? After all, five years were so few compared to the more than forty that had passed since he first drove into the graveled entrance of Miss Myrna's. Everything had been new then. Miss Myrna's father had died the year before, and she had invested her small inheritance in this bright dream, only to see her hopes doomed when the new highway was built farther south. Why, he had once asked, had she stayed here?

"Oh, I suppose the desert gets a hold on you," was Miss Myrna's vague answer.

The truck he drove then was neither more nor less battered than the one he drove now. There had been four German shepherds in the back, his slightly famous canine quartet of obedience champions, and they were all bound for Hollywood to become movie stars. Tucked away in the coat pocket of the decent blue suit that hung wrapped in newspapers was a letter from the great film producer who had, by accident, seen his dogs perform at an obedience trial.

And, oh, but that quartet was beautiful! Heidi, who could clear a fifteen-foot broad jump at a height of four feet, sailing like Pegasus; Inga, who took commands so fast she seemed to read his mind; and the two magnificent males, both dual champions for obedience and beauty, Donner and Blitzen. What a show they put on—tracking, leaping, retrieving, scaling a wall.

There had been so many puppies since then, but those four, his first loves, remained unchallenged in his heart. He could still feel Donner's soft nose gently touching his arm to awaken him in the morning; he could still see his dark golden gaze studying him gently, thoughtfully. Donner was the studious one, the quiet scholar of the quartet, just as Heidi was a loving clown, while Inga, who was fussy and precise, had no sense of humor whatsoever. Blitzen, a roughneck who disgraced them all with horseplay, made up for this by his adoration of Cappy.

So, after their first victories, they were going to be Hollywood stars. Cappy had believed such things then.

The first time he entered the restaurant its dimness had blinded him after the glare of the sun outside. A bell hanging over the door tinkled and, as at a signal, a pack of small dogs raced from behind the counter, a herd of miniature poodles swirling about him, snapping at his boots, leaping straight into the air as if they had springs for paws, meanwhile still in full cry.

A woman's voice shouted, "Annette, Cecile! Yvonne! Marie! Shut up, all of you! Be quiet, Emilie!"

Then he looked at the woman behind the counter, looking into that strange, arresting face he would never forget, yet could never describe or define. At first glance her features were too severe, the eyebrows stern, the hair skinned back too primly in a tight bun. The nose and cheekbones that were too strong also gave her an exotic look. She had knowingly emphasized this with small gold ear loops and a touch of gaudy eye shadow.

"I hope you like dogs, mister," she said. "Because dogs are something we have plenty of."

"I like dogs," he told her emphatically.

Two years later he returned, defeated, hating himself because his dream of Hollywood had proved infantile and he had learned he could not cope with the fierce world, he was ignorant and defenceless. Blitzen, the loving roughneck, was dead, and when he looked at the three survivors of his wonderful quartet, he felt pain and desperation because they were almost as thin as he was.

Miss Myrna helped give him back his confidence, made him feel that he was a man again. She represented the landmarks of his life, although he had seen her infrequently. She had admired him in his army uniform, dithering over his captain's bars, and listened to his unabashed bragging about the dogs he was training for war. Miss Myrna had known Ben, his son, but had never met his wife, although after his wife's death he had come here and felt less lonely for a while.

And now the last visit.

Taking the marigolds from his cap, he gathered them into a rough bouquet. He suddenly found he was tired, worn out from the long drive, and his bones ached from running with Blaze.

And he was hungry, even imagining he smelled the aroma of hot coffee from the restaurant. But climbing down from the cab, he felt that the dog's needs must come before his own. So he went to the back of the van and opened the door.

375

Thunder rolled across the sky and Blaze, watching Cappy through the door, pricked up his ears, but gave no other sign.

"So you're not spooked by the thunder, fellow? That's good," said Cappy. Deftly, he mixed the food in a metal dish. "I see you're hungry. Well, so am I."

Cappy unfastened the door of the cage, unworried about the dog, knowing that in these circumstances he was identified in Blaze's mind as the bringer of food. Still, he put the pan on the floor before opening the door.

Cappy glanced around the interior of the van. "Well, I guess there's no reason for you to go back in that cage right away. You can have the run of the van for a while."

David, crouched in the cupboard, heard the words but did not understand their meaning. He did not even realize that the dog was not in his cage when his grandfather left the van closed and locked the door behind him.

CHAPTER 3

CAPPY, seeing her through the screen door, stopped at the threshold, surprised. Like a gauze curtain, the wire mesh softened and slightly blurred his view of the room beyond. Miss Myrna, slender as a girl, stood behind the Formica lunch counter, frowning through thick glasses as she poured salt from a cardboard box into a shaker. Except for the heavy glasses, which he had not seen before, she appeared unchanged by the years, her black hair as thick and lustrous as ever, her forehead unlined. At her ears and wrists gold gypsy loops sparkled in the cold fluorescent light.

Pushing open the door he heard the tinkle of a bell, then the shrill barking of a pack of tiny dogs. They swept from behind the counter. Six dogs? No, seven charged toward him, yelping excitement and welcome. Their delicate paws and sparkling eyes were poodlelike, but over the years Miss Myrna's pack had evolved into a breed apart.

Still concentrating on filling the saltshaker, she gave a nod of automatic greeting. "I hope you like dogs, mister. Because dogs are something we have plenty of."

As the words echoed across forty years, Cappy waited silently, feeling for that moment young again, almost boyish as he stood holding his unruly bouquet of wild flowers.

"Cappy!" she cried then, hurried from behind the counter, and embraced him. Artfully Miss Myrna slipped the thick glasses into her apron pocket.

Later she prepared his supper, served him in one of the two booths, and sat opposite him with a mug of coffee delighted at his praise of the food, touched by his gift of flowers.

"And you look wonderful," he told her.

"Tell me everything," she said. "It's been almost five years since you were here, hasn't it?"

Outside rain began to fall, big drops splashing against the plate glass windows. "Ben and Alice were in an accident," he said at last. "She was killed. He died over a year ago."

"I know. You wrote me a note. What about your grandson? David?"

"Yes, David. He's fine. I saw him and his aunt yesterday morning. I judged some trials in San Francisco last week."

"I'll bet David was proud of his grandpa!"

"I couldn't say." Cappy shrugged. "He didn't come, had other things to do." He studied his plate, then added, "I suppose Nadine arranged the other things. She knows I never liked her sister, and doesn't forgive me for it. It doesn't matter. The boy and I haven't anything in common. He's more like Alice than like Ben."

"Why, Cappy! You sound as though you have something against the boy."

"Oh, I don't dislike him," he said. "I quarreled with Ben about his marriage—you know that. I expected him to finish medical school, wanted him to bring a wife home one day—a wife who'd fit into the plans Ben and I made for Rancho San Pascual. Well, Alice changed everything, and I was bitter. I don't hold that against David, of course. Although I admit he doesn't seem to have much backbone. Mostly I just don't know him, and it's too late to get acquainted now. Better leave things alone."

"Too late? It's never too late for anything important."

She brought him a wedge of cherry pie and took away the dirty dishes, then joined him again.

"Now tell me about your real family. I mean the four-footed ones," she said, chuckling. "Last time you had a beautiful puppy with you—I remember the silver in his coat. You called him Starfall."

"Yes. Starfall." Cappy avoided her eyes. "He turned out fine."

"I suppose he's winning all kinds of ribbons and siring puppies you're selling for a fortune."

"Yes, he did well, a fine guard. Two daughters are seeing-eyes." Cappy could not quite conceal the catch in his voice. "They've *all* done well. Things have never been better."

"Cappy, what happened?" Her voice was sharp. "Something's wrong. I hear it in your voice, I feel it. Tell me!"

He had not intended to talk about what had happened. Yet why had he come here if not to unburden himself? In the last six months he had talked to no one about his loss. He was a man who lived only with himself and the thought that anyone might pity him was unendurable. Nor did he believe anyone else could comprehend the tragedy that had befallen him. But now he was able for the first time to talk about what had happened.

"They're gone, all of them. Dead, destroyed. Fourteen German shepherds as beautiful as God ever created. The work of a lifetime—wiped out in an hour. I still can't believe it."

He spoke quietly, with almost no emotion, but his jaw had a hard, tense set.

"It started with such a little, unimportant thing. Something went wrong with the drains in the kennel runs. Water was backing up. So I moved the dogs into the old barn I built years ago when Ben and I had horses. It was warm and dry. I really didn't think much about it since they'd only be there a couple of days." Closing his eyes, he drew a long breath.

"I had this lovely bitch, Shenandoah. She'd had her second

litter by Starfall, and—oh—those five puppies were beautiful. I was keeping one, a little pixie called Star Shadow. I'd sold the other four by mail, and that morning I was driving to the airport to ship them to their new homes. And I was also shipping Blaze to David in San Francisco. Blaze was from a different whelping."

"Blaze?" she asked.

"Yes, my final problem. I'll tell you later." He shook his head, then went on with his story. "So I took the five puppies in sky crates and drove three hours to the airport. Everything went wrong and it was almost dark when the last pup got off. I was tired and decided to stay in the city that night. There was no reason for worry. Mrs. Littlefoot—she's my housekeeper—and her nephew would take care of things at home."

Cappy paused, looked at the rain streaming down the windows. "It was five minutes after three when the phone rang in my hotel room. It was Mrs. Littlefoot, sobbing and mumbling, but I finally understood her. The stable had somehow caught fire. It was gone in ten minutes, burned like a matchbox. The floor and walls were brick, so I'd never thought of fire. I never thought about the shingle roof and the rafters and wooden stalls and loft."

He leaned against the booth, closing his eyes. "They were trapped inside, all of them. Starfall and Shenandoah and the six pups. Cheyenne was killed, so was my beautiful Astrid and Lancer . . . and all the others. Gone . . . all gone."

His voice trailed to silence, and he sat motionless, resting his forehead on his hands. No one on earth could imagine what he felt when he saw the embers, still smoking in the pale dawn. These were the charred ruins of his life, so long to build, so fast to vanish.

Miss Myrna allowed him his moments of grief, then said, "So how are you starting over?"

"Starting over?" He stared at her. "There's no way to start. Everything's finished. I'm finished."

He could not explain to her that beginning again was not a simple matter of buying new breeding stock. The animals that had perished were the culmination of generations of work, not just

379

good shepherds, but *his* good shepherds. Even if he were allowed time to recreate them, he felt too bitter, too tired.

Impulsively Miss Myrna took his hand, opened the closed fingers. She did not look at his palm, but felt the ridges and creases.

"No, there's no future to read in my hand," he told her.

Her eyes seemed strangely bright, their gaze intent upon him. "There will be love and happiness you have not expected, but you must not be afraid to take what comes."

Gently he withdrew his hand. "Thank you, Gypsy," he said. "You mean well."

Miss Myrna tilted her head toward the parking area. "How good to see your van out there again. But it's strange to think that for once there aren't any dogs in it."

"But there is a dog. Blaze, the pup I sent David. I'm taking him back."

"Taking back your grandson's pup? Why, Cappy?"

"He didn't keep it," said the old man gruffly. "His aunt doesn't like dogs, and I suppose David didn't stand up to her."

"Well, then you'll still have one dog at the ranch."

"I won't keep him except long enough to find out if it's safe to turn him over to someone else." Cappy frowned. "Poor Blaze! Too dangerous to keep and too beautiful to destroy. Would you like to see him?"

"Yes, very much."

"All right. Just as soon as I've had some coffee and the rain stops."

"Fine," she said, going to the big metal urn and picking up a mug. "There's no hurry."

DAVID, huddled against the wall of the van, felt a new surge of fear as he realized that the dog's eyes were now watching him.

The interior was so dark that he could see only vague shapes and outlines, but a beam from the driveway lights entered the window from the cab, making a gray patch on the floor where the dog rested his head on his heavy paws. Above the black muzzle and glint of white teeth David could discern a gleam of the open eyes. They revealed that Blaze had awakened again, that the tranquilizing drug was rapidly losing its effect.

David sensed that the animal was troubled, but he could not imagine the dog's inner conflicts.

Blaze knew for certain that here was one of the miniature people who had tormented him in the past, an enemy to be attacked and destroyed. At the same time another voice, almost stilled by what he had suffered, whispered that this creature was one of those special beings to whom he owed gentleness and protection. He did not know what to do, and lay quietly, waiting.

So the dog and the boy watched each other, neither moving.

When Cappy had left, locking the van behind him, David had not realized for a moment that Blaze was no longer locked in his cage. Then, with fear like a cold shock, he heard the animal pacing and snuffling near the rear door. David held his breath, squeezing into the corner behind the burlap curtain, making himself as small as possible.

Minutes passed, an eternity, then the dog seemed to sleep, his breathing deep and even. Edging the curtain aside, David peered cautiously at Blaze. He felt terribly afraid of the dog, and from all that Cappy had said, he knew how dangerous the animal could be. But mixed with this fear, David harbored an almost desperate longing for the dog to like him. Earlier today, looking from behind the curtain, he had seen Blaze racing and bounding in the desert—the wonderfully free and most beautiful animal David had ever seen. He had thought that even he himself could run like that if only Blaze ran beside him.

And, after all, Blaze was *his* dog, belonged to him. Blaze should love him. They should be companions and friends. Yet he knew better. He looked for a safer hiding place.

Near the ceiling was a narrow wooden shelf, and if he could reach it by climbing on top of the cupboard, then squeezed back, would he be out of reach? How high could the dog jump?

David edged forward silently. Steadying himself, he put his hand on the top of the cupboard, then gasped as his fingers touched an empty tin cup, which fell to the floor with a clatter. Suddenly, terrifyingly, the dog growled.

David's mouth went dry, his heart pounded as he tried to remember what his grandfather had said. "They want you to talk, they like to hear your voice . . . The words don't matter . . ."

He would talk to Blaze, make him know he was a friend. Blaze *had* to understand. *Please, Blaze, don't hurt me!*

David trembled as he waited. The growl became a snarl, until the van echoed with furious barking. Then without warning, the burlap was ripped from its rod. Blaze slashed the cloth with his teeth, rending it, then hurled the tattered curtain aside to turn to face his human enemy.

David, dodging away from the knifelike teeth, had instinctively leaped from the cupboard and stood with his back to the screened window of the cab, arms outstretched against the wall as though pinned there. Quivering he forced out the words. "Blaze . . . Now there, Blaze. You won't hurt me, will you, Blaze? Remember I'm David . . . We're friends, Blaze, friends . . ."

CAPPY finished his coffee and stood up. "Rain's stopped. It's time I let that ruffian out for some air, so if you want to see him, come along."

She looked doubtful. "Maybe I'd be safer seeing him through the window. Can't you bring him up here?"

"You can sit in the cab. I don't want him getting wind of that pack of varmints you keep."

She touched a switch and an extra floodlight brilliantly illuminated the parking area where the van stood some distance away. "Still the same truck?" She squinted ahead. "I recognize the sunflowers."

"Yes. Ben painted those crazy flowers the last summer he was home."

They were approaching the van from the rear. Cappy lifted his head sharply when he heard furious barking erupt inside. "Well, my friend seems to be on guard."

Miss Myrna did not notice the uncertainty in his voice. Something in Blaze's barking seemed wrong to him. Dogs did not merely bark: they called, greeted, requested, complained, and applauded. Then there was the whole lexicon of warnings. It struck him now that this barking meant dangerous business.

Cappy quickly handed Miss Myrna a key from his ring. "Get in the cab and close the door. I want to talk to this fellow before we're face to face. Something has made him hysterical."

Then Cappy halted, eyes wide, a look of unbelief on his face. Faintly but unmistakably he heard a high-pitched voice, a child's voice, speaking inside the van. The wooden wall muffled all the words except "Blaze," which was repeated again and again.

Cappy rushed toward the door and unfastened the padlock. He rattled the door handle loudly, then waited a second or two before speaking. "Blaze, Blaze, old fellow," he called, "What's the matter? I've come back, so it's all right now. Easy, Blaze, just take it easy now."

The silence in the van seemed ominous. He eased the door open slowly, an inch at a time. The dog, angrily wheeling back and forth in the narrow aisle, seemed hardly aware of Cappy. His attention was riveted on a small prisoner he had cornered against the cab. The little boy's face lay hidden in shadow.

"You there, son! Don't move a finger." Cappy spoke in the same calm, cheerful tone he used to the dog. "Blaze! Hey, Blaze!"

Ignoring Cappy, the dog stopped his frenzied pacing and lowered his body to a crouch, ready to spring, his tail lashing.

"You now, Blaze!" he shouted, clapping his hands sharply. The dog half turned his head, realized Cappy was there. *"The Camptown ladies sing this song, doo-dah, doo-dah . . ."* Cappy sang lustily. His hand drifted to his shirt pocket, searching for the liver bait he carried there, then he remembered it was inside the cab. But on the floor, near the door of the van, sat Blaze's empty food dish. Cappy picked it up carefully, tapped it against the cage.

"Blaze, come on now, boy. See what I've got for you."

The dog stood quietly, then turned toward him, confused, unwilling to give up his attack, yet fascinated by Cappy.

"We can't wait all night, Blaze, boy! Blaze, boy! . . ."

Slowly the dog came toward him. Cappy extended his hand, holding it lower than the dog's muzzle and with the palm upward. When Blaze reached him, he gently scratched the dog's chest while with the other hand he pushed the food dish far into the open cage.

"Go on, Blaze. Time for bed, in you go. Now that's a good boy!" He cajoled the dog with his voice and his hands, urging him on with gentleness. And Blaze, assured by Cappy's words and easy touch, went peacefully into the cage, turned around twice, and lay down comfortably while Cappy latched the door.

"Oh, thank God, thank God!" exclaimed Miss Myrna, and for the first time Cappy realized she had been watching just behind him, a large rock in each hand.

The boy in the van took a step forward, then crumpled to the floor.

"David! Oh, God, David! How—?" Cappy lifted the boy in his arms, carried him from the van, David's body seemed surprisingly frail and thin. Bewildered, Cappy said to Miss Myrna, "It's David, Ben's boy. I didn't know—oh!"

"Take him inside, Cappy," she said. "Come now. It's starting to rain." She snapped the padlock on the door of the van.

As they started toward the lunchroom, David looked up at Cappy, his dark eyes big, and spoke in a whisper. "I wasn't much afraid of him. Just tired of standing there—but I wasn't afraid. Blaze wouldn't really bite me."

Cappy, still dazed, did not answer, but Miss Myrna patted David's hand. "Of course, you weren't afraid, anyone could see that."

Cappy, without realizing it, held David closer. "You've been in there all the way from San Francisco?" he asked.

"Yes."

"Why didn't you tell me you were there?"

"I was afraid of you."

"I see. Not afraid of Blaze, but afraid of me?" To Cappy's surprise the boy nodded. "Why did you run away, David? Why?"

"I don't know. Maybe I just came to be with my dog."

"No more questions tonight," said Miss Myrna. "Some hot food and a good bed for this young man."

An hour later Cappy was slowly pacing the floor of the lunchroom when Miss Myrna returned from putting David to bed in one of the cabins.

"You were gone a long time," said Cappy. "Did he talk to you?"

"Yes." She smiled. "You can forget calling his aunt. She thinks he's at some camp and she's away for two or three weeks herself, so no one's worried."

Miss Myrna put on her glasses and, sitting at the counter, began to deal and redeal a worn pack of cards, turning up three at a time and placing them in a star-shaped design. "Your grandson's as stubborn as you are. Scared as he was, he wanted to go back to the van and talk to Blaze—to show there weren't any hard feelings." Cappy sat on the stool next to Miss Myrna. "The cards tell me something," she said. "It says here that in a very little while a certain little boy is going to slip out of his room and say good night to that dog."

"Just let me catch him trying it! He's done his share of mischief for the year!"

"No, Cappy. Let him do it if he wants to. There's no harm. It's sort of like getting back on a horse after you've fallen, isn't it?"

"Well, he ought to ask permission," said Cappy gruffly. "Did he tell you why he stowed away in the van?"

"He told me he was going with you to the ranch—that he and Blaze were going to live there."

"*What?* His aunt'd never allow it. Besides, I've forgotten anything I ever knew about little boys and I don't intend to learn again."

"Oh, I think they're something like your German shepherds. If you give them enough care and patience, they turn out fairly well." Taking his hands in hers, she held them tightly. "Keep him as long as you can, Cappy."

He shook his head. "Once I talk to his aunt, back he goes! But right now I don't seem to have much choice."

Miss Myrna rose. "You'll leave early in the morning?"

"Yes. We'll say good-bye then."

"No, I'll be asleep. You get your own breakfast—and the boy's, of course."

"The boy's? Cook *his* breakfast?" Cappy's face was a portrait of shock.

From the rear of the building came a sharp barking muffled by a closed door. Miss Myrna turned toward the window. "Listen, someone's crossing the gravel, the dogs always know."

"It's David. He's slipped out of his cabin." Cappy took a step toward the door, then stopped. "Well, as you say, no harm done."

A moment later Blaze sounded a loud warning in the van. "We'll have an hour of this now," grumbled Cappy.

A cloud moved westward revealing the moon and in the faint light Cappy could just distinguish a small figure in polka-dot pajamas standing near the van. He sighed. A ridiculous situation, Cappy thought, and he resolved to bounce the boy back to San Francisco at the first airport.

Yet at the same time, watching now and remembering David standing so unflinching before the raging dog, Cappy felt a wistfulness, though it was not sadness but contentment, a feeling he had known before, although he could not remember when.

CHAPTER 4

CAPPY awakened at dawn, fresh and vigorous. He shaved carefully around the edges of his beard, and found himself humming. At six o'clock he decided it was time to rout David from his bed in the next cabin.

But he found David already dressed and waiting on the step outside his own cabin.

"I thought we'd want to start early so we could get home tonight," said David cheerfully.

Home? Cappy shook his head. "With that antique I'm driving, I'll be lucky to see Rancho San Pascual by tomorrow afternoon. Now go to the kitchen and find yourself something to eat. I'll be

387

along shortly—when it comes to getting breakfast, it's every man for himself," he said sternly. "I'm going down to the van to clean the cage and feed Blaze."

"How often does he eat?"

"He only needs one meal a day. I'm feeding him two or three times because it's a way for us to get better acquainted."

"Can I come along and help?"

"Not this time. I'm in a hurry."

David nodded, hid his disappointment. "Okay. Then I'll get breakfast, Grandpa."

Cappy winced. "Hold it right there, David! By blood and law I'm your grandfather, it's true. But I am *nobody's* grandpa. My name is Cappy. You remember that."

"Yes, Cappy. Yes, sir!" David gave a sharp little military salute, about-faced, and headed toward the restaurant.

Blaze was in a playful mood, all traces of last night's anger having vanished. Cappy let the dog run free, trusting that no strange animals would wander near. The dog returned willingly to a clean cage, and Cappy went to the lunchroom, thinking not very happily about day-old doughnuts and canned fruit juice.

David was waiting for him. "I've scrambled some eggs for you, Cappy, and made toast and squeezed oranges."

"How did you learn to scramble eggs?"

"Aunt Nadine hates to get up early when Uncle Arthur isn't home. I take care of myself."

Cappy nodded. "Good eggs. A lot better than I can make."

David washed the dishes while Cappy wrote an awkward note to Miss Myrna, ending as he always ended such notes with "See you soon," and wondering if he would. He left the note on the counter, then put money in the open cash register for their food and lodging.

A few hours later they were crossing the Arizona Plateau. Cappy had tried twice to telephone Nadine in San Francisco, but there had been no answer.

"I told you, Cappy. She's away. She and Uncle Arthur won't be home for weeks." The boy had not let Cappy know why they were away, and had evaded all questions about his own flight from home.

"You know it's not right your running off like this," said Cappy. "The people at that camp where you should have gone must be terribly worried. At the next town I'll call them. What did you say the name of the camp was?"

"I didn't say." David eyed him suspiciously. "Cappy, are you planning to put me on a plane in Flagstaff and try to send me to the camp?"

"Well, I suppose that's the only right thing to do," said Cappy.

They rode for a while in silence, avoiding each other's eyes.

"All right, David," Cappy said, turning the truck into the drive of a service station. "Tell me the name of the camp. I won't send you there, but I have to phone them."

"You promise?" David's eyes were suspicious.

"When I tell you I'm going to do something or not do it, it's *always* a promise. And you make certain it's the same way when you talk. Clear?"

"Clear, Cappy." From his pocket he took a crumpled piece of paper. "Here's the number."

It was almost dusk when they left the highway and took a winding dirt road that eventually brought them to a hacienda where they were to spend the night.

In the morning Cappy and David were again up with the sun and driving into the clear morning toward distant peaks tipped with snow, reminding David of the white world and his father. But these thoughts were pushed aside by excitement as each hour brought them closer to Rancho San Pascual.

"Why does it have that funny name? San Pascual?"

"Because in this part of the world a saint called San Pascual protects sheep and shepherds."

"I see. And the dogs from San Pascual were mostly dogs for sheepherding?"

"No, only some of them. German shepherd dogs herd sheep naturally, and there aren't any better herders in the world. But some ranchers want smaller dogs that are cheaper to feed, or they have very small flocks and can't buy the best dogs. Mostly I bred puppies for pets and for guide dogs for the blind and for use as guards."

They drove on, skirting the suburbs of a city. "Over there's the airport," said Cappy firmly. "It's from there you'll take off for San Francisco one day before long."

The village near the range lay at the foot of a mountain and a map of it would have resembled a tic-tac-toe game, four straight streets intersecting to form a square in the middle. A mission church faced this plaza and so did the general store, a saloon, the post office, a two-story brick barn that was the feed store. It was a poor town, but a modestly pretty one, the inhabitants unembarrassed that the geraniums on the windowsills were potted in tin cans or that chickens roamed the streets.

Cappy drove slowly past the plaza, nodded to passersby and saluted the elderly men in broad-brimmed hats and high-heeled boots who lounged on the porch of the Hotel Hacienda.

When they left the town and the foothills, the truck wheezed as the road climbed toward aspen forest on the southern ridge of the great mountain.

The canyon gradually broadened and softened into a green valley with scattered stands of pine and spruce. Between the groves stretched winding meadows tall with grass. Then, on the right and almost at the edge of the road, rose a high stone wall. As they passed big double gates of lacy ironwork, David glimpsed a lawn surrounding a swimming pool and beyond it a landscaped garden. A small sign above the gate said "Spirit Canyon Lodge."

"A hotel?" David asked.

"No, just an expensive new house with a fancy name. A rich widow from the city built it this year."

A jeep was approaching from the opposite direction, and Cappy pulled aside in the shadow of the wall to let the vehicle pass on the narrow road. "And this is the same lady," he said.

Instead of passing, the jeep pulled up beside them. "Oh, Captain Holland," a woman's voice twittered, "do wait just a minute!"

David stared first at the jeep, which was decorated with pink fringe and plastic daisies, then at its two occupants, who impressed him as being extraordinary. The man at the wheel was sallow faced and dark haired. Everything about him was narrow or thin—his moustache looked like two single slashes from a black crayon, and so did his eyebrows, which were set above hawk's eyes in a hawklike face. A slender hand with tapering fingers rested elegantly on the windowless door of the jeep, the wrist tightly encased in the French cuff of a gray silk shirt. The hand glittered —cuff link, watch, and a ring winking like diamonds in the sun.

The woman in the passenger's seat wore an enormous sun hat. Her hair cascaded in ashen waves below her shoulders. Beneath the coatings of makeup she had a rather pretty, doll-like face. David had no idea of her age, but it had to be far from young.

"Well, Captain Holland, how nice to see you back! I hear you've been on the West Coast piling up some kind of honors," she cried.

"Good afternoon, Mrs. Bradley." Cappy nodded politely, touching the peak of his cap.

"I suppose you've met Carlos Jones?" she asked, indicating the driver.

"I have." Cappy looked at the man, his face like flint. Jones muttered an inaudible greeting, then became preoccupied with the inspection of his own fingernails.

Seeming unaware of the animosity between the two men, Mrs. Bradley rattled on. "Carlos has been helping me find stones for my little Japanese garden. Captain Holland, a week from Sunday I'm having a housewarming for the Lodge. I've sent you an invitation, of course. A swarm of people from the state capital will be here, but I'd feel just devastated if my nearest neighbor didn't attend. You will come, won't you?"

"I will remember the date," said Cappy.

"Oh, good!" she exclaimed. "I've had a feeling that you're positively antisocial at times, Captain, and I do hope it's not personal with me because I'm such a cat fancier."

"Loving dogs doesn't preclude loving cats, Mrs. Bradley. I'm fond of almost all animals."

391

"Then I must show you Flossie!" Reaching below the seat, Mrs. Bradley lifted up a bundle of white fluff that straightened itself into the shape of a very plump and very irritable Persian cat.

"Isn't she gorgeous! Flossie-wossie!"

"Phsst!" it hissed, white fur bristling.

"I have six of them now, and Flossie's the prettiest."

Suddenly Blaze, catching a scent, burst into enraged barking, leaping forward to clatter the metal door, then banging against the wooden panel. Mrs. Bradley's smile dissolved.

"A dog?" she shouted above the noise.

Cappy nodded gravely, and Mrs. Bradley thrust the spitting Persian into concealment on the floor of the jeep.

Carlos Jones now seemed to take an interest in the van. For an instant Jones's eyes and Cappy's met, then Jones looked away.

"Well, we must be going," said Mrs. Bradley uneasily. "Until a week from Sunday, Captain!" For the first time she took notice of David. "Bye-bye, little man!" She smirked, and David knew instantly that she was ill at ease with children.

As the van and the jeep drew away from each other, David asked, "Who are they? Do you think she really has six cats?"

"Not now, David. I don't want to talk about them just now. It would take the edge off my homecoming. Just one thing. You stay clear of Carlos Jones."

"He's funny looking," David said.

"As funny as a rattlesnake in your closet. I've had trouble with him. He used to organize commercial dogfights. He had a ring in an old corral."

"Dogs fighting in a ring? Wow! That must be exciting! Championship kind of fights? I'll bet Blaze would be a champ!"

"Would you like that?" Cappy asked quietly. "Would you like to see Blaze covered with some weaker dog's blood? Would you want him to commit murder when it's not natural to him?"

"Cappy, you don't mean the dogs fight to death!"

"Death or the next thing to it. And they only do it because some evil man like Carlos Jones has trained them by torture and brutality." There was quiet rage in Cappy's voice.

A moment later Cappy stopped the van, letting the engine idle. They were at the top of a little rise, a low hill where the stream had cut a waterfall whose mists made a rainbow in the sunshine. Farther down the road a stone bridge spanned the white water and four willow trees marked the entrance to a driveway winding toward an adobe house with a rambling log porch and a stone chimney where vines wove their way to the roof tiles. Near the house stood another low building constructed of old faded bricks. On two sides of it, shaded by ash trees and softened by shrubbery, wire-mesh fences outlined kennel runs that were now deserted.

David smiled as he saw a tall whirring windmill rising above a brick springhouse, and there were sunflowers just as his father had once told him there were, and a big tree that once had held a tree house. Near it split rails formed a circle that David took to be a corral, and far past the corral on a slope two tiny girls in straw hats and calico dresses were tending a flock of sheep. It was just as he had imagined the scene.

"Rancho San Pascual," said Cappy. "I like stopping just here for a moment when I've been away for a while. This is the prettiest place in the world."

They drove over a cattle grid at the bridge, and the clanking of its pipes seemed to be a signal that started a loud and dismal howling audible all the way from the house.

"I didn't think there were any dogs here," said David.

"There aren't," Cappy answered, then chuckled. "I don't count old Xenia. She's the house dog, the one who's always slept at the foot of my bed—or on my bed."

"She must be beautiful."

"No, not especially. Coat's thin, hindquarters too high. Ears aren't the best, either."

"Well, then why's she so special?"

Cappy considered this as they drove to the house. "Well, Xenia knew from the day her eyes opened that she loved me most, that she was my dog. And once I realized that, it didn't much matter that she wasn't very pretty and couldn't do much."

Blaze, hearing Xenia, began his own baying, increasing his volume to match old Xenia's as she hobbled from the house. To Cappy it sounded like home.

MRS. LITTLEFOOT, a widow for as long as anyone could remember, had come to Rancho San Pascual a quarter of a century ago as a laundress, then stayed to nurse Cappy's dying wife, and had reigned as cook and housekeeper ever since. Her black hair, now flecked with gray, hung in two thick plaits that dangled halfway to her waist and were tied with little bows to match the flower print dresses she always wore on weekdays.

Since one of her ancestors had been Spanish, Mrs. Littlefoot considered herself a "native," along with the majority of people who lived in Spirit Canyon and in the three villages near it. The other inhabitants were either Indians, like many of her cousins, or Anglos, like Cappy.

Mrs. Littlefoot betrayed neither surprise nor pleasure at David's arrival, yet he felt that in her silent way she welcomed him, even though she only said, "You have your father's eyebrows and ears, so I know what to watch out for. And so skinny! Like your father, God remember him. You will drink a big glass of goat's milk every day."

She led David to a long narrow room with a tiled roof supported by aspen beams. Tall windows had sills just above the floor, and looking out David saw Cappy standing near a kennel run talking to Blaze, who sat quietly in his new home.

Mrs. Littlefoot gestured toward a wardrobe. "Hang your clothes there. Now I must cook supper. If you need anything, I will be in the kitchen." Then she hesitated, put her hand on his shoulder, studied him, nodded approval, and left.

Glancing toward the floor beside his new bed, David recognized the rainbow rug about which his father had told him when he talked about his life on the range as a young boy. His father's dog had slept there—his father's dog, his father's bed. For a second the white mountain returned to him, its snow dazzling, then it faded when he heard his grandfather calling him.

"Yes, Cappy! Coming!" he answered, stepping through the unscreened window.

Cappy stood at the door of the brick building that housed the kennels. "I want you to feed Blaze, then we'll take a walk with him before supper."

"Can I, Cappy? Will he let me?"

"Yes, I think so. I'll be with you."

The kitchen in the kennel building gleamed with stainless steel and enamel. David inspected scales and measuring containers, dust-proof cabinets and bins. The room was like a scientist's laboratory, nothing at all like the kitchen in the house where everything was casual, a little run-down.

"You measure out the food mixture like this, David. Add some ground meat. Here the meat's usually ground scraps of mutton because this is sheep country."

Cappy mixed the food, then turned it out into a metal pan. "Never, never use a plastic dish for food or water for a German shepherd. Remember that!"

"Why not, Cappy? On television—"

"What you *don't* see on television are dogs being cut open by a veterinary surgeon because they've chewed up a plastic dish. Sharp pieces are like broken glass inside them. Come, we'll feed him in the yard since we've got only one dog."

"What about Xenia?"

"Xenia eats in the kitchen near the stove. She wouldn't touch a bite anywhere else."

Cappy left the dish of food behind, just inside the kennel door, then opened a low gate to release Blaze from the fenced run. The dog bounded and barked, a whoop of delight at being reunited with Cappy; he jumped, trying to put his paws on Cappy's shoulders, and seemed not the least offended when Cappy clipped him sharply with a raised fist, knocking him aside. "Down, Blaze! Down!"

But Blaze eyed David with suspicion and would not approach him. "Sit on the ground," said Cappy, and David sat. The old man sauntered over to David and joined him, also sitting on the ground. "Talk to him, David." David began talking, but at the sound of his voice, Blaze barked. David's heart sank.

"That bark isn't a warning," Cappy said. "Listen to it! That's a confusion bark. Blaze doesn't know how to behave. So he's barking to hide his confusion."

Suddenly Blaze raced in a wide circle, still barking, although his tone had changed. Still going full speed, he leaped into the air, then rolled over on the ground twice, paws wildly kicking the air.

"An actor!" exclaimed Cappy. "He's showing off for us."

His performance over, Blaze came confidently to Cappy, his tail wagging, proud of his new accomplishment as an entertainer. He ignored David.

"Good boy! Good fellow!" Cappy praised him, then said to David. "Touch him now. Scratch him under the chest bones. Be firm and not the least shy."

David put out his hand, not quite able to disguise his timidity. Blaze was so very big standing over him as he sat on the ground. But then his hand was actually in the dog's fur as though he had plunged it into a great mat of fine silk. Blaze, gazing into Cappy's face, paid no attention yet seemed contented, so David scratched a little harder, digging in his fingers, feeling under the thick hair and smooth skin a heavy breastbone, and it was like touching rock. Then the dog slowly turned his great head and looked down at him, studying him with a judicious gaze.

"Blaze, Blaze," David whispered. The dog's eyes seemed deep and knowing. After a moment he put his head on David's shoulder, and David felt the broad, moist tongue lightly touching his ear.

"I think this is the start of a friendship," said Cappy. "Now give him his dinner, but move slowly. Don't surprise him in any way."

As David went to get the food dish, Cappy called to him, "Put the dish on the ground fast. He hasn't got any table manners yet, and if you keep moving that slowly, he might knock you down by accident when he rushes the food."

As Cappy suspected, David had a narrow escape when Blaze smelled food and dashed to get it. They stood together, watching

Blaze, Cappy frowning and shaking his head in disapproval. "He goes for food like a pig. Lord, he needs civilizing!"

David nodded. "When do we begin, Cappy?"

"Begin what?"

"Civilizing him." David did not dare look at Cappy, and the next few seconds seemed the longest of his life.

Cappy studied Blaze. The dog had finished eating and now stood alert, watching his human companions. His coat and ruff glowed jet and tawny in the thickening light; his eyes, now shadowed, were no longer dark gold but two bright points of obsidian.

Of the German shepherds Cappy had bred, Blaze now struck him as the most beautiful he had produced in a lifetime, the nearest to perfection. Blaze was the culmination but he had come too late and his mind had been twisted and harmed. He looked from the dog to the waiting boy. These two were the final products of his life—a boy he did not understand and a dog he distrusted.

Blaze walked slowly to David's side and sat waiting.

"I think we should start tomorrow morning," Cappy said at last.

MRS. LITTLEFOOT served them supper at the big round table in the kitchen, filling their plates with a pungent stew. She herself ate standing at the draining board. Xenia, lying in a corner, was waiting impatiently for the aroma of coffee being poured, which was a signal that the meal was over and she could approach and lie at Cappy's feet.

"What's the news of the canyon?" Cappy asked.

Mrs. Littlefoot considered the question. "Carlos Jones is back and has gone to work for the Woman." Since Mrs. Bradley was this year's topic of gossip there was no need to name her.

"I know. I passed them on the road."

"He is living in a cabin on her land. It is dangerous to have such a man for a neighbor," she said. "He will end worse than his father who was shot while stealing rabbits from a pen."

"Don't worry," he answered. "I'll watch out."

When Mrs. Littlefoot poured coffee, Xenia came confidently to the table, and Cappy automatically scratched behind her ears. She rubbed her head against his knee, blissful, and David imagined Blaze sitting beside his own chair, magnificent and devoted. But Cappy had already explained that Blaze must never be allowed in a room with Xenia, because she would be jealous and would probably attack Blaze, who was far too strong and rough for her.

After supper Cappy went through his small accumulation of mail, tossing Mrs. Bradley's coy cocktail invitation in the wastebasket.

David watched Mrs. Littlefoot cook liver Cappy had ordered so he could reward Blaze tomorrow when the dog did well in training. At nine o'clock Cappy tried to telephone the apartment in San Francisco, but again there was no answer, and at nine-thirty David went to bed in the long narrow room.

He was tired, yet not ready for sleep, and for a long time he stared into the darkness. Then, suddenly, he knew what to do. Slipping from the bed, he went to the window and opened the shutters Mrs. Littlefoot had fastened against the night. A cool wind had flooded down from the peaks of the sierra, and it billowed the thin curtains.

He stepped over the low sill and moved into the moonlight and shadows. Stiff grass pricked the bare soles of his feet as he ran across the yard toward the kennels. And there Blaze was waiting for him, sitting tall eared and expectant, alert at the gait of his run. David slipped back the bolt while Blaze, unmoving, watched him. "Come, Blaze! Come with me!"

Then they were running together in the night, around the dim circle of the empty corral, past the windmill and the shuttered well house. They ran as David had only imagined they could run, his own body light as air, his legs strong and well mended. Laughing happily David bounded with Blaze across the meadow, flew to his own window, and let Blaze hop into his room. While David entered after him, put on the lamp and closed the shutters, Blaze inspected the corners, peered under the bed, and checked the wardrobe. When David sat on the faded rainbow rug, Blaze, after turning around twice, lay down beside him. He remained there quietly after David turned out the light and slipped between the covers of his bed and rested his head on the white pillow. He fell asleep. His hand dangled from the side of the mattress, came to rest on Blaze's back. The dog stirred in sleep but did not awaken.

CHAPTER 5

AT SIX-THIRTY Cappy, unaware of the change in Blaze's sleeping place, opened the door of David's room and took one very quiet step inside. The room, its shutters bolted, was almost dark, but in the dim light from the partly open door he saw David's tousled head on the pillow and the dog, asleep on the rug.

Cappy realized with some consternation that David had spirited the dog into the house, once again showing more determination and independence than good judgment. They must have had quite a night, to judge from how heavily both the boy and the dog now slept, Cappy thought. Well, this would be David's last nocturnal adventure at San Pascual.

Cappy decided to let the boy sleep a little longer, and started to turn away. When he touched the door, a hinge creaked and the high-pitched sound came faintly to Blaze's ears, causing him to half open his eyes. A door that had not been open last night was strangely open now, and silhouetted against the light Blaze saw a menacing figure, a man who lurked in the room. Blaze did not recognize the intruder. Even as a growl was forming in his throat, he charged to attack.

Cappy had sensed what was about to happen and snatching up a wooden chair that stood beside the door, he blocked the assault before Blaze was fully in action, but even so the dog's power knocked him backward against the wall.

"Blaze!" he yelled. "Blaze!" The dog, pulling back for a new assault, instantly recognized the voice. He blinked, then the bristling fur smoothed, and he trotted forward happily, eager to wish his friend good morning.

David sat up in bed, eyes wide. "What happened?"

399

Cappy, after opening the shutters, glowered at both the boy and the dog. "Well, it's nice to start the day with a little surprise! I came in unexpectedly and Blaze jumped me."

"I'm sure Blaze didn't mean any harm. I suppose if you'd knocked on the door, he'd have expected you."

"*Expected me!*" Cappy's mouth opened, he turned red, then smothered the explosion he'd meant to let loose. No, he had not thought of knocking. "Then next time I'll knock," he said gruffly. "But you'll make no other changes in arrangements around here without consulting me. Do you have that straight, young fellow?"

"Yes, sir," said David reasonably.

After breakfast they went to the corral, which Cappy called "the training ring." Blaze frisked beside them, ran off to pursue a butterfly, carefree and well meaning as a puppy.

"Don't hope for much," Cappy warned David. "It's hard to salvage a dog—or a child—who's been abused too long."

But at first everything went so well that Cappy wondered if he had misjudged Blaze. The dog sat smartly at Cappy's left while a slip-chain collar was put over his head, seeming almost at military attention except for his wagging tail. Cappy left the collar on for only a few minutes, then removed it and showed David how it worked. "The steel links are light but strong. The slip collar gives you control—once you understand how to use it."

"I thought training collars had spikes or points on the inside to make the dog mind," said David.

"Not at San Pascual! Suppose you'd been trained with torture equipment. How would you feel about the world? Ready to chew it up, I'll bet."

Cappy had David put the collar on Blaze. "Now the leash. It's flat leather and just as long as I'm tall. Too long for you, but don't ever twist it around your arm."

He showed David how to hold the leash while Blaze romped and frisked with energy that never seemed to flag.

"Blaze seemed to know a leash, so we won't worry about its being unfamiliar to him. But remember, he weighs more than you do, and he's got four feet to give him power and balance. You can't handle him by pulling the leash, so you *jerk* it, don't pull it."

"Jerk, don't pull," David repeated.

"When he does well, praise him. When he goes wrong, yell 'Phooey!' as loud as you can."

David called and Blaze trotted to his side, and sat quietly while David fastened the harness snap of the leash on the proper collar ring.

"Just take an easy little walk," said Cappy.

They walked around the ring and David, confident of Blaze and finding the leash too long, let it twist around his arm.

"David, don't let the leash—"

Blaze moved ahead, enough that the collar tightened sharply. He felt the restricting pull of the line, and a hateful memory surged in him—the strangling chain that slid along the wire in George Blount's yard. As the thing around his throat tightened, he fought it, hurling himself wildly ahead. At the same time, he turned his head to slash at the leash, struggling to bite through this maddening, confining strap.

Blaze's first lunge threw David to the ground, and unable to let go of the twisted leash, he found himself dragged across the ring face down.

Cappy threw himself on top of David to pin the leash to the ground with the weight of his body. For a few seconds the dog struggled, then with a faint snap the steel slip chain broke, freeing Blaze, who went dashing in frantic circles around the ring.

Cappy got to his knees. "Are you all right, boy?"

"Uh, huh," murmured David, gingerly touching his arm where the leather had burned his skin. Scratches smarted on his cheek and forehead, and when he touched his chin, he brushed away fine gravel.

"Let's go to the house and wash," Cappy told him. "We'd better disinfect these scratches. Mrs. Littlefoot can mend that shirt of yours."

When Cappy stood up, he realized that this evening every joint in his body would ache. Something in his left shoulder seemed pulled loose and both his kneecaps were skinned. He was too old

401

for this, too old to be fighting and throwing himself on the ground. He should never have started this hopeless work.

Blaze approached, his world right again, and nuzzled Cappy's hand, then lay down, rolled over, and kicked his paws in the air playfully.

That afternoon Cappy, despite stiffening joints, decided to try again with Blaze, to work for an hour, although he had little hope that the dog would respond. David could watch, but Cappy would handle Blaze himself.

But after a few minutes of walking Blaze around the corral, Cappy forgot his aching bones. Blaze, now calm and assured, showed not the least skittishness, even in accepting the leash after being allowed to inspect it carefully and drag it after him.

"That's what I should have done this morning," said Cappy. "You let a puppy discover the leash for himself. But I didn't think of Blaze as a puppy—my mistake!"

Blaze sat with his head cocked, ears alert, and eyes sparkling as he concentrated on every word Cappy spoke. Until the past few days no human had ever spoken to him except to shout, so now it seemed soothing and reassuring to hear quiet voices.

But even more important than his discovery of language was his discovery of love. When he had first met Cappy he had felt a tugging of emotion, and a little later a not quite sure sense of belonging. Yesterday this new feeling had expanded to include David, and then last night, after running with David in the meadow, he had gone to sleep contented, knowing he had at last come home.

Cappy, too, felt an unfamiliar contentment as he worked with Blaze while David, sitting on a rail of the corral, watched admiringly. He felt refreshed and vaguely realized that despite his aches, this was the first time in months that he had not the faintest sense of being a little run down. He was doing what he had always loved most, working with an eager, intelligent dog on a fine, clear day.

The allotted hour went by, became an hour and a half, then almost two hours before Cappy looked at his watch. "That's enough. In fact, it's far too much. You never let training become hard work."

At supper that evening they talked over every detail of what had happened during the day. Mrs. Littlefoot watched them without saying a word, standing at the draining board.

After the table had been cleared and Xenia had received her proper attention, Cappy brought out an old manual and showed David drawings of various hand signals used in dog training. They went through the entire book, practising every gesture, while Xenia, half asleep, watched them, now and then thumping her tail to show she approved and even understood a few commands, although she had no intention of obeying any of them.

At bedtime David, with permission tonight, went to the kennel run to bring Blaze in to sleep on the faded rug by the bed.

That night Cappy forgot to try calling San Francisco, and Mrs. Littlefoot, although she noticed this, did not remind him.

THE next few days David learned about this new world he had entered, a small universe bounded on one side by the swift, shallow stream and on the other three by rambling wire fences that marked out the extent of Rancho San Pascual. David and Blaze could walk these limits in half an hour.

The dog and the boy were always together, for contrary to what Cappy had feared, once Blaze had given his devotion, he was constant and steady.

Surprisingly, David never felt lonely, although his world had only three inhabitants besides himself—Cappy, Blaze, and Mrs. Littlefoot. Xenia did not count, for she had retired into her private sphere, interested only in watching and sometimes stiffly following Cappy. She tolerated Mrs. Littlefoot and ignored David.

On the edge of this world a few other creatures loitered or passed. Every day David saw at a distance the flock of grayish sheep tended by the two small Indian girls, but they never came close to the San Pascual boundaries. Twice he saw Mrs. Bradley's flower-bedecked jeep on the road, but too far away for him to know if the hawk-faced man, Carlos Jones, was driving.

403

One afternoon David went down to the river intending to catch a trout, a doomed ambition because Blaze quickly discovered the joy of leaping into the shallow water and splashing it with his head, scaring off any fish.

At sunset, they went back to the house. Cappy was sitting on the back steps, looking thoughtfully at the changing sky. He was shortening a training leash, making it the right length for David to handle. David sat beside him and after a silence Cappy said, "Your uncle telephoned about an hour ago."

David's heart seemed to lurch. "From San Francisco?"

"No. From a hotel at Lake Tahoe. He'd called that camp where you're supposed to be. They told him to try here."

"How is Uncle Arthur?" David asked cautiously.

"Mad enough to spit nails! For a minute I thought he was going to catch the next plane, come here, and drag you to California by the scruff of your neck, young man. But I persuaded him not to make any violent moves."

Arthur Wheeler's anger had surprised Cappy, who had always regarded him as affable but shallow, a harmlessly vain man with a salesman's show of confidence. But David's defection had struck

Arthur as a personal attack and, as Cappy suspected, even as an accusation of failure.

"What did Uncle Arthur want?"

"That's a fool question!" Cappy spluttered. "He wanted to know if you are, by some chance, still alive. Your uncle does have a certain interest in your health and whereabouts, although you're not exactly popular with him right now."

David avoided Cappy's glare. "Does he want me to go to that camp? To go back to San Francisco?"

"He doesn't care about the camp—except he's not overjoyed about the money wasted on camp fees. But of course he wants you to go back to San Francisco. What would make you think anything else?" Cappy hesitated. "But angry as your uncle sounded, I thought we'd better give him a while for his temper to cool," he continued. "So I told him I needed you here this summer to help train Blaze. You can stay here until a week before school starts in October. That is, if you want to."

"I want to," said David, hardly breathing. Until October? That was a time in the unimaginable future that might never come. And he wanted to tell Cappy that he loved him, but he could not seem to make the words come right, and Cappy was suddenly acting strange and uneasy, avoiding his eyes.

CHAPTER 6

THE next Sunday turned out to be a memorable day in David's life—a day no one in Spirit Canyon would ever forget—but at Rancho San Pascual that morning there were no portents of what was to take place.

Mrs. Littlefoot was unusually talkative as she leaned against the draining board sipping coffee from a mug. "The Woman has hired half the village to work at her party today," she said. "Yesterday a truck from the city brought a load of fancy things and a statue carved from a block of ice! There will even be an orchestra!"

She finished the breakfast dishes quickly, then tied her hat on with a long scarf of black silk and left for Mass at the village church.

"We won't work with Blaze today," said Cappy. "This afternoon we'll take him on a walk down to the waterfall."

Something had been on David's mind. "Cappy, could Blaze learn to track? I mean like tracking down burglars by following their scent."

"I wish you wouldn't always think of Blaze doing police or guard work," said Cappy. "Yes, he could do that. But I'd rather see him as a search-and-rescue dog saving people who were lost."

"Rescue, then. Could we teach him?"

"We could but we won't. If we spent a full hour every day just on tracking, it'd take about four months for Blaze to be a really good tracking dog. And you'll be back in school in San Francisco long before that." Cappy, seeing David's face, looked quickly down at his Sunday newspaper. A moment passed and without glancing up, he said, "Tell you what. Tomorrow we'll start playing a hide-and-seek game with you and Blaze. It isn't really training for tracking, but it's something like it. You know, some dogs don't need training. They track naturally, once they get the least idea of what you want."

THAT afternoon, when they started for the waterfall, Cappy unsnapped the leash, rolled it and clipped it to his belt. "He needs some freedom to explore."

It was a beautiful day, bright with clear skies. A trout, a flash of silver, broke the surface of the stream beside them, then vanished in white foam. Blaze, forgetting dignity, plunged his muzzle into the water and splashed David's trousers as usual.

"We'll go just a little farther," said Cappy, standing on the bank. "Just to the edge of Mrs. Bradley's place, then go back home."

They were already quite close to Spirit Canyon Lodge, and David saw a line of big, expensive cars parked just off the road.

Cappy was just deciding that he should put Blaze on leash when David distracted him by exclaiming, "Look, Cappy! It's the little girls."

407

A track branching from the road on their left led up a slope along Mrs. Bradley's stone wall. The two small Indian girls, dressed in their usual calico skirts, were struggling to bring their flock of sheep, more than half a hundred, down to the grassy bank of the stream.

At the moment the sheep reached the road Cappy unclipped the leash from his belt and was about to call Blaze back. But by then it was too late.

Blaze, like David, had seen sheep far away at the blurred limits of his vision, yet he was familiar with their scent. Even at a distance, this rich scent never failed to stir a vague instinct in him, an ancestral memory implanted in his brain and blood.

And now, at the immediate sight and smell of the sheep, that formless instinct took shape. With a yelp Blaze charged ahead, pressing stragglers back into the flock, brushing aside one little girl who tripped over the long stick she carried. The girl shrieked in alarm, inciting the nearer sheep, who pressed hard against those ahead of them until suddenly the leaders stampeded, charging down the road. But in seconds it became a controlled stampede, banked on the left by the wall of Spirit Canyon Lodge and on the right by Blaze, who raced along the edge of the ovine torrent, barking fiercely but joyfully, euphoric in fulfilling his natural mission and utterly deaf to Cappy's shouted commands and David's yelling.

Blaze darted just ahead of the flock, and there he found open gates with grass, water, and shelter beyond. Barking with the satisfaction of work well done, Blaze turned the torrent through the portals of Spirit Canyon Lodge to join Mrs. Bradley's patio cocktail party.

Mrs. Bradley lingered at the railing surveying the gala scene. Below her the narrow green lawn framing the swimming pool teemed with guests sipping cocktails, nibbling hors d'oeuvres, while others prowled the sumptuous buffet table seeking more substantial fare. So crowded was the enclosed patio that waiters with trays of food and drink had to elbow through, but that was just as Mrs. Bradley had planned it.

For today's fete she had bagged three members of the state legislature, a brace of judges, a family flock of exiled Iranian nobility, a lumber tycoon, and a mining magnate. These, plus eighty other persons of note, had made the journey to Spirit Canyon to enjoy her famous hospitality. She enjoyed the role of Famous Hostess and regarded party giving as a competitive contact sport.

Carlos Jones was making his society debut as a singer and guitarist today, and he climbed upon a high stool, flexing his long fingers to limber them for performance.

The leader of the band, resplendent in gold lamé, spoke into the microphone after a fanfare. "Ladies and gentlemen, we are honored—"

And then catastrophe struck.

A grayish tidal wave swept away the cocktail party, and Mrs. Bradley, gripped by a horrid fascination, stood paralysed, gazing upon pandemonium beneath a crepe paper cloud. The guests, utterly routed by the avalanche of sheep yet hemmed in on all sides, had no retreat except to pile upon one another. A maypole with gay streamers whirled away, enmeshing five musicians in its web, as plastic plates sailed through the air like Frisbees, raining morsels of deviled egg, caviar, olives, and herring in cream sauce upon the bedlam below.

Unfortunate guests lingering at the buffet table suddenly found themselves wallowing on top of it, grasping at quicksands of salads, helpless against the oil slick of gravy that gelled on their summer casuals.

Then the entire table was overthrown in the crush, collapsing at the same instant the portable folding bar folded and let loose a deluge of scotch, an eruption of soda.

Carlos Jones, high on his perch, was among the first casualties of the merino charge. Tumbling backward, he splashed into the swimming pool, taking the guitar and the stool with him, his salvation since they floated and he could not.

Around him the pool was awash with guests and floundering sheep.

Most of the scene hardly registered on Mrs. Bradley, but one detail impressed her powerfully. In the middle of the open gates, erect on his haunches and proud as a field marshal, sat a German shepherd dog. Lifting his head slightly, he inspected the conquered patio, then uttered one short but very positive bark of triumph.

It was then Mrs. Bradley went into hysterics.

SUPPER at Rancho San Pascual that night was eaten in silence.

David did not know how he should feel, what was expected of him. It seemed only proper that they should all be mortified by Blaze's misbehavior, but it was hard to be ashamed when he was secretly bursting with pride in Blaze's natural talent as a sheepherder.

Cappy finally spoke. "Anyway, she can't sue us. Our hides are saved by the gate and fence ordinance. This is grazing country—if Mrs. Bradley leaves a gate open, it's her own fault if sheep or cattle trespass."

"My nephew heard people say that Blaze should be shot or poisoned," said Mrs. Littlefoot darkly.

"Yes, I heard that repeated. But I'm sure it didn't mean anything. Everybody was a little hysterical at the time." Cappy looked down at the coffee Mrs. Littlefoot was pouring for him. "You can hardly blame them. They had a few things to be hysterical about." The corners of Cappy's mouth twitched, then he forced his lips into a firm line. "Tomorrow, I'll call on Mrs. Bradley and offer my . . . uh . . . condolences, you might say."

Suddenly Mrs. Littlefoot could contain herself no longer. Her sense of dignity seldom permitted her to smile, let alone laugh, but now she burst into such uproarious laughter that she had to cling to the draining board. "That Blaze is the devil's own dog!" she cried, pounding her thigh.

Then Cappy and David were laughing so hard the table shook. Xenia barked in happy excitement, her tail waving in the air.

Despite their laughter, Cappy did not feel easy until after he had talked with Mrs. Bradley the next morning. He returned to

San Pascual greatly relieved. "She's a good sport," he said. "I never suspected she had much sense of humor, but she has."

Mrs. Littlefoot nodded but looked grim, and David forgot all about Marcella Bradley because of the excitement of a new game they were learning.

THEY started the hide-and-seek training with teaching Blaze to chase and retrieve a ball, a special ball made of rubber so hard that it resisted the powerful pressure of Blaze's jaws. Once Blaze grasped the idea of finding the ball, Cappy explained, they would gradually change the game to finding David, who would hide holding the ball.

"The command will be '*Blaze, find David,*'" Cappy said, and made a sweeping, circular gesture as a hand signal. "It's very hard for a dog to learn the name of a person, so we're using the ball to help him identify you."

David was absolutely certain Blaze knew his name, but did not argue.

The lessons were not easy, and in the next few days David learned patience above everything else. On Friday Cappy began using one of David's sandals, having Blaze sniff it just before the search command and signal were given.

"Tracking," said David with satisfaction.

"Only in a way. To teach tracking properly we'd use a harness and a long lead. It would be much slower."

That afternoon Blaze found David unerringly three times—behind the shed, in the springhouse, and under the bridge.

"A few more lessons, and he'd be a real search-and-rescue dog," said David proudly.

"Umm." Cappy did not disillusion David by telling him that it took a year of training for a good German shepherd to become proficient and reliable in rescuing lost persons.

It had been a happy and quiet week; nothing unusual happened until late Saturday night. At midnight Blaze suddenly awakened David with loud barking. The shutters were open and moonlight streamed through the window where Blaze stood alert on guard duty. Seeing that David was awake, Blaze stopped barking and waited, poised for action.

When an engine came to life on the road near the house, the dog barked again, and David hurried to the window just in time to see a vehicle—he thought it was Mrs. Bradley's jeep—pass the turn-off at Cappy's bridge and continue on toward the village. Since Blaze, day or night, ignored the few cars and trucks that passed on the road across the stream, David decided that the jeep had stopped for a moment. But it had vanished down the road, so David went back to bed.

"It was funny," he told Cappy the next day. "I didn't realize it last night, but there weren't any headlights. No taillight, either."

"Not too unusual," Cappy said. "Some of the trucks and cars canyon people drive never have lights."

"If it was Mrs. Bradley, why would she be coming from the upper canyon? You said almost nobody lived there."

"Her driver takes that road as a shortcut to the city. It's very dangerous, a rock-slide area. But some people will risk their lives to save five minutes."

It was a warm, lazy Sunday, and in the afternoon David took Blaze to the stream where he made another futile attempt to catch a fish.

Because the day was warm, Blaze felt less frisky than usual, and he lay contentedly beside David, now and then lifting his head to gaze into the boy's face with quizzical eyes. Cappy often spoke of the love that existed between humans and dogs. Now, as David reached out and touched Blaze's black and tawny coat, he felt a wash of this love, a deep yet undemanding companionship and understanding, a love without rivalry or question or limit.

David rested his head against Blaze's back and studied the sky through the leafy strands of a willow tree, watching a circling hawk. He felt love and security, and he was puzzled that happiness should be such a quiet feeling.

A few minutes later he wound in his fishing line and unbaited the hook. Blaze was investigating the nearby bushes and seemed to be chewing something. David payed no attention.

"Home, Blaze. Home!" It was a new command, and David repeated it twice as they ambled toward the house.

Cappy was in the kennel kitchen, boiling a broth he would use to moisten meal, stirring a three-day supply in a big kettle. He turned when David and Blaze entered.

Earlier Cappy had been watching David and Blaze at the bank of the stream, marveling at how both the boy and the dog had changed and blossomed in less than a month. David was no longer pale and silent, no longer so withdrawn into the world of his imagination. In fact, when David was alone with Blaze he became downright talkative; Cappy often heard David outside the window chatting with Blaze so naturally that Cappy almost expected the dog to take up the conversation. And Cappy was proud of his newly confident grandson.

Kneeling, Cappy inspected Blaze's forepaws. "Nice dark nails," he said, "but they need trimming. Tomorrow you get a pedicure, Blaze old boy."

He looked into Blaze's face, scratching him lightly under the muzzle. Suddenly, Blaze shuddered and his fur ruffled. He lifted his head, stretching the neck into an ugly parody of alertness, shoulders straining, front legs frozen.

Blaze cried out, a scream of terror, ending in a sound of strangling. The stiff legs gave way and Blaze collapsed, lay sprawled on the linoleum, his whole body suddenly flaccid yet trembling.

Cappy recognized what he was seeing, yet for a moment the memories aroused by the dog's convulsion paralyzed him, left him unable to act. It could not be, he thought desperately, this was too terrible to happen!

"Blaze!" David was shouting. "Oh, Cappy, what's happened to him? What's wrong?"

"Be quiet!" Cappy recovered his senses, but his voice was a hoarse whisper. "Not a sound—do you understand?"

David nodded dumbly, but he understood only that a terrible thing was happening. He reached out to touch Blaze, to give love or comfort, but Cappy caught his wrist. "No, let him alone."

For a few seconds Blaze twitched and shivered, then, as though he had touched an electric wire, his whole body writhed. He rolled over on his back and his spine arched so sharply that only the top of his head and the tip of his backbone rested on the floor, his muscles drawn up in such a ghastly contortion that David pressed his fists against his mouth to keep from screaming while tears streamed down his face. Only moments before they had been frolicking on the path, and now this nightmare.

Blaze went limp again, but his eyes rolled wildly, and small spasms shook him like violent sobbing.

Cappy moved swiftly to the medicine cabinet, meanwhile speaking softly to David. "Go to the house and tell Mrs. Littlefoot to call Doctor Matson or Doctor Gomez in the city. If she can't reach them, any other vet should come. Say it's an emergency—Blaze has been poisoned with strychnine. And, David, no noise."

"Strychnine?" asked David faintly.

"Yes. It's a poison usually used against rats. Now hurry on, David, we can't waste any time."

Cappy did not say that for Blaze time had probably run out already, and by the time any doctor came from the city it would be far too late. Blaze, he supposed, would die in the next half hour, and it was a heartbreaking waste of an innocent life. Then, fighting off despair, Cappy began to do what he could.

David stumbled on the sill of the kitchen door, hardly able to gasp out his message but Mrs. Littlefoot understood instantly and went to the telephone where she consulted a list of names and numbers thumbtacked to the old desk.

"Will a doctor come right away?" David asked with a chalky face as she began to dial.

"Yes, one will come quickly," she answered. She dialed number after number, reaching only answering services who promised to try to reach a veterinary surgeon.

David watched her with growing terror, until she said, "Quickly now! Pump some rainwater from the cistern, put it on the stove and set it boiling. Add salt and keep stirring it slowly. Put the oven on low heat in case we need to warm blankets or towels."

David rushed to these tasks, not suspecting what he did was useless work invented by Mrs. Littlefoot to divert his mind and occupy his hands until this first panic abated. She knew how desperately he needed to feel he was helping Blaze.

The water was boiling steadily when Mrs. Littlefoot put down the phone. "Go to your grandfather," she told David. "A doctor will come soon."

David turned back in the kitchen doorway. "Mrs. Littlefoot, have you seen other dogs that ate this? Swallowed strychnine?"

"Of course. It was frightening, but they were better in a day or two."

She told this lie because she could not bear to speak the truth to him. Almost always those who swallowed strychnine died quickly, whether dogs or cats, rats or humans.

The air in the kennel hung heavy with the chloroform Cappy had used to keep Blaze quiet, to try to stave off the deadly convulsions. David, sitting tense and quiet on a stool in the corner, fought off the waves of sickness the smell brought. The western windows were now tinted with crimson, the light of sunset deepening into night. From far away David heard a muffled roll of thunder, an approaching storm. Blaze appeared to shudder at the sound, and David clasped his hands together, his lips forming silent words. "Don't die, Blaze. Please, Blaze, don't die!"

Cappy swabbed up the last of the fluids and particles he had flushed from the dog's stomach. He tiptoed to the steel counter and examined what he had found—two morsels of meat, both of them studded with grains of poisoned wheat, lethal grains sold in stores everywhere as rat killers. So the worst Cappy had suspected was true. Blaze had not eaten one of the few deadly plants that sometimes grew in the canyon; he had been deliberately poisoned by someone.

Cappy felt David's eyes upon him, questioning, and he gestured. Together they slipped outside, moved a little distance from the kennel.

"Blaze is dying," said David. His voice had taken on the lonely, withdrawn note Cappy had not heard for weeks.

He put his arm around David's shoulders, realizing again how fragile the boy's body was. "No, he's still alive, David. Every moment he lives counts now. It's more than an hour since the first seizure, and that's a good sign, a reason for hoping."

"Why did she do it?" David asked suddenly.

"What do you mean?"

"Mrs. Bradley. I saw her jeep on the road last night, and today Blaze was chewing something down near the bridge."

"David, we can't blame anybody unless we're sure—and we don't know."

David was silent a moment, considering this. Then he said, "I'd better go back inside, Cappy. I don't want Blaze to be alone now."

David lay on a blanket not far from Blaze. They watched into the night, each passing minute seeming an eternity and each one filled with dread. Nearly three hours passed, and Blaze lay still, as though lifeless.

They heard the engine of a car on the road and Cappy, realizing a vet had probably arrived from the city, went out to meet him.

THE young vet soon saw that Blaze had survived the worst, but decided to stay the night so he could examine the dog thoroughly when there was no further danger of spasms. "The heartbeat's fine," he said. "No apparent damage. This fellow must be made of steel."

By order of the vet Blaze spent most of the next three days confined in a crate Cappy removed from the van. The poison had passed from Blaze's body, but he needed long hours of rest to recover from the racking convulsions that had wrenched every muscle to breaking point.

Since Xenia was too old, Cappy borrowed a hound from a friend in the village, and the hound, wearing a muzzle to protect it from any tempting but lethal titbit, helped Cappy and David search the ground near both banks of the stream.

"What can we do?" David asked, anguished. "What if she comes back again with more poison?"

"David! We don't know who did this"

"Maybe a high fence," David went on. "With fine holes like screen so nothing could be pushed through them. Or a wall."

Cappy shook his head. "No fence shorter than the Great Wall of China can stop them. Usually dog poisoners are sick people. Maybe they think they're acting because of revenge or fear or because a barking dog kept them awake all night. You can't guard against every possible attack by fences and walls."

"But we have to do something!"

"Yes, we'll do something. As soon as Blaze is strong enough, we'll teach him not to pick up strange food. Hard lessons—but there's no choice."

A week later training began. Joey, Mrs. Littlefoot's fourteen-year-old nephew, arrived with his friend Sam Raindancer. Both rode tough little mountain ponies and wore fringed shirts and beaded hatbands. David thought they resembled the advance scouts of an Indian war party.

Cappy cut a long switch, leaving a cluster of leaves at the thin end. Then he explained what they were to do while he made marks on the ground to show where to stand, where to fall back when the time came. He brought Blaze from the kennel, using an extra long leash.

Blaze, suspicious of strangers, gave a threatening growl when he saw Joey, but relented a little when he caught scent of a bit of meat Joey carried in his left hand. Approaching, Joey offered the morsel, then dropped it on the ground and stepped back. The instant Blaze lowered his head to sniff the unexpected gift, Joey whacked Blaze across the muzzle with the switch he had concealed behind his back. At the same time Cappy jerked the leash, shouting, "No!"

Blaze gave a yelp of surprise, for the switch with its leaves was more startling than painful. When he tried to lunge for Joey, Cappy pulled him up short. They repeated this at intervals six times that morning, Joey alternating with Sam Raindancer, and the last two times, when Blaze refused the bait, Cappy patted and praised the dog lavishly, rewarding him with a tiny piece of liver.

Joey and Sam returned several mornings, and sent friends to play the role of deceitful giver.

"This is the easy part," said Cappy. "We're teaching him not to accept bribes. It will be harder for him to learn he mustn't take gifts found on the ground with no stranger nearby."

Working in rubber gloves so his own scent would not cling to any object, Cappy baited small mousetraps with bits of meat. The springs of the traps were too weak to injure Blaze's nose, yet strong enough to deliver a sharp tweek, and the closing trap broke a little bag of quinine to give both the meat and the probing nose a bitter squirting. Cappy also cut slits in larger pieces of mutton and stuffed these pockets with the fieriest chili Mrs. Littlefoot could obtain. He closed the slits to hold in the odor, and hid these tongue-burning treats where Blaze was sure to find them.

Cappy and David planted bait along a marked course where they walked Blaze, jerking the leash sharply and shouting "No! No!" whenever he lowered his head to pick up these discoveries.

"I think we're winning the battle," Cappy said one day after Blaze passed three temptations without succumbing. "But we'll never be completely safe, David. Refusing food he finds goes against Blaze's nature, so the training's never certain."

CHAPTER 7

AUGUST came, the golden weeks of late summer in Spirit Canyon —hushed afternoons when even the aspens did not rustle and the circling hawk seemed to swim through the heavy light. Melons lay ripe in Cappy's garden, and Mrs. Littlefoot decorated the table with blue columbines. Blaze mastered close heeling in figure-eights and David caught a trout.

A fire marshal, a big man in heavy boots, came to post warnings. He stayed to lunch, complaining about the lack of rain and the carelessness of campers. After he had gone, Cappy stood gazing at the blackened foundations where the barn had stood.

In the middle of the month Cappy went away overnight to

judge an obedience trial, and no dog he saw was as quick or as eager as Blaze.

David moved through the magical August days with a boy's heedlessness of time. He learned how to cut a two-note willow whistle and had his first ride on Joey's pony. He lived joyfully in the present, thinking no further ahead than making plans for the next morning. The past did not intrude upon him even when Cappy compelled him to write postcards to Aunt Nadine and Uncle Arthur.

But with passing days, Cappy felt a growing apprehension. The summer was ending, it was time for David to return to San Francisco, time to be ready for the start of school. He dreaded the boy's leaving, blamed himself for allowing his affections to be so deeply touched—a thing he had once sworn would never happen again. Yet he did not question the rightness of David's departure. The boy belonged with Nadine and Arthur, the point had been settled long ago, and one did not go back on a settlement.

But the unbearable prospect was separating Blaze and David. Their separation would seem more bitter because it would be unnecessary. Arthur Wheeler's apartment was large, and a nearby park offered open space for running and play. Despite their size, German shepherd dogs made excellent pets in apartment houses because they were stable, not prone to howling, and unlike some breeds did not become unhappy when they could not roam. The problem, as Cappy saw it, was not the dog; it was Arthur and Nadine with their fears and prejudices.

If only they could see David and Blaze together, Cappy thought. The sight of the boy with the dog should melt a heart of flint, Cappy told himself.

He pondered the problem, reached a decision, and on the last day of August, a Sunday, called San Francisco when David was out playing, and found Arthur Wheeler at home.

"I think you and Nadine should come here to get David," Cappy told him, hiding his motive. "David would feel more assured, more wanted, if you were actually here."

"But that's impossible," said Arthur. "Nadine can't travel. The baby's expected the first week in October. Well, if it's absolutely necessary, I'll come and get David on Tuesday."

"That's the best thing! We'll meet you at the airport. You spend the night here at the ranch and return the next day."

"Well, I suppose it's the best thing. By the way, Cappy, I've been meaning to send you a cheque for David's room and board while he's been with you. The insurance company pays his living expenses, as you must remember. Of course, I'll have to deduct the money paid to the camp he never attended, then there'll be his plane fare and mine and—"

"Don't worry about it, Arthur! We'll see you Tuesday."

Cappy hung up, a little disturbed by the final turn their conversation had taken. He had known that David had been left financially secure, but he had never considered how important this money might be to Arthur. At least, Cappy thought grimly, Arthur could not object that it would cost too much to feed Blaze. The money was David's, and there was quite enough of it.

Cappy said nothing to David that evening or during the day on Monday. Twice he tried to introduce the subject, but his mouth went dry, and somehow the circumstances seemed wrong. Then, when he knew no more delay was possible, he steeled himself.

After supper they went to the porch. Cappy forced himself to bring up an unwelcome subject. "I have good news, David. Your Uncle Arthur's arriving tomorrow."

"Tomorrow?" David seemed stunned. "For a visit?"

"He's coming to take you home. He and your Aunt Nadine have missed you very much, and now that summer's ending—"

"Home?" The boy still did not appear to understand. "He's coming to take me away?" David's hand suddenly rested on Blaze's shoulder.

"Well, school will be starting next week, I suppose, and—"

Suddenly David gave a muffled cry. He leaped to his feet and ran into the house, letting the screen door slam behind him, and raced through the kitchen and down the hall to his room.

Cappy sat quietly, filled with a sense of futility, blaming himself for not having prepared David better for this news.

Cappy realized that Blaze was upset by David's strange behavior, and he tried to comfort the dog, scratching him behind the ears and talking gently. But he failed at that, too, and Blaze left him to find David's window and scratch at the shutters. Cappy heard them open to admit the dog, then close again quickly.

Cappy entered the kitchen where Mrs. Littlefoot, who had overheard everything, carefully hung up her damp dish towel and did not turn to look at him. He meant to go to David's room, to talk further with the boy, but in the hall he hesitated. The worst question had not yet been asked. *What about Blaze?* Cappy had no answer, and suddenly anger welled in him. Let Arthur Wheeler tell David whatever must be told. He himself could not deliver the blow of saying the dog must stay behind.

In the morning David answered Mrs. Littlefoot's call through the closed door, but did not appear for breakfast. Cappy found David, fully dressed, sitting on the edge of his bed with Blaze lying watchfully on the rug.

"It's time to leave, time to go to the airport to meet your Uncle Arthur," Cappy said.

"You go. I don't want to." David's face was pale, but the small jaw had a firm set.

Cappy considered the situation. "All right," he said. "I won't force you to go, although I hoped you would, because I'm taking Blaze with me."

David looked up quickly, alarmed.

"I want your uncle to meet Blaze right away, to see how well behaved he is."

David nodded, looking away. "I don't want to go."

"Very well. But you're not to leave the property until we get back, and I'll expect you to show your uncle some good manners when he arrives."

Cappy left, taking Blaze with him. After he had gone, Mrs. Littlefoot tried to lure David to the kitchen with a promise of apple pie, but he hardly answered her.

"I'm going into the village—to the store. Is there anything you'd like me to bring you?"

"Nothing."

A few minutes later her motor scooter coughed to life and she rode off, leaving David alone.

He sat silently on the bed, staring down at the rug. Tonight would be his last night at Rancho San Pascual. Until this second he had not quite comprehended the fact that he must leave, and at the same instant he understood why Cappy had taken Blaze to meet Uncle Arthur. Blaze was on trial, and David had little doubt about Uncle Arthur's decision.

He stood up then and went slowly to the kitchen, knowing vaguely what he must do. From a drawer he took the cloth bag with a drawstring and packed it with the few things he would need—bread and cheese, fishing line and hook with his best lure. He took one of the special whistles only dogs could hear and stuffed a pocket with dog biscuits.

He would not need anything else. There were nuts and berries in the upper canyon. He would find a cave or a big hollow tree for shelter and stay only a few days or at most a week. Only until Uncle Arthur had gone back to San Francisco. Uncle Arthur, who so often described himself as a busy man, could hardly wait for ever. David took a folder of forbidden matches for lighting campfires, and left the house.

Half an hour later he paused to drink from the stream, scooping up water that tasted like leaves. His sense of adventure had now pushed aside all other feelings. Full of confidence he walked on. A moment later the stream veered away from the road. David came upon a long straight stretch, then stopped in sudden alarm. He looked left and right, not knowing where to hide. Ahead, some distance away, was Sam Raindancer on his pony. Sam would certainly question him, probably force him to go back home.

David was so concerned about Sam Raindancer that he did not hear a vehicle approaching behind him, until the honk of a horn made him leap for the side of the road. Mrs. Bradley drew up beside him. She was alone. She leaned across the seat of the jeep and opened the door.

"Need a ride, young fellow?" she asked.

He stared at her made-up doll's face.

"Hop in," she said, smiling. "I won't bite you."

David climbed into the jeep, impelled not by her invitation but by the sound of the trotting pony. The jeep offered refuge—Mrs. Bradley would appear to be taking David for a ride, and Sam was not likely to question this. As the vehicle started forward, David slumped down in the seat, hoping to escape detection. A moment later, they passed Sam.

"You're Davy Holland, aren't you?" Mrs. Bradley asked.

"David." He forced out the correction, keeping his face turned away from her, wondering how soon he could escape without arousing suspicion.

"David, is it? And where are you going, if I may ask?"

David spoke the first words that came to mind. "Up near the Three Caves. I have a friend lives there."

"Well, I'm glad I found such a nice boy." She sounded determinedly cheerful. "It makes me feel better on a morning when I'm so upset I shouldn't be driving alone to the city."

"The city? You're going the wrong way!" David exclaimed.

"No. I'm taking the shortcut through the upper canyon. I hope you know all the turnoffs, because I've never driven this road alone before."

David looked at her warily. She was taking a route Cappy said was dangerous.

Mrs. Bradley, who had not been watching the road, kicked the brake pedal and they both tilted forward sharply. "Here—this is what I mean." The road divided a few feet ahead of them, one branch climbing a shoulder of the mountain, the other plunging into a forest in a lower valley.

"Which way?" she inquired. "Since your grandfather lets you wander up here, I suppose you know the road?" She fished a spray can from a bag on the seat beside her, then squirted herself with a gray mist that smelled overpoweringly of lilacs.

"Not the road to the city," David replied at last. "I'll get out here. My friend lives over there." He gestured toward the left fork. "Good-bye Mrs. Bradley."

But the jeep was already in motion before he could open the door. "Don't be silly, David Holland. I'll drive you there. It won't take a moment."

When the road diverged again, David nodded to the left, while he frantically tried to devise a way of graceful escape. By now they followed a winding track with deep ruts on the sides and high weeds in the center.

A low branch brushed the windshield, sprang away, and matted foliage almost barricaded the track, making it impossible to see more than a few yards ahead.

"Mrs. Bradley, you'd better turn back," said David. He was suddenly quite frightened. "I don't think this is the right way. Maybe I made a mistake."

"Oh, dear! Well, I suppose we'll find a place to turn around in a minute."

But there was no such place. The track twisted and wound, climbed, then dipped, but never widened enough to permit the jeep to turn around. Twigs broke off as the heavier branches were forced aside, and stripped leaves fell through the open window into David's lap. He had lost all sense of direction.

Mrs. Bradley swerved, skirting a sudden outcropping of granite that loomed like a reef hidden in the forest. With no warning the track ended, dropped off into a dry creek bed, and the jeep's front wheels plunged over the bank before Mrs. Bradley could stop. She was thrown against the steering wheel. David hit the dashboard. The front wheels spun helplessly in the sand of the creek, the rear were in the air, a foot off the ground. The jeep could go no farther.

Mrs. Bradley sat absolutely still for a moment. David reached over and turned the key.

"Maybe you should set the hand brake," he advised cautiously.

"What? Oh, yes." But she did nothing, only managing a wan smile. "Does your friend live near here? Could we walk to his house and telephone the village garage?"

David was astonished she did not know that she herself and Cappy owned the only two telephones in Spirit Canyon.

"Your friend?" she repeated. "Where does he live?"

"I don't know, Mrs. Bradley. But there's a house near here."

"How do you know?"

"I can smell smoke," he said, and climbed from the jeep.

They found a path on the far side of the creek bed, a deer trail. David could no longer smell smoke, only the lilac scent of Mrs. Bradley, and he wished she had stayed at the jeep.

They struggled along a little farther. Soon they saw the brighter, unbroken sunlight of a clearing ahead, and the aroma of smoke became sharp.

David felt the sudden warmth of the sun as he moved from the shade into the open, and for a moment the brilliance blurred his vision. Yet he sensed instantly that something was wrong—the clearing seemed too small to be the site of a cabin, and the smoke was too diffused to come from a chimney. Then he saw the apparition.

A phantom figure, a man swathed in cobwebs, stood a few yards away, his back to David. In one hand he held a burning brand of pitch pine, in the other a ragged length of cloth that he whirled in the air, dissipating smoke rising from the trunk of a hollow tree. Nearby was a bucket of water and several wet burlap bags. David realized that the strange gray shroud was made not of cobwebs but of old window curtains, begrimed with smoke.

David stared, more puzzled than frightened. He could make nothing of this baffling scene until he heard the angry buzzing of bees. Then he realized this was no ghost but simply a man smoking out wild bees to take their honey. The man was fanning the air so the smoke of his unlawful fire would not attract attention from afar.

The figure turned. They stared at each other in astonishment, then the honey thief took a menacing step forward, lifting high his torch. At that moment Mrs. Bradley pressed through branches and entered the clearing to see the grotesque figure advancing on David. Lifting her head she uttered a blood-curdling scream, then snatched the spray can of lilac scent from her bag, pointed it like a weapon, squirted a long stream, and screamed again.

Suddenly a cloud of maddened bees burst from the smoking tree. The man shrieked in panic, hurled the flaming pine brand in David's direction, then whirled to flee through the undergrowth.

Clasping hands, David and Mrs. Bradley retreated blindly, David pulling his stumbling companion after him, running along a vague trail he supposed was the route they had followed before.

Meanwhile, the burning pitch pine seemed to splutter out. But one coal still smoldered near the bare roots of a thorn bush.

DAVID and Mrs. Bradley ran on as best they could, branches scratching their hands and faces, tearing at their clothes. Mrs. Bradley began to make little whimpering sounds of fright.

"Please stop crying, Mrs. Bradley." David said. "It doesn't help. We have to figure out how to get back to the road—or maybe find the stream and follow it."

"Oh, where are we?" she asked. "Aren't we almost back to the jeep? When we get back to the jeep, we'll keep blowing the horn. Then someone's sure to find us."

She tried to smile, but there was a helpless note in her voice that worried David. She was the grown-up, she should take charge, yet he felt she was counting on him to decide which of these crisscrossing, almost invisible trails to follow.

"This is terrible!" she cried, looking at her slender gold watch. "We've been wandering in this wilderness for two hours."

Two hours? Cappy would be home now, David thought, home and coming to find him.

The trees separated and on both the right and left loomed great cliffs of granite, dark towering walls forming a gigantic corridor. Here the trees were sparse, scrub growth was starved by the rocks.

"What a dreadful place," murmured Mrs. Bradley.

FOR Cappy Holland the return trip from the airport to San Pascual with Arthur Wheeler was a trying experience. Their meeting had gone wrong from the first moment.

Blaze, properly on the leash and with ears at attention, had stood gallantly at Cappy's side, a model of canine beauty and deportment. But Arthur visibly blanched when he saw the dog.

"Hello, hello!" he exclaimed and started to clap Cappy on the shoulder, but glanced at the dog and changed his mind. "Good to see you, Cappy," he finished uncertainly.

"Arthur!" Cappy returned the greeting, explained that David was waiting at the ranch, and then tried to introduce Blaze.

"He sure is big," said Arthur, approaching no closer. "I'll bet he eats ten pounds of meat a day! Well, where's your car?"

During the long trip to Spirit Canyon Cappy made attempts to explain David's devotion to Blaze, but he realized he was having no success.

"Sounds like an unhealthy affection. The boy's just been alone too much," said Arthur complacently. "But now he'll have a little brother for a companion."

When they arrived at San Pascual Cappy was not surprised to find that David had gone out. "He's playing somewhere," he told Arthur. "He'll be along as soon as he realizes Blaze is here. Remarkable how devoted they are!"

But Arthur did not hear this last remark because old Xenia, after inspecting the newcomer, growled her opinion, causing Arthur to move uneasily to the other side of the table.

In the yard Cappy shouted for David, then paused to greet Sam Raindancer who was chopping wood near the springhouse.

"Seen David, Sam?"

"Yes, sir. Maybe two hours ago when I was on my way to work here. He was going toward the upper canyon."

"The upper canyon?"

"That's right. He was with Mrs. Bradley—in her jeep. I waved to him, but he didn't notice me."

Baffled, Cappy returned to the house where Mrs. Littlefoot, looking worried, stopped him at the kitchen door. "There is a lot of cheese missing," she said in a low voice. "And I know what mouse has run off with it."

Fortunately Arthur had gone to the guest room to unpack his

427

overnight bag and did not hear Cappy telephone Spirit Canyon Lodge, where the housekeeper told him that Mrs. Bradley had left that morning to keep an appointment in the city and, yes, she had driven toward the upper canyon.

"Thank you," said Cappy, hanging up.

Obviously David had run away. Perhaps he should have anticipated this, but it had seemed unlikely that David would leave without Blaze. Despite this, the boy had fled and accepted a ride from Mrs. Bradley, unlikely as this seemed.

But the upper canyon road, the so-called shortcut to the city! This was what he could not put from his mind as he paced between the telephone and the window. The whole upper canyon, to those who did not know it, was a treacherous wilderness. Avalanches thundered down its gray slopes, flash fires could turn its hundred cul-de-sacs into furnaces, but most dangerous of all was that the upper canyon was simply wilderness. No one knew how many men and women—prospectors, homesteaders, hunters, and innocent picnickers—had wandered until they found death in that hostile land.

Striding across the kitchen, Cappy told Mrs. Littlefoot to serve Arthur's lunch. "Say I've gone to fetch David." He moved swiftly through the yard to the kennel and unlocked Blaze's run. "Come on, boy, we're taking another ride." The dog looked at him and whined a question.

"That's right, Blaze. We're going where David is."

THE corridor between the cliffs was rougher than David had first supposed. Rocks were strewn everywhere; vines, thin but tough, seemed like trip wires; and patches of stunted undergrowth, wreathing dead tree trunks, lay in formidable tangles. Mrs. Bradley moved hesitantly beside him, smiling wanly when he nodded encouragement.

"You're walking much better," he told her. "You hardly wobble at all."

She seemed grateful for his praise. Then, without warning, she staggered, pressing one hand to her forehead. "I'm afraid I am a little faint. I'm on a diet, I haven't had a bite to eat since yesterday noon, so I suppose I'm giddy from hunger."

David reached into the bag that hung from his belt. "Here, have a piece of cheese."

She eyed the cheese ravenously. Her arm, seeming to have a will of its own, darted out and seized the titbit. Without another word she wolfed it down, then silently accepted the slice of bread he gave her.

"I'm hungry, too. We can eat over there—there's shade." He pointed to a huge boulder of mottled granite just ahead.

"Of course! A picnic." The thought of food seemed to restore her considerably.

As they moved toward the boulder, David took the bag from his belt and took stock of their provisions. Not much for two people, he thought. He wished he had brought water.

A terrifying sound erupted at David's feet, a rasping alarm. David stared down into the small beady eyes of the snake that lay coiled a yard away, and he was petrified. Rooted to the spot, he could only look at the horrible thing, seeing the curved white fangs and the little tongue darting between them. Again it buzzed its warning, ready to strike, and still he stood staring, mute and paralyzed.

Shrieking, Mrs. Bradley hurled her shoulder bag, completely missing. But the reptile saw a gray and white shape hurtling downward. It struck, its powerful body lashing out in a smooth, uncoiling thrust, the head veering at David's ankles to sink fangs into the leather, piercing the bag as though it were cotton.

David hurled himself away. Flight was his only thought. From the corner of his eye he saw that the snake was already coiled again, ready to attack.

They ran from it, staggering and lurching over the rocks. Bruised and panting, swallowing air in gulps, they reached a grove of aspens, and there Mrs. Bradley collapsed, unable to run another stride. For a few minutes neither could speak, then David said, "Thank you."

She nodded, still catching her breath.

"I lost the bread and cheese," David told her, suddenly humbled.

"I'm not hungry now anyway." She swallowed hard, cleared her throat, then tears began to stream down her cheeks. "This is the worst day of my life!"

David stared at her, despising himself because this woman, his enemy, had saved his life. Worse, he felt sorry for her now. "It's terrible being lost," he said gently. "But we'll find our way."

"It's not just that! This terrible day started when I found Taffy and Fluffy, my kitties, dead! Poisoned! That man Jones must have done it. He threatened me yesterday when I fired him, told me I'd better watch my cats. But I didn't pay any attention, didn't believe he'd actually harm an innocent little animal. How could anybody do such a thing? Oh, it's wicked!"

David, watching her weep, knew she would not have hurt Blaze and he felt ashamed. Reaching out timidly to touch her hand, he said, "I'm sorry, Mrs. Bradley. I understand how you feel."

They dipped water from the brown puddle at the spring, enough to wet their lips, but the water was too muddy to drink.

Before they continued, David found a broken branch thick enough to use as a weapon.

CHAPTER 8

FOLLOWING David's morning route proved far easier than Cappy had feared. The canyon road, dirt with sparse gravel, told a clear story. The hoof marks of Sam Raindancer's pony were sharply stamped, and only one vehicle, which had to have been Mrs. Bradley's jeep, had left recent tire marks in the soft dirt along the right shoulder. In several places David's small running shoes had imprinted the dust with corrugated tracks.

Cappy rounded a curve and came to a place where the jeep had pulled to the edge of the road. Cappy suspected this was where David had accepted a ride, a suspicion confirmed a hundred yards farther where tire marks veered right and hoof marks moved left, indicating that the pony and jeep had passed each other at this point.

Now Cappy drove more rapidly. "They went along here, Blaze," he said. "They didn't stop, they passed this trail to the Raindancer ranch. See? Then they came to the fork and . . . oh, no!"

The jeep tracks went left instead of right, following an overgrown, washed-out road. It led nowhere except into deep wilderness.

Cappy drove down the road at a snail's pace. It was simple to follow the jeep now—it had left scars in disturbed leaves, in dust, in fallen pine needles. But taking the van farther into the forest was a risky venture. "We'd better follow on foot, Blaze," Cappy told the dog, shutting off the ignition and dropping the keys into his pocket. He removed a small compass from the dashboard and clipped it to his watch strap. Blaze bounded to the ground as soon as Cappy opened the door.

Cappy followed the broken twigs and stripped leaves, the deep scratches on bark. A large granite outcropping loomed ahead, and Cappy noticed that the jeep, swerving to circle it, had scattered a thick mound of dry pine needles and cones. The ground was sloping slightly downward, and he guessed that they would soon find a dry watercourse.

Blaze, suddenly alert, moved ahead of Cappy, rounding the rock formation, then gave a summoning bark. Seconds later Cappy saw the immobilized jeep helplessly straddling the creek bank. He rushed forward, but even before reaching the open doors he knew that David, at least, was not there, for Blaze sat calmly awaiting Cappy's next move.

Cappy picked up a pocket comb from the floor. "David's. Must have fallen out of his pocket." Sniffing the comb, Blaze wagged his tail eagerly.

Clear tracks of two different sets of shoes led plainly across the dry sand of the creek. "Now why would they walk in that direction? David should know enough to walk downstream, downhill. Somewhere this creek has to find a river! But instead they followed this miserable deer trail."

Then, before he had gone a dozen steps forward, Cappy learned the answer. "Smoke! The boy smelled this smoke and knew there had to be a cabin or a camp right over there!"

Cappy felt a surge of relief. David was safe, in a few minutes they would find him. But then, only a little farther along the tangled trail, his new confidence began to waver as he realized the smoky aroma was not what it should have been. Slowly the truth dawned on Cappy—a ground fire lay ahead, creeping among the dead leaves and needles.

Cappy plunged through a thicket and burst into the clearing. At a glance he realized what was happening. On two sides the clearing had charred without flame, without sparks; he saw only thin curls of almost transparent smoke, and on the ground lay heaps of white ash. Now the air hung absolutely still, but with the least breath, the surrounding acres would go up blazing like a gigantic torch.

He saw a half-empty bucket of water and some rags. He moved quickly toward it—it might be enough to wet his own clothes and Blaze's fur. In his haste, he did not watch the ground, and suddenly his right boot sank, sending him sprawling. He hit his head on the root of a dead stump, lay stunned for a few seconds, then Blaze was licking his face.

"I'm all right, old fellow," Cappy said.

But he was not all right. The least pressure on his right knee brought unbearable pain. He tried to hop, but the sprained knee rebelled at supporting the weight of his upraised foot, and he collapsed on the ground again.

For a moment he sat perfectly still, head bowed. "There is a way," he said. "I have only to find it."

There was no hope that he could go on searching the wilderness for David and Mrs. Bradley. Even without the injured knee he had no right to do so. His duty was to get back and raise an alarm; the people of the canyon had to be warned.

But there was David—David lost somewhere in the wilderness and in terrible danger when these embers burst into a raging fire, sweeping the canyon. This would happen soon, he knew it.

"Blaze, come! " he commanded, forcing himself to stand for a moment. "Sit!" Cappy spread his hands in front of the dog's eyes as he did at home when they played hide-and-seek. Then he took David's comb from his shirt pocket and offered it to Blaze, gave him the scent.

"Blaze, find David!" he said, sweeping his arm in a great arc. The dog did not move. In the dark eyes Cappy saw a struggle to understand, a desperate wish to know and obey.

Cappy's knee throbbed, but he held himself upright and tried once more, presenting the comb, gesturing, commanding in a voice that now was almost a shout. "Find David, Blaze! Find David—find him, Blaze. "

Blaze hesitated, eyed the smoking ground, listened to the faint snap of burning. Slowly, slowly he moved toward the deer trail, stepping cautiously as he skirted the gray coals that dotted the clearing. Then he turned back, paused with his eyes, dark and tragic, holding Cappy's. That look, full of obedience and farewell, spoke words Cappy would remember for the rest of his life.

"Find him, find him," Cappy gasped as the dog vanished into the thicket. Then he began crawling.

How far back to the van, he wondered? Two miles? And he dragged himself a few more inches.

BLAZE found easier footing a hundred yards away. Hesitating, he lifted his head, letting one particular combination of scents register, winnowing out many others. It was David's scent mixture he defined now; a certain odor of his body, another of his hair.

Blaze moved on carefully, head lowered, disturbed by the powerful lilac scent left by Mrs. Bradley. This was not a natural smell, so it made him wary. Yet, Blaze stubbornly followed David's scent, eager to join his friend.

No breeze stirred, and the whole overcast sky seemed to bear down upon the canyon, cupping it like a great bell of dark glass. Blaze moved ahead rapidly.

Then a vast hissing, a rushing, a roaring sound like an explosion, shook the leaves. Blaze halted, turned back with his head lifted, every nerve tingling. The smoldering ground fire behind him had burst to flaming life, shooting upward, a fire storm exploding in the dry foliage above, a blast of heat that consumed ten acres of leaves, twigs, and small branches in one searing flash, leaving the heavier trunks, blackened, to stand like torches.

A huge cloud of heated air spiraled a mile upward into the clouds, causing flurries of wind to blow back and forth through the canyon. At Blaze's feet a dust devil of pine needles fluttered upward to the lower branches of a great cottonwood.

A new and deep emotion stirred in Blaze. Before he had wanted to find David; now a realization of danger told him he *must* do it.

But the scent was fainter as he tried to move on. Using his eyes, which he had hardly relied on until now, he found a bit of turned earth where Mrs. Bradley's sharp heel had implanted itself. It puzzled him that here, where odor should be strong, he sensed almost nothing. Then he detected a drifting of the scent, a drifting to the left that followed the wind currents toward a tangle of briars.

Head low, he followed this new track until David's scent flowed into his nostrils as powerfully as ever.

Blaze began anew, following another sort of track, one that did not cling to the trees or to ground David had actually touched, but a totally invisible track of scent particles floating in the air and descending to earth on a route not the same as David's but parallel to it.

When the barriers were impassable, he gave up battling for each step and circled, recovering the trail at a farther point where it might be easier, fighting his way, tearing through undergrowth, briars, and the low-branched spruce trees that barred his way. And because of the circling, in the next hour Blaze traveled ten times the distance David had actually walked. Behind him Blaze could hear the fire roaring, hear the groans of twisting tree trunks, the crash of branches.

Then at last he broke from the timber and was free in rocky, almost open country. Here he lost the scent, but found it again at a little distance from a huge outcropping of granite that now lay deep in the shadows of the late afternoon.

THE rattlesnake, after its attack upon David and Mrs. Bradley, had retreated, hiding for a long time in a deep crack in the rocks. He had wound himself into a taut coil as he felt the movements of a large animal approaching. Feeling the vibrations of its steps, he decided the newcomer was an unusually heavy coyote, not prey for him, but not a danger, either.

The intruder came straight toward him. Lifting the vibrators on his tail, the snake sounded a sharp, unmistakable warning.

Blaze hesitated, perplexed.

Instinct warned him that this reptile was as lethal a creature as he had ever encountered and the only safe course was retreat. Yet the passage between rocks that the snake guarded cried out David's presence. Crumbs of biscuits had fallen just ahead, cheese and bread that David had touched lay at Blaze's feet. He knew he had to go forward.

He barked fiercely, a terrible threat to drive the long-fanged creature away, but it only buzzed defiance, lifting its evil head higher. Blaze crouched, ready to lunge, then the head came hurtling toward him, so close that the fangs brushed the tips of his chest hair, but Blaze had darted aside and back at the exact instant of the strike, and now moved back and forth a little farther away as the snake instantly drew its coils together again.

Now Blaze understood how it attacked, knew its speed and striking distance. He began to jump to the left, then to the right, snapping and feinting until the infuriated reptile lashed out once more.

Its recoiling was a little slower this time, and knowing this, Blaze reared up on his hind legs as though to hurl himself onto the rattler, but instead, at the crucial instant, lunged to the left as the snake shot forward, trying to bury its fangs near the dog's heart, a strike that meant instant death. The rattler's head had not quite touched the ground when Blaze, attacking from the side,

seized the snake just behind the head, crushing the base of the skull with his jaws. The reptile's long, muscular body whipped and lashed.

With a violent toss of his head, Blaze hurled the snake away, watching it writhe over the rocks, sliding down the slope. The dog lay panting for a moment, then forced himself to rise and continue on his errand through the passage he had won.

Darkness came quickly, a black overcast night except to the east and north, where the sky was edged with crimson and yellow. The moon was full and whenever the clouds parted briefly the whole canyon was illuminated.

Blaze rested near the muddy spring. His coat was a tangle of

brambles, his right forepaw swollen from a thorn he had just dislodged with his tongue. For half an hour he had lain here, working at the paw and recovering his strength. The fire seemed no nearer and he felt no heat. But the wind told him that the flames were creeping along the ground. Animals that lived in the corridor were already in flight; a doe plunged into the clearing near the spring and leaped over Blaze as though he were a log, and a complaining raccoon hurried on its way, ignoring the dog.

Blaze rose, trotted a little way from the spring, then paused, undecided. No familiar scent came to him. He leaped to a shelf of rock a few feet above him, and began to climb, hoping for a draught of air higher up that would tell him where to go. Yellow eyes suddenly blazed into his, only inches away, and a snarling, spitting face confronted him, the face of the bobcat whose den he had approached. Two kittens cowered behind her, and at this moment the bobcat, small compared to Blaze, had the courage of a tigress.

"Sccrrtt!" she screamed at him, slashing at his face with her claws.

Hooked nails raked him near the left eye and along his muzzle. Wobbling, he fell back, losing his balance, and he rolled over the edge of the rock shelf, turning helplessly on the sharp stones until his body came to rest on the floor of the corridor.

THE carved Swiss clock chimed two, but Cappy, sitting near the telephone with his leg propped up, had no thought of sleep. His radio, turned low, crackled with reports and warnings each time the fire shifted or advanced. It had devoured most of the upper canyon by now.

Cappy marked each change on an ordinance map tacked to the table beside him. And each time he drew a new red line on the map he thought, "Is David in new danger?" Could, God forbid, he have wandered into the old Lodestone Mine section, now a square mile of inferno where nothing lived? Or had he gone toward the Three Caves, a neck of the canyon that might flame up at any minute?

The lower canyon remained untouched by fire and seemed safe, but neighbors living farther away were injured, homeless, or missing.

A few minutes earlier Arthur Wheeler had staggered in, face flushed, hands blistered after managing half a shift as a fire fighter. He asked if there was news of David, then collapsed on the guest room bed, and now lay snoring, exhausted.

Mrs. Littlefoot gave the ranger who drove Arthur home a thermos of steaming coffee and he took it to his comrades who were struggling a few miles away. She then began packing two large baskets with food, towels, soap, and bandages for the temporary shelter in the village school.

Cappy watched her for a moment, then said, "If the boy comes through all right, he's going to live with us."

She nodded, having known this for hours, and went on wrapping sandwiches. "You have done some things today, and still you are waiting. Look now at who sleeps and at who sits watching. Do you need anything before I go?"

Cappy shook his head, tired. "Just hope for a miracle, as I do," he said quietly.

After she had gone, Cappy sat alone, haunted by his fears for David, and at the same time trying to ponder the strange thing that had happened today.

He recalled the crawl through scrub and timber, the painful crossing of an anthill where the insects seemed tipped with acid; there had been moments when he thought he could not drag himself an inch farther. He remembered the grotesque struggle to back the van to the road and drive it, and after all that these desperate hours of waiting for news of David.

David *had* to come back safely—David and Blaze. They had to come back because now was the time to begin life again, to rebuild, to look forward.

IN THE flickering light of a small fire David stared at a handful of dry dog biscuits. "I suppose if we wet them so they were soft, they might not taste too bad."

Mrs. Bradley coughed and rubbed her eyes. The wood smoke was bothering her more than she admitted. "I'm sure those biscuits will be delicious," she agreed.

They had found a cave high on the canyon slope just before dark, had literally stumbled into it, for its mouth was hidden by bushes. David had almost reached exhaustion, and Mrs. Bradley had declared she could not lift one foot after the other. Both had agreed to shelter here until morning.

The cave was large and clean; a little trickle of water dripped from its ceiling. They were weak from hunger and very footsore, yet the worst thing was the terrible gloom. In the fading light David remembered the matches in his pocket; he scraped together moss and dry twigs, and built a small fire near the entrance.

"You're supposed to set a circle of stones around the fire," Mrs. Bradley said, her expression far away.

"Is that right? How do you know, Mrs. Bradley?"

"I was a girl scout." Her face puckered but she did not weep again. "A century ago I was a girl scout—and I can't even find my way home!"

David softened the dog biscuits with water, and Mrs. Bradley ate one without tasting it. "Good!" She gulped. "May I have another, please? They're a little bit like liverwurst."

David left her and returned to the mouth of the cave where he broke off the bushes so he could watch the slow and terrible growth of the fiery arc to the east.

An hour went by and another. Mrs. Bradley dozed and so did David, but each time his eyes opened, the fire had crept closer and had widened. It was, he supposed, slowly cutting off their way home. Yet he did not think he could run from it any longer.

It saddened him to think that Cappy and Blaze had not come for him. During the last hours he had believed at almost every minute they would appear to take him home. He would have wept—but Mrs. Bradley was there and he could not let her suspect that he was weak and frightened.

Burying his head in his hands, stifling all sound, he let the deep sobs shake his shoulders.

Then he felt something hard in his pocket pressing against his leg, and he took out the steel whistle that only dogs could hear. Putting the whistle to his lips, he blew a short and a long blast, a short and a long—the signal he used to call Blaze from afar at San Pascual.

Closing his eyes, he nodded, the smoke making him sleepy. He drifted into a dream, knowing he must soon rouse himself because Mrs. Bradley needed him. But for a moment he was hiding in the cool shadows beneath the bridge, the water flowed gently over his bare feet, soothing him. Nearby Blaze searched for him, hide-and-seek, but he made no sound. Then Blaze, with a jubilant bark, found him, licking his face and hands, kissing him.

David awoke from his dream and looked up into Blaze's face. Blood had dried on the dog's muzzle, the flesh was raw and angry near the left eye, and when David reached up to touch Blaze's chest, to make sure he was real, his hands touched more dry blood and knots of brambles.

"Blaze! You came for me, Blaze!" His heart swelled until it seemed to be breaking.

BLAZE led David and Mrs. Bradley carefully down the slope, skirting the edge of the fire, and when the woman hung back or seemed too tired to go on, he went to her and nudged her gently with his nose as he would have encouraged a lagging sheep, and once when she tried to sit on the ground, he growled and would not permit her to linger.

"I think the dog's lost," she moaned.

"No," David told her. "He can follow the scent home. It's called backtracking and Blaze knows all about it."

But even as he reassured her, David's own confidence suffered a jolt. A fine, thin rain began to fall, enough to dampen the land, but certainly nothing to discourage the roaring fire on their left. Indeed, above the fire the rain turned to white steam before it touched the flaming treetops.

But would the rain wash away the trail Blaze was following? David was afraid it would, for it seemed impossible that Blaze could detect scent through the moisture covering the ground.

Blaze, limping but still hurrying his charges along, felt his strength returning with the new coolness, and the moisture held the scent particles to the ground and glued them to the surfaces of the rocks, the bark of the stunted trees. He was not, as David believed, backtracking. The old route lay engulfed in fire. Of the thousands of trees they had passed that day not one now stood except as a blazing or blackened stump. Blaze now led them along another route that would bring them to water, to the canyon stream that marked the way to San Pascual.

THEY WALKED THROUGH THE night and into the dawn. Eventually they found themselves no longer alone in the canyon. Above them helicopters hovered in the pale sky, and parachutes blossomed as fire fighters were dropped into the wilderness like invading troops behind enemy lines, men who would be cutting breaks and setting back fires.

When they reached the lower canyon road it was crowded with men driving mules laden with all kinds of equipment.

Weary though they were, neither David nor Mrs. Bradley asked these men to help them reach home. With Blaze, they had come this far on their own, emerging from the very heart of the burning canyon, and now they would finish the last two miles alone. They limped, they were bedraggled and soot blackened, they were half blinded from smoke—yet they walked proudly. They had done something.

They paused at the top of a little rise and David gazed down on Rancho San Pascual. The windmill turned peacefully, the house with its stone chimney looked strong and secure; it was even more beautiful than it had seemed to David on that day when he first saw it, a summer ago, a lifetime ago, when he was a child.

At the cattle grid, Mrs. Bradley, numb and staring straight ahead but with her chin high, allowed David to take her arm in case she should stumble. He cupped her elbow, and they moved ahead, their slowness and stiffness lending them an odd elegance, a tall woman and her tiny escort entering a ballroom.

Raising his head, Blaze barked to proclaim their return, telling old Xenia and Mrs. Littlefoot, telling Cappy who sat by the telephone, his head in his hands, and telling the canine ghosts that played forever in the fields of San Pascual that he had brought his charges home, that he had not failed them.

Robert Somerlott spent four years of his childhood in the south-western U.S.A., the rugged country described in *Blaze*. It was there, on a sheep ranch in Colorado, that his lifelong passion for German shepherds was born, a passion which later led him to establish a successful breeding farm which has produced a number of champions in both obedience and conformation.

After completing his studies at the University of Chicago, young Robert Somerlott went to California, where he worked as an actor and theater director for fifteen years. In 1963 he moved to Mexico and his home in a small town with the romantic name San Miguel de Allende. "I went to Mexico hoping to find the time and inspiration to write, to become an independent author," he recalls of this risky venture. His first short stories met with immediate success, and *The Flamingos* established his reputation as a novelist.

Robert Somerlott

"Like most of my stories, this novel is set in Mexico. Throughout the years I have always drawn on my knowledge of Mexican history and archaeology," says Somerlott who is above all interested in Mayan culture. As a well-known specialist in this field he regularly lectures at a Mexican university.

Despite all these activities, Robert Somerlott still makes time for his German shepherds. This book is his tribute to them and will certainly help to fulfil the author's foremost aspiration: to help man better understand his four-legged friends.

DEAD FIX

by Michael Geller

When jockey Ken Eagle meets
jockey Tricia Martin, sparks fly...
and they're not the sparks of romance.
Ken is a top-ranked rider, Tricia
a talented upstart with a mysterious
past and a chip on her shoulder.
The two are rivals, locked in
competition in the glamorous and
ruthless world of thoroughbred racing.
In this sport where corruption and
greed can lie just below the surface,
victory must be won at all costs...
perhaps even at the cost of
a human life.

1

I WATCHED her fall.

It was October at Belmont. The overcast sky had held off the rain but the gusts of cold Canadian air that swirled worthless mutuel tickets with deserved disdain gave notice that winter was impatient.

The ninth race was a contest for four-year-olds who had won only one race in their careers. Tricia was on the favorite, Telno, and I had a fainthearted sprinter ironically named Mr. Courage.

I had gone for the lead and held it comfortably going into the turn. Then, as if on cue, Mr. Courage shortened stride and spit out the bit. That was his modus operandi and I was specifically employed to see that he didn't repeat this habit. Ken Eagle was a leading jock on the New York circuit: I was supposed to be able to make quitters run like champions. Well, not this time.

We drifted back to sixth as Tricia came from dead last on the outside. Telno was full of run. There was no mistaking the determination of the gelding, and Tricia helped him by staying low and distributing her weight evenly. She rose with his rhythm and urged him along with soft hands on the reins.

On past performance, there was no good reason for Telno to be the two-to-one favorite. The horse's record was mediocre, and he seemed more at home in longer races than the three-quarters of a mile contest he was entered in today. But the betting public knew that Telno had changed hands. He was now trained and owned by Orlando Marcano, and a Marcano horse was like money in the bank.

Tricia was five lengths in front of me. The two horses sharing the lead were running as a team on the inside and she chose to go around them. The crowd anticipated the stretch run. Telno would be sweeping by majestically, leaving the others in his wake. It happened every day. The crimson silks of the Marcano stable were seemingly invincible.

I heard the leg snap. Over the muted thunder of three-dozen hooves the sound was a staccato pop. Telno stumbled badly. Tricia reached down on the reins to try to help him up but it was as if he had fallen down an invisible flight of stairs.

Tony Violet, directly behind her, had no time to pull out of the way. He and his mount plowed into Telno and also went down. Another horse tried to leap over the tangle, its jockey bailed out, and he fell clear of the carnage.

I managed to pull Mr. Courage to a halt. I don't remember tying his reins to the rail or running to the fallen horses and riders. My eyes were on Tricia. She was lying face down in the dirt and she wasn't moving.

Telno was thrashing about in agony, trying to get up. His left front leg was a ghastly flapping appendage of splintered bone and blood. I had to move Tricia. Telno might roll over on her or kick her with his wild flailings.

Tony Violet crawled over. "I'll keep Telno down," he said, grabbing the loose reins and immobilizing the doomed animal.

I gently got my hands under Trish's shoulders and moved her clear. With a small measure of relief, I could see she was breathing. The fibreglass helmet worn under her bright silk cap was dented, but it had surely saved her from an even worse injury. Trish's eyes were closed, the right one puffed with blood pouring from a slash just over the brow. Her right hand was bleeding and from the angle I guessed there was a break.

"Are you okay, Tony?" I asked.

"Yeah, I think. How's the girl?"

"Bad."

"She'll be okay," he said. "She's tough."

Tricia Martin had to be tough. She took on the men at their own game and held her own. Having the skills to be a jockey was only part of it. If you showed weakness, the backstretch crowd could grind you down for fodder. But I knew the other side of her as well . . . warm, vulnerable, wary of her new success, and frightened of failing.

The ambulance was there in seconds. They got her on a stretcher and I tried to intercept the looks on the attendants' faces. One of them was a confirmed long-shot player named George. He was usually garrulous but today he was uncharacteristically subdued.

"I'm going to ride with her, George," I told him.

"You're not allowed to, Ken. We'll be taking her over to Long Island Jewish Hospital. You can meet us there."

"I'm going," I insisted. I climbed in, still holding my helmet and my whip.

We rode through the back gate and in seconds we were on the parkway. Behind us, another ambulance would be carting Telno away to be humanely destroyed.

No matter how many times you see a horse go down, the impact stays the same. I had no doubt that Orlando Marcano was responsible for Telno's death. Whatever trick he used on his horses to make them win also masked their pain and their natural instinct to protect themselves. This was not the first time that a Marcano horse, seemingly in good condition, had broken down, and Telno was the second horse that had to be destroyed.

Bob Diamond, Orlando's regular rider, had escaped injury the last time. This time, Trish wasn't so lucky.

I WAITED in a private room that the hospital staff used to interview job applicants. It was a square little room, big enough for a desk, two chairs, and a computer terminal. I had poked my head out a couple of times to see if I could get any information. The receptionist, who guarded the swinging doors of the emergency room as if it were the Tower of London, gave me a chilly look each time and told me that as soon as there was any information, they would let me know. That was two hours ago.

I had done my time in hospitals over the years. I had damaged my kidneys, broken my jaw, cracked ribs, and had my back broken. It was typical for someone who had been racing for over twenty years.

There was a light tap on the door and it startled me. Before I had a chance to react, my agent, Gus Armando, walked in.

Gus was my height with the face of a bulldog and the tenacity to match. He was a quick-to-smile fireplug who had made the transition from jockey to trainer to agent, and proved the lie about nice guys finishing last. I had been a one-dimensional rider when I met Gus back in Pennsylvania. My reputation, earned busting quarter horses in Texas, was that I could bring home a speed-burner but didn't have a chance with any horse that liked to come from behind.

Gus took me under his wing and taught me all he knew about pace and timing. And when he realized that he could never be a successful trainer on the minor-league racing circuit, he took me with him to New York where he called on his lifelong contacts to give me a shot on their horses. Over the years we had done well together, culminating with my receiving an Eclipse Award as top jockey in the country.

Gus's cut of my earnings was more than enough to keep him occupied with the two things he enjoyed most—fast cars and faster women. He was the only agent I'd ever had and our agreement was based on a handshake over a bottle of tequila.

"What have you heard?" Gus asked me. "They've got some battle-ax out there who won't let me inside."

"I know, I've tried a few times myself."

He knew my feelings for Trish. We had gone out together a few times; me, Trish, Gus, and whoever his blonde-of-the-week was. The last one I remembered was named Greta. He handed me a small bag he was carrying. "Here, I got something for you."

I pulled out my jeans and the blue crewneck I had left in my locker. As I changed, Gus fished in his pocket for my wallet and two gold rings.

"Thanks, Gus. Did you see my watch?"

He shrugged. "No, it wasn't in your locker. You're sure you brought it?"

"Maybe I left it home."

It was a special watch for me. My fourteen-year-old daughter, Bonnie, had given it to me for Father's Day. The face had a picture of Pegasus with the tips of his wings pointing out the hours and minutes. On the back was the inscription *#1 Dad*. I had worn it for luck every day since I had gotten it. It figured that today would be the day I forgot to take it.

"This was Marcano's fault, Gus. Somebody better figure out a way to stop that bastard."

"They will."

"Believe me, Gus, if they don't . . . I will!"

The door opened again. This time an intern walked in, wearing hospital greens and looking as old as my daughter.

"Mr. Eagle?"

"Yes, I'm Ken Eagle."

"Would you come along with me, sir? We'd like to try something and you could be a big help."

We walked past the receptionist and through the ER doors. They were doing a brisk business. Nurses and doctors scurried from one room to the next. Heart monitors peeped, respirators chirped, orderlies mopped. The smell of disinfectant permeated the air.

Tricia was in a separate room, hooked to an IV while two doctors and two nurses looked down at her gravely. The older doctor came forward and introduced himself to me as Dr. Sid Reissman.

"Here's what we have, Mr. Eagle. Tricia has a broken wrist, a fractured rib, and a severe concussion. We are concerned that there may be other internal injuries and we're particularly concerned about the spine."

"There's a chance something happened to her spine?"

I thought of Trish in a wheelchair for the rest of her life, paralyzed. No, that couldn't happen!

"It's a possibility we'd love to rule out. That's why we called you in. She's in a shallow coma and won't respond to us, but sometimes when these patients hear a voice they recognize . . . Would you mind calling to her? Just call her name."

I moved close to the bed. "Trish, it's me, Ken. Trish, can you hear me?"

She didn't move. Her usually lively blue eyes were dull and lifeless, open and staring at nothing.

"Try a little louder," Reissman suggested.

"Trish! *Trish!*"

Still nothing.

"Yell at her. Tell her to get up," Reissman said.

"Trish! Trish! Come on, get up! *Get up, Trish!*" I screamed at the top of my lungs.

She moved then. Her head tilted to one side and her eyelids fluttered. You could see her trying.

"Tell her to move her toes," Reissman said.

One of the nurses folded over the blanket covering her legs. We all watched as I yelled at her again. The toes of her right foot moved. Reissman and the others smiled.

WE WOULDN'T have seen Marcano if Gus hadn't decided he wanted to buy a box of cigars. The gift shop was closed, and I explained to Gus that they don't sell cigars in a hospital anyway. That led us to the front lobby and right to the fringe of an impromptu news conference Marcano was holding with reporters who were covering Tricia's condition.

"Come on," Gus whispered, pulling me toward the exit.

"No, I want to hear this."

Orlando Marcano was a squat man, always nattily dressed, with black, oily hair and a Pancho Villa mustache. He favored colors like beige and navy that coexisted with his olive complexion. And he liked gold. He wore three gold rings on his right hand, and another three on his left. Around his neck was a heavy chain, with a solid gold "O" initial. Around the track he was known as the "Big O."

Marcano enjoyed fielding the press. I had read, at least fifteen times, his explanation for his phenomenal success: *I work sixteen hours a day with my horses. I hire only the best people and give my horses the best of everything. I spare no expense. When I make my horses happy in the barn, they make me happy on the track. I have no magic formula. I just do my work.*

The truth was that Marcano probably put in less effort with his horses than most. For six years he had been just another trainer, winning an occasional race. For the past two years, he had been able to accomplish things previously reserved only for God.

A case in point was Bottled Water. I had ridden Bottled Water for trainer Jack West, who was as capable as they come. As a three-year-old, the horse had been considered a possible stakes winner, and Jack had given her every chance to bloom. Finally, Jack and her owners decided that they had been aiming too high and they dropped Bottled Water into a thirty-thousand-dollar claiming race.

Claiming races gave every horseman a chance to buy an animal at the price level it was racing for. They ensured that horses wouldn't steal purses by being too strong for the competition. You could be assured that if a horse was entered in a thirty-thousand-dollar race, by and large that horse was worth about thirty thousand dollars.

Bottled Water won several races at this level and then tailed off with a series of injuries. By the time I rode her, she was entered for fifteen-thousand-dollar races, and not coming close to winning those. Jack West was, in fact, quite happy when Orlando Marcano claimed B.W. for fifteen thousand dollars.

Four days later, the horse raced in a seventy-five-thousand-dollar claiming race. Not only did she win, but she finished in a time that was only four-fifths of a second off the track record.

"What happened out there with your horse, Orlando?" Hal Epstein from *Newsday* asked the first question.

"From where I stood, it looked to me that he stepped into a hole and that caused his leg to break. I want to find out from the girl what happened. I hope she's going to be okay."

"Do you think a more experienced rider would have done better?" That was Dave Siegel from the *Daily News*.

"Well, Bobby Diamond rides most of my horses, and you don't see this happening." Orlando shrugged. "When Bobby got a week's suspension I looked around and she was the hot rider, so I took a chance. Maybe I made a dumb move."

"You lying son of a bitch!" I shouted.

They all turned.

After a few seconds of embarrassed silence, Epstein pointed his tape recorder in my direction. "What's he lying about, Eagle?"

The other reporters followed suit and pointed their mikes at me.

"Shut up, will ya?" Gus whispered to me.

But I wasn't going to listen. Telno's and Tricia's blood was on Marcano's hands. "Orlando knows damn well that that horse's leg snapped because he shouldn't have been running!"

"You're crazy!" Marcano answered. "That horse's never been so good in all his life."

"That horse was an accident waiting to happen. Last week the whole backstretch saw him hobbling like a cripple."

"How come the vet passed him?" a guy from the wire service wanted to know.

Before a horse can race, the track vet checks him out at the starting gate.

"Because the vet couldn't find anything. The horse wasn't limping then, so the vet couldn't scratch him."

"That's because he was feeling healthy and good. That's because I make him happy," Orlando smiled.

"That's because he was drugged!"

The reporters exchanged looks. It was out in the open . . . finally. Everyone on the racetrack was talking about it. Any horse that Marcano started was made the immediate favorite regardless of how poorly that horse had done for someone else. Bobby

Diamond was winning races in bunches now, thanks to Orlando, challenging me and Tony Violet for top jockey honors.

Marcano's eyes narrowed. "You got big problems now, Mister!" he hissed. "Everybody knows my horses get tested for drugs each time they run. Everybody knows track security raids my barn maybe two, three times a week, and they find nothing. They search my car, my house, they find nothing."

"If he is using drugs, how's he doing it, Eagle?" Siegel pushed the mike in my face.

"I don't know. He's got something new, something that doesn't show up in the drug tests. Whenever he claims a horse from someone, it wins. And if anyone takes a horse back from him, the horse reverts to a cripple."

Marcano laughed. "Maybe Eagle's got other things than drugs on his mind. Maybe Tricia Martin told him she doesn't love him anymore or maybe he's angry because Bobby Diamond is now the top jockey."

Marcano was goading me and in the state I was in, it worked. I lunged for him and Gus strained to hold me back.

"I'm going to get you, Marcano," I screamed. "There's a girl up there who almost died because of you. I'm going to find out what you give those horses and I'm going to nail you."

In my anger, I hadn't noticed the photographer. I didn't even see the flashbulb go off. At any rate, the back page of the tabloids the next morning showed Gus holding back a wild man, *me,* and the caption was: I'LL NAIL YOU, MARCANO!!

2

TUESDAY was a dark day at the track with the advent of Sunday racing. It gave me a much needed day off.

Ordinarily, I would still get up early to exercise someone's Stakes prospect, or to ride a special project for Joe Herrera. Joe was the Cuban-born trainer whose stable had first call on my services. Between Gus's ability to get me good horses, and Joe

Herrera's powerful stable, I was always within the top two or three for the championship.

Today, I was taking the morning off. It gave me a chance to sleep late: seven-thirty was way past my normal waking time. I got up, read all about myself in the papers, received an *I told you so* call from Gus, and admitted to him that I had made an ass of myself.

I wondered if Ann and Bonnie would be reading about me in the Los Angeles papers.

My ex-wife Ann had suddenly started to take her mother-role seriously a couple of years ago. She was being interviewed for a national magazine and her manager suggested she take the edge off her usual bitchiness by having the reporter see her with her daughter. After the interview they went to a restaurant, and surprise! Ann found that she was really very fond of Bonnie.

I didn't buy the sudden reversal at first. I still remembered her speech the day she told me she was leaving:

"I know I'm supposed to go through heartwrenching agonies but frankly, Ken, I've thought about it and I think she'd be better off with you. I love her, but not like you do. And Bonnie doesn't figure into my plans just now."

That was Ann ... Mother-of-the-Year. Her acting career was picking up steam then. She had the second lead in some Off-Broadway thing that garnered her some good reviews, a stint on a daytime soap, and more recently, a top-notch second lead in a network miniseries.

At twelve years of age, Bonnie was enthralled with her mother's success. When Ann offered to take her out to L.A. for a few months, my knee-jerk reflex said nothing doing! Then I saw Bonnie's sad face and thought better of it. Now, the time in L.A. had become an annual thing.

Right after the disaster of Ann leaving me, I floundered around from one regrettable affair to another. Then I met Tricia.

Tricia Martin was the top jockey for two years straight at a small New Mexico racetrack. She moved to the Northeast and established herself as a capable jockey at Suffolk Downs, and then had a terrific winter at Hialeah in Florida. Racing people whom I respected reported that if she came to New York she would do very well.

I had heard that before. New York is the capital of racing in North America. A week doesn't go by without some fuzzy-cheeked sixteen-year-old coming to town heralded as the reincarnation of Steve Cauthen. I watched them come...and I watched them go.

From the looks of her, Tricia Martin would be no exception. She was a fresh-faced brunette, with a wholesomeness that belonged on a breakfast cereal box. She was tanned a deep shade of brown with occasional freckles, sparkling teeth and quick, intelligent blue eyes. The rest of her was on the verge of curvy yet just this side of skinny. She was just too pretty to be any good. That was my first impression.

My second impression was that Tricia Martin was a nasty piece of goods. I had walked over to her in the paddock to introduce myself, but she ignored my outstretched hand.

"Yeah, I've heard of you, Eagle," she said. "You're supposed to be the hotshot around here. Well, I'm letting you know that I'm going to be the number-one rider. I'm going to take your title away."

She walked away leaving me with my jaw hanging open like a two-dollar suitcase.

Bobby Diamond, who had witnessed the encounter, was wearing a big grin. "Friendly gal, isn't she?" he drawled.

"Do you believe that? She looks so sweet."

"Sweet as a Texas rattler. I'm giving that lady a wide berth," Bobby said. "J. C. Tanner used her on a couple of his horses. He told me that a wet-eared apprentice cut her off in the stretch and after the race she went after the kid with a butcher knife." Bobby tilted his Stetson way back on his head.

"How did J.C. do with her up at Suffolk?" I asked him.

"He said she's the best rider they had up there. She knew where the wire was and didn't care who she trampled getting there."

"Just what we need here . . . another daredevil rough rider." I shook my head.

"Trainers and owners just want to see their numbers on the board. But if she starts crashing a few good-looking two-year-olds, she'll be on her way back to wherever the hell she comes from."

"And where is that?"

Bobby looked at me with surprise. "Don't you read the track press guide? That's the big mystery. She won't tell anybody where she's from or anything about her past. All they had down for her was that she's twenty-six and 'exploded on the racing scene.'"

"Maybe she'll become civilized after she's been around a little while," I told him.

"I wouldn't count on it."

Bobby was right on that one, but I had to find out the hard way.

THE FIFTH race on the card was for horses that had never won more than one race. Tricia was riding a speedburner. I had Clicker, a come-from-behind type animal who let everything else get a long lead and then ran like the wind. If you tried to rush her early, she'd just loaf along and look at the daisies.

Tricia moved out to a long lead and I was lying fourth. At the head of the stretch, Clicker went into overdrive and at the eighth pole we were second with Tricia's horse tiring. I saw there was still daylight on the rail and that I could gun Clicker along the inside even though Tricia was starting to drift in that direction. I made my move and was almost clear when I felt something on my right stirrup, and then my right leg.

Tricia was using an old and dangerous trick. Most riders lengthen their left stirrup a bit more than the right one, so that when horses move onto the steeply banked turns, the rider is leaning toward the inside. Tricia had lengthened her left stirrup for a different reason. Jocks hate to be passed on the inside. If a horse has to beat you, you want him to lose some ground by swinging to the outside. What Tricia did was to stick her leg out and lock mine, preventing me from getting past her.

I drew my hand back and punched her mid-calf. Her leg came off mine, and Clicker jetted past her while I fought to keep my balance. We came in two lengths in front.

I had to wait to be weighed in. When you started a race required to carry one hundred and thirteen pounds consisting of yourself, a saddle, and occasionally a pound or two of lead bars that made up the difference, the stewards expected that at the end of the race you weighed in at about the same amount. That requirement out of the way, and the happy picture with the owners recorded for posterity, I tore after Tricia and caught up with her in the tunnel leading to the jockeys' quarters.

I grabbed her shoulder and spun her around. She was in lavender silks, her cap off and her luxurious brown hair cascading down her neck. The color of the silks brought out the blue of her eyes and I thought to myself that no one so thoughtless and crude deserved to be so beautiful.

"What did you think you were doing out there?"

"Leave me alone, will you? You won!"

"Yeah, I won, but I could have gotten killed."

"But you didn't, did you?" She brushed past me.

"What are you going to tell the stewards?" I called after her. "They won't let you get away with that stuff."

"They won't know anything unless you rat to them."

I wouldn't have to rat on Tricia Martin. She'd done it to herself. About an hour later I was handed a note stating that my presence was "requested" in the hearing room. It was signed by Stewards Berry, Dwyer, and Mifflin.

Tricia was used to minor-league tracks and hunt meetings, but not much got past the stewards in New York. The track had built-in towers populated by keen-eyed patrol judges. In addition to the side-shot taping of the races, the stewards also reviewed head-on shots of the horses coming down the stretch. Tricia's leg-lock maneuver would be picked up without any trouble.

It was a stupid trick, and it could cost her plenty if she was suspended. The Pine Knot Stable's good-looking four-year-old, Painted Pine, was entered in Saturday's Stakes race, and Tricia had been named as the horse's jockey. The purse was worth a hundred thousand for the winner. The jockey's cut was ten percent.

Tricia was already in the waiting room when I arrived. She averted her eyes and I was content to thumb through a magazine until we were called into the hearing room, where the three stewards sat behind a massive conference table.

Over the years I had been in this room about thirty times. It was a pretty clean record. Most of my infractions had been of the traffic-violation kind. I'd failed to keep a straight course ... I'd whipped left-handed and bored into another horse ... I'd failed to clear the field before crossing to the rail ...

Mifflin started the videotape. We watched as the head-on camera caught Tricia's move. It was an open-and-shut case.

"You want to say anything, Miss Martin?" Dwyer asked.

Tricia looked up defiantly. "No."

Berry was shaking his head. "Young lady, we won't put up with tricks like that around here," he said forcefully.

The stewards were going to throw the book at her. I could see it on their faces.

Mifflin looked at me. "Do you have anything to say, Eagle?" It was a matter of course to get my comments for the record.

"Yes, sir, I do."

Dwyer looked up at me, surprised. Ordinarily, the victimized party kept his mouth shut and let the stewards mete out punishment.

"I'm afraid that a lot of what you saw on the screen was my fault. You can't see it clearly on the films, sir, but when I went around the turn my foot slipped out of the iron. I was fishing around trying to get it back in when I locked up with Miss Martin."

"Oh, so that's how it happened," Dwyer said. From the look on his face I could tell he wasn't buying it.

"Yessir. I would hope that considering what happened didn't affect the outcome, and no one got hurt, perhaps we could forget about any disciplinary action. It was an accident."

Dwyer was wavering. "Well, if you say so, Eagle. Let's just understand that no matter what happened out there today, it isn't going to be repeated." He looked directly at Tricia. "Is that understood?"

"Yessir," Trish mumbled.

"Yessir," I echoed.

"I'll go along with a warning," Berry added.

"Warning noted," Mifflin wrote it down.

"Watch those irons," Berry told me. It was his way of letting me know that I wasn't fooling him either.

We walked out to the waiting room. I didn't expect any thanks from Tricia, and she didn't surprise me.

Two DAYS later, on Saturday, she won the Commodore Stakes with a well-judged ride on Painted Pine.

She was waiting for me near my car in the Belmont parking lot. "Here," she said, handing me an envelope.

"What's this?" I thumbed through the envelope and counted five one-hundred-dollar bills.

"I wouldn't have won the race today if it hadn't been for you bailing me out with the stewards. I don't like to owe anybody anything. That makes us even."

I handed the envelope back to her. "No sale," I told her. I got in the car and started the engine.

She leaned over and stuck her head in the window. "Tell me, Eagle. Why did you do it? Why'd you save my bacon?"

"Because you're a talented rider, and if you *are* going to challenge me for the rider's title, you won't be able to do it on a suspension. I hope you're not too stupid to learn you can't get away with those tricks around here, okay?"

"Yeah . . . Okay. But I still owe you, Eagle."

"Good. Buy me a cup of coffee some time."

Why *did* I cover for her with the stewards? I kept asking myself that same question. It couldn't be that I found her attractive. Ken Eagle didn't fall for a woman that way.

That wasn't the reason either why I went out of my way to say hello to her in the mornings, or find a seat next to her in the cafeteria, or hang around to watch her exercise Tanner's horses.

No way!

EVENTUALLY Trish did get "civilized." Her success on Painted Pine started the ball rolling. She was picking up some good horses and winning her share.

The Jockey Standings listed her in eighth place with nine wins. Tony Violet was two ahead of me with twenty-three wins; and Bobby Diamond, having an incredible year riding mainly for Marcano, was barking at my heels with eighteen winners. Hector Rodriguez was in fourth place with twelve victories so Trish was only three wins off Hector and fourth place.

She would have been doing much better had it not been for Orlando Marcano and Bobby Diamond. Orlando and Bobby were winning at a clip approaching fifty percent, and that was happening over an extended period of time.

I was happy for Bobby. He had knocked around for years making a living but not really doing well. Now he was a celebrity. Bobby seemed almost embarrassed by his new success. He had no idea how Marcano was creating his "miracles." "I just sit on the horse's back and try not to fall off before we hit the finish line," he said.

For all his talk about giving Trish a wide berth, on a couple of occasions I saw them talking together and laughing about something. Ken Eagle jealous? Ridiculous!

Trish started saying hello to people, and once or twice she smiled at me as we passed going out to mount up in the paddock. Once, she was aboard a particularly canny horse who lulled you into thinking that he was going to behave and then did whatever he could to throw you. I brought my horse over to Trish's as we were both getting into the starting gate.

"Watch out for that one," I told her. "He'll go along as smooth as silk and then he'll try to flip you."

The starting gate is the most dangerous spot on the racetrack. You're locked in a steel cage on the back of a fourteen-hundred-pound animal who could pin you against the bars and squash you like a bug. I was in the stall next to Trish's and watched her out of the corner of my eye. She was crouched low, holding the reins and set for any kind of trouble.

The horse seemed to be waiting patiently for the gate to open. There was no sign of nervousness. And then he tried to flip. His front legs climbed up the gate as he tried to turn himself over on Trish. She held onto his mane for all she was worth, and the assistant starter standing just outside the gate was finally able to grab the horse's head and steady him down. In one second it seemed, the horse was back to its placid state.

Trish looked over to me and raised her whip in salute. "That's another cup of coffee," she said.

Neither of us won that race, but Trish seemed happy just to get off in one piece. She was waiting for me at the door of the jockeys' quarters after the race.

"How about collecting on what I owe you?" she asked me.

Did I catch a touch of seductiveness in her tone? Just wishful thinking, Eagle.

"Sure."

We went to the Argo Diner, which was far enough away from the track so people wouldn't be trying to overhear what we were talking about. When the racing public saw two jocks talking, it signaled a betting coup in the works. They would strain to pick up a name of a horse and brag that they'd gotten the word that so-and-so was a sure thing.

We took a quiet table. Trish suggested that we order dinner and said she would be happy to pick up the check. I pretended to be trying to decide on what fattening and expensive dinner I would have. That got a laugh. No one ever went broke taking a jockey out for a meal.

My weight had to stay between one hundred and ten and one hundred and twelve pounds. It was absurd to think that a pound more was going to make the slightest bit of difference in the outcome of a race, but weight was something trainers could control, so they insisted on that edge.

I ordered lettuce and tomato on toast, Trish had a small salad, and we both drank only water.

Trish was in excellent spirits and I found myself talking more than I had intended. She asked me about Ann. It seemed that Trish liked soap operas and had read somewhere that Ann Page of "Emergency Hospital" was my ex-wife. I found myself telling her about Ann and Bonnie, and the trials and tribulations of a father raising a teenage girl. It suddenly dawned on me that I was prattling on and Tricia wasn't doing any of the talking.

"Now, what about you?" I asked. "What's happened? A couple of weeks ago you were a bitch on wheels."

"On horseback," she quipped. Then, "I guess I was scared. Ever since I was a kid, all I ever wanted to be was a jockey. I've mucked out stalls, walked hots, been an assistant groom, an exercise rider. Now I've finally ridden successfully all over the country, but it doesn't mean a thing if I can't do it in New York. And I'd heard all kinds of stories about how the top jockeys stay together and do anything they can to hurt a newcomer's chances."

"That's just sour grapes."

"I know that now. In fact, I've gotten more help here from people in a short time than I ever did anywhere else."

I wondered if that included Bobby Diamond.

"You've gotten friendly with Bobby, haven't you?" I tried to sound breezy, conversational.

"He's a good guy. You know he's been talking to Marcano about me? He thinks he can get him to give me some horses to ride."

"You don't want to do that."

"I don't? Are you crazy! What a chance that is."

"Marcano's horses are drugged. You can never tell when they're going to break down."

"Yes, but—"

"No buts. Look, Marcano's a menace. He drugs horses and then he runs them into the ground. When he finishes with them, they're absolutely useless."

Trish shrugged. "That's not my problem. I've got a job to do, and that's what I worry about."

465

I could see I wasn't getting anywhere so I changed the subject and asked her about the "mystery," as Bobby termed it, of her roots. I brought it up with a half-smile, anticipating a good-natured answer.

Instead, Trish's eyes narrowed and an edge came into her voice. "There are some things I'd like to keep private, okay?"

"Yeah, sure."

The waitress set down our coffee and mercifully the tension of the moment was eased.

FOR THE next couple of months I got to see quite a bit of Trish Martin, both on and off the track. We went out to dinner occasionally and because she had never been to New York before, I took special delight in squiring her around town, showing her the museums and theaters. The cold, hard shell that she still showed to much of the world began to soften.

Then Bobby Diamond was set down by the stewards because he "failed to maintain a straight course," and Marcano asked Trish to pilot his stock.

She was ecstatic, but I was scared. "You know how I feel about you riding Marcano's cripples."

She laughed. "You're just a worry wart. I think you're nervous that I'm going to take that riding title away from you."

I was nervous about more than the title. Trish had become the focal point of my life . . . and I was in love with her.

Trish Martin was a very easy woman to fall in love with. She was beautiful, bright, and knew how to make a man feel like a man. Before Trish, my relationship with women had left a lot to be desired. Which wasn't hard to understand, considering my limited social experience.

I grew up on a moderately successful farm in Pike's County, Pennsylvania. My father managed to turn a profit but it was by no means a lucrative business. The ledger sheets weren't helped either by my father's insistence that he was going to make a big score at Liberty Bell and Keystone racetracks.

His interest in horses was perhaps why he encouraged me at a very early age to learn how to ride. While other kids were tooling around on their toy scooters, I was cantering around the fields on the back of Clarissa, a gentle mare with the disposition of an old hound dog.

At the age of thirteen, it became obvious that I wasn't going to follow in the footsteps of my older brother, Mike, a strapping six-footer who was an All-State guard on our champion high-school basketball team. I measured a whisker over five-three, and all the prophecies that I'd soon "shoot up like a weed" turned out to be wrong. Although I had the coordination and speed to be a good athlete, it seemed that every sport gave the advantage to the taller, beefier guys.

My lack of height hurt me even more socially. Girls didn't care to be seen with a boy who was shorter than themselves.

It was during those dark days as a teenager that my parents surprised me one Christmas morning with an aging but genuine thoroughbred who had seen better days on the track and now was costing his trainer more in feed bills than he was returning in purses. My father had the idea that if he trained me to ride Inky's Longshot, he wouldn't have to put up with the "crooked" jockeys who sabotaged all of his selections.

I threw myself into training with a dedication that I had never before shown about anything. Suddenly, here was something that I could do better than anyone else, including my older sibling. Training meant waking before dawn, taking care of Inky's Longshot, exercising the horse, doing my own exercises to strengthen my upper body and legs. Then after school, there were several hours of actual riding. Supper and schoolwork came next and then a self-imposed eight o'clock curfew in order to be able to get up fresh the next morning.

But it wasn't long before we realized that whatever competitive desire Inky's Longshot once had was long gone. Even an optimistic diehard like my father had to admit that Inky would never race again.

One of the men who worked on the farm had ridden quarter horses out West, and he suggested that I start my career as a professional jockey by apprenticing on the quarter-horse circuit. Abner had friends in the El Paso area and he could place me with a family who would look after me while I learned the trade.

So by the age of sixteen, I was lying about my age and riding quarter horses in Texas and New Mexico. By nineteen, I was the leading jockey in races won and purse earnings. I was making more money that I ever knew existed, sending home a thousand dollars a week to my parents and going through the rest like a hot knife through butter. I drove a Porsche and wore six-hundred-dollar suits. My celebrity status even fostered an entourage of female "jockey groupies."

I moved from Texas to the Pennsylvania circuit, where my father finally had a chance to wager on his son, the only honest jockey in the bunch. Sad to say, I probably didn't improve his bankroll noticeably because my horses paid short prices and Dad couldn't break the habit of chasing longshots.

Then Gus Armando took me under his wing and we left the minor leagues to try our luck in the big time of New York racing. I had almost immediate success in New York and it was here that my playboy exploits hit full stride. I flitted from woman to woman, from affair to halfhearted affair, and through it all, if I ever allowed myself time to think, I never could shake off a feeling of loneliness.

Then I met Ann.

I had won the Boojum Stakes on Had To Be and his appreciative owner, Nate Coleman, invited me to a celebration party at Sardi's. Nate, who was backing a soon-to-open Broadway show, invited three members of the cast to join us. One of the three was Ann Page.

The chemistry was there right from the start. Ann was like no other woman I had ever known. She was stunningly attractive, the embodiment of the class and style of New York and I, in comparison, was the stumbling country bumpkin.

I was all of twenty-four years old and I fell hopelessly in love. Ann taught me to appreciate the theatre, ballet, fine restaurants. She became my friend and teacher, as well as my lover. When we married, I knew that for the rest of eternity I would never find another woman like Ann.

It was quickly obvious that she didn't feel the same about me. She became bored and restless. She told me that she hated my hours and the smell of horses that stuck to my clothes.

Her career was going sideways, and during the darkest time of that period she told me she was pregnant but intended to abort the child. Her agent had lined her up for a spaghetti western in Italy, and having a baby would cost her the part.

I offered her all the money I had in the bank, one hundred thousand dollars, if she had the child. I thought a baby would bring us back together. Finally she agreed, deciding she would use the money to invest in a show in which she would have the starring role.

Things weren't helped by the fact that the girl who had taken her part in the western—while Ann's show had bombed—got rave notices.

Shortly thereafter, Bonnie was born. Ann, once back on her feet, started searching for her elusive "vehicle," the play that would make her a star. It was just a matter of time before our marriage was over.

To say I took it badly was the understatement of the century. I lost my desire to ride and saw my weight balloon ten pounds. I became mean and surly, carrying a chip on my shoulder with Ann's name on it, and ready to fight anybody or break down weeping at the slightest provocation. I failed to show up for assignments, and once I even punched a horse who had beaten me in a close race. My services as a jockey were becoming less and less in demand.

Somehow or other, I survived. Bonnie was living with my parents, and I came to realize that I had to fight back to win a life for me and for the little girl I loved. With Gus's help, I bounced back from the bottom. I put myself on a regimen of fresh air and exercise, and in the end I came back stronger both mentally and physically. A year later I had my second Eclipse Award as the top jockey in the nation.

It was a remarkable comeback, but the scar left by Ann was deep. When I began dating again I found I couldn't help holding back a part of myself to ensure that I wouldn't be hurt.

Then Trish Martin came into my life with her mixture of toughness and innocence and I knew I hadn't felt the same about any woman since Ann. But the situation I had experienced with Ann was reversed. Now I was the New York sophisticate eager to introduce the rough-hewn country girl to the pearls that were in the Manhattan oyster. I became her teacher and guide and thoroughly enjoyed her wonder and enthusiasm.

Trish's feelings for me were difficult to assess. She told me that she loved me, but there seemed to be something that she couldn't quite express. Our relationship progressed in an erratic line that mystified and frustrated me. We would find ourselves distant on one date, and as close as possible on another.

We talked about it and Trish told me she just needed more time. She was not used to really trusting a man, or anyone for that matter. I told her I understood. I had to understand—I loved her. I loved her far too much not to be concerned about her riding for Marcano.

3

I WAS thinking about that particular conversation as I left for the hospital. There would be no riding title for Trish this year. At the very best, Dr. Reissman told me, she wouldn't be able to get on a horse for at least two months. It would be six weeks before she could think about taking the cast off her wrist.

Trish's room was on the fifth floor. It was bright and airy and filled with flowers from well-wishers. Marcano had sent a floral horseshoe.

When she saw me, Trish broke into a smile. She still had the bandage around her head but her color was close to normal.

"You look terrific," I told her. "How do you feel?"

"Like somebody's been tap-dancing on my skull."

"That's to be expected with a concussion. You'll have headaches for at least a couple of days."

"There was no warning, Ken. One moment we were going fine, and the next moment I was down."

"I know. Marcano's horses don't feel any pain. They run until they drop. Telno had to be destroyed," I told her.

"I thought so. I was hoping that he could be saved."

You couldn't ride horses, be around horses, and not feel for them. Each had his own personality. Each became part of a stable's family.

There was a knock on the opened door and I turned to see Bobby Diamond. He stood in the doorway carrying a large box of candy.

"Hi, Bobby," Trish called.

I wasn't the only one who got the big smile, I thought.

He was wearing what for Bobby had become a uniform: the flannel shirt, jeans, denim jacket, and the ever-present Stetson. In honor of the hospital visit, perhaps, he wore a string tie with a silver bucking-bronco clip.

He flashed me a smile. "Hi, Ken. Let me run over and say howdy to the little lady."

He crossed to the other side of the bed and leaned over, giving Trish a peck on the cheek. I watched the way she looked at him. There was no getting around the fact that Bobby was a nice-looking man with a Marlboro-man image.

"How's she doin', Ken?"

"She looks like she's ready to ride the hurdles."

"Sure, with half a head on my shoulders and one hand. You picked a good week to get suspended," Trish kidded.

Diamond shook his head sadly. "Dumb racing luck."

"I call it Marcano luck."

"Come on now, Ken," Bobby said. "It could have happened on any horse."

I wondered if he really believed that. Maybe it made him feel better. After all, he was the one riding Marcano's string and he had already had one close call.

471

"Trish, you should see today's paper," Diamond said laughing. "Ken looks like one of those wrestlers being held back by his manager."

"Really, Ken?"

"Yeah," I answered sheepishly. "I guess I made a fool of myself. Marcano was talking in the lobby downstairs and I just couldn't help it."

She reached out and took my hand. "Ken, you're okay."

There was an uncomfortable silence as Trish and I stared at each other. Bobby broke it with a cough. "Well, I guess I have to be gettin' along. You get better real quick. Don't forget to save me a few of those chocolates."

I heard the door close behind me but I wasn't really paying any attention. I was holding Trish's hand and looking in her eyes.

THE RAIN hit Belmont about fifteen minutes before the first race. It was heralded by a series of thunder claps and the track, which just a few minutes ago had been a finely manicured strip consisting of a clay base and a mixture of rich loam, would soon be a hard, sand-packed road with pools of water.

On such days you wanted to be on a horse who could get the lead. You gunned your horse to the rail with the knowledge that speed held up longer on a wet track. And the lead horse could kick back mud and sand into the faces of the horses trying to catch him.

I had often been stuck on a horse trying to chase a speed demon in the rain. Jockeys wore up to fifteen pairs of clear goggles that could be flipped up, one by one, during the course of a race. Horses had their own windshield-wiper system in the form of a membrane that blinked from side to side over the eye. But they still hated to have those clods hurtling back at them and more often than not, the more talented horses lost coming from behind on an off-track.

I checked the *Daily Racing Form* and looked over the past races of the horses I was riding. One looked like a cinch in the third race: he was a speed merchant that would leave everything in his wake. The other three were a mixed bag in terms of chances to win. There was a horse in the ninth race that was a complete washout, I thought. I wondered why Gus had booked me that one.

My horse in the third won easily. I lost with the next three, coming in in the money with only one of them; and my ninth race "loser" made a shambles of his field and won by ten. He proved once again that jockeys were terrible handicappers.

I changed and made my way to the car. I planned to visit Trish and make an early evening of it.

A gray-uniformed Pinkerton security man was waiting by the gate talking to one of the hawkers who sold salted pretzels. When he saw me, he stopped the conversation and walked over. "Nice price on that one in the ninth," he said, shaking his head.

"Did you have it?"

"Nah. I bet you made a hit, though."

"Hell, no. I was the most surprised guy on the track."

"No kiddin'? Jeez, you can't figure this game."

"You're right about that," I told him. I made a move to my car.

"Oh, Mr. Eagle. You know my boss, Mr. Demaret. He said he'd like to have a word with you before you left today. He'd appreciate it if you'd come down with me to his office."

"Sure," I said. I had some time to kill before hospital visiting hours.

Track security was below ground level in a winding tunnel that extended under the grandstand. We passed a large imposing door guarded by two Pinks with drawn guns. I knew that to be the counting room where the money was tallied before being taken to the bank.

Demaret's office was the next room down. My escort knocked twice and waited for a buzzer that released the lock.

The inner office was large. It was carpeted in blue with modern furniture and it had a bevy of female secretaries typing on word processors. One of them, a tall blonde, walked over. "Hi, I'm Nancy. Would you step this way, Mr. Eagle?"

I was led to a green frosted door with the name ART DEMARET

on it in neat, two-inch letters. Inside the office, Demaret was on the phone talking softly. Nancy motioned for me to have a seat, closed the door behind her and left.

Demaret was in his late fifties and had a lined, handsome face topped by a thatch of gray hair cut in a short crew. He put down the phone, stood up, and shook my hand. "Thanks for stopping by, Mr. Eagle."

"Call me Ken," I told him.

"Fine, Ken. You look like a man who appreciates plain talk, so let me give it to you. I'm also not terribly fond of our friend Orlando Marcano. I think he's found a way to beat the system, and I think that's bad for everybody. After a while, the public says, 'Why bother puttin' in a bet . . . the whole thing's fixed.' And that puts me and you out of a job."

He stood up and walked to a small refrigerator next to a row of filing cabinets. "How about a cold one, Ken?"

I shook my head and watched as he snapped open the top and drank it straight from the can. He had large meaty hands and the beer can got lost in them.

"So what's on your mind?" I asked. "You know I agree with everything you're saying. I think Marcano is killing racing."

"Sure you do, and you're not shy about talking to the press." He reached into his desk and pulled out a copy of the *Daily News* with my picture on the back page. "What the hell do you think you're accomplishing? All that happens is I get more pressure, and all my guys look like jerks."

"I didn't intend—"

"Yeah, I know." He held up his hand and took another swig from the can. "I know just how you feel. I'd love to pop off about that son of a bitch too. But stories in the paper about him using drugs just makes it harder to nab him. The public loses confidence and he's going to be even more careful. The only chance I got is if he makes a mistake."

I felt bad for Demaret . . . but not that bad. "The fact is, Art, this has been going on for a couple of years now."

"Don't I know it! We've raided his barn, we've had his horses' feed and water tested, we've searched his car. And do you know what we came up with? Headaches! At first I thought it was a battery. They've transistorized cattle prods into the size of matchbook covers. Diamond sticks it on the rump of his horse, and the sucker'll run through a brick wall."

"Bobby Diamond wouldn't do that," I said.

"I wouldn't rule out my own mother if she was involved with Marcano," Demaret said angrily. "But I know it ain't a battery. It's got to be some long-lasting drug that doesn't show up in any lab tests. I can't figure out what it is he's using, but I'm sure as hell going to keep trying."

"Anything I can do?"

"Just keep your mouth shut and your eyes open."

"I'll remember that," I told him.

I got up and walked to the door.

"Hey, Eagle. Did you have anything down on that bomb you rode in the ninth?"

"Not a penny," I shrugged.

"Too bad," he said, shaking his head and taking another pull on his beer.

THE RINGING came from a long distance away.

I was driving down a dirt road that had turns just like a racetrack. Ann was in the backseat and she was laughing, and then she became Tricia. She was leaning over now to tell me something but I couldn't hear her because of the incessant ringing that seemed to be getting louder.

Then I woke up. The phone was still ringing as I pulled myself together and lifted the receiver. I noticed it was two a.m. on the clock radio.

"Mr. Eagle?" The voice was muffled.

"Yes, who is this?"

"A friend. I saw what you said about Marcano in the paper."

"How did you get my number?" I asked. My phone was unlisted.

"Forget about that. Do you want to see how he juices the

horses? I can tell you about it, but this is the only time I'm going to call you. You got to come now, by yourself, or the deal's off."

"What kind of deal?"

"You bring me five hundred bucks and I'll show you how he does it."

"Why now? What about tomorrow?"

"It's got to be tonight. Now!"

I did want to find out how Marcano was drugging his horses. I wanted to prevent what happened to Trish from happening to Bobby or anyone else. I had a bank card, and I could get five hundred from a machine.

"All right. Where?"

"The bridge in Sheepshead Bay. Be there in an hour. Bring the money, and no one else!"

He hung up.

MY APARTMENT was a duplex on the East Side in the low thirties. Once a six-story walk-up, it had been converted into a fashionable co-op.

My car was in the underground garage. I was still driving a Chevy that had seen seventy thousand miles. Each month I promised myself a new car, but I never seemed to find the time to actually do it.

I opened the garage door with my remote and jammed on the brakes as a strong flashlight was aimed into my eyes.

"Oh, sorry, Mr. Eagle."

It was Chester, the building's doorman, who doubled as garage watchman.

"Out a bit early," he said.

"I've got an errand to take care of, Chester."

"Okay, sir. Have a nice evening," he said, touching the brim of his cap.

I found a Citibank and pressed buttons to dispense the money; then I turned down the FDR Drive, through the Battery Tunnel, and around the horn of Brooklyn to Sheepshead Bay.

Sheepshead Bay is a very picturesque spot in Brooklyn that features along its wooden piers a substantial fishing fleet. The bridge my caller was referring to is a small wooden affair large enough for three people abreast. It connects the Bay with the small peninsula of the exclusive Manhattan Beach area.

I found a parking spot and waited. From where I sat I had a perfect view of anything that came over or near the bridge. I waited for over an hour . . . nothing. I got out of the car and walked over the bridge to the other side. Still nothing.

A policeman crossed opposite me as I headed back to my car. He looked at me in that funny way cops look at you late at night when they're trying to decide whether or not to question you. I was spared making up some story when he passed me by.

Out in the Bay, the boats groaned and creaked with the currents. A bright moon lit up the surface of the inky water. I made a mental note to take Bonnie out on a fishing trip one day when she got back.

I nosed the Chevy back on the Belt toward eastern Long Island and Belmont. It was three forty-five. Was this someone's stupid idea of a joke? How did he get my phone number?

MORNING is a good time to be around a racetrack. Exercise riders lead their horses out on the deep exercise track under the watchful eyes of the trainers. There's a cacophony of sound in the backstretch: aside from the whinnying of the horses, other mainstays of the stable are vying for attention and food, including cats, dogs, goats, and even monkeys. Horses are very sociable creatures and love the company of a smaller animal in their stalls. Many impossibly difficult stallions become docile with the addition of a stable pet.

That morning there was a touch of a fall chill that seemed to put all the animals on their toes. Joe Herrera asked me to take out Viceroy for a five-furlong breeze.

"Get him back in a minute-one and change."

The "change" referred to the fifths-of-a-second splits that made all the difference between winning and losing.

Viceroy was doing well and wanted the bit. I let him out a

notch around the far turn and then reined him in slightly to let him know this was just practice. Herrera, stopwatch in hand, nodded slightly as we passed him at the eight-furlong pole.

Unless they were just starting out and trying to impress a trainer, jockeys generally didn't exercise horses. I did it for Herrera for two reasons. First, I was always fighting my weight: I just had to look at food to gain. Exercising horses helped me keep the weight off so I often volunteered, to Joe's delight.

The second factor had to do with knowing Joe's stock. Horses remembered you in the afternoon if you exercised them in the morning and more importantly, you remembered them. It gave me an edge to know which horse was ouchy, which was on the muscle, and which were culls or rogues.

I walked Viceroy back to shed row and waited until his groom took him in tow. Then I made my way back to the block-long corrugated building known as "the kitchen" which in actuality was a large cafeteria.

It was here that trainers, grooms, exercise riders, jockeys, and agents all broke into different groups like adolescent cliques. Here, people were hired and fired, gossip exchanged, and betting coups hatched.

I ordered a cup of coffee and a slice of dry toast and sat down near the door. Generally, Joe and Gus would join me and we would discuss the day's racing card. Neither of my friends seemed to be around.

I was two bites into my toast when I spotted Herrera. The refugee from Castro's Cuba, who had been a champion trainer in his own country and then had duplicated that feat in America, was usually unflappable. Today, however, something had gotten to him. He looked slightly lost, deep in thought.

"Joe, over here," I called to him.

He seemed to sleepwalk his way over to my table.

"What's wrong? You look like you're in a fog."

"You didn't hear nothin'? It's all over the track."

"I've been exercising your horses. What's all over the track?"

"Somebody killed Orlando Marcano."

TRISH KNEW ABOUT IT. I CALLED her after leaving the track. Bobby Diamond had already given her the news. Diamond always seemed to be in there pitching.

I tried to find out from Trish if she had any details.

"Bobby said he was stabbed to death." She sounded very upset. "He was found in his home by his housekeeper."

"How is Bobby taking it?" I asked her.

Bobby was the closest thing Marcano had to a friend at the track. Other trainers detested Orlando, and anyone who'd ever had any financial dealings with him walked away calling him a swindler. Even after his murder, you weren't hearing the usual hypocritical platitudes.

"When he called I could hardly hear him, he was talking so low."

I sighed. I didn't like the man, but to die like that . . .

"I'm getting out of here by the end of the week, Ken. The doctor said I could be discharged after some routine tests."

"That's great! But where will you stay? I mean, you'll need someone to help you with your arm in a cast, and all. Is there anyone who—"

"No!" She cut me off emphatically. Her past was a door that she didn't want opened.

"All right, you'll stay with me until the cast comes off."

"That might take more than a month."

"So what? Bonnie is with her mother for the rest of this school term. It's a big enough apartment."

"I don't know."

"Well, just think about it then. You'd really be doing me a favor. I'm kind of lonely."

"I'll let you know." She seemed preoccupied.

Marcano's death must have hit her harder than I'd thought it would. I hung up the phone and walked to my car.

CHESTER had a worried look on his face when I pulled up to the garage. "There are a couple of cops upstairs waiting to talk to you, Mr. E. They asked me a couple of things. About how long I knew you, things like that. I hope I didn't do anything wrong."

"No, of course not. Someone I know got himself murdered last night. I'm sure it's routine."

"Oh, okay, sir." Chester seemed relieved.

I took the elevator to the third floor. There were two of them waiting for me in front of the apartment. A thin man wearing a beige raincoat and a rainhat, and a taller man, beefy with a large mustache.

The thin man spoke first. "Mr. Eagle, I'm Detective Fusco. This is my partner, Detective Barrad. We'd like a word with you."

"You have badges?" I asked, and waited while they showed me their department shields. "Come on in," I said.

They looked around, taking everything in as if they were prospective buyers. I led them to the living room and sat down with them on the couch.

"Nice place," Barrad said.

"Thanks."

Barrad let Fusco do the talking.

"You knew Orlando Marcano, didn't you?" He made a face. "What am I saying? Of course you knew Mr. Marcano. You were trying to slug him. I saw that picture in the paper."

"I think the whole world saw that picture," I said.

"From what I hear, he deserved to be slugged," Fusco said affably.

"Slugged, yes. Killed, no. What's what happened to Marcano have to do with me?"

"Do you mind telling me where you were last night, Mr. Eagle?" Fusco asked.

"Here . . . most of the night."

"And when you weren't here?"

"I had to go out early to meet someone."

"Really? You went to meet someone at three in the morning? Your doorman saw you leave."

"That's right." I was feeling more and more uncomfortable.

"Did you see Marcano last night?"

"No."

"You're sure about that?"

"Yes."

"One of the beat cops near Marcano's house identified you as being in the neighborhood," he said calmly.

I remembered the cop on the bridge. "Where did Marcano live?"

"Manhattan Beach."

I felt the cold hand of fear grip at my throat.

"Mr. Eagle, do you want to tell me who you met last night?"

"I didn't meet anyone. I got a call from someone to meet him at Sheepshead Bay. He never showed up."

Fusco nodded. "That's too bad. Oh, by the way, did you lose this?"

He flashed out a watch from his pocket. It was the Pegasus watch Bonnie had given me for Father's Day.

"Yes, I did lose it, as a matter of fact. Where did you find it?"

"It was clutched in Marcano's hand when his housekeeper found him."

I was reeling. I was being framed and the noose was getting tighter and tighter. "I don't understand," I said weakly.

Barrad got out of his chair. "You mind if I look around the place, Mr. Eagle? I can get a warrant but if you didn't do anything wrong, you shouldn't have any objections." He pulled a piece of paper out of his pocket. "Please sign this form. It says you gave us the right to have a look-see."

I read it and signed.

"How do you think he got a hold of your watch like that?"

"I'm being framed, Fusco."

"Who would want to do that to you?" Fusco asked as if genuinely concerned.

"I don't know. Someone got me out of the house with a fake phone call. I lost the watch. I don't know who, or why, but—"

"Vinny, see you a minute," Barrad called.

"Excuse me, Mr. Eagle." Fusco walked over to my bedroom door. I heard them talking to one another, then they both came back into the living room.

"Jerry found this in your closet. It was tucked in the back, behind the shoes."

I looked at what they were holding. It was my shirt, a simple cotton polo that I hadn't worn for at least a month. It wasn't folded neatly like the rest of my shirts: this one had been rolled up into a ball. It was covered with fresh bloodstains.

Fusco brought out a pair of handcuffs. "Mr. Eagle, I'm placing you under arrest for the murder of Orlando Marcano. You have the right to remain silent. Anything you . . . "

4

I SPENT the next three hours in a twelve-by-fifteen holding pen. It was a bit short on amenities. A bolted-down wooden bench, a two-tiered bunk bed, and a commode built into the orange brick wall made up the decor. They had brought me down here after taking my possessions and fingerprinting me.

The cell had been built for at least two but I was alone. Maybe murderers were always assigned private cells, while drunks and pickpockets got crammed in four or five to a room. Maybe Fusco thought I was too dangerous to be allowed near the other prisoners.

In a way, I was grateful for the time to sort things out. I went over everything that had happened and tried to make some sense out of it.

I'd been half-asleep when I'd answered that phone call beckoning me out to Sheepshead Bay. The voice was muffled as if someone were talking through a handkerchief. I couldn't even tell if it was male or female.

Fusco had said that Marcano's housekeeper had found the dead man with my watch clutched in his hand. How was that possible? I believed I'd had the watch the day that Tricia fell—I had asked Gus about it at the hospital. He didn't have it with him when he brought my clothes from my locker at the track. Anyone in the jockeys' room could have opened my locker and taken it that day.

Had I had the combination lock on? I'd have to ask Gus if he'd opened it. Gus knew the combination.

How many other people knew it? I had never gone out of my way to hide it. Bobby Diamond had the locker to my left and J. J. Alvarado was on my right. I had known them both for years. They would never open my locker, even if they knew the combination.

Then there was the not-so-small matter of how my shirt had got covered with blood. Had that shirt also been in my locker? I thought about that. It was possible that I had worn it several weeks ago and left it in the locker instead of taking it home. When the watch was taken, the shirt could have been taken also. But how had it gotten back to my apartment just in time for Barrad to pull it out of my closet?

"You want to stand up please, Mr. Eagle?" The officer who had locked me in was standing at the door.

"Fusco wants to see you upstairs," he said, swinging it open. "Place your hands behind your back. We have to cuff you again, that's the regs."

I noticed he kept one hand on his holstered gun as he snapped the cuffs on my wrists.

I preceded him up the narrow staircase to the second floor and down a drab gray corridor. My jailer opened a warped brown door with the words DETECTIVE DIVISION on it, walked me to a set of cubicles and stopped by the one that had DETECTIVE VINCENT FUSCO etched on the glass door.

"Your prisoner's here, Vince," he said, ushering me in.

"Okay, Walter," Fusco said as the man left.

He motioned for me to sit down opposite him. We were sitting at a long, cigarette-burned oak table under a row of six-foot fluorescents. There was a mirror on one wall of the cubicle. I guessed it was one-way glass.

Fusco read my mind. "That's a see-through mirror. For your protection and ours, this session is being videotaped. We can't have anybody accusing us of using a rubber hose on you."

He reached in his pocket for a pack of Marlboros and offered me one. I shook my head no.

"I read somewhere that I get a phone call."

"That's been taken care of," he said somberly.

The door opened again and this time a tall, dark-haired woman entered. She carried a chair and put it down.

She ignored Fusco. "Mr. Eagle, I've been engaged by Mr. Gus Armando to represent you. My name is Arlene Kirshbaum." She extended her hand. "I have many years of experience as both a prosecutor and a defense attorney. That's why Mr. Armando hired me. However, if you feel you might be more comfortable with someone else, I would understand completely."

She waited for my response before she sat down. She was an attractive woman, large-boned with chiseled, angular features and sharp, blue-green eyes. She seemed tough and knowledgeable and I had faith that Gus knew what he was doing.

"I'm sure you'll do fine, Ms. Kirshbaum," I managed with a weak smile.

Her face softened for an instant and she sat down. "Don't worry, we'll have you out of here in no time."

Fusco fenced with Kirshbaum for a few minutes as he tried to establish that there was bad blood between me and Marcano. He asked me about the shouting match at the hospital and then he started asking me about my feelings for Tricia.

"It must have gotten you real angry to see Miss Martin banged up," he said, "especially when you blamed him."

"I was very angry, but not angry enough to kill anybody."

Fusco pulled up a black attaché case from the floor and placed it on the table. He opened the snaps and drew out the white cotton polo shirt, the watch Bonnie had given me, and some stark, gruesome photos of the murdered Marcano.

"It may interest you to know, Mr. Eagle, that the blood on the shirt matches Marcano's. Is it your shirt?"

"Don't answer that!" Kirshbaum warned.

"It's okay. I know it's my shirt," I said.

"No." She shook her head. "You know that it appears to be a shirt like one you own."

"What about the watch?" Fusco wanted to know.

"It appears to be my watch," I told him.

"So it *appears* that your watch finds its way into Marcano's hand. It *appears* that your shirt, covered with Marcano's blood, finds its way into your closet. It *appears* that your automobile finds its way into Marcano's neighborhood." Fusco frowned. "You know, Ken, I really understand how you feel. I mean, Tricia Martin is all broken up in the hospital. Marcano is sitting on top of the world. You have a riding title that's being threatened by this fellow. Hell, I think anybody might flip out. I think a jury would understand that, Ken, I really do."

"Perhaps I can save us all some time," Arlene said. "Ken, did you kill Marcano?"

"No."

"Ken, have you told the detective that you don't know how your watch and shirt got involved in this case? Have you told the detective you were called to meet Marcano?"

"Yes."

"Okay, Detective Fusco? I think that's plain English. Now why don't you drop the charges. The case you have against my client is an obvious frame-up."

"I really don't think—" Fusco started.

"Oh come on, Detective Fusco. I've read what you and your partner submitted on your DD5s. You found the bank receipt from the cash machine in Ken's pocket. The time on the receipt corroborates his story about getting a call and shows that Ken was on his way to Marcano's house after Marcano had already been killed."

"The coroner's report doesn't say that. The time estimate was inconclusive," Fusco answered coolly.

"What about the telephone company's report?" Arlene countered. "They say someone called Eagle from Marcano's house. It was obviously the killer setting Eagle up."

"That's your interpretation."

"What's yours?"

"Marcano called Eagle to talk. They argued. Eagle decided he had had enough. He drove over to Marcano's house—"

"And Marcano just opened the door and invited him in." Arlene rolled her eyes. "In the middle of the night, no less."

Fusco took the photos of Marcano and placed them in front of me. "Look at these, Eagle. Somebody got into Marcano's house, somebody who knew him because there was no sign of forced entry. And then he buried a six-to-eight-inch knife in Marcano's belly. Until somebody can show me different, I say you did it."

"How did you know to look in Eagle's closet for the shirt?" Kirshbaum wanted to know.

"That's police business," he said gruffly.

"Come off it, Detective. You got a tip. Are you going to tell me that Ken killed Marcano and then called you with information about where to find the knife and shirt he used?"

"We haven't found the knife as yet," Fusco said.

"I'm sure you will. It'll be planted the same way the shirt and watch were," Arlene told him. "Now I think you'd better drop the charges before I'm forced to initiate a five-million-dollar false-arrest suit. This man is a public figure and this unwarranted arrest could destroy his reputation and his ability to earn a living in his chosen profession."

"All right, take it easy . . . take it easy," Fusco said. "There's a lot of things in this case that don't add up. I wasn't comfortable about the tip we got . . ." It had slipped out and Fusco looked embarrassed.

"I thought so. If Eagle had killed Marcano do you think he would have told somebody about it?"

"I've seen a lot of smart people do very stupid things." Fusco tapped the table for emphasis.

"I'm not a killer, Fusco," I said softly.

He stared at me and held my eyes for several seconds. "Maybe you're not," he sighed. "I'm going to drop the murder charges, counselor. Eagle, I want you to make a list of anyone who had access to your apartment. I don't care who they are or how close to you they are. If you get any ideas about this case, talk to me directly." He handed me a card.

"And I don't want you getting any ideas that you're in the clear.

486

You're still a suspect and that means you make yourself available. You go on a trip somewhere, I want to know about it."

"He'll be a good boy," Arlene said. "Cut to the chase and let us get out of here."

Fusco made a half-nod toward the door. I was up and out in a flash with Kirshbaum at my heels.

I turned to thank her but she cut me off.

"Don't say anything until we're out of the building. Big Brother has ears all over."

IT WAS a cool evening with a strong hint of an impending rainstorm. I took a deep breath and enjoyed breathing the air of a free man.

"Come on," Arlene said. "I've got my car parked down the block. Gus said I was to take you back to his apartment."

"How did you know you were going to get me off?"

"Hey, come on, that was a piece of cake. Fusco was just fishing. He knew all along he had a handful of wet tissues."

"I wish I'd known it."

She had a late-model Galant that she drove as if they made you pay for using the brake. We got to Gus's apartment on Madison in less than eight minutes.

Gus lived on the top floor in an apartment that wasn't as big as the Astrodome, but didn't miss by much. He had recently decided that he was going to move again, so most of his furniture had been put in storage. We left a trail on the white llama rug and followed Gus into the dining room.

"Are you okay?" he asked, his thick black eyebrows knitting together in concern.

"I guess . . . I'm just bewildered by it all. It just doesn't make sense."

"Oh, I think it makes perfect sense to the person who killed Marcano," Kirshbaum said. "You were ripe for the plucking with that picture of you in the paper and the way you popped off against the guy."

I fidgeted in my Louis-the-something-or-other chair. It was

heavy oak with a velvet seat pad that seemed to be scientifically designed to be as uncomfortable as hell.

"I hate your chairs," I told Gus.

"At nine thousand dollars apiece, they're for looking at . . . not sitting on. I'll give you something that'll take your mind off your keester."

He walked over to the bar and poured bourbon into three glasses.

"You're telling me something, aren't you, Gus? Doesn't bourbon have calories?"

Gus handed us our drinks before he spoke. "I was talking to Demaret from Security. He kind of thought it might be a good idea if you took a vacation for a week or two until things quieted down. There's no reason for you to have to put up with any abuse from the fans or anyone else."

"What's that supposed to mean?"

"There have been some death threats against you," Kirshbaum explained. "Why take any chances?"

"Death threats?"

"Demaret thinks they may be from members of Marcano's family." Gus shrugged. "Anyway, you can drink your bourbon without guilt."

"Look, Gus, I'm not running away from anything. Call Herrera and tell him I'll be back tomorrow morning."

Gus and Arlene exchanged glances.

"I told you he was going to say that," Gus said. "Ken, the fact is that you don't have any Stakes races coming up for a couple of weeks, and a rest would be good for you."

"Sure, just sit back and let someone else take the title."

"Look, if you're rested, you can come back and in three days make up all the ground you lost. You know that as well as I do. And I'll tell you something else. An experience like this can't help but prey on your mind. If you lose a couple of nose-finishes, people are going to say you've got your mind on the Marcano murder. You'll start getting fewer and fewer mounts and your vacation could become permanent."

What Gus was saying made sense. Trainers latched onto any excuse to explain to owners why their charge didn't win.

"All right. I'll take a week off," I said. "I'm going to need the time to find out who was behind the frame."

Gus sighed. "I've already hired someone to take care of that. I would like to see you out of New York and on a real vacation somewhere."

"Damn it, Gus! You know I'm not going to be able to relax until I know who was behind this. I'm also not too comfortable about having some high-powered detective trampling around asking questions and making a nuisance of himself."

"I promise I won't do too much trampling," Arlene said.

Gus smiled at my confusion. "Arlene got her law degree from Harvard and then became an FBI agent. She's got a top-notch track record, Ken."

Arlene slowly sipped some whisky and then placed her glass on the table. "Any objections, Ken?"

I shook my head. I had already seen Arlene Kirshbaum in action wearing her lawyer's hat, and I had been impressed. I figured I could do a lot worse.

"I think the key to this thing is my locker," I told her. "The only thing I can figure is that someone got the combination, or maybe I never closed it. Then they took out the polo shirt and watch, but how did they get the shirt back into my apartment?"

"No doubt you also had keys in your pocket," Arlene suggested. "There are twenty to thirty hardware stores that make duplicate keys in the vicinity of the track. All they would have to do is make a dupe and then return the keys."

There was a long pause as we all tried to fit the pieces together. I finally stood up.

"I ought to call Ann and Bonnie and let them know I'm okay. Then I'll call Trish at the hospital and see how she's doing."

"Ann called earlier," Gus said. "I told her you were being released. Bonnie doesn't know anything, and Ann said she wasn't going to tell her."

"There's a problem with Trish, though," Arlene said.

I felt my body tense. "What's wrong with her? Were there complications with the concussion?"

"She's disappeared from the hospital, Ken," Gus said. "It seems that when the nurse came in to give her breakfast, she was gone. She just walked out on her own, didn't tell anybody where she was going."

"I spoke to her at the hospital. She was supposed to stay with me while she recuperated. Maybe she's home sleeping."

"I tried your apartment and her apartment," Gus said. "I left messages all over the track."

"Maybe she's staying with family," Arlene offered.

"I doubt that. My impression was that there was some trouble between Trish and her folks."

Gus looked decidedly uncomfortable. "I don't like the fact that nobody's heard from her," he said. "And I don't like the fact that she disappeared right after Marcano got killed. I might be letting my imagination run away with itself, but I think Arlene should check up on what happened to her."

Arlene nodded.

Outside the sky was inky black with tinges of pink along its western flanks. I suddenly felt very tired.

"I have to sack out for a couple of hours, Gus. Is your guest room free?" Gus's apartment could have been listed in guide books as a stopover for stewardesses.

"Coast is clear," he said, smiling.

I shook hands with Arlene Kirshbaum and thanked her for all her help.

By the time my head touched the pillow, I was asleep.

I WOKE up with a start, not remembering for the moment that I was in Gus's guest room. The alarm clock said 8:45 p.m. I stretched and sat up.

Gus had left a note for me on the mirror. He had a date (of course) and he'd had to leave. He wanted me to make myself at home and he'd written that he had ordered something up for me from the corner diner.

The "corner diner" turned out to be one of the most expensive restaurants in the city. I lifted the covers off the heated plates and allowed myself the luxury of breathing in the fragrant aroma. If I had been riding tomorrow, that would have been all I could do, but since I was on vacation I grabbed a fork and dug in.

There was shrimp cooked in an aromatic sauce of garlic, tomatoes and chopped onions. I couldn't place one of the ingredients until I took a couple of bites. Coconut milk! A small tossed salad rounded off the main meal, and there were two desserts—a fruit mousse, light and delicious, and a crumbly confection of coconut and brown cane sugar. I washed it all down with Gus's special blend of mocha coffee, which he'd thoughtfully kept warm on a hotplate.

I finally pushed myself away from the table, dashed some cold water on my face, and I was ready to take on the world.

I tried Trish's number and let it ring ten times. Nothing. Then I wrote Gus a note thanking him for his hospitality, rode the elevator down the forty-four floors to the lobby and grabbed a cab to my place.

I called the management company and told them I needed the lock changed. Ten minutes later I pulled out of the garage and headed toward the Midtown Tunnel to Queens.

In the back of my head, I had mental pictures of Trish Martin lying on the floor of the house she had rented, unconscious because of the concussion or loss of blood caused by internal bleeding. The thought caused me to press a little harder on the accelerator. I took Queens Boulevard into Forest Hills and then after a couple of missed turns, found myself on Tricia's block.

It was a middle-class neighborhood consisting mostly of one-family brick houses with postage-stamp front gardens. When she'd arrived in New York, Tricia had searched for a furnished apartment within hailing distance of Aqueduct and Belmont race-tracks. She'd been fortunate enough to connect with a middle-aged couple who spent most of their time in Florida, so instead of an apartment she had a whole house to herself.

The house was completely dark. I paused in front of the door before I pressed the bell, trying to hear any sounds inside. There was nothing. I rang the bell and then I used the heavy knocker. I tried it again a minute later. If Trish was home, she wasn't willing or able to answer the door.

There was a bay window on the porch and I peered through it, shielding my eyes from the reflected glare of the street light behind me. I could make out general shapes of furniture but that was all.

Tricia had invited me in a number of times during the months we had been seeing each other. I knew there was a rear door that led into the kitchen. As I walked across the dark driveway I could see Tricia's car inside the wooden carport.

Without the light of the street lamps the back porch was almost pitch-black. I walked up the steps, feeling my way along the handrail, and reached the door. I tried knocking again and then looked in the kitchen window. My eyes were adjusting to the darkness and I could make out a little of the hallway that led into the dining area. It was then that I saw it.

Toward the end of the hallway there appeared to be something on the floor. It looked for all the world like a pair of legs with the main part of the torso blocked from sight by a partially opened closet door.

I walked back to the door and tried to budge it by ramming it with my shoulder. It was made of thick wood with two sets of locks and it didn't take a genius to figure out that my shoulder would break long before the door did.

I went back to the window and tried it. It was locked shut. Glass at least I could deal with. I took off the windbreaker I was wearing, wrapped it around my fist like a boxing glove, and punched in the pane of glass just under the lock.

Too late the thought hit me that the house might have an alarm system. Ken Eagle arrested for murder on Wednesday, arrested for breaking and entering on Thursday. I held my breath for a second, anticipating sirens. But nothing happened.

I gingerly drew my hand back, shook off the glass from my jacket, and then reached in to open the lock. It slid to the side easily enough, which allowed me to raise the window. I was just about to step over the sill when something hard and cold pressed against the back of my neck.

"If you move an eyelash I'll blow your head off! Put your hands up against the wall."

The voice sounded familiar to me. I did as I was told as he frisked me for weapons.

"Turn around, slowly," he warned, then: "What the . . . it's you, Eagle!"

"Bobby!"

It was Bobby Diamond, packing a mean-looking pistol.

"What are you doing here?" I asked him.

"Never mind that. How come you're bustin' into Trish's place?" he asked in a low whisper.

I pointed through the window. "Look over there."

"Hell, it must be Tricia."

He climbed through the window with me right behind him. We crunched through the glass and down the narrow hallway.

"Put a light on, Ken," he said as he bent down next to the body.

I fished along the side of the wall and came to a light switch. I flicked it on just as Diamond started laughing. I looked over his shoulder.

Trish Martin's "body" turned out to be a pair of slippers on the floor next to a half-cord of firewood.

"False alarm," Bobby said, smiling.

"I guess you know that Tricia left the hospital on her own this morning."

"That's why I came here to check on her," Bobby said. "I pulled up to the curb and saw someone sneakin' down the alleyway. I never figured it'd be you."

I tried to beat back the pangs of jealousy I was feeling. I didn't like the fact that Bobby seemed as concerned about Trish as I was.

"Look, Bobby, let's make sure she's not somewhere else in the house."

Together we went through the two-story house and convinced

ourselves that Trish wasn't there. If Bobby hadn't been with me, I probably would have looked in the desk drawers to see if there was any clue to where she might be. With him around, though, it would look like spying. When Tricia turned up, Bobby would score a lot of points telling her I had gone through her things.

There was one thing, though, that I couldn't pass up. A small black telephone book was on a shelf over the phone. I waited until Bobby turned his back and pocketed the book. If Tricia was okay, I'd give it back to her and take the flak. If she stayed missing, the information in the book could be valuable.

We left the house together, but not before Bobby called a friend who promised to put a new pane of glass in the kitchen window. We said we'd keep each other informed if we heard anything.

IT WAS close to eleven, and considering the kind of day it had been I should have been out on my feet. Instead, I was wide-awake with all kinds of thoughts jumping around in my head. As I drove homeward I played out one scenario after another, balancing reason and logic against the utterly confounding facts of Marcano's death. The big fear that kept resurfacing was that Trish had been lured out of the hospital on some pretext and then the same person or persons who'd gotten Marcano had also . . .

I took a deep breath and tried to concentrate on what was real. *There are three main points here, Eagle, so let's not read any more or less into them. The first is that Marcano was killed . . . the second is that the killer tried to frame me . . . and the third is that Tricia Martin picked herself up and left the hospital without telling anyone where she was going.*

I couldn't face going home. On a sudden impulse, I turned off the expressway at the next exit and drove to Long Island Jewish Hospital. There might be someone at the hospital that Trish had spoken to, a nurse or a doctor who knew what had happened to her.

I pulled into the hospital lot and parked my car. Through the glass-fronted doors of the hospital I could see a surly-looking security guard whose table and chair blocked off access to the elevator banks. There was no way he wouldn't stop me, so I walked around to the side of the building and made my way into the Emergency waiting room. Somehow I had to get to the fifth floor, where Trish's room had been.

The intake nurse stationed by the door was busy helping a nervous young woman fill out an insurance form. There were nine other people in the room, some of them obviously in pain. Two large swinging doors led into the actual emergency rooms and to the left of them was a corridor.

I went down the corridor past a men's room, and a couple of rooms with NO ADMITTANCE warnings on the doors. Then I saw a bank of three gray-doored service elevators. The only problem was another guard sitting in front of them reading the *Daily News*.

I watched as the elevator doors opened and two women stepped in. The guard kept his eye on the elevator until the doors closed and then he went back to reading his paper.

How could I get past him? As it turned out, I didn't have to. He suddenly got up and started walking in my direction. I quickly retraced my steps and headed back down the corridor. When the guard opened the door of the men's room and went in, I darted back to the elevators and pushed the button to open the doors. Inside, I pressed five, and breathed a sigh of relief as the doors closed.

Unlike the main elevators that stopped in front of the nurses' station, the service elevator opened near an empty lounge. The closest room was 527 and I recalled that Trish had been in 541. I doubted if there would still be anything in the room that could point the way to Trish. My best bet would be to find someone, a patient or a nurse, who might have seen something out of the ordinary.

"Can I help you?" A tall woman in a nurse's uniform came around the corner of the corridor and fixed me with a cold stare. The nameplate on her chest said MCARDLE.

"Hi, I wanted to talk to someone about my sister," I said, mustering up a semblance of self-assurance. "Her name is Tricia Martin."

"Visiting hours are from twelve to two, and from six to eight. You shouldn't be here," she said sternly.

"I was hoping I could see someone who might be able to tell me what became of her. It seems she checked out on her own and—Look, Miss McArdle, it's urgent. My sister might be in danger. I thought that if I spoke to her nurse or her doctor they could tell me if Trish said anything about where she was going."

A doctor had walked over to the nurses' station and was listening to my explanation. He was about forty, heavyset, with an old-fashioned handlebar mustache.

"Well, Mr. Martin, I wish I could help you, but I can't," said McArdle. "To talk to the nurses you'd need permission from the hospital administrator, and she's gone home. I really am sorry," she added, seeing the disappointment on my face.

"I'm on my way down," the doctor said. "I'll take Mr. Martin with me."

I was going to say something but the doctor put his finger to his lips behind McArdle's back. I read his nametag. It said: DR. ACKERMAN.

"Thank you, Doctor Ackerman. Good night, Mr. Martin."

Dispirited, I got into the elevator with Ackerman. He waited until the doors closed. "You should never argue with nurses," he said, smiling under his handlebar.

Ackerman stopped the elevator at the third floor. He stuck his head out the door and looked conspiratorially in both directions. "Come along with me," he said.

"This isn't the lobby," I told him.

"Of course not. You want me to help you, don't you? Then come on."

I followed him down the quiet hall to an empty waiting room. "This is the intensive-care area. There's twenty-four-hour visiting on this floor, so no one will bother you. Now, what do you need to know, Eagle?"

"You know me?"

"Sure. I spotted you immediately. You've won a few bucks for me down the highway of broken dreams. I spoke to Tricia, too, while she was here. I asked her for a hot tip. She told me to stick it in a toaster," Ackerman laughed.

I smiled, too. That sounded like the old Tricia.

"She's a friend of mine and I'm concerned. It's not like her to just go. She could be in trouble."

Ackerman nodded. "From what I heard, she just had breakfast and split. You stay here and I'll check it out for you. I'll take a look at the charts."

"Thanks."

Ackerman waved me off. "Don't mention it."

I spent the next fifteen minutes thumbing through a magazine and catching snippets of conversation of the two families that were assembled to support their stricken loved ones. One of the people in intensive care was a fifty-five-year-old father of four. The other family had an eighty-year-old grandmother dying of cancer. Ackerman couldn't get back soon enough as far as I was concerned.

At last I looked up and saw Ackerman motioning to me at the door.

"Okay, here's the scoop," he said. "I spoke to a friend of mine who worked a double shift yesterday. It seems that your friend never said a word to anyone about taking off."

"Did anyone see her go?"

"No. She had breakfast, and then she was gone. By noon, someone realized that she was gone for good."

I shook my head. "I'm back at a dead end again."

"Yeah, but there's a twist. This gal, Jean, the friend I mentioned before, was on call for Tricia during the night. She said she popped into Trish's room about one-thirty or two a.m. and Trish wasn't there. She didn't think too much about it, figuring Trish couldn't sleep and had gone to stretch her legs. Then another patient started having chest pains and Jean was called in to help. Much later she decided to go back and see how Tricia was. As she turned down the corridor she thought she saw Tricia dressed in street clothes running into her room. Not only that, but the elevator door was closing as if someone had just gotten off. Jean walked into the room and Trish was under the covers, but there were clothes on the floor as if she had just taken them off."

"Did she say anything to her?"

"No. This isn't a prison. Tricia obviously didn't want her to know she had left the floor so Jean saw no reason to pursue it."

"When did this happen?" I asked him.

"It had to be a little after four," he replied. "What do you make of it?"

I couldn't come up with any answers that made sense so I thanked Ackerman for his trouble and left the hospital the same way I had come in.

The drive home at night took half the time it would have during the day. By now I was very tired. I just wanted to sack out and take my chances with a new day.

The apartment was dark except for the blinking red light of the answering machine. I pressed play and heard the voice of Arlene Kirshbaum.

"Hi, Ken, it's Arlene. I've got some interesting stuff about Marcano. Give me a call if you get in before twelve. Otherwise call me first thing in the morning."

It was after twelve, and I was too bushed to talk to anyone. I didn't bother to get undressed. I put my head on the pillow and fell asleep.

5

I AUTOMATICALLY woke up at four-thirty the next morning, but forced myself to go back to sleep after setting the alarm for eight. After a force-of-habit breakfast of orange juice and dry toast, I telephoned Trish's house (no answer), then dialed Arlene Kirshbaum, who answered on the first ring.

I told her about my visit to Trish's and the events at the hospital.

"Interesting," was her reply. "Trish was out of the hospital at just about the same time you were called to Sheepshead Bay."

"I doubt there was a tie-in," I said.

"Probably not." She didn't sound too sure. "Anyway, I've got some interesting news about your friend Marcano. It seems the Big O was heavily in debt."

"How could that be? He was the most successful trainer on the grounds."

"He forgot a small matter of paying taxes for the years nineteen-eighty through eighty-five. Add the fact that the man believed in pampering himself at every turn, and throw in the name of a character known around the racetrack as Bath Beach Frankie, and you've got a big financial problem."

Bath Beach Frankie was a well-connected loan shark who catered to the racing trade.

"I know Frankie," I told Arlene. "I'll go have a talk with him. Maybe I can get a line on Orlando and find out who tried to frame me."

"Maybe you should just take it easy and let me dig," she suggested.

"No, Arlene, I'm driving myself crazy. I've got to do something to keep my mind off Tricia."

There was a pause on the other end as Arlene tried to muster an argument to talk me out of getting involved.

"All right, but be careful," she finally said. "And, Ken, it might be a good idea for us to compare notes. I have an office on Broadway near the State Building. Can you meet me at six?"

I told her I could and wrote down the address. Then I remembered the phone book I had taken from Trish's house and told Arlene about it.

"Bring it along," she said. "It might be helpful."

I hung up and looked for the small, black leatherbound book. It contained thirty numbers in all. One-third of them were New York businesses. There was a hairdresser, a bunch of fast-food takeout places, a neighborhood grocery, and a pharmacy. There were also seven numbers and names I recognized besides my own: Diamond, Marcano, Mike Westbrook, and four other people Trish knew from the track.

It was the last dozen or so numbers, however, that I found interesting. They all had a 404 area code, which I looked up and found was a rural Georgia exchange. These people had to be part of the past Trish had chosen to bury.

I felt torn. Should I respect Trish's privacy and forget I had those numbers? Another part of me argued that Trish might be in trouble and I had to do something to help her. Before I could change my mind, I took the phone and dialed the number of Oliver and Gloria Pusey.

It rang five times before someone answered. "Yeass?"

"Hello, I'm calling from New York. My name is Ken Eagle and I wonder if you could help me."

"Sure, if'n I can," she said in a smooth Georgia accent.

"I'm trying to locate Tricia Martin."

"Sorry, I don' know any Tricia Martin."

"Is this the Pusey residence?"

"Yeass, it is, but I don' know anybody named Tricia. If yo'll hold on, I'll ask my husband." There was a rustling on the line. "Ollie, honey, you know a gal named Tricia Martin? A fellow from New York is on the wire asking for her . . . No, Mr. Eagle, he don' know her either. Are you sure you've got the right Puseys? We got kinfolk in Atlanta named Jess and Steve."

"No, that's okay. It's my mistake."

I called the rest of the numbers. Half of them didn't answer or directed me to leave a message on the machine. The people I talked to had never heard of Tricia Martin.

I tucked the telephone book into my pocket. Maybe Arlene could figure out what was going on.

I KNEW where to find Bath Beach Frankie. Every morning at precisely nine a.m. his gray limousine pulled into the same space in the Aqueduct parking lot. It was here that Frankie and his lieutenant, a hulk of a man everyone called Homeboy Looie, held court. It was rumored that you could borrow anything you needed from Frankie, up to a cool million, as long as you could dig up the nominal fifty-points-a-week interest.

I parked my car next to the block-long Continental and waited for its chauffeur to walk over to me.

"Ken Eagle." He registered surprise at seeing me. "You here to see Bath Beach?" he asked.

"If he can spare a few minutes. I have to ask him something about Marcano."

I saw the chauffeur's eyes spark for a brief second. He was a compact five-feet-nine, no neck, with greasy black hair.

"I gotta check with Bath Beach. You wanna step out of the car?"

I got out.

"Sorry, Eagle, but we got a lot of very weird people around. Frankie's orders." He frisked me for weapons.

"Stay here a sec." He tapped on the rear window of the car and it rolled down an inch. The windows were darkly tinted and there was no way to see inside. The chauffeur nodded and called me over. He opened the door for me and I climbed in.

Although I had known Bath Beach Frankie through mutual acquaintances, this was the first time I had ever been to his "office." The spacious rear compartment was separated from the driver by bulletproof Plexiglass. Frankie had a bar, TV, stereo, telephone, and a fold-down marble table, which now held a silver coffeepot and fine china cups and saucers. There were two black leather bench seats. I sat down and sank into the plush foam rubber. Frankie and Homeboy sat across from me.

"Some coffee, Eagle?" Frankie offered.

He was a studious-looking man with thick glasses and an acne-scarred complexion. Homeboy was half his age, about twenty-five. He had a big head with uneven and missing teeth that made him look like a Halloween jack-o'-lantern. He was Frankie's muscle and he fit the part. Even sitting, he was imposing, with forearms and biceps that stretched the material of his black polo.

"Do you know Mr. Eagle, Looie?" Frankie asked.

"I seen him around," Homeboy grunted.

"I'll pass on the coffee, Frankie," I said.

"Okay. You don't mind if we have some, then."

He poured and handed a cup and saucer to Homeboy.

As he took it from Frankie, he spilled coffee on himself. "Damn! Why can't we drink from a container? I hate these cups!"

Frankie chuckled. "You can take the boy out of the Lower East Side, but you can't take the Lower East Side out of the boy, eh, Eagle?"

"Whatever you say, Frankie," I said, being amiable.

The loan shark leaned back and took a sip. "You told Joey that you had a question about Marcano. Didn't I hear somewhere that the cops got you on that little number?"

"They made a mistake."

"I'm glad to hear that. Orlando was a dear friend of mine."

"Then you're in very select company," I said.

Frankie started laughing. I must have caught him on a good day. "You're right," he smiled, "I hated the bum."

"I heard he owed you money."

Bath Beach nodded. "You heard right, Ken. Two hundred big ones. His death makes it hard to collect. How about you? What makes you interested in the late Orlando?"

"Somebody tried to stick me with the murder and that doesn't sit well. You know anybody who'd want to kill him?"

"There isn't a soul on the track who could stand the guy. What did your lady friend see in him?"

"Trish?"

"Yah, the Martin girl. They were a hot item for a while."

I sat up in my chair. "What are you talking about, Frankie?" I snapped. "You're full of it! Trish never dated Marcano."

Homeboy put his hand out menacingly. "Watch it, man!"

"Hey, Ken," Frankie shrugged. "What's it to me? I got no reason to lie to you."

It was possible, of course. I hadn't been involved with Trish when she first came to New York. As a newcomer on the scene she would have wanted to be introduced to the leading trainer, Orlando Marcano. But wouldn't Trish have mentioned something if she and Marcano had been seeing each other? I couldn't be sure. There seemed to be two Tricias. One was a frightened, unsure, young woman; the other was a cold, hard, calculating person with a mysterious past. Whatever the truth, I wasn't going to show how I felt to the loan shark and his goon.

"I know a lot of people didn't like Marcano and I was one of them. But who would go so far as murder?" I asked.

"I got no idea. I'm just a businessman trying to earn a living," Frankie said with a straight face.

"Why did Marcano need money from you? He was making it hand over fist."

"He had trouble with the feds. They were skimming his purses and watching him at the betting windows. He also needed a stake for some big deal that he had cooked up."

"Like what?"

"Sorry, that's privileged information. I got to respect my clients, even if they're dead."

"You're a prince, Frankie," I told him. "How come you don't seem upset that Marcano died and you can't collect?"

"I got back my principle; he was just paying off the weekly juice. So what do you say, Eagle. You want to do business?"

"No, I just needed some information."

"Always glad to help a fellow horseman. Now, if you'll excuse me, me and Homeboy have a few things to talk over."

I let myself out of the limo and into the blinding sunshine of the crisp fall day. My visit to Frankie's "office" had raised more questions than it had answered.

I spent the next hour walking along the backstretch and asking about Tricia. I didn't expect to make any progress, and I was right.

At one point Bobby Diamond approached me and the look on his face told me that he had been just as frustrated as me in trying to find Trish.

"You haven't heard anything, have you?" he asked me.

"No, I was hoping you had."

We both leaned against the track rail and watched a two-year-old filly breeze a quarter-of-a-mile in fast time. This was a good one, gliding effortlessly with a perfect gait. The horse pulled up and the owner and his wife came over to the animal. The exercise boy was talking to them with obvious excitement, probably telling them that the filly would win the Kentucky Derby. What would happen later when she would be asked to show her stuff on the track . . . well, that could be an entirely different matter. If you got by the bowed tendons, the split hoofs, the colic, the equine fevers, the bleeding, the rundown inflammations, the incompetent trainers and grooms, then she might have a chance to win a race or two.

The owner patted the young horse's head. Horses are the stuff dreams are made of. Hope always springs eternal on the backstretch. It was said that no one ever committed suicide at a racetrack because there was always a new crop of foals coming along that might change one's life.

I turned around and looked at Diamond. "Bobby, was Marcano going out with Trish?"

He didn't answer at first, and I thought he didn't hear me.

"I can't say for sure, Ken, but they seemed to be a lot closer than they let on," he said finally. "I remember she once called him and I answered the phone at the barn. You know what a loudmouth Marcano is . . . was. Well, when he got on the phone with Trish, he got very quiet, held his hand over the mouthpiece and whispered for at least a half-hour."

"That could have been business," I said.

"It could have," Bobby agreed.

It was obvious, though, that he didn't think so.

Bobby took off for the barn area and I traded pleasantries with some old friends. Then I headed for Security.

It had been Art Demaret who had been watching Marcano the closest over the past year. It stood to reason he might be able to shed some light on who would have wanted Marcano dead.

As I descended to the Security area, I heard the crowd roaring as the horses in the first race neared the finish line. It was a strange sound for me. When you were riding, you heard the sound of hooves and the yelling of the other riders as they urged their mounts on, or as they warned you to get out of their way. It was only after the race that you noticed the crowd.

Demaret's secretary told me that he was very busy, but when I gave my name she showed me in.

Art shuffled some papers and looked at his watch. "I can give you ten minutes, Eagle. What's on your mind?" He lit a cigar, leaned back and waited.

"They pulled me in for the Marcano murder," I told him.

"So I heard. A cop named Fusco called to ask about you. I said you're a hothead and a jerk, but not a murderer."

"Thanks . . . I think."

"Don't thank me. They had already released you. He was just fishing to see if I had anything on Marcano."

"Do you?"

Demaret took a pull on his cigar. "Eagle, I would have thought you'd learned something from the last time you mixed yourself in where you didn't belong."

"It seems to me that someone else mixed me in."

Demaret thought that over. "Why should I tell you anything? Maybe I'm happy to see this Marcano thing finally put to rest. The bastard made me look like the Keystone Kops."

"My guess is that you're still curious about how he got away with doping his horses."

"Maybe I've come around to the idea that Marcano was a master trainer and he didn't juice his horses after all."

"Sure, and now tell me about the tooth fairy. Look, Demaret, I'll make a deal with you. You answer my questions about Marcano, and I'll let you in on something that I found out. Who knows, maybe you can solve Marcano's murder. That might help to polish your image a bit."

He let that sink in. "I'm always willing to listen," he said.

"Did you know that Marcano was in debt up to his eyeballs?"

"Come on, Eagle. Everybody knew he had tax problems."

"I'm not talking about the IRS. I'm talking about Bath Beach Frankie."

"How deep was he?"

"Two hundred thousand."

Demaret gave a low whistle. "You've got my attention."

"He told Frankie that he needed the money for some kind of big deal. Frankie wouldn't tell me what it was."

Demaret nodded. "He was trying to become a partner in a breeding farm in Paris, Kentucky. The deal fell through when one of the partners, a count, or a duke, balked at a lowlife like Marcano getting in on the action. I wondered where he got the money."

"That doesn't make sense. He could have returned the money to Frankie and been off the hook," I said.

Demaret shook his head. "No, the deal dragged on for a couple of weeks. At fifty-percent-a-week interest, he couldn't get even. He couldn't go anywhere else for the money because of the federal lien on his income."

"Who'd want him dead?"

Demaret laughed to himself. "I could make a case for a lot of people. You've got all the trainers and owners. And there had been some pretty intense shouting matches between Bobby Diamond and Marcano. Orlando didn't approve of the way Bobby was riding some of his nags. In fact, the rumor was that Marcano was going to replace him."

That caught me totally by surprise. "I thought they were good friends," I said.

"Marcano had no friends," Demaret said flatly.

"Do you know anything about Tricia dating Marcano?"

Demaret nodded. "They had quite a romance going for a while. I think she fell head over heels for Orlando and he wasn't the type of guy to stay with one woman."

Head over heels! Demaret couldn't be right. It was one thing for Trish to date Marcano, but to be in love with him . . .

I tried to make my voice sound casual. "What do you know about her, Art? She's a mystery."

"I'm checking on her past. There were a couple of incidents at smaller tracks that got her suspended," he told me.

I remembered the story that Bobby had told me about how,

when an apprentice jockey had cut her off in a race, she'd gone after him with a butcher knife.

"But Marcano put her on his horses. How come, if he'd dumped her?"

"Why not? Business is still business. You know how driven that girl is. Hey, are you okay, Eagle?"

I mustered a half-smile. "I'm just trying to figure out where she might be. Nobody has seen her since she left the hospital."

"I haven't heard anything, but I'll let you know if I do."

"I'm not going to hold you up any longer," I said, rising. "Thank you for your help."

"Yeah, sure," Demaret replied.

As the day wore on, the weather turned dark and foreboding. Snow wasn't in the forecast, which was a dead giveaway that a blizzard might hit.

I watched a few races from a table in the restaurant area and went over the things I had learned about Trish and Marcano. Three cups of coffee later I was still loaded with questions and far from any answers.

THE MIDTOWN Tunnel took me into the city and it was just a couple of minutes before six when I pulled into a parking lot and crossed over to Arlene Kirshbaum's office building.

A secretary seated me in a waiting room and let me know that Ms. Kirshbaum was expecting me. The room didn't fit with what I knew of Arlene's personality. There were dark, heavy chairs backed in a satiny type of fabric. The chairs rested on a wine-colored carpet and the walls were mauve and garnished with ornate moldings. A large, gold-filigreed chandelier illuminated the room, and the window was framed by thick, gold drapes. It was the kind of look that would have impressed Gus.

Arlene herself was nothing like the room. I had found her very down-to-earth, with the ability to roll up her sleeves and mix it up when and if she had to.

"Would you follow me please, Mr. Eagle?"

The secretary led me down a corridor and into an office where

Arlene sat at a massive oak desk. We shook hands and I sat down. Her office decor was similar to the waiting room, apart from the ceiling-to-floor library of leatherbound law tomes.

"Do you read any of these?"

"Not only do I read them, I find them interesting. Think there's something wrong with me, Ken?" she asked, grinning.

I shrugged. "I don't know about that, but I will say that this place doesn't seem to be you. People usually stamp their personality on their offices. I wouldn't know this was yours."

"You're very perceptive," she said shaking her head. "I feel like I don't really belong here myself. This office was my father's. He was a very successful attorney who became a state supreme court judge. This was the office I remembered as a little girl. There's so much of Dad here that I find it difficult to change anything. Are your parents still alive, Ken?"

"No, they passed away a few years ago."

The intercom buzzed and Arlene's secretary's voice came over the speaker. "Mr. Mohammad Saif is here."

"Send him in, Carol," Arlene told her.

She saw my puzzled expression.

"Tricia would have had to use a taxi to leave the hospital. So I had my investigator check out the different car services listed by the pay phone at Long Island Jewish. We struck paydirt on Acorn Car Service. This driver, Saif, claims he remembers Tricia Martin."

The door opened and Carol brought in a slight, copper-skinned man in his late twenties. He seemed nervous.

"Have a seat, Mr. Saif," Kirshbaum said pleasantly. "This is Mr. Eagle."

He looked at me for a second and then turned to Arlene. "You pay me for the whole night, yes?"

"I instructed your boss, Mr. Cavanna, that we would pay you what you would earn for an evening of driving."

"I clear one hundred dollar for one evening," he said.

"Mr. Saif, during my career as an investigator, I've had the occasion to drive a cab. On your best night you might take home sixty bucks. However, we'll pay you one hundred if you tell us all you know about a fare you picked up a couple of nights ago."

"Good. I trust. Okay." Saif settled back in his chair. "That night I get call from Cavanna, the dispatch, to pick up woman at Long Island Jewish. The call come maybe one-thirty, two in the morning. I go there, I see little woman, pretty, with arm in cast. She have bruise on face."

"Where did you take her?"

"In Forest Hill area."

"That's where she lives," I said.

"She go in house for maybe ten, maybe fifteen minutes. She come out with a little case."

"A suitcase?"

"Yes. Little, like bag, maybe."

"Okay. Then what happened?"

"She say I take her to Brooklyn." He reached in his pocket and pulled out a piece of folded paper. "Here is address. Cavanna give me to show you."

Arlene looked at it and handed it to me. It was the two cross-streets that intersected near Marcano's house.

"She tell me to wait and then she come back maybe fifteen, maybe twenty minutes later."

"Are you sure about this?" I asked.

"I swear to God. I die now if I not tell truth."

Arlene reached into a drawer and pulled out a manila envelope. She took out five different head shots of young women and laid them out on her desk. "Are any of these the woman you picked up?"

Saif took a pair of glasses from his breast pocket and looked over the photographs. "No, she not here," he said decisively.

Arlene took out five more, different, photographs. I recognized Tricia, and so did Saif.

"Yes! Here she is. This is lady."

"Then where did you take her?" Arlene asked him.

"Back to hospital, and I go back to garage."

Arlene kept Saif for another ten minutes just to go over all the things he had said. After assuring the driver that her secretary would take care of his money, Arlene saw him to the door.

"I don't know what to make of all this," I told her as she slipped back behind her desk.

"Ken, is there anything, even the most obscure thing, that Tricia might have said to you when you spoke to her at the hospital after Marcano died?"

"You mean about where she was the night before? No, not a word. She seemed a little preoccupied but I put it down as shock over Marcano's death. The whole thing is so unlike Tricia."

"Maybe you never really knew her," Arlene said mildly.

I told her what Demaret and Bath Beach Frankie had said about Tricia dating Marcano. Arlene didn't say much. I watched her play with a lock of hair as she listened.

"She never let on to you anything about Marcano?" she asked when I had finished.

"No. I guess you're right, I never really knew her."

I handed Arlene the address book I had taken from Tricia's home and explained to her how I learned that none of the Georgians in it had ever heard of Tricia Martin.

"She's not from Georgia," Arlene said. "We did a check on her from the track records. She was born and raised in Oran Grove, Florida. I find it strange that there isn't anybody in this book from her old hometown."

"Arlene, do you have any idea what's going on?"

She thought about it for a few moments. "I'm not sure, Ken. I think I know what a good district attorney would argue. Are you certain you want to know?"

I nodded.

"Ken, Tricia doesn't have a spotless record. There were a couple of suspensions of her jockey license for fighting, and one for menacing with a deadly weapon. That weapon happened to be a knife. She had her driver's license suspended a few years back for driving while intoxicated."

"I've heard of worse records."

"I'm looking at Tricia the way Vince Fusco would. He'd say that

Marcano found someone else. This enraged Tricia. Then when one of his doped horses fell on her, taking her out of the race for the jockey title, she had to get even."

"I can't believe—"

"Let me finish. She might have been thinking about this for a long time. She had access to your shirt and watch when she was in your apartment, or she could have gotten at your locker."

"You mean, all along she was just setting me up?"

"Ken, these are possibilities. She takes a car from the hospital, goes home, picks up the knife and watch, and then goes to Marcano's house. She kills him and calls you. You said you couldn't tell if the voice was a man's or a woman's."

"But if Saif took Trish back to the hospital, how did my shirt with Marcano's blood wind up in my closet?"

"It needn't have been put there the night Marcano died. Trish had the next morning after she left the hospital to plant the shirt. You were at the track. Then she could have called the police and taken off to parts unknown."

"You won't get me to believe that," I said, shaking my head.

"Look, Ken, you're my client. As far as I'm concerned, the one given in this murder is that you didn't do it. After that, everyone is a suspect. It may not be the best scenario in the world, but it does explain how you could have been framed. I play the hand that's dealt me."

"What now?" I asked dejectedly.

"We try to locate Tricia Martin. I'm going to send one of my investigators to Oran Grove. There may be people there who could shed some light on where she might be."

"Don't send anyone. I'll go."

Kirshbaum shook her head. "I don't think that's a good idea. You don't have the training and your involvement with Tricia is going to cloud your judgment. It might be dangerous."

"I'm going," I said stubbornly.

"That's what I thought you'd say," Arlene sighed. "Take Tricia's picture and this background-check information. You're booked on a USAir flight tomorrow to Orlando. That will put you about an hour from Oran Grove. You better call in every day in case Fusco wants to talk to you."

"Will Fusco be a problem?"

"I'll just tell him you're gone to Disney World," she said, smiling.

6

ORAN Grove was about what you would expect of a town with a population of just a shade under five hundred.

I cruised down Main Street in the rented Plymouth Fury and took note of the town's businesses. There was a gas station, a diner, a pharmacy, two small grocery stores, a church, and the Oran Grove Elementary School. I followed the street down to a small lake, and eventually came to a fork, one way leading in the direction of Titusville. I had been told that Tricia Martin's childhood home was about a quarter of the way to Titusville. It was the weekend and I hoped to find her folks at home.

Fifteen minutes later I was standing in front of a rundown wooden frame house. The front yard was overgrown with weeds. A stone walkway that led to the front door was badly in need of repair. I noticed a pickup truck parked along the side of the house, and a swing made out of an inner tube. I tapped gently on the door a couple of times and heard a dog bark from within.

The woman who answered might have been pretty once but her lank, unkempt hair and her tired demeanor soured her appearance. She could have been thirty, but she looked ten to fifteen years older. At any rate, she wasn't old enough to be Tricia's mother.

"I'm looking for a Mister or Missus Martin."

"I'm Priscilla Martin."

I explained who I was and that I was interested in talking to her about Tricia.

She looked at me in an odd way. "Tricia, huh?" she said.

"You're too young to be her mother," I offered.

"Her mother was the first Mrs. Martin, Jessica. She moved out about ten years ago. I married Charlie after that. These here are our kids." She made a slight gesture indicating a brood of young children who lay on the floor behind her watching television.

"Tricia and I were friends in New York and I was hoping I might ask you a few questions about her."

She stared at me, searching my face. She seemed on the verge of saying something, but she held herself in check. "Charlie!" she called. "Come out here, would you?"

A dark-haired man emerged from a back room and came to the door, looking at me kindly enough. "What can I do for you, son?" he asked.

"I'm Ken Eagle, a friend of Tricia. She had an accident a few days ago and she was in the hospital. I don't want to alarm you, she wasn't badly hurt. The problem is that she left and didn't let anyone know where she was going. I was wondering if she's contacted you at all."

Charlie Martin froze. Then he turned to his wife. "I'm going out for a while with Mr. Eagle," he said, pushing past me toward the pickup truck. "Come on, Mr. Eagle, I'm going to take you to see Tricia."

I slipped onto the cracked leather seat next to him.

Martin stared straight ahead at the wheel. He backed the truck out of the yard and in a couple of minutes we were bouncing along a dusty backroad.

"Tricia's here?"

"Yeah."

Martin was in no mood for conversation. I found myself holding onto the dashboard as he made hairpin turns much too fast.

"Take it easy," I told him after one turn when two of the truck's wheels seemed to lift off the ground. He didn't answer.

We stopped in front of a stone arch with the words SACRED SOULS' CEMETERY carved in its face.

"What is this?" I asked him, annoyance creeping into my voice. "What's going on?"

"Come on," he said, getting out of the truck. I followed him for about fifty feet down one of the finely manicured paths.

"You wanted to see Tricia. Well, there she is." He was pointing to a gray marble tombstone.

I read the inscription: PATRICIA MARTIN—18 YEARS OLD—GOD BLESS HER SOUL.

"Now you tell me what the hell is going on," Martin demanded, sitting down on a neighboring tombstone. "If this is some kind of practical joke, you're going to be one sorry son of a bitch."

"If it is, it's against me . . . not you. I don't know what's going on. How long has your daughter been dead?"

"Nine years in April."

"Mr. Martin, there's a female jockey in New York named Tricia Martin. What I told you about the hospital was the truth. What I didn't tell you was that there is also a murder investigation going on and Trish may be involved. Look, I can show you a picture." I handed him the black-and-white glossy of Trish that Arlene had given me.

"She's not from around these parts," Martin said. "I've never seen her before."

"There isn't any other Martin family around here?"

"Nope."

The two of us turned to look at the solid slab of gray stone.

"How did Tricia die? If you don't mind my asking."

"Auto accident. A fellow driving drunk on the wrong side of the road. My daughter died instantly. I guess we can be thankful for that. The fellow who killed her got off with a couple of years. Then he was killed in a bar fight.

"You said something about a murder investigation."

We were pulling into the Martin's yard as I finished telling Charlie the full story.

He shook his head. "I don't get it. I just don't get it," he repeated.

"WHERE are you?" Arlene wanted to know. "The phone connection isn't too clear."

"In a Holiday Inn on the outskirts of Rome, Georgia. I want to check out the people in Tricia's phone book."

"What happened yesterday in Florida?"

"I found out that the person we've been calling Tricia Martin is an impostor. The real Tricia Martin died about nine years ago at the age of eighteen."

"You mean our Tricia took over this kid's identity?"

"It looks that way, Arlene. She's been Tricia Martin for a long time and I guess she applied for her jockey's licence as Tricia Martin."

"How are you getting along through all this, Ken?"

"I'm numb, but I'm still going to follow through."

Arlene took down the number of the Holiday Inn and warned me, once again, to be careful.

THE OLIVER Puseys of Rome, Georgia, lived in a housing development called Happy Haven. Happy Haven was composed of identical-looking brown-and-gray townhouses, seven blocks of them, built around a lake and a clubhouse.

I had called Mr. and Mrs. Pusey earlier in the day and told them I was the same Ken Eagle who had spoken to them from New York. I explained that I was in town investigating the disappearance of a young woman and asked if they could spare a few minutes of their time.

Gloria Pusey turned out to be an attractive redhead in her mid-thirties. She wore a simple yellow print housedress and she answered the door with a dustrag in her hand.

"Won't you come in, Mr. Eagle."

I followed her into a contemporary living room. The floor was highly polished wood with a couple of tasteful throw rugs. A brown sofa stood near an upright piano opposite the door.

"Can I get you a cup of coffee?"

"Well, if it's no trouble."

"None at all." She went on talking from the kitchen. "Oliver isn't here. He just went out to the hardware store. He's always got some job going."

When she came back with the coffee I told her the story which had by now become second nature to me. Trish Martin, a friend and fellow jockey, had suffered a concussion in a riding accident. She'd left the hospital without telling anyone where she was going and we were very concerned about her.

"Well, I sure would like to help, but . . ."

"I know, you don't know any Tricia Martin. Perhaps you'd be kind enough to take a look at this photograph."

I handed her the picture and watched her reaction. "Mister Eagle, there must be some mistake. This isn't any Tricia Martin. This is my sister—Courtney Reed!"

"Your sister? Are you sure?"

"Of course I'm sure. I should know my own sister!"

"What's this about Courtney?"

I hadn't heard the man walk in. Gloria's husband was a heavy-set man with a stubble of beard. He came over and extended his hand. "I'm Oliver Pusey. You must be Mr. Eagle."

"Make it Ken."

"I take it you know my sister-in-law, Courtney."

Before I could answer, Gloria cut in. "How serious was this head injury?"

"I think she's all right. We're just trying to locate her to be sure."

"How did it happen, Ken?" Oliver wanted to know.

"She was riding a race and fell off her horse."

"A race?"

Oliver and Gloria exchanged puzzled glances.

"He says Courtney's a jockey in New York, Oliver."

Oliver shook his head. "There's something wrong here. Courtney isn't a jockey, and she isn't in New York. We got a call from her about a month ago. She was leaving the States for Kenya. She's in the Peace Corps," Oliver explained.

"Kenya?" I heard myself say.

"That's in Africa," Gloria explained, trying to be helpful. "Courtney's been in the Peace Corps . . . got to be about five or six years now."

"She comes by to visit when she's between assignments," Oliver said. "They send her all over."

"Show him the postcards and letters, hon," Gloria told her husband. Oliver nodded and walked into the bedroom.

"I guess there's some kind of mix-up with those photos. Courtney's doing just fine now."

"Now?"

Gloria smiled. "Well, it ain't no secret that my sister was a hell raiser. My momma and daddy took her out of an orphanage when she was six and they just couldn't do much with her. She ran off a couple of times before her thirteenth birthday, and when she was eighteen she ran off for good with this young fellow that came through town."

Oliver sat down next to his wife. He placed a number of postcards and letters on his lap, looked them over quickly, and then handed them to me.

The postcards were from countries in Europe, as well as from New Zealand and Australia. I checked the postmarks, and they looked genuine, as did the handwriting—it seemed definitely to be Trish's. The letters were from major U.S. cities. I noticed that the stationery came from hotels that were situated near racetracks. There were paragraphs describing Peace Corps training, but a Peace Corps volunteer wouldn't jaunt around all over the place. She'd stay in the country she was assigned to.

I finished my coffee and thanked the Puseys for all their trouble. Not knowing what else to say, I agreed with them that there must have been some kind of mix-up and promised that I would get back to them when I finally had the facts.

There were several other names in the address book that Tri . . . Courtney had listed. But now I debated whether I would find out anything new if I got in touch with them.

When I arrived back at the hotel, the desk clerk called me over. "Mr. Eagle, you got a long-distance phone call from someone named Kirshbaum. She asked you to call her back."

I dialed New York.

"Hi, Ken. Have you got a name for our mystery lady?"

"I've got a name, Courtney Reed, R-e-e-d. The only trouble is her sister and brother-in-law have postcards and letters that she's sent them over the last six years describing her exploits as a volunteer in the Peace Corps."

"The Peace Corps? Are you kidding? They've got to be phony. If it's the same woman."

"I'm sure it is. The letters I can explain. Trish wrote them from hotels near racetracks—I've stayed in a couple of them myself. But how was she able to send the postcards?"

"That wouldn't be a problem. I know of places that will make up any kind of postmark you like, and add the foreign stamps. All you need is twenty bucks apiece. Courtney Reed, huh? I'll run a check on her. You did very well, Ken—maybe I should offer you a position with the firm."

"I'll hold you to that when I retire from the track. Now you tell me what's up. You could have waited for my news."

"Okay, the other shoe has dropped. You're off the hook for the time being. But Miss Courtney Reed, aka Tricia Martin, isn't so lucky. Fusco has a warrant out for her. They found the knife used on Marcano stuck in the mattress of her hospital bed."

GUS PICKED me up at the airport at noon the next day and drove me to my apartment. He told me the details of how the knife had been discovered by an orderly who was mopping the room and started to clean under the bed. When he looked underneath he saw the knife, which had been thrust into the underside of the mattress.

"I guess there's no doubt that it was the knife used in the Marcano murder," I said, thinking aloud.

"The police are convinced it is," Gus concurred, lighting one of his malodorous cigars.

My thoughts drifted to the good times I had spent with Tricia/Courtney. "You know, Gus, I just can't believe that I could be such a poor judge of character."

"From what you've just told me, Courtney Reed has made a practice out of fooling people."

"This could still be a frame-up, Gus. Someone did it to me, they could be doing it to Courtney, too."

519

Gus sighed. "Suit yourself, Ken. But let's say that your theory is correct. What do you do now? You can't find the woman, you've got no hard evidence . . ."

"I'm not sure, but there's a big piece of the puzzle that's still missing and I think it may be the key."

"Namely?"

"The person who helped Marcano dope his horses. We know that Orlando was being watched. Hell, he was under a microscope! So somebody else had to be juicing up his horses and it had to be someone he trusted."

"You think this person killed him?"

"I just think that whoever it was could give us a leg up on solving this thing and since Marcano had been doping his stock for a long time, it couldn't have been Courtney."

Gus thought it over. "You're not thinking it was Bobby Diamond, are you?"

"I'm not ruling him out. Demaret told me that he and Marcano were on the outs. Marcano was going to give his horses to Courtney to ride. And don't forget, Gus, Bobby had access to my locker. He could have taken my keys."

Gus shook his head. "I've known him for years. He's not the kind of person who would do anything like that. I'll tell you what I think, Ken. I think the girl made a fool out of you and you just don't want to accept that. You're even trying to bring Bobby into this. It just so happens that Diamond is a rival for the girl's affections. Wouldn't it tie everything into a nice neat bow for you if Bobby Diamond was Marcano's killer?"

"Gus, you know me better than that," I said weakly.

"I do know that it's time for you to get back to work. And your job is not running around the country searching for this girl—leave that to the professionals. You got a leak, you call a plumber. You got a toothache, you go to a dentist. You—"

"Damn it, Gus! That's it!" I said excitedly.

"What's it?"

"That's what we've been doing wrong. We've been talking to people like Art Demaret. Demaret's the wrong person. You said it—go to a professional. If you want to find out how a race is fixed, the person to see is a fixer."

"I'm afraid to ask what that's supposed to mean," Gus groaned.

"Mark Russell."

"Mark Russell! Now I know you're crazy, for God's sake! Kenny, when your parents took you to the zoo, did you beg them to lock you up in the tiger cage?"

"Gus, it makes sense," I reasoned. "If anyone would be able to figure out how Marcano did it, it would be Russell. Anyway it's worth a try. What do I have to lose?"

"Oh, nothing much. Just your life . . ."

MARK Russell, also known as Marco Roselli, or simply as "The Bank," was the man whose money financed all the big bookie operations on the East Coast. People like Bath Beach Frankie worked only with his permission and for a large franchise fee. I wasn't exactly happy at the thought of getting mixed up with a guy like Russell. Make one wrong move and you could end up wearing cement underwear.

Getting in touch wasn't all that easy either. You couldn't just look Russell up in the phone book. Everything had to go through channels. I relayed my interest to Bath Beach Frankie, who promised he would pass it along. He warned me that the request for an appointment made its way up the chain of command and anywhere along that chain, someone might turn thumbs-down and I would be out in the cold. Frankie advised me to stay by my phone.

At 5:45 the phone rang. The voice on the other end told me that Mr. Russell would see me at a place called Pasta Presto on Second Avenue. I was to be there at 6:15 sharp.

I grabbed a cab and made it with twelve seconds to spare.

Mark Russell was sitting by himself in a small booth. Even though I had met him before, I was still surprised by his youth. He didn't look older than thirty and yet he was one of those people who have presence. Although in no way physically imposing, Russell had a kind of assurance in the way he carried himself. He was about five-ten, with short, black curly hair. His chin and nose could have been carved in granite. Only his soft, brown eyes contrasted with the otherwise hard, masculine face. He was wearing tight-fitting jeans and a white cableknit sweater.

Russell handed me the menu. "You're still riding, aren't you, Ken?"

"I've taken a few days off. I should be back in the irons in a day or so."

If he had heard about my involvement in the Marcano murder, he wasn't letting on. He looked over the menu.

"The reason I ask is that everything on this menu might be too fattening for you. I got an idea. I'll have them bring you a bowl of spaghetti with a little bit of marinara. You'll enjoy it. Very little fat, and it's low in calories."

"That sounds great," I told him.

A waiter appeared out of nowhere and took our orders. Over his shoulder I could see the restaurant manager watching very carefully, hoping to please—or at the very least, not displease—Mr. Russell.

"So what's on your mind, Ken?"

I gave Russell a bare-bones breakdown of the Marcano case. He listened attentively, asking appropriate questions and nodding in all the right places.

"So, both you and now your lady friend have been implicated in this thing?"

I nodded.

"Now that I see the whole picture, tell me what you want."

"You have to be aware that Marcano's horses were being juiced," I said to him.

He shrugged. "I heard things. It never really affected my business. I mean, a lot of people were winning by backing Marcano's ponies, but the odds went down so low it didn't matter."

"So you never checked into it?"

"There were other things that took precedence, I guess."

"I was hoping you'd help me find out how he did it."

Russell smiled. "You're thinking of becoming a trainer?"

"No. The way I see it, if I can find out who was involved with Marcano, I may get to his real killer."

Russell thought it over. "Okay, and what do I get out of it?"

I took a couple of bites of spaghetti and tried to come up with some inducement to get Russell to help me. Nothing came to mind. "What can I offer you?" I said eventually.

Russell speared a piece of broccoli with his fork. "It can be open-ended. Let's just say that you owe me one," he said with a disarming smile.

I thought of Gus's image of stepping into the tiger cage. There would be a race that Mark would want to win and I could visualize him asking me to pull my horse, or take a fall off my mount, or God knows what . . .

"I'd feel more comfortable if things were spelled out," I told him.

"Ken, don't you trust me?" He looked annoyed.

"I'm learning from you, Mark. Business is business, and I want to be sure I can meet my obligations."

He smiled. "You don't trust me, but I like the diplomatic way you said it. Look, I have an idea. I've got a yearling in Florida. The horse's name is Ginny's Little Guy. Virginia is my girlfriend and she always wanted a horse, so I bought her one. I'm really a hopeless romantic. Well, what I want from you is a firm commitment that you'll ride him any time I ask you to."

"To win?"

"Of course to win! That four-legged Lamborghini already set me back a million six. I'd like to win some back. You think I'm going to ask you to stiff my girl's horse?"

I would have to okay the arrangement with Gus and Joe Herrera, but I knew that would be no problem.

"You've got a deal, Mr. Russell."

"Good!"

He extended his hand and we shook on it. "Now you finish your meal, and when you walk out of here there'll be a limo waiting. He'll take you to the wizard. I hope you find out what you want, but don't forget, even if you don't, we have a deal. Now I'm off

523

to Lincoln Center for a dose of culture. You take care of yourself," he said as he got up to go.

The limousine was there as Mark Russell had promised. The driver opened the door for me and told me that Mr. Russell had given him directions on his car phone about where to take me. He took a black hood out of his pocket.

"When we get a few miles from where we're going, I'll have to ask you to put this on," he explained.

I told him it would be okay. We headed out of the city and into New Jersey through the tunnel, and then south. We were traveling in the direction of Atlantic City. After about an hour, the driver pulled off at a roadside diner.

"Time to put on your outfit," he said, handing me the hood. "Do me a favor and don't take it off until I tell you to. Otherwise, you might really complicate things," he said ominously.

"The last thing I want to do is complicate things," I said. I placed the hood over my head.

We must have driven another fifteen or twenty minutes. Then the feel of the road changed from smooth highway to a more uneven surface, and finally to a long stretch of gravel. We stopped and I heard the door open beside me. I felt the chauffeur's hand slip under my shoulder and he helped me out of the car.

"When you hear the door close behind you, you can take it off. There'll be someone waiting for you."

I heard a door opening and immediately felt the change of temperature as I was gently pushed forward. I waited for the door to close and then took off the hood.

I wasn't prepared for what I saw. Standing directly in front of me was a black female midget. I took her to be about fifty, but her silver-gray hair and thick, black glasses might have been deceptive.

"What are you staring at? You've seen little people before. You're not so tall yourself," she said good-naturedly. "I'm the wizard Mark Russell told you about. You can call me Sarah. Follow me please and don't touch anything!"

The building was large and modern. We walked along a neon-lit hallway past a number of laboratories. They looked clean and new and the equipment seemed to be state-of-the-art. Someone had invested a lot of money in this place.

Sarah's office was a very simple room with a gray Formica desk and a couple of modern leather chairs. There were two paintings, one a seascape and the other a still life featuring a bowl of fruit. There were no windows anywhere.

"This belongs to Mark Russell?"

"A small nook in the vast Mark Russell empire," Sarah said.

"Yeah, his narcotics empire," I said, shaking my head.

She looked at me as if she was trying to understand what I meant. Then she threw her head back and laughed. "You think we make illegal drugs here like heroin and cocaine? Oh, that's funny." She laughed again. "Not that I would have a problem with making narcotics. I am a genius, you know, so the world's morals don't concern me. It's just that that kind of business isn't worth our time. Oh, my goodness, between securing raw materials, manufacturing, setting up a distribution network . . ."

"Then why all the secrecy? Why did I need to wear this?" I pulled the hood from my pocket.

"That was for my protection. I used to work for the government but we had a falling out. We'd rather not make it easy for them to find me," she explained.

"If this isn't a narcotics factory, then what is it?"

"We make products that no one will ever see. That's where the real money is."

"Weapons?"

"My goodness, Mr. Eagle, you have a very nefarious mind. No, not weapons, we make consumer goods that are so good they can't be distributed. I see you're all confused. You wear shoes, don't you, Mr. Eagle? Most of the people who live on this planet wear shoes. Now let's say for argument's sake that there was a polymer spray that you could apply to the soles of your shoes. This chemical would bind the atoms of the leather so that they would be impervious to wear. One pair of shoes would last a lifetime."

"Does something like that exist?"

"If it did, you wouldn't know about it. You see, the shoe business would be devastated if shoes didn't have built-in obsolescence. The same thing would hold true for the rubber industry: you could have tires that never wear out. Then there's razor blades that never get dull, batteries that last for decades instead of weeks . . . the technology is there. It would, of course, create economic chaos and no one wants that, least of all Mr. Russell. He doesn't have to worry about getting a product to market and distributing it and all the other headaches. The wizard just mixes her chemicals, comes up with the magic elixir, and we show it to representatives of the targeted industry. The formula is paid for, locked deep in the corporate vaults, and we move on to our next challenge."

"Is that what you're in it for? The challenge?"

"Well, you're right in assuming it's not the money. I could make all the money I ever wanted in an instant." She stared into my eyes. "Do you really want to know?"

"Yes."

"Well, there are certain works of art that appeal to me, and sometimes, unfortunately, they belong to someone else. Mr. Russell, through his contacts and power, is able to acquire what I need. Like me he has no moral restraints." She was smiling.

"Now let's get back to you. What brings you to the wizard?"

It was hard to think of this little woman as an art thief, but that wasn't important. I told her about Marcano—how he had turned the racing world inside out by claiming a poor-to-mediocre horse from another trainer and then making that same horse into a world beater.

"I could name at least fifteen or twenty different substances that could do that," she said evenly.

"What about escaping detection?" I told her of the elaborate post- and pre-test drug screening procedures.

"A good chemist can get around that. You'd have to change some molecules on a proportional basis and you might have to add a substance or two as a screen."

"There's one other thing. The horses are mild before the race and come out of the starting gate like tigers."

"Then the drug is administered within minutes of the start," she said matter-of-factly.

I shook my head. "The horses are watched. They make video-tapes of every step the horse takes outside the paddock."

"The drug I'm thinking of requires a hypodermic needle, say, about seven inches long."

"No. No way. There's no way they could stick a horse with something like that in full view of twenty thousand people and two dozen racing officials."

Sarah put her hands on her hips. "Well, then there's no drug that fulfills the criteria you've set up for me."

"Are you sure? What about something new?"

"Mr. Eagle, don't insult me! If I say there's nothing, there's nothing. Are you sure you've given me all the facts?"

"As much as I know."

"Let's see . . ." Sarah looked up at the ceiling and tapped her fingers on the edge of the desk. "We've got to worry about detection, the drug is fast-acting, and it's administered without a hypo . . . No, there's no single drug that can meet all those specifications."

I sighed deeply. "I guess that's it then."

Ignoring me, Sarah began pacing. "Synergism!" she said suddenly.

"Beg your pardon?"

"Synergism," she said again. She noticed my blank look and began to explain. "Synergism is when two discrete agencies in cooperate action produce a total effect greater than the sum of their effects taken independently."

"Which means . . . ?"

"Two and two equal eight."

I stared at her dumbly.

"Mr. Eagle, you take an antihistamine and it makes you drowsy, perhaps a level-two measure of drowsiness. A shot of whiskey would also give you level-two drowsiness. If, however, you take the two substances together, expecting to boost your tiredness to a four, you might be surprised to find that the level has been raised by the interaction of the two substances to a level eight or ten. That's a synergistic response. Now . . . let me see, let me see." She began pacing again. Finally, she nodded. "Yes! I see how it was done. Very elementary, and yet very clever. The drug they use is a man-made synthetic for heroin called fentanyl. We don't see much of it here in the East, but it's a favorite of the California crowd. Horses' systems react very differently to heroinlike compounds. People get tired and slow down, but horses think they're prancing young colts. That's what they slip the horse just before the race."

"That wouldn't require a large needle?"

"Ah, here's the good part. Sometime within three weeks before the race, the horse is injected with corrasalin. That's a long-acting drug that can stay in the horse's system for up to a month. Corrasalin is indistinguishable from the horse's own adrenalin and won't show up on any test. By itself, it won't do a thing, but combine it with fentanyl and you've got rocket fuel!"

"Wouldn't that show up?"

"Yes, but you'd have to test right after it was administered. After the race would be too late. You see, the fentanyl gets right into the bloodstream and stimulates the heart and lungs. Then during the race it's expelled through sweat and breathing vapor. There'd be nothing in the urine, saliva, or blood."

"But you said that the drug was given just before the race. How could they do that in full public view?"

"That's no problem. With corrasalin in the horse's system, a scratch of fentanyl would react synergistically. They could use a tack needle. I'll show you what they look like."

She pressed a button on the phone. "Lee, get hold of some fentanyl and prepare it for me in a tack needle, and give Jefferson two cc's of corrasalin."

Less than twenty seconds later there was a knock at the door. A young man walked in, half-bowed to Sarah, and handed her a cork. Then he walked out, bowing slightly again.

"Move your chair closer," she said to me. "We keep it in a cork to prevent sticking ourselves accidentally."

She pulled it away from the cork and reached into her desk drawer. She handed me a magnifying glass. "Look closely. You see what looks like a thumbtack. The top is flesh-colored, that's to match the color of your palm. The head is coated with adhesive so it can stick to your palm with the needle pointed out. With the glass you can see the pin part. That amber color is the fentanyl. Now, if you're a CIA agent, you go over to your victim with the tack needle in your palm and slap him on the back. A split second later he's out cold or dead, depending what drug is being administered. The needle part breaks right off in the victim's skin where it's designed to melt at a temperature of ninety-eight degrees."

"So all a jockey has to do is pat his horse with this thing?"

"That's all."

There wasn't a jockey in the world who didn't pat his mount gently to reassure it or to encourage it.

"Could a civilian get his hands on these needles?" I asked her.

"They don't sell them in department stores, but they can be purchased . . . in California. Now, I'll show you the effects. Follow me," she said leading the way into the hall. She held the fentanyl between her thumb and index finger.

We passed several more doors until we came to one with BIOLOGICAL SPECIMENS on it in neat black letters. Sarah opened it and we entered what looked like a large pet shop. There were at least fifty different-sized cages holding dogs, cats, snakes, guinea pigs, rats, and some exotic-looking creatures I couldn't place. The smell brought back my boyhood days on the farm.

We stopped in front of a large cage. A mid-sized German shepherd barked once, sheepishly, as if his heart wasn't really in it. He brought his head close to the bars to try to sniff us.

"No treats today, Jefferson."

The mention of the name drew my attention. "Are you thinking of injecting this dog?" I asked her.

"Of course. He's already had some corrasalin. We'll give Jefferson the fentanyl and then measure his motor responses on the treadmill."

"Is it really necessary?" The dog was licking my hand. I remembered the wild, panicked eyes and flaring nostrils of Marcano's doped horses. I didn't want to see that transformation in Jefferson. "Can it be dangerous?"

"There's always some danger in the unknown, but until we carry out the experiment, all we have is a theory."

"I'll take your word for it," I told her.

Jefferson seemed to appreciate my concern. I got two fingers through the bars and patted the top of the dog's head.

"As you wish," Sarah said, her tone implying she thought I was being very silly. I watched her place the cork she had taken from her pocket on the business end of the tack needle.

"Can I take that with me?" I asked. "It may turn out to be important evidence."

She thought about it. "I have no objections, but you would be well advised to forget where you got it."

I nodded my thanks and ever so gingerly took the needle from her.

"You don't have to treat it so daintily. As long as the cork is on the needle, you can keep it right in your pocket. In animals it sends them up, but if you were to get stuck, you'd react the way humans do to heroin."

"You mean nod out?"

"Well, it would certainly be more than a 'nod,' but it wouldn't be lethal."

I still treated the fentanyl with respect. "I appreciate your help," I told Sarah. "Quite frankly, I never expected that you would be able to tell me so quickly what I wanted to know. I'm tremendously impressed."

"Well, we all do what we can. You ride horses, and I solve the riddles of the universe." She smiled. "It was very nice meeting you. And now, if you'll get your hood ready, I'll take you back to the outer door."

7

CHESTER, my doorman, was impressed to see me stepping out of the limo. I had to explain to him that I hadn't hit the lottery. He told me that the building management company had been around to change the cylinders of my lock and he handed me two shiny new keys for my door.

I made my way upstairs and let myself in to my apartment. Gus had left a message on my machine, and from the sound of his voice, it seemed to be important.

"Ken, Arlene Kirshbaum was trying to get you but she didn't want to leave a message. She called me and I told her I'd get in touch with you. I'm afraid there's some bad news about Courtney Reed. Don't get nervous, she's all right. I mean, I guess she's all right, no one has seen her since she took off. The bad news is about her past. It seems that when Arlene ran it down, she found out that Courtney and an accomplice were wanted for an armed robbery that resulted in a murder about ten years ago. Look, Ken, I'm awful sorry . . ." There was a brief pause. "I'll be home late tonight if you want to talk."

I stared at the machine for a good two minutes and tried to sort out my feelings. Tricia Martin, or Courtney Reed, or whatever her name was, had taken me for a ride. Was the woman I had fallen in love with an armed robber and involved in a murder?

I could see clearly now what Arlene had meant about not getting too close to the case. I saw that what I had been really trying to do the last few days was to find another suspect besides Courtney, instead of trying to find the truth. I had been ready to pin the whole thing on Bobby Diamond.

"You should have your head examined, Eagle," I said out loud in disgust.

I got up and walked to the kitchen. Angrily, I picked an apple out of the refrigerator and devoured it along with a handful of vitamin pills. How long had she been planning this? The whole time Tricia was with me, was she thinking of ways to frame me for Marcano's murder? What a lovesick puppy I'd turned out to be.

I trekked back to the living room and switched on the TV. For five minutes I watched a new show but couldn't get into it. I turned the TV off and paced around the house for a while.

I wanted to confront Courtney. I wanted to tell her what I thought of her. I wanted to ask her how she could repay my feelings with such cold-hearted deceit.

I took out her address book and looked it over again. There had to be someone here who knew where she was hiding. The people in the book were all links to her past. I noticed that on the inside cover of the black leather book, Courtney had written: J. Phillip, Sullivan County, R.E. Brokers. It started me thinking.

I grabbed the phone and got the area code for Sullivan County, then called information. I asked about a listing for J. Phillip.

The operator informed me that it was an unlisted number, so I asked about a business called Sullivan County Real Estate Brokers.

"That's on Field Street. Please hold for the number."

I copied it down and tried it. I knew it was way past business hours but sometimes you could catch someone working late in a real-estate office. I let it ring ten times, then gave up.

Certain things were coming back to me. We had once discussed the relative merits of living in a warm climate or a cold one. Courtney liked the cold. She had told me that if she ever had any time to herself, she was going to rent a cabin "up north."

"Nothing beats sitting by a roaring fire while a snowstorm howls around outside," she had said.

If you liked the cold and were looking to get lost, Sullivan County in the Catskill Mountains was as good a place as any.

THE MORNING found me in no less black a mood, but at least I had some hope of finding Courtney.

I waited until nine o'clock to call the Sullivan County Real Estate people but no one was in the office yet. It was hard to think of people not starting work until after nine. On the race-

533

track, half your day was over by nine a.m. I was about to try the number again when the phone rang. It was Arlene Kirshbaum.

"I guess Gus got the message to you?" she asked.

"Yes. I feel like I've been taken."

"Well, if it makes you feel any better, it's obvious you weren't the only one."

I told Arlene about the real-estate lead I had developed.

"You think she rented a place up there?"

"That's my hope," I told her.

"What's the name of the real-estate outfit?"

"I'm going to keep that to myself. I need to follow this up."

Arlene didn't sound happy about it. "Ken, you're paying good money for my advice and you'd do well to take it. Courtney Reed's wanted for armed robbery and she's implicated in two murders. That's a pretty somber chain of events, especially for a young woman who hasn't seen her thirtieth birthday yet."

"You're telling me it could be dangerous?"

"I'm telling you that you might be killed!"

Arlene's words had a chilling effect on me. I'd never considered that I could be in danger: the thought of Courtney actually causing me physical harm was just too farfetched. But then again, perhaps Marcano had felt the same way.

"You might be right, Arlene. Look, I don't even know if this lead is going to pan out, but . . . I'll be careful."

"You better be *very* careful. Gus is very fond of you, and I'm very fond of Gus. You wouldn't want to do anything to nip a romance in the bud, would you?"

I smiled. No wonder my agent had been so closemouthed about the latest development in his love life. Arlene Kirshbaum certainly broke the mold of Gus's Blonde-of-the-Week Club. I heartily approved.

"Well, if you put it that way, I'll take every precaution."

"I'd rather you took a gun. Do you have one?"

"No."

"Okay, at least let me have someone tail you until—"

"No tail, Arlene. I mean it!"

"Don't bite my head off. I've got to leave the office now. Whatever goes down, I want a phone call from you."

"Yes, Mommy," I kidded.

"Ken, nobody likes a wiseass," she said, but jokingly.

I TRIED the real-estate office again, and this time they answered.

"Sullivan County Real Estate, how can I help you?"

I had spent a restless night practicing my story. "I'd like to talk to Mr. Phillip," I said.

"We don't have a Mr. Phillip," the girl said.

"No J. Phillip?"

"Well, we do have a Jean Phillips," she told me.

You had to admire the mental agility of the receptionist to make that farflung connection.

"Yes, that's who I mean. Jean Phillips. Is she in?"

"Who may I say is calling?"

"She doesn't know me. My name is Mike Joseph and I'm with the bank."

A moment later a woman got on the phone. She sounded older, very professional. "Jean Phillips here. How may I help you, Mr. Joseph?"

"Please call me Mike. We've had a young woman come in to apply for a loan—"

"Excuse me. What bank did you say you were with?"

How stupid of me not to anticipate that. Jean would know every bank in the area.

I took a shot. "Fidelity."

"Fidelity?" She sounded puzzled.

I'd blown it.

"Oh, you mean Statewide Fidelity. We just call it Statewide."

I was back in business.

"You say someone came in for a loan?"

"Yes, the young woman mentioned that she had just done some business with you folks. We just need to verify her address. Let me see, I *know* I had that application. I was away for a week and when I came back my desk was a mess."

535

Jean laughed. "Believe me, I can relate to that. Do you remember her name?"

"Y'know, I had it here right in front of me. She was a pretty young girl in her late twenties . . . brown hair. She had a cast on her right arm."

"Oh, you mean Karen North, the girl who was in that skiing accident," Jean said. "She rented the Eaton house. That's over on Califon and Joy Road over in Monroe."

"Karen North, right!" I wrote down the address. "That's the information she gave us. Thanks for your help," I told her.

"That's okay. If you need anything else, just call or drop us a note. And say hello to Dotty, the teller, for me."

"I sure will," I said. I thanked her and hung up.

I WONDERED how Courtney was able to rent a place so easily without identification. The one thing I'd have to come to grips with was that she was an accomplished liar. Maybe she'd shown up with a bagful of cash and that had been enough to answer any questions or doubts anyone may have had.

I had a map of New York State in my car's glove compartment and I pulled it out and looked it over. Monroe was a scoot up the thruway. Without traffic, it would take about two hours. I drove over to the East River Drive and followed the signs north.

IT WAS a cold gray day with the colors of the clouds matching the shades of the slabs of rock that bordered either side of the road. What was I going to do when I finally saw Tricia/Courtney/Karen? I felt like throttling her, but I knew I wouldn't. I suppose I needed to see her to vent my anger.

Okay, Eagle . . . then what? Are you going to call Fusco and have him *haul her off to jail?*

Maybe there was some explanation for her actions . . . *Cut it out, Eagle! This is the girl who set you up.*

About a mile from Monroe I stopped to ask for directions. Joy Road was a two-laned highway that I took for four miles. Califon was an unpaved road that had been cut through a forest. It seemed dark and mysterious, even more so now because of the threatening sky.

About twenty feet from the intersection was a red aluminum mailbox with the name EATON. I pulled off on the side of the track and got out of the car.

There was a footpath behind the mailbox and I followed it about forty feet to a clearing. I could see a small, wooden cabin with bright, yellow-painted windows and a cedar door. There was no smoke rising from the chimney and no sign of a car. From all appearances, the place was deserted.

I waited quietly for a few minutes wondering how I could best approach the cabin without being seen. If Courtney had driven off somewhere, she'd see my car when she returned. Maybe the best thing for me to do would be to hide it farther down the road.

It turned out that I didn't have to make that decision. When I turned around, I was staring down the barrel of a Browning automatic.

"How did you find me, Ken?" Courtney Reed asked.

She was wearing jeans and a brown suede jacket. Her right hand was in a cast from her wrist to her elbow. Her left balanced the gun that was pointed at my chest. She had never looked so beautiful . . . or more deadly.

"You left the name of your real-estate company in your address book. I followed it up."

She nodded. "Pretty stupid of me. Who else knows?"

"Why, are you going to kill us all?"

"*I'm* not killing anyone," she said. "I was taking a walk when I saw your car coming up the hill. I waited for you to get out and I followed you."

"Are you going to keep that gun pointed at me?" I asked.

"That depends. What did you think you were doing?"

"I was going to talk to you. I was going to let you know what a bitch I think you are," I said bitterly.

"*I'm* a bitch?" She dropped the gun to her side. "Why couldn't you just leave things alone? We could have had so much but you had to . . ."

"I had to what?"

"Come on. You know as well as I do."

"What? Spell it out for me."

"Marcano, damn you! Why did you kill him? Did you think you were doing it for me?" she asked sadly.

"I didn't kill Marcano."

She bristled. "You expect me to believe that?"

I didn't understand what she was up to. She was turning things around. But why? And she really seemed to mean it.

"What makes you think I killed Orlando?"

Her eyes opened wide. "Are you crazy? You told me you were going to kill him. I tried to stop you!"

"When was this?"

"What do you mean, *when?* You phoned me the night Marcano was killed. Stop trying to confuse me."

She pointed the gun again. "I want you to get out of here!"

"If you thought I killed Orlando, why didn't you tell the cops? Why did you run out?"

"I was trying to protect you, that's why!"

"And how about protecting Courtney Reed?"

Her head jerked as if she'd been hit.

"Oh, God," she sighed.

Her eyes closed and her knees seemed to buckle. I reached out to steady her. She didn't fight when I took the gun from her hand. I broke it open. It wasn't loaded.

"Let's go inside," I told her. "I think I could use a cup of strong coffee."

THE EATON house was furnished in early Americana with straight-backed rockers, heavy oak tables and Civil War maps on the walls. We walked through a sitting room into a bright kitchen with flowered wallpaper and gingham curtains. I sat at the table while Courtney put the coffee on.

"How much do you know about Courtney Reed?" she asked me.

"Armed robbery, accessory to murder . . ."

Her whole body seemed to sag.

"Do you also know that it all happened when I was sixteen years old?" Her voice sounded tired and bitter.

"I don't know all the details."

"I was sixteen and living with people in Georgia who'd taken me out of an orphanage. They raised me not because they wanted a daughter but because they wanted cheap labor on their farm. I wasn't their child, I was their slave. When I was fifteen, I ran away for six days. The Georgia Highway Patrol picked me up and brought me back. Alice, that's my adopted mother, whipped me so bad with a razor strop that I couldn't stand up for four days. My adopted father said, 'Why'd you whip her so damn hard for? Now I got to git up early and do the damn milkin'.'"

"What about Gloria?"

"You know my sister?"

"I spoke to her."

"Gloria was all right, but what could she do? They were working her skinny butt off, too. But at least they weren't always mean to her. I never heard a kind word from those people.

"On the way home from school one day, a man offered me a ride. I'd been told not to accept rides from strangers, so naturally I did it just for spite. Every day this fellow, John, would come along in his shiny new car and drive me back to my prison. He told me he was a salesman and that he was heading for Florida in another week. He said I could go with him and if he had a good trip selling his hardware, maybe we could get married."

"You believed that?"

"I was only sixteen! I would have run off with the devil if he'd promised I wouldn't have to go back to that farm."

"What happened?"

"It turned out John—his name was John Jordan—was no salesman. He was an escaped convict. We'd drive to a Seven-Eleven and John'd walk out all smiles with a wad of bills in his pocket. He told me he'd made a big sale. What he'd really done was rob the place. I had no idea John was on a three-state crime spree."

"When did you find that out?"

"The day some store owner came running out shooting at us with a shotgun. John tried to bluff me with a story but then he finally told me the truth. He told me I was wanted by the cops as much as he was. That night we checked into a motel and while he was in the bathroom, I thumbed my way out of there."

"You could have gone to the police and explained."

"Who was going to believe me? Even if they had, I'd just have been sent back to the farm. Then I read in the paper that one of the people John had held up had been shot and killed, so I knew I couldn't go to the police. I bought a bus ticket and wound up in New Mexico. I always loved to ride, so I started mucking stalls on the track. I went from that to exercise girl and then I became a jockey."

"As Tricia Martin?"

"She was some girl I read about in a newspaper who'd gotten killed in an auto accident. She was about my age and I remember thinking I wished it had been me instead of her."

"You didn't have a problem getting a license or proving who you were?" I asked skeptically.

"I did whatever I had to do," she shrugged.

She poured us both cups of coffee and sat down at the table across from me. She seemed drained. "There were times when I thought I'd go back and straighten everything out, but I knew it'd be the end of my riding career. That was something I couldn't give up. Then I met you, and I thought maybe things were finally breaking my way . . . but you turned out to be another Johnny Jordan."

"I didn't kill Marcano," I insisted. "All I know is that someone tried very hard to set me up."

"What about your call to me at the hospital?" she snapped. "You told me you were going to kill Marcano!"

"That call wasn't from me! It was part of the frame!"

"It was you! I tried calling you back but you had already left. I got out of my hospital bed to try and stop you."

"That's why you went to Marcano's house?"

"Yes!"

"Then why did you go home first? The car service driver said he took you to your house where you picked up a bag."

"I went to get my car," she explained. "I didn't want the driver to see me try and stop you. I thought I could manage the stick shift, but I couldn't. I was forced to keep the rented car but I made him park away from Marcano's house."

"And what was in the bag?"

"A pair of jeans, the sweater I'm wearing now, and my makeup case. What did you think I took?"

"I don't know. My watch and shirt, I guess."

Everything she said made sense, but . . .

"Why didn't you tell me you had been dating Marcano?" I asked defensively.

"I *had* to date Marcano. I was ashamed to tell you, okay?"

"Had to? Why? So you could have a chance to ride his stock?" I said bitterly.

"No, I did it for Demaret. He'd found out, somehow, about John Jordan and me. He threatened to expose me if I didn't help him discover how Marcano was doctoring his horses. He wanted me to get close to him and get the information and report back. I went out with Marcano less than a month and I couldn't find out anything."

"Demaret let you just walk away?"

"Yes. He turned out to be very nice. He told me he'd find some other way to catch Orlando. He was the one who warned me that the police were going to question me and that they might find out about my past."

"That's why you ran out of the hospital?"

"That and the fact that Art had told me the police had picked you up for the murder. I was afraid they'd ask me about your phone call threatening to kill Orlando."

"Listen, Trish—Courtney. You're going to have to believe me. The only time I called you was the next morning. I was awakened myself by a caller who said he or she could expose Marcano. That's how they drew me out of the house. Are you sure it was my voice?"

She nodded. "Definitely. It really bothered me the next morning when you called as if nothing had happened." She paused. "There was something, though. You sounded kind of funny, like you were drugged."

Now, thinking back on it, I remembered how odd she had sounded when I called her that morning. As if she was waiting for me to say something.

In spite of my inner warnings, I was buying her story.

"Let me understand this. You thought you heard my voice and I told you that I was going to kill Orlando."

"I could never forget it. You—or someone who sounded exactly like you—said, 'I'm going to kill Marcano' and then hung up. I guess I just panicked. I called a car service, stopped off at my house for my car, and then I went to Marcano's."

"What happened when you got there?"

"Nothing. Absolutely nothing. The house was dark and I didn't see your car. When I rang the doorbell there was no answer. I tried looking through the window on the porch and as far as I could see, everything looked completely normal. I figured that whatever you were going to do, it wasn't going to happen that night."

"And then what?"

"I had the driver take me back to the hospital. The next morning Bobby called to give me the news about Orlando. Later he came by the hospital for a couple of minutes to look in on me. After that, you called."

"When did you see Demaret?"

"He came in a few minutes after your call. He told me that he had spoken to a detective and that they were going to pick you up for questioning. He asked if I knew anything at all about what might have happened to Marcano. He said he'd do whatever he could to help me, but that with my background, I'd better not lie."

Outside, the snow that had been threatening all day fell from the sky in large powdery flakes.

I wanted to believe her. Her recounting of the events was possible, even plausible. Yet there was still that nagging doubt. Who else could have set me up?

"I haven't asked you this before, and maybe you might feel it's none of my business . . ."

"You can ask me anything you want," she said.

"Just what kind of relationship did you have with Bobby Diamond?"

She gave me a half-smile. "Bobby is just a good friend—no more."

Her answer pleased me, but I tried not to show it. "How did he get along with Marcano?" I asked.

"Why?" Her eyes narrowed. "You don't think Bobby had anything to do with—"

"I told you before, I don't know. I heard that Marcano was thinking of taking him off his stock permanently."

Courtney played with a lock of her hair, weighing her words carefully. "I'm no snitch, Ken. But—Bobby was always talking about Orlando. He said that no matter what he did, Orlando would find fault with him. Orlando expected every horse he saddled to be a winner. If they didn't win, he blamed Bobby. Everybody at the stable knew they were having problems."

"Did Bobby ever threaten to do anything about it?"

"Ken, you know Bobby couldn't hurt a fly. He said things the way we all do, but I never took him seriously for a moment."

I nodded. The Bob Diamond I knew was a hard-working jockey who for the first time in his life was getting a taste of the spotlight. The fact that Marcano might have wanted to replace him didn't seem a strong enough motive for murder.

In just the few minutes we had been talking, the snow had covered the ground. I walked toward the door.

"I think I'd better get back, otherwise I could get stuck. Do you have a phone number here?"

She reached for a piece of note paper with the phone number of the Eaton residence. I looked at the number she had given me before pocketing it.

"You're not going to run off again?"

She smiled sadly. "No. No more running. I'm tired of living in fear." She touched my sleeve. "Ken, I'm sorry I didn't have faith in you. I should have known you couldn't do anything so horrible. Do you forgive me?"

"There's nothing to forgive. That phony call would have been hard to ignore. And let's face it, I wasn't thinking such nice thoughts about you either."

"Maybe we can gain each other's confidence back now. I want your trust more than anything in the world, Ken. You've been the best thing in my life," she said, her eyes moistening. "Please believe me. I had nothing to do with Orlando's death."

"I do believe you," I said. But even as I said it, something was trying to break through my consciousness. It was the same feeling you got trying to remember a name and just as you almost had it, it would slip away.

8

THE STORM, which had already dropped about three inches of snow on the ground, was tapering off to intermittent flurries. Crossing into the city over the George Washington Bridge, I started a bout of yawning that didn't end until I hit the Harlem River Drive. It dawned on me that if I didn't get a dose of caffeine in my system I was going to conk out at the wheel.

I pulled into a diner and fortified myself with two cups of coffee. Then I used the outside pay phone to call my answering machine. I thought there might be a message from Arlene.

Instead the first voice I heard was an angry Gus. I was never around when he called he said. He was having lunch with Arlene and if I could join them, they'd be at P.J. Clark's on Fifty-fifth around two-thirty. I checked my watch. If I didn't hit heavy traffic, I could just make it.

Gus was pacing in front of P.J.'s entrance when I arrived, looking for all the world like an expectant father. His face broke into a broad smile when he saw me.

"You're impossible to reach, do you know that?"

"You're not exactly a shut-in yourself," I told him. "Where's Arlene?"

"She's inside. I just came out for a second to see if I could spot you. I wanted to say . . . I'm sorry about Courtney Reed. I would have rather told you about that in person."

"Don't worry about it. I just came from talking to her."

"You what?"

"Come on, let's find Arlene and I'll fill you both in."

Arlene was sitting in a booth sipping a martini. She slid over on the long bench to make room for Gus, and I sat opposite the lovebirds. It was surprising to see how much younger and lovelier Arlene looked. The relationship with Gus was obviously agreeing with her.

"How did your hunch pan out?" she asked me.

"I just this minute got back from talking to Courtney."

Gus gave Arlene a puzzled look. "Wait a second!" he said to her. "You knew about this, too. What's going on?"

"Lawyer-client privilege, dear. Ken and I both decided we didn't want you to worry. What happened?"

I shrugged my shoulders. "I'm sorry, guys. I believe her."

Gus exploded. "You are the most naive—"

"I know," I interrupted. "The fact is that she explained everything and I'm really convinced she's innocent."

We ordered, and between forkfuls of salad, I spent most of the next half-hour filling them in on what had happened.

Arlene and Gus listened quietly. At first, Gus's disgusted expression showed that he mistrusted Courtney but when I'd finished, he seemed to be coming around.

Arlene looked thoughtful. "For whatever it's worth, her story about John Jordan seems to be in line with the information I'm receiving from Georgia. He was a very smooth character, I'm told. He had a history of picking up young girls and getting them involved in his holdups."

"How much trouble is Courtney in as a result of that?" I asked.

"It's hard to say right now. We're talking about a case that's

545

been buried for ten years. If the story she told you checks out all the way, I think she might get off with a few years' probation. I'm going to stress the *if* part."

"Hey, hold on for a second," Gus chimed in. "What about the knife from under her hospital bed?"

"That could have been planted by someone who came to visit her. All they had to do was wait for the right moment, reach underneath, and stick the knife in the mattress."

"Yeah, but Ken, a lot of people visited her . . . including me and you," Gus said.

I looked at both of them. "I think we can narrow it down. I have two suspects in mind. The first one is Bobby Diamond. He and Marcano had bad blood between them. From what I hear, Marcano was going to put another jockey on his horses, probably Courtney."

"I can't believe that of Bobby," Gus said, shaking his head.

"Quite frankly, Gus, neither can I. But he had a motive and he could have worked the frame as easily as Courtney."

"I see you've already dismissed the lady as a suspect," Gus sighed.

"Who qualifies as your second suspect?" Arlene asked me.

"Art Demaret."

"Demaret? From track security? What do you base that on?"

"He had some strong motives." I counted them off on my fingers. "He was worried about losing his job, and Marcano was making a complete fool out of him. With Marcano dead, he might feel all his problems would be solved. And he was one of the last people to visit Courtney before the knife was discovered."

"Sure, but there's no way to determine how long it had been planted there," Gus said.

"Gus, I know that. I'm just trying to think of people who might have hid the knife under the bed."

"Well, then to be completely fair, Ken, we shouldn't leave out Courtney. She *is* the most obvious. If she did kill Marcano, she could have put the knife in her bag and then . . ."

"She could have, Gus, but she didn't."

My next stop was Art Demaret's office at the racetrack. It was almost post time for the Eighth Race feature and Nancy, Demaret's secretary, told me the boss was watching the race from the third floor in the clubhouse.

I thanked her and rode the elevator to the owners' boxes. Demaret was sitting up close to the rail, four tickets firmly clutched in his right hand.

The horses were coming around the turn and down the homestretch. I spotted the silks of the stable Joe Herrera trained for. Tony Violet was in there pinch-hitting for me and he had the lead. With forty yards to go, one horse closed a lot of ground on the outside. Violet and the other jock, J. J. Alvarado, were in a furious whipping, driving finish. The winner would have to be ascertained by a photograph.

One of the owners with whom I had a nodding acquaintance called out to me. "How did you see it, Eagle?"

"I'd have to say it was the 'eight.'" I identified the horse farthest from the rail.

Demaret looked back from the first row. "I hope you're wrong, Eagle. I think Violet got him home on the inside."

We all stared at the toteboard. Upstairs, the stewards were reviewing the photo. The placing judge would be calling down the results to the computer technician who controlled the infield tote.

The sign lit up OFFICIAL. The final order of finish was 8—5—7—1.

Demaret ripped up his tickets and tossed them over his shoulder. "If you'd been riding, Eagle, you would have nailed it on the wire," he said.

It wasn't true, but I accepted Demaret's compliment with a smile. "May I have a brief word with you, Art?" I asked him.

"Sure. How about a cup of coffee in the cafeteria—that is, if I can still afford it after that race."

It was late in the afternoon now and the crowds in the cafeteria had thinned. There were a few souls left, staring into their coffee, making up lies to tell the wife, or trying to figure out a

547

way to get train fare home. The floors were littered with worthless stubs, cigarette butts, and printed matter filled with the unrealized predictions of false prophets.

Demaret and I took a table near the cashier and because we were both part of the track family, the manager brought over our coffees and told us they were on the house.

"When's your vacation going to be over?" Demaret asked.

"In a day or two, I suppose."

"Well, you better get back fast. Your pal, Violet, is making a strong run for the rider's title. But I guess you're not here to discuss your career, Eagle. What can I do for you?"

I decided to be up front. "What does the name Courtney Reed mean to you?" I asked him.

He didn't even twitch. "What's it supposed to mean to me?" he asked easily.

"Come off it, Art," I said quietly. "She told me that you'd spotted her."

Demaret stared at me dully. Finally, he leaned back in his chair. "I guess I should have reported her. I didn't. I saw a kid who had gotten a pretty bad start and I thought of my own daughter just a couple of years younger than her. Maybe I'm getting soft, Eagle. I gave her a chance to keep up her masquerade."

"You used her to help you investigate Marcano."

"I don't deny it. Look, Ken, I would have used anyone to trap that Marcano bastard."

"You really hated him, didn't you?"

Demaret laughed. "Yeah, I hated him. I hated him professionally. I hated him the same way I hated the opposing team when I played baseball."

"Do you mind telling me how you knew who Tricia was?"

Demaret shrugged. "Before I got this job I was the FBI agent in charge of the Southern regional office. We had been after this John Jordan for months. The girl's picture came across my desk and we had a bulletin out on her. Mainly, we wanted her to testify against Jordan. In the end we didn't need her because somebody whacked Jordan with a two-by-four in the prison yard . . .

By the way, how did you know that I used her to help me get close to Marcano?"

"She told me."

"Recently?" he asked, cocking his head.

He reminded me of a big dog trying to pick out a strange sound.

"Yeah, fairly recently. She told me that she came to you and said she wasn't going to spy for you anymore."

"Maybe I told her I didn't need her anymore, or maybe she wanted to quit . . . it doesn't matter now. Marcano's secret is buried with him."

"No, it's not. Tell your friends in the lab to come up with a test for fentanyl," I told him.

"Fentanyl." He laughed silently to himself. "You armchair detectives really tickle me. You know what the problem is with your fentanyl, Mr. Smartass? You need a hypo full of the stuff. And how do you administer it? Me and my men had our eyes on everyone who came in contact with Marcano's horse before the race. Or maybe you think we'd miss a hypodermic," he said sarcastically.

"All you would need is a couple of drops."

Demaret sighed. "You want to run that by me again?"

"All you would need is a couple of drops. And the needle could be as small as a thumbtack if the fentanyl is given in conjunction with a drug called corrasalin. Corrasalin can be injected up to a month before the fentanyl. It acts like a booster."

I had been carrying the tack needle around with me since leaving Sarah's lab. I took it out of my pocket and let Demaret inspect it. He held it to the light and then handed it back.

"How the hell do you know about this stuff? What are you, some kind of chemistry freak?"

"Find the right person to ask the questions, and you wind up with the right answers."

"If that's supposed to be a dig at me, it's off the mark," Demaret said angrily. "I had some top people in on this case. That included chemistry professors from—"

"I wasn't riding you, Art. The reason I'm telling you this is so that someone doesn't do it again."

He thought about that, and finally nodded. "Okay, Eagle. I'll have this corasalin checked out with the fentanyl. If it turns out to be the jackpot, I owe you a thank-you. And Eagle . . . since you seem to know so much about it, do you have any idea if there was anybody else in on it with Orlando?"

"You checked out all the horses before they went to post. Did Marcano saddle every one?"

It was customary for a trainer to walk out to the paddock with his horse and rider. The trainer would check the horse's equipment and give the jockey any last-minute instructions. Sometimes a trainer had two horses riding in the same race, or had out-of-town commitments. When that happened, he'd leave the post-time chores to an appointed assistant. In Marcano's barn, 'Judge' Phil Pearl handled those assignments.

"There were seven races where a Marcano horse came in first with Pearl saddling the stock," Demaret said. "But if Marcano had an accomplice it was not Phil Pearl. He is the last person to be involved with something shady."

Demaret was right. Phil Pearl was an eighty-year-old black man who had spent his entire life on one backstretch or another. In all that time, you would have been hard-pressed to find anyone willing to say a bad word about him. His reputation for honesty had earned him the nickname of "The Judge."

"That leaves Bob Diamond," I said.

I could almost see the wheels spinning in Demaret's brain.

"That's an interesting notion," he said at last. "Maybe I should talk to him about it."

ART DEMARET couldn't force Bobby Diamond to talk to him: as the track security man, he had no subpoena power. But what he could do if Diamond refused to cooperate was influence the track stewards to strip him of his racing license under the detrimental-to-racing clause.

Like umpires in baseball or referees in football, the three track stewards made judgment calls and upheld the rules. Unlike their counterparts in other sports, the stewards also issued rulings and punished infractions that had nothing to do with the actual running of races. For example, they issued fines for profanity and they could suspend you for passing bad checks. The stewards also made the determination of whether an individual had done anything "detrimental to the sport of racing."

This system of judge and jury had no relation to jurisprudence, but it worked. It was the reason that Bob Diamond came when he was summoned to Demaret's office.

As usual, he was wearing jeans, a fancy cowboy shirt and the ever-present Stetson.

"I was summoned by His Majesty," Diamond told Nancy. Then he spotted me sitting there. "Hey, Ken, he's got you down here, too?"

"Apparently so," I shrugged.

"You can go right in, Mr. Diamond," Nancy told him.

"Sorry to get ahead of you, Ken, but that's the breaks. Thank you, little lady," he told Nancy. It was typical of Diamond, who stood five-four at most, to call the almost-six-foot Nancy "little lady."

I tried to sort out my mixed feelings about Bobby Diamond. He had never been anything but friendly and courteous to me, but if he had been doping Marcano's horses, then I wanted him to be caught and punished. Modern racing was totally dependent on the trust of the general public. A betting scandal always generated comments such as: "See, you can't win. I told you it was fixed." Needless to say, if that attitude took hold, there'd be less purse money, fewer horses, fewer tracks, and ultimately fewer jockeys.

The voices behind Demaret's glass-paneled office door gradually grew louder and more heated. I could make out who was yelling, but not what was being said.

Nancy and I exchanged glances.

"Sounds like they're having a tiff," she said.

"A tiff? It's more like a war."

Suddenly the door swung open. Diamond stormed past me, and slammed the outer office door behind him.

"Oh, dear," Nancy said.

I knocked on Demaret's door.

"Yeah, come in, Eagle."

Demaret had some balled-up tissue paper in his hand and he was dabbing at an ugly brown stain on his shirt and tie.

"That little son of a bitch spit tobacco juice at me," he said angrily. "I could wring his neck."

"I take it he didn't appreciate your line of questioning."

"Yeah, you could say that. He wouldn't say a thing."

"Do you want to venture an opinion?" I asked Demaret.

"I'll give you an opinion. Guilty as charged! I've interviewed hundreds of suspects during my career and he's as guilty as they come. I'm going to contact Vince Fusco. Hang on."

He pushed a button on the intercom. "Nancy, get me Vince Fusco."

He looked up at me. "I'll ask Fusco to get a warrant so we can have a look-see in all of Mr. Diamond's hiding spots. If he's the keeper of the juice, we'll find it."

I DROVE back to my apartment alternately feeling like a rat for turning Bob in and angry that he might have tried to frame me.

I was about to call Courtney when the blinking light on the answering machine caught my attention. I turned the contraption on and her voice came over loud and clear.

"Hi, Ken. I hope you don't mind, but I miss you terribly and I'm coming over. I was able to rent a car with an automatic transmission, so driving won't be a problem. I hope you're home, and I hope you still care about me."

There was a slight pause. "Because I care about you *very* much," she said huskily.

ANY RESOLVE I had fortified myself with melted shortly after Courtney walked through my door. Her eyes were red from crying.

"I hated being away from you. A hundred times I wanted to call you and I just stopped myself. I love you, Ken. When I thought you killed Marcano it just brought back John. It was like a crazy *déjà vu*. I should have known better. I should have known you could never do that."

I didn't tell her how deep my suspicions had been of her. There was no reason to do so, and it would have been hard to talk while we kissed.

We made love almost desperately, as if we were afraid we'd lose each other. Later, I absently caressed the nape of her neck while she lay sleeping under the covers of my bed.

When this was all over, I wanted to get away alone with Courtney Reed. It would be important to have some time together where we could get to know one another without any masks or mysteries about our pasts.

The buzzing of the apartment intercom caught me by surprise.

"Are you expecting anyone?" Courtney mumbled sleepily.

"No, I'll see who it is," I told her.

I pressed the "talk" button. "What is it, Chester?"

"Two gentlemen here to see you, Mr. Eagle. A Mister Demaret and a Detective Fusco."

I couldn't imagine what they wanted here.

"Okay, Chester, send them up."

I turned to Courtney, who was standing in the doorway. "Is it possible they tracked you here?"

She shook her head. "No. It has to be something else. I'll stay in the bedroom." She closed the door.

Fusco and Demaret lumbered into the apartment. There was nothing else in the world that these two could be but cops. They both wore beige raincoats, dark slacks, and drawn expressions.

"We're not going to stay long," Fusco said. "I asked Demaret to come over here with me, Eagle. Since I was the one who hauled you downtown, I think it's only right that I come by here tonight and tell you I'm sorry. We just came from Diamond's house and it looks as if the Marcano case is wrapped up."

"Diamond's dead," Demaret said bluntly. "He killed himself."

"Yeah, and before he pulled the trigger, he had the decency to take responsibility for killing Orlando," Fusco added.

I kept looking from Demaret to Fusco and back again. "I'm not sure I understand what you're telling me," I said finally.

Demaret nodded. "After you left my office, I called Detective Fusco and asked him to meet me at the track. He came to my office and we discussed my suspicions. Fusco was able to get a warrant over the phone and we were about to leave my office to look over Diamond's place.

"All of a sudden, Nancy buzzed me. She said Mr. Diamond was on the phone. I took the call and he told me I was right about him doping the horses. He and Marcano had been partners and the partnership had gone sour. Marcano was greedy, always looking for more and more dough. Bobby wanted to be cautious. He realized that he could do better without Orlando, so he worked out a plan to get rid of him. When you popped off at Orlando at the hospital, he figured that was his chance. I told him to tell this to Fusco and I handed him the phone."

Fusco continued the story. "I took the phone from Demaret and the next thing I hear is a bang."

"He shot himself?" I asked quietly.

"We went to his house and there he was. He still had his coat and gloves on. The phone was hanging off the table," Demaret told me.

"You might want to know that we found some vials of fentanyl and some other stuff that is probably that corrasalin substance you mentioned to Demaret. We also found this."

Fusco tossed over a set of keys to me. "Match them with your own keys and I guarantee they'll be duplicates."

I found my old set of keys and Fusco compared them. "Perfect match," he said. "That's how he got your shirt, and if he didn't get your watch out of your apartment, he got it from your locker. You were set up, pal. No question about it."

Demaret stood up and put his hand on my shoulder. "It's all over now, Eagle." He looked a bit uncomfortable. "You mind if I ask a favor of you?"

"What is it, Art?"

"Well, the fact that you came up with the way the horses were being juiced doesn't do you any good. If I could put in my report that I figured out how it was done, it could mean whether my contract gets renewed or not. If you have a problem with that, I'll understand."

"No, I've got no problem with it."

"Thanks, Eagle. You really are a good guy," he said.

I tapped Fusco on the shoulder. "Detective Fusco, where does this leave Tricia Martin?" I asked.

"You mean Courtney Reed, don't you? I'm not as stupid as I look despite what our friend Ms. Kirshbaum might think. Reed's clear on this Marcano thing but she still has to straighten out some federal warrants."

"I intend to do everything I can to get the charges dropped," Demaret told me as they left.

He was giving me notice that my helping him would mean him helping Courtney.

When they had gone, I went to the bedroom.

"You heard?" I asked Courtney. I was still dazed.

She was sitting on the edge of the bed, staring out of the window. "I just can't believe it," she whispered. "Bobby's dead. He tried to frame you."

I sat down next to her and put my arm around her. We sat like that for a few moments, both of us lost in our thoughts of Bob Diamond.

"Thank God it's over," Courtney said. "At least it's over."

THE CELEBRATION dinner party was Gus's idea.

We were ushered to a special table at the Helmsley Palace and treated to one of the most sumptuous meals I had ever eaten. It was a veal dish that Gus swore I'd be able to square with my scale the next morning. Courtney ordered the same, but she cheated with a baked potato smothered in butter.

"I've still got five weeks before this comes off," she said, raising the cast. "I'll work off the calories by then."

We settled back with coffee and for the first time in a long while I felt happy and relaxed.

"I have a couple of items I'd like to share at this time," Arlene said, smiling warmly. "I spoke to Fusco and with some of my Southern associates and the word I'm getting is that the federal government might not prosecute Ms. Reed. I think you can put the past behind you, Courtney."

Courtney reached over and squeezed Arlene's hand. "I don't know how I can thank you," she said.

Gus picked up his glass of champagne. "Here's to better times coming down the homestretch."

We all joined in the toast.

"You know what I don't understand, though, Ken? How did Bobby imitate your voice, and why?" Courtney asked.

"I wanted to ask Arlene about that myself," I said.

We all waited as the ex-FBI agent and lawyer put down her glass. "We might never know for sure. He could have given the police another anonymous tip that you'd received a mysterious phone call. When the police questioned you, he was sure you would say it was Ken."

I nodded. "You see, darling, he never thought you would get out of your bed and actually try to head me off. He also had no idea that you would disappear rather than implicate me."

"I could still swear it was your voice, though, Ken."

"It might very well have been. It's a very easy thing to do," Arlene explained. "All you need is two tape recorders. Bobby could have taped a conversation with Ken, and then spliced out certain words from one tape and put them on another. That would account for the metallic quality you said the voice had."

"Okay," Gus said. "I got all that part. What I don't understand is why Diamond wanted to stick it to you, Ken. You two never had a fight or anything."

"I figured it out," I told them. "I think Bobby was in love with Courtney. By pinning Marcano's murder on me, he got rid of his rival."

"But he was so nice," Courtney said wistfully.

"Sometimes it's hard to tell the good guys from the bad guys," I said.

"*Amen!*" Arlene chimed in agreement.

I PULLED up in front of Courtney's house and started to park in her driveway.

"Ken, would you be angry if I didn't invite you in?" she asked. "Maybe it's the champagne, but I have a terrible headache."

"Headache? We're not even engaged yet," I kidded. "Sure, no problem. You just get a good night's sleep."

In a way I was glad that Courtney was going to sleep early. It meant that I could sack out myself and get a good start in the morning. I decided I would go to the track and start exercising some horses in order to get back in riding shape. A few days and I would be ready to go full tilt minus the two or three pounds I had picked up during my "vacation."

It was going to be harder for Courtney to get back into the swing of things, especially if she kept eating baked potatoes with butter. I smiled to myself.

Courtney had said the cast was coming off in five weeks. That could mean at least another month before the hand and arm were in good enough shape to ride. It was a real shame the fall had happened just when Courtney was hitting her full stride as a professional jockey.

Unbidden, her fall off Telno came to mind with perfect clarity. Courtney had almost been killed. It was pure luck that she was all right. And Telno, that veteran campaigner had had to be destroyed because of Bobby and Orlando . . .

The suddenness of the realization made me jam on the brake. Something was wrong! It just didn't make sense.

I ignored the horns of the other motorists and turned my car around in the direction of Courtney's house. There had to be an explanation . . .

I pulled into her driveway and walked up to the door. I tried the bell and then used the heavy brass knocker in case she was sleeping and didn't hear the bell. But she wasn't sleeping.

"Ken! What are you doing back here?" she asked, surprised. She was still wearing the beige outfit she had worn to dinner.

"We have to talk," I told her. "Can I come in?"

"What . . . oh yes. Of course."

I followed her into the living room. There was a small fire burning and the room was warm and inviting.

"Sit down, Ken. You look very upset."

I sat next to her on the sofa. "I was on the way home and for some reason, I thought about the fall you took on Telno."

"That shouldn't have upset you. I'm fine now. She reached out and held my hand."

"No, it's something else. Look, Court, Marcano didn't saddle Telno. He was in the trustees' room for some reason."

"That's right. He was being interviewed by some cable station. Phil Pearl gave me a leg up, so what about it?"

"Bobby Diamond was on suspension," I told her.

"Of course he was, silly. That's the reason I was riding."

"Don't you see, Court? If Marcano wasn't there, and Bobby wasn't there, who injected the horse?"

Courtney stared at me blankly. "No one did, I guess."

"He *was* tanked up. I know that horse. I rode him myself at least six or seven times. He was flying before he went down."

"Superior jockey," Courtney said, smiling.

"Court, this is serious."

"What's serious? Horses get good all of a sudden."

"No!" I insisted. "That horse was drugged. You must have felt something different about him."

"Honestly, I didn't Ken, I've been on lots of horses who—"

"Not like that! And certainly not on Telno. Tomorrow, I'll get the tapes of that race and check it."

"Ken, why are you so obsessed with this?" Courtney reached out and took my hand. "Can't we forget about it for now?"

I stood up. "Don't you see how important this is? If it wasn't Marcano or Bobby who gave Telno the fentanyl, it had to be someone else. That means someone else was in on it."

"I really don't care! I don't care if one person or ten people were involved in some stupid betting scheme. It's over. Bobby's dead and it's over!"

I looked at her. She was more beautiful than a woman had a right to be.

"Come on, Ken, relax." she smiled. "There's a fire going, a nice cozy couch . . . Maybe we don't need to go upstairs."

It came to me out of the blue. *"Demaret!"* I yelled.

"What?"

"Art Demaret. He was always around every Marcano horse. He insisted on giving them last-minute clearance himself. It would be the easiest thing in the world for him to inject them with fentanyl."

"Ken, that's ridiculous. Bobby did it! He confessed."

"Fusco didn't hear the confession. Demaret told Fusco what Bobby had said. How do we know Bobby was involved at all? Demaret had the same access as Diamond to my locker. He could have been the one who played that tape to fool you in the hospital. Courtney, Demaret may have killed Bobby!"

"Bobby committed suicide!"

"Did he? What did Demaret say? He was still wearing his coat and gloves. How convenient that he was wearing gloves so there would be no powder burns on his hand."

I sat back down on the sofa and leaned my head back. "There's only one problem."

Courtney put her head on my shoulder. "And what might that be?" she asked softly.

"Nancy. Demaret's secretary. She buzzed Demaret with Fusco sitting there and said she had a call from Diamond. She knew him well enough to recognize his Texas drawl."

Courtney was kissing me, little baby kisses running up and down my cheek. "What does that mean?"

I thought about Bobby in the waiting room outside Demaret's office. I thought of the brown stain on Demaret's shirt where Bobby had spit on him. There had been something wrong right from the first about Diamond's supposed suicide. That just wasn't Bobby.

"It means Bobby was murdered . . . but not by Demaret. Fusco did hear the actual shot, and Nancy really did hear Bobby's voice."

"Who did it, darling?" she said, putting her free arm around my neck and giving me a long hard kiss.

"I don't know," I whispered.

"Yes, you do," she said, kissing me again.

Her fingers were undoing the buttons of my shirt. I was aware of her body close to mine, her hot breath on my face.

I pushed her back. "You," I whispered, and I knew it was true.

"Make love to me, Ken. I need you to make love to me."

I held her back. "Did you kill Marcano, too?"

"Yes," she smiled at me. It was a slow, evil smile. "What are you going to do about it?"

"You *and* Demaret. You both set me up."

"That was our intention. I'm glad it didn't work out that way. This is much neater."

"You must be crazy!" I told her.

"Sure, I'm crazy. I lost ten years of my life living in fear, pretending to be someone I wasn't. I can have it all now . . . and so can you. We've made a lot of money, Ken, and some of it belongs to you . . . if you'll keep your mouth shut."

"No!"

"Yes, Ken. You're in love with me. You know you'll never meet another woman who is as perfect for you as I am. Yes, I murdered and I lied, and I tried to set you up, but you're going to forgive me, darling. Because now I'm in love with you, too."

I nodded slowly. She was so sure of me, so damn sure. "You're right. I'm helplessly in love with Trish and Courtney. I could never do anything to hurt them. My only problem is I have no idea who *you* are."

"What does that mean?"

"It means you can save your breath. I'm going to call the police."

I began walking toward the door.

"Touch that doorknob and I'll shoot you right here!" a male voice warned.

I spun around.

Art Demaret had stepped out from the small hall that led to the kitchen. A large revolver was in his hand, aimed at my head.

I DIDN'T know much about guns, but this one had a mean snub nose and at that range, Demaret couldn't miss. Even if I'd had the inclination, it was no time for heroics.

Courtney took the gun from Demaret. "Finish splitting the money," she told him. "I'll keep him here until you come back."

"You really weren't thinking about splitting with him, were you?" he asked her.

"Why not, Art? If he said he'd keep his mouth shut, I'd have believed him. I meant everything I said, Ken, every word." She smiled, shaking her head. "You don't know how sorry I am."

Demaret got up slowly. He was going to say something to Courtney but then thought better of it. He walked through the hall back into the kitchen. It was obvious she was running this show.

"Why, Court?" I asked. "Why did you do it?"

"You couldn't understand," she said simply.

"Try me. You had everything going for you. Your career was taking off. You were riding well . . ."

She gave it a few moments' thought. "When I woke up in the hospital I realized that I'd come within an inch of dying. I got to thinking, Ken, about how I had wasted my life. I saw this as a second chance and I was going to have it all this time.

"When you popped off in the newspaper, well . . . that made the timing perfect. Mr. No Guts over there was supposed to do it, but he chickened out at the last minute so I had to take care of Orlando. I don't feel bad, though. He deserved it."

"So the call that came into the hospital was—"

"Demaret chickening out—but I wasn't going to waste the opportunity. It nearly worked, too, except I got so flustered I walked out of there with that stupid knife. Hiding it in the mattress was really dumb . . ."

"What about Diamond?"

"I liked Bob," she said sadly. "He just got in the way."

"You made it look like a suicide," I said. "Was that your idea?"

"That was easy enough. Art told me what had happened and I figured that we'd make Diamond the fall guy. I told Bobby I was afraid that Marcano's killer was out to get me next. He offered me his gun and was even sweet enough to load it for me. He said it would give me protection.

"When he told me about the charges Art had made against him, I talked him into going back with me to refute them. I had him call Demaret knowing that Fusco was in the office. When Art gave Fusco the phone, I pulled the trigger. Then I took off my gloves and put them on Bobby's hands."

"You don't show the least bit of remorse," I said.

"Why should I?" she snapped angrily. "It's a tough world out there! I want my piece of it."

As if on cue, Demaret came back into the living room carrying two suitcases.

"Half a million dollars, split two ways," he told her. "Pick whichever one you want."

"Art," she said, "I trust you, but give me a little peek."

He opened one of the cases. I could see pile after pile of hundred-dollar bills.

"That's the money you made from drugging Marcano's stock," I said.

"Very good, Eagle. What else do you know?" Demaret said cockily.

"What I don't know is why Marcano needed you two as partners. He was the one who originally came up with the corrasalin and fentanyl scam. Or was it you, Art?"

"No, you got it right again. Marcano had been playing this tune for two years. I only came aboard the last eight or nine months. I just want you to know that I discovered how he was doing it long before you did, Ken. I tailed him to San Francisco and video-taped him making a buy of fentanyl. I showed Orlando the video, and told him I was going to throw the book at him. His only out was to make me a partner. In return I tipped him off before every search and I ran interference for him when I injected the horses in front of everybody." Demaret laughed.

"It sounds like you had a good thing going," I said.

I wanted to keep them occupied. Courtney was looking at the money. If I could move a little closer to Courtney it might be possible to make a successful grab for the gun.

I didn't have any illusions. I was going to be the next victim. Just like Diamond, I had gotten in the way.

"Sure we had a great thing going, but I didn't know how bad Marcano was when it came to money. He wanted gold . . . and cars . . . he even wanted to get involved in that breeding operation along with a group of Saudi princes and European aristocracy. The man didn't know how to stop spending."

"If he spent so much, where did this half-million come from?"

I was about to make my move when Courtney abruptly closed the case and stood up.

"Art came up with the idea. He and Orlando deposited half of their winnings in a special vault that required two keys. Art had one and Marcano the other," Courtney explained.

"Come on, Courtney, we're wasting time," Demaret told her nervously. "We've got to take him upstate now."

"Why upstate?" I asked.

Demaret and Courtney exchanged glances. I didn't have to be told this was one trip I wasn't going to return from.

Demaret took the gun from Courtney. "I better hold this in case he gets any ideas about jumping you."

"You think you can use it?" she asked sarcastically.

"Don't worry. If he tries anything, I'll blast him."

Courtney walked over to the front window and looked out. "The neighborhood looks pretty clear now," she said. "Let's give it another few minutes to be sure."

"Did you really recognize her from the days you were in the field, Demaret, or was that a lie, too?"

"No, that was legit. I figured I could use her help—Marcano had an eye for the ladies and she's a very beautiful woman. I put them together."

"You wanted her to get his vault key?"

"That's right. She did a great job."

"That was good practice for you so you could steal mine," I told her.

She shrugged. "I do what I have to. At least you were more fun than Marcano."

"I'll cherish that thought in the time I have left," I said bitterly.

"I'm sorry it had to be this way, Ken, but it was your choice. Keep him covered, Art. I'll bring my car into the driveway. We'll come back later and take care of *his* car."

"Just hurry up!" Demaret told her.

Courtney closed the door behind her.

"Don't get any ideas, Eagle. I couldn't kill Marcano, but that doesn't mean I won't do you. I'm not spending the rest of my life rotting in prison."

"It's still not too late for you, Art. You didn't kill anyone. And how long will it be before she decides that you're the one who's in the way?"

"Eagle, just keep quiet and make it easier on all of us."

"How do you justify it to yourself, Art? How do you make the transition from FBI agent to thief?"

Demaret laughed to himself. "Before I got involved with Marcano, I had the grand total of thirteen hundred bucks in the bank. A guy is supposed to be able to show more than that after a lifetime of work! And do you know how the Racing Board was going to reward me for my years of service? Because I couldn't nab Marcano right away they were going to boot me out on my ass. How's that, Eagle? I had the choice of busting Marcano and getting a pat on the back or cutting myself in for millions."

"Why did he have to be killed?"

"He brought it on himself, dammit! We had our own mint, Eagle. It was easier than printing money. All Marcano had to do was slip one over maybe once every two weeks, but the greedy bastard had some kind of sickness that compelled him to spend and spend. It was like he had a death wish. 'Here I am, look at me.' I heard they were going to check into his taxes."

"You could have walked away from him."

"Sure, and put my faith in some judge who was going to make an example of me for violating the public trust."

"So you decided he was expendable."

"It was him or me. I told Courtney she was helping out in an investigation, but she saw right through that. Once she got the key, she held out on me until I agreed to cut her in."

"So you made her a partner just like that?"

"Look, Eagle. Courtney is one smart woman. She showed me how it could be done without getting caught."

"Yeah, I know about that," I said ruefully.

Courtney had managed to get my keys, make dupes, and return them. That had given her access to my apartment where she'd taken my shirt, and after she went down with Telno it was Demaret who'd gone to my locker and taken my watch. When Demaret backed out at the last minute, Courtney went to her house to pick up the items he had left for her. Then she calmly had the driver take her to Marcano's house where she'd stabbed him to death . . .

We heard the car pulling into the driveway. Demaret very carefully put on his coat and waited as I zipped up my parka.

"Come on, Eagle, move!"

The car was a Pontiac automatic. Demaret opened the rear door and I slid onto the back seat. As Courtney looked around to see if anyone was watching, Demaret got in next to me and closed the door.

"You better not take the thruway or any other road that requires a toll," Demaret warned.

"I've already thought of that," Courtney snapped. "I'll take route seventeen." She sounded annoyed at his questioning of her plans.

"You really let her take over, don't you, Art?" I prodded.

"I warned you once to shut up," Demaret said dully.

He was right. I was wasting my time. They were accomplished, cold-blooded killers. They were taking me to Courtney's desolate cabin and they were going to kill me. I fought to push down the panic. *Think positively, Eagle. You can't let fear paralyze you.* I had to be ready for something to break my way. But what?

Perhaps the car would go into a skid and I could pounce on Art. Maybe Courtney would pass a light and get pulled over by a patrol car. I kept anticipating the possibilities, but the car continued tooling along at fifty-five.

We were out of the city now. Taking me to the cabin was a good idea from their point of view. They could shoot me and bury my body in the woods. Maybe a decade from now a construction crew would come across a skull and some bones.

I knew my disappearance would spark an investigation. But Courtney would swear that I had dropped her off, and that was the last time she had seen me. Demaret would offer to lend a hand in the inquiry and manage to thwart any real chance of progress. They'd get away with it, I decided.

Courtney would stay close to Gus and use him to land my old spot with Joe Herrera's stables. Arlene would win the total acquittal of all charges against her and after a while, the only person who would still remember me would be my daughter, Bonnie.

Bonnie would have to grow up without a father. I would miss her wedding. I wouldn't see my grandchildren born . . . Then I shook myself. *Take it easy, Eagle! Stop with the imagination and stay with facts and reality. You're not dead yet. Hang in there!*

I recognized the area we were going through. There was a stretch of about nine miles of straight road and then we'd veer off onto the country road to Courtney's cabin.

Although more snow had fallen upstate, the roads were clear. We went up Joy Road, came to the fork, and then Courtney guided the car onto the Eaton property and shut off the engine. "All right, Art, get him inside," she ordered Demaret.

Art carefully stepped out of the car and waited until I was in front of him. He nodded toward the house. "Come on. Get going."

No one had shoveled the walk, so Courtney blazed a trail that Art and I followed. When we got inside, she closed the door behind us. "Stay here with him, Art."

She walked into the next room, then I heard her dialing a number on the phone.

"Hi, darling," she breathed. "I know it's late but I wanted to apologize for not inviting you in. My headache is gone and I sure wish you were here. Call me first thing in the morning."

"Giving yourself an alibi?" I asked when she came back.

"It's like dressing up, Ken. Sometimes it's the accessories that make the outfit."

"Now what?" Demaret asked her.

"I'll keep the gun on him," she said, taking it. "You get the shovel that's on the back porch. Then come around to the car again."

Demaret walked off, and Courtney took me outside.

"Are you really going to kill me, Courtney?"

"I've gone this far, Ken. There's no turning back."

Demaret came up behind us carrying a large iron shovel.

She returned the gun to him. "Just follow me and stay close." She opened the trunk of the car and took out a long flashlight.

We walked single file into the woods, Courtney shining the light in front of her. I followed the pool it made, and Demaret followed me. In some areas, the snow had blown in two-foot drifts. In other spots, well protected by the closely spaced trees, the ground was only lightly dusted.

We came to a small natural clearing. Courtney sat herself down on a large rock and shined the light on a patch of ground in front of her.

"Start digging!" she said ominously. Demaret handed me the shovel.

Digging my own grave was more than I could handle. "What if I don't?" I asked her. "What will you do? Kill me?"

"I'll kill you, but before I do I'll make you suffer. I can put a bullet in each of your kneecaps to demonstrate that some deaths are a lot easier than others. And then Art will do the digging anyway, so what do you gain?" Courtney said cruelly.

I started digging. The ground was cold, but not frozen. After breaking through the top soil, it got easier. I lost track of time, and after a while I was standing in a shallow grave that was about two feet deep.

"How much more of this?" Art asked in a bored voice.

"He's got to go about another foot. The way he's slowing down, we'll be here for hours. I'd spell him myself it if wasn't for this damn arm."

"Well, there's nothing wrong with my arm," Demaret said, handing her the gun. "Give me the shovel, Eagle."

I gave him the shovel and stepped out of the hole. Demaret went at the ground with hard regular strokes. Eventually Courtney stood up, walked between me and the pit and took a look over Demaret's shoulder.

"Maybe another ten shovelfuls, Art, and that should do it."

I counted them down as the big man scooped up the earth and deposited it on the edge of the hole. Ten . . . nine . . . eight . . . It was as if my blood was slowly, shovel by shovel, being drained from my body. Two . . . one . . .

"Okay, that's great," she told him.

Demaret threw the last load of dirt over the edge and started to climb out.

"Hell, Art, don't bother getting out," she told him.

"What?"

The shot sounded like an explosion. In the stillness of the woods the sound was amplified, bouncing off trees and rocks and echoing like a thunderclap. Demaret's head snapped back like elastic as he fell backward into the grave, knocking the shovel in with him.

"That brings it down to one little Indian," Courtney said. "Nice of Art to leave his money at my house."

"A half-million beats a quarter-million," I said dryly.

"Exactly. You don't seem very surprised."

"I knew you wouldn't let him walk away with the money if you could help it. Art should have known better too. How will you explain his disappearance?"

"I don't have to explain anything," she said smugly. "No one knows we were here. I'll be the broken-hearted lover and lead the fight to find out what happened to you guys. Maybe I'll even put up some reward money."

"You think you have all the answers."

"I think I'm better off than you at the moment."

There had to be something I could do! Suddenly, I came up with a plan.

"*Oww!*" I doubled over in pain, clutching my stomach.

"Come on, Ken. What the hell are you up to?"

I put my hand in my pocket and then drew it out quickly. "I must have a muscle cramp," I groaned.

"Well for God's sake don't die on me over there, I need you in the grave. Damn you, *get in there!*" she ordered.

I moved slowly and reluctantly, but I knew my only chance was to do what she wanted. I climbed into the three-foot-deep ravine. Demaret was lying at my feet, his lifeless eyes staring skyward. A bloody third eye was in the center of his forehead.

The moon was behind Courtney's head and the brown tendrils of her hair were lit by its pale light, giving her an almost supernatural appearance. She stood looking down at me and angling the gun at the top of my skull.

"You're not going to be able to cover us up with your arm in the sling."

"I can use my left hand, Ken. It'll take time, but I've got the rest of my life to rest up. It was nice of you to think of me, though."

She looked around. "Where's the shovel?"

"It's under Demaret," I told her.

I'd said it too quickly. It sounded planned.

"Is it really? Well, why don't you hand it up to me, Ken. Hand it up *very* slowly and put it in my right hand. I'll keep the gun on you with my good hand, so don't try anything."

I pulled the shovel from under Demaret and slowly lifted it up to her.

"Put the handle right here in my hand," she instructed.

I held it up and watched as she grasped it. In less than a second she collapsed to the ground—unconscious.

Jefferson and Courtney probably weighed about the same. The fentanyl in the lab dog's tack needle attached by adhesive to the shovel handle had done its job well.

9

SOMEHOW, I made it through the week. It was a week that found me repeating the story of what had happened to police, district attorneys, track officials, and reporters. It was a week of very little sleep and miles of pacing around the apartment.

I knew Gus was worried about me. He and Arlene made repeated visits and Gus kept asking me in a nervous sort of way, "You're all right, aren't you, Ken?"

I tried to reassure him that he didn't have to worry. I wasn't going to collapse the way I had after my breakup with Ann, not this time. But how could I have fallen in love with a woman like Courtney Reed, a woman who could murder three of my track colleagues? It seemed inconceivable.

Arlene tried to comfort me. "I've seen a lot of Courtney Reeds in my time," she sighed. "They're crafty and very good at what they do. They have a set of rules that's very different from the set most of us live by. If they think you took their parking space, they'll shoot you to death."

"Yes, but—"

"Listen, Ken," she interrupted, "we don't usually think of evil as being young and pretty. Evil is ugly: trolls, witches, vampires. When it comes in a package like Courtney, it's twice as deadly."

"She took me in so easily," I said weakly.

"Welcome to the human race, Ken. The rest of us make mistakes, too." Arlene smiled.

"I don't want to talk about that bitch anymore," Gus said. "I got some of my own business I have to talk about. Number one, when the hell are you going to get back to work?"

I hadn't told Gus that I couldn't bring myself to go back to the track. At least not yet. There were too many memories.

"I'm going to need some more time, my friend."

"You need to get to work!" Gus told me, waving his cigar. "Okay, I got some more business . . . I'm gonna marry Arlene."

"What?" Arlene and I chorused.

"You heard me, I'm gonna marry you," he told her. "You have a problem with that?"

"In the middle of a conversation, you just throw that in?" Arlene said in amazement. "That's not my idea of sweeping me off my feet, Gus Armando."

"Yes or no? What do you say?"

"Yes," she said.

"Now I'll be romantic." Gus smiled. He pulled a ring box out of his pocket and gave it to Arlene. She seemed to be in a state of shock as she opened the lid. It was a pear-shaped diamond.

"My God!" Arlene gasped. "Gus, it's beautiful!"

She threw her arms around him and they sealed the engagement with a kiss.

I did everything I could to show my enthusiasm, but somehow my words sounded forced. Gus and Arlene's happiness just made me feel even more alienated and alone.

I CUT myself off from the outside world. The Sullivan County real-estate people were able to rent me the Eaton place. When I gave them my name, eyebrows were raised, but in the end, they agreed. Why there? I wasn't sure I knew. There were plenty of other places without the dreadful associations, but I needed to be there. For some reason, it was important.

I disconnected the phone, telling Gus it would only be for another week or so. But the weeks stretched to over a month.

I jogged, chopped wood, enjoyed the sights and sounds of the country. At night I watched the stars and let the heavens put everything in perspective.

A LIMOUSINE appeared early one morning. It was a long, black stretch with a chauffeur who opened one of its doors.

My guest was Mark Russell.

"Jeez, you look like hell. What happened? You forget how to shave?" he asked me.

"It's my mountain look," I told him.

"Whatever turns you on, kid." He shrugged. "Your agent told me you might not ride again."

"I was thinking of calling it quits."

"Rethink it!" Russell advised.

"I wouldn't be any good to you on a horse."

"I'll take a shot with you. I think you're the best. I also think I got the horse that's going to win the Kentucky Derby."

"Not with me, Mark. I'm through. You want to beat me up, go ahead."

Russell ignored me. "I've got something to show you." He tossed a set of Polaroids on the table. "You tell me that's not the most beautiful animal you ever saw."

I gazed at the pictures. The horse was magnificent. It had the long neck and tapered body of a classic distance runner; its black coat shined with vitality.

"That's Ginny's Little Guy?" I asked.

"That's Ginny's Little Guy," he said proudly.

"Can he run?"

"We clocked him yesterday morning. He did a half in forty-five; and five furlongs in fifty-seven."

"That's racehorse time," I told him.

Was that my voice rising in excitement?

"I want you to exercise him tomorrow morning. You in shape under all that hair?"

"I'm in great shape. I've been running, and—"

"Well, let's get the hell out of here," Russell said.

I nodded. "You really think this is a Derby horse?"

"Guaranteed!" Mark Russell said.

I followed him to the limo, looking at the Polaroid shots of the young horse. I hadn't noticed before what a beautiful morning it was turning out to be.

When jockey Ken Eagle makes his middle-of-the-night visit to Sheepshead Bay in the borough of Brooklyn, he passes very near the home of author Michael Geller. Once a quiet fishing village, Sheepshead has grown into a bustling urban neighborhood with rich ethnic traditions and a unique charm that appeals to the celebrated mystery writer. A lifelong New York resident, Geller feels deep attachment to that city and its surrounding areas, which he depicts so vividly in his novels.

Michael Geller

But Geller's civic concern goes beyond fiction. He is active in local politics, and in addition to writing "whenever and wherever I can," he has a distinguished full-time career in city service. His current position as Director of Substance Abuse and Alcoholism Prevention for New York City's Board of Education explains his inside knowledge of illegal substances, like the horrendous designer drug fentanyl, which plays a vital role in *Dead Fix*. Fentanyl is real, Geller explains — only too real; corrasalin, on the other hand, is a product of his imagination.

An avid sportsman, Geller has played semipro basketball and baseball in the minor leagues. He developed an interest in horse racing as a young man while he was laid up recovering from an accident. "Handicapping was a lot more interesting and challenging than doing crossword puzzles," he says with a laugh. And he got to be quite good at it. Before long he had acquired an interest in a racehorse and was beginning to feel the call of the racing circuit when the horse died tragically in a stable fire. Marriage and then family responsibilities brought Geller back to reality and he settled in Brooklyn, where his glory dreams live on in the adventures of Ken Eagle.

Charter members of the Eagle fan club are Geller's wife Merilee, his son Alan, and two daughters, Bonnie and Courtney.

The original editions of the books in this volume are published and copyrighted as follows:

Such Devoted Sisters
Published by Viking Penguin, a division of Penguin Books USA Inc.
distributed by Penguin Books Canada Ltd., at $25.99
© 1992 by Eileen Goudge

Rules of Encounter
Published by St. Martin's Press
distributed by McClelland & Stewart Inc., at $29.99
© 1992 by William P. Kennedy

Blaze
Published by Viking Press
© 1981 by Robert Somerlott

Dead Fix
Published by St. Martin's Press
© 1989 by Michael Geller

ILLUSTRATORS
John Berkey: *Such Devoted Sisters*
Bob McGinnis: *Rules of Encounter*
Peter Klaucke: *Blaze*
Mitchell Heinze: *Dead Fix*

181 219 9211